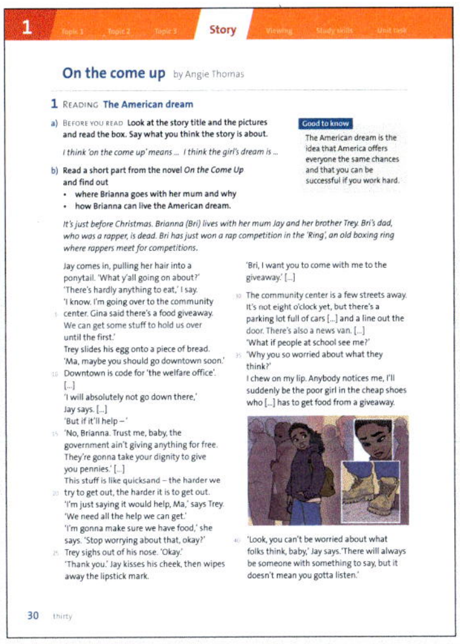

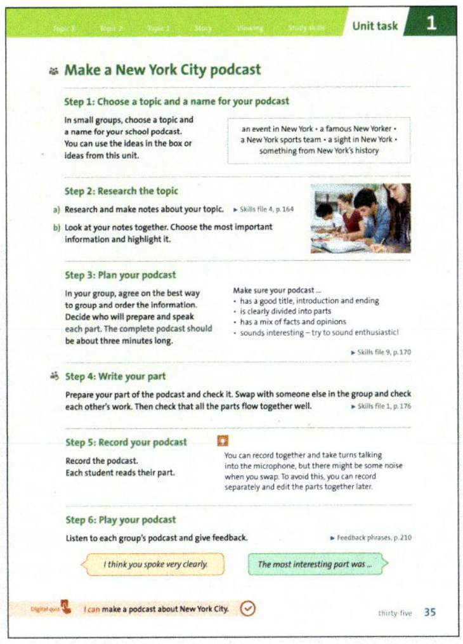

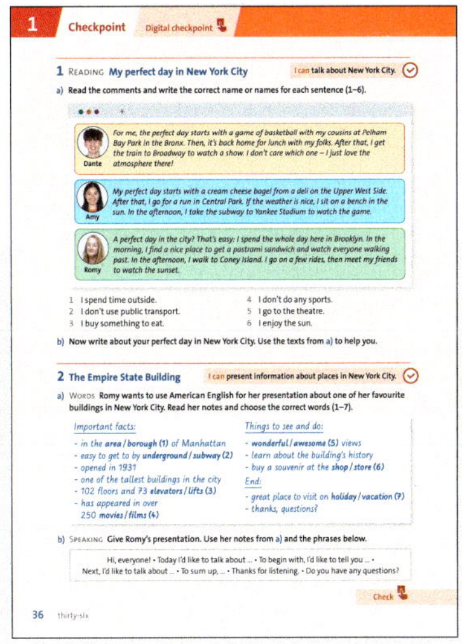

Spannende Storys

Nach den *Topics* kannst du unterhaltsame Geschichten und Romanauszüge über Jugendliche in den USA (Units 1–4) und Kanada (Unit 5) lesen sowie Filme sehen.

Study skills* und *Unit task

Auf der *Study skills*-Seite übst du wichtige Lern- und Arbeitstechniken wie z. B. online zu recherchieren. In der *Unit task* erstellst du ein größeres Produkt und wendest das in der Unit Gelernte an.

Im *Checkpoint* wiederholst du

Hier überprüfst du, wie gut du die Lernziele der Unit erreicht hast.
Im Anschluss findest du ein *Text file* zum Thema der Unit (Units 1–4) sowie ein *Bilingual module* (Units 1 und 4).

Diese Verweise führen dich in die *Diff bank* am Ende der Unit

▶ More help	▶ More practice	▶ Challenge
Hilfen zu den Aufgaben	weitere Übungen	weitere Übungen mit höherem Schwierigkeitsgrad

Diese Lernangebote findest du im hinteren Teil des Buches

▶ Skills file	▶ Language file	▶ Wordbank
eine Übersicht über die Lern- und Arbeitstechniken	die wichtigsten Sprachregeln	zusätzliche Wörter zu bestimmten Themen
Let's talk	**Vocabulary**	**Dictionary**
Redewendungen nach wichtigen Themen und Situationen geordnet	eine Liste der neuen Vokabeln einer Unit mit hilfreichen Tipps	eine alphabetische Wörterliste zum Nachschlagen (Englisch – Deutsch)

ADVANCED
lighthouse 4

Im Auftrag des Verlages herausgegeben von
Martin Bastkowski, Schellerten; Berit Schaarschmidt, Aschaffenburg *sowie* Sonja Mahne, Basel; Ulrike Rath, Aachen

Erarbeitet von
Rebecca Kaplan, Mauer;
Rebecca Robb Benne, Kopenhagen;
Zoe Thorne, Royston;
Jennifer O'Hagan, Bristol *(Checkpoints)*;
Ulrike Rath, Aachen *(Skills file)* und
Hartmut Tschepe, Berlin *(Language file)*

In Zusammenarbeit mit der Englischredaktion
Klaus Unger (Projektleitung), Katrin Heinecke (koordinierende Redakteurin), Doreen Arnold, Lisa Ahmadi, Chiara Castellano, Michael Dunkel, Melina Frick, Stella Hunger, Chelsea Ledvinka-Heß, Julian Theo Wacker *sowie* Ingrid Raspe, Düsseldorf *(Vocabulary, Dictionary E–D)*

Beratende Mitwirkung
Christian Fesler, Eppelheim; Nikolas Grote, Hannover; Stefanie Kelly, Villingen-Schwenningen; Sandra Mercatoris, Ilvesheim; Lara-Sophie Räuschel, Hamburg; Karina Schöpflin, Sprockhövel; Christina Sieber, Schorndorf; Andriana Zaroti, Krefeld *sowie* Vertr.-Prof. Dr. Christian Ludwig, Berlin; Prof. Dr. Michaela Sambanis, Berlin

Illustrationen
Harald Ardeias, Schelklingen; Irina Zinner, Hamburg

Fotos
Chocolate Films, London

Umschlaggestaltung
Rosendahl, Berlin

Layoutkonzept
Klein & Halm, Berlin

Layout und technische Umsetzung
zweiband, Berlin

Druck
Mohn Media Mohndruck, Gütersloh

www.cornelsen.de

Soweit in diesem Lehrwerk Personen fotografisch abgebildet sind und ihnen von der Redaktion fiktive Namen, Berufe, Dialoge und Ähnliches zugeordnet oder diese Personen in bestimmte Kontexte gesetzt werden, dienen diese Zuordnungen und Darstellungen ausschließlich der Veranschaulichung und dem besseren Verständnis des Buchinhaltes.

Dieses Werk berücksichtigt die Regeln der reformierten Rechtschreibung und Zeichensetzung.

Die Webseiten Dritter, deren Internetadressen in diesem Lehrwerk angegeben sind, wurden vor Drucklegung sorgfältig geprüft. Der Verlag übernimmt keine Gewähr für die Aktualität und den Inhalt dieser Seiten oder solcher, die mit ihnen verlinkt sind.

Bei diesem Buch handelt es sich um eine Prüfauflage. Es ist nur für Prüf- und Testzwecke der Lehrkraft im Rahmen des Unterrichts vorgesehen und darf nicht weiterverbreitet bzw. in Ausschnitten oder Teilen vervielfältigt, verbreitet sowie verkauft werden. Rückmeldungen zur Prüfauflage sind an den Verlag erbeten auf **www.cornelsen.de/Produktbewertung**.

Die **Cornelsen Lernen App** ist eine fakultative Ergänzung zu *Lighthouse Advanced*, die die inhaltliche Arbeit begleitet und unterstützt. Als solche unterliegt sie nicht der Genehmigungspflicht.

Alle Drucke dieser Auflage sind inhaltlich unverändert und können im Unterricht nebeneinander verwendet werden.

1. Auflage, 1. Druck 2025
ISBN 9783060367078 broschiert

1. Auflage, 1. Druck 2025
ISBN 9783060367085 gebunden

Produktnummer 1100031760 E-Book

ADVANCED lighthouse 4

Cornelsen

Inhalt

	I can ...	Kompetenzen	Sprachliche Mittel	Seite
Welcome to the USA				
	... talk about the USA.	**R/L/S** Einer Karte, Fotos und einem Podcast Informationen über die USA entnehmen und wiedergeben · Sich über Aktivitäten bei einem *summer camp* austauschen **R** Ein USA-Quiz lösen **W** Informationen zu den USA auf einem Poster sammeln	**Voc** *activities in different states · facts about the USA · activities at a summer camp · hobbies and interests*	10

Unit 1
NYC: The world in a city

	I can ...	Kompetenzen	Sprachliche Mittel	Seite
Lead-in	... talk about New York City.	**L** Informationen über *sights* in NYC verstehen **V/S/IC** Einem Film über NYC Informationen entnehmen	**Voc** *sights in NYC · places in a city · The picture shows ... · I can see ...*	16
Topic 1 Out and about in New York City	... present information about places in New York City.	**L/S** Dialoge über New York verstehen **IC** US-Währung erkennnen und benennen **R/S** Einer Karte und Sachtexten Informationen über die *boroughs* in NYC entnehmen und wiedergeben **My task** Argumente für eine New York-Reise präsentieren **Background file** Times Square	**Voc** *talking about an exchange · British and American English · sights and activities in NYC · arguing for something* **G** *present tenses (revision)*	18
Topic 2 New York: A diverse city	... talk about diversity in New York City.	**R/S** Inhalte einer Grafik wiedergeben **L/IC** Dialogen Informationen über NYC und Einwanderung entnehmen **R** Biografien berühmter Persönlichkeiten verstehen **My task** Einen Artikel über Diversität in New York City schreiben	**Voc** *talking about charts · numbers and percentages · neighbourhoods in NYC · ethnic groups in NYC* **G** *simple past and present perfect (revision)*	22
Topic 3 A city of sports	... ask for and give help.	**R/IC** Einem Blogpost über Sport Informationen entnehmen **W** Bewerbungsfragen für ein Austausch-programm beantworten **L** Durchsagen verstehen **M/IC** Touristische Informationen sprachmitteln (E→D) **R/S** Wegbeschreibungen geben **My task** Rollenspiel: schwierige Situationen höflich auflösen	**Voc** *sport words · polite phrases · asking for and giving directions* **G** *gerunds (ing-form)*	26
Story On the come up	... understand a text about poverty and dreams.	**R/W/S** Eine Geschichte über den *American dream* verstehen und über die Gefühle der Protagonisten sprechen **S/GG** Sich darüber austauschen, was man (nicht) zum Leben braucht	**Voc** *feelings · welfare, poverty and dreams: People need ... / It's nice to have ..., so that you can ...*	30
Viewing Chris the comic book writer		**V/IC** Filmszenen verstehen **S/LS** Über Lebensträume sprechen	**Voc** *superheroes · comic books · dreams*	33
Study skills Plan a project	... plan a project.	Ideen für einen Podcast sammeln und die Umsetzung planen · Problemlösestrategien brainstormen	**Voc** *planning phrases · talking about a project*	34

	I can ...	Kompetenzen	Sprachliche Mittel	Seite
Unit task Make a New York City podcast	... make a podcast about New York City.	**W/MK/S** Themen sammeln und online recherchieren · Eine Struktur festlegen · Einen Podcast vorformulieren und einsprechen **S** Feedback geben	**Voc** *sights, activities, events and people in NYC · podcast phrases · linking words · feedback phrases*	35
Checkpoint	Kompetenzen und sprachliche Mittel (Unit 1) üben, Lernfortschritte erkennen			36
Text file	United – a magazine for young people across the USA: 9/11 · After 9/11 **Bilingual module** US timeline			40
Diff bank	Partner B, More help, More practice, Challenge			44

Unit 2 The South-East: Changing times

L Listening · **R** Reading · **S** Speaking · **W** Writing · **M** Mediation · **V** Viewing · **IC** Intercultural competence · **MK** Medienkompetenz · **LS** Life skills · **GG** Global goals · **Voc** Vocabulary · **G** Grammar

	I can ...	Kompetenzen	Sprachliche Mittel	Seite
Lead-in	... talk about the South-East of the USA.	**V/IC/S** Einem Film über Nashville Informationen entnehmen **R/IC/S** Informationen über Orte und Aktivitäten im Südosten der USA verstehen und sich dazu austauschen	**Voc** *You should visit ... because ... · You can ... there because it's ... · Nashville seems/looks ...*	50
Topic 1 #Everyday Racism	... take a stand against racist behaviour.	**L/S** Ein Gespräch und eine Meldung über Alltagsrassismus verstehen und reflektieren **My task** In einem Post eine diskriminierende Erfahrung und die Reaktion darauf schildern **Background file** French influences in New Orleans, Louisiana	**Voc** *American slang · opinion phrases · feedback phrases* **G** *past progressive*	52
Topic 2 Black lives	... talk about justice.	**R** Sachtexte über Rassentrennung und die Bürgerrechtsbewegung verstehen **L/S** Einen Song über *Black Lives Matter* verstehen und sich darüber austauschen **R/GG/S** Über Sachtexte zum Engagement von Prominenten sprechen **My task** Über Möglichkeiten, für Gerechtigkeit zu kämpfen, diskutieren	**Voc** *slavery, segregation and the fight for justice · opinion phrases* **G** *past perfect*	56
Topic 3 Let the good times roll!	... make recommendations.	**M** Einen Artikel über Karneval in New Orleans sprachmitteln (E→D) **L/S** Einem Gespräch über typische Gerichte im Südosten der USA Informationen entnehmen **R/L** Einen Artikel über New Orleans verstehen · Beschreibungen typischer Musikstile Hörproben zuordnen **My task** In einem Text oder Video Orte und Aktivitäten empfehlen	**Voc** *adverbs of degree: extremely, quite, really, ... · describing food and music · recommendation phrases · feedback phrases*	60
Story Hurricane!	... talk about extreme weather experiences.	**S** Sich über Extremwetter austauschen **R/IC** Eine Geschichte über Hurricane Katrina verstehen und über die Gefühle des Protagonisten sprechen	**Voc** *weather words · feelings*	64

	I can ...	Kompetenzen	Sprachliche Mittel	Seite
Viewing Storm chasers		V/IC Filmszenen verstehen LS Über Risiken und Gefahren und ihre Vermeidung sprechen	Voc *extreme weather · risks and safety*	67
Study skills Write a summary	... write a summary.	Regeln und Wendungen für das Schreiben von Zusammenfassungen kennenlernen	Voc *linking words · wh-questions*	68
Unit task Write a review	... write a review.	W Eine Rezension zu einem Buch, Film oder einer Serie verfassen S Feedback geben	Voc *linking words · recommendation and opinion phrases · feedback phrases*	69
Checkpoint	Kompetenzen und sprachliche Mittel (Unit 2) üben, Lernfortschritte erkennen			70
Text file	United – a magazine for young people across the USA: Black history · Juneteenth			74
Diff bank	Partner B, More help, More practice, Challenge			76

Unit 3
Texas: Teen life

	I can ...	Kompetenzen	Sprachliche Mittel	Seite
Lead-in	... talk about Texas.	L/IC Informationen aus einem Podcast über Texas in einer Tabelle sammeln V/IC Einen Film über eine texanische Kleinstadt verstehen	Voc *talking about towns/ cities and activities*	82
Topic 1 Small-town life	... talk and write about small-town life.	L/IC Einem Interview Informationen über die Unit-Charaktere und ihre Heimatstadt Fredericksburg entnehmen S Vor- und Nachteile vom Leben in der Kleinstadt diskutieren R Einen Artikel über eine Kleinstadt verstehen My task Einen Artikel über den eigenen Heimatort schreiben	Voc *opinion phrases · discussion phrases · phrases for an article* G *conditional sentences type 2*	84
Topic 2 School life	... describe school life in the USA.	R/IC/S Einem Interview Informationen über eine texanische Highschool entnehmen und mit deutschen Schulen vergleichen L/S Einen Song verstehen und beschreiben L/M/IC Ein Telefonat über einen Abschlussball verstehen und sprachmitteln (D→E) R Einem Dankesbrief Redemittel entnehmen My task Einen Dankesbrief verfassen	Voc *school words and phrases · words and phrases for talking about music · phrases for saying thank you*	88
Topic 3 Thinking about the future	... talk about jobs and future plans.	R/IC Einem Dialog über Zukunftspläne Informationen entnehmen S Über eigene Zukunftspläne sprechen R/IC/S Sich zu Jobanzeigen austauschen L/S/W Sich um einen Ferienjob bewerben My task Ein Video erstellen Background file Driving in the USA	Voc *When I graduate, I think I'll / I want to ... · job adverts · I'd like a flexible / ... job.* G *The will-future (revision)*	92

	I can ...	Kompetenzen	Sprachliche Mittel	Seite
Story Moxie	... talk about clothes at school.	R Eine Geschichte über die Kleiderordnung und den Kampf gegen Sexismus an einer US-Schule verstehen S/W/LS Eine faire Kleiderordnung entwickeln	Voc *clothes words · discussion phrases · All students should / can / ... wear ... · Shirts / Skirts / ... must / mustn't be ...*	96
Viewing High Tech High School		V/IC Filmszenen verstehen S/GG Sich über Merkmale einer guten Schule austauschen	Voc *school words and phrases · discussion phrases*	99
Study skills Communicate better	... use strategies to communicate better.	Tipps zum aktiven Zuhören verstehen und umsetzen · Ein Gespräch durch Fragen aufrechterhalten · Verständnisprobleme klären	Voc *encouraging words: Go on. / Right. / Really? · I'm not sure I got that. / Do you mean ...?*	100
Unit task Do an interview about school	... do an interview.	W/S Ein Interview über amerikanische und deutsche Schulen planen, einüben und durchführen · Feedback geben	Voc *encouraging words · discussion phrases · questions · feedback phrases*	101
Checkpoint	Kompetenzen und sprachliche Mittel (Unit 3) üben, Lernfortschritte erkennen			102
Text file	United – a magazine for young people across the USA: Hartford Moves (Lektüreauszug)			106
Diff bank	Partner B, More help, More practice, Challenge			110

Unit 4 California: State of contrasts

L Listening · R Reading · S Speaking · W Writing · M Mediation · V Viewing · IC Intercultural competence · MK Medienkompetenz · LS Life skills · GG Global goals · Voc Vocabulary · G Grammar

	I can ...	Kompetenzen	Sprachliche Mittel	Seite
Lead-in	... talk about California.	R/S/IC Fotos von Orten in Kalifornien vergleichend beschreiben V/IC Einen Film über Los Angeles verstehen	Voc *phrases for describing pictures: The photo of Death Valley shows a mountainous landscape ...*	116
Topic 1 The future is now	... have a discussion about AI.	L Einem Telefonat Informationen über die Nutzung von KI entnehmen S/W Einen Prozess erklären und eine Anleitung schreiben R Einen Chat über die Nutzung von KI für Hausaufgaben verstehen und beurteilen My task Argumente für und gegen KI sammeln und darüber diskutieren	Voc *First, the idea for a game is chosen. Next, the game is designed ... · discussion phrases: Don't you think that ... You have a point that ... I hear what you're saying, but ...* G *simple present passive*	118
Topic 2 My people	... talk about Native American history.	R/IC/S Einem Essay über die Geschichte indigener Völker Informationen entnehmen und diese reflektieren L Eine Präsentation über das Leben des Yurok-Volkes verstehen · Einen Cartoon beschreiben und erklären M Einen Leserbrief sprachmitteln (D→E) My task Einen Cartoon beschreiben und erklären	Voc *numbers, percentages · definitions: It's a bird which was introduced to California again. · phrases for describing pictures* G *simple past passive*	122

	I can ...	Kompetenzen	Sprachliche Mittel	Seite
Topic 3 The Redwoods	... talk about nature in California.	**R/IC** Einem Reiseblog Informationen über den Redwood National Park entnehmen **L** Ein Gespräch über Regeln im Umgang mit Bären verstehen **My task** Einen Reiseblog-Eintrag schreiben **Background file** Hollywood, California	**Voc** *nature, wildlife, animals · rules* **G** *subordinate clauses*	126
Story Please help!	... understand a story about problem-solving.	**R** Eine Geschichte über einen Waldbrand verstehen · Die Folgen von Ereignissen benennen **L/S/LS** Die Problemlösung am Ende der Geschichte verstehen · Sich über kreative Problemlösungen austauschen	**Voc** *nature words · chat language*	130
Viewing Swimming in the desert		**V/IC** Filmszenen verstehen **S/GG/W** Ein Poster zum Thema Wassersparen erstellen	**Voc** *saving water: Switch off ... / Only use ... when ...*	133
Study skills Talk about charts	... talk about charts.	**MK/R/S** Diagramme zu Waldbränden in Kalifornien, zur Nutzung von künstlicher Intelligenz und zum Thema *Native Americans* vorstellen und erklären	**Voc** *numbers, percentages, charts: This pie charts shows ... / ... gallons of water are used for ...*	134
Unit task Prepare and give a presentation	... prepare and give a presentation.	**W/S/MK** Eine Präsentation vorbereiten · Seinen Vortrag einüben und halten **S** Feedback geben	**Voc** *phrases for presentations · charts · feedback phrases*	135
Checkpoint	Kompetenzen und sprachliche Mittel (Unit 4) üben, Lernfortschritte erkennen			136
Text file	United – a magazine for young people across the USA: I love languages! · Making a language body map **Bilingual module** Climate change in California			140
Diff bank	Partner B, More help, More practice, Challenge			144

Unit 5 Canada: The northern neighbour

L Listening · **R** Reading · **S** Speaking · **W** Writing · **M** Mediation · **V** Viewing · **IC** Intercultural competence · **MK** Medienkompetenz · **LS** Life skills · **GG** Global goals · **Voc** Vocabulary · **G** Grammar

	I can ...	Kompetenzen	Sprachliche Mittel	Seite
Lead-in	... talk about Canada.	**S/L/V** Einer Karte, einem Text, Fotos und einem Podcast Informationen über Kanada entnehmen **V/IC** Einen Film über Vancouver verstehen	**Voc** *describing locations on a map · In this photo you can see ... · Vancouver seems / looks very ...*	150
Story The amazing adventures of Jack London: Forty Mile	... understand a longer story extract.	**R/W** Einen längeren Lektüreauszug verstehen · Ein Lesetagebuch führen **R/W/S** Ein Poster zu einem der Charaktere erstellen und vorstellen · Eine kurze Rezension schreiben · Feedback geben	**Voc** *My character is / likes / feels / ... because ... · feedback phrases · discussion phrases*	152
Diff bank	More practice			160

Anhang

Die Angebote des Schulbuchs sind nicht obligatorisch abzuarbeiten. Die Auswahl der Übungen und Übungsteile richtet sich nach den Schwerpunkten des schulinternen Curriculums.

Skills file 162

SF 1 Vokabeln lernen und strukturieren 162
SF 2 Unbekannte Wörter erschließen 163
SF 3 Im Wörterbuch nachschlagen 163
SF 4 Im Internet recherchieren 164
SF 5 Kommunikationsstrategien anwenden 165
SF 6 Einen Vortrag vorbereiten und halten 166
SF 7 Bilder beschreiben 168
SF 8 Diagramme beschreiben und erklären 169
SF 9 Einen Podcast erstellen 170
SF 10 Hörtexte und Filme verstehen 171
SF 11 Lesetexte verstehen 172
SF 12 Einen Artikel verfassen 173
SF 13 E-Mails und Briefe schreiben 174
SF 14 Eine Zusammenfassung / Rezension schreiben 175
SF 15 Texte überprüfen und verbessern 176
SF 16 Mediation 177

Language file 178

LF 1 Die Wortstellung *(Revision)* 178
LF 2 Die einfache Gegenwart *(Revision)* 179
LF 3 Die Verlaufsform der Gegenwart *(Revision)* 180
LF 4 *Simple present* oder *present progressive*? 180
LF 5 Die einfache Vergangenheit *(Revision)* 181
LF 6 Das *present perfect (Revision)* 182
LF 7 *Present perfect* oder *simple past*? 183
LF 8 Das Gerundium 184
LF 9 Die Verlaufsform der Vergangenheit 185
LF 10 Das *past perfect* 186
LF 11 Die Steigerung der Adjektive *(Revision)* 187
LF 12 Adverbien der Art und Weise *(Revision)* 187
LF 13 Gradadverbien 188
LF 14 Die Zukunft mit *going to (Revision)* 188
LF 15 Das *present progressive* mit Zukunftsbezug *(Challenge)* 189
LF 16 Die Zukunft mit will *(Revision)* 189
LF 17 Bedingungssätze Typ 1 *(Revision)* 190
LF 18 Bedingungssätze Typ 2 190
LF 19 Modale Hilfsverben *(Revision)* 191
LF 20 Das Passiv 192
LF 21 Adverbialsätze 194
LF 22 Relativsätze *(Revision)* 195
Grammatical terms 196
Wichtige Schreibregeln im Englischen 198

Wordbanks (nach Themen sortierter Wortschatz, z. B. Umgangsformen, Extremwetter, Jobs und Zukunftspläne, Diagramme) 199

Let's talk (Redewendungen für wichtige Situationen, z. B. Wegbeschreibungen, Konfliktlösungen, Präsentationen) 204

Feedback phrases 210

English numbers 211

The English alphabet, English sounds 212

Vocabulary (Lernwortschatz Unit für Unit) 213

English-German Dictionary (alphabetisch geordnetes Wörterverzeichnis Englisch-Deutsch) 262

List of irregular verbs 300

Ähnliche Wörter im Englischen und Deutschen 303

Typical tasks (Übersicht über häufige Arbeitsanweisungen) 304

Quellenverzeichnis / Sources 306

Continents, countries and regions 310

Welcome to the USA

1 SPEAKING A beautiful country

a) **Look at the map and the photos. Where can you ...**

1 find alligators and crocodiles? *In Florida!*
2 go surfing on big waves?
3 see famous actors and other stars?
4 ride a snowmobile?
5 admire the shapes of the Grand Canyon?
6 see cowboys and lots of cattle?
7 explore Manhattan Island?

b) **Choose one of the photos.**
Describe it to a partner and explain why you like it.

► Skills file 7, p. 168

2 LISTENING & SPEAKING **Which city or state?**

a) Write the names of the city or states in the photos. Listen to a podcast from a website for exchange students. Note at least one fact about each city or state.

b) Listen again and check or complete your notes. Then compare with a partner.

c) WALK AROUND Your partner writes the name of a state on a sticky note and puts it on your forehead. You do the same. Don't look! Walk around and ask questions to find out the state.

A: *Does this state have beaches?* – B: *Yes, it does. / No, it doesn't. / Sorry, I don't know.*
A: *Can you do / go / see / ... there?* – C: *Yes, you can. / No, you can't. / Sorry, I don't have a clue.*
A: *Am I from Alaska / Hawaii / ...?* – D: *Yes, you are. / No, you aren't.*

A quiz about the USA

1

How many states are there in the USA?

A 40 B 50 C 60

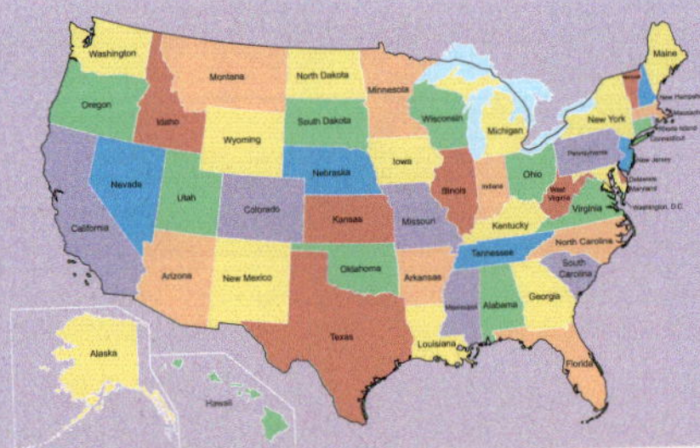

2

What's the capital of the USA?

A Washington, DC
B New York City
C Los Angeles

3

Who is the leader of the USA?

A the prime minister B the king
C the president

4

Which of these isn't a type of American money?

A pound
B dollar
C cent

1 READING Do the quiz!

a) How much do you know about the USA? Do the quiz and find out.

b) Check your answers at the bottom of the page.

☒ c) Write your own quiz question about the USA. Collect the questions in class and do a class quiz.

1 B • 2 A • 3 C • 4 A • 5 B • 6 C • 7 B • 8 C • 9 A • 10 B

8–10 points: Great! You know a lot about the USA!
4–7 points: Well done! Are you ready to learn more?
0–3 points: Try again after you've finished this unit. You'll know much more then.

5

How many times could Germany fit inside the USA?

A 4 times
B 28 times
C 50 times

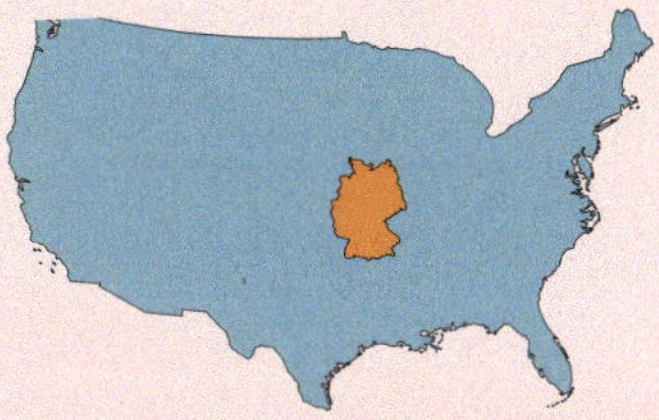

6

If it's 6 o'clock in New York, what time is it in Los Angeles? The map on the last page of this book can help you.

A 5 o'clock
B 4 o'clock
C 3 o'clock

7

What do the stars on the American flag stand for?

A the stars of Hollywood
B the number of states
C the clear skies

8

What's the population of the USA?

A 100 million
B 200 million
C over 330 million

9

Which two states are separate from the rest of the USA?

A Alaska and Hawaii
B Rhode Island and Hawaii
C Alaska and Rhode Island

10

What are sweets called in the USA?

A chocolate
B dessert
C candy

2 WRITING & SPEAKING **Graffiti posters about the USA**

films • food • music • people • places • sports

a) Make six groups – one for each of the topics in the box. Each group writes their topic on a piece of paper. In one minute, write as many words about the topic as you can.

b) Swap papers with another group and read their notes. Add more notes about the new topic in one minute. Correct any mistakes that you find.

c) Keep swapping until you get your poster back. Look at all the notes on your poster. What was new to you? What surprised you? What would you like to know more about?

I didn't know that ... / I was surprised that ... / I would like to know more about ...
Is it true that ...?

At summer camp in the USA

Students from all over the USA spend their summer at the

Lakeview Adventure Camp, California.

Name	Amy Wu
Age	14
From	New York City
Interests	sports, cooking, photography
Why I'm here	I live in a city, but I love being outdoors and I'd like to learn some new sports. I'm also looking forward to the camp food!

Name	Troy Freeman
Age	14
From	New Orleans, Louisiana
Interests	reading, church, fishing, band
Why I'm here	I'm here with my older sister. I want to learn new skills and spend time in nature. The camp is by a lake, so I'm hoping there are lots of fish in it!

1 READING Meet the campers

a) BEFORE YOU READ **Have you ever been to a summer camp?**

Yes What did you do?

No Would you like to go to a summer camp? Why or why not?

b) **Scan the profiles on pages 14–15. Find the places where the four campers are from on the map on the last page of this book.**

c) **Read the profiles. What are the campers hoping to do at camp?**

d) **Tell a partner which person you'd like to meet and why.**

I'd like to meet Amy / Troy / ... because ...

Good to know

Summer break in the USA is eight to twelve weeks long. Summer camps are free-time programmes of outdoor and creative activities for kids and teens during that time. They can last from one to eight weeks. Counsellors look after the campers, who live together in cabins.

Meet some of our campers this year!

Name	Diego Perez
Age	14
From	Fredericksburg, Texas
Interests	science, robots, video games
Why I'm here	I'm not a very good swimmer, so I don't like water sports, but I'd like to do something to get fit. I'm also looking forward to just hanging out and sitting around the campfire.

Name	Tiana Moore
Age	15
From	Eureka, California (originally from the Yurok Reservation near Eureka)
Interests	music, dance, making jewelry
Why I'm here	I'd like to make some new friends from different parts of the USA. I'm mostly interested in creative activities, but I also enjoy ball sports.

2 LISTENING & SPEAKING Camp activities

a) Listen to a camp counsellor. Which kinds of activities (A–F) can you do at the camp?

A outdoor activities B sports C languages
D coding E music F creative activities

b) Listen again and write down the specific activities. Then compare with a partner.

c) With your partner, decide on the best activities for Amy, Troy, Diego and Tiana. Their profiles can help you.

What activity would be good for Amy? – I think she would enjoy ... because ...

d) What would the best activities be for you? Tell your partner. *I would like to do / go / try ...*

Digital quiz I can talk about the USA.

Unit 1
NYC: The world in a city

1 LISTENING Famous sights in New York City (NYC)

a) BEFORE YOU LISTEN **Match the sights in photos A–E to the correct names in the box below. There are two extra names.**

Broadway • the Brooklyn Bridge • Central Park • Museum of Modern Art (MoMA) • One World Trade Center (One WTC or Freedom Tower) • the Statue of Liberty • Times Square

b) **Listen to a tour guide and check your answers from a).**

c) **Listen again and take notes on the five sights. Then compare with a partner.**

d) **Find out more about the two extra sights from a).**

Nach dieser Unit kann ich ...

- über die Stadt New York sprechen und eine kurze Präsentation halten
- amerikanisches und britisches Englisch unterscheiden
- um Hilfe bitten und Hilfe anbieten
- über Armut und Träume sprechen
- ein Projekt planen

Unit task

- einen Podcast über New York erstellen

1 Union Square

2 the subway

3 Annalise at Van Leeuwen's

4 Washington Square Park

5 the West Village

6 Koreatown

2 VIEWING A different New York

a) BEFORE YOU WATCH Look at photos 1–6 from a video about New York City. What do they show?

Picture 1 shows ... I can see ...

► Skills file 7, p. 168

b) Watch the video. Which place do you find most interesting and why?

c) Watch again. Write at least one thing about each place.

1: farmers' market, ...

d) Which side of New York City do you prefer: the tourist attractions on p. 16 or Annalise's tips on p. 17? Tell a partner and give reasons.

► More practice 1, p. 45

► Workbook, p. 8

Digital quiz I can talk about New York City.

Out and about in New York City

1 LISTENING Amy, Dante and Romy

a) BEFORE YOU LISTEN Romy is an exchange student from Germany. What do you know about exchanges? In pairs, discuss what can be good and bad about an exchange.

Amy Dante Romy

b) Listen to the conversation. Take notes on:

1 how Dante knows Romy
2 Romy's family background
3 how Romy likes being an exchange student
4 Romy's general opinion of New York City.

c) Talk about Amy, Dante and Romy's plans for the day. Say where they will go, what they will do and why.

d) Copy the table below, then listen again. Match each picture (A–E) to its borough and add one piece of information about each borough.

A The Staten Island Ferry

	Borough	Picture	One piece of information
1	Bronx	*D*	*biggest ...*
2	Brooklyn		
3	Manhattan		
4	Queens		
5	Staten Island		

B Chinatown

C the High Line

D roller coaster

E zoo

e) Tell a partner which place from d) you would you like to visit and why.

2 Words British and American English

a) Romy sometimes forgets to use the American words for things. Listen. Match the American words in the box to the British words and pictures (1–6).

French fries • pants • sneakers • store • subway • vacation

1

holiday

2

underground

3

shop

4

trainers

5

trousers

6

chips

b) Listen again and check. ☒ Which two words can cause problems and why?

c) Some words have different spellings in American and British English. Read the words in American spelling below and write the British spelling of each word. You can use a dictionary.

1 center	3 color	5 jewelry	7 gray
2 favorite	4 meter	6 traveled	8 TV program

▸ More practice 2, p. 45

☒ d) Look at words 1–4 in c). Can you make rules for two different groups of letters in British and American English? Use an online dictionary to look up other words you know with the same groups of letters. Do your rules work?

▸ More practice 3, p. 45

e) Romy gets confused about the names of American coins. Look carefully at each coin and find its value or name.

Good to know

Each of the four American coins below has a name. Either the coin's name or its value is on each coin, but not both. There are also 50-cent and dollar coins, but you will probably never see one: They're mostly for coin collections.

1 One nickel is ... cents.

2 One penny is ... cent.

3 A ten-cent coin is called a ...

4 ☒ There are 100 cents in a dollar. A 25-cent coin is called a ...

▸ More practice 4, p. 46

f) Start a page for American versus British English. Write words under headings like *city, food* or *money* or make a mind map. Add new words later from the unit. Add words in another language that you know.

French: (pommes) frites, ...

▸ Skills file 1, p. 162

3 Reading New York City's boroughs

a) **Before you read Look at the map. With a partner, talk about geographical features like rivers.** *Manhattan is an island.*

b) **Look at the map and write the name of the borough or boroughs:**

1 Amy lives here.
2 Dante and Romy live here.
3 These two boroughs are islands.
4 The famous Yankee Stadium is here.
5 JFK and La Guardia airports are here.
6 The Brooklyn Bridge connects them.

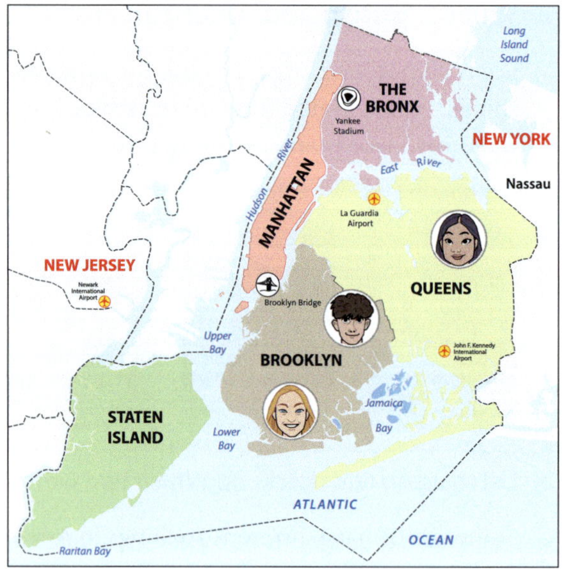

c) **Read about Manhattan in a website guide. Take notes.**

Three rivers divide **Manhattan** from the other boroughs. It measures only 22.6 square miles (58.5 square kilometers), but there are lots of important sights to see. Visitors get a great view of New York City from One World Trade Center and we always recommend a visit to the 9/11 Museum. At Ground Zero you can see where the two towers of the old World Trade Center stood.

d) **Make groups of four (partners A–D). Read your texts on p. 44 and take notes on your borough.**

e) **Use your notes to tell your group about your borough. Take notes on the other three boroughs for an overview of New York City's five boroughs.**

REVISION Present tenses: ▸ Language file 2–4, pp. 179–180 ▸ More practice 5, p. 46 ▸ Challenge 1, p. 46

My task

4 Your trip to New York City

▸ Digital help

a) **Your class has won the lottery! You want to visit New York City, but need to convince your English teacher. As a group, collect sights and activities from pages 16–19 and 44–45.**

b) **Say why this trip is a good idea. Discuss ideas, choose the best ones and prepare a presentation (three minutes). You can use the sights and activities from a).** ▸ Skills file 6, p. 166

On this trip we can practise our English / find out more about famous sights / ... ▸ More help, p. 47

c) **Give your presentation. Which group had the best arguments?** ▸ Feedback phrases, p. 210

▸ Workbook, p. 8

Digital quiz **I can present information about places in New York City.**

Background file

1 READING Times Square

a) BEFORE YOU READ **Look at the photo of Times Square. How is it different from that on p. 16?**

b) **Read the text and**
- say how Times Square got its name
- say if the lights have always been on and why (not)
- name a famous tradition in Times Square.

Times Square in 1908

Times Square is one of New York City's most famous and exciting places. However, it didn't always have this name: Until 1904 it was Longacre Square and was the centre of the city's horse business. When the city introduced public transport and electric lights in the 1880s, the area started to become busier and more popular, with new shops, offices and theatres. The name of the area changed to Times Square in 1904 when the newspaper *The New York Times* built a skyscraper here. Times Square became famous for its lights, theatres, and endless fun.

In the 1930s, the USA had big problems. People didn't have enough money to go to the theatre; many theatres closed. Cheap restaurants and dance halls opened in Times Square. The area was attractive to criminals and became dangerous.

During World War Two, Times Square had to switch off its famous lights and electric signs to save electricity and be safer during the war. Times Square's reputation stayed bad for many years. The streets were dirty, and homelessness and drug addiction were big problems.

In the 1990s, the city began working hard to make it better. It bought the old theatres and helped bring in good shows. In the early 2000s, the city closed off most of the area to traffic and put in big red stairs where people can sit.

The ball drop just before midnight

One of the biggest events is a tradition that *The New York Times* started in 1907. On New Year's Eve, a big ball with lights slowly drops from the top of the old New York Times building. About one million people come to Times Square to celebrate and watch pop stars sing and dance.

It's very crowded: If you want a space, you need to arrive in the afternoon – and there are no toilets! If you leave, you can't come back. And New York City can be very cold in winter.

Today, Times Square is a spot for everyone to enjoy. Thousands of tourists come to see the bright, colourful signs, get tickets for a Broadway show and go to the area's shops and restaurants.

c) WRITING **Imagine you spent New Year's Eve in Times Square. Write your Californian friend an email and tell them:**

- when you arrived
- about the people there
- about the weather
- if you enjoyed it
- what you did while you waited
- tips for other visitors.

New York: A diverse city

1 Listening Romy's school project

Top 10 languages spoken in NYC as a first language

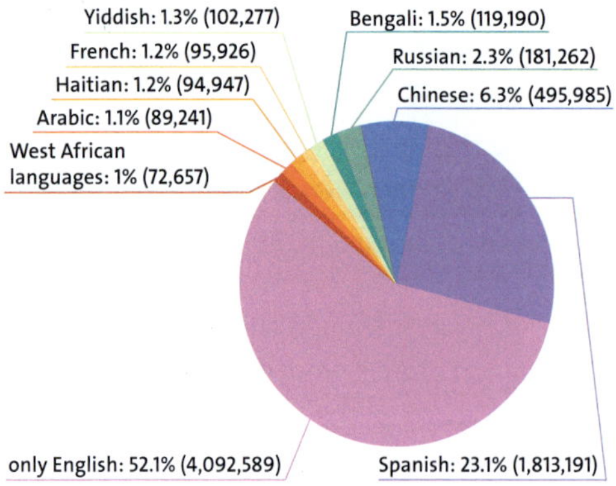

Source: https://data.census.gov (s. Quellenverzeichnis)

Source: https://data.census.gov

Good to know

New York City is one of the most ethnically diverse places in the world and people speak about 800 languages in the city!

Remember

2.7% = two **point** seven per cent
two ~~comma~~ seven per cent
fifty-six thousand = 56,000
(~~56.000~~)

a) Before you listen **Look at the chart in the box. What are the four most spoken languages in New York City?**

▸ Skills file 8, p. 169 ▸ Wordbank 5, p. 203

The (second/third) most spoken language is ...
... per cent of New Yorkers speak ...

▸ Challenge 2, p. 47

b) **Romy is talking to Dante and his parents about a school project. Listen and answer the questions.**

1 What does Romy have to find out about?
2 Who should she speak to and why?

c) **What other information about the neighbourhoods do you remember? Make notes.**

d) **Listen again and match the neighbourhoods to the information.**

1 ...,

1 Little Italy
2 Washington Heights
3 Harlem
4 Williamsburg
5 Flushing

A This is a very musical area.
B This area has people and businesses from lots of different Asian countries.
C This area isn't as big as it was before.
D This area has become famous because of a film.
E Romy has eaten Jewish food in this area.

2 LOOKING AT LANGUAGE Revision: The simple past and the present perfect (form)

Read the quotes from the conversation in 1, then copy and complete the table.

Simple past	Present perfect
'My parents lived in Little Italy when they first came to New York City.' 'My host dad and I went there last weekend.' 'He came over from China in the 1970s.'	'I haven't seen that yet, but I want to!' 'We've seen a few concerts there.' 'Have you been to Williamsburg before?' 'He's started writing a book about his experience.'

Verb	Simple past	Present perfect
live	...	have / has lived
start	started	have / has ...
come	...	have / has come
go	...	have / has gone
...	saw	...
be	...	...

We use **have / has been** if the person has gone somewhere and come back.
We use **have / has gone** if they're still there.

REVISION The simple past and the present perfect: ▸ Language file 5–7, pp. 181–183 ▸ More practice 6 + 7, p. 47

Good to know

In British English it's important to use the present perfect:
Have you eaten yet? I've already finished.
Americans often use the simple past instead of the present perfect with *yet* or *already*:
Did you eat yet? I finished already.

3 LISTENING A new New Yorker

a) BEFORE YOU LISTEN **Look at the photo. It was taken on a ship. When do you think it was taken? Who do you think the people in the photo are? How might they be feeling?**

b) **Listen to Amy's grandfather. How did he feel when he came to New York City?**

c) **Listen again and complete what happened at these times.**

1 In 1892, Ellis Island ...
2 In the 1920s, there were laws so that ...
3 In 1954, Ellis Island ...
4 In the 1970s, ...

▸ Workbook, p. 10

4 LOOKING AT LANGUAGE Revision: The simple past and the present perfect (use)

a) Read the quotes from the conversation in 3. Which are simple past and which are present perfect? ☒ Say how you know. Which clues helped you?

1 People have always come to New York City ...
2 In 1892, that became the place ...
3 They didn't go via Ellis Island.
4 I've just started writing it.
5 Have you seen Ellis Island yet?
6 Back then, lots of people came from Ireland ...
7 They passed laws in the 1920s ...
8 I've loved this city since the moment I arrived.

b) Choose 'simple past' or 'present perfect' to complete the rule in the box.

When you talk about a finished action, especially if you say when it happened, use the ...
When you talk about something that affects you now, or if you use *just, yet, since, always* or *ever*, use the ...

▸ Language file 7, p. 183

5 Coming to the United States

Choose the correct form of each verb.

1 Mr Wu lived / has lived in New York City since the 1970s.
2 Mr Wu's family didn't have / hasn't had an easy life in China.
3 In the past, people have come / came to the USA via Ellis Island.
4 Romy didn't visit / hasn't visited Ellis Island yet.
5 The Statue of Liberty was always / has always been an important symbol of welcome.
6 In 1965, the USA passed / has passed a law to give new rights to Chinese Americans.
7 The population of New York City just went / has just gone below 8.5 million people because immigration to the city dropped / has dropped.

▸ More practice 8, p. 48

6 SPEAKING Find someone who ...

a) WALK AROUND **Copy the table. Walk around and ask and answer questions. Write the name of one student for every question. ☒ If your partner says 'yes', ask a question in the simple past.**

Have you ever been to the USA? – Yes, I have. – When did you go to the USA? / Where / What ...?

... has been to the USA.	... has played soccer.	... has watched an American film.
... has eaten Korean food.	... has been to a concert.	... has sung in front of an audience.
... has met someone famous.	... has been abroad.	... has found money.

b) Tell the class something interesting that you learned in a).

Mahmoud has been to the USA. / Nobody has eaten Korean food!

7 READING At home in New York

For her project, Romy read two articles about famous New Yorkers. Read the articles and decide if 1–6 are about Lin-Manuel Miranda, Jonquel Jones or both.

1 born in New York City
2 speak(s) another language
3 lived in several different countries
4 proud of their background
5 not sure where they want to live next
6 got prizes for their work

Songs of diversity

Lin-Manuel Miranda is an award-winning songwriter, rapper and actor who has written two musicals about New York City, including *Hamilton*, in which actors of colour play the founders of the USA. He is also behind the music for films like *Encanto* and *Star Wars*. His parents left Puerto Rico for New York City, where Miranda was born and grew up in a Hispanic neighborhood. Both sides of his background are important to him: He speaks Spanish as well as English and spent summers in Puerto Rico as a child. He talks about his love of New York City in his songs. For example, in 'Cheering For Me Now', he sang: 'I came here with nothing / like hundreds before me / and millions behind me. / You know you can find me in New York / where everyone's different, / but share the same island. [...] / Where else can you wander / and hear every language?'

Proud to be herself

Some people call Jonquel Jones the best women's basketball player in the world. She was born and grew up in the Bahamas, but moved to the USA when she was 14 to follow her dream of becoming a professional basketball player. Jones has played for lots of different teams, some in other countries, and joined New York Liberty in 2023. She has won several awards, for example women's basketball Most Valuable Player in 2021. Jones is proud of her background and what she loves about New York is the freedom to be herself: a Black gay woman who doesn't like to wear dresses. She has said in interviews that not everyone has accepted those sides of her. When she was younger, she tried to look like other girls, but 'that wasn't me. [...] I was trying too hard to be something I wasn't.' In her new home city, everyone is welcome. Wherever she lives in the future, New York City is her home for now.

My task

8 YOU CHOOSE Romy's project

▶ Digital help

Help Romy to write an article about diversity in New York City for her school magazine (80–100 words). You can use information from tasks 1, 3 and 7 on pages 22, 23 and 25. Write about A, B or C.

A a borough of New York City and who lives there
B a food that immigrants brought to New York City
C a famous New Yorker and their family background

Remember that an article needs ...
- an interesting title
- an introduction
- quotes or statistics
- a good ending.

▶ More help, p. 48 ▶ Skills file 12, p. 173

▶ Workbook, p. 10

Digital quiz

I can talk about diversity in New York City.

A city of sports

1 READING Sports in New York City

a) BEFORE YOU READ **Try to answer the quiz questions about American sports.**

1 What's the American national sport?
2 What's the most popular sport on TV in the United States?
3 What's the sport that most people play in the United States?
4 What's the biggest tennis competition in the United States?
5 What big run takes place every year in New York City?

b) **Read Amy's blog post and check your answers from a).**

https://www.example.com/AmysNYCBlog

Time for sports

For all those who don't know much about American sports (like my friend Romy from Germany), here's a short summary. The American national sport is baseball. In New York City, the Yankees play in the Bronx and the New York Mets play in Queens. Although I live in Queens, I'm a Yankees fan because it's a family tradition. (And Yankee Stadium has the best hot dogs. 😊)

The most popular TV sport is American football – actually, we just say 'football'. We call British football 'soccer'. New York City has two teams in the National Football League (NFL). I'm not crazy about football, though – it can be dangerous!

The sport that Americans play the most is basketball. My favourite team, New York Liberty, plays in the Women's National Basketball Association. Although I'm not very tall, I really enjoy playing basketball. A lot of New Yorkers play on the courts in the park or on the streets.

Tennis is a sport that I don't play, but I like watching the big games. The US Open (the biggest tennis competition) takes place in Queens. My favourite sports event is the New York City marathon from Staten Island to Central Park. I'm good at running and I hope to run it one day.

A

B

C

c) **Read Amy's article again and correct sentences 1–5 below.**

1 The Yankees play in Queens.
2 British-style football is called 'British football' in the USA.
3 People in New York City usually play basketball in sports centres.
4 The US Open takes place in different boroughs every year.
5 The New York City marathon takes place in Manhattan.

2 LOOKING AT LANGUAGE **Gerunds (*ing*-form)**

a) **The words in blue in these sentences from Amy's article are gerunds. Look at the examples and choose the correct words for the rules in the box.**

1 Reading about sports might be helpful for others.
2 Understanding the rules is hard!
3 I **like** watching the big games.
4 I really **enjoy** playing basketball.
5 I'm not **crazy about** watching football.
6 I'm **good at** running.

A **gerund** is the *ing*-form of a verb, but we use it like a noun. A gerund can be the **subject** or **object** of a sentence.
In sentences 1–2, it is the ...
It can also be the ... after certain verbs (3–4) or after adjective + preposition (5–6).

▶ Language file 8, p. 184

b) **Read the opinions about sport (1–6).**
Tell your partner which ones you agree or disagree with. Say why or why not.

1 I like keeping fit.
2 Playing team sports is fun.
3 Kids should start playing sports early.
4 I'm against having more school sport.
5 Sport isn't important: I'm good at doing other things.
6 I suggest running if you want to get fit.

3 The Super Bowl

Complete what Amy tells Romy. Form the correct gerunds with the verbs in the box.

~~celebrate~~ • check out • dance • eat • have • make • watch • win

Celebrating (1) the Super Bowl (the NFL championship game) is an American tradition and my family always watches it together. Both teams play hard and focus on ... (2) the game. ... (3) fun is the main thing for the audience, of course. But the Super Bowl is about more than football! We especially like ... (4) the half-time show. There are always awesome singers who are great at ... (5) too. I also recommend ... (6) the special TV ads with famous people and cute stories. During the game, a lot of families eat snacks like chips and popcorn, but we eat dim sum. Although they take some time to make, my dad loves ... (7) dim sum – my favorite food. Days before the game, I dream about ... (8) my dad's dim sum – which can be translated as 'touch the heart'.

▶ More practice 9, p. 48

4 WRITING **A student exchange with the United States**

You want to take part in an exchange programme. Answer the questions. Use gerunds.

Tell us more about yourself: What do you like doing?
What are you good (and not so good) at doing?

▶ Skills file 13, p. 164

▶ Workbook, p. 12

5 Listening **On the subway**

Good to know

Most New York City subway lines have letters, but some lines have numbers. You say the letter or number first: the A line, the 5 train, ... The subway runs 24 hours a day. A single ticket for two hours cost $2.90 in 2024.

a) Before you listen **Read the box. Say what's different from the public transport in your area.**

In my area, we don't have ... / We only have ...
The underground in ... runs ... / The buses run ...

b) **The three friends have tickets for a Yankees game. Romy is at the subway station in Brooklyn. Listen. Match announcements 1–5 to the main information (A–E) below.**

A You can change to other lines.
B A train is coming into the station.
C Don't step into the space between the train and the platform.
D The police can look through your backpack.
E The doors are going to close.

c) **Listen to the announcements again and answer the questions.**

1 Which train does Romy take?
2 Which trains can you change to at Canal Street?
3 At which station does Romy get off?
4 Which train do Romy and Amy need to take to Yankee Stadium?
5 Do Romy and Amy need to change on the way to the stadium?

6 Mediation **Using the subway**

Romy is mediating between a German tourist and Amy. In groups of three, complete the dialogue. Then act it out.

Tourist Ganz schön schwierig, diese U-Bahn!
Romy **Hallo, können wir Ihnen helfen?**
Tourist Oh – sehr gern, danke! Wenn ich einen Einzelfahrschein kaufe, kann ich damit umsteigen?
Romy **He wants to know if he ...**
Amy Yes, he can use the ticket for two hours and change once.
Romy **Sie können ...**
Tourist Und wie lange fährt die U-Bahn? Es ist ja heute Sonntag.
Romy **...**
Amy The subway runs 24 hours every day.
Romy **...**
Tourist Na, prima! Und wissen Sie, welche Linie ich nach Chinatown nehme?
Romy **...**
Amy He needs to take the 4 or 5 train to Canal Street. It's four stops.
Romy **...**
Tourist Vielen Dank und einen schönen Tag noch!

► Skills file 16, p. 177

7 Speaking Let's ask

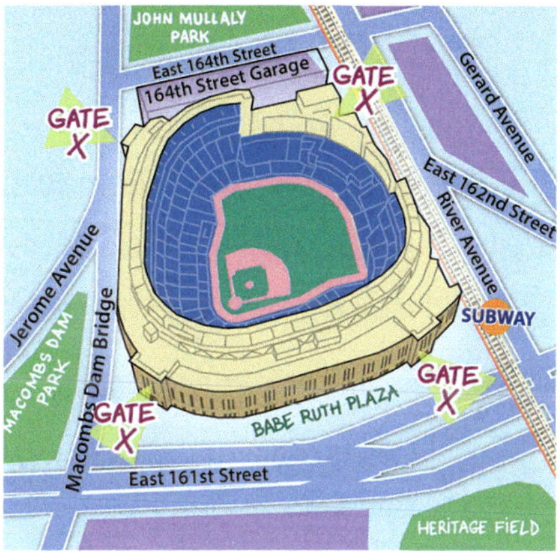

a) **Amy and Romy arrive at the subway station and want to meet Dante at gate 4. Look at the map and read the dialogue. Which gate is gate 4?**

Amy	I don't understand which way we go to get to gate 4. The map on my phone isn't very clear.
Romy	Let's ask somebody. ... Excuse me, could you help us, please? Could you tell us how to get to gate 4 of Yankee Stadium?
Woman	Sure. Take the exit for East 161st Street over there. Then go straight on along the street. It's the second gate on the right.
Amy	Thanks for your help.
Woman	No problem!

b) **Find the polite phrases in a).**

c) **Politely ask for directions from the subway to the top left-hand gate (partner A) and the top right-hand gate (partner B).**

▶ Wordbank 1, p. 199

d) **Partner B: Look at p. 44.**
Partner A: Ask partner B politely ...

- where the nearest hot dog stand is
- how much a hot dog costs
- where the nearest restroom is.

e) **Partner A: Look at the information on the right. Answer partner B's questions.**

▶ More practice 10 + 11, p. 49

Good to know

Americans say 'restroom' for public toilets and use 'bathroom' for a toilet in a home.

- Yankees team store: Great Hall, gate 6 (near ticket office)
- veggie burger: first level near gate 2
- cost of veggie burger: $10.50

My task

8 Showtime At a sports event

a) **You're at a sports event. Look at the box and decide who is A and who is B. Then think what you can say in each situation. Be polite.**

▶ More help, p. 49 ▶ Wordbank 1, p. 199

b) **Role-play the two situations. Use props like a phone and a paper ticket.**

☒ c) **Think of another difficult situation at a sports event and make a role-play about it.**

d) **Act out one of the situations for the class.**

1

Partner A: You're at the gate and your phone is dead, so you can't show your ticket.
Partner B: You're the person who checks tickets at the gate. Send partner A to the customer service area to get help with their phone.

2

Partner B: You're in the stadium, but somebody is in your seat.
Partner A: You're the person in the seat. At first you're annoyed, but then you check your ticket: You're in the wrong seat.

▶ Workbook, p. 13

Digital quiz I can ask for and give help. ✓

On the come up by Angie Thomas

1 Reading The American dream

a) Before you read **Look at the story title and the pictures and read the box. Say what you think the story is about.**

I think 'on the come up' means ... I think the girl's dream is ...

b) **Read a short part from the novel *On the Come Up* and find out**
- **where Brianna goes with her mum and why**
- **how Brianna can live the American dream.**

Good to know

The American dream is the idea that America offers everyone the same chances and that you can be successful if you work hard.

It's just before Christmas. Brianna (Bri) lives with her mum Jay and her brother Trey. Bri's dad, who was a rapper, is dead. Bri has just won a rap competition in the 'Ring', an old boxing ring where rappers meet for competitions.

Jay comes in, pulling her hair into a ponytail. 'What y'all going on about?'

'There's hardly anything to eat,' I say.

'I know. I'm going over to the community center. Gina said there's a food giveaway. We can get some stuff to hold us over until the first.'

Trey slides his egg onto a piece of bread.

'Ma, maybe you should go downtown soon.'

Downtown is code for 'the welfare office'. [...]

'I will absolutely not go down there,' Jay says. [...]

'But if it'll help –'

'No, Brianna. Trust me, baby, the government ain't giving anything for free. They're gonna take your dignity to give you pennies.' [...]

This stuff is like quicksand – the harder we try to get out, the harder it is to get out.

'I'm just saying it would help, Ma,' says Trey. 'We need all the help we can get.'

'I'm gonna make sure we have food,' she says. 'Stop worrying about that, okay?'

Trey sighs out of his nose. 'Okay.'

'Thank you.' Jay kisses his cheek, then wipes away the lipstick mark.

'Bri, I want you to come with me to the giveaway.' [...]

The community center is a few streets away. It's not eight o'clock yet, but there's a parking lot full of cars [...] and a line out the door. There's also a news van. [...]

'What if people at school see me?'

'Why you so worried about what they think?'

I chew on my lip. Anybody notices me, I'll suddenly be the poor girl in the cheap shoes who [...] has to get food from a giveaway.

'Look, you can't be worried about what folks think, baby,' Jay says. 'There will always be someone with something to say, but it doesn't mean you gotta listen.'

I stare at the news van. She acts like it's easy *not* to listen. 'Can't we –'
'No. We're gonna go in here, get this food, and be thankful for it. Otherwise, it won't be that there's *hardly* food to eat. There won't be *any* food to eat. Okay?'
I sigh. 'Okay'. [...]
We get in line, and not a minute later four more people are behind us. There are all kinds of folks in line, too, like moms with their kids and elderly people on walkers. Some of them are in coats, others have on clothes and shoes that look like they belong in the trash. [...]
I look at my shoes. Jay says *'Head. Up.'*
For what? This isn't anything to be proud of. [...]

There are tables around the gymnasium with clothes, toys, books, and foods. One of the volunteers takes some information from Jay, gives her a box, tells us to make our way around. [...] Near the basketball hoops, a Black Santa gives kids candy from his bag. [...]
'C'mon.' Jay pulls at my arm. 'We're only getting food. That's all we need. Some of these other folks aren't so lucky.'
The first table is full of canned goods. These two elderly ladies – one Black and one white – are behind the table. They wear matching Christmas sweaters.

'How many in your household, dear?' the Black one asks Jay. Her table partner watches me with the smallest smile, and the look in her eyes makes me wanna scream.
Pity.
I wanna tell her that this isn't how it normally is for us. We don't usually get in long lines at community centers and beg for food. We sometimes have an empty fridge, yeah, but it always filled back up.
I wanna tell her to stop looking at me like that. That I'm gonna fix this one day. That I wanna get out of here.
'I'm gonna walk around,' I say to Jay. [...]

Santa wears dark sunglasses that hide his eyes [...]. That's Supreme, my dad's old manager. [...] 'My momma took me to all kinds of giveaways like this when I was small,' Supreme says.
'My mom hasn't taken me to any giveaways.'
'Ah, a first-timer,' he says. 'First time always the hardest. Especially with those sympathetic looks folks give you. You learn to ignore them eventually.'
Impossible.
'Listen, I ain't come over to get in your business,' he says. I [...] thought I'd show my respect. You did a great thing in the Ring.'
'I know.' No, I don't, but I have to act like I do.
'I saw something in you that I ain't seen in a long time,' he says. 'We folks [...] call it "It". Nobody can explain what "it" is, but we know It when we see It. You got It. [...] Shame you ain't doing nothing with It.
'What you mean?'
'I looked you up. You ain't got no music out there or anything. [...] You gotta make music. That's what I told Dee-Nice. Now look at him. [...] Same thing with your daddy. All it took was [...] the right song at the right time [...].'

The right song. 'How do you know if something is the "right song"?'
'I know hits when I hear 'em.' [...] He starts to walk away. [...]
'Wait,' I say. Supreme turns around.
I take my phone from my pocket. 'I have a song.' [...] 'I'd like your opinion.'
'All right.' He takes some earbuds from his pocket. 'Let me hear it.' [...]
After the longest three minutes of my life, Supreme takes his earbuds from his ears, unplugs them from my phone, and gives my phone back to me. I swallow. 'That bad?'
The edges of his lips turn up and slowly form a full smile. 'That's a hit, baby girl.'
'For real?'
'For real! [...] If I talk to the right people, you could be on your way.'

Good to know

We use a capital letter for 'Black' when we are talking about a person.

▶ Quellenverzeichnis, p. 309

2 What happens

Read the story again and finish the sentences.

1 Trey thinks his mum should go downtown because ...
2 When Bri thinks 'the harder we try to get out, the harder it is to get out', she's talking about ...
3 At a giveaway you can get ...
4 Supreme speaks to Bri because ...
5 Supreme tells Bri to ...
6 Supreme thinks Bri's song is ...

3 How Brianna and her mother feel

Read the story again and write ...

1 how Bri's mother feels about going to the welfare office.
2 how Bri feels when she sees the news van.
3 what Bri feels like when she stands in line.
4 why Bri's mother tells her to keep her head up.
5 how Bri feels when the volunteer at the table looks at her.
6 what Bri thinks when Supreme says that she will learn not to mind people's sympathetic looks.

Good to know

Welfare programmes in the USA help families in poverty. They can get money and food stamps to buy food.

4 GLOBAL GOALS No poverty

a) THINK **Think about Bri's family situation and what 'no poverty' means. Make notes under the two headings 'What people need to have or do' and 'What is nice to have or do'.**

b) PAIR **Compare and explain your ideas.**

c) SHARE **Discuss your ideas with the class.**

People need ...

It's nice to have ... / to ... (so that you can ...).

▶ Workbook, p. 14

Digital quiz I can understand a text about poverty and dreams.

Chris the Comic Book Writer

1 Comic book reader

BEFORE YOU WATCH Do you read comic books, graphic novels or mangas?

No Why not?

Yes Tell your partner what your favourite comic or who your favourite character is.

2 VIEWING Chris's dream

a) Watch the video. Say what Chris's dream is and how he makes it come true.

b) Watch the video again. Copy and complete the profile about Chris's comic book project.

Character	1 Name of superhero
	2 Costume
Comic book project	3 Artist
	4 Writer
	5 Number of pages
	6 Advertisement / Promotion (Promo)
Result	7 What's the result?

c) Answer the questions.

1 What do you think of Chris's superhero?
2 How hard do you think it was for Chris to make his dream come true? Give reasons.

3 LIFE SKILLS Make your dreams come true

a) THINK Think about a dream you have and how you could make it come true.

b) PAIR Tell a partner.

I want to be a famous dancer / create an app / develop software ...

c) SHARE Share your dream in a group of four. Comment on the dreams of other students.

Wow, that's awesome!

I'm sure you'll do it!

Ask other students questions about their dream.

How long has this been your dream? / ...

Plan a project

1 Before you start

a) Look at the cartoon below and and read the caption. Why does the beaver think they need a project manager? Tell a partner.

b) Look at the project description below. Use the blue keywords from the box in 2 and take notes:

• topic: New York City • size: ... • time: ...

In groups of three, make a short podcast (about three minutes long) about New York City. You will need to choose a New York topic, research it, write and edit a script, and record and edit your podcast. You have two weeks. Please send your podcast by email.

CartoonStock.com

'I think we need a good project manager to coordinate our efforts ...'

2 Divide the project into parts

a) Work in groups of three. Look at the project in 1. List all tasks that need to be done.

• choose a topic, ...

b) List what material you need to do the project. Use your own ideas.

• recording equipment, quiet space, ...

c) Talk about roles for this project.

Everyone needs to ...
One person / Two people can write / talk / record / edit ...

d) Talk about the time for each task.

We need to meet ... / We'll need an hour to ... / ...

Before you start a project, you need to know ...
- the **topic**
- the **size** of the product
- how much **time** you have to complete it
- if you're going to do the project **alone or as a group**
- the **form** of the final product.

Good to know

A project manager is the leader of a team. They make sure that the team members do their jobs and that everything happens on time.

3 Problem-solving strategies

List possible problems and brainstorm solutions.

If someone is ill, you can ... /
If there's bad communication ...

bad communication
illness time
technical problems
arguments

Digital quiz | I can plan a project.

Make a New York City podcast

Step 1: Choose a topic and a name for your podcast

In small groups, choose a topic and a name for your school podcast. You can use the ideas in the box or ideas from this unit.

an event in New York • a famous New Yorker • a New York sports team • a sight in New York • something from New York's history

Step 2: Research the topic

a) Research and make notes about your topic. ▶ Skills file 4, p. 164

b) Look at your notes together. Choose the most important information and highlight it.

Step 3: Plan your podcast

In your group, agree on the best way to group and order the information. Decide who will prepare and speak each part. The complete podcast should be about three minutes long.

Make sure your podcast ...
- has a good title, introduction and ending
- is clearly divided into parts
- has a mix of facts and opinions
- sounds interesting – try to sound enthusiastic!

▶ Skills file 9, p. 170

Step 4: Write your part

Prepare your part of the podcast and check it. Swap with someone else in the group and check each other's work. Then check that all the parts flow together well. ▶ Skills file 1, p. 176

Step 5: Record your podcast

Record the podcast.
Each student reads their part.

You can record together and take turns talking into the microphone, but there might be some noise when you swap. To avoid this, you can record separately and edit the parts together later.

Step 6: Play your podcast

Listen to each group's podcast and give feedback. ▶ Feedback phrases, p. 210

I think you spoke very clearly.

The most interesting part was ...

Digital quiz

I can make a podcast about New York City.

1 READING My perfect day in New York City

I can talk about New York City.

a) Read the comments and write the correct name or names for each sentence (1–6).

Dante

For me, the perfect day starts with a game of basketball with my cousins at Pelham Bay Park in the Bronx. Then, it's back home for lunch with my folks. After that, I get the train to Broadway to watch a show. I don't care which one – I just love the atmosphere there!

Amy

My perfect day starts with a cream cheese bagel from a deli on the Upper West Side. After that, I go for a run in Central Park. If the weather is nice, I sit on a bench in the sun. In the afternoon, I take the subway to Yankee Stadium to watch the game.

Romy

A perfect day in the city? That's easy: I spend the whole day here in Brooklyn. In the morning, I find a nice place to get a pastrami sandwich and watch everyone walking past. In the afternoon, I walk to Coney Island. I go on a few rides, then meet my friends to watch the sunset.

1 I spend time outside.
2 I don't use public transport.
3 I buy something to eat.
4 I don't do any sports.
5 I go to the theatre.
6 I enjoy the sun.

b) Now write about your perfect day in New York City. Use the texts from a) to help you.

2 The Empire State Building

I can present information about places in New York City.

a) WORDS Romy wants to use American English for her presentation about one of her favourite buildings in New York City. Read her notes and choose the correct words (1–7).

Important facts:

- in the **area / borough (1)** of Manhattan
- easy to get to by **underground / subway (2)**
- opened in 1931
- one of the tallest buildings in the city
- 102 floors and 73 **elevators / lifts (3)**
- has appeared in over 250 **movies / films (4)**

Things to see and do:

- **wonderful / awesome (5)** views
- learn about the building's history
- buy a souvenir at the **shop / store (6)**

End:

- great place to visit on **holiday / vacation (7)**
- thanks, questions?

b) SPEAKING Give Romy's presentation. Use her notes from a) and the phrases below.

Hi, everyone! • Today I'd like to talk about ... • To begin with, I'd like to tell you ... • Next, I'd like to talk about ... • To sum up, ... • Thanks for listening. • Do you have any questions?

Check

3 Mediation At a cafe

I can talk about diversity in New York City.

You and your grandma are in a cafe in Manhattan. Your grandma doesn't speak English very well, so you mediate for her. Complete sentences 1–5.

Oma Hmmm, das riecht aber lecker hier!
Juan Guten Tag and, erm, willkommen!
Oma Sie sprechen Deutsch, das ist ja toll!
Juan Oh, I'm sorry, I only know a few words of German.
Du Er sagt, dass er ... (1).
Oma Ach so, okay. Hat er Deutsch in der Schule gelernt?
Du My grandma would like to know ... (2).
Juan Oh no. But when you live in New York, you meet a lot of people from a lot of places. Some are born here, some are on vacation, others have lived here for years – like me!
Du Er sagt, dass ... (3).
Oma Stimmt, wir haben ja gemerkt, dass es in New York Restaurants vieler verschiedener Nationalitäten gibt. Das Essen hier ist also mexikanisch?
Du My grandma asks if ... (4)?
Juan Well, we describe our menu as Mexican-Asian, just like our family. My wife is Vietnamese and I'm from Mexico. We offer dishes from both cultures here.
Du Er beschreibt die Küche als ... (5).
Oma Da bin ich aber gespannt. Ich nehme ich das Tagesgericht, bitte.

4 Writing A blog post about Little Italy

a) **You're in Little Italy, Lower Manhattan, and want to write a blog post. Read the information on the right and think about the following:**

- the area
- what you can see, hear and smell
- if you like it there and why.

b) **Write 100 words or more. Use the information in the box on the right and the phrases below to help you.**

Hi, everyone! I'm on holiday in New York City and I'm visiting Little Italy at the moment. ...

This area is popular with ... • In the past ... • Today ... • I can see / hear / smell ... • I (don't) like it here because ...

Past:
- 1880–1920: many Italian immigrants arrived
- working-class neighbourhood
- first pizzeria in the USA opened here

Present:
- getting smaller as Chinatown gets bigger
- expensive neighbourhood
- traditional Italian cafes and restaurants

Check

5 On the subway

I can ask for and give help.

a) LANGUAGE **Read the conversation between Dante and a tourist. Complete sentences 1–6 with the correct gerunds of the verbs in the box.**

be • get • travel • read • visit • walk

Tourist Excuse me, could you help me, please? Could you tell me if this is the right train for me? I want to go to the Museum of Natural History.

Dante Well, you're on the right line, but you're going in the wrong direction. You need to get off at the next stop and take the D train to Bedford Park Boulevard.

Tourist Ah, I see. I don't know how I made that mistake. I love ... (1) big cities and I'm usually good at ... (2) subway maps.

Dante No worries. ... (3) by public transportation can be hard! Is it your first time in New York?

Tourist It is, yeah. I already knew a lot about it from films, but I really enjoy ... (4) here in real life!

Dante It sure is a great city. If you have time, I recommend ... (5) off the subway at Columbus Circle and then ... (6) to the museum. Then you can see some of Central Park too.

Tourist Great idea! Thanks so much for your help.

Dante No problem!

b) SPEAKING **You're travelling on subway line 7. Decide who is A (a tourist) and who is B (a New Yorker). Make a dialogue. Use the phrases in blue from a) to help you.**

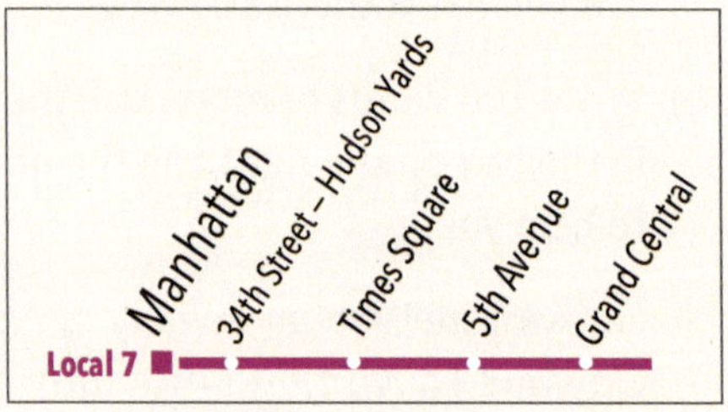

Partner A:
You start. You're a tourist and you want to go to Times Square. You didn't understand the announcement and you're worried you have missed your stop.

Partner B:
You live in New York City and you often travel on the subway.
You answer the tourist's questions.

Check

6 Listening Mr Wu's dreams

I can understand a text about poverty and dreams.

a) Mr Wu arrived in New York in the 1970s. What do you think his dreams were for his new life? Compare your ideas with a partner.

b) What were Mr Wu's dreams? Listen to Romy's conversation with him and choose the correct pictures (A–E). There are two extra pictures.

c) Listen again and answer the questions.

1 Why did Mr Wu want to see his parents happy?
2 What does Mr Wu say about his old school in China?
3 When did Mr Wu meet his wife?

d) Imagine you have just moved to New York City. What are your dreams? Tell your partner.

7 Speaking The High Line

I can make a podcast about New York City.

a) You're making a podcast. Complete sentences 1–6 in Parts A and B with the correct phrases from the box.

b) Work with a partner. Decide who will read part A and who will read part B. Practise saying your part. Give each other feedback, then swap roles.

c) Record your podcast. Listen to another pair's podcast and give feedback. Then swap roles.

Phrases

Finally, let's talk about ... • Firstly, we'd like to tell you ... • Hello and welcome to all our listeners! • Next, we'd like to talk about ... • Today, we're going to talk about ... • Well, that's all for now.

Part A

... (1). You're listening to 'Out and about in New York City' where we talk about our favourite places in the city. ... (2) the High Line. ... (3) a bit about its history. In the past, the High Line was a train line, but trains stopped travelling on it in 1980. In 2009, it became a public park.

Part B

... (4) what makes it special. There's no park in New York City which is quite like the High Line. It's a calm, beautiful, green spot in the middle of this busy, crowded city and it has amazing views of the Hudson River. ... (5) when you can visit the park. It's open every day from 7 a.m. until 8 p.m. and it's free to get in. ... (6). We hope that you enjoyed our podcast!

Check

United[1]

A magazine for young people across the USA

9/11: The day that changed New York City *by Dante Rossi*

Every year in New York City we remember 9/11 (September 11, 2001), the day when a group of terrorists took over two planes full of people and flew them into the two towers of the old World Trade Center. Almost 3,000 people died, including the travelers on the planes, workers in the towers and many brave firefighters, paramedics and volunteers who came to the rescue. Helaina Hovitz, then twelve years old, was at school near the World Trade Center on that terrible day. She wrote about how she tried to get home with her neighbor Charles and his mother Ann.

Helaina's story

(from: 'What the 20 years since 9/11 have been like for a survivor' by Helaina Hovitz)

Now, of course, you know what happened next. The whole world knows what happened. But in real time, we — 11, 12, 13-year-olds — had no idea. When we went outside, it looked like we had walked onto the set of a disaster film. We were almost directly under the towers, which were yet to collapse[2], feeling the heat on our faces. Rather than running uptown[3] like everyone else was, we ran further into the chaos. We were hoping to get home, which was just three blocks away from the towers on the other side of town. [...]

We didn't make it home before the first tower fell, nearly an hour after being hit. Suddenly, voices shouted 'Get inside! Quick!' and a group of people pulled Ann, Charles, and me inside a building with a giant[4] lobby, where we waited a few minutes [...].

Back outside people were running, falling over shoes, backpacks, and body parts, screaming and crying. Underneath[5] several inches of ash were things that people wore that day and had now left on the street. For the next hour, we continued to try to get home, walking through the bleeding bodies of people covered in[6] soot[7] and ash [...].

In the days that followed, our neighborhood became a war zone [...]. We lived with unreliable electricity, little food, water, and medication[8], and the wreckage[9] from the towers was still on fire. [...] I was ducking[10] when I heard planes passing[11] above me, then crying, panicking, sometimes running back and forth[12] with nowhere to really go. Nightmares[13] and flashbacks[14] took over my days and nights. Lower Manhattan was destroyed, never to return as it was.

► Quellenverzeichnis, p. XXX

[1] **united** *vereinigt, verbunden* [2] **which were yet to collapse** *die noch einstürzen würden* [3] **uptown** *der nördliche Teil von Manhattan* [4] **giant** *gigantisch* [5] **underneath** *unter* [6] **covered in** *bedeckt mit* [7] **soot** *der Ruß*

After 9/11: Bringing people together

After the shock of 9/11, events and festivals have brought people in New York City closer together. People meet, dance and have fun. Here are my two favorite festivals!

River to River Festival

The first River to River Festival was held in 2002, right after 9/11. The idea was to use the power of art to make people in Manhattan feel more united and happier.
The amazing art (e.g. light shows, paper art, sculptures with found materials) and performances (e.g. concerts, storytelling, dance) make people think, smile and dance!
The festival takes place in June in downtown Manhattan and all events are free.

Mermaid Parade

The Mermaid Parade is one of New York City's greatest summer events and a must-do New York activity! It takes place at Coney Island, Brooklyn, where there are cool beaches and two great theme parks. You can dress as a mermaid or just put on your favorite costume, walk in the parade and party on the beach. If you don't like costumes, you can help as a volunteer and watch all the fun!

[8] **medication** *die medizinische Versorgung* [9] **wreckage** *die Trümmer* [10] (to) **duck** *sich ducken* [11] (to) **pass** *hier: vorbeifliegen* [12] **back and forth** *hin und her* [13] **nightmare** *der Albtraum* [14] **flashback** *der Flashback, die Erinnerung*

US timeline

... till 1,000 BC

- About **12,000 BC**[1]: The first Americans probably crossed a land bridge from Asia.
- About **1,000 BC:** The Vikings arrived in north-east Canada.

1400–1500

- By **1400:** About two million Native Americans belonging to hundreds of different tribes lived in North America.
- **1492:** Christopher Columbus sailed[2] to America. Europeans began to found **colonies** on the east coast.

1600

- **1619:** Europeans enslaved[3] Africans and brought them to the colonies. **Slavery** in the USA continued for over 200 years.
- **1620:** The English **Pilgrims** arrived and started Plymouth Colony.
- **1621:** The first Thanksgiving

1700

- **1775–1783:** The 13 American colonies fought a war to be independent of Britain.
- **1776:** ■■■
- **1777:** The first national flag had 13 stars and 13 stripes[4] – one for each of the states.

- **1789:** George Washington became the first president of the USA.

1 Important dates in US history

a) Pictures A–H show events from US history. Match them to the blue dates on the timeline and give reasons for your choice. Use your book or the internet for help.

b) Research one event from US history and present it to the class.

c) Name one event in US history that you think is important that is not in the timeline.

Use your words and phrases

I think A is from the year ... because it looks ... / it shows ...
I choose ..., which was when ...
In 2024, ... become president.

A

Same-sex marriage became legal in the whole country.

B

Thomas Jefferson and 56 others signed the **Declaration of Independence**.

C

Ellis Island immigration centre opened.

D

Rosa Parks didn't give up her bus seat for a white person.

[1] **BC (before Christ)** *vor Christus* [2] (to) **sail** *segeln* [3] (to) **enslave sb.** *jn. versklaven* [4] **stripe** *der Streifen*

1800

- In the **1800s**, about forty million immigrants came to the USA from Europe. Many of these immigrants crossed America from east to west. **Settlers** fought and killed many Native Americans and took their land.
- **1830s: ■■■**
- **1861–1865:** The northern and southern US states fought each other over slavery in the **Civil** War.
- **1865:** The South lost the Civil War and slavery became illegal.
- **1872:** Yellowstone National Park opened as the first national park.

- **1892: ■■■**
- By **1900,** there were fewer than 250,000 Native Americans. They had to live on reservations.

1900

- **1906:** San Francisco **earthquake**
- **1917:** The USA entered the First World War (1914–1918).
- **1920:** Women got the right to vote.

- **1941:** The USA entered the Second World War (1939–1945) after Japan attacked[1] Pearl Harbor, Hawaii.
- **1955: ■■■**
- **1963: ■■■**
- **1964:** The US government passed the Civil Rights **Act**. It ended **segregation** in schools and public places and gave Black people the right to the same jobs as white people.
- **1965–1973:** The USA fought in the Vietnam War.
- **1969: ■■■**

2000

- **2001:** On September 11th, terrorists flew two planes into the World Trade Center in NYC.
- **2003:** The USA began a 'war on terror' and sent soldiers to Iraq and Afghanistan.
- **2005: ■■■**
- **2008:** Barack Obama became the first Black US president.
- **2013:** The Black Lives Matter movement was founded after the shooting of several unarmed[2] Black people by police officers.
- **2015: ■■■**
- **2024:** Thousands of people supporting ex-president Donald Trump attacked the US **Capitol** on January 6th.

Key terms

- act *das Gesetz*
- Capitol *das Kapitol, Sitz des Parlaments*
- civil *Bürger-, bürgerlich*
- colony *die Kolonie*
- Declaration of Independence *die Unabhängigkeitserklärung*
- earthquake *das Erdbeben*
- pilgrim *der/die Pilger/-in*
- same-sex marriage *die gleichgeschlechtliche Ehe*
- segregation *die Trennung*
- settler *der/die Siedler/-in*
- slavery *die Sklaverei*
- Thanksgiving *das Erntedankfest*

E

The US government sent five Native American tribes west on the Trail of Tears[3]. Thousands died.

F

The first person to walk on the moon was an American: Neil Armstrong.

G

Martin Luther King Jr. held his famous speech 'I have a dream ...'.

H

Hurricane Katrina destroyed over a million homes in New Orleans.

[1] (to) **attack** *angreifen* [2] **unarmed** *unbewaffnet* [3] **Trail of Tears** *(der) Pfad der Tränen*

Partner page

▸Page 20

3 READING New York City's boroughs

d) **Partner A–D: Read about your borough and take notes on it.**

A: The Bronx is one of the most creative boroughs in New York City and is famous as the home of hip-hop. Many hip-hop artists were born or grew up here, as well as famous scientists, including Nobel Prize winners. You can also find a great zoo, the New York Botanical Garden and Yankee Stadium in the Bronx.

B: Brooklyn is the borough with the largest population. Some people call it the trendiest borough. You can walk around the neighborhood and look at street art or check out the view from the Brooklyn Bridge. A lot of New Yorkers visit the beach and the piers at Coney Island and go on the rides there.

C: Staten Island is great for outdoor activities such as hiking and picnics – when it isn't raining! The mountain of trash in Freshkills Park was once higher than the Statue of Liberty, but now the city is making the area into a beautiful green space. Snug Harbor Cultural Center and Botanical Garden is also a great place to be.
You love scary fun? Then we recommend their ghost tour!

D: Queens is the largest New York City borough by size. It has some great museums, such as the New York City Hall of Science and the Museum of the Moving Image which shows movies in two movie theaters. One of the best beaches is in Queens: People swim or surf at Rockaway Beach every day.

▸Page 29

7 SPEAKING Let's ask

d) **Partner B: Look at the information on the right. Answer partner A's questions.**

e) **Partner B: Ask partner A politely …**
- where the Yankees team store is
- where you can get a veggie burger
- how much a veggie burger costs.

Good to know

Americans say 'restroom' for public toilets and use 'bathroom' for a toilet in a home.

- nearest hot dog place: top level, between gate 4 and gate 6
- cost of hot dog: $6.75
- nearest restroom: main level

Diff bank

▸ Page 17

More practice 1 READING Food in New York City

a) Read the New York City food guide below. Write down where you would go to eat each type of food.

Five top tips for New York City food

1 Let's start with breakfast! Chicken and waffles is a mixture of savoury and sweet foods: fried chicken on waffles with butter and maple syrup. This dish comes from the South, but you can try it in one of New York City's many diners.
2 You can find them everywhere in New York City – in the street, in parks and in restaurants: hot dogs New York-style with mustard, sauerkraut and onions. So good!
3 Jewish immigrants brought bagels to New York City. Today nothing says 'New York' more than a bagel with cream cheese – with or without salmon.

4 If you're hungry at lunchtime, try a pastrami (beef) sandwich. Pastrami came to New York City from Romania, but now you can find it in delis all over the city – as well as lots of other great sandwiches.
5 Ready for dessert? Then take a break in a cafe and enjoy New York cheesecake.

b) You're in New York City. Would you like to try one of the dishes above? Say why or why not.

▸ Page 19

More practice 2 Are you an expert now?

Find eleven British words or spellings and write the American words or spellings.

I'd love to go to New York City on holiday! The city has all my favourite things: great theatres, hamburgers with chips everywhere and amazing shops with cool clothes. I'd like to use the New York City underground to do my shopping: I need some new trousers and some trainers in a bright colour. I'd like to travel across New York Harbour with the ferry and look round some neighbourhoods in different boroughs.

More practice 3 A teen travel podcast

a) Listen to two tourists talking about their week in New York City on a teen travel podcast. Which one speaks American English and which one speaks British English? How can you tell?

b) Listen to American and British speakers saying the same words. For each word, write the number and then 'A' for American or 'B' for British.

▸ Page 19

More practice 4 American money

How much money is there in each picture? Write the number with the dollar sign ($) before it.

1

2

3

▸ Page 20

More practice 5 Real New Yorkers

REVISION **Present tenses**

1 Use the **simple present** to talk about facts or things that happen often, rarely, or never.
*We always **recommend** a visit to the 9/11 Museum. Manhattan **measures** only 58.5 km².*

2 Use the **present progressive** for actions now, around now or for a short time.
*The city **is making** the area into a green space. Staten Island is great when it **isn't raining**.*
We don't use verbs such as **like**, **need**, **recognize**, **want** in the -ing form.

▸ Language file 2–4, pp. 179–180

Amy has written a blog post about New Yorkers. Choose the correct verb.

My German friend Romy **lives / is living (1)** in New York City for a year and she **wants / is wanting (2)** to know what 'real' New Yorkers are like. Well, everybody is different, but **do you recognize / are you recognizing (3)** these things? And can you add some more?

★ A real New Yorker **always walks / is always walking (4)** fast.

★ A real New Yorker **never goes / is never going (5)** to Times Square.

★ People **often cross / are often crossing (6)** the street when the lights are red. A real New Yorker **doesn't think / isn't thinking (7)** 'Why **do those people jaywalk / are those people jaywalking (8)**?' And if **you look up / you're looking up (9)** the meaning of 'jaywalk' now, you're not a New Yorker at all!

Challenge 1 The Empire State Building

Simple present or present progressive? Complete Romy and Dante's sentences.

Dante Hi, Romy! What ... **(1 you / do)** today?
Romy I ... **(2 book)** my online ticket for the Empire State Building. The website ... **(3 say)** that it ... **(4 have)** 102 floors and 1,872 steps!
Dante ... **(5 you / plan)** to walk? Visitors ... **(6 usually / take)** the elevator!
Romy The lift? No, I ... **(7 not plan)** to walk. But ... **(8 you / know)** that every year people ... **(9 run)** up the steps in a tower race? I ... **(10 think)** that's cool!

More help 4 My task Your trip to New York City

b) **Say why this trip is a good idea. Discuss ideas, choose the best ones and prepare a presentation (three minutes). You can use the sights and activities from 4a) on p. 20 as examples.**

On this trip we can	practise our English in places like parks / shops / ticket offices / ... find out more about New York City's culture / food / history / people / ... visit museums / visit famous buildings like ... / ...

▸ Page 22

Challenge 2 Bilingual programs

Look at the chart about bilingual programs in New York City schools. Write a paragraph that answers these questions:

What information does it give you?
What do you find most interesting?
What surprised you?

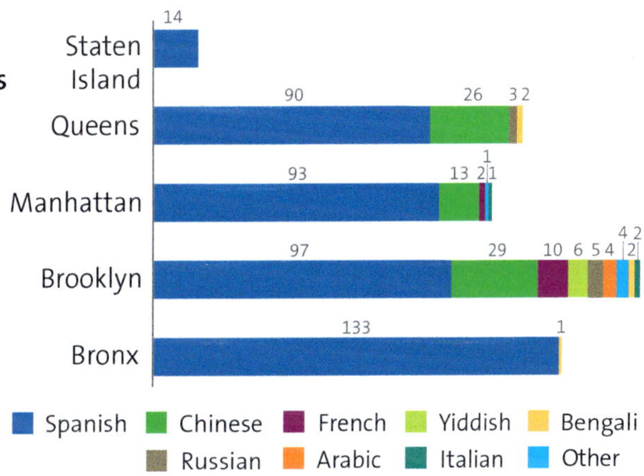

Source: NYC Department of Education: https://data.cityofnewyork.us/Education/2021-2022-Bilingual-Program-List/6iwb-7euj/about_data

▸ Page 23

More practice 6 Dante's grandparents

Read what Dante says about his grandparents. Write the verbs in the simple past.

My grandparents ... (1 be) born in New York City like me, but their parents ... (2 come) from Italy, and their Italian background ... (3 be) important to them. Grandma and Grandpa ... (4 live) in a part of the city called Little Italy and ... (5 have) an Italian restaurant. It ... (6 not be) big and they ... (7 not make) a lot of money, but everyone ... (8 love) it. Grandpa ... (9 cook) the meals and Grandma ... (10 take) the customers' orders. Everyone ... (11 say) their food was the best in the city! Unfortunately, the restaurant ... (12 not stay) in the family: They ... (13 sell) it when they ... (14 be) too old to work.

More practice 7 Class projects

Look at the list. Write what Romy and Dante have and haven't done for their projects.

Romy / Dante has / hasn't ...
They have / haven't ...

Romy	Dante	
✓	✓	Find books about New York City in the library.
✗	✗	Speak to a person who immigrated to New York.
✓	✓	Make an outline.
✓	✗	Do online research.
✗	✓	Take photos around the city.

▸ Page 24

More practice 8 **Ellis Island**

☒ **Look at the brochure. Write the verbs in the simple past or the present perfect. Say how you decided to choose the verb forms. Which clues or words helped you?** ▸ Language file 7, p. 183

Explore Ellis Island: A journey through America's immigration history

Everybody knows Liberty Island with its famous statue, but ... **(1 you / see)** the island next to it? As the door to the USA for immigrants, Ellis Island may be even more important to America's history. In the 19th and 20th centuries, millions of immigrants ... **(2 come)** to America because they ... **(3 want)** a better life, and most of them ... **(4 start)** that new life at Ellis Island.

Registration ... **(5 not be)** easy. For some, it ... **(6 last)** between a few days and several weeks, although most people ... **(7 leave)** the island after a few hours. Doctors and other workers ... **(8 check)** the immigrants' health, history and personal information. For many years, we ... **(9 collect)** thousands of stories and objects so that people today can learn about this important part of the city's history. Millions of Americans ... **(10 visit)** the island and ... **(11 research)** their family's history here. Don't miss the new show about the American dream that ... **(12 just open)**! Book your guided tour today.

▸ Page 25

YOU CHOOSE **More help** **8** MY TASK **Romy's project**

Help Romy to write an article about diversity in New York City for her school magazine (80–100 words). You can use information from 1, 3 and 7 on pp. 22–25. Do A, B or C.

Introduction: In this article, I'll explain ... / Did you know that ...? **Quotes/Statistics:** A A large / The largest ... population in New York City is in ... / The number of ... went up / down. / One important statistic is ... B A popular food in New York City is / are ... Immigrants from ... brought it / them to New York City. C One famous New Yorker is ... He / She says ... In the future, he / she will ... **Ending:** To sum up, ...

▸ Page 27

More practice 9 **About Romy and Dante**

Look at the notes below. Write about Romy, Dante, or both. Use gerunds. *Romy loves ...*

Romy Cook (14)			Dante Rossi (14)		
What I love doing			What I love doing		
What I'm interested in			What I'm interested in		
What I don't like doing			What I don't like doing		

▸ Page 29

More practice 10 At the hot dog stand

a) Complete the dialogue with polite phrases.
More than one answer is possible.

Customer	Hello, ... (1) I have a hot dog with mustard a and onions, please?
Assistant	Sure. ... (2) you like sauerkraut?
Customer	Yes, ... (3). ... (4) I have some ketchup too?
Assistant	... (5). Here you are. That's $6.75.
Customer	... (6). Could you ... (7) me where the nearest restroom is?
Assistant	Sure. It's on the top level, just up those stairs.
Customer	... (8).
Assistant	... (9).

▸ Wordbank 1, p. 199

b) Check with a partner. Then read your completed dialogues together.

More practice 11 LISTENING The game

a) BEFORE YOU LISTEN Read the information in the box. Make a prediction about the score of the game: the New York Yankees against the Los Angeles Angels.

Good to know

A baseball game usually has nine parts which are called 'innings'. There are three bases and a home base (where players start and finish). Players can score 'runs', and teams score one each time they run to all three bases and back to home base.

b) Listen to a radio report about the game.

1 Who won and what was the score?
2 Whose prediction was correct or the closest to the result?

c) Listen again. In which innings did the two teams score their runs?

SHOWTIME More help 8 MY TASK At a sports event

a) You're at a sports event. Think what you can say in each situation. Be polite!

Situation 1

B Can I see ...?
A Oh no. My phone ...!
B Sorry, you can't ... Maybe you can ...?
A ...

Situation 2

B Is this number ...? I think you're in my seat.
A No, sorry, this is ...
B Can you check ...?
A OK ... Oh, ...

Unit 2

The South-East: Changing times

A Listen to country and metal in Nashville, Tennessee

B Go hiking in the green hills of Georgia

C Ride the tram in New Orleans, Louisiana

D See the old town of Charleston, South Carolina

1 VIEWING **Sights of the South-East**

a) BEFORE YOU WATCH **Look at photos A–H and describe them. Have you heard of any of the places?**

► Skills file 7, p. 168

b) **Watch the video about a famous city in the South-East. Say which places A–H you see in the video.**

c) **Watch again. What can you say about Nashville? Think about places, activities and the atmosphere. Then tell your partner five things.**

In Nashville, there is/are ... / you can ...   Nashville seems/looks ...

d) **Would you like to visit Nashville? Why or why not?**

Good to know

The Mississippi is the second longest river in the USA: It flows from Minnesota in the north to New Orleans in the south of the USA.

Nach dieser Unit kann ich ...

- über den Südosten der USA sprechen
- zu rassistischem Verhalten Stellung nehmen
- über Gerechtigkeit sprechen
- Empfehlungen aussprechen
- mich über Extremwetter austauschen

Unit task

- eine Rezension schreiben

E

Take a boat trip on the Mississippi River

F

Visit malls and theme parks in Atlanta, Georgia

G

Visit Lane Motor Museum in Nashville, Tennessee

H

Watch concerts and hockey in Nashville, Tennessee

2 SPEAKING Where should you visit?

Take turns to play roles from the box below. Say which places in the South-East your partner should visit and why. Use the photos in 1 to help you.

You love music. • You're a sports fan. • You want to go shopping. • You want to take cool photos for social media. • You're interested in nature. • You're interested in history. • You enjoy exploring cities. • You're interested in cars.

I love music / want to go shopping / ... Where should I visit?

You should visit Nashville / Atlanta / ... because you can ... / it's ... / there's ...

▸ More practice 1, p. 76

▸ Workbook, pp. 26–27

Digital quiz **I can talk about the South-East of the USA.**

#EverydayRacism

1 Speaking Kisha and Troy

a) **Partner B: Look at p. 76.**
Partner A: Read the information about Kisha and answer partner B's questions. Then ask partner B about Kisha's brother Troy: his age and interests.

b) **Do Kisha and Troy have the same or different interests?**

Kisha Freeman, 16 (New Orleans)
In my free time, I love dancing in a dance group and debating in the school debate club. I also like writing stories and drawing and, most importantly, meeting my friends.

2 Listening Kisha's experience

a) Before you listen **Kisha is telling Troy about an experience she and her friend Maria had. Look at the picture and say what you think happened.**

b) **Listen and check your ideas from a).**

c) **Listen again and complete the summary.**

Kisha and ... go to ... They want to ...
A security guard ... He wants to ... because ...
Later Kisha writes ... and posts ...

3 Words American slang

a) **Match the American slang words and expressions 1–8 from 2 with their meanings A–J. There are two extra meanings.**

1 What's up?
2 mad
3 (to) check sth. out
4 guy / dude
5 yeah
6 Way to go!
7 rent-a-cop
8 (to) have someone's back

A to look at sth. carefully
B yes
C Great work!
D What's happening?
E How are you?
F security guard
G man / boy / person
H angry
I to support someone
J Go in that direction!

Good to know
What's the difference between *slang*, a *dialect* and an *accent*? Words which you use in informal speech or writing, especially by a specific social group, are *slang*. A *dialect* is the form (words, pronunciation, grammar) of a language used in a certain area. An *accent* is the way you pronounce words.

b) **What other American slang words do you know?**

► Workbook, pp. 28–29

4 BEFORE YOU LISTEN In someone else's shoes

a) Imagine you've had Kisha's experience from 2. What would you do? Tell a partner.

I think I would ... / I wouldn't ...

b) Discuss what you think happened after Kisha posted about her experience in the shop.

I think that ...
If you ask me, ...

5 LISTENING & SPEAKING What happened next?

a) Listen to a news story and choose the correct answers.
Then listen again and check.

1 Kisha's post
- A got racist comments online.
- B didn't get many views.
- C was very popular.
- D had a lot of mistakes in it.

2 A big group of young people
- A complained to the store.
- B protested at the store against racist discrimination.
- C recommended the store to their friends.
- D was shopping at the store today.

3 Some of the shoppers said that
- A they don't care about the protest.
- B they will join the protest.
- C they will stop shopping in that store.
- D they don't see the problem.

4 At this store
- A nothing like this has ever happened before.
- B there have been many similar situations.
- C the same kind of thing recently happened.
- D there have been many protests.

5 After the protest,
- A the store said sorry.
- B Kisha got a gift card.
- C the security guard lost his job.
- D the store promised to train its guards better.

b) Why was the security guard's behaviour racist? What do you think about Kisha's reaction? Think for a minute and then tell a partner your opinion. Give reasons.

In my opinion, the security guard's behaviour was racist because ...
I think Kisha's reaction was ... because ...

▶ More help, p. 77

6 Looking at language **The past progressive**

Read the sentences with the past progressive from 2b). Then complete the rule in the box.

1 We were in the department store and we **were looking** at clothes.
2 A security guard **was following** us the whole time **while** **we were shopping**.
3 The rent-a-cop **was waiting** for us **when** we **came out**.

We use the **past progressive** for something that happened over a period of time in the past.
We were looking at clothes.

We make the **past progressive** with … / … and the *-ing*-form of the verb.

It is often used with the conjunctions ***when*** and ***while*** to talk about two past actions.
We use the conjunction … if both actions were happening at the same time.
We use the conjunction … if one shorter action (in the **simple past**) happened while a longer action (in the **past progressive**) was happening.

► Language file 9, p. 185

7 Troy's social media post

Complete Troy's post with the verbs in the past progressive.

Hi! I want to tell you about a racist experience that I had. I *was walking* **(1 walk)** along the street with some Black friends. We … **(2 chat)** and we … **(3 laugh)** when two cops stopped us. We … **(4 not do)** anything wrong, but they said we … **(5 act)** strangely. They wanted to search us for drugs. While they … **(6 search)** us, one of my friends called his mom, who's a lawyer. He … **(7 look)** at the cops while he … **(8 explain)** the situation to his mom and finally the cops just walked away. Have you or somebody that you know had a racist experience? What did you or that person do about it?
Post on your socials! **#EverydayRacism**

► More practice 2 + 3, p. 77

My task

8 Your social media post

► Digital help

a) **Think about an experience with racism or other forms of discrimination that you or someone else has had. It can also be something that you have read or heard about. What did you or that person do about it?**

b) **Write a social media post and explain what happened. Troy's post in 7 can help you.**

You won't believe what happened to my friend. While she was …

► More help, p. 78

c) **Read your partner's post and give feedback: Do you understand what happened? Do you have any questions?**

► Feedback phrases, p. 210

d) **Write a one-line comment on your partner's post.** *I'm so glad that other people supported him.*

► Workbook, p. 28

Digital quiz — **I can take a stand against racist behaviour.**

Background file

1 Reading French influences in New Orleans, Louisiana

a) Before you read **What happens when people bring their language and culture to a new place? Talk about your experiences and what you know from Unit 1.**

b) **Read the text.**

The British weren't the only Europeans who were looking for more land and resources abroad. In the late 17th century, French explorers arrived in an area that was home to thousands of Native Americans. But the French took over the land and named the place 'Louisiana' after King Louis XIV.
The French and the Native Americans traded goods and influenced each other in many areas such as food, language or religion but it wasn't without conflict. The French built towns for themselves along the Mississippi River to use the water for travel and trade. One of these towns was New Orleans, the capital of the French colony. In 1803, the USA bought the territory from France in the Louisiana Purchase. Today, all or parts of 15 US states are on this land that was Louisiana at the time.

The French influence is stronger in New Orleans than anywhere else in the USA. You can still notice it today – in language, culture, names and food. When the French built the city of New Orleans in 1718, they named the streets after French royal people. Today, the old part of New Orleans is known as the French Quarter. You also find the French Market with an artists' and a farmers' market there. In New Orleans there are lots of French restaurants too. And there are still many words from the French language such as beignet, Café du Monde, flambé, Mardi Gras, praline, Vieux Carré. Over the years, the different cultures of Native Americans, French and African communities were mixed and today New Orleans is a vibrant and open city with a diverse culture.

c) **Complete the sentences with information from the text.**

1 'Louisiana' came from the name of the French ...
2 ... were already living in Louisiana when the French arrived.
3 The capital of the French colony was ...
4 The French sold Louisiana to ...
5 The ... of the French can still be seen today.
6 The French Market is in the ...

Black lives

1 Reading A fight for change

a) Before you read **Read the information in the box and look at the photo. Describe the photo and explain how it shows an example of segregation.**

The photo shows ...
It's an example of segregation because ...

Good to know

Over 400 years ago, slave traders took millions of Black people from Africa to work in America as slaves under horrible conditions. They got no money and had no rights. **Slavery** officially ended in 1865, but many states, especially in the South, made laws about **segregation** of Black and white people in public places. They weren't allowed to use the same school, hospitals, waiting rooms or public toilets. Segregation lasted until the 1960s in many places. Many Black people fought against this injustice.

A police officer putting out a segregation sign at the train station in Jackson, Mississippi, in 1956.

b) **Read the text below. Who is Ruby Bridges? Why did she need bodyguards as a child?**

In 1960, when Ruby Bridges was six years old, she started as the first Black student at an all-white school in New Orleans. The school had made Ruby take a very hard test, but she did well and got a place. Until then, Black children and white children hadn't gone to the same schools in the South, even after the US Supreme Court passed a new law against segregation in schools in 1954. But in 1960, many white parents in the South still hadn't accepted the new law. Ruby's parents thought the fight was important – not just for Ruby, but for all Black children.

On Ruby's first day (and many days after that) bodyguards took the little girl to school and back home again. Outside the school, white people threw things and shouted racist comments at Ruby. All the white parents had taken their children out of the school before Ruby started. Only one teacher had agreed to teach her. Ruby did lessons alone for the first year. She ate lunch alone and she played alone. Many years later, in 2011, Ruby Bridges met Barack Obama – he was the USA's first Black president. This was possible because brave people like Ruby and her parents had fought for Black rights.

▶ More practice 4, p. 78

c) **Imagine you're Ruby on her first day and in her first year at this school. How do you feel?**

▶ Workbook, p. 30

2 Looking at language The past perfect

a) **Look at the sentences from the text in 1b). Say which of the actions in each sentence happened first: the actions in blue or the actions in red?**

1 All the white parents had taken their children out of the school before Ruby started.
2 This was possible because brave people like Ruby and her parents had fought for Black rights.

b) **Look at the past perfect verbs in a) and complete the rule.**

We use the past perfect to describe an action that happened before another action in the past. We make the past perfect with ... and the past participle (the verb + *-ed* or an irregular form).

▶ Language file 10, p. 186 ▶ Irregular verbs, pp. 300–302

3 The Little Rock Nine

a) **Complete the text with the verbs in the past perfect.**

In 1957, three years after a new law *had banned* **(1 ban)** segregation in schools, nine Black students in Little Rock, Arkansas, wanted to join an all-white high school. Until then they ... **(2 go)** to a school far from their homes. Before their first day at the new school the nine students ... **(3 take part)** in training for difficult situations. But the state governor of Arkansas ... **(4 tell)** state soldiers to stop the students. The US president didn't agree with this. So after the nine students ... **(5 try)** to get into the school for a month, the president sent 1,200 US soldiers to protect them. After the Black students ... **(6 start)** classes, the racist discrimination and terrible violence continued. However, the Little Rock Nine stayed strong and graduated a few years later.

b) **Read the completed text. What's it about? Why are the Little Rock Nine important for the fight for Black rights?**

4 Black Lives Matter

Complete the information with the past perfect of the correct verbs in the box.

arrive • decide • do • not do • kill • look • ~~shoot~~ • use

There is still a lot of racism in the USA today. Three Black women started the Black Lives Matter movement in 2013. The year before a man *had shot* **(1)** Black teenager Trayvon Martin dead. The man said Trayvon ... **(2)** suspicious to him, although Trayvon ... **(3)** anything wrong. After the courts ... **(4)** not send the man to prison, many people protested. But still the racist violence against Black people continued. In 2020, a shop assistant called the police and said that a Black man, George Floyd, ... **(5)** a fake $20 note. One of the four cops who ... **(6)** at the store was later responsible for his death. Floyd's last words before he died were 'I can't breathe'. Millions of people saw videos of what the cop ... **(7)**. After many protests, the white cop who ... **(8)** Floyd went to prison.

▶ More practice 5 + 6, p. 79 ▶ Challenge 1, p. 79
▶ Workbook, p. 31

5 Song **Black Lives Matter**

Dax is a Canadian-Nigerian rapper, singer and songwriter who lives in the USA.

a) Before you listen **Look at the information about the singer. What songs do you know about social problems?**

b) **Find the song on the internet. Listen and read the lyrics below. Choose the statement that best describes the message of the song.**

A Black lives are more important than others.
B We should fight against the cops.
C We should all take action against racism.
D We all need to breathe.

c) **Listen again. Read the sentences below. True (T) or false (F)? Correct the false sentences.**

1 Everything is OK the way it is.
2 Skin colour shouldn't matter: We are all humans.
3 Everybody should work together to make life better.
4 The singer doesn't dream.
5 Small children care about skin colour.
6 Hate is something which we are born with.
7 Treat others well and they will treat you well too.

***MLK =** Martin Luther King Junior (1929–1968), an important person in the fight for Black rights in the 1960s, made a famous speech called 'I have a dream'.

...
I can't breathe, I can't breathe.
Ay, ya, I can't breathe.

Change is what we really need,
cut me open, cut you open,
red's the color every single human
being bleeds.
Let's come together, cops, citizens
and in between,
and rally for the rights of everybody
in humanity:
Black, blue, white, green, playing
for the same team.
I'm no MLK but, boy, that doesn't*
mean I can't dream.
Black Lives Matter shouldn't anger
you or make you scream.
All lives matter 'cause we aren't
treated equally.

Remember when we were kids and
didn't see color and when we
played in kindergarten and I called
you my brother.
Then we grew up and they taught
us we should hate on each other,
even though we one and the same
and we all came from our mothers.
I hope y'all understand hate is not a
trait, it was learned, man.
Equality is the quality we need
inside this earth, man.
Give and receive, it's the karma that
you earn, man.

d) **What do you think of the song? ☒ Which parts of the lyrics do you like best and why?**

I like the phrase ... because they are about change and hope / they show ... ▶ Wordbank 2, p. 200

6 Global goals Peace and justice

a) **Read about two sportspeople who fight for justice. How did/do they do this?**

Serena Williams

Serena Williams is one of the greatest tennis players of all time. She is also an activist and businesswoman who has always used her name and her money to support Black women and fight for justice. When Williams started playing tennis in the 1990s, there weren't many professional Black players. Williams has often experienced racist comments and behaviour, even today. However, she always speaks out and has become an example for many other young Black players. She says that technology, for example the use of phones to film racist events, has helped give Black people a voice.

Colin Kaepernick

Colin Kaepernick was a popular NFL football player for five years with the San Francisco 49ers. In the USA, every game starts with the national anthem and usually everyone stands to show respect. But 2016, Kaepernick knelt to protest against police racism and violence. Other athletes supported him, but Kaepernick also got a lot of hate. People said he didn't respect his country and sports events weren't the right place to protest. After Kaepernick left the 49ers in 2017, he was never able to get another job in the NFL: No teams wanted him, although he had been one of the best players. But his protest has become an important symbol in the fight for justice.

b) **Do you pay more attention to issues when famous people talk or write about them? Is it OK for famous people to protest at big events? Why (not)?**

My task

7 Fight for justice

a) Think **What's the best way to fight for justice? Look at the ideas in the box and decide what's the most effective. You can also add other ideas.**

b) Pair **Discuss your ideas with a partner and agree on your top three (1 = most effective).**

► More help, p. 80

c) Share **Discuss your ideas with the class.**

Our number 1 is ... because ...

Ideas

- doing role-plays against racism at school
- complaining to a school, shop or company
- having a protest in the street or in a school, shop or company
- signing an online petition
- writing a social media post or a letter
- uploading a video of discrimination

Digital quiz I can talk about justice.

Let the good times roll!

1 MEDIATION Mardi Gras

a) Read the article about Mardi Gras in New Orleans. When is it and why is it special?

New Orleans is **almost** ready for Mardi Gras which means 'Fat Tuesday' in French. Many countries celebrate Carnival, but nobody parties like New Orleans! It's an **extremely** big event and brings over a million people to the city each year: That's **not at all** easy to organize! The party season begins **quite** early in January, when people bake special cinnamon cakes called King Cakes and decorate them with yellow, green and purple icing. The person who finds the small plastic baby inside has to buy the next cake, so the food never stops. The main Mardi Gras celebration is in February and lasts five days. The city is full of music, costumes and **really** bright colours, including millions of **very** colourful necklaces which people throw at the parades. Does that sound fun to you? It's too wild for some people!

b) Write a short article about Mardi Gras in German for your school magazine. Use information from the article in a). You don't have to include every detail.

2 WORDS Adverbs of degree

Adverbs of degree change how strong an adjective is.

a) Look at the blue adverbs of degree in 1a). Write them in order of how strong they are, from least to most.

not at all, ...

b) The adverbs *fairly* and *pretty* have the same meaning as one of the blue adverbs in the text. Which is it?

Good to know

Americans usually use the word *pretty* instead of *fairly* or *quite* in informal speech, e.g. *pretty early*.

c) Complete sentences 1–4 with an adverb from a) to give your own opinion. Say why. WALK AROUND and talk to different partners about the sentences.

1 I find festivals ... fun because ...
2 Crowds are ... stressful to me because ...
3 Carnival is ... important in my area because ...
4 King Cake sounds ... delicious because ...

▸ More practice 7, p. 80 ▸ Language file 13, p. 188

▸ Workbook, p. 32

3 Listening Grandma's cooking

a) Before you listen **Look at the photos of New Orleans foods. Which do you think might be ...**

1 sweet 2 spicy 3 vegetarian 4 salty 5 crunchy 6 cold?

A

B

C

D

b) Listen to Troy, Kisha and their grandma and match the names of the dishes (1–4) to the photos (A–D) in a).

1 gumbo
2 po'boy
3 beignets
4 cornbread

c) Listen again and choose the correct ending (A–D).

1 Gumbo is
A Troy's favourite dish. B not at all spicy.
C great for vegetarians. D with sausages.

2 Po'boys are
A with rice. B extremely sweet.
C too spicy for Kisha.
D sometimes too bland for Kisha.

3 Grandma's beignets are
A too salty for Troy. B really soft. C covered with nuts. D very creamy.

4 Grandma's cornbread is
A not at all tasty. B a little sweet and salty. C bland. D too heavy.

Good to know

Po'boy is a short form of *poor boy*. The sandwiches got their name in 1929 from a New Orleans restaurant that belonged to two brothers. They gave free sandwiches to workers who were on strike. Every time a worker came into the restaurant for a free sandwich, one of the brothers shouted, 'Here comes another poor boy!' In the local accent, *poor boy* sounds like *po'boy*.

d) Tell a partner which food(s) in a) you would and wouldn't like to try and why.

I'd like to try ... / ... sounds delicious ... *I'm not sure about ... because ...*

► More practice 8, p. 80
► Workbook, p. 33

4 READING New Orleans – city of music

a) BEFORE YOU READ **Read each of the statements below. Do you agree or disagree? Talk to a partner partner and give more information.** ▶Wordbank 2, p. 200

1 Music is a big part of my life.
2 I play or would like to play a musical instrument.
3 I listen to music when I'm angry or sad.
4 I like lots of different kinds of music.

b) **Read Troy's article about Mardi Gras in New Orleans for a website for young tourists. Which two statements in a) are true for him?**

Mardi Gras starts tomorrow and I'm so excited because I'm going to play in the parade for the first time!

I've played the trumpet in my school band for three years now, but this year my teacher Mr Benoit says that I'm finally ready to join the older kids and play in the street. I can't wait! We've all practised really hard for months.

Of course, we play traditional New Orleans jazz in our band. It's not really my thing, but it's a big part of our culture and I enjoy playing with everyone else. And if you're a jazz fan, you'll love it! It's hard to get away from that kind of music in the city. Even when it's not Mardi Gras, we have small parades all year round for weddings, funerals and all kinds of events. Bands walk and play music in the street. You should check it out!

But don't forget all the other music that we have here. There's country music, rock music, hip-hop and the only music that I really like: funk! I listen to it every day when I'm chilling out in my room or doing homework. If you're visiting New Orleans, I can recommend walking around the French Quarter to hear all the street musicians or going to one of the hundreds of music clubs. Don't miss the parties on Bourbon Street where musicians make up songs together – it's a must-see!

Check out some of my New Orleans music clips and let me know what you think!

c) **Read sentences 1–6. True (T) or false (F)? Find the lines in the text that give you the information about each sentence. Correct the false sentences.**

1 Troy plays in the Mardi Gras parades every year.
2 Troy's instrument is the trumpet.
3 Troy likes the music that his band plays.
4 The small parades are only for happy events.
5 Troy mostly listens to music at home.
6 Troy doesn't recommend visiting Bourbon Street to hear music.

5 Listening & reading **Troy's music clips**

a) Before you listen **Which styles of music does Troy mention in his article?**

b) **Listen to the music clips (1–5) and match them to Troy's descriptions (A–E).**

A You'll hear a lot of hip-hop like this in music clubs. It has a strong beat from the drums and rapped lyrics.

B You get this kind of country music, bluegrass, a lot in the Southern states. It's sometimes quite slow, but it can be fast as well and there are always lots of violins and guitars.

C This is metal, a kind of rock music. It has lots of electric guitars and drums in it. And it's really loud and fast, so it feels angry.

D This song is called *Down by the Riverside* and it's a classic New Orleans song in the traditional jazz style. Every musician in the city can play it! It's upbeat and often has lots of trumpets.

E This is funk, my favourite kind of music. It often has electric guitars and keyboards. It really makes you want to move to the music.

c) **Tell a partner which of the five music clips you liked best and why. What other styles of music do you know?** ▸Wordbank 2, p. 200

I liked the ... song because the rhythm / melody is ... / the instruments are ... / it makes me feel ...

My task

6 Local recommendations

▸ Digital help

a) **Find the phrases that Troy uses to give recommendations in 4). Look at lines: 10–11, 15–16, 17, 19, 21, 22 and 23.**

b) You choose **Do task A or B.**

A **Write an article like Troy's in 4. Give recommendations for things to do, see and listen to and eat in your area. Is there a local festival you can recommend?** ▸ Skills file 12, p. 173

B **Make a short video with recommendations for things to do, see, listen to and eat in your area. Is there a local festival you can recommend?**

Use the phrases from 4 to help you give the recommendations. Give reasons. ▸ More help, p. 80

c) **Swap with a partner and check their work, then give feedback. Which recommendations do you like best?** ▸ Feedback phrases, p. 210

You used lots of different recommendation phrases. You gave interesting information about ...

Next time, you could use more adverbs of degree to improve your descriptions.

▸ Workbook, p. 34

Digital quiz

I can make recommendations.

Hurricane!

1 Before you read Extreme weather

a) Match pictures A–E to definitions 1–5 in the box.

Good to know

There are about twelve hurricanes every year in the USA, mostly in the South-East. Homes frequently lose power during storms because most power lines are above ground. In 2005, Hurricane Katrina hit New Orleans. Nearly 2,000 people died and thousands lost their homes.

A

tornado

B

thunder and lightning

C

hail(stones)

D

flood

E

hurricane

1 water covers area that is usually dry • **2** hard balls of ice from the sky • **3** a big storm with extremely strong winds • **4** a storm that moves in a circle • **5** bright lights and loud noises in the sky

b) Tell a partner what extreme weather you or people that you know have experienced. You can also talk about extreme weather that you have seen online or on the news.

▸ Wordbank 3, p. 201 ▸ Challenge 2, p. 81

2 Reading Where's Zahra?

Read the story about Hurricane Katrina. Say who Zahra is and why Tyler is looking for her.

It was very quiet. The sky was a strange green colour and black clouds were gathering.

'Are you ready, Tyler?' his dad asked. 'We'll only be at your aunt and uncle's tonight.'

'But what about our house, Dad? Will it be OK?' asked Tyler.

Hurricane Katrina was on its way and people in their part of New Orleans had got a warning that they should leave the area until the storm had passed.

'Our house will be fine,' said his dad. 'Don't worry, Tyler. While you're packing, I'm just going to see if Miss Elektra and Zahra need a ride.'

Miss Elektra was their neighbour. Her daughter Zahra was fourteen like Tyler and they had grown up together. Last year he had tried to kiss her, but Zahra had just laughed. 'Tyler, you're my favourite person ever, but you're like my brother!'

'All OK,' said his dad when he came back. 'Miss Elektra's sister is on her way and she'll be here soon. Let's go!'

At his aunt and uncle's house, Tyler lay in bed and listened to his heart. It was beating loudly. The weather report said that the house was outside the path of the hurricane, but he could hear thunder, heavy rain and wind blowing violently against the house. Suddenly his phone rang.

'Hey Tyler,' said his friend Darius. 'Crazy out there, right?'

'Yeah,' said Tyler. 'Good thing we left early. When did you leave?'

'Late,' said Darius. 'We had to pick up Mom from work first. But we weren't the last ones – your neighbours were still there.'

'What do you mean?' asked Tyler. He didn't understand. 'They left hours ago.'

'Well, the lights were on in their kitchen and I saw Zahra,' said Darius.

'Oh no ... Sorry, dude, I have to go,' said Tyler.

Tyler called Zahra's number. No answer.

'Come on,' said Tyler. 'Pick up!'

Still no answer. Tyler ran downstairs. His dad and his uncle were watching TV.

'Dad!' said Tyler. 'We have to go back, they're still there!'

'Hey, slow down,' said his Dad. 'Who are still where?'

Tyler explained. His dad looked worried, but he shook his head slowly.

'We can't go anywhere in this,' he said. 'I'm sorry, Tyler. Maybe the sheriff's office can help.'

After Tyler's dad had tried to get through to the sheriff's office in New Orleans, he checked the internet. 'The phone lines are down,' he said. 'And the power there is out too.'

Tyler couldn't sleep that night and watched the news on TV. The hurricane was a bad one. Thoughts went around and around his head. What if ...?

In the early morning, Tyler and his dad drove home in silence. The closer they got to New Orleans, the worse things looked. Trees and pieces of houses were everywhere and cars were on their sides. Many of the roads were

full of water from the floods. Tyler tried to breathe, but panic was rising inside him.

'Hey,' said his dad and stopped the car. 'It's OK, just breathe ... That's it.'

In their street, some of the new houses were fine, some had no roofs and some of the older ones were totally destroyed. Tyler breathed a sigh of relief – their house was OK. But the hurricane had taken off the roof of their neighbours' house – and the door was open.

'Zahra!' shouted Tyler. He and his dad ran into the house. Miss Elektra was sitting on the kitchen floor, holding her foot. She looked tired. 'I'm OK, but my foot is hurting a bit,' she said. 'My sister couldn't get through yesterday because of the floods, but she's on her way now. We're going to stay with her for some time. Could you go and find Zahra, please? She ran out after Popcorn and hasn't come back yet. I'm worried about her.' Popcorn was a very big dog with sad eyes. Zahra had found him in their yard one day, scared and hungry. She had adopted him and they'd been together since then.

Tyler and his dad ran into the street and called Zahra's and Popcorn's names. Nothing. 'Please let her be OK,' thought Tyler. They walked to the next block. And there suddenly were Zahra and Popcorn.

The dog barked happily when he saw his neighbours. Tyler threw his arms around Zahra. He was laughing and crying at the same time.

'It's OK, Tyler,' said Zahra. 'I was really scared when the roof came off, but we're all fine.'

'Happy to hear it,' said Tyler's dad. 'But I'm sure a lot of other people weren't so lucky. Let's tell your mom that you're safe and then check on our other neighbours. We all need to help each other now.'

3 Tyler's story

Read the story again and put the events in the correct order. *1C; 2 ...*

A Tyler gets a phone call from his friend Darius.
B Tyler and his dad find Zahra and Popcorn who are fine.
C Tyler and his dad leave their house to stay with family before the hurricane.
D Tyler sees that the roof of Zahra's house is gone.
E Tyler and his dad drive back home the next morning.
F Miss Elektra is hurt and Zahra and Popcorn aren't at their house.

4 Feelings and reactions

Complete the sentences about Tyler's feelings and reactions. You can use words from the box or your own ideas. There may be more than one possible answer.

confused • couldn't breathe • happy • panicked • relieved • scared • shocked • worried • ...

1 While they were packing to leave, Tyler was ...
2 When his friend called him, Tyler at first.
3 When he was in the car, he ...
4 When he saw his house, ...
5 When he saw Zahra's house, ...
6 When he found Zahra and Popcorn, ...

5 Freeze!

a) **Make groups. Choose a scene from the story. Describe what is happening or what has just happened and how the people feel. Look at 4 for help.**

Let's take the scene where Tyler and his dad are driving to ...

I think we should choose the scene where Tyler was really worried about ...

b) **Show your scene as a freeze-frame. Students from the other groups say what is happening or what has just happened.**

► More help, p. 81
► Workbook, p. 35

Digital quiz — I can talk about extreme weather experiences.

Storm chasers

1 An unusual job

BEFORE YOU WATCH Tell a partner what you think storm chasers do and why. Do you think it's a dangerous job?

2 VIEWING Reed and his team

a) Watch the video. Check your answers from 1 and name the different kinds of weather you see in the film. ▸ Skills file 10, p. 171

b) Read and copy sentences 1–8 into your exercise book. Watch the video again: What did Reed and his team do? Tick the things that happen. Then compare with a partner.

1 They follow a tornado.
2 They drive across Oklahoma.
3 They drive into the tornado.
4 Reed phones the local TV channel.
5 Reed live-streams the tornado.
6 Somebody in the team gets hurt.
7 The storm breaks part of the car.
8 They leave when it gets too dangerous.

c) Would you like to be a storm chaser? Why or why not?

3 LIFE SKILLS Protect yourself when you take risks

a) Talk about the questions 1–3.

1 Why do you think Reed and his team do this job?
2 What risks do they take?
3 How do they protect themselves?

▸ More help, p. 81

b) Tell your partner about a risk that you sometimes take or that you have taken in the past. Explain how you protect or protected yourself.

I ride my bike quite fast, but I wear a helmet and I watch carefully for cars.

Last year I went rock climbing, but I was with a guide and we used a rope.

Write a summary

1 Get a general idea

What's the main idea of the story on pages 64–66 about? If you don't remember, skim the story again.

► Skills file 11, p. 172

Remember
When you skim a text, you look at it quickly for the general ideas. Headings, photos and captions can also help you.

2 Take notes

a) Take notes on the key events in the story. You can look at 3 on p. 66 for help.

b) Compare your notes with a partner. Do you have similar notes?

3 Writing a summary

a) Read the summary of the first half of the story and compare it with your notes from 2a). Do you have the same or different information?

b) Answer the questions about the summary.

1. How long is the first half of the summary compared to the first half of the story (until line 70): a bit shorter or a lot shorter?
2. What tense is the summary in: past or present?
3. Does the summary add information that is not in the story?
4. Does the writer of the summary give their opinion?
5. Does the summary include whole sentences from the story or only the writer's own words?

A summary of 'Hurricane!'

The story 'Hurricane!' takes place in New Orleans during Hurricane Katrina 2005. The main characters are Tyler and his dad and their neighbours Zahra and her mum.

Tyler and his dad leave their house before Hurricane Katrina to stay with family outside New Orleans. Zahra and her mum plan to stay with an aunt.

However, late at night, Tyler gets a call from his friend and realizes that Zahra is still at home. He tells his dad, but the phone lines are down and power is out in New Orleans.

c) A summary needs an introduction. What information *(who, what, when, where, why)* does the introduction to the summary of 'Hurricane!' include? Find useful phrases.

d) A summary should be easy to read. What linking words in this summary make it flow?

e) Summarize the second half of the story (lines 71–116). Compare your version with the one on p. 81.

► Skills file 14, p. 175

Digital quiz — I can write a summary.

Write a review

Step 1: Think of a book, film or series

You are going to write a review of a book that you have read or of a film or series that you have seen. First brainstorm ideas.

In a **review** you tell the reader about a book, film or series and give your opinion. The review has two parts:
- a short summary
- your opinion or recommendation.

Step 2: Make notes and write a summary

a) What's the book, film or series about? Write an introduction. Use the phrases from 3c) on p. 68.

b) Make notes on the main events. Then use your notes to write the rest of your summary. Remember to use the present tense and add linking words.

▶ Study skills, p. 68
▶ Skills file 14, p. 175

Step 3: Give your opinion

A summary only includes facts. For your review, add a paragraph with your opinion. Write whether you recommend the book / film / ... and why or why not.

This is a fantastic / terrible ... book / film / series.
If you're a fantasy / romance / ... fan like me, you'll love it! / you should check it out!
I can recommend reading / watching ... It's a must-read / must-see!

▶ My task, p. 63

Step 4: Check your partner's review

Read your partner's review and check that:

- the summary has an introduction
- the summary isn't too long, but contains enough information to make you interested
- the summary is in the present tense and has linking words
- the review includes an opinion.

▶ Skills file 15, p. 176

Step 5: Give your partner feedback

Give feedback on the review and the language. You can use sticky notes or digital comments.

Your review was good and the story of the film sounded really exciting.

▶ Feedback phrases, p. 210

Digital quiz I can write a review.

1 LISTENING A rainy day in New Orleans

I can talk about the South-East of the USA.

a) **Listen to the conversation between Kisha, Troy and their aunt Mae. Put pictures A–F in the correct order. There's one extra picture.**

A

visit St Louis Cathedral

B

visit the Museum of Art

C

try beignets

D

go on a boat trip

E

ride a tram

F

enjoy some live music

b) **Listen again and complete the sentences. Write the missing word.**

1. The weather in New Orleans is often ...
2. There are many ... in the garden.
3. The seats on the tram are really ...
4. Hurricane Katrina nearly destroyed the ...
5. The French Quarter is always very ...
6. Mae doesn't usually eat in ... when she's in town.

c) SPEAKING **Tell your partner which two activities from a) you would like to do and why.**

2 Kisha's email to customer services

I can take a stand against racist behaviour.

a) LANGUAGE **Complete Kisha's email with the correct form of the past progressive.**

Dear Ms Benoit, I'm writing to complain about a racist experience at your store. While my friend and I ... (1 look) around, a security guard ... (2 follow) us. After we had tried on some clothes, the guard ... (3 wait) for us. He asked to see my bag, but he didn't ask to see my friend's bag – maybe because my friend is white? He ... (4 look) in my bag for a long time. I felt very embarrassed while this ... (5 happen) because a lot of people ... (6 stand) around and they ... (7 all stare) at me. Even though my bag was fine, he said he ... (8 still watch) me. I won't return to your store, and I'd like to know what you are doing to stop discrimination.
Yours, Kisha Freeman

b) WRITING **Imagine you're the store manager. Write an answer to Kisha's email.**

Dear Ms Freeman, ... I was very sorry to read about ... Discrimination is ... and we do not ... We are going to speak to ... We are also going to organize ... Best wishes, ...

Check

3 LANGUAGE Avery's text

I can talk about justice.

Avery is writing an introduction to the online school magazine, *Hear our voices*. Complete the text with the past perfect of the correct verbs in the box. There are two extra verbs.

go • hope • kill • know • live • organize • say • write

Hear our voices began in March 2012, one month after a man ... (1) Trayvon Martin. Trayvon ... (2) near our school, and some students ... (3) him or his family. The teachers at our school ... (4) some events to remember Trayvon, but we wanted more than that. Students were angry – and scared. They created an online space for people to share their experiences of discrimination. A few days after the website appeared, over a hundred students ... (5) comments. More than ten years later, the magazine is still a big part of our school. That's not something that we're happy about. Back then, the students ... (6) that people would hear our voices, and things would change, but we're still talking about racism.

4 Voices in the media: Beyoncé and Jay-Z

In 2020, singer/songwriter Beyoncé gave an online speech for university students. She thanked students for telling the world that 'Black Lives Matter.' She also spoke out against sexism and racism, and talked about the problems she has faced in the music industry. She told students that there wasn't enough diversity in the music industry, so she had started her own business to give more people a voice. Her speech has over one million views on YouTube. In the same year, rapper and producer Jay-Z (Beyoncé's husband) paid for pages of adverts in newspapers across the USA. On those pages, he asked people to remember George Floyd and shared a speech from Martin Luther King about speaking out against injustice.

a) READING **Read the text above and correct sentences 1–6.**

1 Beyoncé gave her speech at university.
2 She said that there is lots of diversity in the music industry.
3 More than ten million people have watched her speech.
4 Jay-Z paid for TV adverts.
5 He wrote a speech against injustice.
6 He wanted people to listen to George Floyd.

b) SPEAKING **Talk about Beyoncé and Jay-Z's ways of working for justice: How are they similar and how are they different? You can use the ideas in the box or your own ideas.**

The ideas are similar/different because ... • Beyoncé's / Jay-Z's idea is more / less ... • lots of people can hear / read / see the message • It's easy / expensive / free / ... to ... •

Check

5 Writing A winter holiday

I can make recommendations.

Read the text message from your American friend Zoe. Write back with <u>three</u> recommendations. Give reasons. You can use the sentence beginnings below or your own ideas.

Hey! I'm going to be in your area for a few days in December! Do you have any recommendations?
Zoe 🙂

Hi, Zoe! There are some great things to do in ...
You should check out ...
My favourite is ...
I can also recommend ...
If you're a fan of ..., you should ...
I hope you ...

6 Words Extreme weather

I can talk about extreme weather experiences.

Read the news updates (1–6). Complete the sentences with the correct word from the box. There's one extra word.

destruction • floods • hailstones • power • relief • risk • tornado

1 More than 3000 homes without ...
2 A ... is coming: Stay home!
3 ... turn city streets into rivers
4 Hurricane causes ... across the city
5 Big ... destroy roofs and windows
6 ... as storm passes

7 Mediation A research project

Your friend Amir is doing a presentation about extreme weather events across the world. Read the article below. Write an email to tell him the most important information in German.

Hi Amir, ich habe einen Artikel über die Auswirkungen des ... auf ... gelesen. Das ist ...

Hurricane Ian causes huge destruction on Sanibel Island

Sanibel is a small island and city in Florida with a population of around 6000 people. It's a popular tourist destination because it has many beautiful beaches and lots of different types of plants and animals. In September 2022, Hurricane Ian hit Sanibel. It was one of the worst hurricanes in Florida's history. It destroyed many things across the island – not only houses, businesses and buildings, but also trees and plants. The hurricane also destroyed an important road which connects the island to the rest of Florida. This meant that people couldn't drive to or from the island.

Check

8 STUDY SKILLS Tornado Team

I can write a summary.

'Leo, breakfast in two minutes!'
'OK,' called Leo, 'I'll be there after I've watched this video.'
'No, in two minutes!' called his mom, Tanya. Leo sighed and pressed 'pause' on the new *Tornado Team* video. They were so close to the storm that Harry P's hair was wet, and the car door had nearly broken. Awesome!
'So Mom, I've been thinking,' said Leo, eating his toast. 'Maybe I'll become a storm chaser. It looks like so much fun and I'd definitely have enough work here in Oklahoma!'
'OK – so you're telling me you're going to do something extremely dangerous lots of times. Well, I'm just letting you know that I don't love the idea! I want you to stay safe!
'Oh, come on, Mom! Those *Tornado Team* videos are really cool though, right?'
'Maybe a little,' smiled Tanya. 'Now, hurry up, I need to be at work in half an hour.'

A few days later, Leo was waiting for his mom at her auto repair shop when he saw an update on his phone. 'Tornado warning for Oklahoma – stay home!' He scrolled down. There was already a new post from *Tornado Team*: 'Oklahoma: WE'RE COMING!'

That afternoon, Leo and Tanya started preparing the house for the storm. Leo was putting some food onto the shelves of the safe room when he saw another post from

Harry P: 'Folks, we have car problems. ☹ Sorry, Oklahoma, no tornado for us!' Leo couldn't stop himself. He wrote a comment back to them: 'Hey guys, pretty sure my mom can help with this. She can repair anything!'
'Why are you smiling so much?' asked Tanya.

Half an hour later, a big car arrived in front of their house. 'Hey, Mom, they're here!' called Leo. 'Who is here?' asked Leo's mom, surprised. 'You'll see! I'll get your tools from the garage.'

The next day, there was relief all across the neighbourhood. The worst weather was over and their house was OK. Leo's phone pinged and he saw a message from his friend Ally: 'Have you seen this?' It was a link to a video of yesterday's storm. At the beginning of the video were the words 'Thanks to Leo and Tanya Diaz! We couldn't have done this without your help!'
'Mom!' called Leo, 'I need to show you something really cool!'

a) **Read the story. Complete the sentences.**

The story 'Tornado Team' is about a boy who ... It takes place in ...
The main characters are ...

b) **What are the main events in the story? Discuss with a partner.**

c) **Write a summary of the story. Use your sentences from a) and your ideas from b). The words and phrases in the box can help you.**

Leo watches ... • While he's waiting for ... • Then he sees ... • However, ... • Leo writes ... • After the storm has passed ...

Check

United

A magazine for young people across the USA

Find out about our new national holiday – Juneteenth[1]!

Juneteenth *by Kisha Freeman*

'Juneteenth' became a national holiday[2] in the USA in 2021. I'd like to tell you more about it.

For hundreds of years, enslaved[3] people worked in the USA for no money and had no rights. Slavery officially ended on different days in different states, first in the northern states, then in the South. Texas was the last state to end slavery. This happened on June 19th, 1865, and Black people have celebrated this date as 'Juneteenth' for many years. Some people call this day 'Freedom Day'.

Today people celebrate the day with music, parades, barbecues and other events. It is a day of happiness. I asked my grandma what Juneteenth means to her and she said, 'Respect. Respect and equal rights for everybody. Black is beautiful and we are proud to be Black.'

There's still a lot of racism in the USA, for example in neighborhoods, at work and in the police:

- Many police officers and judges[4] are unfairly hard on[5] Black people. Also, Black people often don't have the money to pay for a good lawyer. That is why in American prisons, there are five times more Black prisoners[6] than white prisoners, although only 12.4% of Americans are Black.
- Black Americans can't get good medical[7] care or they live in areas with more environmental[8] problem. As a result, they live shorter lives and have more health problems than white people.

That's why many Black activists use Juneteenth to protest for equal rights. **Black lives matter!**

Imagine you can create a new national holiday. What would it be and how would you celebrate it?

[1] **Juneteenth** *(von* June *und* nineteenth:*) der 19. Juni* [2] **holiday** *hier: der Feiertag* [3] **enslaved** *versklavt*
[4] **judge** *der Richter, die Richterin* [5] (to) **be hard on sb.** *hart zu jm. sein* [6] **prisoner** *der Häftling*
[7] **medical** *medizinisch* [8] **environmental** *Umwelt-*

Black history *by Troy Freeman*

Every February, Black History Month celebrates the lives of Black Americans. I have just watched a film about an amazing Black woman, Harriet Tubman, and would like to share information to her life and my film review with you.

Celebrate Black History Month with us!

Harriet Tubman was born into slavery around the year 1820 because her family was enslaved on a farm in Maryland. We don't know her exact birthday because white slaveholders[1] treated enslaved people like property[2] – it wasn't important to remember their birthdays. Harriet had to work hard and experienced a lot of violence from an early age on. In September 1849 she escaped slavery and headed north to Philadelphia, Pennsylvania. She joined a network of men and women called the Underground Railroad and helped other people to escape slavery too. She fought for the rights of Black people until she died in 1913.
Today, most Americans would like to see Harriet Tubman on a new twenty-dollar bill[3]! She would be the first African American on a US dollar bill, and the second woman. How amazing is that?

Harriet

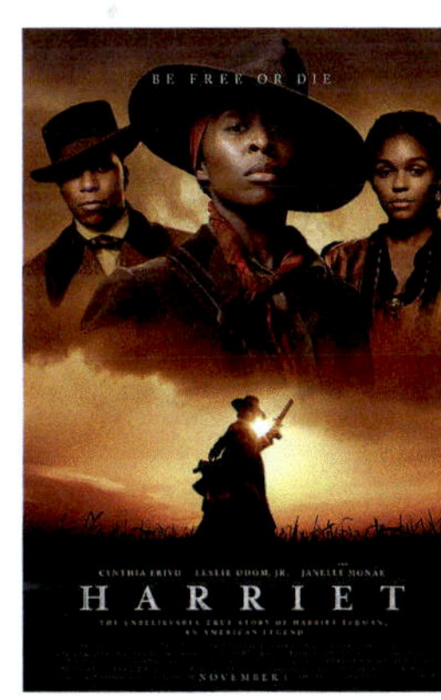

In this film we see Harriet Tubman's escape[4] from slavery and how her enslaver's son Gideon hunts her.
There's a scary scene where Harriet is on a bridge and Gideon, her enslaver's son, and his men come from both sides. Harriet climbs onto the top and says, 'I'm gonna be free or die.' Then she jumps into the river! Luckily, Harriet is fine and she walks 100 miles north to Philadelphia, where she can be free. She decides to help her family and other enslaved people and joins a network of men and women called the Underground Railroad[5]. Following the North Star and the river, they guide enslaved people to freedom in the northern states. It's very dangerous for Harriet, but she says, 'If I'm free, they should be too.'
This is an awesome film and I think Harriet Tubman was a very brave woman. I learned more about her life and about Black history.

★★★★★ I give this film five stars because it's really exciting and the actor Cynthia Erivo as Harriet is fantastic. Watch the movie (or the trailer on the internet)!

Who would you like to see on a Euro bill?

[1] **slaveholder** *der Sklavenhalter, die Sklavenhalterin* [2] **property** *der Besitz, das Eigentum* [3] **bill** *der Geldschein*
[4] **escape** *die Flucht* [5] **Underground Railroad** *die Untergrundbahn,* hier: *das Netzwerk aus geheimen Fluchtwegen*

Partner page

▸ Page 52

1 SPEAKING Kisha and Troy

a) **Partner B: Ask partner A about Troy's sister Kisha: her age and interests. Then read the information about Troy and answer partner A's questions.**

Troy Freeman, 14 (New Orleans)
I'm from New Orleans in the state of Louisiana. I like reading, especially sci-fi books, and fishing – I fish in the Mississippi with my dad. I also play the trumpet in the school band. I go to church with my sister and my parents on Sundays.

Diff bank

▸ Page 51

More practice 1 Atlanta: The place to be

Read the blog post below and answer the questions 1–5 in complete sentences.

1 What state is Atlanta the capital of?
2 Why can paddleboarding on the Chattahoochee River be dangerous?
3 What is *Dragon Con*?
4 What can visitors learn about at the cola brand's interactive museum?
5 What do you think the famous brand of cola from Atlanta is? What information in the text helped you? Use the internet to check your answer.

Atlanta is the capital of our state Georgia. And I think there's no better place in the country for teens! There's so much to do here. Check out my top three activities for teens in the city:

- Atlanta is famous for its malls and busy streets, but if you prefer a more peaceful day in nature, try paddleboarding on the beautiful **Chattahoochee River**. It's very clean: Atlanta gets 70% of its drinking water from the river – but watch out for alligators!
- If sci-fi and fantasy are more your thing, you can't miss **Dragon Con**. Every September, tens of thousands of cosplayers, writers, comic fans and even movie actors come to this amazing event.
- One of the world's biggest and most famous **cola** brands comes from Atlanta: You can visit its interactive museum to find out about the drink's history and its top-secret recipe, learn about the science behind it and try different types of cola from all over the world. How did this product become so important? Get answers here.

▸ Page 53

More help **5** LISTENING & SPEAKING **What happened next?**

b) Why was the security guard's behaviour racist? What do you think about Kisha's reaction? Think for a minute and then tell a partner your opinion. Give reasons.

I think In my opinion,	the security guard's behaviour was racist	because	he only asked … / he didn't … / he said …
	Kisha's reaction was good / great / …		it's important to complain / fight for … / protest / … everybody should know about experiences like these.

▸ Page 54

More practice 2 **Names are important**

a) Complete Maria and Kisha's conversation with the correct verbs from the box in the past progressive.

call • get • have • laugh • say • ~~teach~~ • try • use

Maria Our geography teacher was sick today, so another teacher *was teaching* **(1)** us. She … **(2)** trouble with the names of some of the kids.

Kisha … she … **(3)** their names wrong?

Maria Yeah, totally! I think she … **(4)** hard at first, but then she gave up. Some students thought it was funny and they … **(5)** but other students … **(6)** really mad because she … **(7)** wrong names all the time. She … **(8)** Amihan 'Annie' and Dequan 'Dec'. But she didn't do that with Liam or Amy.

Kisha That's not OK. Names are important!

b) Do you think names are important? Why or why not?

More practice 3 **What were you doing?**

Ask a partner what he or she was doing at certain times on certain days. Take turns and then find new partners. Make sure to use the past progressive!

What were you doing on Sunday at eight o'clock in the morning?

I was sleeping / eating breakfast / …

▸ Language file 9, p. 185

▸ Page 54

More help **8** My task **Your social media post**

b) **Write a social media post and explain what happened. Troy's post in 7 on p. 54 can help you.**

You won't believe what happened to **me / my friend / somebody I know / somebody on the news / ...**

... was/were	... on the bus/tram/underground/... in the street / corridor at school / in a supermarket / on the internet/...
Somebody in my class / at school / in my football club / on the street / ... A security guard A man / woman My trainer	... made a racist / rude / stupid / comment about ... ... called me / my friend a racist name. ... treated me / my friend differently to ... ... hit me / ... ... said / wrote something nasty about me that isn't true. ... said I wasn't good / clever / ... because I'm a girl / Black / ... ... said I was too slow / lazy / ... because I'm ...
I / My friend / ...	felt angry / sad / upset / ...
	asked other people for help / complained to / organized a protest / reported the person / spoke to them / wrote about it online / ...

▸ Page 56

More practice 4 **Ruby Bridges**

a) **Copy the timeline. Put the events (A–F) in the order that they happened in Ruby's life.**

E → ... → ... → ... → ... → ...

A Parents took their children out of the school.
B Ruby started at the new school.
C Ruby met president Obama.
D Ruby took an important test.
E A new law stopped segregation in schools.
F Ruby was alone at the school for a year.

b) **Who is the man in the photo? What was special about him?**

c) Words **Match the words from 1 on p. 56 to make phrases.**

1 start at	A a test
2 pass	B injustice
3 take	C a law
4 fight against	D Black rights
5 fight for	E a new school

▸ Page 57

More practice 5 A day in my life

a) **Think about things that you did yesterday and make notes.** *got up, ate breakfast, …*

b) **Until your teacher says 'stop', play a chain game in groups like this:**

A Yesterday, I got up at ten o'clock.
*B After I **had got up**, I ate breakfast.*
*C After I **had eaten** breakfast, …*

Use the past perfect for the action that happened first.

More practice 6 What had happened?

a) **Complete the sentences about you. Use adjectives from the box (or other adjectives) and the past perfect.**

1 Last week I was … because …
2 Last weekend I was … because …
3 Yesterday I was … because …
4 This morning I was … because …

angry • annoyed • bored • embarrassed • excited • happy • proud • relaxed • surprised • tired • upset • worried

▸ Language file 10, p. 186

b) **Take turns to read out a sentence to your partner.**

Last week I was upset because I had broken my phone screen. What about you?

Challenge 1 Going to a protest

a) **Kisha and Troy went to a Black Lives Matter (BLM) event with friends. Rewrite the sentences in the past perfect to describe events that happened before the protest march.**

1 The organizers asked the city to be allowed to have the event.
2 They invited speakers to talk to the protesters.
3 They spoke about the reasons for the BLM movement.
4 The crowd listened to the speakers.

b) **Complete the text with the simple past or the past perfect.**

1 The day before the event, the teens … (prepare) signs with powerful messages that … (support) the movement.
2 Kisha's friend Marie … (take part in) training on peaceful protests the week before the event. On the way to the event, she … (tell) her friends what she … (learn).
3 When they … (get to) the city centre, a large crowd … (already/arrive).
4 Some teens … (never / go to) a protest before, but they … (feel) it was important to be there.
5 The media … (already / report) on the protest before it … (start).
6 The organizers … (plan) the event for weeks, so everyone … (know) what to do.
7 Several people … (gave) speeches before the protest march … (begin).

▸ Page 59

More help 7 MY TASK **Fight for justice**

I think ... is useful	because	it's an easy way to protest / it gets attention on social media / it makes people understand how terrible racism is / it clearly shows what happened / you can do it at home / ...

▸ Page 60

More practice 7 **The French Quarter**

Write the sentences with the adverb of degree in the correct place.

1 **(really)** The French Quarter is a famous part of New Orleans. You can see its French history everywhere: in the food, the street names and the buildings. 2 **(very)** There are lots of cool things to do there! 3 **(really)** For example, there's always great music on Bourbon Street. 4 **(a bit)** But if you find that too loud, you can do something quieter. 5 **(very)** Why don't you go on a scary ghost tour? 6 **(quite)** Or you can visit the Jazz Museum – it's interesting! 7 **(extremely)** And don't forget the open-air French market, where you can try all sorts of delicious local food!

▸ Page 61

More practice 8 WORDS **Describing food**

a) **Match the words and phrases (1–5) to their opposites (A–E).**

1 soft • 2 tasty • 3 salty/savoury • 4 bland • 5 my favourite	A horrible • B something that I don't like at all • C hard • D spicy • E sweet

b) **In small groups, take turns to say a food. Everyone chooses a word or phrase from a) to describe it. How many foods can you agree on?**

▸ Page 63

More help 6 MY TASK **Local recommendations**

You should / You can / Why not /	check out / eat / go to / listen to / see / taste / try / visit / ...
You mustn't forget / Don't miss / One must-see is / You'll love	the beach / the castle / the festival / the street music / ...
I recommend	going to / seeing / trying / ...

▸ Page 64

Challenge 2 LISTENING **Hurricane Katrina**

Rescue team looking for victims

a) **Kisha did a presentation at school about Hurricane Katrina. Listen. True (T) or false (F)?**

1 Thousands of people got out of the city.
2 The people who stayed in the city were fine.
3 The government handled the situation well.
4 Many Black people never came back to New Orleans.

b) **Listen again and complete the statistics.**

1 ... of the city was underwater.
2 ... of people had to leave the city.
3 ... people had to stay in the city.
4 In 2022, only ... of the New Orleans population was Black.

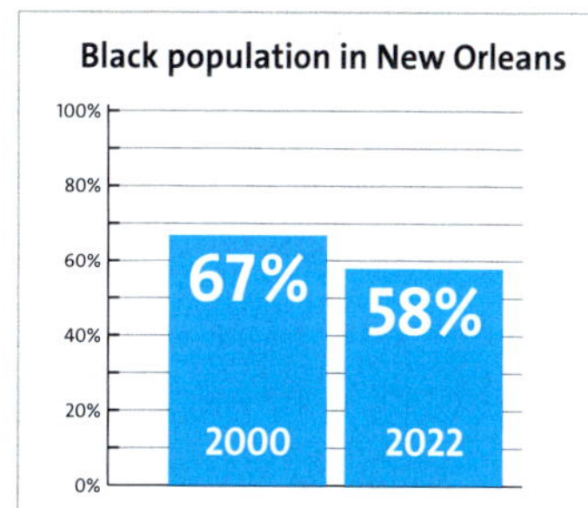

Datenquelle: https://www.data-centerresearch.org/ (siehe Quellenverzeichnis)

▸ Page 66

More help **5 Freeze!**

b) **Show your scene as a freeze-frame. Students from the other groups say what is happening or what has just happened.**

In this scene ..., Tyler is packing because ... / Tyler is lying in bed and ... / Tyler is talking to ... / Tyler and his dad are driving ... / have just found ... Maybe Tyler / his dad / Zahra feels ...

▸ Page 67

More help **3** LIFE SKILLS **Protect yourself when you take risks**

a) **Talk about the questions. You can use the ideas in the boxes.**

1 learn more about storms • like the danger • ...	2 drive into a dangerous situation • flying objects can hit them / break their car • ...	3 use high-tech equipment • leave when it gets too dangerous • ...

▸ Page 68

3 Writing a summary

e) They drive home early next morning and see how much the storm has destroyed. Their house is fine, but their neighbour's house has no roof. Zahra's mum is hurt and Zahra has left to find her dog. Luckily, Tyler and his dad quickly find her and there is a happy ending.

Unit 3

Texas: Teen life

C

The Texan flag

A

An armadillo

B

Over NASA's Space Center, Houston

D

English and Spanish signs at a school

E

A barbecue

1 LISTENING Wonderful Texas

a) BEFORE YOU LISTEN Look at pictures A–E. Say which of them you find most interesting and why.

b) Listen and match each part of the podcast (1–5) to the correct photo (A–E).

c) Copy the table below about Texas. Then listen again and add information to each column. Each column stands for one part of the podcast (1–5).

Other names	Animals	Food	Science and industry	Location
Lone Star State	...	...	...	...

▸ Map of the USA, inside back cover

Nach dieser Unit kann ich ...

- über Texas sprechen
- über das Leben in einer Kleinstadt sprechen
- das Schulleben in den USA beschreiben
- Jobs und Zukunftspläne besprechen
- mich zu Kleidung in der Schule äußern
- Kommunikationsstrategien anwenden

Unit task

- ein Interview führen

F

Downtown in Lufkin, Texas

G

A coffee shop

H

A street mural

I

Ruben on the family ranch

2 VIEWING With Ruben in Lufkin, Texas

a) BEFORE YOU WATCH **Look at pictures F–I. Say what you think the town is like. The words in the box can help you.**

boring • busy • cool • cosy • dangerous • exciting • pretty • quiet • rural • safe

b) **Watch the video and say if your ideas in a) were correct.**

c) **Watch again and answer the questions below.**

1 What are Ruben's favourite indoor and outdoor activities in Lufkin?
2 What does Ruben think of his town?
3 What would you like to do in Lufkin?
4 How is Lufkin different from your town/city?

▸ Workbook, p. 41

Digital quiz **I can talk about Texas.**

Small-town life

1 LISTENING At home in Fredericksburg

Jacob Schmidt, 15 Diego Perez, 14

a) BEFORE YOU LISTEN Look at the pictures of the boys and the sign of their hometown Fredericksburg, Texas. What do you notice about Jacob's family name and the sign?

b) Copy the table below and work in pairs. Listen to an interview with Jacob and Diego for a survey about Fredericksburg. Add the information for Jacob (partner A) and Diego (partner B).

Name	Where he lives in F.	Interests	What he likes about F.	What he doesn't like about F.
...	...	...	...	...

Good to know

In polite conversation, Texan children and teenagers use 'ma'am' when speaking to a woman and 'sir' when speaking to a man. Adults also often use these words when talking to an older person or a stranger.

c) Use your notes to tell your partner about Jacob or Diego. Say why their families moved to Texas.

▸ More practice 1, p. 111 ▸ Challenge 1, p. 111

2 SPEAKING Small towns: pros and cons

a) PLACEMAT Form groups of four. On your own, think what could be positive and negative about small towns (people, transport, activities, places, ...). Write your ideas in your part of the placemat.

Student 1	Student 2
Group result	
Student 4	Student 3

b) Turn the paper and read your group members' ideas.

c) Discuss the ideas as a group. Agree on the two most important positive and negative things. Write them in the middle of your placemat.

d) Tell the class your results. Do you have similar opinions about small towns?

Fredericksburg

3 Reading A town for young people

a) Before you read **Think about where you live. Can you get around easily?**

b) **Read the headings in the box. Then read the article and put headings A–F in the correct places (1–4). There are two extra headings.**

A Council reacts to survey • B Council not open to teens' ideas • C Attractive to teens • D Recent city council survey • E Fredericksburg popular with parents • F Suggestions and criticism

Teens love Fredericksburg! *by Jeff Schwartz*

1 How do young people feel about living in Fredericksburg? And what would they like to change? That's what a recent survey by the city council asked Fredericksburg teenagers.

2 On the one hand, seventy-six per cent of the young people that the council interviewed like living in Fredericksburg. With a population of about 10,000 people, the town offers enough places for young people to hang out, such as the ice-cream shop and the bowling alley, but still has a small-town feel. Most young people like living here because people know and like each other.

A place to hang out

Jacob M. (15) said: 'If I moved to a city, I would miss the friendly people here.'

3 On the other hand, a few young people say that there isn't much privacy in Fredericksburg. If everybody didn't know them, they would feel freer. Other teenagers would like to have better stores with longer opening hours. 'If there were lots of cool stores for teenagers, I wouldn't shop online,' said Diego P. (14). Some teens said it's hard to get around.
'We can't drive yet,' said Luna T. and Steve P., both 14. 'If the town offered a free bus service for teens, we'd see our friends more often.' Mila S. (16) pointed out that cars are bad for the planet. 'My car runs on gas, but if I had a lot of money, I'd buy an electric car.' The good news is that there are already lots of car-charging stations in our town.

4 As a result of the survey, the city council has decided to look more carefully at the transportation situation. It will also include a young person as an adviser on the city council.

c) **Match paragraphs 1–4 in b) to their function (A–D).**

A Conclusion • B Main part: point 2 • C Introduction • D Main part: point 1

▸ Skills file 11, p. 172 ▸ More practice 2, p. 112
▸ Workbook, p. 42

4 LOOKING AT LANGUAGE Conditional sentences type 2

a) Match the two clauses in the sentences from the article on p. 85. *1C, 2…*

1 If I **moved** to a city,
2 If everybody didn't **know** them,
3 If there **were** lots of cool stores for teenagers,
4 If there **was** a better bus service,
5 If I **had** a lot of money,

A we'**d see** our friends more often.
B I'**d buy** an electric car..
C I **would miss** the friendly people here.
D they **would feel** freer.
E I **wouldn't shop** online.

b) **Complete the rule about the two clauses in conditional sentences type 2.**

In conditional sentences type 2 we use
- an **if-clause** to talk about a condition which is possible, but unlikely and
- a **main clause** to talk about the result.

A conditional sentence has two parts:

if-clause (condition)	**main clause (result)**
If + verb in the …	… (or short form …) + infinitive
*If I **moved** to a city,*	*I **would miss** the friendly people here.*

► Language file 18, pp. 190–191

c) **What about you? Complete the sentence in three different ways. Then tell a partner. Do you both have similar ideas?**

If I had a lot of money, I would …

buy • change • give • go to • have • subscribe to • …

► More practice 3, p. 112

5 The town's summer barbecue

Complete the conversation with the correct form of the verb.

Jacob It's the Fredericksburg summer barbecue next Sunday. You're all going to go, aren't you?
Diego We'll be in Austin at Grandpa's. But if we *were* (1 be) in town, we'd definitely go.
Jacob Too bad! Maybe if you … (2 ask) your parents again, they'd let you stay in town. You could sleep at my house.
Diego Thanks, but it's my grandpa's 60th birthday on Saturday. If I … (3 stay) here, he would not be happy.
Jacob I know, but if you … (4 come) back Sunday afternoon, you'd make it. If you … (5 explain) to your parents, they'd probably agree.
Diego I'm not so sure about that, but I'll try. If I … (6 take) the bus to the barbecue, we could meet there. If I … (7 miss) the summer barbecue, I'd miss the town's best summer event!

► Challenge 2, p. 112

6 What would you do?

a) **Partner B: Look at p. 110.**
Partner A: Ask your partner the questions below.

1 If you could live anywhere in the world, where would you live?
2 If you could travel in time, where would you go?
3 If you lived on a desert island, what would you miss about your area?
4 If your town had no electricity for one week, what would you do?
5 If you were an architect, what building would you design?

b) **Partner A: Answer partner B's questions. ☒ Give reasons.**

If I was an animal, I'd be a ... (because ...).

c) **Tell the class one interesting thing about your partner.**

My task

7 WRITING Where we live

► Digital help

a) **You're going to write an article for your school magazine about the place where you live. With your class, brainstorm what's positive and negative for teenagers. Take notes of your classmates' comments for your article.**

b) **Organize your notes:**

- **introduction:** paragraph 1
- **main part:** paragraphs 2 and 3 with pros and cons of your area; suggestion for at least one change
- **conclusion:** paragraph 4.

c) **Use your notes and some of your classmates' comments to write your article. The article on p. 85 can help you.**

What do teenagers think about ...?
One good thing about my town is ...
Felix S. (14) says '...'
On the one hand / On the other hand, ...

Think of a good headline and an interesting introduction for your article. You can also add headings to the paragraphs.

► Skills file 12, p. 173

► More help, p. 113

d) **Swap articles with a partner and give each other feedback:**

- Does your partner's article have an introduction, a main part and a conclusion?
- Does it have a good headline and an interesting introduction?
- Say what you liked about the article.

► Feedback phrases, p. 210

► Workbook, pp. 43–44

Digital quiz

I can talk and write about small-town life.

School life

1 Reading A German exchange student

a) Before you read **For his school newspaper, Diego has interviewed German exchange student Alicja. Look at the photos. Describe them and say what you think is happening.**

▶ Skills file 7, p. 168

b) **Read the interview and check your ideas from a).**

Alicja thinks our school is awesome!

Diego Hi, Alicja! You're in ninth grade – a first-year student or a 'freshman' – and you're here on an exchange from Germany. How is it?

Alicja The school is awesome! Everyone is so friendly. And there are school buses!

Diego Glad you like it. What about the school? You said earlier that you think there is a lot of security.

Alicja Yes. I knew people can carry guns in the USA, but I didn't know there are security checkpoints in schools, like at the airport.

Diego Yeah, it's a bit scary, isn't it? But nineteen kids and two teachers died in a Texas school shooting. So we have more security now.

Alicja I heard about that. How horrible. I'm sorry.

Diego What are your other impressions of the school?

Alicja The cafeteria food isn't great, but it's good that you can buy lunch here. And that thing where students promise to respect the American flag every day in first period – that was new for me.

Diego The Pledge of Allegiance? Yeah, but if you don't want to do it, your parents can write a note.

Alicja Ah, OK. What's really different here is that I'm not with the same kids all day. In Germany, we stay with our class for almost every subject. And we have a class teacher.

Diego A class teacher? We only have those in elementary school.

Alicja In Germany we have them in high school too. What else? I think the school day is long – from 8.15 a.m. to 3.50 p.m., but I have some long school days in Germany too. I love the sports and clubs after school, but then I have lots of homework when I get back. It makes me so tired sometimes!

Diego Yeah, it does, doesn't it?

2 Words School words and phrases

a) **Choose words from the interview on p. 88 for explanations 1–6.**

1 a school year (or a mark)
2 a student in the first year of high school or college
3 where you eat lunch
4 a lesson
5 a promise to respect the USA
6 school for lower grades (till 5th grade)

b) **Use the interview on p. 88 to make a table with differences between American and German schools.**

Category	USA	Germany
1 *school buses*	...	...

c) **Discuss differences between Diego's school and your school. Use your answers to a) and your notes from b).**

3 Song Fifteen

a) Before you listen **Think about your life now. With a partner, talk about what people and things are important when you're a teenager and what challenges there are.**

Country and pop musician **Taylor Swift** was born in 1989. She got her first record deal when she was 15. Like many of her songs, 'Fifteen' is about her own life, including her best friend from school, Abigail, who is also in the video.

b) **Alicja listens to the song 'Fifteen'. Find it on the internet. Listen and say what it's about. Choose the correct topics and compare with a partner.**

being young • boys and girls • bullying • friends • love • problems with parents • school

c) **Listen again. Choose the correct answers. Then check with the lyrics on p. 113.**

1 On her first day at school, Taylor feels nervous / confident / angry.
2 Taylor is in the first / second / third year of high school.
3 At 15, when somebody tells you they love you, you believe / thank / don't believe them.
4 Abigail and Taylor love school / are good students / want to leave school.
5 Taylor's first date is with Abigail / goes well / doesn't go well.
6 At 15, Taylor knows / doesn't know / doesn't believe that she will do more important things than dating this guy.

d) **Describe the music of the song and say how it makes you feel.**

It's catchy / sad / slow / upbeat / ...   It makes me feel that 15 is a great age / ...

▸ Wordbank 2, p. 200
▸ Workbook, p. 45

4 MEDIATION Time for junior prom!

a) Alicja is on the phone to her sister Marta. Oscar, Alicja's date to junior prom, is listening and asking questions. In the pauses, take notes in English on:

1 who usually goes to prom
2 who students go with
3 promposals
4 what students wear to prom

b) Listen again. In the pauses, tell a partner in English how Alicja explains the topics in a) to Oscar. Use your notes to help you.

▸ Skills file 16, p. 177

5 LISTENING At prom

a) BEFORE YOU LISTEN Look at the photos on this page. Describe the clothes that Alicja, Oscar and the students in 4 are wearing. Say if you like them or not.

b) Alicja tells Jacob and Diego about prom. Listen and say what the best thing was for her.

c) Listen again. True (T) or false (F)? Correct the false sentences.

1 Alicja and Oscar went alone.
2 They travelled to prom in a limo.
3 The prom theme was 'red carpet'.
4 The prom princess was the captain of the soccer team.
5 Diego is going to interview the prom princess.
6 The prom prince was no surprise.

REVISION The going to-future: ▸ Language file 14, p. 188 ▸ More practice 4, p. 114

d) Your class is going to have a prom at your school. In pairs, decide on a prom theme and what you're going to wear. Then discuss ideas with the class.

How about ... as a prom theme? / We could wear ...
Our prom theme is going to be ... / We're going to wear ...

▸ Workbook, p. 46

6 Reading **Thank you!**

a) Before you read **You went abroad for a year and want to thank your host parents, brothers and sisters. What would you thank them for? Collect ideas.**

b) **Read the letter and compare it with your ideas in a).**

Dear host family

I would like to thank you for letting me stay with you this year. I had an amazing time in America because of you! You made me feel like part of your family and that meant the world to me.
I loved attending an American high school. One of the best parts was going to prom. It was like a dream for me. I'll always remember that special night.
Thank you again for everything. I hope we can keep in touch. If you visit Germany, you're welcome to stay with my family!

Love
Alicja

c) **Read the letter again and find useful phrases for thank-you letters.**

I would like to thank you for ...

d) **In how many languages can your class say thank you?**

My task

7 Writing **My thank-you letter**

▸ Digital help

a) **You're going to write a letter to a person who helped you. Think of at least two ideas and make notes: What would you like to thank them for?**

fix my bike / ...

b) **Write your letter. The phrases from 6c) can help you.** ▸ Skills file 13, p. 174

c) **Swap your letters with a partner. Give your partner feedback:**

- Did you partner's letter have a greeting at the beginning and end?
- Did your partner thank his or her friend for at least two things?
- Did your partner use some of the useful phrases from 6c)?

▸ Feedback phrases, p. 210

d) **Correct and rewrite your letter. Give it to the person that you would like to thank.**

▸ Workbook, pp. 47–48

Digital quiz **I can describe school life in the USA.**

Thinking about the future

1 LISTENING After graduation

Good to know

In the USA, it's expensive to go to college / university. The tuition (the money that you pay for the lessons) and fees (the money that you pay e.g. for activities and healthcare) for a normal public college are about $26,000 (€24.000) a year and can be $56,000 (€52.000) for a private college. In addition, students must buy expensive books and most live at the college and pay for a room and food. US universities offer scholarships to students who are excellent at sports or don't have a lot of money. Most students stay in college for four years.

a) BEFORE YOU LISTEN **Stand on a line of agreement about your future after you graduate. One end of the line means 'I know exactly what I want to do' and the other end means 'I don't know at all'. Then talk to your neighbour about your position.**

b) **Listen to the conversation. Where should Jacob and Diego stand on the line in a)?**

c) **Read the sentences below. Then listen again and decide whether each sentence is about Jacob or Diego.**

1 He wants to live in a city.
2 He has a plan for how he'll pay for college.
3 He wants to have his own business.
4 He can see disadvantages of going to college.
5 He is worried he won't have enough money for fun activities.
6 He wants to save some money to buy something special.

Jacob

Diego

REVISION The will-future: ► Language file 16, p. 189 ► More practice 5, p. 114 ► Challenge 3, p. 115

2 SPEAKING My options

a) **Look at the different options in the box of things that you could do in the future. Check that you know what they mean. Then choose the two things you would most like to do and the two things you wouldn't like to do at all.**

b) **Compare with a partner. What's the same and what's different? ☒ Give reasons for your choices.**

We both want to ... / I also want to ...
Neither of us want to ... / I don't want to ... either.
I'd like to ..., but you wouldn't like that. /
You'd like to ..., but I wouldn't like that.

- do an apprenticeship
- do volunteer work
- get a job
- go to university
- go to a vocational school
- join the army
- live abroad
- travel

► Workbook, p. 49

3 Reading Finding a job

a) Before you read As a class, brainstorm weekend or summer jobs that young people in your area can do to earn money.

b) Jacob and Diego are looking at job adverts. Form groups of four.
Partner A: Read advert A. Tell the group the main points: what, when, how much.
Partners B, C and D: Look at p. 110.

A

Are you strong and hard-working and looking for a Saturday job? We're looking for a reliable person (13+) to help clean out the stables each weekend at our farm.

FARM HELP WANTED

We can offer $8 an hour, plus one free riding lesson every week.
If you're happy to be out on the farm, rain or shine, call us today.

c) Read the speech bubbles. As a group, decide which job would be best for each of them and why.

I'd like to work outside – I don't want to be indoors all day! I need regular hours so I can save some money every week. I'm free on the weekends.

I don't mind working with kids because I look after my little sister quite often, but I don't really like animals. I'm often busy so I don't want to work every day. I'd like a flexible job.

d) Tell your group which of the four jobs you would like best and why. ► More practice 6, p. 115

4 Asking about a summer job

a) Listening Jacob is contacting an employer from 3 about the job that he is interested in. Listen to the conversation and say which job Jacob is applying for.

b) Read phrases 1–8 from the conversation and listen again. Copy and complete the phrases.

1 I'm ... farm help on Saturdays.
2 Can I ask ...?
3 We pay ... work.
4 ... I start?
5 Sounds ...
6 What time ...?
7 I'll be there ...
8 ... to meeting you in person.

c) For each phrase, write the number from b) and 'A' for applicant or 'E' for employer.

d) Speaking Use the phrases from b) to act out the conversation with a partner. Swap roles.

5 READING A message about a summer job

a) Diego has written a text about the job he is interested in. Read the message.

► More help, p. 115

b) Talk about what's good about Diego's text and what he should change.

c) Rewrite Diego's text, using complete words and sentences from 4 or your own ideas. Leave out the emojis.

d) Imagine you're the parent who is looking for a babysitter. Write an answer to the corrected message from Diego.

Hey!! 😊 Saw ur ad 4 a babysitter. 🍼 👶 I ❤️ kids n I'm rlly interested! Can start any time. 🕐 Lmk when works 4 u to meet IRL! Thx! 🙏

When you write to a future employer, you shouldn't be too informal, even in a text for a summer job. Using correct spelling and grammar makes you seem reliable.

6 SPEAKING & WRITING Applying for a job

a) Contact the employer of the job you picked in 3d) on p. 93. Write an email (partner B) or a text (partner C) or make notes for a conversation (partners A and D). Use words and phrases from tasks 4 and 5 on pages 93 and 94 or your own ideas.

b) Ask a partner to read your message or to role-play your conversation with you.

c) Listen to your partner's feedback. Correct your message or repeat the role-play.

► Feedback phrases, p. 210

My task

7 Hello, future me!

► Digital help

a) Make notes about what you think you'll do in five or ten years. Think about:
• family • hobbies • home • job • school • work.

► More help, p. 115 ► Wordbank 4, p. 202

b) YOU CHOOSE Do task A or B.

A Use your notes to record a video time capsule. Talk to your future you and say what your predictions are. Name the video with the date in the future. Watch it in five or ten years and check if you were right.

B Write a message to your future you about your predictions. There are websites that will send you the email in five or ten years.

Hello, future me! I think that in five / ten years, I'll be rich / …

► Workbook, p. 50

Digital quiz I can talk about jobs and future plans.

Background file

1 Reading Driving in the USA

a) Before you read **Talk about the pros and cons of cars as a form of transportation.**

b) **Read the text.**

Freedom, adventure, fun: Cars are an important part of the American way of life. There are practical reasons for this: The USA is huge and many areas do not have good public transportation. If you want to go shopping, get to work or visit friends and family, driving may be your only option.

However, driving is becoming less popular with teens. Ride-sharing services that you use with an app make it faster, easier and cheaper to get to places without your own car. Teens today often hang out with their friends online, which means that they don't need to meet in person. In order to reduce accidents by teenagers, getting a driver's license has also become more difficult. The percentage of teenagers aged 16–19 with a driver's license went from 64% in 1995 to less than 40% in 2021.

Most US schools offer driver's ed courses. In many states, your parents are allowed to teach you. You have to take a written test and a road test. Each US state sets its own driving age, but in general it is lower than in Germany. States with a lot of countryside usually have lower driving ages than states with many big cities. In some states, you can learn to drive at 14 and get a provisional driver's license at 15. 'Provisional' means that there are rules about the passengers in the car and the hours when you're allowed to drive.

Like in Germany, traffic drives on the right in the USA. While many rules are the same, there are a few important differences.

- US road signs often have words (e.g. 'No stopping') in addition to symbols.
- Signs are given only in miles.
- Highway speed limits are generally lower. The average is about 70 miles (113 km) per hour. The Texas State Highway 130 has the highest speed limit in the country: 85 miles (137 km) per hour.
- In many places you're allowed to turn right carefully at a red light.
- Roundabouts are uncommon in many places.

c) **Match each sign (A–F) with its meaning (1–6).**

1 You can't drive into here.
2 You can only drive in this direction here.
3 You may not drive faster than fifty-five miles per hour here.
4 A road is closed: You have to use this road instead.
5 There are train tracks ahead.
6 If you park your car here, the city will move it.

A 

B 

C 

D 

E 

F 

Moxie by Jennifer Mathieu

1 School clothes

a) Before you read **Discuss the following questions with a partner.**

1. What is or isn't OK to wear at your school? Use the box and your own ideas.
2. Are the rules the same for everyone?
3. Do you think the rules about clothes are fair at your school? Why or why not?

crop tops • football shirts • rude T-shirts • shorts • short skirts or dresses

Good to know

'Bullshit' is a swear word used to say that something is unfair, untrue or annoying. Most American schools don't allow students to use this or other swear words.

b) **Read a short part of the novel *Moxie* and find out**
- what happens to some of the students in the story
- how this school treats boys and girls.

Vivian (the narrator) and her friends Claudia, Lucy and Sara go to East Rockport High School in a small town in Texas. Lucy has recently moved there from Houston, a big city. Claudia has just told Vivian about a boy called Jason, who is wearing a rude T-shirt.

We slide into American history and take our seats at the back. As the bell rings Mrs Robbins announces a quiz on our reading from last night, and all of us groan. [...] As she starts giving out the papers, there's a knock on the door, but the person doesn't wait for Mrs Robbins. The door opens and Mr Shelly, one of Mr Wilson's assistant principals, comes in. [...]

'Doing a dress-code check, Mrs Robbins,' Mr Shelly barks, letting his eyes run over us. Mrs Robbins sighs and waits, then jumps back a bit like the rest of us when he says, 'Lady in the back. Is that you, Jana Sykes? Stand up, dear.' [...]

Of course we all turn and look, and Jana Sykes stands up uncertainly, shrugging her shoulders. As it turns out, her shoulders are the problem.

'Jana, those straps to your shirt are pretty thin, aren't they?' [...]

'Um, they're ... straps?' Jana says. [...]

'Jana, come with me. We need to get you changed.'

'They're about to take a quiz,' Mrs Robbins says.

'I'll have her back in a minute,' Mr Shelly answers. [...] But Jana never does come back.

All through our morning classes, girls get pulled out by administrators and counselors. Sometimes it's Mr Shelly who does it and sometimes it's other assistant principals. In my second period math class, Jasmine Stewart and Kelly Chen get pulled out for their pants being too tight although they don't seem extra tight to me.

In fourth period chemistry, Carly Sanders gets told her shirt is inappropriate. It's just a T-shirt with a scoop neck. [...]

I look down at my boring jeans and plain gray T-shirt. Each time an administrator called out a girl she had to stand up like some doll on display as the administrator scanned her carefully. When Kelly Chen had to stand in math class, her cheeks turned pink so quickly that I felt myself going red out of sympathy. I'd rather die than have the whole class's eyes on me analyzing my clothes and body. [...]

After the bell rings, Lucy and I go to the cafeteria to meet up with Claudia and the other girls. Lucy is still talking about the dress-code checks.

'This whole thing is just so gross and sexist,' she says. [...] 'I mean, it's totally random. These girls have to stand up and allow themselves to be looked at and have this ... like ... public *shaming*.' She spits out the last word.
'I know, it's gross,' I answer, waving to Claudia who is waiting for us near the entrance to the cafeteria.
'So this has happened before?' Lucy asks.
'Yeah, several times last year. Whenever the administration decides we're breaking the rules with our clothes or whatever.'
'But Jason whatever-his-name-is is allowed to wear rude T-shirts every day of the week, yeah?'
I don't have to answer because she already knows what I would say.
Claudia joins us at the door [...]. 'Y'all, Sara is really upset.'
'Why?' I ask.
'Just now in French class,' Claudia explains. 'Mr Klein came in and took her away to make her change her top.' [...]
Just then we spot Sara coming toward us, dressed in an ugly East Rockport gym shirt that's much too big. There are grass and dirt stains as old as the school in the orange material.
'Hey,' Sara says, sitting down. Her voice is soft, almost a whisper. Nobody knows what to say. Sara puts her paper bag lunch on the table, opens it, and pulls out a carton of chocolate milk. Then a shaky breath slips through her lips and she's about to cry.
'Sorry,' she says. 'I had to change. Mr Klein was so rude about it. He accused me of wearing an outfit that could distract the boys.' She can't stop herself from crying now.

Meg, Kaitlyn, Claudia and I begin a chorus of 'I'm sorrys', and Meg reaches over to squeeze Sara's shoulders. But Lucy just slams her hands down on the cafeteria table so loudly we jump.
'This is bullshit,' she says, and none of us answer. We just stare at Lucy as Sara wipes her eyes [...]. 'I mean it,' Lucy continues. 'It is.

Making girls change their behavior and their appearance because boys are supposedly unable to control themselves? That is one of the oldest tricks in the book.' She falls back against her chair as if she's tired. The other girls are staring at her, almost a little nervous, but I'm listening carefully to every word. Lucy's little speech sounded like it could have come out of one of my mom's zines. It's so exciting.

'At my old school in Houston, the administration never could have gotten away with this without a fight,' she continues. 'The girls […] would have found some way to fight back.'

'I know, Lucy, but this isn't Houston,' Claudia answers, and there's something in her voice. Annoyance, maybe? Frustration?

'Trust me, I know this place isn't Houston,' Lucy answers.

▸ Quellenverzeichnis, p. 000

2 Characters in the story

Read the story again and write which character best fits each sentence.

1. This person has the first dress-code check.
2. This person doesn't think the clothes look inappropriate.
3. This person is embarrassed by the idea of having a dress-code check.
4. This person has to wear horrible clothes.
5. This person is the angriest about the situation.

3 LIFE SKILLS Treat people fairly

a) **In the story, Vivian creates an anonymous magazine to fight sexism at her school. Look at the picture below and say what she asks students to do. What do you think about her idea? Discuss with a partner.**

b) **In small groups, write a list of clothes rules for Vivian's school that are fair to all students and help everyone to feel comfortable and included.**

Boys / Girls / All students should / can (not) wear …
Dresses / Shorts / Skirts / T-shirts should (not) be / must (not) have …

▸ Workbook, p. 51

Digital quiz — I can talk about clothes at school.

High Tech High School

1 Imagine

BEFORE YOU WATCH **Look at the title of the video and the photos. What do you think could be different about this school? Discuss with your partner.**

I think students at the school ...
Maybe this school has ...

2 VIEWING A different type of school

a) **Watch the video and choose the best description of High Tech High School (A, B or C). Did you guess correctly in 1?**

A Students use technology all the time to help them learn.
B Students can choose what they learn at school.
C The students do all their exams online.

b) **Watch the video again. True (T) or false (F)? Correct the false sentences.**

1 Students at this school use textbooks in their lessons.
2 The teachers are there to help, but not to lead the lessons.
3 Some students in the video are working on a science project.
4 The students are worried about being ready in time.
5 The students get good grades for their projects.

c) **Make a list of differences between your school and High Tech High School. Use the ideas in the box.**

d) **Write at least four sentences about what you like and don't like about High Tech High and compare with a partner.**

building • exams • grades • homework • lessons • school subjects

3 GLOBAL GOALS Quality education

a) **Put these features of a good school in order of how important they are to you. Is anything missing?**

b) **In small groups, make notes about your dream school and present it to the class. Vote for the best school.**

- everyone equal
- teachers care about students
- no bullying
- lots of clubs
- interesting lessons
- latest learning technology

Communicate better

1 Listen and show respect

a) You're going to tell a partner what you think about school. Make notes on your favourite subjects, homework, clothes at school, phone rules, ...

b) Read the tips on how to listen. Work in groups of three and talk about yourselves. One person talks and one person listens. The third person watches and uses the box as a checklist. Then swap roles.

Go on. *Really?* *Right.*

That's interesting.

When you listen
- Sit up straight.
- Make eye contact.
- Look friendly and interested.
- Use encouraging words.
- Focus on what the speaker is saying, not on what you want to say.
- Be patient and don't interrupt.

2 Ask questions to find out more

a) With a partner, think of questions you can ask after the yes/no questions (1–4).

1 Do you eat in the school canteen?
1 Do you like school sports?
3 Do you walk to school?
4 Do you usually go home after school?

b) Take turns to ask and answer the questions in a).

3 Make sure you understand

a) If you haven't understood, you can ask and check. Look at the phrases in the green speech bubble.

b) Work in pairs. One of you is an American exchange student and the other a German student.
German student: Explain the German school system, the types of school, the school day, security, ...
American student: Use a phrase from the green speech bubble to check you understood correctly. Then swap roles.

In Germany there are different types of high school.

I'm not sure I understood / got that.
Do you mean ...?
So you mean ...?
Tell me more about ...

► Skills file 5, p. 165

Digital quiz I can use strategies to communicate better.

Do an interview about school

Step 1: Choose roles

What are advantages and disadvantages of the German and the American school system? You're going to do an interview for the school newspaper to find answers to this question.
Work in pairs:
Partner A: American exchange student
Partner B: Interviewer.

Step 2: Make role cards

Partner B: Look at the role card below. **Partner A:** Look at p. 111.
Prepare the role card for your role and make notes.

Partner B: Interviewer
1. Say hello and introduce the topic and the student.
2. Ask questions about school life in the USA: the school day • transport to school • a dress code • special celebrations in the school year.
3. Ask what the American student thinks of the German school system.
4. Sum up the interview and thank the student.

Step 3: Practise your role

a) All American students (A) meet in one group, all interviewers (B) meet in another group. Help each other with information about the topics on your role cards. ▶ Study skills 2 + 3, p. 100

b) Study your role alone and practise what you can say. Check how to pronounce words and prepare useful phrases.

Step 4: Do the interview

a) Present your interview to another pair. Listen and ask questions. ▶ Study skills 1 + 2, p. 100

b) Give the other pair feedback on their interview.

- Did the interviewer ask interesting questions?
- Did the American student answer the questions with interesting information?
- Did the audience pay attention?

▶ Feedback phrases, p. 210

Digital quiz I can do an interview.

1 Listening Tessa's Texas

I can talk about Texas.

a) Listen to a new episode of Tessa's podcast about Texas. Choose the best title (A–C) for this episode.

A Comments about the show

B Your questions answered

C 1000 followers!

b) Copy and complete the table. Write short answers.

Name	From	Wants to know more about ...	Tessa's answer (one fact)
Lucy	...	...	
Salim	...	...	
James	...		

c) Listen again and fill in any missing details.

d) Speaking What do you already know about Texas? What would you like to know more about? Tell your partner.

2 If we moved to Wimberley, Texas

I can talk and write about small-town life.

a) Language Read Aaron's blog. Complete the conditional sentences type 2 with the correct form of the verb in brackets.

Hi, guys, I've just come home after a weekend visiting my cousins. They live in a small town called Wimberley. It's a very friendly place with nice little shops and cafes and lots of great places to go swimming and hiking, but only about 3,000 people live there – so it's not like Houston! I keep thinking how different my life would be if we ... (1 move) there.

If I ... (2 go) to school in Wimberley, I'd soon know most of the kids in town. And if I ... (3 know) a lot of people, I'd feel pretty safe. But it could also be boring! If I ... (4 get) bored, I'd go swimming and hiking. But if I ... (5 need) a job, it would be pretty hard to find one in town.

b) Writing What would your life be like if you moved to a small town like Wimberley? Write a comment to Aaron. Use these sentence starters.

If we moved to a small town like Wimberley, ... *If we had a house there, ...*
If my old friends came to visit me, ... *If there was an airport, ...*

Check

3 WORDS Matteo's first day

I can describe school life in the USA.

Complete the dialogue with the correct words from the box. There are two extra words.

administrator • bell • cafeteria • freshman • grade • period • principal • prom • responsible • senior

Alicja Hey, you must be Matteo! You're from Italy, right?
Matteo Oh, hi. Yes, I am. I'm new here.
Alicja I know! I'm Alicja. I'm here to help you. I'm from Germany and near the end of my exchange. I'm a ... (1).
Matteo: What's that?
Alicja: Sorry, that's a student in the fourth year of high school. You're in your first year, so you're a ... (2).
Matteo Thanks. I have so many questions!
Alicja No problem! First I'm going to take you to Ms Garcia's office. She's an ... (3), has a lot of information and can help you with your questions.
Ms Garcia Hello, Alicja. Ah, is this our new ninth ... (4) student?
Matteo Yes, I'm Matteo.

Ms Garcia Welcome to Westfield High, Matteo! We don't have a lot of time. First ... (5) starts in ten minutes. You need to be there when your teacher takes attendance.
Alicja That's when your teacher checks to see who's here every day.
Ms Garcia Oh, and one more thing: Ms Bell, our ... (6), would like to meet you at 2 p.m.
Alicja That's the person who is ... (7) for the whole school. Don't worry, she's pretty cool. Right, it's nearly nine. I'll take you to your first class. Would you like to meet for lunch in the ... (8)?

4 WRITING Alicja's blog post

Alicja wants to write a blog post at the end of her exchange year. Write her text. Use her notes below and your own ideas. Write about 100 words. You can start like this:

I'm nearly at the end of my exchange year at Westfield High ...

my exchange year in Texas

feelings
- *nervous (at the start)*
- *proud (now)*

challenges
- *long school days – tired!*
- *spending birthday away from family*

highlights
- *prom with Oscar*
- *friendly people*

Check

5 Mediation A voice message

I can talk about jobs and future plans.

Listen to the voice message from Alicja's sister Marta. Complete the dialogue.

Oscar Hey, is everything OK? You look a bit worried.
Alicja Well, not really worried. I've just listened to a voice message from my sister. She's feeling ... (1).
Oscar Oh, I'm sorry. Has something happened?
Alicja Well, she has to decide really soon if ... (2).
Oscar Where does she want to travel to?
Alicja She'd like to ... (3), but ... (4).
Oscar That sounds difficult. Maybe you should call her back now? I can come back later.
Alicja Thanks, Oscar. I think that would ... (5).

6 Study skills Planning the prom

I can use strategies to communicate better.

a) **Oscar and Hazel are on the prom planning committee. Complete their conversation with the correct words and phrases (A–I) from the box. There are two extra words or phrases.**

Hazel I have a pretty cool idea for the prom!
Oscar ... (1)? ... (2) are you thinking?
Hazel Well, we're in Fredericksburg ... erm ...
Oscar ... (3).
Hazel The town was founded by Germans. So our theme could be Germany!
Oscar ... (4) with German food and drinks?
Hazel ... (5)!
Oscar ... (6) your idea.
Hazel Everyone could wear German costumes too.
Oscar A German prom theme is a good idea, but I'm not sure about the costumes.
Hazel ... (7) don't you think that costumes are a good idea?
Oscar Kids dress in their best clothes for the prom. It's not a costume party. But I like the German theme!

A Do you mean • **B** Go on • **C** I'm not sure I understood that. • **D** Really • **E** That's right • **F** Tell me more about • **G** That's interesting. • **H** What • **I** Why

b) **Practise the conversation with a partner. Remember to ...**

- sit up straight
- look interested and friendly
- make eye contact.

Check

7 Reading A survey in the school magazine

I can talk about clothes at school.

a) **Read the article. Choose the correct heading (A–F) for parts 1–5. There's one extra heading.**

A What next? B Students want changes C No to uniforms! D Unfair rules

E Administrator explains F A question from our exchange students

1 As many of you know, Ethan and Leah from the UK are visiting our school this year. One thing that they find surprising is the freedom that we have in the States to wear what we want at school. Last month, Leah asked me, 'Could you imagine introducing uniforms at this school?' I thought it was a good question, so we did a survey. The results were pretty interesting!

2 You probably won't be surprised to hear that most of us aren't interested in having uniforms at school. In fact, only 9% of students thought it would be a good idea, with many students writing that their clothes are an important part of their personality. However, one student in 9th grade wrote that uniforms 'could help to stop bullying because we'd all look the same.'

3 But that doesn't mean most of us are happy about how we dress at school. When we asked if you feel good about what you can wear to school, only 38% of students said 'yes'. The main reason for this was the dress code. Nearly 60 % of students said that they think that clothing is something very personal, and not something which the school should decide for you. And 40 % of students said that they think the dress code should be different for different seasons.

4 Students also told us that they think some teachers are stricter about the dress code than others. One student in 11th grade wrote, 'It feels like the rules aren't the same for everyone', and a student in 9th grade said, 'I always have to take off my cap, but there are older students in our school who wear caps all the time and get away with it. That's so frustrating!'

5 We shared the results of our survey with the principal. She told us that she's going to hold a meeting to improve the dress code. It's taking place next Monday at lunchtime in room 16, and all students are invited.

b) **Complete the sentences with the correct word or number.**

1 Ethan and Leah think that American students have more ...
2 ... per cent of students would like to wear uniforms at school.
3 62 per cent of students aren't so happy about the ...
4 ... per cent of students think that the weather should make a difference to what you can wear.
5 One student finds it ... when older students get away with wearing a hat.
6 Next week there will be a ... about the dress code.

c) **Choose an orange statement and discuss it for your school. Say why you agree or why not.**

Check

United

A magazine for young people across the USA

My reading tip *by Diego Perez*

I love reading and I just finished *Hartford Moves*. Iris Quinn, the main character, is in trouble. At school, somebody has sprayed the words 'All lives matter' over a wall mural. The principal, Mr. Barnes, thinks that Iris is responsible for the graffiti. Iris talks to her friend Lalo, and the two of them create a plan. They walk into the cafeteria and see Kellyann and J.J.

'All lives matter' sounds fair, but it's a negative reaction to 'Black lives matter'. People who say that 'all lives matter' don't accept that Black people experience racist violence.

Hartford Moves *by Marc Proulx*

'Are you sure you want to do this?' I asked. 'There's nothing else I'd rather do,' Lalo said. I was nervous, but I badly[1] wanted to sort this out. Maybe Lalo's idea wasn't the best, but it was the only one we had. We walked in and scanned the cafeteria.

'There,' said Lalo, looking at a table on the left side. [...]

I took a deep breath. *Let's play this cool*, I thought. Kellyann and J.J. were sitting next to each other and didn't notice when we walked up to the table.

'Hey, is that vegetarian lasagna?' I said to Kellyann. 'That's my favorite too. Isn't that funny?'

We sat down opposite them. J.J. had his mouth[2] full of food. He looked at Lalo like he was from another planet. Lalo looked back at him.

'Hola,' he said. Neither[3] of them reacted.

'How was the bowling on Saturday?' I asked, not really interested in their answer.

'You missed it. It was awesome,' J.J. said.

[1] **badly** hier: *unbedingt* [2] **mouth** *der Mund* [3] **neither** *keiner, keine*

Kellyann gave me a cold look. 'I heard you got into trouble,' she said. 'Something about some graffiti?'
I let her enjoy the moment. 'Yeah,' I said. 'The principal thinks I painted over the wall mural. They found a bag of mine with spray paint in it. I can't explain it.'
I paused for a bit of dramatic effect, then looked straight at both of them. 'You don't know anything about that, do you?' I asked. [...]
'Me? I don't know anything about any graffiti. Or your gym bag,' Kellyann said.
Lalo and I looked at each other.
'Sorry, did you just say "gym bag"?' I said. 'What makes you think I'm talking about my gym bag?'
Kellyann's eyes searched around. 'Did I say gym bag?'
I turned to J.J. 'She did say gym bag, didn't she?' He looked at me with a stone face.
'I definitely heard gym bag,' Lalo said.
'Who asked you, gay-boy?' J.J. said, his voice hard.
His words surprised me. I wondered[1] how Lalo felt. Was it the first time someone had said that to him? Lalo's reaction was beautiful. He smiled.
'I don't need your permission[2] to talk, white boy.'
I looked at Kellyann. 'I think you know more about that graffiti than you say you do,' I said calmly.
Kellyann looked surprised. [...]
'Maybe,' she said. 'Maybe you deserved[3] it. Anyway, it's true what it says on the wall, so what's the problem?'
J.J. smiled. 'Don't you like my handwriting?' he said.
I sat back. 'Wow. So you're both admitting[4] it.'
'We're not admitting anything,' Kellyann said.
'Nope[5],' J.J. said.
'I just heard you,' I said. 'And Lalo is my witness[6].'
'Yup[7],' Lalo said.
Kellyann's cold blue eyes looked at me.
'Well, J.J. is my witness and I'm his. You can't prove[8] it,' she said. 'So get your thin ugly butt[9] out of here and take fat-boy with you.' [...]
'At least I don't try to hide behind cheap make-up,' I said.
Her face went tomato red. [...]
I could feel what was coming next.
'You little shit,' she said. 'Here's your freaking[10] vegetarian lasagna.' [...]

What do you think happens next?

[1] (to) **wonder** *sich fragen* [2] **permission** *die Erlaubnis* [3] (to) **deserve** *verdienen* [4] (to) **admit** *zugeben* [5] **nope** *nö* [6] **witness** *der Zeuge, die Zeugin* [7] **yup** *jawoll* [8] (to) **prove** *beweisen* [9] **butt** *der Hintern* [10] **freaking** *verdammt*

With one quick movement[1] she tried to dump[2] her lunch on me. [...]
I blocked the tray[3] with both hands and everything on it flew back at her. [...]
The cafeteria went silent. All eyes were on Kellyann. She's normally someone who likes attention, but I think this time was different. Tomato sauce and mozzarella cheese were on her face and all down her neat[4], expensive blouse. The rest of her lasagna was sitting warmly in her lap[5].
She looked shocked. [...]
The next voice I heard was Mrs. Gonzalez's.

Mr. Barnes's office had begun to feel familiar[6]. He was sitting at his desk and didn't seem to mind letting us all stand.
Kellyann and J.J. stood further away.
Kellyann looked uncomfortable and shaken. She wasn't wearing her lunch any more, but she was a mess[7], with red spots on her blouse and skirt and cheese in her hair.
Lalo was standing next to me. He looked amazingly calm and relaxed, like he knew exactly why he was there.
Mrs. Gonzalez had already given her view of the events in the cafeteria. Once again, it didn't make me look very good. I was sure I was in trouble again. [...]
After hearing Mrs Gonzalez, Mr. Barnes got up, walked around his desk and stood between the four of us. He had his arms crossed and was holding his reading glasses in one hand. He looked at Kellyann and J.J., then at Lalo and finally at me.
He kept looking at me. He seemed tired.
Then he turned again to Kellyann.
'Miss Moore, what's your side of the story?' he asked.

Kellyann started slowly. She was choosing her words carefully. She painted a picture of herself and J.J. as unfortunate victims who hadn't been doing anything wrong.
She looked upset, like her feelings had been hurt. She was a good actor.
J.J. nodded[8] the whole time, like he would have told it exactly the same way.
Mr. Barnes nodded[8] too. He turned back to me.
'Why do I get the feeling that she's telling the truth, Miss Quinn?' he said.
'Because you don't know the full story, Mr. Barnes,' I said. Lalo looked over at me.
Mr. Barnes lifted his tired eyebrow[9].

---

[1] **movement** *die Bewegung* [2] (to) **dump** *auskippen, wegwerfen* [3] **tray** *das Tablett* [4] **neat** *sauber, schick*
[5] **lap** *der Schoß* [6] **familiar** *vertraut* [7] (to) **be a mess** *völlig verdreckt sein* [8] (to) **nod** *nicken* [9] **eyebrow** *die Augenbraue*

'Tell me then. What part of the story am I missing?'

'The part about my locker[1]. You see, it doesn't work. Anyone can open it,' I said. 'It's been like that for weeks. Only three people know about it: Jason Lee and these two.' […]

'So what are you saying, Miss Quinn?' he asked.

'One of them could have taken my gym bag out of my locker and put the spray cans in it, so that it looked like I had painted the graffiti,' I said. 'It had to be someone with racist views. Someone who wasn't happy with me. Like Kellyann. On Friday I disagreed with her view of Black activism and told her I didn't want to go bowling with her.'

Kellyann's mouth dropped[2] open. 'That's *so* not true.' […]

'These guys have already admitted it,' I said. 'That's what the scene in the cafeteria was all about.'

'I didn't admit anything!' Kellyann said.

'Me neither[3]!' J.J. said.

'Lalo Mendez is my witness,' I said.

Mr. Barnes looked at Lalo. 'Is that true, Mr. Mendez?'

Lalo nodded.

'That's a lie!' J.J. said. 'I was there. Kellyann didn't say anything like that.'

'J.J. didn't either,' Kellyann said.' I'm his witness.'

They looked at each other and at Mr. Barnes confidently.

Mr. Barnes rubbed[4] his eyes and sighed.

'It sounds like it's your word against theirs, Miss Quinn,' he said.

Lalo spoke for the first time. 'Not exactly,' he said.

He reached into the pocket of his bomber jacket and pulled out his cell phone. He held it up and tapped the screen. A recording started. There was cafeteria noise and the sound of voices, including my own. We heard the whole conversation.

Mr. Barnes listened, both of his eyebrows slowly rising. Kellyann's face was frozen. J.J. looked at the floor. […]

Lalo stopped the recording. The room was silent. […] Finally, Mr. Barnes spoke.

'Miss Quinn, Mr. Mendez, you can go now,' he said.

▶ Quellenverzeichnis, p. 00

How does this ending make you feel? If you liked this chapter, read the rest of the book!

[1] **locker** *das Schließfach* [2] (to) **drop** *fallen* [3] **Me neither.** *Ich auch nicht.* [4] (to) **rub** *reiben*

Partner page

▸Page 87

6 What would you do?

a) **Partner B: Answer partner A's questions. ☒ Give reasons.**

If I could live anywhere in the world, I'd live in ... (because ...).

b) **Partner B: Ask your partner the questions below.**

1 If you were an animal, what would you be?
2 If you were a superhero, what would your superpower be?
3 If you could meet a famous person, who would you like to meet?
4 If you spoke perfect English, what would you use it for?
5 If you were a politician, what would you change in your area?

▸Page 93

3 READING Finding a job

b) **Partners B–D: Read your advert below. Tell the group the main points: what, when, how much.**

B

Wanted: Garden help

My mother has a large garden just outside Fredericksburg and finds it difficult to keep it tidy. I'm looking for a reliable and flexible person who can help out from time to time, for example with cutting the grass. Pay is $7.50 an hour and the hours will change with the weather. If you're interested, please email us.

C

Babysitter wanted

We're looking for an experienced person (at least 13 years old) to babysit our five-year-old son once or twice a month in the evenings. We need someone friendly and responsible to read to him and put him to bed when we're out. We can pay $9 an hour and will also give you snacks! To organize a meeting in person, please send a text.

D

Part-time job

We are a family-run hairdresser's in Fredericksburg looking for help on Saturday afternoons. The hours are 2 p.m. to 5 p.m. each week. The job will include cleaning the floor and making tea or coffee for customers. The pay is $8.50 an hour, plus free haircuts. If you are tidy and have a friendly personality, visit us for more information.

▸ Page 101

UNIT TASK **Do an interview about school, Step 2: Make role cards**

Partner A: American exchange student

1 Say hello.
2 Answer the interviewer's questions about school life in the USA, for example about:
- the school day (how long? after-school activities?)
- transport to school (walk / cycle / bus / car / ...?)
- the dress code in school (clothes, hair, make-up)
- a special celebration in the school year.

3 Answer the interviewer's questions about your experiences and your opinion of school in Germany.
4 Thank the interviewer.

Diff bank

▸ Page 84

More practice 1 A German-Texan town

a) Read about Fredericksburg's German roots. Take turns to explain the blue words in English.

Lindenbaum: This is a kind of tree.

In 1846, German immigrants founded the town of Fredericksburg. Even today, it still has a German feel. Some places have German names – for example, there's a restaurant called **Der Lindenbaum**. For more German food, try the **Altdorf Restaurant & Biergarten**. For three days each October, the town celebrates **Oktoberfest** in the **Marktplatz** with musicians in **Lederhosen** and **Dirndl**. Another German festival is **Saengerfest** with the many German choirs in the area. And of course every year there's **Weihnachtszeit**. Admire the beautiful **Weihnachtspyramide** and enjoy the holiday season!

b) In class, talk about how immigrants have changed Germany in a positive way.

Challenge 1 German words in English

c) English also uses German words. Read the descriptions and write the German words.

1 a feeling of worry or being scared
2 a type of German sausage
3 a celebration or festival
4 a child with amazing abilities
5 someone who looks like another person
6 a ghost that makes a lot of noise and breaks things
7 a feeling of being happy when something bad happens to another person
8 broken

▸ Page 85

More practice 2 WORDS Write like a reporter

Complete sentences 1–6 from an article with the useful phrases from the box.

as a result of • On the other hand • pointed out • sixty-five per cent • That's what we asked • The good news is

1 How could our town be better? ... our class.
2 On the one hand, ... of the students in our class like our town.
3 ..., some students think that the town is a bit boring.
4 Leoni ... that there aren't a lot of places for young people.
5 ... that our town will look at our suggestions.
6 We hope that the situation will improve ... our suggestions.

▸ Page 86

More practice 3 If I lived in ...

a) **Write conditional sentences type 2 with ideas from the boxes or your own ideas.**

If I lived in Nashville, I'd hear lots of great music.

1 If I lived in Nashville, ...	I'd go	alligators.
2 If I lived in Texas, ...	I'd be	surfing.
3 If I lived in New York City, ...	I'd have	on the subway.
4 If I lived in Alaska, ...	I'd hear	lots of great music.
5 If I lived in Hawaii, ...	I'd see	very cold.
6 If I lived in Florida, ...	I'd travel	a barbecue.

▸ Language file 17, p. 190

☒ b) **Choose three more places anywhere in the world and write similar sentences.**

Challenge 2 My classmate's life

a) **Think of a classmate and complete the sentences for him/her. Use the correct form of the verbs in brackets.**

1 **(go)** If you *went* on holiday, I think you *would go* to *(Hawaii / ...)*.
2 **(learn)** If you ... another language, I think you ...
3 **(choose)** If you ... another first name, I think you ...
4 **(try)** If you ... a new sport, I think you ...
5 **(have)** If you ... a tattoo, I think you ...
6 **(get)** If you ... a pet, I think you ...

b) **Take turns to read out a sentence to each other. How many sentences can you agree on?**

▸ Language file 17, p. 190

▸ Page 87

More help **7** My task **Where we live**

c) **Use your notes and some of your classmates' comments to write your article. The article on p. 85 can help you.**

Introduction	What do teenagers think about living in ...?	
Main part (1)	On the one hand,	... is a great place to live because ...
	What I like about my town	is the park / the sports centre / ... are the outdoor activities / ...
Main part (2)	On the other hand, my town	is a bit boring because ...
		doesn't have a cinema / a skatepark / a swimming pool / places to hang out / ...
Conclusion	All in all, my town	isn't such a great place to live. / doesn't have ..., but it's still a good place to live. / ...
	To sum up, my town	is an awesome / ... place for teenagers.

▸ Page 89

3 Song **Fifteen** by Taylor Swift

c) **Check your answers with the lyrics below.**

You take a deep breath and you walk through
the doors.
It's the mornin' of your very first day.
You say 'hi' to your friends you ain't seen in a
while, try and stay out of everybody's way.
It's your freshman year and you're gonna be
here for the next four years in this town,
hopin' one of those senior boys will wink at
you and say
'You know, I haven't seen you around before.'

'Cause when you're fifteen and somebody
tells you they love you,
you're gonna believe them.
And when you're fifteen, feelin' like there's
nothin' to figure out,
well, count to ten, take it in.
This is life before you know who you're gonna
be at fifteen.

You sit in class next to a redhead named
Abigail
and soon enough, you're best friends,
laughin' at the other girls who think they're
so cool.
We'll be outta here as soon as we can.
And then you're on your very first date and he's
got a car
and you're feelin' like flyin'.
And your mama's waitin' up and you're thinkin'
he's the one.
And you're dancin' round your room
when the night ends, when the night ends.

'Cause when you're fifteen and somebody
tells you they love you,
you're gonna believe them.
And when you're fifteen and your first kiss
makes your head spin around –
well, in your life, you'll do things greater than
dating the boy on the football team.
I didn't know it at fifteen.

▸ Page 90

More practice 4 Oscar's plans

REVISION The going to-future
We use the **going to-future** to talk about plans in the future.
We often use time words and phrases like *tomorrow, at the weekend, next Saturday.*
We form the going to-future with ***am / is / are* + *(not) going to* + infinitive**.
*Our prom theme **is going to be** James Bond. We**'re going to wear** fancy clothes.*

▸ Language file 14, p. 188

a) Diego is interviewing Oscar. Write the questions and answers. Use the *going to*-future.

Diego So it's the weekend soon, Oscar. What ... (1 you / do)?
Oscar Well, ... (2 I / volunteer) at the hospital on Saturday as usual. On Sunday ... (3 I / do) some work for my parents' cafe downtown.
Diego Cool. ... (4 you / make) sandwiches and coffee?
Oscar No, ... (5 I / not work) in the cafe. I'm learning about the business.
Diego Great. And ... (6 you / celebrate) being prom prince?
Oscar Yeah, ... (7 I / have) a party in the cafe on Saturday evening.

b) Talk to a partner about your weekend plans.

What are you going to do at the weekend? — On Saturday / Sunday I'm going to ...

▸ Page 92

More practice 5 What will they do?

REVISION The will-future
We use the **will-future** to talk about ideas and predictions for the future.
We often use words like *maybe, probably* and *hopefully.*
We form the will-future with ***will / won't* + infinitive**.
How **will he pay** for college? He's worried he **won't have** enough money.

▸ Language file 15, p. 189

Complete Diego's sentences with a verb from the box in the will-future. There are two extra verbs.

be • do • feel • go • have • help • learn • rain • work

1 My sister says maybe she ... a mechanic when she's older.
2 Hopefully I ... to drive this summer. My parents can teach me.
3 I don't think it ... today – there should be dry weather all day.
4 We probably ... (not) out this weekend because we ... tired after a long week.
5 ... you ... me with my homework, Jacob? I'm finding it really hard!
6 I ... on the farm with you afterwards if you like.

Challenge 3 After graduation

We can also use the **present progressive** to talk about plans for the future (time words and phrases, e.g. 'tomorrow' or 'next Friday').

Read each sentence. Write 'P' if it's about the present or 'F' if it's about future plans.

1 My sister is going abroad in summer.
2 She's already packing her bags.
3 My parents are visiting her in July.
4 I'm going with them.
5 We're all feeling a little sad.
6 We're having a party before she leaves.

▸ Page 93

More practice 6 LISTENING A radio advert

a) **Listen to the advert and choose the correct answer A, B or C.**

1 The job is for a A fitness studio B newspaper C baseball team.
2 The business is looking for someone to A deliver their product B clean C listen to music.
3 The working hours are A weekends B evenings C mornings.
4 The pay A is $25 an hour B is $25 a day C can change.
5 The person for this job should be A reliable B always on time C fast.

b) **Talk for one minute about why you would be a good person for this job.**

I already have some work experience. In the past, I ...

▸ Page 94

More help 5 READING A message about a summer job

a) **Abbreviations and emojis for social media:**

❤ = love	LMK = let me know	Thx = thanks
4 = for	n = and	u = you
IRL = in real life	rlly = really	ur = your

More help 7 MY TASK Hello, future me!

a) **Make notes about what you think you'll do in the future.**

In the next five / ten years,	I (don't) think I'll hopefully I'll maybe I'll I probably won't	be / become get go learn / be able to live look	famous / a nurse / ... good results / married / ... on holiday / to college / out with friends / ... drive / (speak) another language / ... abroad / ... with my friends / ... very different / ...

Unit 4
California: State of contrasts

A

Hollywood, Los Angeles

B

Fire lookout

C

Sequoia National Park

D

Silicon Valley

1 SPEAKING **Californian contrasts**

artificial • busy • coastal • dry • flat • green • modern • mountainous • natural • quiet • rural • traditional • urban

a) **Take turns and describe photos A–H to a partner. Use the words in the box or your own ideas. Your partner says which photo it is.**

In the background / foreground of photo ..., I can see a mountainous / ...
The scene in this photo looks really busy / ...

☒ b) **Choose two photos and compare them.**

The buildings in the photo of San Francisco are more modern than ...
The photo of Death Valley shows a dry landscape, whereas ...

▸ More practice 1, p. 145

Nach dieser Unit kann ich ...

- über Kalifornien sprechen
- eine Diskussion über Künstliche Intelligenz führen
- über die Geschichte der *Native Americans* sprechen
- die Natur in Kalifornien beschreiben
- Diagramme auswerten und präsentieren

Unit task

- eine Präsentation über Kalifornien erstellen und halten

E
Death Valley

F
Santa Monica Beach, Los Angeles

G
Market in Olvera Street, Los Angeles

H
San Francisco

2 Viewing **Welcome to Los Angeles (LA)**

a) Before you watch **With a partner, write sights, activities etc. that you might expect to see in a video about Los Angeles.**

b) **Watch the video and tick any things from a) that you see. Is there anything unexpected?**

c) **Watch again and say if each sentence is true (T) or false (F). Correct the false sentences.**

1 Julia is American.
2 10 million people come to Griffith Park each year.
3 Echo Park is an Italian neighbourhood.
4 Julia's neighbour Woody loves baseball.
5 It's very easy to drive around LA.
6 Julia shows us a beach in the morning.

▸ More practice 2, p. 145

▸ Workbook, p. 58

Digital quiz I can talk about California.

The future is now

1 LISTENING Riley's family

Riley's dad, Mike

Riley Walker, 14

Riley's mum, Nicole

a) BEFORE YOU LISTEN **Look at the pictures of Riley's parents. Make predictions about ...**

1 what they do in their jobs.
2 who lives in ...
- the small town of Eureka.
- the city of San Jose in Silicon Valley.

Good to know

Silicon Valley in California is an area with thousands of tech companies. They develop social media apps, artificial intelligence tools and other high technology.

b) **Listen to a phone conversation between Riley and her mum. Which of your predictions in a) were correct?**

c) **Listen again and answer the questions.**

1 Who does Riley live with?
2 Why is Riley's dad happy?
3 What does Riley want to do next weekend?
4 What is Riley's mum working on?

2 LOOKING AT LANGUAGE The simple present passive

a) **Listen to the conversation in 1 again and complete the sentences.**

1 It ... optimized with artificial intelligence.
2 The game ... designed to adapt to the player.
3 The player's results ... analysed.
4 The next level ... made a bit harder.
5 The level ... chosen just for me.
6 A game like this ... developed so quickly.
7 The game ... launched.
8 Then all the bugs ... fixed.

b) **Complete the rule about the simple present passive.**

Active: A programmer **tests** the demo. **Passive:** The demo **is tested**.
We use the passive when we want to focus on the **action** and not so much on **who** does it.
We make the simple present passive with a form of the verb *to be* in the simple present tense: ... , ... or ... and the past participle of the verb (the third form).

► Irregular verbs, pp. 300–302 ► Language file 20a), p. 193

3 Artificial intelligence

Complete an online article about artificial intelligence. Use the correct form of the verbs in brackets.

We can use 'by' in passive sentences to explain who does the action.

Artificial intelligence (AI) is a tool that is *built* **(1 build)** by humans, but it allows computers to 'think'. In the past, computers could only follow instructions. Today, if a computer is ... **(2 feed)** with information, called data, it can learn and create new ideas. This technology is ... **(3 use)** in lots of different ways and new tools are ... **(4 develop)** all the time. Posts you see on social media are ... **(5 choose)** by AI, and millions of AI texts are ... **(6 write)** and pictures are ... **(7 create)** every day. Illnesses are now often ... **(8 find)** earlier because of AI. All of this can be very useful, but AI is ... **(9 not welcome)** by everyone. Some people say that it's harder and harder to know what is fake. They also worry that jobs are ... **(10 lose)** to AI and that more mistakes are ... **(11 make)** when humans are ... **(12 not include)** enough in decisions.

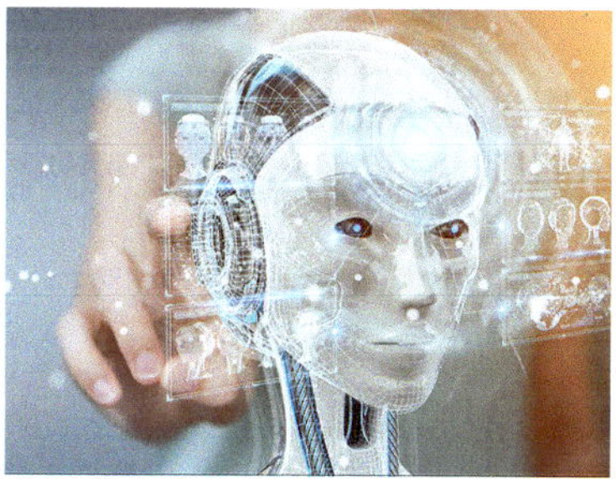

▸ Language file 20a–b), p. 193 ▸ More practice 3, p. 146

4 SPEAKING & WRITING Developing a game

a) **Partner B:** Look at p. 144.
Partner A: Read the notes. Tell your partner step 1 for developing a video game. Use the passive.

The idea for the game is chosen.

Then listen to your partner and take notes on step 2.
Take turns to complete all the steps.

Step 1: idea for game – choose
Step 2: ...
Step 3: characters and levels – design
Step 4: ...
Step 5: music and sound effects – add
Step 6: ...
Step 7: any bugs – fix – programmers
Step 8: ...

b) Use your notes in a) to write a description of how a video game is developed. Use the passive and some of the linking words in the box.

Firstly, • Secondly, • Next, • After that, • Then • Finally,

c) Compare your description with your partner's and check each other's work.

- Have you used the passive correctly?
- Have you used full sentences?
- Have you used linking words?

▸ More practice 4, p. 146

▸ Workbook, p. 59

5 Reading Riley's problem

a) Before you read **Do you sometimes use AI for your homework? Why (not)? Tell a partner.**

I / never / always use ... because ...

b) **Read the chat between Riley and Tiana. What happened and why is Riley angry?**

c) **Decide if sentences 1–5 are about Riley, Tiana or both.**

1 She had a problem at school today.
2 She uses AI to help her sometimes.
3 She agrees with the teacher.
4 She gives a reason for her opinion.
5 She changes her mind at the end.

d) **What do you think about what Riley did and why? Tell your partner.**

I think what Riley did was wrong / not so bad / ... because ...

I can't believe that I got detention today! 😠

Oh no, what happened? 😮 *Did you talk in class again?*

No, Mr Gomez said that I cheated on my history essay because I used AI to write it! 🙄 *Isn't that stupid?*

I'm sorry that you got detention, but if you ask me, that IS kind of cheating. 😬

Are you serious? EVERYONE uses AI!

For research, sure, we all do – but not to write the whole thing! You didn't do your homework – a computer did! 🤗

I guess you have a point. 😔

6 Listening Can you believe your eyes?

a) Before you listen **Look at the two pictures. Guess which one is real and which is made by AI. Give reasons. Find the answer on p. 311.**

I think photo A/B is real because the deer ...
The colours / details / legs / ... look ...
The light is ...

b) **Listen to the conversation between Riley and her dad. What does he think about AI?**

c) **Listen again and complete the sentences.**

1 A company emailed Riley's dad to say that they don't need ...
2 He thinks the photo they showed him is not ...
3 He says the company just wants to get ... photos.
4 He's annoyed because they use photographers' photos to train ...
5 But when they do this, they don't ... them.
6 He thinks being a photographer is not ...

7 Opinions

a) Read speech bubbles 1–6 and decide who might say them: Riley's mum or her dad.

1 Don't you think that *AI is a big problem for people in creative jobs?*

2 You have a point that *AI isn't always reliable.*

3 But can't you see that *AI is a really useful tool for a lot of industries?*

4 The reason why I think that *AI should be banned is that it takes people's jobs.*

5 I hear what you're saying, but I still don't think that *AI is really dangerous.*

6 I don't see it that way at all *because AI is a disaster for people like me.*

b) Copy and complete the table with the phrases in blue. ☒ Add more examples.

Checking opinions	Agreeing	Disagreeing	Giving reasons
…	…	…	…

My task

8 Let's discuss

▸ Digital help

a) Make notes about the pros and cons of using AI. You can use your work from pages 118–121 to help you.

▸ More help, p. 146

b) Work in groups of three. Each student prepares a role:
Student A: You think AI is a positive thing.
Student B: You think AI is a negative thing.
Student C: You're going to lead the discussion and ask for opinions.

Use your notes in a) and the phrases in 7b) to help you.

c) Talk to other students with the same role (A/B/C). Share your arguments, questions or phrases.

d) Have the discussion in your first group. Another group listens and takes notes:
- Did students A and B give reasons for their opinions? What reasons did they give?
- Did students A and B use good phrases to agree, disagree and give reasons?
- Did student C lead the discussion and ask for opinions?
- Did all students speak clearly and confidently?

▸ Skills file 5, p. 165

e) **Give feedback. Then swap.**

▸ Feedback phrases, p. 210

▸ Workbook, pp. 60–61

Digital quiz

I can have a discussion about AI.

My people

1 Reading The Native American story

a) BEFORE YOU READ **Tiana and Riley are learning about Native American history. Read Tiana's speech bubble and say whose land you think the white settlers took and what a 'reservation' is.**

b) **Read Tiana's essay and check your answers from a).**

Yurok people at a protest, 2024

In the USA, there are 9.7 million Native Americans and around 600 diverse tribes. My mom's family belongs to the biggest tribe in California, the Yurok. We were given the name 'Yurok' by Europeans, but we call ourselves 'Oohl'.

When European people came to America over five hundred years ago, my ancestors were already here. They fished, hunted animals like buffaloes and wild turkeys and grew vegetables like corn and beans. They had a special connection to nature – to the trees, the animals, water and sky.

Europeans colonized America and took Native land for themselves. Thousands of Native people were killed by white settlers and soldiers and millions died of diseases which were brought by Europeans. Later, many Native Americans were forced to leave their tribal lands and live on reservations – areas of land which were chosen and owned by the government. About forty per cent of children from Native families, like my great-grandmother, were sent to boarding schools where their cultural identity was taken from them and where many children died. Native people still have trauma today. Only a fifth of Native Americans live on reservations today.

Many tribes have fought to get their land back. Ninety per cent of the Yurok's tribal land was taken from us, but we bought back some land and some land was returned to us by the US government. A council was formed in 1994 to govern the tribe. We continue to fight to protect our traditional way of life. Our message for the world: We're still here!

c) **Read the essay again and find these numbers. What are they about?**

A 9,700,000 B 600 C 500 D 40% E ⅕ F 90%

► English numbers, p. 211

d) **Explain how Native Americans have changed their situation.**

They have fought to … / They continue to fight to …

e) **Talk about your feelings about specific parts of Tiana's essay.** *When I read …, I felt …*

► More practice 5, p. 147

2 Looking at language The simple past passive

Read sentences 1–6 and complete them. Then complete the rule in the box below.

1 Thousands of Native people ... killed by white settlers. (lines 15–17)
2 Millions died of diseases which ... brought by Europeans. (lines 17–19)
3 Many Native Americans ... forced to leave their tribal lands. (lines 19–20)
4 Their cultural identity ... taken from them. (lines 26–27)
5 The Yurok's land ... taken from us. (lines 32–33)
6 Some land ... returned to us by the US government. (lines 34–35)

Remember
We often use the passive when we focus on the **action** and not on who did it.

We make the simple past passive with ... / ... and the past participle.
Remember: If we want to say **who** did the action, we use ... + person or thing.

▸ Language file 20c), p. 193 ▸ Irregular verbs, pp. 300–302

3 The Yurok and the condors

Read and complete the website information with the correct form of the simple past passive.

Californian condors are some of the largest birds in the world. For the Yurok people, condors are sacred birds and their feathers and songs play an important role in Yurok ceremonies. In the past, this bird *was found* (1 find) along the whole west coast of the USA. But when the area ... (2 colonize) by Europeans, many condors ... (3 kill) or their eggs ... (4 steal). Additionally, many of their homes ... (5 destroy) by people. When only thirty condors were left in California, the condor ... (6 list) as endangered species. In 1987, the last wild Californian condors ... (7 catch) to breed new birds. In 2008, a programme ... (8 create) by the Yurok with an important goal: to bring the condor back to the area. And they have been successful: In 2022, there were around 300 wild condors in California.

4 Words What is it?

a) **Read definitions 1–5 from pages 122–123. Take turns to say the correct word.**

1 A place where Native Americans were forced to live by white people is ... – a reservation
2 Name that was given to Tiana's tribe by settlers is ... – ...
3 Something that was brought by Europeans that killed a lot of Native Americans is ... – ...
4 A bird which was introduced to California again is ... – ...
5 Something which was taken from condors by Europeans is ... – ...

b) **Partner B: Look at page 144. Partner A: Look at p. 148.**

▸ More practice 6, p. 147 ▸ Challenge 1, p. 148

5 LISTENING Native Americans today

a) BEFORE YOU LISTEN Tiana is giving a presentation to her class about the Yurok people. Look at her slides and say what you can see.

b) Listen and write notes with more details about the pictures.

c) Listen again and add more details. Then compare with a partner.

▶ Challenge 2, p. 148

6 A cartoon about Native Americans

a) Look at the cartoon and describe the people, the place and the actions. The words in the box can help you.

astronaut • crater • dark • earth • feather • flag • headdress • moon • space • spacesuit • star • tent • weapon

I can see two people. They are on ... The astronaut is putting ...

Use the **simple present** to describe where people and things are in a cartoon and what they look like. Use the **present progressive** to describe their actions and what they are wearing.

b) Look at the speech bubble and explain what it means. Think about what you have learned about Native American history.

The Native American says 'again' because ...

c) Give your opinion on the message of the cartoon.

I think this cartoon is funny because ...
In my opinion, it isn't funny, but ...

CartoonStock.com

Good to know

Cartoons are often funny because they use a surprising or shocking image for a serious message. Many use stereotypes – like the traditional look of the Native Americans in this cartoon.

▶ Skills file 7, p. 168

7 MEDIATION Respect other cultures

a) Tiana met Max from Mainz at summer camp. He wants to tell her about a comment that he read on social media. Help Max mediate.

Hi, Tiana
I just read a comment about a Carnival costume. A girl called Pia wrote that she saw ... She knows that ... A headdress like this ... You shouldn't wear ... At the end Pia says that ... What do you think?
Max

Beim Karnevalsumzug in Mainz habe ich einen Jugendlichen gesehen, der als *Native American* verkleidet war. Soweit ich weiß, zeigt das *Native Americans* gegenüber keinen Respekt. Besonders der Kopfschmuck ist für sie heilig und ein wichtiges Symbol ihrer Kultur. Man sollte den Kopfschmuck deshalb nicht einfach aus Spaß tragen. Ich bin mir sicher, dass der Junge niemanden damit verletzten wollte, aber ich finde, es wäre besser gewesen, wenn er dieses Kostüm nicht getragen hätte. Wie seht ihr das?

Pia (15), Mainz

b) Why did Pia think that wearing a Native American headdress for fun wasn't OK?

A Native American headdress is / isn't ...

☒ c) Talk about styles (hair, clothing, music etc.) from other cultures that people sometimes use. Discuss whether you think it's OK to wear styles from other cultures. Give reasons.

My task

8 Describing a cartoon

▸ Digital help

a) Look at the cartoon and write a description. Include an explanation of its meaning using the ideas from 7. Give your opinion. You can use the words in the box or your own ideas. Write 100 words or more.

▸ Skills file 7, p. 168

The cartoon shows ... The man on the left is asking ... His question ...

culture • expression • fancy • fashion statement • feather • headdress • insensitive • (to) look • religion • (to) wear • white • (to) use

b) Check your writing. Then read and check your partner's text. Is the language correct? Do you understand the explanation and the opinion? Give feedback.

▸ Feedback phrases, p. 210

▸ Workbook, pp. 62–63

Digital quiz — I can talk about Native American history.

The Redwoods

1 Reading The Redwood National Park

a) Before you read **Tiana, Riley and Riley's dad are going camping. Have you ever gone camping? What was it like? What do or don't you like about camping?**
Walk around **and tell different partners.**

I camped in the garden with my friends and we had breakfast in the tent. — That sounds fun!
I haven't gone camping. I wouldn't like to go camping because ... — I agree.

b) **Riley found a travel blog before her trip to the Redwood National Park. Read it and look at the pictures: What do you find most interesting?**

Tony's travel blog: The Redwood National Park

The Redwood National Park is home to some of the oldest and tallest trees on earth: Redwoods can grow to over 300 feet (91 m)! My family and I went on a forest walk with a ranger and she told us about the tallest tree in the world, which is in this park – it's 380 feet (nearly 116 m) high. That's taller than the Statue of Liberty! The ranger also told us that the Yurok tribe live near here and they help to protect the trees and the condors in the forest. We saw a lot of wildlife. Although we didn't see any bears (more than a hundred black bears live in the forests), we spotted a raccoon and two porcupines. We stayed in a cabin at a campground in the park. We built a great campfire, told scary stories and made s'mores. For those of you who aren't from the USA: S'mores are two sweet crackers with melted marshmallows and chocolate in them — like a sandwich. They taste so good you want some more! It was an amazing trip because I saw and learned so many new things.

c) **Read Tony's blog again. True (T) or false (F)? Correct the false sentences.**

1 Some trees in the national park are over 90 m high.
2 The Statue of Liberty is smaller than the tallest tree in the park.
3 You can't see bears in the forest.
4 It's called a s'more because people always want to eat another one.
5 Tony enjoyed the trip because the weather was great.

2 LISTENING Are you a bear expert?

a) BEFORE YOU LISTEN Riley sees this sign. What do you think you should do if you meet a black bear? Copy the table. Tick (✓) or cross (×) tips 1–10 in column A.

	A	B
1 Leave food outside.	×	
2 Make some noise.		
3 Stay calm.		
4 Run away.		
5 Wave your arms.		
6 Scream and shout.		
7 Move slowly to the side.		
8 Climb a tree.		
9 Hit the bear in the face.		
10 Use bear pepper spray.		

b) Listen and check your answers from a). Tick (✓) or cross (×) tips 1–10 in column B in your table. Did you get seven or more answers correct? Then you're a bear expert!

c) Complete the sentences from the conversation in b) with the correct conjunction. Then listen again and check your answers.

1 Avoid bears unless / although / whenever possible.
2 They often come to campgrounds if / so that / unless they smell food.
3 Bears don't usually attack people although / because / unless a mother bear has cubs or it is eating.
4 We'll talk, sing and clap because / so that / if they know we're coming.
5 Wave your arms slowly or hold up a jacket so that / because / unless you look bigger.
6 Don't climb a tree if / although / because bears can climb trees!

▸ Language file 21, p. 194

3 LISTENING Bears at the campground

Tiana and Riley meet some other campers. Complete their story with conjunctions from the box.

although • because • if • so that • unless • whenever

Hey, I'm Fred and this is my girlfriend Andi. Be careful here ... (1) we saw a black bear yesterday! They don't usually come to the campgrounds ... (2) people leave trash here. And someone did that yesterday. It makes us so mad ... (3) we see that! ... (4) nothing was damaged and we weren't hurt, we were a little scared! Please make sure to put your trash in the special cans here ... (5) the bears can't smell it. Let us know ... (6) we can help you with anything!

▸ Challenge 3, p. 149

4 Making films in the Redwoods

Many studios use the Redwoods to make films and TV shows. Complete the sentences with the simple present passive or the simple past passive.

Use the **simple present passive** to describe what happens in a book, film, play or TV show. Use the **simple past passive** to explain how something was made or done.

E.T.: The Extra-Terrestrial
E.T. is *left* (1 leave) in the forest here by his friends. Many forest scenes *were filmed* (2 film) at night.

The Lost World: Jurassic Park
In this film, dinosaurs ... (5 bring) back to life on an island. State parks ... (6 choose) for some of these scenes.

Star Wars: Return of the Jedi
The forest ... (3 use) as Planet Endor. The planet ... (4 inhabit) by creatures that look a little like teddy bears.

After Earth
The main characters of this film ... (7 play) by real-life father and son Will and Jaden Smith. Only a few people ... (8 allow) to be there during filming, to protect the local birds.

My task

5 My travel blog post

► Digital help

a) YOU CHOOSE You're going to write a post for a travel blog (100 words or more). Do task A or B.
A Write about a real or imaginary trip to Redwood National Park.
B Write about a trip to a natural area that you visited with your family or class.

b) Think of ideas for your travel blog post:
- Where did you go?
- What did you see and do?
- Was it a day trip? If not, where did you sleep?
- Was it a good or bad trip? Why?

► More help, p. 149

c) Write your post. Tony's blog post on p. 126 can help you. You can add photos.

d) PEER CONFERENCE In small groups, exchange your blog posts and give feedback. Did the posts answer all the questions in b)? Were they interesting?

► Feedback phrases, p. 210

► Workbook, pp. 64–65

Digital quiz I can talk about nature in California.

Background file

1 Reading **Hollywood, California**

a) Before you read **What do you know about Hollywood? Answer questions 1–6.**

1 What industry is Hollywood famous for?
2 In what decade did this industry begin?
3 What city is Hollywood in?
4 What's the name of a Hollywood street?
5 What symbols are in some Hollywood pavements?

b) **Read the text. Check your answers from a) and correct them if necessary.**

Today it's famous as the film capital of the world, but a little more than a hundred years ago Hollywood, California, was still quiet countryside. A couple who bought the land in 1887 heard the name from a friend, liked it, and gave it to the area.

The first film made in Hollywood was a 1910 Western called 'In Old California'. Hollywood's first film studio was started in 1911 and many more soon followed. Lots of land, light and warm weather year-round made it an attractive location for the industry. In just a few years, almost all US films were made here. Its most recognizable sight, the huge Hollywood sign, was put up in 1923.

Hollywood is not actually an independent city: It's a neighbourhood of Los Angeles. Hollywood Boulevard and Sunset Boulevard are two of its most well-known streets, filled with theatres, shops and sights – for example the stars on the Hollywood Walk of Fame – that attract visitors from around the world.

It's not just about movies either. Hollywood is also a popular location for live music and other performances. The Hollywood Bowl, an outdoor theatre, hosts hundreds of concerts and events for music lovers each year.

Hollywood is also a symbol for creativity and dreams. Its history and importance in the entertainment industry make it a fascinating destination for visitors and an exciting place for people to live and work.

c) You choose **Use the internet to research a celebrity who has a star on the Hollywood Walk of Fame. Do task A or B.**

A Make a short digital presentation about your celebrity.

B Make a poster about your celebrity.

Include information about

- **your celebrity's life and career** • **what the star was given for (film, music, ...)**
- **when it was placed** • **photos/videos from the ceremony when the star was placed.**

Wildfire

1 Camping again

a) BEFORE YOU READ **Look at the group chat and answer the questions.**

1 Who is Tiana writing to?
2 Where did Tiana meet them?

Lakeview campers

Amy Troy Diego Tiana

Hi, everyone!
Just to say I am going camping again! This time with my friend Riley and her dad in Redwood National Park. Hope it's as good as our camp last summer! Take care ❤

b) **Read the story. What happens and why does Amy write to Tiana and their friends in the end** (p. 132)**?**

After their first day in the national park, Tiana, Riley and her dad made a fire at their campground.

'Remember,' said Riley's dad, 'whenever you make a campfire, you always stay near it when it's burning. And of course, you have to use the fire pits at the campground: You're not allowed to make a fire in the middle of the forest when it's dry and hot and the temperature is over 86°F. So today it's OK.'

Good to know

In the USA, the temperature is measured in Fahrenheit (°F). In Germany, we use Celsius (°C).
86°F are 30°C. (°C = (°F - 32) x 5/9)

They cooked some food over the fire and talked about their day while they were eating.

'I can't believe how tall these trees are,' said Riley. 'They make me feel tiny! It's beautiful when you stand in the forest and look up.'

'I know, right?' said Tiana. 'For us Yurok, redwoods are very important, so we try not to hurt them. When we need wood, we find trees that have already fallen.'

When they had eaten, Riley, Tiana and her dad looked at some of the photos they had taken that day. 'I took lots of great photos of wildlife,' said Riley's dad. 'Look at this condor!'

Riley laughed. 'That bird is so ugly, Dad. But it's a great photo.'

'Yes, it is,' said Tiana. She yawned. 'Sorry – I'm so tired.'

'Let's put the fire out and get some sleep,' said Riley's dad. 'We've got an early start tomorrow.'

In their tent it was quiet and soon all three of them were asleep. Suddenly Tiana woke up – and smelled smoke. 'Something's burning,' she thought. She opened the tent and looked out. The forest was on fire!

Tiana shouted loudly to Riley and her dad. 'Fire! Wake up!'

'It was probably a spark from a campfire further in the forest,' said Riley's dad. His voice was calm, but his eyes were worried. 'Go to the car quickly. It's good that we're the only campers.'

As they drove through the forest, Riley called 911 to report the fire. 'They know about it already, Dad. There are firefighters in the forest.'

'We're lucky, girls, the road is clear,' said Riley's dad. But a little further on they weren't so lucky. The road was blocked by a tree. It was a fairly small tree, but they couldn't get past it.

'What do we do now?' asked Riley. She was starting to panic. 'Is there another road?'

'Riley, it's OK,' said her dad. 'I'll take a look.' He got out of the car and looked at the tree. Then he ran back. 'It looks like the firefighters have the fire under control on this side of the road. I'm going to ask them for help.'

'It's dangerous out there!' said Riley. 'You could get hurt!'

'I'll be back in a few minutes and I promise I won't take risks,' said her dad. 'Don't worry.'

'I'm scared too, Riley. But I'm sure, your dad knows what he's doing,' Tiana said.

Riley's dad went into the forest and Tiana tried to distract her friend. 'Look up there. Can you see the condor in the sky? I think it's watching us.'

Riley gave a small smile. 'It's probably just looking for food.'

The condor flew down to a tree near the car and watched them with its red eyes as the girls waited for Riley's dad.

'Where is he?' said Riley after five minutes. 'I'm going to find him.' She tried to get out of the car, but Tiana held her back. 'Just wait a little longer,' she said. 'Then we'll both go.'

At that moment, Riley's dad came out of the forest. With him were two firefighters. 'Cole and Ana are going to help us move the tree,' he said.

The firefighters and Riley's dad put a thick rope around the tree and tied it to the back of the car. Riley sat in the driver's seat while the three adults pushed the car, but the tree didn't move. Then slowly the car moved forward and pulled the tree to the side of the road so that the car could drive through.

'Thanks for your help,' Riley's dad said to the firefighters. 'And thanks for your awesome work fighting the fire.'

'You're welcome,' said Ana. 'But the fire is moving north-east now and it's getting stronger.'

Tiana got out of the car. 'It's moving north-east?' she asked worriedly. 'Where exactly?'

The woman checked her screen. 'Toward the Yurok reservation,' she said. 'The people there were told to leave. I hope they listened.'

Tiana took a deep breath and suddenly the condor flew away.

The next day, Amy wrote to her friends again:

Amy

OMG Tiana, are you OK? And the reservation? The fire was all over the news! 😦

Tiana

🙏 *Thanks, Amy, we're OK. The fire got really close to the reservation, but the tribe helped firefighters turn the fire in a different direction. But we're so sad about the forest. So much of it was destroyed.* 😭

Diego

Tiana, we're here for you. What can we do? 😦

Troy

We'll set up a crowdfunding page. Send us some more info. Stay strong! 💪

Good to know

Crowdfunding is a way to collect money on social media. It can be for a personal, social or business project.

2 What was the result?

Read the story again. Write what happened as a result of each action or event 1–5.

1 A spark came from a campfire. → *A fire started in the forest.*
2 There was a tree on the road. → ...
3 Two firefighters came to help. → ...
4 The fire moved north-east. → ...
5 Amy wrote to her friends. → ...

3 Planning a camping trip

a) **You're going camping. List 25 things you will need. Look up words you don't know.**

b) **Compare your list with a partner. Agree on the ten most important things.**

4 Life skills & listening Think creatively

a) **Tiana's friends helped creatively. Listen. How much money did they collect?**

b) **Listen again and write what each friend did.**

1 Amy, a photographer, organized an online exhibition of her ...
2 Diego, a robot builder, held a robot ...
3 Troy, a trumpet player, gave a concert with the choir from his ...

c) **Now you want to crowdfund to help a friend. What are your ideas?**

▸ Workbook, pp. 66–67

Digital quiz   I can **understand a story about problem-solving.**

Swimming in the desert

1 The title of the film

BEFORE YOU WATCH **Read the film title. What kind of film would you expect to see? What do you think the film is about?**

Good to know

California has three deserts. A desert gets less than ten inches (25.4 cm) of rain in a year – while New York City gets an average 49,5 inches (about 126 cm) of rain per year.

2 VIEWING Making a river

The film is set in the town of Agua Dulce in California. Angie doesn't speak and uses sign language or writes things down, so a narrator tells her story.

a) **Watch the first part of the film. Choose the best words.**

1 In the past, there was more / better / less water in the area.
2 A soft drinks / bottled water / truck company bought up the wells and their water.
3 Now the landscape is very hot / green / dry.
4 Lots of people are moving away from / moving to / staying at Agua Dulce.

b) **Watch the second part of the film. Put the key events in the correct order.** *1D, 2 ...*

A Angie's grandfather and other people help to fill the river with water.
B Angie wants to make a new river with the water from her grandfather's well.
C Angie's grandfather sells his well to the bottled water company.
D Angie's mum leaves Angie with her grandfather. He isn't very nice to Angie.
E Angie is angry with her grandfather: She writes rude messages and leaves the office.

c) **Why do you think Angie's grandfather changed his mind?**

I think he felt ... / he realized that ... / he wanted to ...

d) **Do you think the ending is possible or is it just a fantasy ending? Discuss with a partner.**

3 GLOBAL GOALS Climate action

Find the official website for the global goals and their suggestions for climate action. As a group, choose one thing that you can do. *We could / should stay informed ...*

Talk about charts

1 How to explain a chart

A chart is a drawing that shows numbers. It is often easier to understand than an explanation in words. For example, a chart about wildfires in California can help you talk about the danger to nature there (landscapes, trees and wildlife). There are different kinds of charts, e.g. bar charts, column charts, line charts or pie charts.

a) Introduce the chart: Say what kind of chart it is, what it is about and name the source.

This column chart shows ...
The source of the data / numbers / statistics is ...
The data / numbers / statistics are from ... (year)

Good to know

In the USA, land is measured in acres. In Europe, we use square kilometres (km^2).
1000 acres = 4.047 km^2

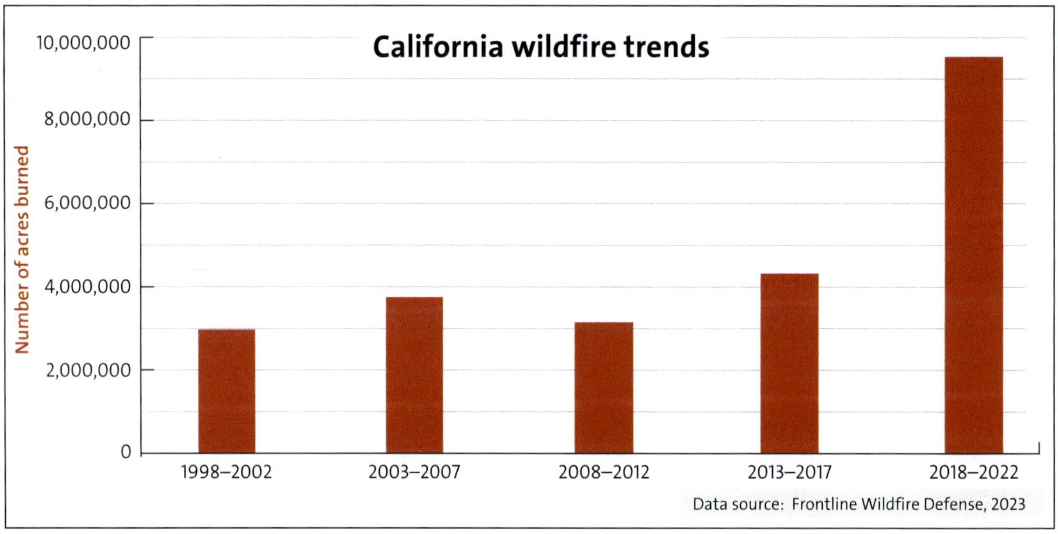

Datenquelle: https://www.frontlinewildfiredefense.com (siehe Quellenverzeichnis)

b) Talk about the numbers.

In the years from ... to ..., ... acres of land were burned.
This number went up/down in the years from ... to ...
More/Fewer acres of land were burned in the years ... than ...
The chart shows that the number of acres burned has increased / decreased in the last 25 years.

▶ English numbers, p. 211 ▶ Wordbank 5, p. 203 ▶ Skills file 8, p. 169

2 Talk about other charts

Now talk about charts on artificial intelligence (AI) and Native Americans.
Partner B: Look at p. 144. Partner A: Look at p. 149.

Digital quiz I can talk about charts.

Prepare and give a presentation

Step 1: Choose your topic

Choose a topic from this unit for your presentation:

Artificial intelligence

Native Americans

Californian nature

Step 2: Think of ideas

a) In groups of students with the same topic, exchange ideas from the unit pages and make notes. You can also do some research. You can structure your ideas with the help of a mind map for example.

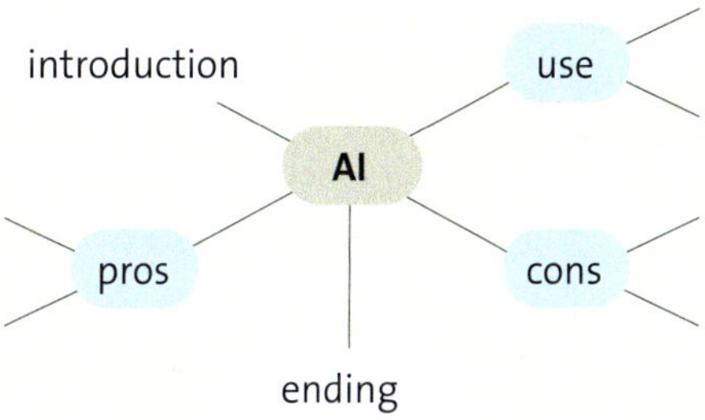

b) To support your ideas, choose a chart from pages 134, 144 or 149.

▸ Skills file 4, p.164 ▸ Skills file 8, p.169

c) Use headings to structure your ideas. Decide who is going to present each part.

Step 3: Make notes, check and present

a) Prepare your part of the presentation with slides and/or note cards and check it.

b) Practise your presentation as a group.

c) Present your presentation to a group who chose a different topic. Use Touch – Turn – Talk.

Touch your slide or poster to show what you are talking about.
Turn to the group and look at them.
Talk using your short notes.

▸ Skills file 6, p.166

Step 4: Give feedback

Listen carefully to the other presentation and give feedback.

- Were the ideas interesting?
- Did the presentation have a good structure?
- Did the group explain the slides, pictures and chart well?
- What did you like most?

▸ Study skills, p.100 ▸ Feedback phrases, p. 210

Digital quiz

I can prepare and give a presentation.

1 California in one picture

I can talk about California.

a) LISTENING Listen to Riley's conversation with her dad. Put pictures A–F in the correct order. There are two extra pictures.

A

B

C

D

E

F

b) Listen again. True (T) or false (F)?

1 The competition wants to find the most shocking photo of California.
2 The photos have to show the urban and rural sides of the state.
3 Riley prefers pictures of buildings.
4 Mike thinks people in California love nature.
5 Mike thinks pictures should be beautiful.
6 To Riley it's important to show people of different ages.

c) SPEAKING Which photo in a) do you think sums up California? Tell the class. Give reasons.

I would choose photo ... It shows ... I think this photo sums up California because ...

2 SPEAKING Should we use AI?

I can have a discussion about AI.

a) You and your partner want to write an article about a recent school trip. Look at the reasons for and against using AI (A–D). Which of them use the simple present passive?

A we can save time

B sometimes wrong information is given by AI

C our writing skills aren't practised

D we can focus more on research and interviews

b) Make a table for and against AI. Complete it with reasons A–D from a). Add two of your own reasons.

c) Now have the discussion with your partner. **Partner A:** You want to write the article using AI. **Partner B:** You disagree. Use the ideas from a) and the phrases below. Then swap roles.

I think we should/shouldn't use AI because ... • I hear what you're saying, but ... • You have a point that ... • But can't you see that ... • I don't see it that way at all because ...

Check

3 The Hoopa tribe

I can talk about native American history.

a) LANGUAGE **For her essay about Native American history, Tiana is reading about the Hoopa tribe. Complete the information with the correct form of the simple past passive.**

The Hoopa are a Native American tribe in northern California, along the Trinity and Klamath rivers. While most Californian tribes *were forced* **(1 force)** to leave their land by European settlers, the Hoopa ... **(2 allow)** to stay. In 1864, a document ... **(3 sign)** with the American government. It said that the Hoopa land belongs to the Hoopa tribe. This meant that their land ... **(4 protect)** and settlers couldn't take it from them. However, the Trinity and Klamath rivers, which are important to the tribe, ... **(5 not include)**. As a result, between 1911 and 1963, eight dams were built on the two rivers to create electricity. The water quality ... **(6 affect)** by the dams – water levels went down and temperatures rose, so that the natural homes of many salmon ... **(7 destroyed)**. In 2002, thousands of salmon ... **(8 kill)** because of this.

b) WRITING **Tiana wants to write a paragraph about this photo of a Hoopa man. Use the photo and Tiana's notes to write her text. Use the simple past passive for two of the sentences (*).**

*famous photo, *taken 1923*
foreground: Trinity River, background: forest
Hoopa man – fishing
Trinity River, Klamath River: important to Hoopa tribe
*before dams *built: lots of salmon; today: fewer salmon*

c) MEDIATION **Tiana shares an online article with her German friend Max from Mainz. Complete the dialogue with his little brother. Tell him three important details from the article.**

Max	Wie cool!
Bruder	Was denn?
Max	Tiana hat mir einen Artikel geschickt. Einige Dämme im Klamath-Fluss in Kalifornien sind zerstört worden.
Bruder	Warum das denn?
Max	...

Hi Max! How are you? Check out this article: It's the news that we've hoped for!!

Klamath River: four dams destroyed
After many years of debate, four of the six dams along California's Klamath River have been destroyed. This action was taken to save the river and protect the local wildlife, especially salmon. Native American tribes, including the Yurok and the Hoopa, first protested against the dams in 2002, when thousands of salmon were killed. Native Americans are hopeful that the number of salmon will rise now that the dams are gone because the fish can return to their natural homes and find cooler water.

Check

4 At Pinnacles National Park

I can talk about nature in California.

a) WORDS **Read definitions 1–6 and find the correct words in the text below.**

1 It's a place where visitors sleep in tents.
2 It's a fire that moves over a large area.
3 It's a very small piece of fire.
4 It's created when something burns.
5 It's a word for animals in natural conditions.
6 It's a small grey and brown animal.

Welcome to our campground! Please read the following information carefully.

- There's sometimes a high risk of wildfires. A single spark can destroy our forest. Campfires are only allowed when there's no fire danger. Check online for updates.
- If you see smoke, you must report it as soon as possible.
- Don't feed the wildlife. Animals like raccoons can become aggressive if they start to look for food from campers.

b) WRITING **Look at Matt's mind map and write his blog post about his trip to Pinnacles. Don't forget to include linking words and adjectives. You can start like this:**

I recently visited Pinnacles National Park in central California with …

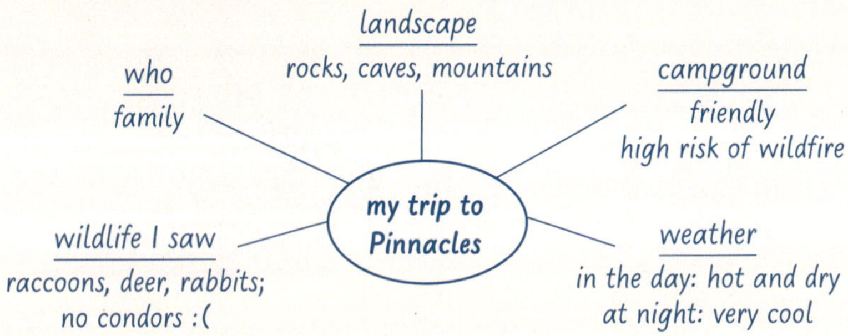

5 STUDY SKILLS Condors in California

I can talk about charts.

Riley has found a chart about condors for her geography homework. Copy and complete her text with the correct word.

The **chart / drawing (1)** shows how the number of condors in California has changed over **32 / 42 (2)** years. The **source / writer (3)** of the statistics is the US Fish and Wildlife Service and the **information / numbers (4)** are from 1980–2022. Since 1980, the number of condors in California has **gone down / risen (5)**: In 1980, there were **a few / no (6)** condors in California. By 2000, there were nearly 200, but **all / most (7)** of them were in zoos. In 2022, there were nearly 600 condors and **less / more (8)** than half of them were in the wild.

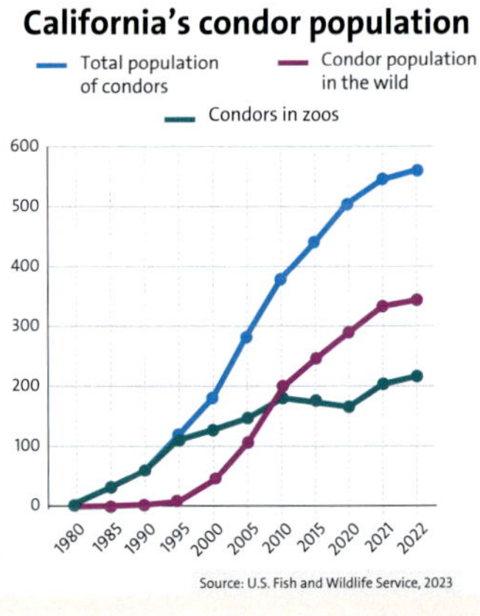

Datenquelle: https://www.fws.gov/media/california-condor-population-graph-1980-2022 (siehe Quellenverzeichnis)

Check

6 READING An interview with the firefighters

I can understand a story about problem-solving.

For her blog, Riley has interviewed the two firefighters at Redwood National Park.

Lots of you already know that I had a pretty scary experience when I was camping at Redwood recently. Well, today I finally spoke with Cole and Ana, the awesome firefighters who helped us.

Riley First of all I want to say thank you for agreeing to do this interview for my blog. And more importantly, thank you for helping us to move the fallen tree from the road that night.

Cole No problem. We were just doing our job and we're happy that you guys got home safely.

Ana And we're really excited to do this interview! We are often visiting high schools to talk about fire safety, but this is our first interview!

Riley Oh great! So I would love to hear about your work. What's it like being a firefighter in California right now? And would you recommend it as a job?

Cole I would definitely recommend it – it's such an important job and you can really make a difference in people's lives. But it's very challenging, and it gets more challenging every year.

Riley That's because the number of fires keeps rising, right?

Ana Right. We're not getting enough rain, and the land is very dry, so it burns easily. I'm sure you talk about climate change at school. It's a very big problem, and not just for Californians.

Riley I hope this isn't rude, but I don't understand how you can enjoy firefighting when the fires are getting worse and worse.

Cole Well, we're really focussed on the solutions, and that's how we stay positive. It's something that Ana and I talk about a lot. Did you know that around 95% of wildfires are actually started by human activities – things like campfires and smoking? If we want to change people's behaviour, we need to tell them about the dangers.

Ana And that's why we like going into high schools, doing tours of the fire station, and having conversations like this!

Riley I'm sure that helps. Is there anything else that gives you hope?

Ana Well, AI is something that we're pretty excited about right now. It's used more and more to help us understand what direction a wildfire will move in. And it can even identify and report a fire before a human has noticed it. This can really help us to stop fires before they get out of control.

a) **Read the interview. True (T) or false (F)? Correct the false sentences. Say where in the text you found the information.**

1 Cole and Ana often do interviews with high school students.
2 Cole thinks that firefighting is getting easier every year.
3 Climate change is having a big effect on the weather in California.
4 Cole and Ana often talk about how to improve the situation in California.
5 Most wildfires begin because of lightning.

b) **Answer the questions with short answers.**

1 What do Cole and Ana do to try and stop fires from happening?
2 How can new technology help with firefighting?

Check

United

A magazine for young people across the USA

What languages do you and people in your family speak?

I love languages! *by Tiana Moore*

Aiyekwee!
That's 'Hello' in the Yurok language – the language of the Yurok tribe in California. The last person who spoke **Yurok** as a first language died in 2013. But before he died he made lots of recordings and taught other people the language. At my school, the Eureka High School in California, there is a Yurok language program and I have also learned some Yurok phrases from my mom. However, I speak English with my dad, and we all speak English too when we're together.

A lot of people all over the world speak **English** as a first or second language. If you go traveling, you'll always find someone who will speak at least a little bit of English! And what's best: On the internet you can connect with different people in English and talk about your favourite music, shows and games. It's really cool to find out how other kids live!

At school I have **Spanish** lessons too which I really like. A lot of people speak Spanish in California and the USA and you can hear Spanish and see Spanish signs all over California.

Some of the kids in my class speak Spanish at home with their parents and with each other at break time. My friend Rosa and her two brothers were born here, but their parents are from Mexico. Rosa and her brothers speak Spanish at home with their parents, but they speak English together. And Rosa says she feels more American than Mexican. I try and speak Spanish with Rosa, although I feel a bit embarrassed about my terrible accent! I also make a lot of stupid mistakes, but that's how you learn a language, right?

How many different languages are there in your class?

[1] **¡Hola!** (Spanish) *Hallo!* [2] **Se habla español.** (Spanish) *Man spricht Spanisch.*

Making a language body map

We did an activity at school where we made a body map with the languages that we know or that we would like to learn.

- First you think about when you use each language or why you like it.
- Then you draw an outline[1] of a human body and match each language to a part of the body.
- Choose a different color for each language and write a key.
- Finally, color in your body map.

Khalil's language body map

My friend Khalil speaks three languages: English, French and Arabic. All three languages are important to Khalil for different reasons. This is his map and what he told me about it:

The heart[2] in my body map is red — this is Arabic. My family's language is Arabic because my mom and dad come from Morocco. My mom has a big family and I love it when we all meet, have a meal together and speak Arabic.

I colored the legs in my body map red too because I speak Arabic with my dad when we play soccer together?

The head in my body map is yellow for English. This is because I speak English at school and learn things there. My hands are also yellow because English is the language that I write best.

I'm also learning French at school, and since my mom can speak French really well, she helps me with my homework. She sometimes cooks French dishes – I love that, so my stomach[3] is blue.

I feel very lucky to speak three languages! In the future, I'd also like to learn Korean because I like the sound of the language and I love K-pop[4]!

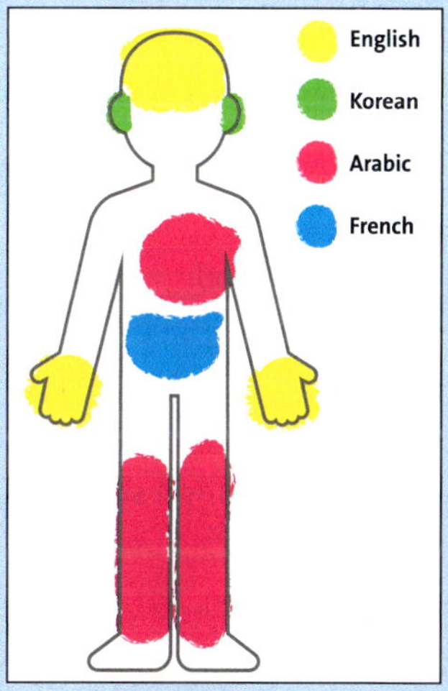

What would your language body map look like?

---

[1] **outline** *Umriss* [2] **heart** *das Herz* [3] **stomach** *der Magen, der Bauch* [4] **K-pop** *die koreanische Popmusik*

Effects of climate change in California

Human activities like burning **fossil fuels**, cutting down[1] trees and factory production[2] create **greenhouse gases** which trap[3] heat from the sun. This **causes** temperatures to rise – an **effect** that we call **climate change** or **global warming**.

People love California's warm weather, but climate change often makes some parts of the state too warm. **Environmental disasters** are often on the news. Just in July 2023, 358 maximum temperature **records** were **reached** or **broken** and an unbelievable 129°F (53.9°C) were measured in Death Valley, a California desert (see photo on p. 117).

Lake Oroville, California, in 2019

Lake Oroville, California, in 2021

Extreme heat causes droughts[4], which **increase** the risk of wildfires. Wildfires not only destroy nature: They also kill people, burn buildings and cause serious air pollution. And wildfires cost Californians billions of dollars each year for firefighters, medical care[5] and repairs. Droughts also mean that there is less water to create **hydropower**, so that California needs more fossil fuels. And more power is needed: To **cool off**, Californians often use **air conditioning**, but when too many people use it at the same time, the state sometimes runs out of[6] power.

It might sound strange, but climate change causes droughts *and* flooding. The air can hold more water when temperatures are high. When it finally rains, a lot of water comes down and can cause floods. These floods can damage homes, roads and other infrastructure[7] and make it hard to grow food.

Glaciers are important sources of water for rivers and lakes. The rising temperatures cause them to melt early in the year. Little or no new ice forms, which further **reduces** the size of the glaciers. So when they melt, there is less water.

Climate change **significantly** affects Native American communities in California. Many of these communities use natural **resources** like fish and plants, which are hurt by **environmental** changes. Salmon, for example, which are important for many Native American **diets** and cultures, can't live as well in warmer water. It is important for people to work together to reduce greenhouse gases and solve these problems to protect the environment and the people who live in the state. Climate change is creating many challenges for California. But there's reason for hope: California already produces more **renewable energy** (like wind energy or **solar** energy) than any other US state except for Texas.

[1] (to) **cut down** (trees) *(Bäume) abholzen* [2] **factory production** *die Fabrikherstellung*
[3] (to) **trap** *(ein)fangen, einschließen* [4] **drought** *die Dürre* [5] **medical care** *die medizinische Versorgung*
[6] **run out of** (sth.) *jm. geht etwas aus* [7] **infrastructure** *die Infrastruktur*

1 Understanding the text

Read the text on p. 142. Complete each sentence with the correct word or words (A, B or C).

1 In 2023, it was extremely A rainy B hot C flooded in Death Valley, California.
2 High temperatures make it easier for wildfires to start because they A cause rain B make the environment drier C cause glaciers to grow.
3 When too many people cool their homes at once, there is sometimes A not enough power B too much power C a decrease in the temperature outside.
4 Melting glaciers A feed rivers B damage roads C cause earlier winters.
5 Native American communities in California are affected by climate change because A they aren't near water B it damages natural resources and lands C they don't use electricity.

2 Thinking about climate change

a) In groups, talk about the five types of environmental disasters in blue on p. 142. Say which type is the most serious for you and say why.

b) Discuss ways to reduce the number of these environmental disasters. Decide which one is easiest / hardest to reduce and list your reasons.

Use your words and phrases

I think that ... is the most serious because ...	
We can reduce the number of ... by	managing / saving ... / using less ... / using more solar and wind energy / ...
I think that ... is the hardest to reduce because	we need ... / people don't want to ... / companies use ...

c) Look for 'UN weather kids USA' online and watch Kaylee's very special weather report. Name her suggestions against climate change.

Key terms

- air conditioning *die Klimaanlage*
- (to) cause (sth.) *etwas bewirken / verursachen*
- cause and effect *Ursache und Wirkung*
- climate change *der Klimawandel*
- (to) cool off *(sich) abkühlen*
- diet *die Ernährung, die Diät*
- *disaster die Katastrophe*
- environmental *Umwelt-*
- fossil fuel *der fossile Brennstoff*
- glacier *der Gletscher*
- global warming *die Erderwärmung*
- greenhouse gas *das Treibhausgas*
- hydropower *die Wasserkraft*
- (to) reach / break a record *einen Rekord erreichen / brechen*
- (to) reduce *reduzieren, verringern*
- renewable energy *erneuerbare Energie*
- resource *die Ressource, der Bestand*
- significant(ly) *signifikant, bedeutend*
- solar *Sonnen- / Solar-*

Partner page

▸ Page 119

4 Speaking & Writing Developing a game

a) **Partner B:** Listen to partner A.
Take notes on the missing step 1 for developing a video game. Then read the notes and tell your partner step 2.
Use the passive. Take turns to complete all the steps.

The main features of the game are decided.

Step 1: ...
Step 2: main features of game – decide
Step 3: ...
Step 4: code for the game – write
Step 5: ...
Step 6: demo of game – test
Step 7: ...
Step 8: game – launch

▸ Page 123

4 Words What is it?

b) **Partner B:** Look at the answers in blue. Write sentences with the simple past passive to describe them. Don't show your partner!

1 big birds / which / hunt / by Native Americans – **turkeys**
2 something / which / return to / or buy back / by tribes – **tribal land**
3 places / where some Native American children / send – **boarding schools**
4 long green vegetables / which / grow by Native Americans – **beans**

c) Listen to partner A's sentences and say the correct words.

d) Read out your sentences from b). **Partner A** says the correct words.

▸ Page 134

2 Talk about other charts

a) **Partner B:** Explain the bar chart on this page to partner A:

1 Introduce the chart.
2 Explain the numbers.

▸ English numbers, p. 211
▸ Wordbank 5, p. 203 ▸ Study skills 8, p. 169

b) **Partner B:** Listen to partner A who is going to explain a chart to you. Take notes. Say if you don't understand.

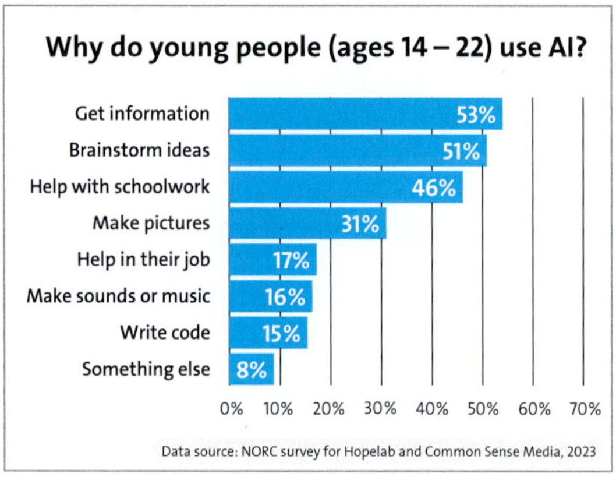

Datenquelle: http://www.commonsensemedia.org (siehe Quellenverzeichnis)

Diff bank

▸ Page 116

More practice 1 WORDS **Antonyms**

a) **Find pairs of antonyms in the word cloud.**

Antonym = the opposite (e.g. warm ◄► cold)
Synonym = the same (e.g. big ►► large)

b) **Write antonyms for these words.**

1 boring
2 rude
3 dark
4 near
5 patient
6 big
7 stupid
8 long

▸ Page 117

More practice 2 **San Francisco**

Read quotes 1–5 from a tour of San Francisco and match them to photos A–E.

1 'San Francisco is an easy city to walk around – if you like a good workout! It has more hills than any other city in the world except La Paz in Bolivia. That's why on this tour, we're going to take one of the famous San Francisco trams, which are called cable cars.'

2 'On your left, you can see a famous sight in San Francisco: the Golden Gate Bridge. It's 1.7 miles (2.7 km) long and connects the city to another part of California on the other side of the water. Isn't it beautiful?'

3 'San Francisco has always been an important city for LGBTQ people. We have the biggest Pride march in the USA! We also became home to the country's first openly gay politician, Harvey Milk, in 1977 and the first gay wedding in 2004.'

4 'If you look out at the water, you'll see another famous San Francisco sight: the old prison, Alcatraz. It's been closed since 1963, but you can still take a ferry and visit it because it's now a museum.'

5 'Our next stop is a San Francisco must-see: Pier 39. It's *the* place to be, right by the water. You'll find shops, restaurants and an aquarium here and look – wild sea lions resting in the sun! There's no other city in the world like this one!'

A

B

C

D

E

▸ Page 119

More practice 3 Riley's school day

Complete the sentences with the simple present passive. Don't forget to use *is / are / isn't / aren't*.

1 Riley *is driven* **(drive)** to school by her dad.
2 Students ... **(check)** by security guards before they can go inside.
3 This is to make sure that guns ... **(not bring)** to school.
4 The national anthem ... **(play)** at the beginning of each school day.
5 Riley's favourite subject, PE, ... **(teach)** by Mrs Gibson.
6 Riley is happy when the basketball games ... **(win)** by her team.
7 For lunch, she brings sandwiches which ... **(make)** by her dad.
8 Riley doesn't like the lunch that ... **(cook)** at school very much.

▸ Language file 19a), p. 193

More practice 4 WORDS Action verbs

Choose the best verb from the box for the blue words or phrases.

decide • design • fix • launch • test • write

Action verbs describe what you do (for example when you build a game) and they can be in the active or passive. They don't need to be about movement: Think, sleep and sit are all action verbs.

1 It's important to **repair** any bugs before you **start selling** a product.
2 First, programmers **choose** what kind of game to build.
3 I'd love to learn how to **create** code.
4 Companies have special people to **see if there's a problem with** a new product.
5 Today, artists often use computers to **draw or plan** video game characters.

▸ Page 121

More help 8 MY TASK Let's discuss

a) **Make notes about the pros and cons of using AI. You can use your work from pages 118–121 to help you.**

😊

- AI can be helpful for correcting texts / driving / health / video games...
- AI can generate images / create new things and ideas / ...
- AI is something that everyone can use / ...
- AI can give feedback directly ...

😟

- Some people might trust AI too much / ...
- AI might mean that some people lose their jobs
- It's hard to know what is fake or real ...
- AI uses other people's work / can make mistakes / ...

▸ Page 122

More practice 5 Thanksgiving

a) **Look at the pictures and read the article. Answer the questions.**

1 What's Thanksgiving about?

2 Why do some people not celebrate Thanksgiving?

> Each year, on the fourth Thursday of November, Americans celebrate Thanksgiving. There are huge parades in New York, Chicago, Philadelphia, Houston and other cities.
>
> Families and friends come together at home. In some families, each person says what they are thankful for that year before the Thanksgiving meal. Families traditionally eat turkey with vegetables like sweet potatoes and corn, followed by pumpkin pie for dessert.
>
> But what are Americans actually celebrating? In 1620, people from Plymouth in England founded a colony called Plymouth in America. Legend says that the Native Americans who lived there, the Wampanoag tribe, helped the settlers to grow food. After the settlers had picked their first fruit and vegetables in 1621, the settlers and Native Americans celebrated together for three days.
>
> Today not all Americans celebrate Thanksgiving. After the colonization and killing of Native Americans by white settlers, this happy celebration seems wrong to them.

b) **In small groups, say what you are thankful for this year.**

c) **Do you think it's right for Americans to celebrate Thanksgiving? Discuss with a partner.**

▸ Page 123

More practice 6 Lucky and unlucky

Write about Tiana's day. What would she say? Use the simple past passive.

1 My bike was stolen at school.

▸ Language file 19c), p. 193

my bike – steal – at school

it – return – the next day

I – choose – for the soccer team

my soccer team – beat

my computer files – delete

the files – save – by mum

▸ Page 123

4 Words What is it?

b) **Partner A: Look at the answers in blue. Write sentences with the simple past passive to describe them. Don't show your partner!**

1 big animals / which / hunt by Native Americans – buffaloes
2 a yellow vegetable / which / grow by Native Americans – corn
3 a group / which / form / by Yurok to govern the tribe – council
4 something / which / write / by Tiana about Native American history – essay

c) **Read out your sentences from b). Partner B says the correct words.**

d) **Listen to partner B's sentences and say the correct words.**

Challenge 1 The foxes and the sun

a) **Tiana's grandfather told her a Yurok legend. Complete it with the simple past passive of the verbs in the box.**

burn • choose • ~~create~~ • kill • make • rescue • see

The foxes were angry with the sun, so a plan *was created* (1) about what to do. Twelve brave foxes ... (2) by the others to catch the sun and strong ropes ... (3) to hold the sun down. The foxes watched as the sun went down in the sky. When the sun was at the top of a hill, the foxes caught it and held it down with the ropes. But the foxes ... (4) by a group of Native Americans and they ... (5) by them. The Native Americans cut the ropes and the sun ... (6). Today you can still see where an extremely big spot ... (7) into the ground by the sun.

b) **How did the foxes catch the sun and what was the result?**

▸ Language file 19c), p. 193

▸ Page 124

Challenge 2 Living in two cultures

a) **Tiana lives in two cultures: the American culture, and the Native American culture of her tribe. Sometimes she's happy about this and sometimes it can be hard for her. Do you or your friends live in two or more cultures? Talk about your situation.**

It's a gift because ...	It's hard because ...
I can speak ...	my parents / some people say ..., but I think ...
I experience ...	my parents / some people don't understand ...
I learn ...	sometimes I am bullied / called names like ...
I am more open to / tolerant of ...	I am criticized for ...

b) **Discuss your ideas in class.**

▸ Text file, pp. 140–141

▸ Page 127

Challenge 3 Campfire safety

Complete the campfire safety tips with suitable conjunctions.

1 You do not need a license for a campfire ... you make it at a campground.
2 Check for fire warnings ... you want to make a fire.
3 ... you can find an area away from trees, do not make a fire.
4 Put a circle of rocks around your campfire ... nothing around it can catch fire.
5 Don't put things like cans into the fire ... it's dangerous.
6 ... the fire may be out, put water on it to make sure.

▸ Page 128

More help 5 MY TASK My travel blog post

b) **Think of ideas for your travel blog post:**

What did you see and do?	I saw a beautiful beach / forest / lake / ... I saw a bear / a deer / a fox / lots of wildlife / ... I went climbing / hiking / kayaking / swimming / ... I climbed a mountain / made a campfire / took lots of photos / ...
Where did you sleep?	I slept in a cabin / tent / hostel / ... It was a day trip, so I slept a home.
Was it a good or bad trip? Why?	It was an awesome / a fantastic / a really cool / ... trip because ... It was a boring / dangerous / terrible / ... trip because ...

▸ Page 134

2 Talk about other charts

a) **Partner A:** Listen to partner B who is going to explain a chart to you. Take notes. Say if you don't understand.

b) **Partner A:** Explain the pie chart on this page to partner B:

1 Introduce the chart.
2 Explain the numbers.

▸ English numbers, p. 211
▸ Wordbank 5, p. 203 ▸ Study skills 8, p. 169

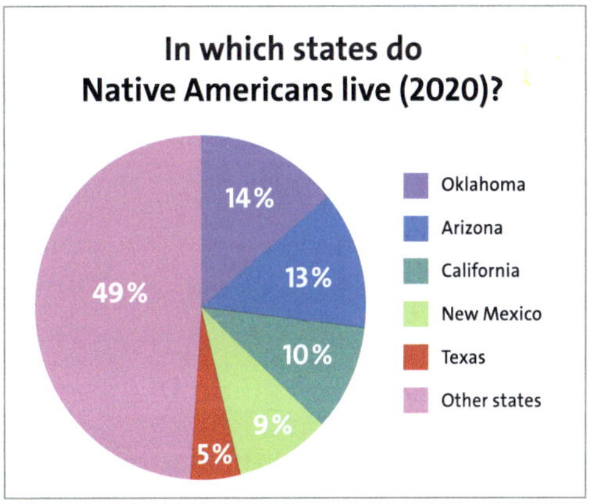

Datenquelle: https://www.census.gov (siehe Quellenverzeichnis)

Unit 5
Canada: The northern neighbour

B

maple leaf flag

A

Orcas, whales with teeth

Population of Canada: **41 million**
Born abroad: **23%**
Native people: First Nations, Inuit and Metis (people with native and European background): **5%**
French spoken as a first language: **22%**
French spoken as a first language in the province of Quebec: **84.1%**
Native languages: about **70**

Source: Statistics Canada, 2021 Census (s. Quellenverzeichnis)

C

Niagara Falls – waterfalls in south-east Canada

1 Speaking **A beautiful country**

Copy the table. Look at the map, the box and photos A–G and make notes about Canada in your table. Then use your notes and talk to a partner about Canada.

Location & size	Population	Languages	Cities	Flag	Sports	Nature & wildlife
north of ...	...	...	...	...	...	...

2 Listening **A quick guide to Canada**

a) Listen to the podcast. What fact was most interesting to you?

b) Listen again. Add information to your table from 1 and compare with a partner.

Nach dieser Unit kann ich ...

- über Kanada sprechen
- einen längeren Auszug einer Geschichte verstehen

E

A game of lacrosse

F

A moose, the world's largest deer

D

Mountains in the Yukon in north-west Canada

G

The city of Vancouver

3 Viewing **Exploring Vancouver**

a) Before you watch **Find Vancouver on the map on** p. 312 **and describe its location.**

b) **Watch the video with Flora and Note. What is Flora's connection with Vancouver and what does she think of the city?**

c) **Watch again. Pay attention to what you can do and eat in Vancouver.**

d) **What activities and food can you remember? Tell a partner.**

You can go to the beach ...

e) **What is your impression of the city?**

Vancouver seems like a diverse / ... city.

▸ More practice 1, p. 160 ▸ More practice 2, p. 161

▸ Workbook, p. 82

Digital quiz I can **talk about Canada.**

The amazing adventures of Jack London: Forty Mile

by David Fermer and Till Nachtmann

1 READING My reading log

a) BEFORE YOU READ **Start a page for a reading log including the title and authors above. Use the information on this page and answer questions 1–3 in complete sentences.**

1 Where is Dawson City? Find it on the map on p. 312. *Dawson City is …*
2 Why is Jack London Smith in Dawson City and why does he go to Forty Mile?
3 Who helps Jack?

b) **Look at the title and the pictures on pages 152–158. What do you think the story will be like? Write one or two sentences. Give reasons.**

I think the story will be sad / … because …

c) **Jack, Shania and Skookum are in Forty Mile and have found the lost film in a museum. Read the information below and the story extract on pages 153–158. In your reading log, note down personal reactions and questions.**

Skookum is funny! / I'd be scared too. / …

Good to know

In 1896, gold was found in the Klondike, a region in the Yukon, Canada. More than 100,000 Americans left their homes to look for gold in what is known as the Klondike Gold Rush. Only a third reached their destination.

Jack London Smith is a 14-year-old British teenager named after the American writer Jack London. In 1897, the writer travelled to Dawson City in the Yukon to look for gold. 120 years later, Jack and his parents go there to find a lost film about the Gold Rush. They learn that the film-maker died in a town called Forty Mile.

Shania is a First Nations girl from Jack's school. Shania and Jack decide to look for the film on their own. Shania offers to take him to Forty Mile in her parents' motorboat. Her dog Spitz comes too.

Skookum goes to school with Jack and Shania. Shania says he's a fox because he always tries to trick tourists and get money from them. Skookum thinks they can make a lot of money if they find the film.

Hal Swanson helps the kids to find the film in Forty Mile. He lives in an old mine called Clinton Creek with his dogs. A wolf has just killed his dog Betsy and he wants to hunt the wolves.

1 Complete the sentence: Jack wants to tell his parents about the film, but can't phone them because …

2 Jack decides to leave a note for his parents. Help him write it.

We go back to the boat.

Shania says the trip back to Dawson will take a bit longer because of the current, but we should be back before dark.

I take out my phone. I want to tell my parents about finding the film, but there's no reception.

"Yukon has the worst reception in Canada," Shania explains. "You have to be in a town to make a call around here."

It's not important. I can call my parents when we're back in Dawson.

Shania unties the boat.

"Shoot!" says Skookum. "I left my picklock in the church!"

Skookum goes back to the church to look for his picklock. I watch him disappear into the bushes. He's a bit like Hal Swanson – without the beard.

Spitz barks.

"OK, Spitz! Get in," says Shania.

1 Explain why Skookum comes back so quickly.

2 How does Skookum feel when he sees the wolf and runs to the boat? Write the numbers of the lines that tell you this.

A few minutes later, Skookum comes running out of the bushes, waving his arms in the air.

“Quick! Get in the boat!” he shouts.

For a moment, I wonder if this could be another Skookum joke, but I can hear the panic in his voice, and everything about him says danger.

Something comes out of the bushes behind him.

A grey-haired dog.

“Wolves!” says Shania.

Then everything happens really quickly. Shania and I grab the boat and push it into the water. When I look over my shoulder again, I see the wolf in the bushes, watching us.

“Go, go, go!” Skookum screams, running towards us.

We jump into the boat. Shania falls over as she rushes to the back. Skookum runs into the water, splashing around like a fish on a hook.

“Give me your hand,” I say.

Skookum grabs my hand. I pull him onto the boat.

“Drive!” he shouts.

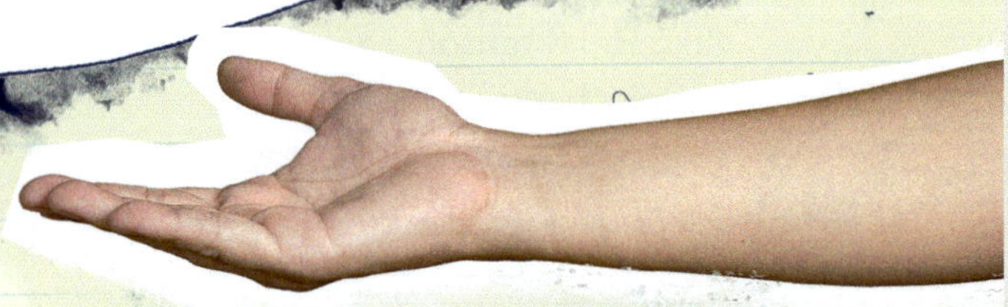

1 Write what happens in lines 1–15.

2 What do you think the kids should do next?

Shania swings the outboard motor into the water. I hear something crack. She pushes START. The motor screams and kicks up a whirlpool of water before dying.

"Please, no!" she says and lifts the outboard out of the water. Two of the three blades are broken. "Oh no! My dad's going to kill me!"

"What happened?" Skookum asks.

"I hit a rock."

I see something black in the water. "Is that petrol?" It's dripping from the motor.

Shania puts the propeller back into the water and presses START again. The motor doesn't even make a sound.

I look over to the beach. The wolf has come out of the bushes and is walking over the beach towards us, sniffing the ground at the place where we left. He seems perfectly calm.

"What do we do now?" Skookum says.

Shania has tears in her eyes.

"How should I know?"

1 Write down the kids' two options and name the problem with each option.

2 Do you have another idea? Write down what you think their best option is and why.

The wolf stands on the beach, his front paws in the water, watching us drift away on the current. He sniffs the air. One of his eyes is white.

We drift past the church and the police station. The Yukon is almost 2,000 miles long. North of us is Alaska.

"How far is the next town?" I ask.

"Just over the border," Shania says, drying her tears. "About eighty miles downriver."

I do the maths in my head. If the current carries us at, say, four miles an hour, it will take us twenty hours to get there. That would be lunchtime tomorrow.

Is that our best option?

The white-eyed wolf loses interest in us. He sniffs at the air one last time, turns around and goes back into the forest.

"We should go back to the beach," I say.

"Are you crazy?" says Skookum. "That wolf just tried to eat me!"

"Wolves don't eat people," Shania says. "They're more scared of us than we are of them."

"Tell that to Hal Swanson's Betsy."

"We should stay here," I say. "Shania's parents are expecting us back before nightfall. They can find us here."

"I say we stay in the boat and paddle back to Dawson," says Skookum.

"Against the current? With our hands?"

Even Skookum knows that's not possible.

"OK," he says. "What if White Eye decides to take a trip to the beach again? Like 'Hey, guys this is my beach, so get the hell out of here or I'll eat you'."

"We make a fire," I say.

Skookum nods grimly. "OK. But if the rescue team isn't here before midnight, that wolf is going to have us for breakfast."

1 Complete the sentences: To make sure the wolf has gone, the kids ... Then ...

2 Explain why Jack thinks that Skookum's sense of humour is back.

Chapter Nine – Clinton Creek

We decide to wait before going back to the beach. We paddle on the spot just to keep our position. It's hard work.

In the end, it's Skookum who gives up first. "Can we go back to the beach now? I think our friend is gone."

We paddle to the shore. Shania sends Spitz on land first. She throws him the rope while the three of us watch for any sign of the wolf.

Nothing.

I get out of the boat and pull us onto the beach. We carry the boat onto the grass.

"I'll get some wood," I say. "Spitz, come with me."

I feel safer with Spitz around.

I come back to the beach with my arms full of wood.

Shania uses dried leaves to start the fire. Soon the wood is burning, and we watch the red glow against the grey sky.

We take off our wet socks and shoes and put them as near to the fire as we can. Skookum takes off his coat and trousers and hangs them on a stick over the fire.

"Would this be the right time for a campfire ghost story?" Skookum says. "Something about a pack of werewolves maybe?"

"No thanks," I say, although I'm glad Skookum has his sense of humour back.

I take out some food.

We eat.

1 Write what mistake Shania and Jack made.

2 Write what you think happens next.

"We should go to Clinton Creek," Shania says.

Skookum gives her his 'are-you-mad?'-look again. "Why? What for?"

"What Jack said about my parents on the boat, it's not true."

"What did Jack say?" Skookum looks at me, panicked.

"That they know where we are," Shania says in a whisper.

"You can't be serious!?" I say. "Your parents let you take the boat out and didn't even ask where you were going?"

"I told them we were going to hang out on the river."

"Well, this is fantastic!" Skookum says sarcastically. "Just great! Do your parents know where we are?" he asks me.

I shake my head.

"Great! What a nightmare."

"Maybe there's a landline up in Clinton Creek," Shania says.

Skookum laughs sarcastically. "Yeah, right! Hal has no front teeth, but I'm sure he's got a phone. Hey, maybe he's even on Instagram!"

I agree with Shania. It's worth a try. To be on the safe side, I take out my multitool and scratch a message into the side of the boat:

If anyone does come to the beach looking for us, that's the first thing they'll see.

We wait for Skookum's clothes to dry. I take some ash and rub it into Spitz's fur. The wolves will smell him before they smell us. We put some more wood onto the fire and set off on the trail.

2 Character posters

a) In pairs, make a character poster for either Jack or Shania. Use the example on the right and an outline of a person to make notes about your character:

- what you know about him / her
- what he / she is like
- what this character does or says
- what others say about him / her
- what he / she likes or doesn't like
- how this character feels at different points in the story and why
- questions you have.

You can use the information on p. 152 and your reading log to help you.

b) Explain your character poster to a pair who made a poster for the other character.

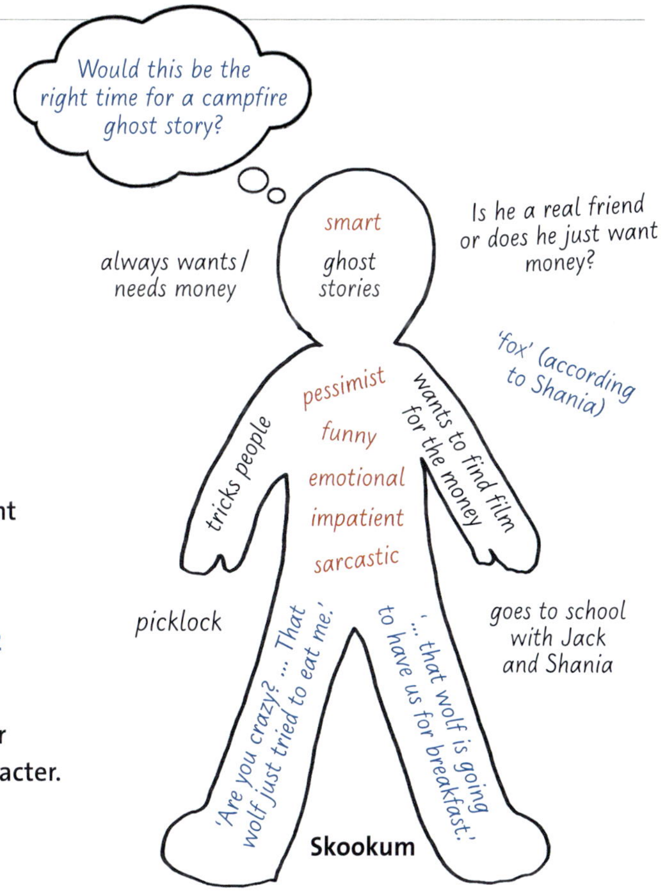

3 Writing **My review**

a) Write a short review of this extract. Begin with a short summary, then write your opinion. The questions below will help you think about the book.

- Did you like the extract and would you like to read the rest of the book? Why or why not?
- Look at your answer to 1b) on p. 152. Was the book like you expected? What was different?
- What was your favourite scene and why?
- How many stars (1–5) would you give this extract?

▶ Skills file 14, p. 175 ▶ Study skills, p. 68

b) Swap your review with a partner. Read your partner's review and comment on it.

I gave it two / four stars.

I (don't) agree. I really liked / didn't really like the story because ...

c) You still have questions about the story and the characters? Read the book and find answers!

Digital quiz

I can understand a longer story extract.

Diff bank

▸Page 151

More practice 1 READING **Life in the Arctic**

a) BEFORE YOU READ **Describe the picture below. What are the people doing?** ▸Skills file 7, p. 168

Not all Inuit live in traditional communities or even in Canada. These teens attend a youth camp to learn about their culture.

Caribou

Seal

b) **Read the article and say where Lucy lives in summer and in winter. Say why.**

Lucy Ninguik lives in Kuujjuaq, a traditional Inuit community in northern Canada. There are no roads to the village, but there is an airport which connects it to other places in the region. Food has to be flown into Kuujjuaq so it's expensive and not always fresh.

Three generations of Lucy's family live together in a small house. In winter, when the temperature is about -9°F (-23°C), the sea is frozen and the family uses snowmobiles to get around. 'But it's pretty warm in summer – about 55°F. That's 13°C,' says Lucy, smiling. In summer, Lucy's family moves to their cabin in the wilderness to hunt. 'I love being there,' says Lucy. 'I love being part of nature.' For Inuit families like Lucy's who don't live in a town or city, hunting and fishing are part of life. The family's main foods are fish, caribou meat and berries. In other areas, Inuit hunt seals and whales.

'We respect our land and when we kill an animal, we usually use every part of it', Lucy's father explains. 'We only kill what we can eat and what we really need.'

c) **Read the article again and choose the correct ending (A, B or C).**

1 You can get to Kuujjuaq by A car. B plane. C plane or car.
2 The climate is A freezing cold all year. B very hot in July and August. C almost never hot.
3 Lucy's family eats food that A they hunt and catch. B is vegetarian. C is from a store.
4 Lucy's family A sells meat to other families. B throws away the skin and bones of animals. C doesn't waste any part of the animals that they kill.

d) **Tell a partner how Lucy's life is different to yours. Would you like to live like Lucy (for a while)? Say why or why not.**

More practice 2 Q & A with Dayo

a) **Read the questions and answers. How did Dayo feel about moving to Toronto and how does he feel now?**

Q Dayo, you've been in Toronto for two years now. Where did you grow up?

A I grew up in Lagos, Nigeria. I was part of a big family. ... (1) I was happy there, but then my father lost his job. My dad's brother lived in Toronto and always told him what a friendly, multicultural city it was. So when I was eleven, my father moved to Toronto. He got a job, but he only got a visa for himself at first. He worked really hard to bring us to Canada.

Q How long did that take?

A Three years. My mother became ill, but she wanted my dad to stay in Canada and get our papers. Luckily, my aunt lived with us and looked after my mother. ... (2)

Q How did you feel when you got your papers to live in Canada?

A ... (3) I was excited, but also a bit scared. I didn't want to leave my friends.

Q Do you like living in Toronto?

A At first it wasn't easy moving to a new city and our apartment wasn't very nice. ... (4) My father worked two jobs and my mother was still sick. I didn't have many friends at first and sometimes I felt alone. I had to learn a different way of life and start at a new school. Also, we arrived in winter and it was very cold! But everybody was really friendly. ... (5) Now I'm doing well at school and have made some friends. I still miss Nigeria, but I feel very lucky to have a good life in Canada with my family.

Toronto seen from Lake Ontario

b) **Read the Q & A again.**
Put the missing information (A–E) in the correct places (1–5). *1C, ...*

A My uncle and our neighbours were very kind and helped us.
B But I worried about her and I missed my father too.
C My aunts, uncles and cousins lived near us.
D It was a dream come true for my family to be together again.
E It was very small and in a bad neighbourhood.

Inhalt

		Seite
SF 1	Vokabeln lernen und strukturieren	162
SF 2	Unbekannte Wörter erschließen	163
SF 3	Im Wörterbuch nachschlagen	163
SF 4	Im Internet recherchieren	164
SF 5	Kommunikationsstrategien	165
SF 6	Einen Vortrag halten	166
SF 7	Bilder beschreiben	168
SF 8	Diagramme beschreiben	169
SF 9	Einen Podcast erstellen	170
SF 10	Hörtexte und Filme verstehen	171
SF 11	Lesetexte verstehen	172
SF 12	Einen Artikel verfassen	173
SF 13	E-Mails und Briefe schreiben	174
SF 14	Eine Zusammenfassung/Rezension schreiben	175
SF 15	Texte überprüfen und verbessern	176
SF 16	Mediation	177

MK Die mit diesem Symbol gekennzeichneten Abschnitte enthalten Hinweise und Tipps, die dir dabei helfen, elektronische Medien beim Englischlernen einzusetzen.

Erklärfilm Dieses Symbol zeigt dir, dass du einen Erklärfilm zu diesem Thema in der App findest.

SF 1

Erklärfilm

Vokabeln lernen und strukturieren

▸ Unit 1 | pp. 19, 45 ▸ Unit 2 | pp. 78, 80
▸ Unit 3 | pp. 89, 112 ▸ Unit 4 | pp. 123, 145

Neue Vokabeln lernst du am besten an einem ruhigen Ort. Je öfter du sie übst, desto besser kannst du sie dir merken.

Wie merke ich mir neue Wörter besser?

Einzelne Wörter merkst du dir leichter in sinnvollen Zusammenhängen. Hierfür gibt es mehrere Wege:

- Notiere zu einer neuen Vokabel einen Beispielsatz oder passenden Ausdruck *(phrase): bottle → a bottle of water*
- Erstelle Wortfelder zu einem Oberbegriff:
  nature *→ wild animals: bear, ... → pets: dog, ...*
  → plants: tree, ...
  Nutze dafür Mindmaps oder Tabellen, die du ergänzt.
- Erstelle Wortfamilien: *friend, friendly, friendship, ...*
- Sammle Gegensätze *(antonyms: warm → cold)* und Wörter mit der gleichen Bedeutung *(synonyms: big → large)*.
- Stelle britische und amerikanische Wörter gegenüber.
- Nutze weitere Sprachen:
  biscuit (English) → bisküvi (Türkçe)

Checkliste Vokabeln lernen

- ✓ Lerne nur fünf bis zehn Vokabeln auf einmal.
- ✓ Lerne jeden Tag zehn Minuten.
- ✓ Lerne mit einem Freund oder einer Freundin.
- ✓ Lerne in sinnvollen Zusammenhängen.
- ✓ Lerne unterwegs mit einer Vokabeltrainer-App oder mit Karteikarten.
- ✓ Schreibe schwierige Wörter mehrmals auf.
- ✓ Sprich die Wörter und nimm dich mit dem Handy auf.
- ✓ Wiederhole die Wörter, bis du sie kannst.

SF 2

Unbekannte Wörter erschließen

▸ Vocabulary | pp. 225, 233, 247

Du kannst englische Texte verstehen, auch wenn du nicht alle Wörter kennst. Diese Tipps helfen dir, die Bedeutung von Wörtern auch ohne Wörterbuch herauszufinden:

Checkliste Wörter erschließen
- ✓ Kennst du ähnliche Wörter in anderen Sprachen?
- ✓ Kennst du ähnliche Wörter aus derselben Wortfamilie?
- ✓ Gibt es Vor- oder Nachsilben, aus denen du die Bedeutung ableiten kannst?
- ✓ Können dir der Kontext, Bilder oder Bildunterschriften beim Verstehen helfen?

Wortfamilien und Wortbildungsregeln

Ein Wort gehört immer zu einer Wortfamilie. Wenn du ein Wort aus der Wortfamilie und ein paar Regeln zur Wortbildung kennst, kannst du die Bedeutung ableiten:

Vorsilben		
un-	Aus einem positiven Adjektiv wird ein negatives.	*happy → unhappy*
Nachsilben		
-er	Aus einem Tätigkeitsverb wird eine Person.	*(to) support → supporter*
-ful, -less, -y, -al	Aus einem Nomen wird ein Adjektiv.	*care → careful, help → helpless, risk → risky, magic → magical*
-ness	Aus einem Adjektiv wird ein Nomen.	*fit → fitness*
-tion, -ation, -ment	Aus einem Verb wird ein Nomen.	*(to) collect → collection* *(to) explain → explanation* *(to) argue → argument*

SF 3

Erklärfilm

Im Wörterbuch nachschlagen

Die Wörter im Dictionary (ab S. 262) sind alphabetisch aufgelistet. Neben oder unter dem Haupteintrag (z. B. **name**) findest du oft auch noch zusammengesetzte Wörter (z. B. **first name**) oder Redewendungen (z. B. **call sb. names**).

name [neɪm]:
1. der Name 1
call sb. names jn. beschimpfen 3
family name der Familienname, der Nachname 1 **first name** der Vorname 1 **What's your name?** Wie heißt du? 1
2. (be)nennen 3

Die Ziffern 1, 2 usw. zeigen, dass ein Wort mehrere Bedeutungen hat (z. B. **free**: 1. kostenlos, 2. frei) oder als unterschiedliche Wortarten vorkommt (z. B. **act**: 1. die Tat, 2. handeln). Lies also immer den ganzen Eintrag und entscheide dann, welche Bedeutung die richtige ist.

In Online-Wörterbüchern stellst du nur die Suchrichtung (E – D oder D – E) ein und tippst dann das Wort ein. Auch hier werden dir oft mehrere Bedeutungen angeboten, aus denen du auswählen musst.

Durch einen Klick auf das Lautsprechersymbol kannst du dir ein Wort anhören.

SF 4

Im Internet recherchieren

▶ Unit 1 | p. 35 ▶ Unit 2 | p. 63 ▶ Unit 4 | p. 135

Suchen

Gib nicht nur einen Suchbegriff ein, sondern zwei oder mehrere (z. B. *New York + activities + teens*).

Auswählen

Nicht alles, was du findest, ist wichtig und richtig. Deshalb prüfe: Von wem stammt die Seite? Wie verlässlich ist die Information? Ein Online-Lexikon ist vermutlich sachlicher als ein Chat-Forum. Achte auf die Endung der Internetadresse:

- **.com** (kommerziell) oder **.uk** (britisch) können persönliche Absichten verfolgen und sind daher nicht immer sachlich oder neutral. Prüfe diese Seiten gut.
- **.gov** bedeutet, dass es eine offizielle Seite der (amerikanischen) Regierung ist – in der Regel kannst du auf die Richtigkeit der Informationen vertrauen.
- **.edu** verweist auf Webseiten von Bildungseinrichtungen – auch diese Seiten sind meist verlässlich.

Vorsicht bei Wikipedia. Das Online-Lexikon wird von Freiwilligen geschrieben und kann Fehler enthalten.

Unseriöse Quellen erkennst du z. B. an extremen oder unpassenden Überschriften, fehlenden Angaben zum Autor / zur Autorin, fehlenden Belegen oder einem veralteten Datum.

▶ Skills file 11, p. 172

Verlasse dich nicht auf nur eine einzige Internetseite, sondern ziehe zwei oder drei heran.

Sichern

- Mache dir Notizen oder drucke wichtige Seiten aus und markiere wichtige Textstellen. Gib die Inhalte in deinen eigenen Worten wieder.
- Wenn du Informationen, Texte oder Bilder einer Webseite verwenden möchtest, nenne immer den Urheber oder die Urheberin und die Internetadresse. Schreibe auch das das Datum der Veröffentlichung und wann du die Webseite zuletzt aufgerufen hast.
- Wenn du Sätze oder Satzteile wörtlich übernehmen möchtest, kennzeichne sie als Zitat durch Anführungsstriche und nenne die Quelle.

Setze Lesezeichen für Webseiten, die du später wiederverwenden möchtest.

So zitierst du richtig:
'New York City is the best place in the world for teens.'
Quelle: *Wu, Amy (11.10.2022): 'My New York', http://united.example.com*, aufgerufen am 16.10.2024

SF 5

Kommunikationsstrategien anwenden

▸ Unit 3 | p. 100 ▸ Unit 4 | p. 121

Wie drücke ich aus, was ich denke?

In einem Gespräch oder einer Diskussion sagst du, was du über ein Thema denkst, und nennst Gründe oder Beispiele, die deine Aussagen unterstützen.

I believe / think that ...
In my opinion, ...
If you ask me, ... because ...
For example, ...

Wie reagiere ich angemessen?

Frage die anderen auch nach ihrer Meinung und gehe höflich und respektvoll auf das ein, was sie sagen.

What do you think?
That's interesting. / Go on.
I agree. / That's a good point.
I see it a bit differently.
I'm not sure here.

Frage nach, wenn du nicht sicher bist, ob du etwas richtig verstanden hast oder wenn du noch mehr über das Thema erfahren möchtest.

I'm not sure I got that.
Do you mean ...?
When / Where / Why / ... ?

Zeige durch deine Körpersprache Interesse am Thema: Sitze aufrecht, halte Blickkontakt und höre aufmerksam zu. Unterbrich andere nicht.

▸ Let's talk 8, p. 208

Wie gebe ich Feedback?

Gegenseitige Rückmeldungen z. B. zu einem Vortrag, einem Text oder einer anderen Arbeit helfen dir und deinen Partnern oder Partnerinnen, Leistungen besser einzuschätzen und zu verbessern.

Feedback-Kriterien werden im Vorfeld in der Klasse besprochen, damit alle wissen, worauf sie bei der Erarbeitung achten müssen. Für eine gelungene Rückmeldung halte dich an folgende Tipps:

- Steige positiv ein und beschreibe, was gut war.
- Nenne Kritikpunkte: Was genau ist wie zu verbessern?
- Steige positiv aus: Worauf kann man aufbauen?

Feedback-Burger

Wie reagiere ich auf Feedback?

Bleib gelassen! Höre aufmerksam zu und prüfe in Gedanken, was du nachvollziehen und annehmen kannst. Frage nach, wenn du etwas nicht verstehst. Bleib offen und lass das Gehörte auf dich wirken. Du brauchst dich nicht zu verteidigen oder zu rechtfertigen!

▸ Feedback phrases, p. 210

SF 6

Einen Vortrag vorbereiten und halten

▸ Unit 1 | pp. 20, 36 ▸ Unit 4 | p. 135

Um einen guten Vortrag vor der Klasse halten zu können, musst du ihn sorgfältig vorbereiten und üben.

Informationen suchen, auswählen, sichern

▸ Skills file 4, p. 164

Nutze verschiedene Medien, um Informationen zu sammeln: das Internet, Bücher, Zeitschriften oder Zeitungen. Prüfe deine Informationen und Quellen sorgfältig. Kopiere wichtige Seiten und Quellenangaben in eine Datei oder drucke sie aus.

Checkliste Text markieren
Du kannst die wichtigen Stellen
- ✓ mit Textmarker markieren.
- ✓ unterstreichen oder umkreisen.
- ✓ mit Symbolen und Abkürzungen markieren. (? !, →, 😊, ☹).
- ✓ durch Notizen am Rand hervorheben.

Textstellen markieren

Auf Kopien von Texten kannst du Informationen markieren, um sie hervorzuheben und einfacher wiederzufinden. Konzentriere dich dabei auf dein Thema und markiere nur die wichtigsten Informationen. Zusätzlich kannst du dir auch am Rand Notizen machen.

Informationen ordnen

Ordne deine Informationen, z. B. in einer Mindmap, unter Überschriften, in Tabellen oder auf Karteikarten. Überlege, was und wie viel du zu jedem Punkt sagen möchtest.

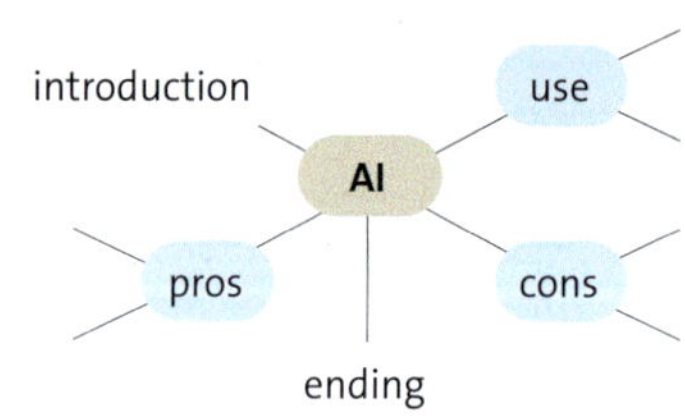

Strukturiere deinen Vortrag

Überlege dir, wie du deinen Vortrag strukturieren möchtest, und sammle nützliche Redewendungen für jeden Teil.

- **Einleitung:** Nenne dein Thema. Überlege, wie du das Interesse deines Publikums wecken kannst, z. B. mit einer Frage, die zum Nachdenken anregt. Gib deinem Publikum zu Beginn deines Vortrags einen Überblick über den Inhalt.
- **Hauptteil:** Nenne nacheinander deine Hauptpunkte. Leite jeden neuen Punkt ein und erzähle mehr dazu.
- **Schluss:** Schließe mit einer Zusammenfassung und bedanke dich fürs Zuhören. Erkundige dich, ob jemand Fragen hat.

I'd like to talk about …
The question is: …

To begin with, I'd like to tell you about …
Secondly, …
Finally, …

To sum up, …
Thank you for listening.
Do you have any questions?

Die Inhalte veranschaulichen

Gestalte nun dein Poster oder deine Folien gemäß deiner Struktur. Veranschauliche deine wichtigsten Punkte durch Bilder oder Diagramme. Beschreibe und erkläre sie. Nenne auch Beispiele, die deine Aussagen verdeutlichen.

Notizen erstellen

Bereite nun Karteikarten mit kurzen Notizen vor, um während deines Vortrags möglichst frei zu sprechen.

- Strukturiere deine Karteikarten genauso wie deine Präsentation.
- Schreibe keine ganzen Sätze, sondern das, was für dich wichtig ist, in Stichpunkten auf *(keywords)*.
- Hebe die wichtigsten Begriffe optisch hervor, z. B. durch Überschriften, Absätze und Farben. Du kannst auch kleine Erinnerungen zum Ablauf deines Vortrags notieren, z. B. wann du welches Medium einsetzt.
- Schreibe Ziffern anstelle von Zahlen, z. B. „15“ statt „fifteen“, und verwende gängige Abkürzungen.
- Nutze auch Symbole, z. B. Smileys für Gefühle, Flaggen für Länder, Strichzeichnungen für Personen.

Deinen Vortrag üben

Übe deinen Vortrag vor dem Spiegel oder nimm dich mit dem Smartphone auf. Oder übt zu zweit und gebt euch gegenseitig Tipps, wie ihr euch verbessern könnt. Gib die Inhalte mit deinen eigenen Worten wieder. Verwende kurze, verständliche Sätze und vermeide schwierige oder unbekannte Begriffe. Erkläre diese, wenn es notwendig ist. Achte auf die Zeit.

Deinen Vortrag halten

Überprüfe zu Beginn, ob alles vorbereitet ist. Dann schaue dein Publikum an und warte, bis es ruhig ist. Sprich langsam, laut und deutlich.
Zeige während deines Vortrags auf deine Folien oder dein Poster. Lies den Text darauf nicht einfach ab.
Gib deinem Publikum Zeit zum Lesen oder erläutere deine Inhalte mit eigenen Worten oder Beispielen.

Checkliste Computerpräsentation

- ✓ Wähle ein einfaches Folienlayout.
- ✓ Verwende eine Schriftgröße von mindestens 16 Punkt.
- ✓ Beschränke dich auf wenig Text.
- ✓ Wähle nur ein Bild oder Diagramm pro Folie.
- ✓ Schreibe die Adresse der Internetseite dazu, von der du das Bild oder Diagramm hast.
- ✓ Gib alle Quellen, die du verwendet hast, am Ende der Präsentation an.

► Skills file 7, p. 168
► Skills file 8, p. 169

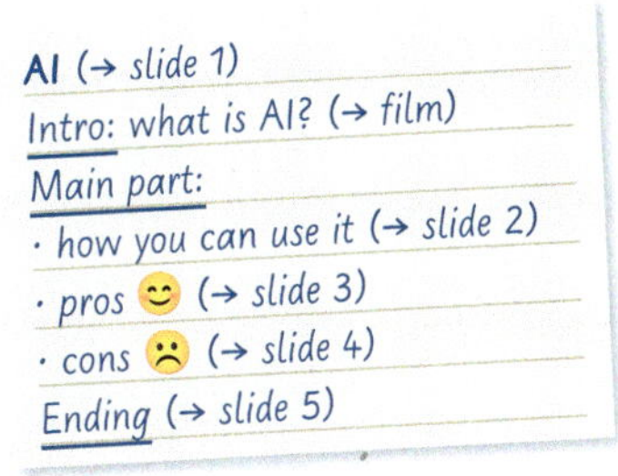

Es gibt auch Apps, mit denen du deine Notizen anfertigen kannst, wenn es deine Eltern erlauben.

Let me explain this word.
It's somebody who ...
It's something that ...

This chart shows ...
In this chart you can see ...

A good example of this is ...

SF 7

Bilder beschreiben

▸ Intro | pp. 10–11 ▸ Unit 1 | p. 17 ▸ Unit 2 | p. 50
▸ Unit 3 | p. 88 ▸ Unit 4 | pp. 116–117, 124, 125

Wie gehe ich vor?

Erwähne zuerst, was du beschreibst, z. B. ein Foto oder einen Cartoon, und die dargestellte Situation.

I want to talk about this cartoon. I can see two people. They're on the moon.

Was ist wo abgebildet?

Kümmere dich danach um die Details. Sage, wo sich was im Bild befindet. Wichtige Personen und Dinge befinden sich meist im Vordergrund.

In the foreground *I can see the moon with craters.* ***On the left*** *there's an astronaut with the flag of the USA.* ***In the middle*** *I can see a Native American in front of a tent.* ***The background*** *shows a dark sky with stars.*

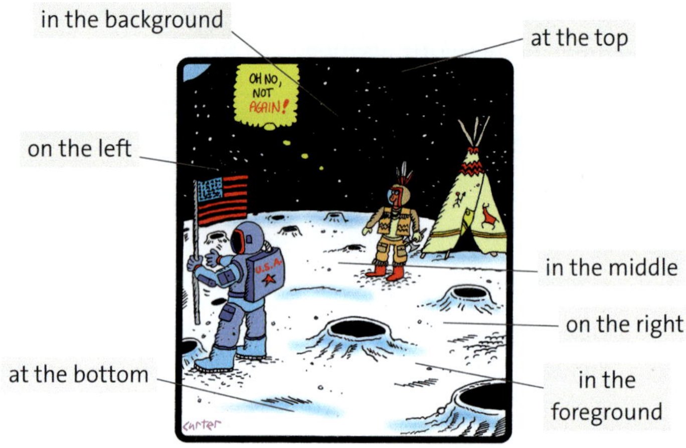

CartoonStock.com

Wer macht was? Was geschieht?

Beschreibe die Personen und ihre Handlungen genauer:

The astronaut *is wearing a spacesuit. He's pushing the flag into the ground.* ***The Native American*** *is wearing a headdress. He's holding a weapon is his left hand and he's looking at the astronaut.*

Was bedeutet es? Was denkst du?

Bei einem Cartoon findest du häufig auch eine Bildunterschrift *(caption)*, Sprech- oder Gedankenblasen *(speech bubble, thought bubble)*. Beschreibe auch diese und erkläre, was sie in diesem Zusammenhang bedeuten:

In the thought bubble the Native American is saying 'Oh no, not again!' He's saying 'again' because ...

Am Ende deiner Beschreibung kannst du noch sagen, was du von der Abbildung hältst und warum:

I think this cartoon is / isn't funny because ...

Wenn du die Positionen von Dingen oder Menschen näher beschreiben willst, kannst du folgende Präpositionen nutzen: *behind* • *between* • *in front of* • *next to* • *over* • *under*

Denke daran: Benutze immer das *present progressive*, wenn du beschreibst, was jemand in einem Bild macht. Andere Dinge im Bild kannst du mit *You can see ...* oder *There is/are ...* beschreiben.

Diagramme beschreiben und erklären

▶ Unit 1 | p. 22
▶ Unit 4 | pp. 134, 138, 144, 149

Mit Diagrammen kannst du Informationen sehr gut veranschaulichen und vergleichen. Sie helfen dir, einen Überblick zu geben oder Entwicklungen aufzuzeigen, z. B. in einem Vortrag.

Ordne das Diagramm ein

Sieh dir zunächst die Überschrift und die Beschriftungen des Diagramms an. Sie geben dir Hinweise auf den Inhalt. Sage, um was für eine Art Diagramm es sich handelt, was es aussagt (Thema), nenne die Quelle und das Jahr der Veröffentlichung:

This bar / column / line / pie chart shows ...
The source of the data / numbers / statistics is ...
The data / numbers / statistics are from the year ...

Beschreibe und erkläre das Diagramm

Schaue dann auf die Einheiten der Angaben: Größen- oder Mengenangaben, Jahreszahlen oder Prozentsätze. Beschreibe die Zahlen im Diagramm, vergleiche sie miteinander und erkläre, was du daran ablesen kannst:

In the years from ... to ..., ...
The x-axis / y-axis shows ...
This bar / column / line / section is for ...
The line shows an increase / decrease by ..
This number went up / down in the years from ... to ...
The number of ... has increased / decreased.
The number of ... fell / grew from ... in the year 2000 to ... in 2024.
25 per cent / One quarter of ...
Nearly nine out of ten people ...
... is greater / less than ...
More / fewer ... of ...

Fasse die Aussagen zusammen

Fasse am Ende die wichtigsten Aussagen zusammen:
To sum up, we can see that ... / the chart shows that ...
The numbers show that ...
As you can see, ...

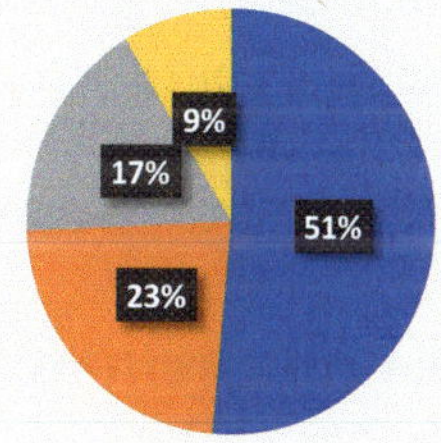

pie chart

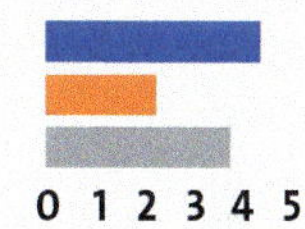

bar chart

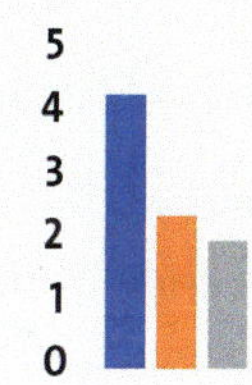

column chart

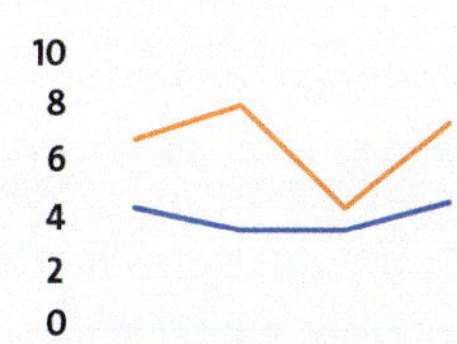

line chart

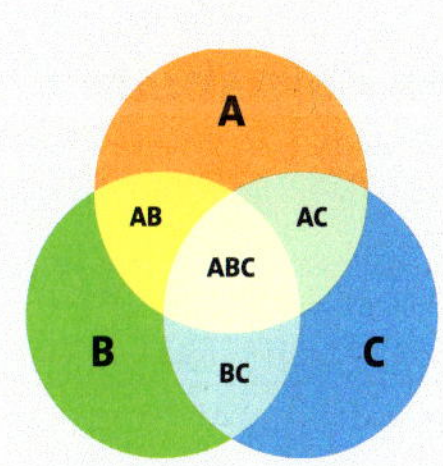

Venn diagram

▶ Wordbank 5, p. 203
▶ Numbers, p. 211

SF 9

Einen Podcast erstellen

▶ Unit 1 | pp. 34–35, 39

Ein Podcast ist eine regelmäßig im Internet erscheinende Audio-Sendung, z. B. auf der Schulhomepage. Sie ist einem großen Publikum zugänglich, das sie nur anhört, wenn der Inhalt interessant, gut recherchiert und unterhaltsam ist. Zudem muss die Aufnahmequalität gut sein.

Sind mehrere Personen an der Erstellung eines Podcasts beteiligt, so müssen alle einer Veröffentlichung im Internet zustimmen. Dies ist im Urheberrecht geregelt.

Die Vorbereitung

Lege das Thema und die Form (Interview, Gespräch, Vortrag, ...) fest. Überlege, wer dein Publikum sein soll. Was könnte für die Zuhörenden interessant und unterhaltsam sein? Formuliere Fragen oder Themen, die du in einem Interview oder Gespräch mit einem Gast besprechen möchtest. Suche für einen Vortrag zu deinem Thema Informationen und wähle das Interessanteste aus.

▶ Skills file 4, p. 164

Je nachdem, wie sicher du dich fühlst, kannst du ein Skript erstellen oder frei sprechen.

Der Aufbau eines Podcasts

Gib deinem Podcast eine Struktur:

- **Einleitung** (30 Sekunden): Nach einem kurzen **Intro** (passende Musik) begrüßt du das Publikum, nennst den Titel deines Podcasts, das Thema der Sendung und deinen Namen. (Begrüße auch deine Gäste.)
- **Hauptteil** (10–20 Minuten): Sprich über das Thema der aktuellen Sendung (mit deinen Gästen).
- **Schluss** (ca. 30 Sekunden): Fasse das Gesagte kurz zusammen. Verabschiede dich (und danke deinen Gästen). Gib eine kurze Vorschau auf die nächste Sendung. Spiel ein **Outro** (passende Musik) ab.

Musikaufnahmen sind urheberrechtlich geschützt. Suche im Internet nach kostenlosen und lizenzfreien Musikstücken bzw. Sounds oder komponiere sie selbst.

Die Aufnahme

Um dich aufzunehmen, reicht in der Regel dein Handy und eine passende App aus. Suche dir einen ruhigen Raum und mache ein paar Probeaufnahmen. Wenn du Gäste hast, könnt ihr entweder in dasselbe Handy sprechen oder euch getrennt aufnehmen und die Teile später zusammenschneiden. Wenn du beim Sprechen Fehler machst, lege einfach eine kurze Pause ein und wiederhole dann deinen Satz. Schneide anschließend die fehlerhafte Stelle heraus.

Hello and welcome to my podcast, Walid's World. *Today ...*

Well, that's all for now!
Thanks for ...
I hope ...
See you next week ...

SF 10

Hörtexte und Filme verstehen

▸ Unit 1 | pp. 16, 17, 33 ▸ Unit 2 | pp. 50, 52, 67
▸ Unit 3 | pp. 82, 83, 99 ▸ Unit 4 | pp. 117, 118, 133

Vor dem Hören / Sehen

Lies dir die Aufgabenstellung genau durch und überlege, was du tun sollst. Finde die Schlüsselwörter in der Aufgabenstellung. Diese zeigen dir, worauf du beim Hören oder Sehen achten musst. Geht es um das allgemeine Thema *(gist)* oder um spezifische Dinge *(details)*?

Stelle dir die Situation bzw. das Thema vor – was erwartest du, dazu zu hören oder zu sehen? Welche Leute sind beteiligt und worum geht es? Was weißt du schon über das Thema und welche Wörter wären wohl typisch?

Beim Hören / Sehen

Versuche, zunächst grob zu verstehen, worum es geht. Konzentriere dich auf die Schlüsselwörter aus der Aufgabenstellung. Oft werden in den Aufgaben Synonyme der Wörter aus dem Hörtext oder Film verwendet.

Achte bei einem Hörtext auch auf die Hintergrundgeräusche. Wenn du ein wichtiges Wort nicht verstehst, dann denke an die Situation, um die es geht.

Bei einem Film helfen dir Bilder, Gesichtsausdrücke und Körpersprache, den gesprochenen Text zu verstehen. Achte daher beim ersten Sehen besonders darauf, wo und wann der Film spielt, welche Personen darin vorkommen und wie sie handeln. Konzentriere dich beim zweiten Sehen mehr auf den gesprochenen Text oder auf Details.

Mache dir Notizen und bleib ruhig, wenn du beim ersten Mal nicht alles verstehst. Hörtexte oder Filme werden im Unterricht meist zweimal präsentiert. Vervollständige deine Notizen beim zweiten Hören bzw. Sehen.

Nach dem Hören / Sehen

Lies noch einmal genau durch, was du geschrieben hast. Passen deine Antworten zu den Fragen? Ergänze fehlende Antworten aus dem Gedächtnis.

Nutze verschiedene Möglichkeiten, um englische Texte zu hören. Wähle etwas aus, das dir gefällt, z. B. dein Lieblingslied oder dein Lieblingsbuch als Hörbuch auf Englisch.

Schaue Filme und Serien auf Englisch. Blende englische Untertitel ein, falls du Probleme beim Verstehen hast. Blende sie aus, wenn du dich sicherer fühlst oder eine Episode schon mehrfach gesehen hast.

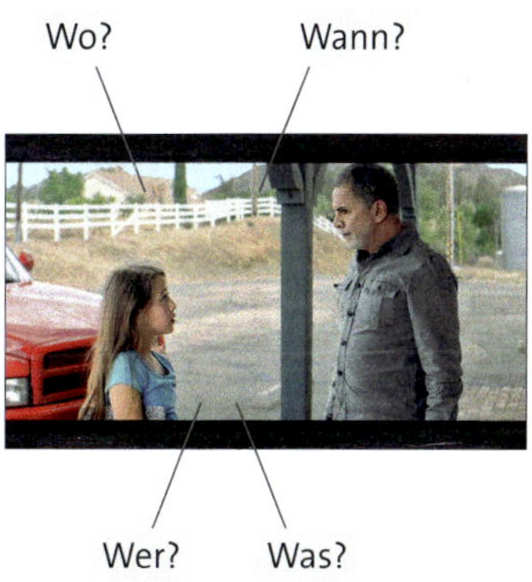

Checkliste Notizen machen

- ✓ Notiere nur wichtige Wörter (Schlüsselwörter).
- ✓ Schreibe Ziffern statt Zahlwörter, z. B. „7“ statt „seven“.
- ✓ Verwende Symbole und Abkürzungen, z. B. „X“ für falsch, „✓“ für richtig und „...“ für Lücken beim Hörverstehen.

SF 11

Lesetexte verstehen

▶ Intro | p. 14 ▶ Unit 1 | pp. 30–32 ▶ Unit 2 | pp. 64–66 ▶ Unit 3 | pp. 96–98 ▶ Unit 4 | pp. 130–132

In diesem Buch findest du viele verschiedene Texte, z. B. Artikel, Dialoge, Geschichten. Die folgenden Tipps helfen dir beim Verstehen der Texte und Lösen der Aufgaben.

Vor dem Lesen

Schaue dir die Aufgaben zum Text an und achte auf Schlüsselwörter. Überlege dir, was du tun sollst und welche Lesestrategie *(skimming, scanning* oder *reading for detail)* gefordert ist.

Skimming *(reading for gist)* hilft dir, schnell einen Überblick über den Inhalt eines Textes zu bekommen. Sieh dir dafür diese Dinge an:

- die Überschrift und Zwischenüberschriften sowie Bilder und Bildunterschriften
- hervorgehobene Wörter (z. B. durch **Fettdruck**)
- den ersten Satz jedes Absatzes, der oft die Hauptidee des Absatzes enthält
- den letzten Absatz des Textes, der oft eine Zusammenfassung des Textes enthält.

Scanning *(reading for specific information)* hilft dir, schnell nach bestimmten Informationen zu suchen:

- Überlege dir Stichwörter. Suchst du z. B. Öffnungszeiten, könnten das Wörter sein wie *open, hours* oder *days*.
- Überfliege den Text und suche nach den Stichwörtern.
- Du kannst dabei mit dem Finger in einer „S-Form" über den Text gehen.
- Lies die Textstelle, die dein Stichwort enthält, um zu sehen, ob du dort die gesuchten Informationen findest. Wenn nicht, scanne weiter.

Reading for detail hilft dir, jedes Detail eines Textes im Zusammenhang zu verstehen, z. B. bei Gedichten, Rezepten, Gebrauchsanweisungen oder Sachtexten mit Diagrammen und Tabellen. Lies jedes Wort und jede Zahl sehr genau. Benutze ein Wörterbuch für unbekannte Wörter.

Je mehr englische Texte du liest, desto größer wird dein Wortschatz und desto schneller und besser verstehst du Texte.

Du musst nicht jedes Wort in einem Text verstehen, um den Inhalt zu verstehen. Um einen schnellen Überblick über den Inhalt zu bekommen, überfliege den Text.

Wenn du mit Texten im Internet arbeitest, kann dein Browser dir viel Arbeit abnehmen: Mit Strg+F (Cmd+F am Mac) kannst du nach deinen Stichworten suchen und nur die Textstellen lesen, in denen ein Stichwort markiert ist.

SF 12

Einen Artikel verfassen

▸ Unit 1 | p. 25 ▸ Unit 2 | p. 63 ▸ Unit 3 | pp. 87, 112

Mit einem Artikel informierst du deine Leserschaft über ein interessantes Thema oder ein Ereignis, z. B. *Diversity in New York City* oder *My hometown – a good place for teens?* Der Stil sollte sachlich, knapp und verständlich sein.

Sammle Informationen

Nutze verschiedene Medien, z. B. das Internet, Zeitschriften und Bücher, und bemühe dich um Objektivität. Du kannst auch Interviews oder Umfragen durchführen. Überlege dir Beispiele und suche Bilder, Fotos, Zahlen und Statistiken, die den Inhalt ergänzen und unterstützen.

▸ Skills file 4, p. 164

Bei Interviews und Umfragen ist es wichtig, dass du von deinen Interviewpartnern das ausdrückliche Einverständnis zur Veröffentlichung einholst. Am besten lässt du dir das schriftlich geben.

Achte darauf, dass du die Äußerungen korrekt und nicht sinnverändert wiedergibst! Nutze wörtliche Zitate.

Strukturiere deine Informationen

- **Einleitung:** Stelle kurz dein Thema *(Who? When? Where? What?)* vor. Mit einer neugierig machenden Frage oder interessanten Aussage kannst du Interesse für dein Thema wecken: *What do teenagers think about ...?, Can you imagine that ...?, Lots of people think ...*
- **Hauptteil**: Gehe auf die Einzelheiten ein und präsentiere Fakten und Hintergründe zu deinem Thema oder nenne Argumente für und gegen eine Position. Ergänze deinen Text um Beispiele, Statistiken und Zitate. *There are two sides to this question.*
  One good thing about ...
  Felix S. (14) says: '...'
  On the other hand, ...
- **Schluss:** Fasse das Wichtigste zusammen und gib einen Ausblick. Wäge das Für und Wider zu einer Fragestellung ab, ohne neue Aspekte oder Argumente zu nennen:
  To sum up, ... / All in all, ...
  In the future, he / she will ...
  The most important thing to remember is ...

Fotos wecken Interesse und lockern deinen Artikel auf und die Bildunterschrift kann neugierig machen. Aber nicht alles, was du fotografierst, darfst du auch veröffentlichen. Es gibt Persönlichkeitsrechte bei Fotos von Personen, Eigentumsrechte bei Aufnahmen auf Privatgelände und Urheberrechte bei Aufnahmen von Kunstwerken oder Designobjekten. Kläre immer die Rechte, bevor du deine Fotos veröffentlichst.

Überlege dir auch eine Überschrift für deinen Artikel – sie sollte kurz sein und Interesse wecken. Bei längeren Artikeln kannst du auch Absätze mit Zwischenüberschriften versehen.

How to explore NYC in one day

The Knicks – what's their secret to winning?

Killer Katrina

Zum Schluss überprüfst du deinen Text inhaltlich und sprachlich.

▸ Skills file 15, p. 176

SF 13

E-Mails und Briefe schreiben

▸ Unit 1 | p. 27 ▸ Unit 2 | pp. 70, 72 ▸ Unit 3 | p. 91

Adresse und Datum

Hier steht die E-Mail-Adresse des Empfängers.
Hier kannst du weitere Empfänger eintragen.
Hier schreibst du ganz knapp, worum es geht.
Hier schreibst du deinen Text.

In englischen Briefen schreibst du deine Adresse rechts oben. Darunter schreibst du das Datum.

To:
Cc:
Subject:

33 Main Street
London NW4 6JZ

12 July 2025

Ms Dora Dal
12 New Street

Aufbau einer E-Mail oder eines Briefs

- **Einleitung:** Beginne mit einer Begrüßung.
  Bei Freunden reicht ein informelles *Hi / Hello, Jim*
  Ansonsten schreibe: *Dear Jane / Mr Jones / …*
  Wenn du den Namen nicht kennst, schreibe:
  Dear Sir or Madam
  Sage im ersten Satz, warum du schreibst:
  I'm writing this e-mail / letter to … oder *This is to …*
  In einem persönlichen Schreiben kannst du nachfragen, wie es der Person geht: *How are you?*
  Du kannst dich auch für die letzte Nachricht bedanken oder dich entschuldigen, falls du länger nicht geschrieben hast: *Thank you for your e-mail / letter. Sorry that I haven't written for so long.*
- **Hauptteil:** Hier schreibst du dem Empfänger Wichtiges, nimmst Stellung oder beantwortest Fragen. Für jedes Thema startest du einen neuen Absatz.
- **Schluss:** Beende deine E-Mail oder deinen Brief mit einem Schlusssatz oder einer Frage sowie einem freundlichen Gruß und deinem Namen.
  Bei Freunden kannst du informell sein: *Best wishes, Paul* oder *Love / Lots of love / All the best, Mia*
  Schreibst du an eine Organisation oder Firma, beende die E-Mail oder den Brief mit *Best regards, Lina Lee* oder förmlicher mit *Yours sincerely (BE) / Sincerely (AE).*
  Zwischen Schlussformel und Name ist ein Komma möglich, aber nicht nötig. Das gilt auch für die Anrede.

Überprüfe deinen Text inhaltlich und sprachlich bevor du ihn verschickst.

Das erste Wort nach der Anrede wird im Englischen großgeschrieben.

Subject: Thank you!
Dear Oscar
This is to say thank you for an amazing prom night!
Thank you for asking me to go with you and for …

That's all for now.
I hope to hear from you soon.
Lots of love
Elif

▸ Skills file 15, p. 176

SF 14

Eine Zusammenfassung/Rezension schreiben

▸ Unit 2 | pp. 68–69, 73

Eine Zusammenfassung *(Summary)* schreiben

Wenn du einen Text zusammenfasst, gibst du die wichtigsten Informationen und Ereignisse in kürzerer Form wieder.

Lies den Text genau

Beginne mit dem *Skimming* des Textes, um dir einen Überblick über den Inhalt zu verschaffen: Überschriften, Bilder und Bildunterschriften sowie der erste Satz jedes Absatzes können dir dabei helfen.

Lies den Text erneut, Satz für Satz *(Reading for detail)*. Mache dir Notizen oder markiere diese Informationen auf einer Kopie des Textes *(Who? When? Where? What? Why? How?)*.

▸ Skills file 11, p. 172

***Who** is the text about?*
***When** does it happen?*
***Where** does it happen?*
***What** happens?*
***Why/How** does it happen?*

Strukturiere deine Zusammenfassung

- **Einleitung:** Beschreibe kurz, worum es geht:
  The story / article / ... by ... is about ... *It takes place in ...*
  The main characters are ...
- **Hauptteil:** Gib die wichtigsten Ereignisse (z. B. einer Geschichte) oder die Hauptpunkte (eines Zeitungsartikels) in deinen eigenen Worten wieder. Fasse dich kurz und schreibe im ***simple present***, auch wenn der Originaltext andere Zeitformen verwendet. Verwende *linking words (and, but, because, ...)*. Verzichte auf Ausschmückungen.

Überprüfe deinen Text am Ende inhaltlich und sprachlich.

Checkliste *Summary*
- ✓ Nenne das Thema und die wesentlichen Inhalte *(Who? When? Where? What? Why? How?)*.
- ✓ Fasse dich kurz!
- ✓ Schreibe im ***simple present***.
- ✓ Verwende deine eigenen Worte, schreibe den Text nicht ab.
- ✓ Verwende keine direkte Rede.
- ✓ Verzichte auf Details, Beispiele oder deine eigene Meinung.

▸ Skills file 15, p. 176

Eine Rezension schreiben

Möchtest du ein Buch, einen Film oder eine Serie empfehlen oder kritisch bewerten, schreibst du eine Rezension. Dafür fasst du zunächst den Inhalt zusammen (s.o.) und schreibst danach einen Absatz mit deiner Meinung. Sage, ob du das Buch, den Film oder die Serie empfehlen kannst und begründe:
This is a really cool / exciting / funny / ... book / film / series.
If you're a ... fan like me, you'll love it!
I can recommend reading / watching ...
It's a must-read! / must-see!

Deine Meinung über ein Buch, einen Film oder eine Serie darf enthusiastisch sein. Wenn du magst, kannst du „Sterne“ vergeben oder Emojis verwenden, um deine Meinung zu verdeutlichen.

★★★★☆

SF 15

Texte überprüfen und verbessern

▶ Unit 1 | p. 35 ▶ Unit 2 | p. 69
▶ Unit 4 | pp. 119, 135

Ein Text ist noch nicht fertig, wenn du ihn zu Ende geschrieben hast. Du solltest ihn mehrmals durchlesen und auch von einem Partner / einer Partnerin anschauen lassen.

Überprüfe und korrigiere deinen Text

Beim Korrekturlesen empfehlen sich mehrere Durchgänge, in denen du nacheinander auf folgende Dinge achtest:

Inhalt:

- Vollständigkeit: Hast du alle Aspekte der Aufgabenstellung beachtet? Sind alle Sätze vollständig?
- Gestaltung: Enthält dein Text alle typischen Merkmale, die du beim Verfassen eines Zeitungsartikels, einer E-Mail oder einer Zusammenfassung beachten musst? Benötigst du z. B. eine Überschrift oder hast du an eine Anrede- oder Schlussformel gedacht?
- Aufbau: Hat dein Text eine logische Struktur mit Einleitung, Hauptteil und Schluss? Hast du Absätze gemacht?
- Lesbarkeit: Ist dein Text verständlich und liest sich flüssig?

▶ Skills file 12, p. 173
▶ Skills file 13, p. 174
▶ Skills file 14, p. 175

Sprache:

- Verwendest du eine abwechslungsreiche und lebendige Sprache und vermeidest Wiederholungen? Beschreibst du Personen, Orte oder Dinge mithilfe von Adjektiven?
- Hast du *linking words* (Bindewörter) benutzt?
- Stimmen Rechtschreibung, Zeichensetzung, Grammatik? Prüfe deinen Text anhand der Checkliste.
- Hast du die richtige Zeitform gewählt? Eine *summary* wird z. B. im *simple present* geschrieben. Bei anderen Textsorten, wie z. B. bei einer E-Mail oder einem Zeitungsartikel, musst du in jedem Satz überlegen, welches die passende Zeitform ist.

Checkliste typische Fehlerquellen

- ✓ Groß- und Kleinschreibung
- ✓ unregelmäßige Pluralformen *(child – children, man – men)*
- ✓ gleicher Klang, aber unterschiedliche Schreibweisen und Bedeutungen *(to – too – two, their – there – they're)*
- ✓ Präpositionen *(by train, in the picture, on the bus)*
- ✓ unregelmäßige Verben
- ✓ Wörter mit stummen Buchstaben *(climb, know, walk)*

▶ Irregular verbs, p. 300f.
▶ Wichtige Schreibregeln im Englischen, p. 198

Partnerkorrektur

Lasse deinen Text auch von anderen Korrektur lesen und hilf anderen, ihren Text zu überprüfen und zu verbessern. Gehe dabei wie oben beschrieben in mehreren Durchgängen vor – erst achtest du auf den Inhalt, dann auf die Sprache. Sprich danach mit deinem Partner / deiner Partnerin über deine Korrekturvorschläge und gib konstruktives Feedback.

Markiere in fremden Texten mit einem Bleistift:

- was dir gefällt: + +
- was unverständlich ist: ?
- was verbessert werden muss: *He lost his Handy.*
- was ergänzt werden könnte.

▶ Skills file 5, p. 165
▶ Feedback phrases, p. 210

SF 16

Mediation

▸ Unit 1 | p. 28 ▸ Unit 2 | p. 60 ▸ Unit 3 | p. 90 ▸ Unit 4 | p. 125

In manchen Situationen musst du zwischen zwei Sprachen vermitteln, um Personen zu helfen, die wenig oder kein Englisch oder Deutsch können. Dies nennt man Mediation. Du überträgst die wichtigsten Informationen von der einen Sprache in die andere, entweder mündlich oder schriftlich.

Normalerweise gibst du bei einer Mediation nur das Wesentliche wieder. Nur bei Gebrauchsanweisungen ist es wichtig, genau zu sein.

Worauf muss ich achten?

Keine Panik vor unbekannten Wörtern
Wenn du für jemandem z. B. während einer Stadtführung vermitteln oder einen englischen Artikel auf Deutsch erläutern möchtest, musst du nicht alle Details übersetzen. Deshalb ist es auch in Ordnung, wenn du nicht jedes Wort verstehst. Es reicht aus, dass du die zentralen Aussagen verstehst.

Gib nur die wichtigsten Informationen weiter
Lasse unwichtige Wörter und Satzteile weg und bilde kurze und einfache Sätze. Z. B.: Ihr besucht britische Freunde und die Tochter spricht über ihren Hund: *I love my dog Teddy. He's the best. Teddy is my best friend. He's really great.*
Dann erklärst du deinem kleinen Bruder: „Emma liebt ihren Hund Teddy, er ist ihr bester Freund."

Achte in Gesprächen auf den Perspektivwechsel
Überlege immer, an wen du dich gerade wendest, und passe die Pronomen entsprechend an. Im Beispiel oben wird aus „I" → „Emma" (oder „sie") und aus „my" → „ihren / ihr".

Oft benutzt man auch einen Einleitungssatz: „Sie sagt, dass sie ihren Hund liebt."

Sage es anders
Wenn du ein Wort nicht kennst, versuche es mit anderen Wörtern zu umschreiben. Wenn dir zum Beispiel das englische Wort für „Onkel" nicht einfällt, kannst du auch sagen *my mum's / dad's brother.*

Achte auf kulturelle Unterschiede
Überlege, was für dein Gegenüber wichtig ist, um die Situation und die Inhalte verstehen zu können. Erkläre kulturelle Besonderheiten.

Checkliste Mediation
- ✓ Gib nur die wichtigen Informationen weiter.
- ✓ Umschreibe unbekannte Wörter.
- ✓ Verwende kurze, einfache Sätze.
- ✓ Achte auf Pronomen: An wen wendest du dich?
- ✓ Bedenke und erkläre kulturelle Unterschiede.

Frage Sam doch mal, wie ihm sein Tag gefallen hat.

Did you enjoy your day?

He/She says/thinks that ...
He/She would like to know ...
He/She asks if ...
Here it says (that) we should ...

Restroom?

Oh, right. That's the American word for public toilets.

Inhalt

			Seite
LF 1	Rev	Die Wortstellung	178
LF 2	Rev	Die einfache Gegenwart	179
LF 3	Rev	Die Verlaufsform der Gegenwart	180
LF 4		*Simple present* oder *present progressive?*	180
LF 5	Rev	Die einfache Vergangenheit	181
LF 6	Rev	Das *present perfect*	182
LF 7		*Present perfect* oder *simple past?*	183
LF 8		Das Gerundium	184
LF 9		Die Verlaufsform der Vergangenheit	185
LF 10		Das *past perfect*	186
LF 11	Rev	Die Steigerung der Adjektive	187
LF 12	Rev	Adverbien der Art und Weise	187
LF 13		Gradadverbien	188
LF 14	Rev	Die Zukunft mit *going to*	188
LF 15	Chl	Das *present progressive* mit Zukunftsbezug	189
LF 16	Rev	Die Zukunft mit *will*	189
LF 17	Rev	Bedingungssätze Typ 1	190
LF 18		Bedingungssätze Typ 2	190
LF 19	Rev	Modale Hilfsverben	191
LF 20		Das Passiv	192
LF 21		Adverbialsätze	194
LF 22	Rev	Relativsätze	195
		Grammatical terms	196
		Wichtige Schreibregeln im Englischen	198

Erklär-film Dieses Symbol zeigt dir, dass du einen Erklärfilm zu diesem Thema in der App findest.

LF 1 Revision

Die Wortstellung *(Word order)*

a) **Aussagesätze *(Statements)***

Subject	Verb	
Jonquel	plays	basketball.
The Diaz	have moved	to NYC.
You	shouldn't ask	Hana.

Last year the Diaz moved to NYC.
Letztes Jahr sind die Diaz nach NYC gezogen.

If you need help, you should ask Lu.
Wenn du Hilfe brauchst, solltest du Lu fragen.

Jonquel often plays basketball.
Jonquel spielt oft Basketball.

Die Wortstellung in englischen Aussagesätzen ist *subject* (Subjekt) – *verb* (Prädikat) – Ergänzung.
Auch wenn der Satz mit einer adverbialen Bestimmung beginnt (z. B. *Last year*; *If you need help*), bleibt die Wortstellung *subject – verb* – ... unverändert.
Häufigkeitsadverbien (z. B. *often*) stehen im Englischen meist direkt vor dem Hauptverb (z. B. *play*). Sie können nicht zwischen Verb und Objekt stehen.

b) **Nebensätze *(Subordinate clauses)***

If they ask me, I'll help them.
Wenn sie mich bitten, helfe ich ihnen.

Auch für Nebensätze gilt die Wortstellung *subject – verb*.

LF 2 Revision

Erklär-
film

Die einfache Gegenwart *(The simple present)*

▶ Unit 1 | pp. 20, 46

I always get up at 7 o'clock.
Ich stehe immer um 7 Uhr auf.

We all love Indian food.
Wir alle lieben indisches Essen.

Where do you live?
Wo wohnen Sie?

Mit dem *simple present* sagst du, was oft, regelmäßig, jeden Tag oder auch selten oder nie geschieht oder was immer so ist (Dauerzustände).
Oft findest du diese Signalwörter in Sätzen im *simple present: always, never, often, rarely, sometimes, usually, every day.*

a) Bejahte Aussagesätze *(Positive statements)*

I / You / We / They	start.
He / She / It	starts.

hurry → hurries
miss → misses
wash → washes
catch → catches

Das *simple present* hat dieselbe Form wie der Infinitiv, also die Grundform des Verbs.

! Bei der 3. Person Singular musst du aber immer ein *-s* an das Verb hängen. Beachte:

- Konsonant (z. B. *-r*) + *y* wird zu *-ies*.
- An *-s, -sh, -ch, -x* hängst du *-es*.
- Sonderformen: ***does, goes, has***

b) Verneinte Aussagesätze *(Negative statements)*

I / You / We / They	don't start.
He / She / It	doesn't start.

Aussagen im *simple present* verneinst du mit ***don't*** oder ***doesn't*** (für die 3. Person Singular). Das Verb nach ***don't / doesn't*** steht immer im Infinitiv: *She doesn't start.*

c) Fragen und Antworten *(Questions and answers)*

Do I / you / we / they start?
Does he / she / it start?
When does he / she / it start? – At ten.

Do they start? – Yes, they do.
Do you like musicals? – No, I don't.
Does he do a lot of sport? – No, he doesn't.

Who loves Amy? – Tim.
Wer liebt Amy? – Tim.

What makes you happy? – Chocolate.
Was macht dich glücklich? – Schokolade.

Fragen im *simple present* musst du mit ***do*** oder ***does*** bilden. Das Verb steht auch hier im Infinitiv: *Does he start?*

Auf Ja-/Nein-Fragen antwortet man nicht einfach *yes* oder *no*, sondern verwendet eine Kurzantwort mit *do* oder *does (not)*:
Yes, they do. / No, he doesn't.

! Wenn du mit *Who* oder *What* nach dem Subjekt des Satzes fragst, bildest du die Frage ohne *do / does*.

LF 3 Revision

Erklär-film

Die Verlaufsform der Gegenwart *(The present progressive)*

▶ Unit 1 | p. 46

Dad **is making** dim sum.
What **are** you **doing** at the moment?
– **I'm working**.
Was machst du jetzt gerade?
– Ich bin gerade am Arbeiten. / Ich arbeite gerade.

Mit dem *present progressive* sagst du, was jemand jetzt gerade tut. Damit beschreibst du auch, was auf Bildern passiert.
Folgende Zeitangaben findest du oft in Sätzen im *present progressive*: *at the moment, now, today*.

a) **Bejahte Aussagesätze *(Positive statements)***

I'**m** You'**re** He'**s** / She'**s** / It'**s** We'**re** They'**re**	**working**.

Das *present progressive* besteht aus zwei Teilen: Form von *be* + *ing*-Form des Verbs.

am ('m) *are ('re)* *is ('s)*	+ *ing*-Form

! Beachte:
take → *taking*
putting, running

b) **Verneinte Aussagesätze *(Negative statements)***

I'**m not** You **aren't** He / She / It **isn't** We / They **aren't**	**playing**.

In verneinten Sätzen stehen *am / are / is* mit *not*:

am not / are not / is not	+ *ing*-Form

c) **Fragen und Antworten *(Questions and answers)***

Am I **working**? – No, you **aren't**.
Are you **working**? – Yes, I **am**.
Where **is** he **going**? – Home.

In Fragen vertauscht man das Subjekt und *am / are / is*: *I am* → ***am I****?*, *you are* → ***are you****?*, *he is* → ***is he****?*

LF 4

Erklär-film

Simple present oder *present progressive*?

▶ Unit 1 | p. 46

Simple present	Present progressive
Tiana often **makes** jewelry.	Look. Tiana **is** just **making** a ring.
Signalwörter: *always, often, never, normally, every day, sometimes, rarely*	Signalwörter: *at the moment, just, (right / just) now, today*

- Mit *makes (simple present)* drückst du aus, dass Tiana regelmäßig Schmuck herstellt, z. B. als Hobby oder Beruf.
- Mit *is making (present progressive)* sagst du, dass Tiana jetzt gerade Schmuck herstellt.

! Verben, die einen Zustand bezeichnen (z. B. *have, hate, know, like, love, prefer, want, remember*) stehen nicht in der Verlaufsform.

LF 5 Revision

Erklär-
film

Die einfache Vergangenheit *(The simple past)*

▸ Unit 1 | pp. 23, 24

Last week I didn't have any homework.
Letzte Woche hatte ich keine Hausaufgaben auf.

Did you watch the Yankees yesterday?
Hast du gestern die Yankees gesehen?

Mit dem *simple past* sprichst du über Dinge, die in der Vergangenheit geschehen sind. Du verwendest es oft mit Zeitangaben wie *yesterday, last week / last year / last summer, two weeks ago, in 2023*.

a) Bejahte Aussagesätze *(Positive statements)*

I / You He / She / It We / They	helped. went.

Last year the rats started their own jazz band.

Die Vergangenheitsform der Verben ist für alle Personen gleich:

- Bei regelmäßigen Verben hängst du *-ed* an das Verb: *walk* → *walked*.
- Bei Verben, die auf *-e* enden, wird nur *-d* angehängt: *arrive* → *arrived*.
- Einige Konsonanten werden verdoppelt: *plan* → *planned*; *stop* → *stopped*.

! Unregelmäßige Formen musst du lernen: *go* → *went*; *have* → *had*; *see* → *saw*.
Du kannst sie auf S. 300–302 nachschlagen.

b) Verneinte Aussagesätze *(Negative statements)*

I / You He / She / It We / They	didn't help. didn't go.

Wenn du sagen willst, dass etwas nicht geschah, setzt du *didn't* vor das Verb. Das Verb steht dann immer im Infinitiv (der Grundform).

c) Fragen und Antworten *(Questions and answers)*

Did they help?
Did she go?
Why did he help? – Because he cared.

Did you help? – Yes, I did.
Did she do a lot of sport? – No, she didn't.

Fragen im *simple past* bildest du mit *did*. Das Verb steht auch hier im Infinitiv: *Did they help?, Did she go?*

Auch in Kurzantworten auf Ja-/Nein-Fragen verwendest du *did (not)*: *Yes, I did. / No, she didn't.*

Who helped you? – My sister.
Wer hat dir geholfen? – Meine Schwester.

What happened? – I had an accident.
Was ist passiert? – Ich hatte einen Unfall.

! Wenn du mit *Who* oder *What* nach dem Subjekt des Satzes fragst, bildest du die Frage ohne *did*.

LF 6 Revision

Erklär-film

Das *present perfect* (The present perfect)

▸ Unit 1 | pp. 23, 24

I **have** never **eaten** dim sum.
Ich habe noch nie Dim Sum gegessen.

Has Leo ever **been** to Rome?
Ist Leo schon mal in Rom gewesen? / War Leo schon mal in Rom?

The train **hasn't arrived** yet.
Der Zug ist noch nicht angekommen.

Mit dem *present perfect* sagst du, dass jemand etwas – irgendwann – in der Zeit bis jetzt gemacht oder nicht gemacht hat. Der genaue Zeitpunkt ist unwichtig oder unbekannt und wird nicht genannt. Oft hat die Handlung Auswirkungen auf die Gegenwart.
Signalwörter: *already, just, ever, never, (not) yet, once, twice, many times*

a) Bejahte Aussagesätze *(Positive statements)*

I / You / We / They	**have finished**.
He / She / It	**has finished**.

Kurzformen:

I**'ve** / You**'ve** / We**'ve** / They**'ve** He**'s** / She**'s** / It**'s**	**finished**.

***Have** you **seen** this? They**'ve started** a new sports club.*

Das *present perfect* besteht aus ***have / has*** und der *past participle*-Form des Verbs.

- Das *past participle* regelmäßiger Verben bildest du aus dem Verb + ***ed***: *walk → walk**ed***.
- Bei Verben, die auf ***-e*** enden, wird nur ***-d*** angehängt: *arrive → arrive**d***.
- Einige Konsonanten werden verdoppelt: *plan → pla**nn**ed; stop → sto**pp**ed*.

! Unregelmäßige *past participle*-Formen musst du lernen: *go → **gone**; have → **had***. Du kannst sie auf S. 300–302 nachschlagen.

b) Verneinte Aussagesätze *(Negative statements)*

I / You / We / They	**haven't finished**.
He / She / It	**hasn't finished**.

In verneinten Sätzen stehen *have / has* mit *not*:

have not (haven't) ***has not (hasn't)***	*+ past participle*

c) Fragen und Antworten *(Questions and answers)*

Where **have** you **been**? – At school.
Has he **booked** the trip? – Yes, he **has**. / No, he **hasn't**.

In Fragen vertauscht man das Subjekt und *have / has*:
*you have → **have you**?, he has → **has he**?*

d) Das *present perfect* mit *since* oder *for (The present perfect with* since *or* for*)*

We **have lived** in Queens since 2023.
Wir wohnen seit 2023 in Queens.

Ella **has been** in our class for two weeks.
Ella ist seit zwei Wochen in unserer Klasse.

Mit dem *present perfect* sagst du auch, wie lange etwas schon andauert. Du verwendest ...

- ***since*** zur Angabe eines Zeitpunkts: *since three o'clock, since May.*
- ***for*** zur Angabe eines Zeitraums: *for two weeks, for ten days.*

LF 7

Present perfect oder *simple past?*

▸ Unit 1 | pp. 23, 24, 48

Present perfect	Simple past
A: I **have been** to the USA. **Have** you ever **been** to the USA? **B:** Yes, I **have**. Signalwörter: *ever, never, already, (not) yet*	**A:** When / Where **did** you **go**? **B:** I **went** there in 2021. Signalwörter: *yesterday, last week, ten years ago, in 2000, when?*
A: How long **has** Alice **lived** in Texas? **B:** Since 2022. Signalwörter: *how long?, since two o'clock, for three hours*	**A:** When **did** she **move** to Texas? **B:** In 2022. Signalwörter: siehe oben

In zusammenhängenden Texten folgen *present perfect* und *simple past* oft aufeinander:

- Mit dem *present perfect* sagst du, dass etwas geschehen ist, aber du nennst keine näheren Umstände, sagst also nicht, wann / wo / wie es geschehen ist.
- Mit dem *simple past* sagst oder fragst du, wann / wo / wie etwas geschehen ist.

- Mit dem *present perfect* sagst oder fragst du, seit wann / wie lange etwas schon andauert.
- Mit dem *simple past* sagst oder fragst du, wann / wo / warum etwas geschehen ist.

LF 8

Das Gerundium *(The gerund)*

▶ Unit 1 | p. 27

Reading can open up new worlds.
Lesen kann neue Welten erschließen.
Vergleiche: Books can open up new worlds.

Die *ing*-Form eines Verbs kann als Gerundium, d.h. wie ein Nomen verwendet werden.

a) Das Gerundium als Subjekt *(The gerund as a subject)*

Dancing is fun.
Tanzen macht Spaß.

Wie andere Nomen kann das Gerundium als Subjekt im Satz stehen.

b) Das Gerundium als Objekt nach Verben *(The gerund as an object after verbs)*

I enjoy / like cooking.
Ich koche gern.

Imagine living by the sea.
Stell dir vor, du wohnst am Meer.

I don't mind helping.
Es macht mir nichts aus zu helfen.
Stop talking.
Hör auf zu reden!

I suggest leaving early.
Ich schlage vor, früh loszugehen.

Start moving.
Fang an, dich zu bewegen!

They continued talking.
Sie redeten weiter.

Wie andere Nomen kann das Gerundium nach bestimmten Verben stehen, z. B.:

enjoy	*begin / start*
finish	*continue*
imagine	*hate*
keep	*like*
mind / not mind	*love*
miss	*prefer*
practise	
recommend	
stop	
suggest	

Nur nach den Verben in der rechten Spalte kann anstelle der *ing*-Form auch ein *to*-Infinitiv stehen, z. B.: *Start to move.*

c) Das Gerundium nach Präpositionen *(The gerund after prepositions)*

Chris is good at dancing.
Chris kann gut tanzen.

I look forward to meeting you.
Ich freue mich darauf, Sie kennenzulernen.

I like the idea of living in New York City.
Mir gefällt die Idee, in New York zu leben.

Wie andere Nomen kann das Gerundium nach bestimmten Wendungen mit Präpositionen stehen, z. B.:

be against	*be sorry for*
be good / bad at	*look forward to*
be crazy about	*worry about*
be interested in	*the idea of*
be scared of	*the risk of*

LF 9

Erklär-film

Die Verlaufsform der Vergangenheit *(The past progressive)*

▸ Unit 2 | pp. 54, 77

People **were waiting** for the next train.
Die Leute warteten auf den nächsten Zug.

What **were** you **doing** there at midnight?
Was hast du dort um Mitternacht gemacht?

Troy called while I **was doing** my homework.
Troy rief an, als ich gerade meine Hausaufgaben machte.

I was on the train with Troy and we **were chatting** about this and that. Other passengers **were checking** messages or **listening** to music on their phones when this guy got up and started to sing. He had a fantastic voice.

Das *past progressive* wird verwendet, um auszudrücken, dass zu einer bestimmten Zeit in der Vergangenheit eine Handlung oder ein Vorgang gerade im Gange und noch nicht abgeschlossen war.

Das *past progressive* wird auch verwendet, um zu sagen, was gerade vor sich ging, als etwas anderes passierte. Das neu eintretende Geschehen steht im *simple past*.

Oft findest du das *past progressive* in Berichten und Erzählungen. Es beschreibt dann die Situation oder „Szene", in der etwas geschah.

a) Bejahte Aussagesätze *(Positive statements)*

I **was**	
You **were**	
He / She / It **was**	**working**.
We **were**	
They **were**	

Das *past progressive* besteht aus zwei Teilen: Vergangenheitsform von *be* + *ing*-Form des Verbs:

was ***were***	+ *ing*-Form

! Beachte:
take → *taking*
putting, running

b) Verneinte Aussagesätze *(Negative statements)*

I **wasn't**	
You **weren't**	
He / She / It **wasn't**	**working**.
We **weren't**	
They **weren't**	

In verneinten Sätzen stehen *was / were* mit *not*:

was not (wasn't) ***were not (weren't)***	+ *ing*-Form

c) Fragen und Antworten *(Questions and answers)*

Were you **working**?
– Yes, I **was**. / No, I **wasn't**.
Where **was** she **going**? – Home.

In Fragen vertauscht man das Subjekt und *was / were*:
you were → ***were you****?*, *she was* → ***was she****?*

LF 10

Das *past perfect* *(The past perfect)*

▸ Unit 2 | pp. 57, 79

The match **had** already **started** when we finally got to the stadium.
I **had** only **been** in New York City two days when I got bad news from home.

Simple past	Past perfect
The Wus **moved** to the USA in the 1970s.	For many years they **had wanted** to leave China.
Their first years in the USA **were not** easy, ...	... but the years before **had been** much harder.

Das *past perfect* wird verwendet, um auszudrücken, dass ein Ereignis vor einem anderen Ereignis in der Vergangenheit stattgefunden hatte oder dass ein Zustand vor einem Zeitpunkt in der Vergangenheit begonnen hatte. Vergleiche:

- Das *simple past* drückt aus, dass etwas zu einem bestimmten Zeitpunkt in der Vergangenheit stattfand.
- Das *past perfect* drückt aus, dass vorher bereits etwas anderes geschehen war.

a) Bejahte Aussagesätze *(Positive statements)*

I / You / He / She / It We / They	**had started** late. **had left** late.

*The rats **had left** when the cat arrived.*

After ten minutes I realized that I **had** already **seen** the film.
..., dass ich den Film bereits gesehen hatte.

I **had been** to the cinema with Jo the year before.
Ich war ... mit Jo im Kino gewesen.

Das *past perfect* besteht aus ***had*** (Kurzform ***'d***) und der *past participle*-Form des Verbs.

- Das *past participle* regelmäßiger Verben bildest du aus Verb + ***ed***: *walk* → *walk**ed***.
- Bei Verben, die auf ***-e*** enden, wird nur ***-d*** angehängt: *arrive* → *arrive**d***.
- Einige Konsonanten werden verdoppelt: *plan* → *pla**nn**ed*; *stop* → *sto**pp**ed*.

! Unregelmäßige *past participle*-Formen musst du lernen: *go* → ***gone***; *leave* → ***left***.
Du kannst sie auf S. 300–302 nachschlagen.
! Im Deutschen wird im Plusquamperfekt „hatte" oder „war" verwendet. Im Englischen steht immer *had*.

b) Verneinte Aussagesätze *(Negative statements)*

I / You / He / She / It We / They	**hadn't started** early. **hadn't left** early.

In verneinten Sätzen steht ***had*** mit ***not***:
had not (hadn't) + *past participle*

c) Fragen und Antworten *(Questions and answers)*

Had you **tidied** your room before the guests arrived? – Yes, I **had**.

In Fragen vertauscht man das Subjekt und *had*:
you had → ***had you***?

LF 11 **Revision**

Erklär-film

Die Steigerung der Adjektive *(Comparison of adjectives)*

a) Steigerung mit *-er / -est (Comparison with* -er / -est*)*

Komparativ (erste Steigerungsform)	**Superlativ** (höchste Steigerungsform)
Troy's smile was **bigger** than Kisha's.	The **biggest** tree in the park is very old.
The airport is **busier** during the holidays.	The **busiest** time is the early evening.
The weather today is **better** than yesterday.	The **worst** part of the film was the ending.

Adjektive kann man steigern und in Vergleichen benutzen.
Bei einsilbigen Adjektiven und bei zweisilbigen Adjektiven, die auf *-y* enden, hängst du ***-er/-est*** an das Adjektiv:
tall → taller / (the) tallest

! Beachte die Schreibung:
- *big → bigger / (the) biggest*
- *busy → busier / (the) busiest*

! Beachte diese Ausnahmen:
- *good → **better** → (the) **best***
- *bad → **worse** → (the) **worst***

b) Steigerung mit *more / most (Comparison with* more / most*)*

Komparativ	**Superlativ**
Lin-Manuel's music is **more creative** than Leo's.	The **most expensive** part of NYC is Manhattan.

Bei längeren (vor allem dreisilbigen) Adjektiven setzt man ***more / most*** vor das Adjektiv:
creative → more creative
expensive → (the) most expensive

LF 12 **Revision**

Erklär-film

Adverbien der Art und Weise *(Adverbs of manner)*

a) Verwendung und Bildung *(Use and form)*

A careful driver drives **carefully**.
Please speak **clearly**.

Adjektiv	**Adverb**
clear	clear**ly**
quick	quick**ly**
nervous	nervous**ly**
happy	happ**ily**
careful	careful**ly**

You speak English very **well**.
A hard worker works **hard**.
A fast runner can run **fast**.

Adverbien der Art und Weise beschreiben, wie jemand etwas tut oder wie etwas geschieht. Sie beschreiben also ein Verb.
Die meisten Adverbien bildet man durch Anfügen von ***-ly*** an ein Adjektiv.

! Beachte die Schreibung:
angry → angrily, happy → happily, full → fully

! Beachte diese Ausnahmen:
- Das Adverb zu *good* ist ***well***.
- Bei ***hard*** und ***fast*** sind Adjektiv und Adverb gleich.

b) **Challenge** **Die Steigerung der Adverbien *(Comparison of adverbs)***

Can you say that again **more slowly**?
Which method works **(the) most effectively**?

I can run **faster** than my brother.
Which animal runs **(the) fastest**?

Milena speaks English **better** than me.
Who in the family sings **(the) worst**?

Adverbien kann man ebenso wie Adjektive steigern und in Vergleichen benutzen. Bei *-ly*-Adverbien verwendest du ***more*** und ***most*** vor dem Adverb.
Bei kurzen (meist einsilbigen) Adverbien hängst du ***-er*** und ***-est*** an das Adverb.
! Beachte diese Ausnahmen:
- *well* → ***better*** → ***(the) best***
- *badly* → ***worse*** → ***(the) worst***

LF 13

Gradadverbien *(Adverbs of degree)*

▶ Unit 2 | p. 60

My exchange family is **really** nice / **very** nice.
The room is **quite** big / not **too** small.
That woman is **extremely** rich.
Do you **really** think that?
I **hardly** recognized Romy.

Gradadverbien – z. B. *a bit, very, quite, really, extremely, hardly* („kaum“), *too* („zu“), *not at all* („überhaupt nicht“) – verstärken die Bedeutung eines Wortes oder schwächen sie ab. So verstärkt *extremely* in *extremely rich* das Adjektiv *rich*. Gradadverbien stehen meist direkt vor dem Wort, auf das sie sich beziehen.

LF 14 **Revision**

Erklärfilm

Die Zukunft mit *going to* *(The going to-future)*

▶ Unit 3 | pp. 90, 114

We**'re going to have** a barbecue tonight.
Wir wollen heute Abend grillen.

Are you **going to be** at the party?
Wirst du auf der Party sein?

Mit *going to* ... sagst du, was jemand vorhat oder plant. *Going to* hat hier nichts mit dem deutschen „gehen“ zu tun, sondern bedeutet „werden“ oder „wollen“.

a) **Aussagesätze *(Statements)***

I**'m** / She**'s** / We**'re**	**going to leave**.
I**'m not** / She **isn't** / We **aren't**	**going to stay**.

Das *going to-future* besteht aus einer Form von *be + going to* und dem Infinitiv des Verbs.

b) **Fragen und Antworten *(Questions and answers)***

Are you **going to ask**? – No, I**'m not**.
Where **is** she **going to live**? – In Texas.

In Fragen vertauscht man das Subjekt und *am / are / is*: *you are* → ***are you****?*, *she is* → ***is she****?*

c) **Challenge** Vorhersagen mit *going to (Predictions with* going to*)*

You're late. We'**re going to miss** the bus.
One day there'**s going to be** an accident if they don't do something about this road.

Mit *going to* ... kannst du auch sagen, was wahrscheinlich (aufgrund bestehender Vorzeichen) bald passieren wird.

LF 15 **Challenge**

Erklär-film

Das *present progressive* mit Zukunftsbezug *(The present progressive with a future meaning)*

▶ Unit 3 | p. 115

Are you **doing** anything tomorrow?
Hast du morgen schon was vor?

Yes, I'**m meeting** my girlfriend in the evening. We'**re going** to the cinema.
Ja, ich treffe mich abends mit meiner Freundin. Wir wollen ins Kino gehen.

Du kannst das *present progressive* verwenden, um zu sagen, dass etwas für die Zukunft fest geplant oder verabredet ist. (Durch eine Zeitangabe wie *tomorrow* oder aus dem Zusammenhang muss deutlich sein, dass es um etwas Zukünftiges geht.)

LF 16 **Revision**

Erklär-film

Die Zukunft mit *will* *(The will-future)*

▶ Unit 3 | pp. 92, 114

I think you'**ll have** a great time in the USA.
Ich glaube, du wirst eine tolle Zeit ... haben.

Wait – I'**ll help** you.
Warte – ich helfe dir.

I'**ll call** you later.
Ich rufe dich später an.

Du verwendest das *will-future*
- für Vorhersagen. Die Sätze beginnen oft mit *I think, Maybe, I'm sure.*
- für spontane Entschlüsse und Hilfsangebote.

! Im Deutschen steht dafür oft das Präsens.

a) **Aussagesätze** ***(Statements)***

It **will** It'**ll**	**be** sunny tomorrow.
It **will not** It **won't**	**be** sunny on Monday.

Du bildest das *will-future* mit ***will*** (Kurzform ***'ll***) und dem Infinitiv des Verbs. Alle Personen haben dieselbe Form: *I'll, you'll, he'll* usw.
In verneinten Sätzen steht ***will*** mit ***not***.
Die Kurzform von ***will not*** ist ***won't***.

b) **Fragen und Antworten** ***(Questions and answers)***

Will it **be** hot? – Yes, it **will**. / No, it **won't**.
Won't you **join** us for dinner? – I'd love to.
When **will** you **start** the new job? – Soon.

In Fragen vertauscht man das Subjekt und *will / won't*:
it will → ***will it****?, you will* → ***will you****?*

LF 17 **Revision**

Erklär-film

Bedingungssätze Typ 1 *(Conditional sentences type 1)*

a) ***if*-Satz und Hauptsatz *(if-clause and main clause)***

If it **rains** tomorrow, I'**ll stay** at home.
Wenn es morgen regnet, bleibe ich zu Hause.

Bedingungssätze bestehen aus zwei Teilen:

- Der Nebensatz mit *if (if-clause)* nennt eine Bedingung.
- Der Hauptsatz *(main clause)* nennt die Folge, also was geschehen wird oder kann.

Zwischen *if*-Satz und Hauptsatz steht ein Komma.

I'**ll stay** at home **if** it **rains** tomorrow.

! Im Englischen setzt man kein Komma, wenn der Hauptsatz vor dem *if*-Satz steht.

b) **Zeitformen im Bedingungssatz Typ 1 *(Tenses in conditional sentences type 1)***

If this **happens** again,	you'**ll be** in trouble.
	you **should call** the police.
	take action as soon as possible.

- Im *if*-Satz verwendest du das *simple present* (z. B. *happens*).
- Im Hauptsatz steht meist das *will-future*. Du kannst auch Modalverben (*should, can* usw.) oder den Imperativ *(take)* verwenden.

LF 18

Bedingungssätze Typ 2 *(Conditional sentences type 2)*

▸ Unit 3 | pp. 86, 112

If I **lived** in New York City, I **would go** (= I'**d go**) to Broadway shows as often as possible.
Wenn ich in New York leben würde, würde ich so oft wie möglich in Broadway-Shows gehen.

If the traffic **wasn't** so bad, we **could drive** to a concert in Brooklyn.
Wenn der Verkehr nicht so schlimm wäre, könnten wir zu einem Konzert ... fahren.

Außer Bedingungssätzen des Typs 1 gibt es auch Bedingungssätze des Typs 2:

- Im *if*-Satz des Typs 2 verwendest du das *simple past* (z. B. *lived, wasn't*).
- Im Hauptsatz steht *would* (Kurzform *'d*) + Infinitiv oder *could* + Infinitiv.

If pigs **could fly**, the world would be very different.
Wenn Schweine fliegen könnten, ...

Could („könnte") kann auch im *if*-Satz stehen.

If I were you, I'd say no.
Wenn ich du wäre, würde ich nein sagen.

Statt *if I / he / she / it was* sagt man auch *if I / he / she / it were*. Merke dir die Wendung *if I were you* („ich an deiner Stelle").

Conditional type 1	Conditional type 2
If it **snows** on the Zugspitze tomorrow, skiers **will be** excited.	If it **snowed** in the Sahara Desert tomorrow, nobody **would believe** it.

! Vergleiche die Verwendung von Typ 1 und Typ 2:

- Mit dem *simple present* im *if*-Satz drückst du aus, dass du es für möglich oder wahrscheinlich hältst, dass die Bedingung eintritt.
- Mit dem *simple past* im *if*-Satz drückst du aus, dass du es für unwahrscheinlich oder unmöglich hältst, dass die Bedingung eintritt.

LF 19 **Revision**

Erklär-film

Modale Hilfsverben *(Modal verbs)*

Can you **help** me, please? – Yes, I **can**.
We **must ask** how much it will cost.
He's ill and **shouldn't go** to school.

Can, ***could***, ***must***, ***needn't***, ***may***, ***might*** und ***should*** sind modale Hilfsverben. Sie haben nur eine Form und stehen mit dem Infinitiv (der Grundform) eines Verbs.

a) Erlaubnis, Verbot *(Permission, prohibition)*

Can I help you?
May / Could I ask you something?
Dad says I **can't / mustn't** go to the party.
You **aren't allowed to** take photos here.

Mit ***can*** sagst du, was jemand tun darf. Wenn du sehr höflich fragen möchtest, ob du etwas tun darfst, verwendest du ***may*** oder ***could***. Um zu sagen, dass jemand etwas nicht tun darf, verwendest du ***can't*** oder ***mustn't***. Bei Erlaubnissen und Verboten kannst du auch *be* ***(not) allowed to*** verwenden.

Challenge I **was allowed to** stay up late last night.
You**'ll be allowed to** bring your own drinks to the concert tomorrow.

Be (not) allowed to hat auch Vergangenheits- und Zukunftsformen.

b) Notwendigkeit, Zwang *(Necessity, compulsion)*

We **must** stop injustice.
I **have to** go now, but I **don't have to** run.
She **needn't** worry. Everything is OK.

Challenge We **had to** call the doctor.
You **won't have to** wait.

Mit ***must*** oder ***have to*** sagst du, was jemand tun muss.
Mit needn't oder ***don't / doesn't have to*** sagst du, was jemand nicht zu tun braucht.
Have to hat auch Vergangenheits- und Zukunftsformen.

c) Fähigkeit *(Ability)*

I **can** bake, but I **can't** cook.

Challenge **Is** Lu **able to** speak English?
I **was able to** dance well when I was young.
We**'ll** soon **be able to** speak Spanish.

Mit ***can / can't*** (Langform: ***cannot***) sagst du oft, was jemand tun oder nicht tun kann.
Mit ***be (not) able to*** kannst du ebenfalls über eine Fähigkeit sprechen. ***Be (not) able to*** hat auch Vergangenheits- und Zukunftsformen.

d) Möglichkeit *(Possibility)*

It **may** rain.
This **might** be a possible solution.
You **could** be right.

Du kannst ***may***, ***might*** und ***could*** auch verwenden, um zu sagen, was möglich ist oder sein könnte.

e) Empfehlung, Rat *(Advice)*

You **shouldn't** eat so much sugar.

Mit ***should / shouldn't*** rätst du jemandem, etwas zu tun oder nicht zu tun.

LF 20

Erklär-film

Das Passiv *(The passive)*

Active	Passive
Mike **plays** baseball.	Baseball **is played** all over the USA. Baseball wird überall ... gespielt.
Companies **develop** new products in Silicon Valley every day.	New products **are developed** in Silicon Valley every day. Im Silicon Valley werden ... Produkte entwickelt.

Man kann einen Vorgang aus zwei verschiedenen Perspektiven beschreiben:

- Ein Aktivsatz drückt aus, wer oder was etwas tut. Das Subjekt des Aktivsatzes *(Mike, companies)* führt eine Handlung aus.
- Ein Passivsatz hebt hervor, mit wem oder womit etwas geschieht. Im Passivsatz wird etwas mit dem Subjekt *(baseball, new products)* getan. Mit einem Passivsatz kann man Handlungen beschreiben, ohne zu sagen, wer die Handlung ausführt.

a) Das Passiv der Gegenwart *(The simple present passive)*

▶ Unit 4 | pp. 118, 119, 146

Bejahte Aussagesätze	
I **am** He / She **is** You / We / They **are**	**respected.**

Verneinte Aussagesätze	
I'**m** He / She **is** You / We / They **are**	**not respected.**

Coffee **is drunk** more than tea.
Posters **are hung** all over town.

Man bildet das Passiv mit einer Form von *be (am, are, is)* + *past participle*-Form des Verbs. Im *simple present* verwendest du also:

am ('m) *are ('re)* *is ('s)* Verneint: *am not ('m not)* *are not (aren't)* *is not (isn't)*	+ *past participle* (z. B. *respected, asked, played, opened*)

! Unregelmäßige *past participle*-Formen musst du lernen, s. S. 300–302.

b) Das Passiv mit *by (The passive with* by*)*

My sister **is taken** to school **by** my dad.
Meine Schwester wird von meinem Vater gebracht.

Artificial intelligence **isn't welcomed by** everyone.
Künstliche Intelligenz wird nicht von allen begrüßt.

The house **is heated by** wind energy.
Das Haus wird mit Windenergie geheizt.

Wenn du in einem Passivsatz sagen willst, von wem etwas getan wird oder wodurch etwas geschieht, verwendest du die Präposition ***by*** („von", „durch").
Die meisten Passivsätze stehen jedoch ohne eine *by*-Angabe, weil unbekannt oder unwichtig ist, wer die Handlung ausführt.

*The cat's food **is** often **stolen by** the clever rats.*

c) Das Passiv der Vergangenheit *(The simple past passive)*

▶ Unit 4 | pp. 123, 147, 148

Alcatraz **was closed** in 1963.
Alcatraz wurde 1963 geschlossen.

The articles **were written** by a team of six.
Die Artikel wurden von einem sechsköpfigen Team verfasst.

Im *simple past* bildet man das Passiv mit ***was / were*** + *past participle*-Form des Verbs.

LF 21

Adverbialsätze *(Adverbial clauses)*

▶ Unit 4 | p. 127

Julie sings	**when she is happy.**
	because she loves music.
	beautifully.

As we got near the airport, we saw a plane come in to land.
Als wir uns dem Flughafen näherten, ...

The phone rang **while I was having a shower**.
..., während / als ich gerade duschte.

I won't go **unless you come with me**.
..., außer du kommst mit.

They are going to have the barbecue **even if it rains**.
..., auch wenn / selbst wenn es regnet.

You must speak loudly and clearly **so that everyone can hear you**.
..., sodass / damit alle dich hören können.

That man talks **as if he knows everything**.
..., als ob er alles wüsste.

Everywhere I went, there were tourists.
Überall, wo ich hinging, waren Touristen.

Nebensatz	Hauptsatz
S V O	S V O
If I help him,	he 'll help me.
Wenn ich ihm helfe,	hilft er mir.

When the cat's away, *the rats will play.*

Adverbialsätze sind Nebensätze, die – ähnlich wie ein Adverb (z. B. *beautifully*) – nähere Informationen zu einer Handlung oder einem Geschehen im Hauptsatz geben. Sie machen einen Text besser lesbar und interessanter.

Adverbialsätze werden durch Konjunktionen eingeleitet, z. B.:

- Adverbialsätze der Zeit mit *after, before, as* („als", „während"), *as soon as, until / till, when, while*
- Adverbialsätze des Grundes oder der Ursache mit *because*
- Adverbialsätze der Bedingung mit *if, unless*
- Adverbialsätze des Gegensatzes mit *although, even if, though, whereas*
- Adverbialsätze der Folge oder des Zwecks mit *so (that)*
- Adverbialsätze der Art und Weise mit *as if*
- Adverbialsätze des Ortes mit *everywhere, where, wherever*

Beachte:

- Wenn der Adverbialsatz am Anfang steht, setzt du ein Komma zwischen Adverbialsatz und Hauptsatz.
- Wenn der Adverbialsatz hinter dem Hauptsatz steht, brauchst du kein Komma.

! Im Englischen haben sowohl Hauptsätze als auch Nebensätze die Wortstellung S-V-O.

LF 22 **Revision**

Relativsätze *(Relative clauses)*

a) Relativpronomen *(Relative pronouns)*

Are you the guy **who / that** developed this computer game?
Bist du der Typ, der dieses Computerspiel entwickelt hat?

This is the girl **who / that** we met yesterday.
Das ist das Mädchen, das wir gestern getroffen haben.

I know a shop **which / that** sells really cool trainers.
Ich kenne einen Laden, der richtig coole Sportschuhe verkauft.

Jin is the girl **whose** parents have opened that new Korean restaurant.
Jin ist das Mädchen, dessen Eltern das neue koreanische Restaurant eröffnet haben.

Mit Relativsätzen kannst du zusätzliche Informationen über eine Person oder eine Sache geben. Man nennt diese Relativsätze *defining relative clauses* (bestimmende Relativsätze). Solche Relativsätze werden im Englischen in der Regel nicht durch ein Komma vom Hauptsatz abgetrennt.
Relativsätze werden durch unterschiedliche Relativpronomen eingeleitet:

- ***who*** für Personen (und Haustiere mit Namen)
- ***which*** für Dinge (und Tiere ohne Namen)
- ***that*** für Dinge (und Tiere ohne Namen) und Personen (für Personen ist *who* gebräuchlicher)
- ***whose*** („dessen", „deren") für Personen, aber auch für Dinge und Tiere. Auf *whose* folgt immer ein Nomen (z. B. *parents*).

*This is the rat **that ate the cheese***
that lay in the house
that Jack built.

b) **Challenge** Relativsätze ohne Relativpronomen *(Contact clauses)*

This is the boy **I met yesterday**.
Das ist der Junge, den ich gestern getroffen habe.

The game **he gave me** is great.
Das Spiel, das er mir geschenkt hat, ist toll.

Relativpronomen als Subjekt	Relativpronomen als Objekt
the girl **who** called das Mädchen, das angerufen hat	the girl **who I called** = the girl **I called** das Mädchen, das ich angerufen habe

Das Relativpronomen kann als Subjekt oder Objekt des Relativsatzes stehen.
Subjekt: *the boy **who** asked → **he** asked*
der Junge, der fragte
Objekt: *the boy **(who)** I asked → I asked **him***
der Junge, den ich fragte

Wenn das Relativpronomen nicht Subjekt, sondern Objekt ist, kann man es weglassen. (Im Deutschen ist das nicht möglich.)

! Wenn das Relativpronomen direkt vor dem Verb steht (z. B. *who called*), dann ist es Subjekt und darf nicht weggelassen werden.

Grammatical terms *(Grammatische Fachbegriffe in diesem Buch)*

action verb	das Tätigkeitsverb	*(to) go, (to) launch (to) write*
active	das Aktiv	*Li went to the party.*
adjective	das Adjektiv	*old, good, popular*
adverb of degree	das Gradadverb	*extremely, quite, hardly*
adverb of frequency	das Häufigkeitsadverb	*often, always, sometimes, rarely, never*
adverb of manner	das Adverb der Art und Weise	*well, carefully, quietly, angrily*
adverbial clause	der Adverbialsatz	*Men were paid $40* ***whereas women only got $30****.*
article	der Artikel	***a / the*** *book,* ***an / the*** *apple*
auxiliary verb	das Hilfsverb	*(to) be, (to) do, (to) have*
comparative	der Komparativ (erste Steigerungsform)	*older, better, more popular*
comparison of adjectives	die Steigerung von Adjektiven	*old – older – (the) oldest*
conditional sentence	der Bedingungssatz	*If it's rainy, I'll stay at home.* (type 1) *If I was rich, I'd buy a house.* (type 2)
conjunction	die Konjunktion, das Bindewort	*although, because, if, when*
contact clause	der Relativsatz ohne Relativpronomen	*a boy* ***I know****; things* ***we eat***
gerund	das Gerundium	***Singing*** *is easy.; I don't mind* ***helping*** *you.*
going to-future	das Futur mit *going to*	*I'm going to eat ...; We're going to watch ...*
if-clause	der Nebensatz mit *if*	*If it rains, ...*
infinitive	der Infinitiv (Grundform)	*(to) do, (to) go, (to) love*
ing-form	die *ing*-Form	***going****,* ***seeing****, ...*
irregular adjective	das unregelmäßige Adjektiv	*bad – worse – worst*
irregular adverb	das unregelmäßige Adverb	*good – well*
irregular verb	das unregelmäßige Verb	*(to) be, was/were, been; (to) do, did, done*
linking word	die Konjunktion, das Bindewort	*because, but, and*
long form	die Langform	*I am, we do not, you are*
main clause	der Hauptsatz	*If it rains,* ***I won't go out****.*
modal verb	das modale Hilfsverb	*can, must, shouldn't*
negative form	die verneinte Form	***don't*** *go,* ***can't*** *go,* ***aren't*** *going,* ***hasn't*** *gone*
noun	das Nomen / Substantiv	*friend, car, competition*
object	das Objekt	*I like* ***cats****.*
passive	das Passiv	*Lots of films are made in Hollywood.*
past participle	das Partizip Perfekt (3. Form)	*loved, eaten, seen, done, gone*

past perfect	das Plusquamperfekt, die Vorvergangenheit	*I **had gone**; it **had been***
past progressive	die Verlaufsform der Vergangenheit	*I **was talking**; he **was reading***
personal pronoun	das Personalpronomen	*I, you, he, she, it, we, they*
plural	der Plural, die Mehrzahl	*book**s**, child**ren**, potato**es**, stor**ies***
possessive determiner	der Possessivbegleiter	*my, your, his, her, its, our, their*
possessive form	die Possessivform (besitzanzeigende Form)	*the **girl's** dog*
possessive pronoun	das Possessivpronomen	*mine, yours, his, hers, ours, theirs*
preposition	die Präposition	***in** the house, **on** the desk, **near** the river*
present perfect	das Perfekt	*He has gone.; Have you seen?*
present progressive	die Verlaufsform der Gegenwart	*I**'m speaking**, she**'s looking**, we**'re talking**, they **aren't listening***
question tag	das Frageanhängsel	*This is nice, **isn't it**?; It hurts, **doesn't it**?; That's not Joe, **is it**?*
question word	die Frage mit Fragewort	***What**'s this? **How** are you?*
reflexive pronoun	das Reflexivpronomen	*myself, yourself, ourselves*
regular verb	das regelmäßige Verb	*(to) move, moved, moved; (to) hug, hugged, hugged; (to) try, tried, tried*
relative clause	der Relativsatz	*someone **who loves**, a shop **which sells***
relative pronoun	das Relativpronomen	*who, which, that, whose*
short answer	die Kurzantwort	*Yes, I do. / No, I'm not. / Yes, she does.*
short form	die Kurzform	*I**'m**, we **don't**, you**'re***
simple past	die einfache Vergangenheit	*it **was**; I **went**; he **talked***
simple present	die einfache Gegenwart	*it **is**; I **go**; he **talks***
singular	der Singular, die Einzahl	*book, child, potato, story*
statement	der Aussage(satz)	*I like oranges. I don't like bananas.*
state verb	das Zustandsverb	*(to) be, (to) become, (to) seem, (to) smell, (to) sound, (to) taste*
subject	das Subjekt	***They** eat dinner.; **The cat** is cute.*
superlative	der Superlativ (höchste Steigerungsform)	*(the) oldest, (the) best, (the) most popular*
tense	die Zeitform	*present progressive, simple past, future*
verb	das Verb; das Prädikat	*(to) go, (to) do, (to) love; I **can hear** you.*
will-future	das Futur mit *will*	*Noah **will** phone, you**'ll** see, he **won't** buy*
word order	die Wortstellung	*subject – verb – object: We know them.*
yes/no-question	die Entscheidungsfrage	*Are you OK?; Will she go?; Did it go well?*

Wichtige Schreibregeln im Englischen

Groß- und Kleinschreibung

Im Englischen wird fast alles kleingeschrieben. Merke dir nur diese Ausnahmen:

- das Wort 'I' (ich);
- Monatsnamen *(January, February, ...)*;
- Wochentage *(Monday, Tuesday, ...)*;
- Eigennamen und geografische Namen *(Tom, Lisa, London, ...)*;
- Länder, deren Bewohnerinnen und Bewohner, Sprachen und Nationalitäten *(Germany, the Germans, German)*;
- das erste Wort am Satzanfang und in Überschriften.

Stumme Buchstaben

Manche Wörter enthalten Buchstaben, die du zwar schreibst, aber nicht sprichst:

b *lam**b***
c *s**c**ience*
d *san**d**wich*
g *desi**g**n*
h *tec**h**nology*
i *frui**t***
k *(to) **k**now, **k**nife*
l *(to) wa**l**k, (to) ta**l**k*
u *g**u**itar, b**u**ilding*
t *(to) lis**t**en*
w *(to) ans**w**er, t**w**o, **w**rong, (to) **w**rite*

Verdoppelung der Endkonsonanten

*(to) sto**p** – sto**pp**ing, sto**pp**ed*
*(to) wi**n** – wi**nn**ing, wi**nn**er*

Anführungszeichen bei direkter Rede

Anders als bei der indirekten Rede – *Lou said she loves her dog.* – wird die direkte Rede durch Anführungszeichen gekennzeichnet: *'I love my dog,' Lou said.*

y wird zu *ie*

- im Plural: *stor**y** – stor**ies**, a pon**y** – three pon**ies**;*

- in der 3. Person Singular: *(to) tid**y** – he tid**ies**;*
- bei der Steigerung von Adjektiven: *bus**y** – bus**ier**, eas**y** – eas**ier**.*

Buchstabenverbindungen

Manche Buchstabenverbindungen kommen häufiger vor. Wenn du sie dir merkst, können sie dir beim Schreiben helfen:

-ee- *(to) see, deep, (to) meet, street*
-ea- *beach, meat, pea*
-igh- *sight, fight, right, night*
-oo- *book, good, look*
-ous *dangerous, nervous, famous*
-tion *station, competition*

Kommasetzung

Im Englischen kannst du oft entscheiden, ob du ein Komma setzt oder nicht.
Sind zwei Hauptsätze durch *and, but, or* oder *so* miteinander verbunden, können sie – je nach Länge des Satzes – durch ein Komma getrennt werden.
*It started to rain, **but** we decided to stay outside anyway.*
Es hat angefangen zu regnen, aber wir sind trotzdem draußen geblieben.
*It was raining **but** I didn't care.*
Es regnete, aber das war mir egal.
Kein Komma steht vor einem Nebensatz mit *that, what, where, why* usw. (auch in der indirekten Rede).

Wordbank 1: Being polite

▸ Unit 1 | p. 29

Offering help & information
Can I help you?
Do you need any help?
Are you OK? /
Is everything OK?

Asking for help & information
Excuse me ...
Sorry to bother you, but ...
Could you help me / us, please?
Could you tell me / us ...?

Asking for permission *(Erlaubnis)*
May I ...
Could I ...
Do you mind if I ...?
Can I sit here? Is this seat free?

Saying yes & no
Yes, of course. / Yes, please.
Sure. / That would be great.
No. thanks.
Sorry, but ...
I'm afraid I can't help you.

Offering food & drink
Would you like ...?
Can I give you ...?
Can I offer you ...?
Can I get you ...?
How about ...?

Asking for food & drink
Can / Could I have ..., please?
I'd like ...
I'll have ..., please.
Can I get ...?
Do you have ...?

Accepting & refusing
(etwas annehmen & ablehnen)
Yes, please.
No, thanks. (I'm afraid I don't eat ... /
I'm completely full.)

Saying thank you
Thanks. / Thank you.
Thanks for your help.
Thanks a lot for ...
I'm thankful for ...

Saying sorry
I'm (so / very) sorry.
It was my fault.
Sorry about that.

Answering to thanks
You're welcome.
No problem.
Any time!
Don't mention it.
I'm happy I could help.
Sure thing!

Accepting an apology
(eine Entschuldigung annehmen)
It's fine.
Don't worry about it.
No worries.
We're good.
Thank you for your apology.

Wordbank 2: Music

► Unit 2 | pp. 58, 62, 63 ► Unit 3 | p. 90

The song has an energetic rhythm.	*Das Lied hat einen dynamischen Rhythmus.*
The tempo is very fast / slow.	*Das Tempo ist sehr schnell / langsam.*
The melody is very catchy.	*Die Melodie ist sehr eingängig.*
The music makes me feel happy / sad.	*Die Musik macht mich glücklich / traurig.*
The lyrics are easy / not easy to understand.	*Der Text ist einfach / nicht einfach zu verstehen.*
The lyrics are catchy / easy to sing along.	*Der Text ist eingängig / leicht zum Mitsingen.*
The song is inspiring / passionate / relaxing / uplifting / ...	*Das Lied ist begeisternd / leidenschaftlich / entspannend / aufmunternd / ...*
The song is annoying / depressing / horrible / weird / ...	*Das Lied ist nervig / deprimierend / schrecklich / seltsam ...*
The singer has a smooth / strong / ... voice.	*Der Sänger / Die Sängerin hat eine sanfte / kräftige / ... Stimme.*
The song is about ... / makes me think of ...	*Das Lied handelt von ... / erinnert mich an ...*
The main message of the song is ...	*Die Hauptaussage des Liedes ist ...*

styles of music					
blues	classical	country	electronic	funk	hip-hop
indie	jazz	metal	pop	rap	rock

I play the ...
bagpipes, trumpet, violin

drums

recorder

piano

electric guitar

saxophone

trombone

Wordbank 3: Extreme weather and natural disasters ▸ Unit 2 | p. 64

There was ...
a flood, a hurricane, a lot of snow, a storm, a tornado, hail, heavy rain, thunder and lightning

Water
There was a tsunami / a storm flood / a flood / ...
Big waves and strong winds hit the coast.
Many towns were flooded.

flood

tsunami wave

Land
There was a landslide / a volcanic eruption / ...
Heavy rain caused a landslide.
A volcano erupted and caused wildfires.

landslide

volcanic eruption

Heat
The temperature rose to 40° Celsius.
There was a drought.
The hot weather lasted for over a month.
A wildfire burned for two weeks.

drought

wildfire

Cold
The temperature fell to minus 15° Celsius.
There was a blizzard / snowstorm / freezing rain / ...
There was ice on the roads. / The roads were icy.

blizzard

freezing rain

Wordbank 4: Job training

▶ Unit 3 | p. 94

I could do an apprenticeship in ...

catering

childcare

plumbing

agriculture

construction

motor service

I could do a qualification in ...

I'd like to work in ... Maybe I'll study ...

computing

hairdressing

hospitality

I would / wouldn't want to work ...
at night, at an airport, at a harbour, at a zoo, at home, in a hotel, in a hospital, in an office, in a shop, in a restaurant, on a farm, outdoors

in a retirement home

in a laboratory

in a factory

in a call centre

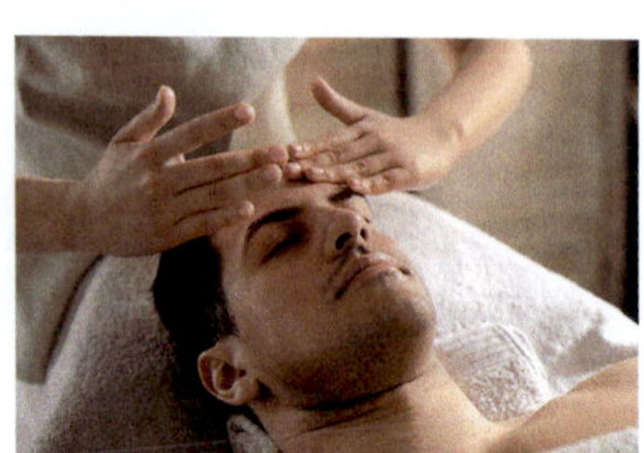
in a beauty salon

as an influencer

Wordbank 5: Charts

▸ Unit 1 | p. 22 ▸ Unit 4 | pp. 134, 144, 149

In this chart you can see … This diagram shows … This chart is about …

types of charts

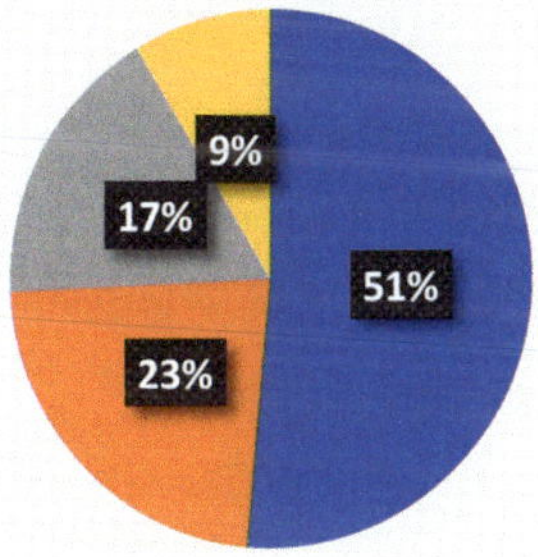

pie chart

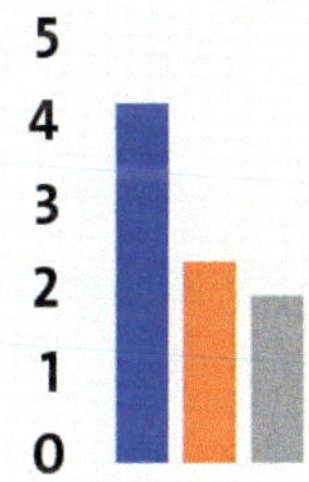

column chart

bar chart

line chart

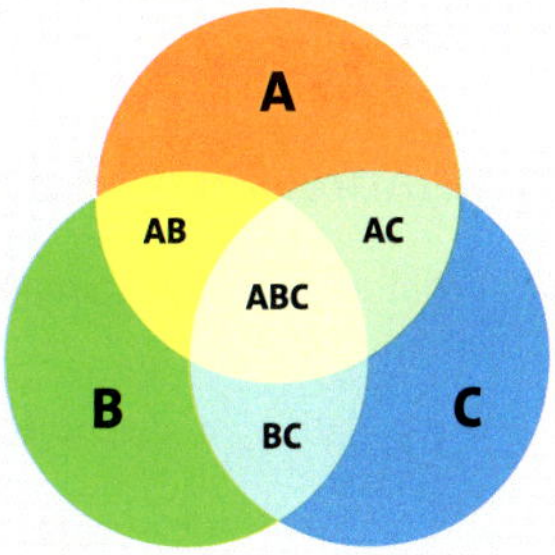

Venn diagram

Talking about charts and diagrams

In presentations

Let me show you this bar chart.
I'd like you to look at this diagram.
In this chart you can see the development of …
The source of the data / numbers / statistics is …
The data was collected …
The numbers / statistics are from the year …

Describing charts

This chart / diagram presents / compares …
The number of … increases / grows.
The number of … decreases / falls / drops.
The line shows an increase / a drop.
The x-axis / y-axis shows …

Comparing charts

These two charts show …
These diagrams are very similar / different.
This chart shows …, but this one …
The pie chart shows how …, whereas the Venn diagram focuses on …
These two charts show very different results.

How to explain numbers

98 out of 100 → almost 100
51 % = fifty-one per cent → over half
45 % = forty-five per cent → under half
23 % → almost one quarter
A low / high number …
Only 5% …

▸ Numbers, p. 211

Hier findest du englische Sätze mit ihrer deutschen Entsprechung.
Achte auf die kleinen Unterschiede.

1 Über Interessen und Dinge sprechen, die einem wichtig sind

	What's your favourite book / sport / ...?	Was ist dein Lieblingsbuch / -sport / ...?
	My favourite sport / ... is ... because ...	Mein Lieblingssport / ... ist ..., weil ...
	What do you like to do in your free time?	Was machst du gerne in deiner Freizeit?
	Are / Is ... important to you?	Sind / Ist dir ... wichtig?
	(My family) is really important to me because ...	(Meine Familie) ist mir sehr wichtig, weil ...
	Do you like ... or do you prefer ...?	Magst du ... oder magst du ... lieber?
	What are your hobbies and interests?	Was sind deine Hobbys und Interessen?
	How long have you played football / ...?	Wie lange spielst du schon Fußball / ...?

2 Sich verabreden und etwas planen

	What are we / you going to do this weekend / on Sunday / ...?	Was machen wir / machst du am Wochenende / Sonntag / ...?
	Are you doing anything (today)?	Machst du (heute) irgendetwas?
	Maybe we could ...?	Vielleicht könnten wir ...?
	Are you free?	Hast du Zeit?
	(Saturday) would be best.	(Samstag) wäre am besten.
	Let's meet at the station / in the park / ... at 7.30 p.m.	Lass uns um 19.30 Uhr am Bahnhof / im Park / ... treffen.
	Sorry, I can't. I'm really busy.	Tut mir leid, da kann ich nicht. Ich bin sehr beschäftigt.
	I'd love to ...	Ich würde sehr gerne ...
	How / What about (later after dinner)?	Wie sieht es (später nach dem Abendessen) aus?

3 Leben in der (Klein-)Stadt

Öffentliche Verkehrsmittel nutzen

	How much does (a bus ticket) cost?	Wie viel kostet (eine Busfahrkarte)?
	This is our stop.	Das ist unsere Haltestelle.
	Do we have to change?	Müssen wir umsteigen?
	We can take the bus / tram / ... from here.	Von hier können wir den Bus / die Straßenbahn / ... nehmen.
	How long does it take by taxi / bike / ...?	Wie lange dauert es mit dem Taxi / Fahrrad / ...?
Unit 1	In my area, we don't / only have (busses).	Wo ich wohne, haben wir keine / nur (Busse).
	The underground / ... runs 24 hours every day.	Die U-Bahn / ... fährt 24 Stunden am Tag.

	You need to take (the 4 or 5 train) to ...	Du musst / Sie müssen die Linie (4 oder 5) zu / nach ... nehmen.
	It's four stops.	Es sind vier Haltestellen.
	You can change to other lines.	Man kann auf andere Linien umsteigen.
	Take the exit for ... street.	Nimm / Nehmen Sie den Ausgang zur ... Straße.
	You need to get off at the next stop	Du musst / Sie müssen an der nächsten Haltestelle aussteigen.
	You're on the right / wrong line.	Das ist die richtige / falsche U-Bahn-Linie.

Nach dem Weg fragen und Wege beschreiben

	Go straight on / across / along / past / ...	Geh geradeaus / über / entlang / an ... vorbei / ...
	Turn left / right.	Biege links / rechts ab.
	Take the first / second / ... road on the right / left.	Nimm / Nehmen Sie die erste / zweite / ... Straße auf der rechten / linken Seite.
	Follow (the river) that way and go past ...	Folge (dem Fluss) und gehe an / am ... vorbei.
	South / North / East / West from ...	Südlich / Nördlich / Östlich / Westlich von ...
	Only a few minutes' walk away from ...	Nur ein paar Minuten zu Fuß von / vom ...
Unit 1	I don't understand which way to go to get to ...	Ich verstehe nicht, wie man zum / zur ... kommt.
	Could you tell us how to get to ...?	Könnten Sie uns bitte sagen, wie wir nach ... kommen?

Essen gehen und in einem Restaurant bestellen

	Would you like some more (water)?	Möchtest du / Möchten Sie noch etwas mehr (Wasser)?
	Enjoy your meal!	Guten Appetit!
	(The falafel) sound good.	(Die Falafel) hören sich lecker an.
	I'm allergic to ...	Ich bin gegen ... allergisch.
	Could I have (a cola), please?	Könnte ich bitte (eine Cola) bekommen?
	I'd like (sparkling water), please.	Ich hätte gerne (Sprudelwasser).
	I'll have (a glass of tap water), please.	Ich nehme (ein Glas Leitungswasser), bitte.
	Can I have it without (tomatoes)?	Könnte ich das / es ohne (Tomaten) haben / bekommen?
	Can you tell me what ... is?	Was ist ...?

4 Global goals

Über Umwelt, Natur(schutz) und Nachhaltigkeit sprechen

	I think it's interesting / surprising / terrible / ... that ...	Ich finde es interessant / überraschend / schrecklich / ..., dass ...
	Why don't we (recycle) ...?	Warum (recyceln) wir ... nicht?
	We think people should recycle / repair old clothes / ...	Wir finden, dass man recyclen / alte Kleidung reparieren / ... sollte.

	It's green because ...	Es ist nachhaltig, weil ...
	What can you do (in your everyday life) to protect nature?	Was kannst du (in deinem Alltag) tun, um die Natur zu schützen?
Unit 4	Don't buy bottled water unless ... Drink ... instead.	Kaufe kein Wasser in Einwegflaschen, außer ... Trinke stattdessen ...
	Use less ...	Verwende weniger ...
	Switch off ...	Schalte ... aus.
	Only use ... when ...	Benutze ... nur, wenn ...

Über Gerechtigkeit und gesellschaftliche Probleme sprechen

Unit 1	People need healthy food / dignity / to feel safe.	Menschen brauchen ausreichend gesunde Lebensmittel / Würde / Sicherheit.
	It's nice to have a phone so that you can contact your family and friends / use apps / ...	Es ist schön, ein Telefon zu haben, mit dem man seine Familie und Freunde kontaktieren / Apps nutzen / ... kann.
Unit 2	It's important to take a (strong) stand against ...	Es ist wichtig, gegen ... (klar) Stellung zu beziehen / sich (deutlich) gegen ... auszusprechen.
	We should treat each other with respect.	Wir sollten einander respektvoll behandeln.
Unit 3	Boys / Girls can('t) wear ...	Jungen / Mädchen können (kein / keine) ... tragen.
	T-shirts / skirts / shorts / ... should (not) be ... / must (not) have ...	T-Shirts / Röcke / Shorts / ... sollten (nicht) ... / dürfen (nicht) ...
	It's important that everyone is equal.	Es ist wichtig, dass alle gleich sind.

5 Miteinander reden

Über Probleme sprechen und Ratschläge erteilen

	Could you help me, please?	Könntest du / Könnten Sie mir bitte helfen?
	What can I do? Please help!	Was kann / soll ich machen? Bitte hilf / helfen Sie mir.
	The problem is that ...	Das Problem ist, dass ...
	You should / could talk to ...	Du solltest / könntest mit ... sprechen.
	I understand that you're unhappy / sad / disappointed / ...	Ich verstehe, dass du unglücklich / traurig / enttäuscht / ... bist.
	I think this is good / bad advice.	Ich finde das ist ein guter / schlechter Ratschlag.

Komplimente machen

	I think you're funny / brave / ...	Ich finde dich witzig / mutig / ...
	I love your shoes / dress / ...	Ich mag deine Schuhe / dein Kleid ...
	I want to tell you that you're great at football / an amazing friend / ...	Ich wollte dir sagen, dass du sehr gut Fußball spielst / ein toller Freund / eine tolle Freundin bist / ...
	Thank you, that's nice of you.	Danke, das ist lieb / nett von dir.
	You're welcome!	Gern geschehen!

Einen Konflikt lösen und sich entschuldigen

	I'm sorry, it was a bad idea to ...	Es tut mir leid, es war eine schlechte Idee ...
	Why did you ....?	Warum hast du ...?
	That's OK.	(Alles) Ist in Ordnung.
	I'm glad you ...	Ich bin froh, dass du ...
	Next time, you could ...	Beim nächsten Mal könntest du ...

Hilfe anbieten, erbitten und annehmen; sich bedanken

	I'd like to ..., but I don't know where to start.	Ich möchte gerne ..., aber ich weiß gar nicht, wo ich anfangen soll.
	I can help you if you like.	Ich kann dir helfen, wenn du magst.
	Could / Can you help me ...?	Könntest / Kannst du mir helfen ...?
	Would you like me to show you how to ...?	Möchtest du, dass ich dir zeige, wie ...?
	I'm OK, thanks.	Alles gut, danke. / Nein, danke.
Unit 1	Excuse me, could you ..., please?	Entschuldigung, könntest du / könnten Sie bitte ...?
	Thanks for your help	Danke für deine / Ihre Hilfe.
Unit 3	Thank you for helping / asking / ...	Vielen Dank fürs Helfen / (Nach-)Fragen / ...

6 Über Technologie im Alltag sprechen

	I believe that (social media) is a positive / negative thing for teens because ...	Ich denke, dass (soziale Medien) einen positiven / negativen Einfluss auf Jugendliche haben, weil ...
	I often / sometimes / never / ... use ...	Ich nutze ... oft / manchmal / nie / ...
	How often do you use ...?	Wie oft nutzt du ...?
	I think one of the problems with ... is that ...	Ich denke, ein Problem von ... ist, dass ...
Unit 4	I think photo ... is real because ...	Ich glaube, das Foto ... ist echt, weil ...
	The colours / details / ... look ...	Die Farben / Details / ... sehen ... aus.
	The light in the picture is ...	Das Licht in dem Foto ist ...

7 Über Berufe und die Zukunft sprechen

Unit 3	I want to go to university / go travelling / get a job / do an apprenticeship ...	Ich möchte studieren / reisen / arbeiten / eine Ausbildung machen ...
	I'd like to live abroad / do volunteer work / ...	Ich möchte gerne im Ausland leben / Freiwilligendienst leisten / ...
	I (don't) think I'll be famous / get married / ...	I glaube (nicht), dass ich berühmt / verheiratet / ... sein werde.
	I probably won't be ...	Ich werde wahrscheinlich nicht ...
	I'd like to work outside / ...	Ich möchte gerne draußen / ... arbeiten.
	I don't mind working (with) ...	Es macht mir nichts aus, (mit) ... zu arbeiten.
	I need regular hours.	Ich brauche regelmäßige Arbeitszeiten.
	I'd like a flexible job.	Ich hätte gerne einen flexiblen Arbeitsplatz.

8 Seine Meinung äußern, diskutieren und Verständnis zeigen

	I'm not really a fan of ...	Ich bin nicht eigentlich kein Fan von ...
	For me that isn't true.	Für mich ist das nicht so.
	In my opinion, it's most important to ...	Meiner Meinung nach ist es am wichtigsten, ...
	If you ask me, I'd say that ...	Wenn du mich fragst, würde ich sagen, dass ...
	I (completely) agree / disagree.	Ich stimme dir (voll und ganz) zu / (überhaupt) nicht zu.
	I see it a bit differently.	Ich sehe das etwas anders.
	Just a minute, please; let me think.	Einen Moment bitte; lass mich nachdenken.
Unit 3	I'm not sure I understood / got that.	Ich bin nicht sicher, ob ich das (richtig) verstanden habe.
	Really? That's interesting.	Wirklich? Das ist interessant.
	Go on.	Erzähl mir mehr.
	Right.	Stimmt.
	So / Do you mean ...?	(Also) Meinst du, dass ...?
	Tell me more about that.	Erzähl mir mehr darüber.
Unit 4	Don't you think that ...?	Findest du nicht, dass ...?
	You have a point that ...	Du hast ein gutes Argument dafür, dass ... Da hast du recht, dass ...
	But can't you see that ...	Aber siehst du nicht, dass ...
	The reason why I think that ...	Ich denke so, weil ...
	I hear what you're saying, but I still don't think that ...	Ich verstehe, was du meinst, aber ich finde trotzdem nicht, dass ...
	I don't see it that way at all because ...	Das sehe ich ganz anders, denn ...

9 Ein Thema (in einem Podcast) präsentieren

Unit 1	Hello and welcome to all our listeners!	Herzlich willkommen, liebe Zuhörer und Zuhörerinnen!
	Hi, everyone! Today I'd like to talk about ...	Hallo zusammen! Heute möchte ich über ... sprechen.
	Firstly / To begin with, I'd like to tell you ...	Zuerst möchte ich euch / Ihnen etwas über ... erzählen.
	Next, I'd like to talk about ...	Dann möchte ich über ... sprechen.
	Finally, let's talk about ...	Zuletzt sprechen wir über ...
	To sum up, ...	Zusammenfassend ...
	(Well,) That's all for now.	(Nun,) Das war's (für heute).
	Thanks for listening.	Vielen Dank für eure / Ihre Aufmerksamkeit.
	We / I hope that you enjoyed ...	Wir hoffen / Ich hoffe, dass ... Ihnen / euch gefallen hat.
	Do you have any questions?	Habt ihr / Haben Sie noch Fragen?

Classroom English

You and your teacher	Du und deine Lehrerin / dein Lehrer
Good morning, Mr / Mrs / Ms ... (bis 12 Uhr)	Guten Morgen, Herr / Frau ...
Good afternoon, Mr / Mrs / Ms ... (ab 12 Uhr)	Guten Tag / Nachmittag, Herr / Frau ...
Sorry I'm late.	Entschuldigung, dass ich zu spät komme.
May I open / close the window, please?	Darf ich das Fenster öffnen / zumachen?
May I go to the toilet, please?	Darf ich zur Toilette gehen?

Homework and exercises	Hausaufgaben und Übungen
Sorry, I don't have my exercise book.	Es tut mir leid, ich habe mein Heft nicht dabei.
I don't understand this exercise.	Ich verstehe die Übung nicht.
I can't do number 3.	Ich kann Nummer 3 nicht lösen.
Sorry, I haven't finished.	Entschuldigung, ich bin noch nicht fertig.
I have ... Is that right too?	Ich habe ... Ist das auch richtig?
Sorry, I don't know.	Es tut mir leid, das weiß ich nicht.
What's for homework?	Was haben wir (als Hausaufgabe) auf?

You need help	Du brauchst Hilfe
Could you help me, please?	Könnten Sie / Könntest du mir bitte helfen?
What page is it, please?	Auf welcher Seite sind wir / steht das?
What's ... in English / German?	Was heißt ... auf Englisch / Deutsch?
Please speak up / speak more loudly.	Könnten Sie / Könntest du bitte lauter sprechen?
Can I say it in German?	Kann ich das auf Deutsch sagen?
Could you write it on the board, please?	Könnten Sie das bitte an die Tafel schreiben?
Could you say / play that again, please?	Könnten Sie das bitte noch einmal sagen / abspielen?

Work with a partner	Partnerarbeit
May I work with Khalil?	Darf ich mit Khalil arbeiten?
May I use your (pen), please?	Darf ich bitte deinen (Stift) benutzen?
Yes, here you are.	Hier, bitte.
It's my / your turn.	Ich bin dran. / Du bist dran.
Let's make / draw a / an ...	Lass uns ein / eine / einen ... machen / zeichnen.
Let's act out the story / the dialogue.	Lass uns die Geschichte / den Dialog spielen.

What your teacher says	Was deine Lehrerin / dein Lehrer sagt
Let's start.	Lasst uns anfangen. / Los geht's.
Listen, please. / Quiet, please.	Hört bitte zu. / Ruhe bitte.
Open your books at page 24, please.	Schlagt bitte Seite 24 auf.
Do exercise 5 for homework, please.	Macht bitte Übung 5 als Hausaufgabe.
Write the correct words.	Schreibt die richtigen Wörter (auf).
Correct the false sentences.	Korrigiert die falschen Sätze.
Where's your book, Dana?	Wo ist dein Buch, Dana?
Try again!	Versuche es noch einmal.

Feedback phrases

Content ☆☆☆

I enjoyed reading your article / blog / ...	
I enjoyed listening to your presentation / talk / ...	
The most interesting part was about ...	Try to make the introduction / the first part / ... more interesting by ...
You included all the points in the instructions.	Next time, remember to include the point about ...
You gave great reasons for your opinions.	Try to give reasons for your opinions.
You used charts to support your ideas.	Don't forget to use charts to support your ideas.

Structure ☆☆☆

Your article / presentation / ... was just the right length.	Next time, you could write more / less.
Your title was interesting / made me want to read it.	Maybe you could find a more interesting title.
Your introduction presented the topic well.	Your introduction could present the topic better.
You structured your article / presentation / ... well.	Try to make the structure clearer. Use paragraphs.
Your conclusion summed up your article / blog / ... well.	Next time, remember to include a title / introduction / conclusion.
You remembered a greeting at the beginning / end of your letter / email.	Next time, remember to include a greeting at the beginning / end of your letter / email.

Media ☆☆☆

Your slides were clear and easy to read.	Next time, make the writing on your slides bigger.
I could see the pictures / charts very well.	You could make the pictures / charts bigger.
Your recording was easy to understand.	Maybe you could speak more clearly on your recording.
You included your sources.	Don't forget to include your sources.
You used good audio-visual effects / music.	Next time, add audio-visual effects / music.

Speaking and presentations ☆☆☆

You looked at the audience / your group.	Remember to look at the audience / your group.
You made eye contact.	Next time, don't forget to make eye contact.
You smiled and looked friendly.	Maybe you could smile more next time.
You spoke clearly.	Try and speak more clearly / more slowly.
You used phrases to buy time when you didn't know a word – well done!	Try and use phrases to buy time when you don't know a word.

Language ☆☆☆

You used lots of different phrases.	Next time, you could use more adverbs.
I understood most of what you wrote / said.	Remember to explain new words.
I didn't notice any / many mistakes.	Next time, use the present tense / the past tense. / Don't forget to use a spellchecker.
Your pronunciation sounded (very) good.	You could check the pronunciation of words in the app / in an online dictionary.

Cardinal numbers

0 **oh, zero, nil** [əʊ, ˈzɪərəʊ, nɪl]
1 **one** [wʌn]
2 **two** [tʊ:]
3 **three** [θri:]
4 **four** [fɔ:]
5 **five** [faɪv]
6 **six** [sɪks]
7 **seven** [ˈsevn]
8 **eight** [eɪt]
9 **nine** [naɪn]
10 **ten** [ten]

11 **eleven** [ɪˈlevn]
12 **twelve** [twelv]
13 **thirteen** [θɜ:ˈti:n]
14 **fourteen** [fɔ:ˈti:n]
15 **fifteen** [fɪfˈti:n]
16 **sixteen** [sɪksˈti:n]
17 **seventeen** [sevnˈti:n]
18 **eighteen** [eɪˈti:n]
19 **nineteen** [naɪnˈti:n]
20 **twenty** [ˈtwenti]

21 **twenty-one** [twentiˈwʌn]
22 **twenty-two** [twentiˈtu:]
23 **twenty-three** [twentiˈθri:]
...

30 **thirty** [ˈθɜ:ti]
40 **forty** [ˈfɔ:ti]
50 **fifty** [ˈfɪfti]
60 **sixty** [ˈsɪksti]
70 **seventy** [ˈsevnti]
80 **cighty** [ˈeɪti]
90 **ninety** [ˈnaɪnti]
100 **a / one hundred** [ə / wʌn ˈhʌndrəd]

101 **one hundred and one**
102 **one hundred and two**
...

Ordinal numbers

1st **first** [fɜ:st]
2nd **second** [ˈsekənd]
3rd **third** [θɜ:d]
4th **fourth** [fɔ:θ]
5th **fifth** [fɪfθ]
6th **sixth** [sɪksθ]
7th **seventh** [ˈsevnθ]
8th **eighth** [eɪtθ]
9th **ninth** [naɪnθ]
10th **tenth** [tenθ]

11th **eleventh** [ɪˈlevnθ]
12th **twelfth** [twelfθ]
13th **thirteenth** [θɜ:ˈti:nθ]
14th **fourteenth** [fɔ:ˈti:nθ]
15th **fifteenth** [fɪfˈti:nθ]
16th **sixteenth** [sɪksˈti:nθ]
17th **seventeenth** [sevnˈti:nθ]
18th **eighteenth** [eɪˈti:nθ]
19th **nineteenth** [naɪnˈti:nθ]
20th **twentieth** [ˈtwentiəθ]

21st **twenty-first** [twentiˈfɜ:st]
22nd **twenty-second** [twentiˈsekənd]
23rd **twenty-third** [twentiˈθɜ:d]
...

30th **thirtieth** [ˈθɜ:tiəθ]
40th **fortieth** [ˈfɔ:tiəθ]
50th **fiftieth** [ˈfɪftiəθ]
60th **sixtieth** [ˈsɪkstiəθ]
70th **seventieth** [ˈsevntiəθ]
80th **eightieth** [ˈeɪtiəθ]
90th **ninetieth** [ˈnaɪntiəθ]
100th **hundredth** [ˈhʌndrədθ]

101st **one hundred and first**
102nd **one hundred and second**
...

Large numbers

6,513 six thousand five hundred thirteen

7,500,000 seven million five hundred thousand

In English, you use a comma (not a point) to divide large numbers into groups of three. You don't say the comma.

Percentages (Prozentsätze)

42% forty-two per cent (of New Yorkers)

90% ninety per cent (of the population)

Decimals (Dezimalzahlen)

0.48 zero **point** four eight
null Komma vier acht

9.7 million
nine **point** seven million
neun Komma sieben Millionen

In English, you write and say decimals with a point (not a comma). Say the point and each number after the point separately.

Fractions (Brüche)

½ a / one half
⅓ a / one third
¼ a / one quarter
⅕ a / one fifth
⅔ two thirds
¾ three quarters
⁵⁄₇ five sevenths
2 ½ two and a half
6 ⅔ six and two thirds

Dates

In most of the world, you write the day first, then the month, then the year **(day/month/year)**, e.g.: 3 April 2025 or 3/4/2025. You say: the third of April, 2025.

In the USA, you write the month first, then the day, then the year **(month/day/year)**, e.g.: April 3, 2025 or 4/3/2025. You say: April third, 2025.

The English alphabet

a	[eɪ]	h	[eɪtʃ]	o	[əʊ]	v	[viː]
b	[biː]	i	[aɪ]	p	[piː]	w	[ˈdʌbljuː]
c	[siː]	j	[dʒeɪ]	q	[kjuː]	x	[eks]
d	[diː]	k	[keɪ]	r	[ɑː]	y	[waɪ]
e	[iː]	l	[el]	s	[es]	z	[zed]
f	[ef]	m	[em]	t	[tiː]		
g	[dʒiː]	n	[en]	u	[juː]		

English sounds

Die Lautschrift zeigt dir die Aussprache von Wörtern und Lauten *(sounds)*.

Einige dieser Laute kommen im Deutschen nicht vor oder werden anders geschrieben. Sie sind hier mit einem Ausrufezeichen gekennzeichnet: **!**. Übe sie mit Hilfe der App.

	[iː]	green, he, sea
	[ɑː]	ask, class, car, park
!	[ɔː]	or, ball, door, four, morning
	[uː]	ruler, blue, too, two, you
	[ɜː]	early, her, girl, work, T-shirt
	[ɪ]	in, big, expensive
	[e]	yes, bed, again, breakfast
	[æ]	animal, apple, black, cat
	[ʌ]	mum, bus, colour
	[ɒ]	song, on, dog, what
	[ʊ]	book, good, put, bully
	[ə]	again, today, a sister
	[i]	happy, monkey
	[eɪ]	name, eight, play, great
	[aɪ]	I, time, right, my
	[ɔɪ]	boy, toilet, noise
	[əʊ]	old, no, road, yellow
	[aʊ]	now, house
	[ɪə]	here, material, really, year
	[eə]	where, pair, share, their
	[ʊə]	tour
	[b]	bike, table, verb
	[p]	pen, paper, shop
	[d]	day, window, good
	[t]	ten, letter, at
	[g]	go, again, bag
	[k]	kitchen, car, back
	[m]	man, remember, mum
	[n]	no, one, ten
!	[ŋ]	wrong, young, uncle, thanks
	[l]	like, old, small
	[r]	ruler, friend, sorry
!	[w]	we, where, one
	[j]	yes, you, uniform
	[f]	family, after, laugh
!	[v]	very, seven, have
	[s]	six, poster, yes
!	[z]	zoo, quiz, his, music, please
	[ʃ]	she, station, English
!	[ʒ]	usually, revision, garage
	[tʃ]	chain, teacher, watch
!	[dʒ]	job, German, project, orange
!	[θ]	thing, three, bathroom, north
!	[ð]	the, weather, with
	[h]	house, who, behind
	[x]	loch

Höre dir in der App jedes Wort genau an und sprich es nach.

Inhalt

Seite

Welcome to the USA 214
Merkboxen: *separate – separately – (to) separate*

Unit 1 NYC: The world in a city 215
Merkboxen: *American English: different words • American English: different spelling – different pronunciation • Mit Artikel – ohne Artikel • Punctuation • welcome – (to) welcome sb. • immigration – emigration • "Pommes frites" and "Kartoffelchips" • (to) run, ran, run • (to) match – match • Verbs and nouns: -tion, -ation*

Unit 2 The South-East: Changing times 226
Merkboxen: *a must • line • Nouns and adjectives • over • total(ly) • American English: different words*

Seite

Unit 3 Texas: Teen life 236
Merkboxen: *Question tags • Students at American high schools • (to) employ / unemployed / (un)employment • education – (to) educate – educational • American English: different words • whatever, whenever, ... • (to) frustrate sb. – frustrating – frustrated – frustration • Verbs and nouns: -ment • Irregular verbs*

Unit 4 California: State of contrasts 248
Merkboxen: *Verbs ending in -ize or -ise • (to) return – return • Temperatures • (to) report – report*

Unit 5 Canada: The northern neighbour 257

Symbole und Abkürzungen

▸ p. 10 ▸ pp. 12/13	Die Seitenzahl zeigt dir, wo das Wort zum ersten Mal in diesem Buch vorkommt.
▸▸ **mainly**	Die doppelten Pfeile weisen auf ein Wort mit gleicher Bedeutung hin, das du bereits kennst.
certain ◂▸ **uncertain**	*Certain* ist das Gegenteil von *uncertain*.
! *German:* **am Himmel** – *English:* **in the sky**	„Vorsicht, hier keinen Fehler machen!"
separate – separately – (to) **separate**	In den Merkboxen findest du wichtige Hinweise zu den neuen Wörtern und Wendungen.

sb.	= *somebody* (jemand)	*adj*	= *adjective* (Adjektiv)
sth.	= *something* (etwas)	*adv*	= *adverb* (Adverb)
infml.	= *informal* (informell, umgangssprachlich)	*conj*	= *conjunction* (Konjunktion)
pl	= *plural* (Plural, Mehrzahlform)	*prep*	= *preposition* (Präposition)
AE	= American English	*BE*	= British English

Hinweise

- Seite 211 enthält eine Übersicht über die **Zahlen**, Seite 212 über die **Lautschriftzeichen**.
- Tipps zum Vokabellernen findest du im **Skills file** auf den Seiten 162–177.
- Die **Wordbanks** (S. 199–203) bieten dir nach wichtigen Themen gesammelte Stichwörter.
- **Let's talk** (S. 204–209) enthält Wendungen für wichtige Situationen, gefolgt von einer Seite Feedback phrases (S. 210).
- Eine **Liste mit unregelmäßigen Verben** findest du auf den Seiten 300–302, und eine Übersicht über **Continents, countries and regions** auf den Seiten 310–311.
- Englische Wörter, die im Deutschen ähnlich sind, findest du auf Seite 303.
- Im **Dictionary** (S. 262–299) kannst du englische Wörter nachschlagen.

Welcome

▸ pp. 10/11	**alligator** [ˈælɪgeɪtə]	der Alligator	 an **alligator** ! Betonung auf der 1. Silbe: **alligator** [ˈælɪgeɪtə]
	crocodile [ˈkrɒkədaɪl]	das Krokodil	 a **crocodile** ! Betonung auf der 1. Silbe: **crocodile** [ˈkrɒkədaɪl]
	snowmobile [ˈsnəʊməbiːl]	das Schneemobil	a **snowmobile** 
	shape [ʃeɪp]	die Form, die Gestalt	noun: **shape** – These toys have strange **shapes**. verb: (to) **shape (**sth. **into** sth.**)** – Can you **shape** an animal from this material? ((etwas zu etwas) formen)
	canyon [ˈkænjən]	der Cañon	There's a river at the bottom of the **canyon**.
	cattle *(pl)* [ˈkætl]	das Vieh, die Rinder	 ! **cattle** ist ein Pluralwort: The **cattle are** in a different field every day.
	state [steɪt]	der (Bundes-)Staat	! **state** = **1.** der (Bundes-)Staat – How many **states** does the USA have? **2.** der Zustand – I was in a **state** of shock when I heard the news.
▸ pp. 12/13	**president** [ˈprezɪdənt]	der Präsident, die Präsidentin	! Betonung auf der 1. Silbe: **president** [ˈprezɪdənt]
	(to) **fit** [fɪt]	passen (zu); sitzen *(Kleidung)*	! **fit** = **1.** *(adj)* fit; **2.** *(verb)* passen (zu) verb: (to) **fit** This dress **fits** me perfectly. – noun: **fit** (die Passform, der Sitz *(Kleidung)*) It's a perfect **fit** for me.

population [pɒpju'leɪʃn]	die Bevölkerung, die Einwohner(zahl)	Twenty per cent of this country's **population** are over 50.
separate ['seprət]	getrennt, separat	

separate – separately – (to) **separate**

adj: **separate** ['seprət]	The library has a **separate** room for children's books.	getrennt, separat
adv: **separately** ['seprətli]	They didn't drive there together (= in the same car), they drove there **separately** (= in different cars).	getrennt
verb: (to) **separate** ['sepəreɪt]	It's not right to **separate** children from their parents.	trennen

candy *(AE)* ['kændi]	die Süßigkeiten	►► *BE* **sweets**
► pp. 14/15 **camp** [kæmp]	das (Zelt-)Lager	**summer camp** = das Ferienlager (im Sommer) **campfire** = das Lagerfeuer
original [ə'rɪdʒənl]	original, ursprünglich	adj: **original** – noun: **original** (das Original) ! Betonung auf der 2. Silbe: **original** [ə'rɪdʒənl]
reservation [rezə'veɪʃn]	das Reservat, die Reservation *(der indigenen Bevölkerung Nordamerikas zugewiesenes Gebiet)*	
jewelry *(AE)* ['dʒuːəlri]	der Schmuck	! *BE* spelling: **jewellery** I have a little box for my rings and other **jewellery** *(BE)* / **jewelry** *(AE)*.
mostly ['məʊstli]	hauptsächlich *(Adv.)*	►► **mainly** Our band plays lots of different music, but **mostly**/**mainly** old pop songs.
counsellor ['kaʊnsələ]	der Berater, die Beraterin; der Betreuer, die Betreuerin	The school **counsellor** will help you if you have problems. ! *AE* spelling: **counselor**
cabin ['kæbɪn]	die Hütte; die Kabine	 a **cabin**

Unit 1 NYC: The world in a city

► pp. 16/17 **trade** [treɪd]	der Handel	nouns: **trade**; *(person)* **trader** verb: (to) **trade (in)** (handeln, Handel treiben (mit)) • She has her own business and **trades in** e-bikes. • Her **trade in** e-bikes is going well.
freedom ['friːdəm]	die Freiheit	the state of being free to live as you choose adj: **free** – noun: **freedom**
liberty ['lɪbəti]	die Freiheit	►► **freedom**

Topic 1

▶ p. 18	**out and about** [aʊt ənd əˈbaʊt]	unterwegs	When I'm in London, I'm **out and about** all the time. There's so much to do!
	general [ˈdʒenrəl]	allgemein	• Let's talk about some **general** questions first before we look at the details. • I like pizza **in general**, but the pizza at that restaurant is horrible. = **Generally**, I like pizza, but ...
	borough *(AE)* [*BE:* ˈbʌrə, *AE:* ˈbɜːrəʊ]	der (Stadt-)Bezirk	a part of a town/city with its own local goverment
▶ p. 19	**value** [ˈvæljuː]	der Wert	**value for money** = das Preis-Leistungs-Verhältnis, der Gegenwert **It's good value (for money).** = Es ist sein Geld wert. / Es ist preiswert.
	either ... or ... [ˈaɪðə]	entweder ... oder ...	Dr Cox could see you **either** at 10.30 or at 4 p.m. on Friday.
	nickel *(AE)* [ˈnɪkl]	das Fünfcentstück	an American five-cent coin
	dime *(AE)* [daɪm]	das Zehncentstück	an American ten-cent coin
	quarter *(AE)* [ˈkwɔːtə]	das 25-Cent-Stück	an American 25-cent coin

American English: different words

British English	American English	
rucksack	**backpack**	der Rucksack
lift	**elevator**	der Fahrstuhl, der Aufzug, der Lift
chips	**French fries**	die Pommes frites
queue	**line**	die Schlange *(wartender Menschen)*
mum	**mom, momma**	die Mama, die Mutti
film	**movie**	der Film
cinema	**movie theater**	das Kino
trousers	**pants**	die Hose
trainers	**sneakers**	die Sportschuhe
shop	**store**	der Laden, das Geschäft
underground	**subway**	die U-Bahn
rubbish	**trash**	der Müll
holiday(s)	**vacation**	der Urlaub

American English: different spelling – different pronunciation

Different spelling

BE: -tre	**AE: -ter**
centre	center
(kilo)metre	(kilo)meter
theatre	theater
BE: -our	**AE: -or**
colour	color
favourite	favorite
neighbour(hood)	neighbor(hood)
BE: -ll-	**AE: -l-**
counsellor	counselor
jewellery	jewelry
travelled, travelling	traveled, traveling

Different pronunciation

	BE: [ɑː]	**AE: [æ]**
ask	[ɑːsk]	[æsk]
can't	[kɑːnt]	[kænt]
plant	[plɑːnt]	[plænt]
	BE: [juː]	**AE: [uː]**
new	[njuː]	[nuː]
student	[ˈstjuːdnt]	[ˈstuːdnt]
Tuesday	[ˈtjuːzdeɪ]	[ˈtuːzdeɪ]
	BE: [ɒ]	**AE: [ɑː]**
body	[ˈbɒdi]	[ˈbɑːdi]
clock	[klɒk]	[klɑːk]
hot	[hɒt]	[hɑːt]

- In American English, you can usually hear the **r** in words like **here, more, sure, shirt, farm, hard, better**.
- In American English, the **t** between two vowels often sounds more like a **d**: **city** [ˈsɪdi], **better** [ˈbedər], **writer** [ˈraɪdər].

▶ p. 20	(to) **measure** [ˈmeʒə]	(aus)messen	• We have to **measure** this room. (ausmessen) • It **measures** 3 x 2 metres. (Er misst ... = Er ist ... groß.) verb: (to) **measure** – noun: **measurement** [ˈmeʒəmənt] (die Abmessung, das Maß, die Maßeinheit)
	km² = square kilometre [skweə]	der Quadratkilometer	The long sides of this playing field are 100 metres long, the short sides are 68 metres long, so the field is 6800 **square metres**. ! **square** = **1.** *(adj)* rechteckig; quadratisch, Quadrat- **2.** *(noun)* das Quadrat; der Platz *(in der Stadt)*
	Ground Zero [graʊnd ˈzɪərəʊ]	*das Gelände des am 11. September 2001 zerstörten World Trade Centers in New York City*	
	botanical [bəˈtænɪkl]	botanisch	connected with plants **botanical garden** = der botanische Garten
	harbour [ˈhɑːbə]	der Hafen	! *AE* spelling: **harbor**

Mit bestimmtem Artikel *the*:

the 9/11 Museum
the Bronx
the Brooklyn Bridge
(! *aber:* Brooklyn)
the Grand Canyon
the High Line
the Staten Island Ferry
(! *aber:* Staten Island)
the Statue of Liberty
the West Village
the Yurok Reservation

Ohne bestimmten Artikel:

Brooklyn
Central Park
Ground Zero
Koreatown
New York City
One World Trade Center
Queens
Staten Island
Times Square
Union Square
Washington Square Park

Background file

▶ p. 21	**entertainment** [entəˈteɪnmənt]	das Entertainment, die Unterhaltung	noun: **entertainment** This band's concerts are good **entertainment**. verb: (to) **entertain** sb. (jn. unterhalten) They know how to **entertain** people. adj: **entertaining** (unterhaltsam) Their shows are very **entertaining**.
	criminal [ˈkrɪmɪnl]	der Verbrecher, die Verbrecherin	• nouns: *(person)* **criminal** – **Criminals** are everywhere and might steal things. *(bad thing that someone does)* **crime** (das Verbrechen; die Kriminalität) **Crime** is a problem in most cities. • adj: **criminal** (kriminell) What can we do against all those **criminal** acts?
	electricity [ɪlekˈtrɪsəti]	der Strom, die Elektrizität	►► (electric) power There is less pollution from cars which use **electricity**.

	reputation [repju'teɪʃn]	der Ruf *(Ansehen)*	someone's **reputation** = the opinion that people have about them, e. g. from past experiences
	drug [drʌg]	die Droge, das Rauschgift	**Drugs** are dangerous. They can kill you!
	addiction (to) [ə'dɪkʃn]	die Sucht (nach), die Abhängigkeit (von)	noun: **addiction** (to) Drug **addiction** is a big problem. – adj: **addicted** (to) [ə'dɪktɪd] (süchtig (nach), abhängig (von)) Many people are **addicted** to drugs.
	New Year's Eve [nju: jɪəz 'i:v]	der/das Silvester	the last day of the year (31st December)
	(to) **drop** [drɒp]	fallen, sinken; fallen lassen	The glass **dropped** to the floor. Don't **drop** another glass! (fallen lassen) verb: (to) **drop** – noun: **drop** (der Fall; der Abwurf) **ball drop** = das Herablassen des Zeitballs *(am Times Square zum Jahreswechsel)*
	crowded ['kraʊdɪd]	überfüllt, voll *(von Menschen)*	adj: **crowded** The shops were very **crowded**. – noun: **crowd** (die (Menschen-)Menge) **Crowds** of people were in the shops.

Topic 2

▸ p. 22	**diverse** [daɪ'vɜ:s]	unterschiedlich, vielfältig	adj: **diverse** – Many people from different countries live here. The population is very **diverse**. noun: **diversity** (die Vielfalt) – I love the **diversity** of the population here.
	ethnic ['eθnɪk]	ethnisch, Volks-	adj: **ethnic** – People from lots of different **ethnic** groups live together in this city. adv: **ethnically** ['eθnɪkli] – The population here is **ethnically** diverse.
	comma ['kɒmə]	das Komma	

Punctuation [pʌŋktʃu'eɪʃn] die Zeichensetzung

.	**full stop** [fʊl 'stɒp]	der Punkt	?	**question mark** ['kwestʃən mɑ:k]	das Fragezeichen
,	**comma** ['kɒmə]	das Komma	!	**exclamation mark** [eksklə'meɪʃn mɑ:k]	das Ausrufezeichen
:	**colon** ['kəʊlən]	der Doppelpunkt	-	**hyphen** ['haɪfn]	der Bindestrich

	Jewish ['dʒu:ɪʃ]	jüdisch	adj: **Jewish** – This is the **Jewish** quarter of our town. noun: **Jew** [dʒu:] (der Jude, die Jüdin) – Many **Jews** live here.
▸ p. 23	**host** [həʊst]	der Gastgeber, die Gastgeberin	**host family** = die Gastfamilie **host dad / host mum** = der Gastvater / die Gastmutter
	law [lɔ:]	das Gesetz; Jura *(Studium)*	• The **law** says that you have to be 17 or older to drive a car in this country. • After school he started studying **law**. **by law** = per Gesetz, gesetzlich

▶ p. 24	**use** [juːs]	der Gebrauch, die Verwendung	noun: **use** – This church is no longer **in use**. (in Gebrauch) verb: (to) **use** – They **use** it as a cafe now. ❗ Aussprache: **use** *(noun)* [juːs] – (to) **use** *(verb)* [juːz]
	(back) then [ðen]	damals	My grandma was born in 1952. Life was a lot slower **(back) then**, she says. ❗ **then** = **1.** dann, danach; **2.** damals
	(to) **pass a law** [pɑːs]	ein Gesetz verabschieden	Several African countries have **passed laws** to stop people from using plastic bags.
	(to) **affect** [əˈfekt]	beeinflussen, betreffen, sich auswirken auf	These changes will **affect** all of us. (to) **be affected by** sth. = von etwas betroffen/beeinflusst sein
	via Ellis Island [ˈvaɪə]	über Ellis Island	When you drive from here to Philadelphia, it's best to go **via** Baltimore. (= Baltimore is on the way from here to Philadelphia.)
	welcome [ˈwelkʌm]	der Empfang; das Willkommen	

welcome – (to) welcome sb.

noun: **welcome**	(to) **give sb. a warm welcome** (to) **get a warm welcome**	jn. herzlich begrüßen herzlich begrüßt werden
verb: (to) **welcome sb. (to)**	**I'd like to welcome you all to our new book club.**	jn. willkommen heißen (in), jn. begrüßen (in)
	Welcome to New York / to the show!	Willkommen in New York / bei unserer Show!
	Thank you for your help. **– You're welcome.**	Danke für deine Hilfe. – Bitte, gern geschehen.

	immigration [ɪmɪˈɡreɪʃn]	die Einwanderung	

immigration – emigration

• (to) **immigrate** [ˈɪmɪɡreɪt]	einwandern	• (to) **emigrate** [ˈemɪɡreɪt]	auswandern
immigration [ɪmɪˈɡreɪʃn]	die Einwanderung	**emigration** [emɪˈɡreɪʃn]	die Auswanderung
immigrant [ˈɪmɪɡrənt]	der Einwanderer/ die Einwanderin	**emigrant** [ˈemɪɡrənt]	der Auswanderer/ die Auswanderin

	soccer [ˈsɒkə]	der Fußball	▶▶ *BE* **football** ❗ In den USA ist mit **football** immer **American football** gemeint. Wenn man über Fußball spricht, verwendet man **soccer**.
▶ p. 25	people/actors of **colour**	die nicht-weißen Menschen/ Schauspieler/innen	people/actors who are not white
	(to) **found** [faʊnd]		verb: (to) **found** – noun *(person)*: **founder** (der/die Gründer/in) ❗ • (to) **found** = gründen: They **founded** a club. • **found** = *simple past des Verbs* (to) **find**: I **found** money in the street.

	Hispanic [hɪˈspænɪk]	hispanisch *(lateinamerikanischer Herkunft)*	a **Hispanic** neighbourhood = an area where people speak Spanish (e.g. because they come from Latin America)
	(to) **wander** [ˈwɒndə]	(umher)wandern, schlendern	(to) **wander off** = weggehen, sich absetzen
	valuable [ˈvæljuəbl]	wertvoll	adj: **valuable** This ring may not be very **valuable**. – noun: **value** But it's of great **value** to me. It's from my grandma.
	(to) **accept** [əkˈsept]	akzeptieren, annehmen	I've asked 20 people to my party and 13 have already **accepted** the invitation. I often find it hard to **accept** other people's strange habits.
	quote [kwəʊt]	das Zitat	noun: **quote** – verb: (to) **quote** (zitieren) If you **quote** Shakespeare, make sure your **quotes** are correct!

Topic 3

▶ p. 26	**league** [liːg]	die Liga *(Sport)*	a group of sports teams who all play against each other to find out which team is the best
	association [əsəʊʃiˈeɪʃn]	der Verband, die Vereinigung	an official group of people who have joined together for special reasons, e.g. teams who play a sport (football, basketball)
	court [kɔːt]	der Platz, der Court *(Tennis, Basketball)*	 a tennis **court**
▶ p. 27	(to) **focus (on)** [ˈfəʊkəs]	sich konzentrieren (auf)	verb: (to) **focus** – The article **focuses on** how young people become victims of racism. noun: **focus (on)** (der Mittelpunkt, der Hauptpunkt, der Schwerpunkt (auf)) Its **focus** is **on** students' experiences with racism in schools. **focus of attention** = das Zentrum der Aufmerksamkeit
	(potato) chips *(pl) (AE)* [tʃɪps]	die (Kartoffel-)Chips	►► *BE* **(potato) crisps** *(pl)* [krɪsps]

"Pommes frites" and "Kartoffelchips"

❗ Nicht verwechseln: *German:* **Pommes frites** = *British English:* **chips**
American English: **French fries**

BE: **chips** / *AE:* **French fries**

German: **(Kartoffel-)Chips** = *British English:* **crisps**
American English: **chips**

BE: **crisps** / *AE:* **chips**

▶ p. 28	(to) **run, ran, run**	fahren, verkehren *(Bus, Bahn)*	

(to) **run, ran, run**		
1. (to) **run**	laufen, rennen	If we **run**, we can catch the bus.
2. (to) **run**	fahren, verkehren *(Bus, Bahn)*	The New York subway **runs** all day.
3. (to) **run on** sth.	laufen, fahren mit etwas *(betrieben werden mit)*	Our car **runs on** diesel.
4. (to) **run** sth.	etwas betreiben, leiten	They **run** their own hotel. It's a **family-run** business. (ein Familienbetrieb)

▶ p. 29	**restroom** *(AE)* [ˈrestruːm]	die Toilette *(in öffentlichen Gebäuden)*	❗ In *American English* wird die Toilette in öffentlichen Gebäuden (Restaurants, Theatern, ...) als **restroom** bezeichnet. In privaten Häusern/Wohnungen heißt es **bathroom**.

Story

▶ p. 30	**ponytail** [ˈpəʊniteɪl]	der Pferdeschwanz *(Frisur)*	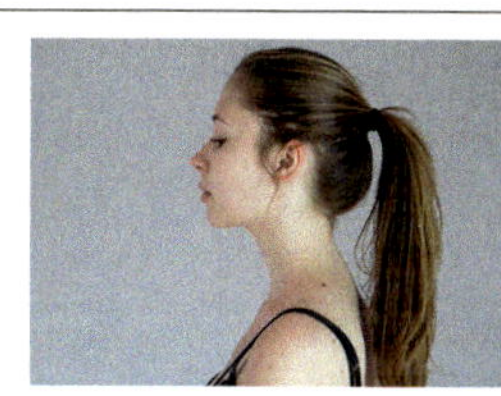 She has her hair in a **ponytail**.

❗ The story is in **informal American English**. Examples:
ain't = is not / are not • **gotta** = got to / have to • **gonna** = going to • **wanna** = want to • **y'all** = you all
You ain't doing nothing with it. = You aren't doing anything with it.
You ain't got no music out there. = You haven't got any music out there.

(to) **go on (about** sb./sth.**)**	die ganze Zeit (über jn./etwas) reden	He **went on and on about** how great his idea was. (= He talked all the time / for a long time about ...)
hardly [ˈhɑːdli]	kaum	It's so dark in here, I can **hardly** see you. ❗ adj: **hard** – It's **hard** work. (hart, schwer) adv: **1. hardly** – They **hardly** work. (kaum) **2. hard** – We work **hard**. (hart)
stuff *(infml)* [stʌf]	das Zeug, der Kram; die Sachen	I have so much **stuff**! I need to take some of these things to a charity shop.
downtown *(AE)* [daʊnˈtaʊn]	im/ins Stadtzentrum	▶▶ *BE* **(in or into) the town/city centre**

welfare [ˈwelfeə]	die Sozialhilfe; die Wohlfahrt, die Fürsorge; das Wohl(ergehen)	• He doesn't have a job and lives on **welfare**. (... lebt von Sozialhilfe) • We need more social **welfare** programmes to support poorer families. (die Fürsorge, die Wohlfahrt) • Our kids' **welfare** is the most important thing to us. (das Wohlergehen)
dignity [ˈdɪgnəti]	die Würde	We should treat the traditions of other cultures with **dignity** and respect.
the harder ..., the more ...	je härter/schwieriger ..., desto mehr ...	**The harder** you work, **the more** money you can make in this company.
(to) **kiss** [kɪs]	(sich) küssen	verb: (to) **kiss** – noun: **kiss** (der Kuss)
cheek [tʃiːk]	die Wange	 her **cheek**
(to) **wipe** [waɪp]	(ab)wischen	 **wiping** the table
lipstick [ˈlɪpstɪk]	der Lippenstift	 **lips** with **lipstick** **lip** = die Lippe
parking lot *(AE)* [ˈpɑːkɪŋ lɒt]	der Parkplatz	(to) **park (a car)** = (ein Auto) parken **car park** *(BE)* / **parking lot** *(AE)* **parking space** = die Parklücke, der Parkplatz 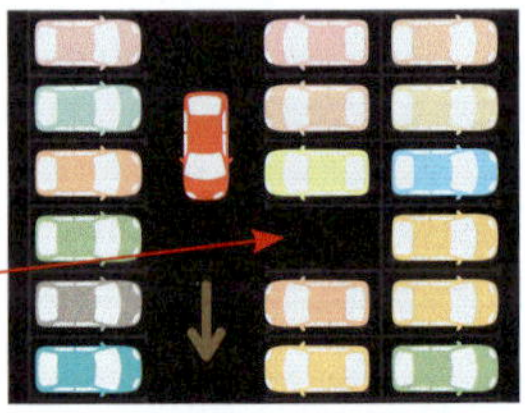
(to) **chew** [tʃuː]	kauen	(to) **chew at/on** sth. = an etwas kauen, auf etwas (herum)kauen **chewing gum** [ˈtʃuːɪŋ gʌm] = der/das Kaugummi
folks *(pl, infml)* [fəʊks]	die Leute	►► **people**
► p. 31 **like**	als ob, als wenn	►► **as if**
otherwise [ˈʌðəwaɪz]	anderenfalls, sonst	We have to hurry, **otherwise** we'll miss the train! The money goes to students who could not go to college **otherwise**.

elderly [ˈeldəli]	ältere(r, s)	a more polite word for "old" adj: **elderly** – noun: **the elderly** (die Älteren, ältere Menschen)
coat [kəʊt]	der Mantel; die Jacke	**coats** 
gymnasium [dʒɪmˈneɪziəm], *pl* **gymnasiums** *or* **gymnasia** [dʒɪmˈneɪziə] (*meist kurz:* **gym** [dʒɪm])	die Turnhalle, die Sporthalle; das Fitnessstudio	• For our sport lessons we go to the school **gym**. (die Sporthalle) • Fitness is important. I'm a member of a **gym** and go there regularly. (das Fitnessstudio) ! Vorsicht – **gymnasium** heißt nicht „Gymnasium".
hoop [huːp]	der Korb *(Basketball)*	a **hoop** 
Santa Claus [ˈsæntə klɔːz] (*kurz auch:* **Santa** [ˈsæntə])	der Weihnachtsmann	**Santa Claus** (*BE auch:* **Father Christmas**)
can [kæn]	die Dose	! • In BE, the word **can** is always used for drinks. To talk about food, the British usually use **tin**. • In AE, **can** is used for both food and drinks. **canned fruit/tomatoes/...** = Obst/Tomaten/... in Dosen
goods *(pl)* [gʊdz]	die Waren, die Güter	things which people or factories produce and which you can buy
(to) **match** [mætʃ]	zusammenpassen; passen zu; (passend) zusammenfügen	verb: (to) **match** – noun: **match** (das Gegenstück, das (zusammenpassende) Paar)

(to) **match** – **match**

verb: (to) **match**	• **These shoes don't match.** • **Which translations match these sentences?** • **Can you match these sentence parts?** • **Match the captions to the photos.**	zusammenpassen, zueinander passen passen zu, übereinstimmen mit passend zusammenfügen zuordnen
noun: **match**	**I think Philip and Laura are a really good match.**	... sind ein gutes Paar.

household [ˈhaʊshəʊld]	der Haushalt; Haushalts-	the people who live together in a house or flat
dear [dɪə]	der Liebling, der Schatz *(auch als Anrede)*	! **dear** = **1.** Liebe/r *(Anrede in Briefen/E-Mails)*; **2.** der Liebling, der Schatz

pity (for) [ˈpɪti]	das Mitleid (mit)	noun: **pity** – I don't want people's **pity**. That's a **pity**. = Das ist schade. **self-pity** [self ˈpɪti] = das Selbstmitleid verb: (to) **pity** sb. (jn. bemitleiden) – I don't want people to **pity** me.
(to) **beg** [beg]	flehen, (eindringlich) bitten; betteln	• (to) **beg** sb. **to do** sth. = jn. anflehen, etwas zu tun • (to) **beg for** sth. **(from** sb.**)** = (bei jm.) um etwas betteln verb: (to) **beg** – noun *(person)*: **beggar** [ˈbegə] (der/die Bettler/in)
fridge [frɪdʒ]	der Kühlschrank	 a **fridge** There are two apples and two bottles of milk in the **fridge**. ►► *short for* **refrigerator** [rɪˈfrɪdʒəreɪtə]
(to) **fill (up)** [fɪl]	sich füllen; (auf)füllen	• (to) **fill up** = sich ganz/komplett füllen (= (to) become full) • (to) **fill** sth. **up** = etwas ganz/komplett füllen (= (to) make full)
(to) **fix** sth. *(infml)* [fɪks]	etwas in Ordnung bringen; reparieren	►► (to) **repair** Your bike is broken? Maybe we can **fix** it. It's difficult to **fix** other people's problems.
(to) **hide** [haɪd], **hid** [hɪd], **hidden** [ˈhɪdn]	verstecken; sich verstecken	I **hid** some money in an old book. Let's **hide** in the wardrobe.
sympathetic [sɪmpəˈθetɪk]	mitfühlend; verständnisvoll	adj: **sympathetic** I hate to feel people's pity and their **sympathetic** looks. noun: **sympathy** [ˈsɪmpəθi] (das Mitgefühl, das Verständnis; die Sympathie) Poor Lynn! We all feel great **sympathy** for her.
(to) **ignore** [ɪgˈnɔː]	nicht beachten, ignorieren	(to) pay no attention to sth. I try to **ignore** people's sympathetic looks.
► p. 32 **earbuds** *(pl)* [ˈɪəbʌd]	der Ohrhörer, der In-Ear-Kopfhörer	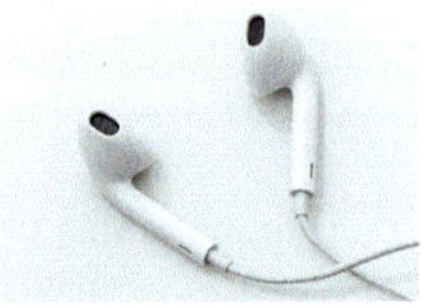 **earbuds**
(to) **unplug** sth. [ʌnˈplʌg]	den Stecker von etwas herausziehen, etwas ausstöpseln	►► (to) **pull out the plug of** sth. noun: **plug** (der Stecker) verbs: (to) **unplug** sth. ◄► (to) **plug** sth. **in** (etwas einstecken, anschließen)
(to) **swallow** [ˈswɒləʊ]	(ver)schlucken	This toy has parts which babies can **swallow**. Chew your food well before you **swallow** it.

	that bad / this good	so schlecht / so gut	►► **so good/bad; as good/bad as this/that** I know they have problems, but is their situation really **that bad**?
	for real	echt, wirklich *(Adverb)*	We're still practising – it's not **for real** yet. I saw a UFO in the sky. – **For real**? (Echt? / Wirklich?)
	stamp [stæmp]	die Marke; die Briefmarke	a **stamp** 

Viewing

► p. 33	**creator** [kri'eɪtə]	der Autor/Zeichner, die Autorin/Zeichnerin; der Schöpfer, die Schöpferin	verb: (to) **create** [kri'eɪt] nouns: **creativity** [kri:eɪ'tɪvəti]; **creature** ['kri:tʃə]; *(person)* **creator** [kri'eɪtə] adj: **creative** [kri'eɪtɪv]
	promotion [prə'məʊʃn] *(kurz auch:* promo [prə'məʊ]*)*	die Werbung; die Förderung; der (berufliche) Aufstieg	• noun: **promotion** She's happy about her **promotion to** manager. (die Beförderung zu) – • verb: (to) **promote** [prə'məʊt] (Werbung machen für; fördern, unterstützen) We want to **promote** our new product. (to) **promote** sb. (jn. befördern) They **promoted** her to manager. (Sie beförderten sie zur Managerin.)

Study skills

► p. 34	**final** ['faɪnl]	endgültige(r, s), letzte(r, s), End-, Abschluss-	**final product** = das Endprodukt adj: **finally** – adj: **final**
	script [skrɪpt]	das Skript, das Drehbuch	Who wrote the **script** for this film?
	(to) **coordinate** [kəʊ'ɔ:dɪneɪt]	koordinieren	verb: (to) **coordinate** How shall we **coordinate** the work in our group? – noun: **coordination** [kəʊ'ɔ:dɪneɪʃn] (die Koordination, die Koordinierung) Good **coordination** is important in a team.

Verbs and nouns: *-tion, -ation*

Die Endungen **-tion** bzw. **-ation** werden verwendet, um Nomen aus Verben zu bilden. Beispiele:

(to) **celebrate**	**celebration** (die Feier, das Fest)
(to) **collect**	**collection** (die Sammlung)
(to) **connect**	**connection** (die Verbindung)
(to) **coordinate**	**coordination** (die Koordination, die Koordinierung)
(to) **decorate** sth.	**decoration** (die Dekoration, der Schmuck, die Verzierung)
(to) **explain** sth. **to** sb.	**explanation** (die Erklärung)
(to) **mediate**	**mediation** (die Vermittlung, die Sprachmittlung)
(to) **motivate**	**motivation** (die Motivation)
(to) **organize**	**organization** (die Organisation)
(to) **prepare (for)**	**preparation** (die Vorbereitung; die Zubereitung)
(to) **present** sth. **to** sb.	**presentation** (die Präsentation, das Referat)
(to) **pronounce**	**pronunciation** (die Aussprache)
(to) **translate**	**translation** (die Übersetzung)

effort [ˈefət]	die Anstrengung, die Mühe	(to) make an **effort** = sich Mühe geben Let's make an **effort** to do a really good job.
strategy [ˈstrætədʒi]	die Strategie	**problem-solving strategy** = die Strategie zur Problemlösung ! Betonung auf der 1. Silbe: **strategy** [ˈstrætədʒi]
technical [ˈteknɪkl]	technisch	**technical** problems = problems e.g. with devices or machines

Unit task

▸ p. 35	**enthusiastic (about)** [ɪnθjuːziˈæstɪk]	begeistert (von)	Jack is **enthusiastic about** cooking. All his meals are delicious.
	(to) **avoid** [əˈvɔɪd]	(ver)meiden; verhindern	(to) **avoid** sth. = etwas (ver)meiden/ verhindern You should always try to **avoid** accidents. (to) **avoid doing** sth. = es vermeiden, etwas zu tun Let's go there early to **avoid** waiting for hours.

Unit 2 The South-East: Changing times

Topic 1

▸ p. 52	**everyday** [ˈevrideɪ]	alltäglich, Alltags-	**everyday life** = der Alltag
	trumpet [ˈtrʌmpɪt]	die Trompete	a **trumpet** 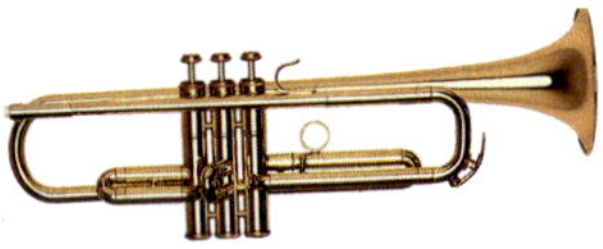
	security [sɪˈkjʊərəti]	die Sicherheit	This is a **security** check. Would you please open your bags? **security guard** = der/die Sicherheitsbedienstete
	dialect [ˈdaɪəlekt]	der Dialekt	! Betonung auf der 1. Silbe: **dialect** [ˈdaɪəlekt]
	accent [ˈæksent]	der Akzent	! Betonung auf der 1. Silbe: **accent** [ˈæksent]
	speech [spiːtʃ]	die Rede, die Ansprache; die Sprache	• nouns: **speech**; *(person)* **speaker** (der/die Sprecher/in) • verb: (to) **speak** She's **giving a speech**. 
	What's up?	Was ist los? / Was gibt's (Neues)?	►► *BE* **What's the matter?** *or* **What's new?**
	dude *(infml)* [duːd]	Mann, Alter *(Anrede)*	Hey **dude**, you're not gonna believe this!
	cop *(infml)* [kɒp]	der Cop *(amerikanische umgangssprachliche Bezeichnung für Polizist/in)*	**rent-a-cop** *(infml)* = die private uniformierte Sicherheitskraft

	(to) **have sb.'s back** [bæk]	jm. den Rücken freihalten *(jn. unterstützen/schützen)*	(to) protect and support sb.
▶ p. 53	(to) **be in sb's shoes** (to) **put yourself in sb.'s shoes**	in js. Haut stecken sich in js. Lage versetzen	(to) imagine you were sb. else Just **put** yourself **in my shoes**! If I were **in your shoes**, I'd help them.
	(to) **complain (to** sb. **about** sth.**)** [kəm'pleɪn]	sich (bei jm. über etwas) beschweren, beklagen; jammern	I **complained to** the shop assistant **about** bad service.
	(to) **protest** [prə'test]	protestieren	verb: (to) **protest** [prə'test] nouns: **protest** ['prəʊtest] (der Protest, die Protestdemonstration); *(person)* **protester** [prə'testə] (der/die Demonstrant/in)
	discrimination (against) [dɪskrɪmɪ'neɪʃn]	die Diskriminierung (von)	noun: **discrimination (against)** – verb: (to) **discriminate against** sb. [dɪ'skrɪmɪneɪt] (jn. diskriminieren = benachteiligen, herabsetzen) **!** *German:* **Diskriminierung von** Frauen/ Schwarzen *English:* **discrimination against** women/ Black people
	reaction (to) [ri'ækʃn]	die Reaktion (auf)	noun: **reaction (to)** – What's your **reaction to** sad films? Do you cry? verb: (to) **react (to)** – How do you **react to** sad films?
▶ p. 54	**lawyer** ['lɔːjə]	der (Rechts-)Anwalt, die (Rechts-)Anwältin	someone who has studied law
	(to) **take a stand (against** sth.**)** [stænd]	Stellung beziehen (gegen etwas)	I think it's important to **take a** strong **stand against** racism. (= make it very clear that you are against racism)
	behaviour [bɪ'heɪvjə]	das Verhalten; das Benehmen	These animals show a strange **behaviour**. **!** *AE* spelling: **behavior**

Background file

▶ p. 55	**influence (on)** ['ɪnfluəns]	der Einfluss (auf)	nouns: *(person)* **influencer / influence** You can still feel the band's **influence** on today's pop music. verb: (to) **influence** (beeinflussen) Even today, they still **influence** musicians all over the world.
	resources *(pl)* [rɪ'sɔːsɪz]	die Ressourcen, die (finanziellen) Mittel	We should stop using **resources** like coal or oil which are bad for our planet. **resource** = das (Hilfs-)Mittel, die Ressource
	century ['sentʃəri]	das Jahrhundert	There are one hundred years in a **century**.
	Native American [neɪtɪv ə'merɪkən]	der amerikanische Ureinwohner, die amerikanische Ureinwohnerin	noun: **Native American** adj: **Native (American)** *(zur indigenen Bevölkerung Nordamerikas gehörend oder sie betreffend)* – a **Native American** dish; **Native** land **native** = einheimisch – native birds/plants **native language** = die Muttersprache

	colony ['kɒləni]	die Kolonie	**!** Betonung auf der 1. Silbe: **colony** ['kɒləni]
	territory ['terətri]	das Gebiet, das Territorium; das Revier *(z. B. bei Tieren)*	The whole of the U.S. was once Native American **territory**. (das Gebiet) These animals will fight to keep their **territory**. (das Revier)
	purchase *(fml)* ['pɜːtʃəs]	der (Ein-)Kauf, der Erwerb	noun: **purchase** – verb: (to) **purchase** sth. (etwas kaufen, erwerben)
	vibrant ['vaɪbrənt]	dynamisch, voller Leben	full of life and energy; exciting

Topic 2

► p. 56	**segregation** [segrɪ'geɪʃn]	die Trennung *(nach Hautfarbe/ Religion/Geschlecht)*	Until the 1960s there was **segregation** in schools. Black and white children couldn't learn together.
	slave [sleɪv]	der Sklave, die Sklavin	Many people from Africa had to work for American farmers, but didn't get any money. The farmers had bought them as **slaves**.
	slavery ['sleɪvəri]	die Sklaverei	Those Africans lived in **slavery**.
	injustice [ɪn'dʒʌstɪs]	die Ungerechtigkeit; das Unrecht	adj: **just** (gerecht) ◄► **unjust** (ungerecht) nouns: **justice** ['dʒʌstɪs] (die Gerechtigkeit) ◄► **injustice** (die Ungerechtigkeit)
	court [kɔːt]	das Gericht, der Gerichtshof	I saw the accident and had to appear **at/in court** to describe what happened.
► p. 57	(to) **ban** [bæn]	verbieten	verb: (to) **ban** – Phones **are banned** during lessons. (... sind verboten) noun: **ban (on)** – There's a **ban** on phones during lessons. (das Verbot (von))
	high school *(AE)* ['haɪ skuːl]	*die Schule für 14- bis 18-Jährige*	*(in the USA)* a school for young people between the ages of 14 and 18
	governor ['gʌvənə]	der Gouverneur, die Gouverneurin	verb: (to) **govern** ['gʌvn] (regieren) nouns: **government** (die Regierung); *(person)* **governor**
	violence ['vaɪələns]	die Gewalt; die Gewalttätigkeit	noun: **violence** – adj: **violent** ['vaɪələnt] (gewalttätig; gewaltsam) **Violence** or **violent** protests won't save the world.
	(to) **graduate (from)** ['grædʒueɪt]	den Abschluss machen (an) *(Schule, Hochschule)*	verb: (to) **graduate (from)** Sean **graduated from** Oxford University last year. nouns: *(person)* **graduate** ['grædʒuət] He is an Oxford **graduate**. (der/die (Hochschulabsolvent/in); *(finishing school/university)* **graduation** He found a good job soon after his **graduation**.
	(to) **matter** ['mætə]	von Bedeutung sein, wichtig sein	Does it really **matter** which team wins? – No, **it doesn't matter**. (Es/Das ist egal.)

	(to) **shoot** [ʃuːt]**, shot, shot** [ʃɒt]	(er)schießen	verb: (to) **shoot** – **shot** nouns: **shot** = **1.** der Schuss; **2.** der Wurf *(Sport)*; **shooting** (die Schießerei) Someone **shot** three people during a **shooting** at a restaurant. **!** *German:* **auf** jn. **schießen** *English:* (to) **shoot at** sb.
	movement [ˈmuːvmənt]	die Bewegung	noun: **movement** – verb: (to) **move**
	suspicious (of) [səˈspɪʃəs]	verdächtig; misstrauisch (gegenüber)	• The man in the taxi looked **suspicious**. (verdächtig) • I was **suspicious of** the strange people at the door. (misstrauisch gegenüber)
	viral [ˈvaɪrəl]	Virus-, viral	(to) **go viral** = sich *(im Internet)* rasend schnell verbreiten adj: **viral** – noun: **virus** [ˈvaɪrəs], *pl* **viruses** [ˈvaɪrəsɪz] (der/das Virus)
	(to) **get away with sth.**	mit etwas durchkommen, mit etwas (ungestraft) davonkommen	What they did was wrong! Don't let them **get away with** it!
	(to) **arrest** sb. **(for** sth.**)** [əˈrest]	jn. (wegen etwas) festnehmen, verhaften	verb: (to) **arrest** sb. – noun: **arrest** (die Festnahme)
	note [nəʊt] (= banknote [ˈbæŋknəʊt])	der Geldschein	►► *AE* **bill** **!** **note** = **1.** die Notiz; der kurze Brief; **2.** (= **banknote**) der Geldschein
	responsible (for) [rɪˈspɒnsəbl]	verantwortlich (für); verantwortungsbewusst	• When my parents are out, I'm **responsible for** my little sister. (verantwortlich (für)) • He always cleans his room and gets up on time. He's a very **responsible** boy. (verantwortungsbewusst)
	death [deθ]	der Tod	noun: **death** – adj: **dead** – verb: (to) **die**
► p. 58	**human** [ˈhjuːmən]	der Mensch	noun: **human** – adj: **human** (menschlich) **human rights** *(pl)* = Menschenrechte **humanity** = die Menschheit; die Menschlichkeit
	(to) **treat sb.** [triːt]	jn. behandeln	No violence please! We should **treat** each other with respect.
► p. 59	**businesswoman** [ˈbɪznəswʊmən], *pl* **businesswomen** [ˈbɪznəswɪmɪn]	die Geschäftsfrau	**businessman,** *pl* **businessmen** = der Geschäftsmann **business person,** *pl* **business people** = die Geschäftsperson
	(to) **speak out** [spiːk ˈaʊt]	(deutlich) seine Meinung sagen, seine Stimme erheben	If you think this is wrong, don't stay silent! Take some action, **speak out** against it! 
	national anthem [næʃnəl ˈænθəm]	die Nationalhymne	Football players sing the **national anthem** before their games.

	(to) **kneel** [niːl], **knelt, knelt** [nelt]	knien	**!** Wie bei **knife** und **know** wird das „k“ von **kneel** nicht gesprochen. Die Aussprache beginnt mit dem Laut [n].
	athlete ['æθliːt]	der (Leicht-)Athlet, die (Leicht-)Athletin	a sportsperson who takes part in competitions
	(to) **be able to do sth.** ['eɪbl]	etwas tun können, in der Lage sein etwas zu tun	We **weren't able to** get tickets. = We **couldn't** get tickets. = We **were unable to** get tickets. **able** ◄► **unable** adj: (to) be **able** – noun: **ability** [ə'bɪləti] (die Fähigkeit)
	(to) **sign** sth. [saɪn]	etwas unterschreiben	If you're against something, one way to show your opinion is to **sign** a **petition**. **!** **sign** = **1.** *(noun)* das Schild, das Zeichen; **2.** *(verb)* unterschreiben
	petition [pə'tɪʃn]	der Antrag, die Petition (*Unterschriftensammlung)*	

Topic 3

► p. 60	(to) **roll** [rəʊl]	rollen	verb: (to) **roll** – noun: **roll** = **1.** die Rolle; **2.** das Brötchen   **rolls** **Let the good times roll.** = Genieß(t) das Leben! / Lass(t) es krachen!
	extreme [ɪk'striːm]	extrem	adj: **extreme** – We had **extreme** weather last summer. adv: **extremely** – It was **extremely** hot. noun: **extreme** (das Extrem) – The weather went from one **extreme** to the other: first it was sunny and hot, then it was cold and rainy.
	fat [fæt]	dick, fett	adj: **fat** – noun: **fat** (das Fett)
	cinnamon ['sɪnəmən]	der Zimt	**Cinnamon** is a spice.
	necklace ['nekləs]	die (Hals-)Kette	a **necklace** 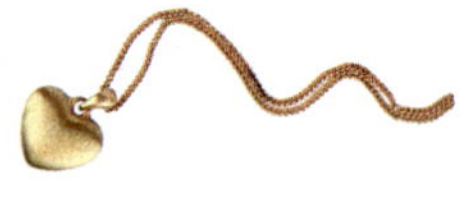 **!** *German* **Kette** = **1. chain** *(z. B. Fahrradkette; Warenhauskette)*; **2. necklace** (die Halskette)
	pretty busy/old/cool/... ['prɪti]	ziemlich hektisch/alt/cool/...	£220? That's **pretty** expensive for a pair of jeans, isn't it? **!** **pretty** = **1.** *(adj)* hübsch; **2.** *(adv)* ziemlich
	fairly ['feəli]	ziemlich, recht	►► **quite**
► p. 61	**crunchy** ['krʌntʃi]	knusprig, knackig	I like rolls when they're fresh and really **crunchy**.
	cornbread ['kɔːnbred]	das Maisbrot	**!** **corn** = *(BE)* das Korn, das Getreide; *(AE)* der Mais

	strike [straɪk]	der Streik	Workers **went on strike / were on strike** for better working conditions. (to) **be on strike** = streiken (to) **go on strike** = in den Streik treten
	bland [blænd]	fade (schmeckend)	The curry still tastes a bit **bland**. Let's put some more salt and spices in.
	heavy ['hevi]	schwer *(Gewicht)*	! *German* **schwer** = **1.** *(von Gewicht)* **heavy** – a heavy box **2.** *(schwierig)* **hard, difficult** – a **hard** exercise, a **difficult** question
► p. 62	**funeral** ['fjuːnərəl]	die Beerdigung, das Begräbnis	Mr Miller died last week. The **funeral** will be tomorrow. 
	(to) **chill out** *(infml)* [tʃɪl 'aʊt]	sich entspannen, abhängen	►► (to) **relax**
	(to) **make sth. up**	etwas erfinden, sich etwas ausdenken	! (to) **make** sth. **up** = **1.** etwas erfinden, sich etwas ausdenken Nothing is true – he **made up** the whole story! a **made-up** character/story/... (eine erfundene Figur/Geschichte/...) **2.** etwas bilden, ausmachen Girls **make up** 58% of the students at our school.
	a must-see *(infml)* [mʌst 'siː]	ein Muss; etwas, was man unbedingt sehen muss	
	a must *(infml)* **(ein Muss)** **a must-have** **a must-do** **a must-read**	 etwas, was man unbedingt haben muss etwas, was man unbedingt tun muss etwas, was man unbedingt lesen muss	
► p. 63	**beat** [biːt]	der Schlag *(z. B. Herzschlag)*; der Beat, der Rhythmus *(Musik)*	noun: **beat** – verb: (to) **beat, beat, beaten**
	drums *(pl)* [drʌmz]	das Schlagzeug	a **drum** = eine Trommel **drummer** = der/die Trommler/in, der/die Schlagzeuger/in
	violin [vaɪə'lɪn]	die Geige, die Violine	a **violin** 
	upbeat *(infml)* ['ʌpbiːt]	optimistisch, zuversichtlich, fröhlich	making you feel positive, enthusiastic and happy
	recommendation [rekəmən'deɪʃn]	die Empfehlung	I'm looking for a good bike shop. Can you make a **recommendation**? noun: **recommendation** – verb: (to) **recommend**

(to) **improve** [ɪm'pruːv]	verbessern; sich verbessern	(to) get better at sth.; (to) make sth. better I hope the weather will **improve** later. What can I do to **improve** my marks?

Story

▸ p. 64 **hurricane** ['hʌrɪkən]	der Hurrikan, der Orkan	a bad storm with very strong winds
frequent ['friːkwənt]	häufig	Storms are quite **frequent** in this area. We have problems with our power lines quite **frequently**.
power line	die (Stark-)Stromleitung	**(phone) line** = die (Telefon-)Leitung

line

- Look at **line** 14 in the text. — die Zeile; die Reihe
- Take the Circle **Line** and change at Waterloo. — die (U-Bahn-)Linie, die (Zug-)Strecke
- There was a long **line** in front of the cinema. — *(AE)* die (Warte-)Schlange
- We had problems with the power **lines** after the storm. — die (Strom-/Telefon-)Leitung

tornado [tɔː'neɪdəʊ]	der Tornado *(Wirbelsturm)*	! Aussprache: **tornado** [tɔː'neɪdəʊ]
thunder ['θʌndə]	der Donner	
lightning *(no pl)* ['laɪtnɪŋ]	der Blitz / die Blitze *(bei Gewitter)*	

thunderstorm (das Gewitter)

hail [heɪl]	der Hagel	noun: **hail** – We ran inside when a bad **hail** shower started. verb: (to) **hail** (hageln) – It **hailed** for over 20 minutes.
hailstone ['heɪlstəʊn]	das Hagelkorn	**stone** = der Stein
flood [flʌd]	die Überschwemmung, das Hochwasser; die Flut	noun: **flood** – There was a **flood** in our town. verb: (to) **flood** (überfluten, überschwemmen) – Many streets **were flooded**. (... standen unter Wasser)

dry [draɪ]	trocken	adj: **dry** The weather was **dry** and sunny. verb: (to) **dry** ((ab)trocknen) Your shoes will **dry** quickly in the sun.

ice [aɪs]	das Eis *(gefrorenes Wasser)*	! *German* **Eis**: Let's eat some **ice cream**. *(Speiseeis)*  When it's very cold, water turns to **ice**. *(gefrorenes Wasser)*  noun: **ice** adj: **icy** (eisig, vereist; eiskalt)

Nouns and adjectives

bag (die Tasche)	**baggy** (weit (geschnitten))	**ice** (das Eis)	**icy** (eisig, vereist; eiskalt)
chat (die Unterhaltung)	**chatty** (gesprächig; geschwätzig)	**mess** (das Chaos, die Unordnung)	**messy** (unordentlich)
cloud (die Wolke)	**cloudy** (wolkig, bewölkt)	**spice** (das Gewürz)	**spicy** (würzig, scharf)
curl (die Locke)	**curly** (lockig)	**sport** (der Sport)	**sporty** (sportlich)
fun (der Spaß)	**funny** (witzig, lustig)	**storm** (der Sturm; das Gewitter)	**stormy** (stürmisch)
health (die Gesundheit)	**healthy** (gesund)	**taste** (der Geschmack)	**tasty** (lecker, schmackhaft)

(to) **gather** [ˈgæðə]	sammeln; (sich) versammeln; *(Sturm)* aufziehen, sich zusammenbrauen	• When you do research, you **gather** information. (sammeln) • Lots of people **gathered** when the film stars arrived. (sich versammeln) • We went inside when dark clouds started to **gather**. (aufziehen)
warning (about/against/of) [ˈwɔːnɪŋ]	die Warnung (vor)	noun: **warning (about/against/of)** – We got a **warning of/about** strong winds. verb: (to) **warn** sb. **(about/of** sth.**)** – They **warned** us **of/about** strong winds. ! *German:* Sie **warnten mich davor, dort hinzugehen.** *English:* They **warned me not to go there.**
(to) **pass** [pɑːs]	vorbeigehen/-ziehen; vorübergehen *(Zeit, Moment, Gelegenheit)*	Time **passes** so quickly. I **pass** 14 shops every morning on my way to school. (= walk/cycle/drive past) We **passed through** several small villages. (fahren/reisen durch) The storm **had passed**. = The storm **was over**. (... war vorbei / zu Ende.)

over

• **Can you climb over that wall there?**	über *(räumlich)*
• **Come over here, please. / Your bike is over here.**	hier herüber / hier drüben
• Can you see that man **over there**?	da drüben, dort drüben
• Would you like to **come over** and play cards tonight?	herüberkommen/rüberkommen *(Besuch)*
• **I'm going over to the** shopping centre now.	hinübergehen/rübergehen
• **We met people from all over the world / from all over Europe.**	aus der ganzen Welt / aus ganz Europa
• *(more than)* **There were over 200 people** in the room.	über/mehr als 200 Menschen
• **The party was over** and everybody went home.	war vorbei

(to) **give** sb. **a ride**	jn. *(im Auto)* mitnehmen	• (to) **ask** sb. **for a ride** = jn. um eine Mitfahrgelegenheit bitten • Do you need a **ride**? = Soll ich dich (im Auto) mitnehmen? noun: **ride** = **1.** die Mitfahrgelegenheit; **2.** die Fahrt; das Fahrgeschäft *(auf Volksfesten, in Vergnügungsparks)* verb: (to) **ride, rode, ridden**
▶ p. 65 **heart** [hɑːt]	das Herz	a silver **heart**  **by heart** = auswendig I don't need the text, I know this poem **by heart**.
(to) **ring** [rɪŋ], **rang** [ræŋ], **rung** [rʌŋ]	läuten, klingeln	My phone is **ringing**. 
(to) **answer the phone**	ans Telefon gehen	• Can you **answer the phone**, please? I'm in the shower. • **No answer.** = Es geht/ging niemand ran. *(ans Telefon)* **!** *German:* **ans Telefon gehen** *English:* (to) **answer the phone** *German:* **(die Haustür) aufmachen, zur Tür / an die Tür gehen** *English:* (to) **answer the door**
(to) **pick up (the phone)**	ans Telefon gehen; zum (Telefon-)Hörer greifen	**!** (to) **pick** = **1.** pflücken; (aus)wählen, aussuchen; **2.** (to) **pick** sth. **up** = etwas aufheben *(vom Boden)*, etwas hochheben (to) **pick up (the phone)** = ans Telefon gehen; zum (Telefon-)Hörer greifen
(to) **slow (down)** [sləʊ]	(sich) verlangsamen, langsamer werden/machen,	►► (to) **make** (sb./sth.) **slower** adj: **slow** – verb: (to) **slow**
The phone lines are down.	Die Telefonleitungen sind zusammengebrochen.	(to) **be down** = außer Betrieb sein, zusammengebrochen sein
The power is out.	Der Strom ist ausgefallen.	►► **There is no power.**
thought [θɔːt]	der Gedanke	verb: (to) **think, thought, thought** – noun: **thought** What are you **thinking**? Tell me your **thoughts**.
panic [ˈpænɪk]	die Panik	noun: **panic** – verb: (to) **panic** (in Panik geraten) **Don't panic.** = Keine Panik. / Immer mit der Ruhe.

	(to) **rise** [raɪz], **rose** [rəʊz], **risen** [ˈrɪzən]	(an)steigen; sich erheben	verb: (to) **rise** – noun: **rise (in** sth.**)** (die Zunahme, der Anstieg (von etwas)) • A lot of islands will be in danger if ... the sea levels **rise**. ... there's a **rise** in the sea levels. • Panic was **rising** inside him. = In ihm stieg Panik auf. / Er bekam Panik.
	roof [ruːf]	das Dach	Fire completely **destroyed** this house. = The house **was** completely **destroyed**. (... wurde total zerstört.)
	(to) **destroy** [dɪˈstrɔɪ]	zerstören, vernichten	

a **roof**

	totally [ˈtəʊtəli]	völlig, total	

total(ly)

adv:	**totally**	The band's new album sounds **totally** different.	völlig, vollkommen, total
adj:	**total**	The **total** cost was £ 100,000.	Gesamt-; totale(r, s)
noun:	**total**	I had to pay a **total** of £ 53.	die Gesamtsumme, die Gesamtzahl

	relief [rɪˈliːf]	die Erleichterung; die Linderung	Our cat was gone for six days, but then he came home again. What a **relief**!

American English: different words

British English	**American English**	
angry (at)	**mad (about)** *(infml)*	wütend (wegen)
garden	**yard**	der Garten
note / banknote	**bill**	der Geldschein
shopping centre	**shopping mall**	das Einkaufszentrum
Well done!	**Way to go!** *(infml)*	Gut gemacht!

▶ p. 66	(to) **adopt** [əˈdɒpt]	adoptieren	verb: (to) **adopt** – Come to our animal home and **adopt** an animal! noun: **adoption** [əˈdɒpʃn] – The **adoption** of animals is very easy. (die Adoption)
	(to) **be relieved** [rɪˈliːvd]	erleichtert	I was so **relieved** when my cat came back home after six days. verb: (to) **relieve** [rɪˈliːv] (erleichtern; lindern) noun: **relief**

Viewing

▶ p. 67	(to) **chase** [tʃeɪs]	verfolgen, jagen	The cat is **chasing** the mouse. verb: (to) **chase** – noun: **chase** (die Verfolgung, die Verfolgungsjagd) **storm chaser** = der/die Sturmjäger/in

Study skills

▶ p. 68	(to) **realize sth.** [ˈrɪəlaɪz]	etwas erkennen, sich einer Sache bewusst werden	verb: (to) **realize** When I got home, I **realized** that I had left my bag on the train. noun: **realization** [riːəlaɪˈzeɪʃn] (die Erkenntnis) The **realization** that my bag was gone made me panic.

Unit task

▶ p. 69	**review** [rɪˈvjuː]	der Bericht, die Rezension *(kritische Besprechung)*	noun: **review** – verb: (to) **review** (besprechen, rezensieren; überprüfen) In a **review** of a book, film etc. (= When you **review** a book, film etc.), you write or speak about your opinion of the book/film.
	fantastic [fænˈtæstɪk]	fantastisch	You're the winner of the competition? Wow, that's **fantastic**! adj: **fantastic** – noun: **fantasy** [ˈfæntəsi] (die Fantasie; die Fantasy *(Literatur-, Filmgattung)*)
	romance [rəʊˈmæns], [ˈrəʊmæns]	die Romanze, die Liebesgeschichte, die Romantik *(Stimmung)*	a romantic film/story; romantic films/stories in general noun: **romance** – adj: **romantic**

Irregular verbs

Infinitive	Simple past	Past participle		Infinitive	Simple past	Past participle	
(to) **hide**	**hid**	**hidden**	(sich) verstecken	(to) **rise**	**rose**	**risen**	(an)steigen, (sich) erhöhen
(to) **kneel**	**knelt**	**knelt**	knien	(to) **shoot**	**shot**	**shot**	(er)schießen
(to) **ring**	**rang**	**rung**	klingeln, läuten	(to) **stand**	**stood**	**stood**	stehen; sich hinstellen

Unit 3 Texas: Teen life

▶ pp. 82/83	**armadillo** [ɑːməˈdɪləʊ], *pl* **armadillos**	das Gürteltier	an **armadillo** 
	weapon [ˈwepən]	die Waffe	You're not allowed to **carry weapons** on a plane. (Waffen mitführen)
	property [ˈprɒpəti]	das Eigentum; die Immobilie; das Gelände	The things that you own are your **property**. (das Eigentum) The sign said "Private **property**." (das Gelände)
	rural [ˈrʊərəl]	ländlich, Land-	We live in a **rural** area. (= in the countryside)
	indoor [ˈɪndɔː]	im Haus/Gebäude, drinnen stattfindend	adj: **indoor** – an **indoor** pool; an **indoor** market; **indoor** sports adv: **indoors** – The house had an indoor pool, so we could swim **indoors**. (drinnen; im Haus)

Topic 1

▶ p. 84	**ma'am** *(AE)* [mæm]	meine Dame, gnädige Frau	! **ma'am** ist kurz für **madam** ['mædəm]
	sir [sɜː]	mein Herr, gnädiger Herr	**Dear Sir or Madam** = Sehr geehrte Damen und Herren *(am Briefanfang, wenn man den Namen nicht kennt)* ! **ma'am/madam** und **sir** werden oft gar nicht ins Deutsche übersetzt. Man benutzt sie als Anrede für (erwachsene) Menschen, wenn man den Namen nicht kennt (z. B. auch für Kunden/-innen im Geschäft).
	(to) **the pros and cons** *(pl)* [prəʊz ənd 'kɒnz]	das Pro und Kontra; das Für und Wider	What are **the pros and cons** of buying a new car now?
▶ p. 85	**council** ['kaʊnsl]	der Rat *(z. B. Gemeinderat)*	the **city/town council** = the government of the city/town (der Stadtrat)
	survey ['sɜːveɪ]	die Umfrage	The council did a **survey** to find out how happy people are in our town. (to) **do a survey** = eine Umfrage durchführen
	criticism ['krɪtɪsɪzəm]	die Kritik	noun: **criticism** – She can't take any **criticism**. (=she doesn't react well to **criticism**) verb: (to) **criticize** sb. **for** sth. ['krɪtɪsaɪz] – Don't **criticize** people just **for** who they are. (jn. für etwas kritisieren)
	On the one hand, ... **On the other hand, ...**	Einerseits ... Andererseits ...	**On the one hand,** Australia is close to Asia. **On the other hand,** it has a strong British tradition.
	bowling alley ['bəʊlɪŋ æli]	die Bowlingbahn	 **alley** = die Gasse
	feel [fiːl]	die Stimmung, die Atmosphäre, das „Feeling"	**small-town feel** = die Kleinstadt-Atmosphäre
	privacy ['prɪvəsi]	die Privatsphäre	noun: **privacy** ['prɪvəsi] – adj: **private** ['praɪvət]
	opening hours *(pl)* ['əʊpənɪŋ aʊəz] / **opening times** *(pl)* ['əʊpənɪŋ taɪmz]	die Öffnungszeiten	**working hours** *(pl)* = die Arbeitszeit(en) (to) **work long hours** = lange arbeiten, Überstunden machen
	(to) **get around**	sich fortbewegen *(mobil sein)*	How do you **get around**? (= move from one place to another) By car, by bike, by public transport?
	(to) **point** sth. **out (to** sb.**)** [pɔɪnt 'aʊt]	auf etwas hinweisen, aufmerksam machen	• Let me **point out to** all of you that the project might become very expensive. • (to) **point at/to** = zeigen, deuten auf Look at this map. Can you **point at** Dublin?
	gas [gæs]	das Gas; *(AE:)* das Benzin	! • German *Gas* is **gas** in BE and AE. • German *Benzin* is **petrol** in BE and **gas** in AE.

	(to) **advise** [əd'vaɪz]	empfehlen; (be)raten	verb: (to) **advise** – I would **advise** you to talk to your teacher about this. nouns: **advice**; *(person)* **adviser** (der Berater, die Beraterin)
	conclusion [kən'kluːʒn]	der Schluss; die Schlussfolgerung	(to) **draw a conclusion, drew, drawn** = einen Schluss / eine Schlussfolgerung ziehen We **drew the conclusion** that ... (... zogen den Schluss / die Schlussfolgerung, dass ...)
► p. 86	**likely** ['laɪkli]	wahrscheinlich	**likely** ◄ ► **unlikely** [ʌn'laɪkli] (unwahrscheinlich) ! (to) **be likely to do sth.** = wahrscheinlich etwas tun (werden) Take a raincoat – it**'s likely to rain**.
	You are ..., aren't you?	Du bist ... / Ihr seid, nicht wahr? / ..., oder?	

***German* "... nicht wahr? / ... oder?" – Question tags** (die Frageanhängsel)

Aussagesatz bejaht → Frageanhängsel verneint:

You are going to go ..., **aren't you?**	Du wirst / ihr werdet ... gehen, nicht wahr? / oder?
It is scary, **isn't it?**	Es ist beängstigend, nicht wahr? / oder?
Yes, **it does**, **doesn't** it?	Ja, das tut es, nicht wahr? / oder?

Aussagesatz verneint → Frageanhängsel bejaht:

We don't want to ..., **do we?**	Wir wollen (doch) nicht ..., oder?

! Bei Frageanhängseln geht es häufig nicht darum, Informationen zu bekommen, sondern ein Gespräch in Gang zu halten.

	(to) **make it**	es schaffen *(mit etwas Erfolg haben)*	• It's difficult, but I'm sure we'll **make it** if we try. • Can you **make** 12.30? Or is that too early? (Schaffst du 12:30? / Schaffst du es um 12:30?)
► p. 87	**desert island** [dezət 'aɪlənd]	die einsame Insel	**desert** = die Wüste ! Nicht verwechseln: **desert** ['dezət] = die Wüste **dessert** [dɪ'zɜːt] = die Nachspeise
	politician [pɒlə'tɪʃn]	der Politiker, die Politikerin	**Politicians** and governments should pass more laws to protect our planet!
	headline ['hedlaɪn]	die Überschrift	headline 

Topic 2

► p. 88	**freshman** ['freʃmən], *pl* **freshmen** *(AE)*	der Studienanfänger, die Studienanfängerin; der/die Anfänger/in in der High School	

Students at American high schools or colleges (four years)

freshman [ˈfreʃmən], *pl* **freshmen**	der Studienanfänger, die Studienanfängerin; der Anfänger, die Anfängerin in der amerikanischen High School
sophomore [ˈsɒfəmɔː]	der Schüler, die Schülerin im 2. Schuljahr
junior [ˈdʒuːniə]	der Schüler, die Schülerin im 3. (vorletzten) Schuljahr
senior [ˈsiːniə]	der Schüler, die Schülerin im 4. (letzten) Schuljahr

	gun [gʌn]	die Schusswaffe, die Pistole	**guns** 
	impression [ɪmˈpreʃn]	der Eindruck	Tomorrow I'll start my new job. I want to make a good **impression**.
▶ p. 89	**college** [ˈkɒlɪdʒ]	die Hochschule	When I finish school, I want to go to **college** and study art.
	category [ˈkætəgəri]	die Kategorie	! Betonung auf der 1. Silbe: **category** [ˈkætəgəri]
	record deal [ˈrekɔːd diːl]	der Plattenvertrag	**record** = die Schallplatte **deal** = das Geschäft; die Vereinbarung
	catchy [ˈkætʃi]	eingängig *(Lied, Slogan)*	a **catchy** melody/slogan/...
▶ p. 90	**prom** *(AE)* [prɒm]	der Schul(abschluss)ball	
	proposal [prəˈpəʊzl]	der Vorschlag, der Antrag; der Heiratsantrag	**promposal** = an invitation to go to prom with sb. (Einladung, als Partner/in mit jm. zum Schulball zu gehen) **promposal** = **prom + proposal**
	carpet [ˈkɑːpɪt]	der Teppich	a **carpet** 
	captain [ˈkæptɪn]	der Kapitän, die Kapitänin	**team captain** = der/die Mannschaftskapitän/in

Topic 3

▶ p. 92	**university** [juːnɪˈvɜːsəti]	die Universität	! Betonung auf der 3. Silbe: **university** [juːnɪˈvɜːsəti]
	tuition [tjuˈɪʃn]	der Unterricht, die Anleitung; die Studiengebühren	! *German:* **die Studiengebühren** – *English:* **tuition** *or* **tuition fees** *(pl)* [tjuˈɪʃn fiːz] **fee** = money that you pay for club membership, advice or services (die Gebühr; das Honorar; der (Mitglieds-)Beitrag)
	scholarship [ˈskɒləʃɪp]	das Stipendium	University students can get **scholarships**. (= money from organizations to help them while they study)

	vocational [vəʊˈkeɪʃənl]	beruflich, Berufs-	**vocational school** = die berufsbildende Schule **vocational training** = die Berufsausbildung
	apprenticeship [əˈprentɪʃɪp]	die Ausbildung, die Lehre	My brother is doing an **apprenticeship** as a hairdresser. **apprentice** [əˈprentɪs] = der Lehrling, der/die Auszubildende
	army [ˈɑːmi]	die Armee	(to) join the **army** = zur Armee gehen ! Betonung auf der 1. Silbe: **army** [ˈɑːmi]
	neither [ˈnaɪðə]	keine/r/s *(von zweien)*	**neither** = keine/r/s (von zweien) **either** = beide; eine/r/s (von zweien) ! **either/neither** + Verb im Singular oder Plural: Should I buy the green bike or the red bike? – I would buy **neither.** / **Neither of them is/ are** very good. – You can buy **either.** / **Either of them is/are** good.
▶ p. 93	**stable** [ˈsteɪbl]	der Stall	a **stable**  (to) **clean out the stables** = ausmisten
	plus [plʌs]	plus	• Bikes are cheap, **plus** cycling keeps you fit! (= ... and *(betont)* cycling keeps you fit!) • **plus** ◀ ▶ **minus** [ˈmaɪnəs] 10 degrees? Do you mean **plus** ten or **minus** ten?
	flexible [ˈfleksəbl]	flexibel	! Betonung auf der 1. Silbe: **flexible** [ˈfleksəbl]
	seven-year-old son	der sieben Jahre alte Sohn	**a five-year-old kid** (ein fünf Jahre altes Kind) = **a five-year-old** (ein/e Fünfjährige/r)
	part-time [pɑːt ˈtaɪm]	Teilzeit-, Halbtags-	**part-time** ◀ ▶ **full-time** [fʊl ˈtaɪm] He has a **part-time** job. = He works **part-time**. She has a **full-time** job. = She works **full-time**.
▶ p. 94	(to) **employ sb.** [ɪmˈplɔɪ]	jn. anstellen, beschäftigen	

(to) **employ / unemployed / (un)employment**

verb: (to) **employ** sb.	Our company **employs** over 100 people.	jn. anstellen, beschäftigen
adj: **unemployed**	I lost my job. Now I'm **unemployed**.	arbeitslos
nouns: **employment** **unemployment**	I'm looking for full-time **employment**. What can we do against growing **unemployment**?	die Arbeit, die Anstellung die Arbeitslosigkeit
(persons): **employer** **employee** [ɪmˈplɔɪiː]	Our company is a good **employer**. It does a lot of good things for its **employees**.	der/die Arbeitgeber/in der/die Arbeitnehmer/in

(to) **apply (to sb. for sth.)** [əˈplaɪ]	sich (bei jm. um etwas) bewerben; etwas beantragen	• verb: (to) **apply to** sb. **for** sth. Six people **applied for** the job. • nouns: **application** [æplɪˈkeɪʃn] We had six **applications** for the job. (die Bewerbung; der Antrag) *(person)* **applicant** [ˈæplɪkənt] We invited all six **applicants**. (der/die Bewerber/in, der/die Antrag-steller/in)
rich [rɪtʃ]	reich	Would you like to be **rich** and famous? (= Would you like to have lots of money?)

Background file

► p. 95	**huge** [hjuːdʒ]	riesig, Riesen-	►► very big
	option [ˈɒpʃn]	die Wahl(möglichkeit), die Option	I had **no option / no choice but** to pay the full price. (Mir blieb nichts anderes übrig, als ... zu bezahlen.)
	ride-sharing [ˈraɪd ʃeərɪŋ]	die Fahrgemeinschaft(en), die Mitfahrgelegenheiten	giving people (whom you might not know) a ride in your car (maybe for a fee)
	(to) **reduce (by)** [rɪˈdjuːs]	reduzieren, verringern (um)	verb: (to) **reduce** We've **reduced** our prices **by** 30–50%! noun: **reduction** [rɪˈdʌkʃn] We have **reductions** of up to 50% this week! (die Reduzierung, die Verringerung)
	driver's license *(AE)* [ˈlaɪsns]	der Führerschein	►► *BE* **driving licence** **licence** *(BE)* / **license** *(AE)* = die Genehmigung, die Lizenz **gun licence** = der Waffenschein
	aged 12 [eɪdʒd]	im Alter von 12 Jahren	►► at the age of 12
	education [edʒuˈkeɪʃn], *infml auch* **ed** [ed]	die Erziehung, die (Schul-)Bildung; der Unterricht	

education – (to) educate – educational

noun: **education** [edʒuˈkeɪʃn]	I got a very good **education** at our local school.	die Erziehung, die (Schul-)Bildung
verb: (to) **educate** sb. [ˈedʒukeɪt]	I think we need to **educate** people to save water.	jn. ausbilden, unterrichten, erziehen
adj: **educational** [edʒuˈkeɪʃənl]	What is your **educational** background? (= What education do you have?)	Erziehungs-, Bildungs-

provisional [prəˈvɪʒənl]	vorläufig	**provisional driving licence / driver's license** = die vorläufige Fahrerlaubnis
passenger [ˈpæsɪndʒə]	der Passagier, die Passagierin, der Fahrgast	I don't like being a **passenger** in a car. I prefer to be the driver.

highway *(AE)* ['haɪweɪ]	die Fernstraße *(oft mit vier oder mehr Spuren)*	a **highway** 
speed [spiːd]	die Geschwindigkeit	noun: **speed** – verb: (to) **speed, sped, sped** [sped] (rasen, zu schnell fahren) The car was **speeding** along the street **at a speed** of 100 km/h. (**mit** einer Geschwindigkeit von ...)
limit (for/to) ['lɪmɪt]	die Grenze (für), die Begrenzung, die Beschränkung (auf)	**speed limit** = die Geschwindigkeitsbegrenzung noun: **limit** verb: (to) **limit** sth. **(to)** (etwas beschränken, begrenzen (auf); etwas einschränken) The number of tickets per person is **limited to** three.
average ['ævərɪdʒ]	durchschnittlich; der Durchschnitt	The **average** age of students in our year is 16.5. I practise the piano two hours a day **on average**. (= im Durchschnitt, durchschnittlich)
uncommon [ʌn'kɒmən]	selten, ungewöhnlich, unüblich	**uncommon** ◄ ► **common** (häufig, weit verbreitet, gewöhnlich) Problems of this kind are not **uncommon** / quite **common**. (= they happen quite a lot)
ahead [ə'hed]	voran, voraus	There's an accident on the road **ahead**! Let's take a different route.

Story

► p. 96 **swear word** ['sweə wɜːd]	das Schimpfwort	(to) **swear** [sweə], **swore** [swɔː], **sworn** [swɔːn] = fluchen; schwören
narrator [nə'reɪtə]	der Erzähler, die Erzählerin	someone who tells a story
bell [bel]	die Klingel, die Glocke	**bells** 
(to) **groan** [grəʊn]	stöhnen	verb: (to) **groan** – He **groaned** when he read the message. noun: **groan** (das Stöhnen) He read the message with a **groan**.

knock [nɒk]	der Stoß, der Schlag, das Klopfen	noun: **knock** – verb: (to) **knock** (stoßen, klopfen) (to) **knock sth. over** = etwas umstoßen (to) **knock (at)** = (an)klopfen (an) (z. B. Tür) **!** Wie bei **knife**, **knit** und **know** wird das „k“ von **knock** nicht gesprochen – die Aussprache beginnt mit dem Laut „n“
principal *(AE)* [ˈprɪnsəpl]	der Schulleiter, die Schulleiterin	►► *BE* **head teacher** **assistant principal** *(AE)* = der/die stellvertretende Schulleiter/in

American English: different words

British English	American English	
canteen	**cafeteria**	die Cafeteria; die Mensa *(an Schule, College, Universität)*
driving licence	**driver's license**	der Führerschein
primary school	**elementary school**	die Grundschule
petrol	**gas**	das Benzin
(school) year	**grade**	die Klasse, das Schuljahr
licence	**license**	die Genehmigung, die Lizenz
lesson	**period**	die (Unterrichts-)Stunde
head teacher	**principal**	der/die Schulleiter/in
rail	**track**	das (Bahn-)Gleis
transport	**transportation**	das Fortbewegungsmittel; die Beförderung

shoulder [ˈʃəʊldə]	die Schulter	**shoulders** 
(to) **shrug (your shoulders)** [ʃrʌg]	mit den Achseln/Schultern zucken	verb: (to) **shrug (your shoulders)** – “I don't know”, he said and **shrugged his shoulders**. noun: **shrug** (das Achselzucken) – “I don't know”, he said with a **shrug**.
(to) **turn out** [tɜːn ˈaʊt]	sich herausstellen; sich erweisen (als)	• It **turned out** that the photo was a fake. (Es stellte sich heraus, dass ...) • The test **turned out to be** easier than I had thought. (... erwies sich als leichter...)
strap [stræp]	der Träger *(z. B. am Top/Kleid)*; der Gurt, der Riemen	 **straps** 
thin [θɪn]	dünn; schlank	When you grow old, your hair gets **thinner**. My sister is tall and **thin**.
(to) **be about to do** sth.	im Begriff sein, etwas zu tun	I **was about to** leave the house when my phone rang.

administrator [əd'mɪnɪstreɪtə]	der/die Verwaltungsangestellte; der Verwalter, die Verwalterin	**(school) administrator** *(AE)* = das Mitglied der Schulleitung **administration** [ədmɪnɪ'streɪʃn] = die Verwaltung, die Schulleitung
chemistry ['kemɪstri]	die Chemie	I like science lessons best, e.g. **chemistry** and biology.
inappropriate [ɪnə'prəʊpriət]	unangemessen, unpassend, ungeeignet	**inappropriate** ◄► **appropriate** (angemessen, passend, geeignet) • Your comment was **inappropriate**. (= You shouldn't say something like that.) • You need **appropriate** clothes for a job in a bank.
► p. 97 **doll** [dɒl]	die Puppe	 a **doll**
display [dɪ'spleɪ]	die Ausstellung, die Vorführung, die Schau	noun: **display** – verb: (to) **display** (zeigen, zur Schau stellen) • Some of my photos are **on display** in our local museum. (... sind ausgestellt ...) • I got the chance to **display** my photos in the local museum. ! Betonung auf der 2. Silbe: **display** [dɪ'spleɪ]
I'd rather ... (than ...) ['rɑːðə]	Ich würde lieber ... (als ...)	Today **I'd rather** drive to work **than** walk – I'm a bit late.
gross *(infml)* [grəʊs]	widerlich	Strawberries with ketchup? Ugh, how **gross**!
sexist ['seksɪst]	sexistisch *(diskriminierend aufgrund des Geschlechts)*	adj: **sexist** – nouns: *(person)* **sexist** (der/die Sexist/in); **sexism** (der Sexismus) • What he said about women was **sexist**. • I didn't know he was a **sexist**, actually! • We must try to stop **sexism**.
random ['rændəm]	zufällig, beliebig	All the books on these shelves are in **random** order – how shall I find what I'm looking for?
like *(infml)* [laɪk]	irgendwie, halt *(bedeutungsloses Füllwort)*	Right now it's ... I don't know ... **like** ... a bit of a hard time.
(to) **shame** sb. **(publicly)** [ʃeɪm]	jn. (öffentlich) anprangern, bloßstellen; jn. beschämen	**(public) shaming** = das (öffentliche) Anprangern, das (öffentliche) Bloßstellen
(to) **spit (**sth. **out)** [spɪt], **spat, spat** [spæt]	(etwas aus)spucken; etwas zischen/fauchen *(in gereiztem Ton sagen)*	"Stop it, you bully!" she **spat out**. (..., zischte/fauchte sie.)
entrance ['entrəns]	der Eingang; der Zutritt	"This door is broken, please use the other **entrance** to the building."  noun: **entrance** – verb: (to) **enter** (eintreten, betreten; einreisen *(in ein Land)*, hineinfahren *(in eine Straße)*)

whatever [wɒtˈevə]	was (auch) (immer)	

whatever, whenever, wherever, whoever, however

- We will help you, **whatever** happens. — ... was immer auch geschieht / egal, was geschieht
- We're allowed to use dictionaries **whenever** we want. — ... wann immer wir wollen
- I'll find you, **wherever** you are. — ... wo immer du (auch) bist / egal, wo du bist
- **Whoever** told you that was wrong. — Wer immer dir das auch erzählt hat, ...
- I want that bike, **however** expensive it might be. — ... wie teuer es auch sein mag / egal, wie teuer ...

! **however** = **1.** allerdings, jedoch – He was born in France. He isn't French, **however**.
2. egal, wie; wie ... auch (immer) – She goes swimming every day, **however** cold it is.

(to) **spot sth.** [spɒt]	etwas entdecken	verb: (to) **spot** – We went hiking on the coast, and dad **spotted** some sea lions. noun: **spot** – Our cat is black with some white **spots**. (der Fleck) This is my favourite **spot** in Wales. (die Stelle, der Punkt)
dirt [dɜːt]	der Dreck	noun: **dirt** – adj: **dirty**
stain [steɪn]	der Fleck	noun: **stain** – The coffee left a brown **stain** on the floor. verbs: • (to) **stain** (Flecken bekommen) – Why does this floor **stain** so easily? • (to) **stain** sth. (Flecken auf etwas machen/hinterlassen) – Who **stained** the floor?
whisper [ˈwɪspə]	das Flüstern, das Geflüster	noun: **whisper** – verb: (to) **whisper** (flüstern) He was scared. "There's someone at the door," he said **in a whisper**. = "There's someone at the door," he **whispered**.
shaky [ˈʃeɪki]	zittrig; wacklig, schwach	After the shock his legs felt **shaky**. And his voice sounded **shaky**, too. adj: **shaky** – verb: (to) **shake, shook, shaken**
(to) **accuse** sb. **of** sth. [əˈkjuːz]	jn. einer Sache beschuldigen, jm. etwas vorwerfen	verb: (to) **accuse** sb. **of** sth. – He **accused** me **of** stealing his bike. noun: **accusation** [ækjuˈzeɪʃn] – I was shocked about the **accusation**. (der Vorwurf, die Anschuldigung)
(to) **distract** [dɪˈstrækt]	ablenken	verb: (to) **distract** – Music **distracts** me when I'm studying. noun: **distraction** [dɪˈstrækʃn] – I hate **distractions** when I'm studying. (die Ablenkung)
chorus [ˈkɔːrəs]	der Chor *(mehrstimmiges Gesangsstück)*; der Refrain *(Lied)*	(to) speak **in chorus** = im Chor sprechen **a chorus of** "I'm sorrys" = ein Chor von „I'm sorry"-Rufen *(Bekundungen von Mitgefühl)*
(to) **reach over**	die Hand ausstrecken, (hinüber) greifen	(to) **reach for** sth. = nach etwas greifen (to) **reach out (your hand)** = die Hand ausstrecken

	(to) **squeeze** [skwi:z]	(zusammen)drücken; (sich) zwängen, (sich) quetschen	verb: (to) **squeeze** – **Squeeze** the bottle to get the honey out. noun: **squeeze** – Give the bottle a little **squeeze**. (das Drücken, der Druck)
	(to) **slam** [slæm]	(hin)knallen, zuschlagen *(Tür)*	verb: (to) **slam** noun: **slam** (der Knall) – I left the room and **slammed** the door behind me. ... and gave the door a good **slam**.
	none (of) [nʌn]	keine(r, s) (von)	**None of** my friends has ever tried German Pumpernickel bread.
► p. 98	**supposedly** [sə'pəʊzɪdli]	vermeintlich, angeblich *(Adverb)*	adv: **supposedly** – These toys are **supposedly** safe, but I'm not sure. verb: (to) **suppose** [sə'pəʊz] – Getting tickets for that show will be hard, I **suppose**. (denken, glauben, annehmen)
	(to) **control** [kən'trəʊl]	kontrollieren, regulieren	verb: (to) **control** – Should parents **control** how much TV their kids watch? noun: **control (of/over)** (die Kontrolle (über)) He lost **control** of the car on the wet road. (... verlor die Kontrolle ...)
	annoyance [ə'nɔɪəns]	der Ärger, die Verärgerung	Speak out and talk about your **annoyance** with sexists and bullies! noun: **annoyance** – verb: (to) **annoy** sb. – adj: **annoying**, **annoyed**
	frustration [frʌ'streɪʃn]	die Frustration	

(to) **frustrate sb.** – **frustrating** – **frustrated** – **frustration**

verb:	(to) **frustrate sb.**	The situation really **frustrated** him.	jn. frustrieren
adj:	**frustrating**	He found the situation very **frustrating**.	frustrierend
	frustrated	He was very **frustrated** with the situation.	frustiert
noun:	**frustration**	He put his **frustration** into clear words.	die Frustration

bathrobe ['bɑ:θrəʊb]	der Bademantel	a **bathrobe**	
male [meɪl]	männlich; der Mann	**man** ◄► **woman** **male** ◄► **female** ['fi:meɪl] (weiblich; die Frau) *(nouns)* Our team has **males** and **females**. (= men and women or boys and girls) *(adj)* Our team has **male** and **female** players.	

Viewing

► p. 99	**examination** [ɪgzæmɪ'neɪʃn], *infml auch:* **exam** [ɪg'zæm]	die Prüfung	I really need to study for my maths **exam** next week. ! *German:* eine **Prüfung machen/ablegen** *English:* (to) **take/do an exam**

textbook ['tekstbʊk]	das Schulbuch, das Lehrbuch	This is the **textbook** for your English lessons at school.
in time	rechtzeitig	! We arrived **in time** for the start of the match. (rechtzeitig für ...) Our train was **on time**. (pünktlich)
quality ['kwɒləti]	die Qualität; die Eigenschaft	noun: **quality** – • Their products are of high **quality**. (... von hoher Qualität.) • For me, kindness is an important **quality** in people. (die Eigenschaft) adj: **quality** (hochwertig, von hoher Qualität) – **quality** clothes/bikes/...
equal ['i:kwəl]	gleich(berechtigt)	adjectives: **equal** ◄► **unequal** [ʌn'i:kwəl] (ungleich) – nouns: **equality** [i'kwɒləti] (die Gleichberechtigung, die Gleichheit) ◄► **inequality** [ɪnɪ'kwɒləti] (die Ungleichheit)

Study skills

► p. 100	**contact** ['kɒntækt]	der Kontakt	! Betonung auf der ersten Silbe: **contact** ['kɒntækt] noun: **contact** – verb: (to) **contact** sb. (Kontakt aufnehmen mit jm., sich in Verbindung setzen mit jm.)
	(to) **encourage** [ɪn'kʌrɪdʒ]	ermutigen, ermuntern; unterstützen	verb: (to) **encourage** – My friends supported and **encouraged** me before my exams. adj: **encouraging** – They were very **encouraging** (ermutigend)

Verbs and nouns: *-ment*

Die Endung **-ment** wird verwendet, um Nomen aus Verben zu bilden. Beispiele:

(to) **announce** (bekanntgeben; durchsagen)	**announcement** (die Bekanntgabe; die Durchsage)
(to) **argue** (argumentieren; (sich) streiten)	**argument** (das Argument; der Streit)
(to) **disappoint** sb. (jn. enttäuschen)	**disappointment** (die Enttäuschung)
(to) **encourage** sb. (jn. ermutigen; unterstützen)	**encouragement** (die Ermutigung; die Unterstützung)
(to) **govern** (regieren)	**government** (die Regierung)

Irregular verbs

Infinitive	Simple past	Past Participle		Infinitive	Simple past	Past Participle	
(to) **speed**	**sped**	**sped**	rasen, zu schnell fahren	(to) **swear**	**swore**	**sworn**	fluchen; schwören
(to) **spit**	**spat**	**spat**	(aus-)spucken	(to) **understand**	**understood**	**understood**	verstehen

Unit 4 California: State of contrasts

► pp. 116/117	**lookout** [ˈlʊkaʊt]	der Wachposten, der Ausguck	 a **lookout**
	artificial [ɑːtɪˈfɪʃl]	künstlich; unecht	Those are not real flowers. They're made of plastic. They're **artificial** flowers.
	coastal [ˈkəʊstl]	Küsten-	Plymouth is a **coastal** town in England. adj: **coastal** – noun: **coast**
	flat [flæt]	flach, eben; *(Reifen)* platt	• The landscape is very **flat** here. (= there are no hills/mountains) • My bike has a **flat** tyre.
	mountainous [ˈmaʊntənəs]	bergig, gebirgig	**flat** ◄► **mountainous** adj: **mountainous** – noun: **mountain**
	urban [ˈɜːbən]	städtisch, urban	**Urban** planners think about the future of towns and cities. **urban** ◄► **rural**
	whereas [weərˈæz]	während, wohingegen	We're very different. Sam loves meat, **whereas** I'm a vegetarian.

Topic 1

► p. 118	(to) **optimize** [ˈɒptɪmaɪz]	optimieren	(to) make something as good as possible
	intelligence [ɪnˈtelɪdʒəns]	die Intelligenz	**artificial intelligence (AI)** = die künstliche Intelligenz (KI) noun: **intelligence** – adj: **intelligent** ! Betonung auf der 2. Silbe: **intelligence** [ɪnˈtelɪdʒəns] – **intelligent** [ɪnˈtelɪdʒənt]
	(to) **adapt** (to) [əˈdæpt]	adaptieren, (sich) anpassen (an); *(Text)* bearbeiten	verb: (to) **adapt** – When we bought our flat, we **adapted** some things to our wishes. noun: **adaptation** [ædæpˈteɪʃn] – We made some **adaptations** to the flat. (die Anpassung, die Adaption, die Adaptation; *(Text)* die Bearbeitung)
	demo version [ˈdeməʊ vɜːʃn] *(kurz auch:* **demo***)*	die Demoversion	This **demo version** isn't perfect yet. noun: **demonstration** [demənˈstreɪʃn] (die Vorführung, die Demonstration) • We'll give you a **demonstration** of how the program works. • There was a **demonstration** (= a protest march) against the plans. verb: (to) **demonstrate** [ˈdemənstreɪt] (vorführen, demonstrieren) We can use this version to **demonstrate** how the program works.

▶ p. 119	**data** [ˈdeɪtə]	die Daten	**!** Auf **data** kann ein Verb im Singular oder Plural folgen: **Data is/are** collected ... (Daten werden gesammelt ...)
	harder **and** harder	immer schwerer/schwieriger	It's getting **harder and harder** to buy a house. Houses are getting **more and more expensive**. (... werden immer teurer.)
	decision [dɪˈsɪʒn]	die Entscheidung	noun: **decision** – verb: (to) **decide**
	bug [bʌg]	das Insekt, der Käfer; der Fehler *(Programmfehler, Gerätefehler)*	**!** **bug** = **1.** das Insekt, der Käfer; **2.** der *(Programm-, Geräte-)*Fehler noun: **bug** – The computer program has a **bug**. It's just the demo version. verb: (to) **bug** sb. *(infml)* – Stop doing that! It really **bugs** me. (jm. auf die Nerven gehen)
	Firstly, ... [ˈfɜːstli] **Secondly, ...** [ˈsekəndli] **Thirdly, ...** [ˈθɜːdli]	Erstens ... Zweitens ... Drittens ...	There's a lot of shopping to do: **firstly**, we need something to eat. **Secondly**, we have to get some juice. And **thirdly**, ...
	(to) **launch** [lɔːntʃ]	starten; einführen *(Produkt auf den Markt bringen)*	verb: (to) **launch** – noun: **launch** (der Start; die Einführung)
▶ p. 120	**detention** [dɪˈtenʃn]	das Nachsitzen *(in der Schule)*	I had **detention** on Friday.
	(to) **cheat (at/on** sth.**)** [tʃiːt]	betrügen, mogeln, schummeln (bei etwas)	verb: (to) **cheat** – nouns: **cheat** (der Betrug, der Schwindel, die Mogelei); *(person)* **cheater** (der Betrüger, die Betrügerin)
	essay (on/about) [ˈeseɪ]	der Aufsatz (über)	What do you think about electric cars? Collect arguments and write a short **essay**.
	mind [maɪnd]	der Geist, der Verstand; die Gedanken; der Kopf *(im übertragenen Sinn)*	• (to) **change your mind** = seine Meinung ändern – Daniel had wanted to go out, but he **changed his mind** and stayed at home. • (to) **make up your mind** = sich entscheiden, sich entschließen (= (to) make a decision) – I can never **make up my mind** about what I want to do.
	detail [ˈdiːteɪl]	das Detail, die Einzelheit	**!** Betonung auf der 1. Silbe: **detail** [ˈdiːteɪl]
▶ p. 121	**disaster** [dɪˈzɑːstə]	die Katastrophe, das Unglück	The test was a complete **disaster**. I only got three points!

Topic 2

▶ p. 122	**people** [ˈpiːpl], *pl* **peoples**	das Volk	**!** **people** = **1.** *(pl)* die Menschen – A lot of **people** are afraid of dogs. **2.** das Volk – the Zulu **people** (das Volk der Zulu) the native **peoples** of Africa (die indigenen Völker Afrikas)

(to) **settle** ['setl]	sich niederlassen, sich ansiedeln	! *German:* Sie **ließen sich** dort **nieder**. *English:* They **settled** there. verb: (to) **settle** – nouns: **settlement** (die (Be-)Siedlung); *(person)* **settler** (der Siedler, die Siedlerin)
tribe [traɪb]	der (Volks-)Stamm	noun: **tribe** – adj: **tribal** ['traɪbl] (Stammes-)
ancestor ['ænsestə]	der Vorfahre, die Vorfahrin	The people in your family who lived before you are your **ancestors**.
buffalo ['bʌfələʊ], *pl* **buffalo** *or* **buffaloes**	der Büffel; der/das Bison	a **buffalo** 
turkey ['tɜːki]	der Truthahn, die Pute; das Putenfleisch	a **turkey** 
(to) **grow** [grəʊ], **grew** [gruː], **grown** [grəʊn]	anbauen; werden	! (to) **grow** = **1.** wachsen – These trees only **grow** in Africa. **2.** anbauen – Farmers **grow** potatoes, carrots and other vegetables here. **3.** werden – Grandma often says she's **growing** old.
(to) **colonize** ['kɒlənaɪz]	besiedeln, aus etwas eine Kolonie machen	! Betonung auf der 1. Silbe: **colonize** ['kɒlənaɪz] verb: (to) **colonize** – nouns: **colony** ['kɒləni] (die Kolonie); **colonization** [kɒlənaɪ'zeɪʃn] (die Kolonisation)

Verbs ending in -ize/-yze or -ise/yse

British English: -ize/-yze *or* -ise/yse	**American English: always -ize/-yze**
(to) **analyze** *or* (to) **analyse**	(to) **analyze**
(to) **colonize** *or* (to) **colonise**	(to) **colonize**
(to) **criticize** *or* (to) **criticise**	(to) **criticize**
(to) **optimize** *or* (to) **optimise**	(to) **optimize**
(to) **realize** *or* (to) **realise**	(to) **realize**
(to) **recognize** *or* (to) **recognise**	(to) **recognize**

(to) **force** sb. **to do** sth. [fɔːs]	jn. zwingen, etwas zu tun	verbs: (to) **force** – We can't **force** people to eat less meat. (zwingen) (to) **force sth.** – We'll have to **force** a decision now. (erzwingen) noun: **force** (der Zwang; die Gewalt; die Kraft) – People don't react well to **force**.
(to) **own sth.** [əʊn]	etwas besitzen	She's the boss here – the **business owner**. She **owns** this business. verb: (to) **own** – noun *(person)*: **owner** – adj: your **own** house/business/...

	great-(great-)grand-mother/grandfather [greɪt ˈgrænmʌðə], [greɪt ˈgrænfɑːðə]	die (Ur-)Urgroßmutter, der (Ur-) Urgroßvater	your **great-grandmother/grandfather** = your parents' grandmother/grandfather
	boarding school [ˈbɔːdɪŋ skuːl]	das Internat	We became friends when we went to the same **boarding school**.
	identity [aɪˈdentəti]	die Identität	My first language is part of my **identity**. (... ist Teil meiner Identität.) nouns: **identity** – verb: (to) **idenitify** **identity card** (= **ID card**) = der Personal-ausweis
	trauma [ˈtrɔːmə]	das Trauma	Victims of **trauma** are people who have experienced terrible shock, stress or extremely scary things in life.
	one fifth [fɪfθ]	ein Fünftel	► English numbers, p. 201
	(to) **return sth.** [rɪˈtɜːn]	etwas zurückgeben, zurückbringen	►► (to) give/bring sth. back

(to) **return – return**

verb:	(to) **return**	
	1. zurückgeben, zurückbringen	I need to **return** these books to the library.
	2. zurückkehren, zurückkommen	I'm looking forward to **returning** to Scotland.
noun:	**return**	
	1. die Rückgabe	You pay £5 for late **return**.
	2. die Rückkehr	I'm looking forward to my **return** to Scotland.

► p. 123	**condor** [ˈkɒndɔː]	der Kondor	 a **condor**
	feather [ˈfeðə]	die Feder *(eines Vogels)*	
	sacred	heilig	This place is **sacred to** the people from this tribe. (... heilig für ... / ... ist ihnen heilig.)
	endangered [ɪnˈdeɪndʒəd]	gefährdet, vom Aussterben bedroht	The European wild hamster is an **endangered species**. There are not many of them left.
	species [ˈspiːʃiːz], *pl* **species**	die Art *(Biologie)*	
	(to) **breed** [briːd], **bred**, **bred** [bred]	züchten; brüten, Junge bekommen, sich vermehren	verb: (to) **breed, bred, bred** – • Female pigs are ready to **breed** when they are 5 months old. (Junge bekommen) • My friend's parents **breed** Irish horses. (züchten) noun: **breed** – This **breed** of dogs is good for people who are allergic. (die Rasse, die Unterart; die Züchtung)
► p. 124	**salmon** [ˈsæmən], *pl* salmon	der Lachs	 a **salmon** **!** Aussprache: [ˈsæmən] – das **l** wird nicht gesprochen.

	astronaut [ˈæstrənɔːt]	der Astronaut, die Astronautin	 an **astronaut** ! Betonung auf der 1. Silbe: **astronaut** [ˈæstrənɔːt]
	crater [ˈkreɪtə]	der Krater	a **crater** 
	headdress [ˈheddres]	der Kopfschmuck	
	stereotype [ˈsteriətaɪp]	der Stereotyp, das Klischee, die Klischeevorstellung	The narrator in this book seems to be just the **stereotype** of a teenager in love.
► p. 125	**expression** [ɪkˈspreʃn]	der Ausdruck	►► a word or a phrase noun: **expression** What does the **expression** "rain cats and dogs" mean? verb: (to) **express** [ɪkˈspres] Can you **express yourself** well in French? (ausdrücken, zum Ausdruck bringen)
	fancy [ˈfænsi]	ausgefallen, extravagant, schick	Did you wear **fancy** clothes to your prom?
	statement [ˈsteɪtmənt]	die Aussage; der Aussagesatz	His sexist and racist **statements** show what kind of person he is. **fashion statement** = das Modestatement *(Botschaft mittels Mode)*
	insensitive [ˈsensətɪv]	gefühllos, unsensibel, taktlos	**insensitive** ◄► **sensitive (to)** einfühlsam (gegenüber), sensibel; heikel *(z. B. Thema)* That was a very **insensitive** thing to say. You should be more **sensitive to** other people's feelings. This is a very **sensitive** topic. Be careful what you say. (heikel)

Topic 3

► p. 126	**wildlife** *(no pl)* [ˈwaɪldlaɪf]	die Tiere *(in freier Wildbahn)*, die Tierwelt	The **wildlife** of Africa is very different from the **wildlife** in Europe.
	bear [beə]	der Bär	

	raccoon [rəˈkuːn]	der Waschbär	 a **raccoon**
	porcupine [ˈpɔːkjupaɪn]	das Stachelschwein	 a **porcupine**
	(to) **melt** [melt]	schmelzen	• Snow **melts** when it gets warmer. • (to) **melt** sth. = etwas zerlassen, auflösen, schmelzen lassen **Melt** the butter in the pot.
▶ p. 127	**unless** [ənˈles]	es sei denn; außer (wenn)	You'll have problems at school **unless** you work harder. (= ... if you don't work harder) ▶▶ **if ... not**
	(to) **attack** [əˈtæk]	angreifen	verb: (to) **attack** – noun: **attack** (der Angriff)
	cub [kʌb]	das (Löwen-, Bären-)Junge	a **lion cub** 
	(to) **damage** [ˈdæmɪdʒ]	(be)schädigen, schaden	verb: (to) **damage** – noun: **damage (to)** *(no pl)* (der Schaden, die Schäden (an)) The fire **damaged** the garage, but there was no **damage** to the house.
▶ p. 128	**play** [pleɪ]	das Theaterstück	noun: **play** = **1.** das Spiel *(das Spielen)*; **2.** das Theaterstück verb: (to) **play**
	(to) **inhabit (a place)** [ɪnˈhæbɪt]	(einen Ort) bewohnen	Few people **inhabit** Alaska: it's too cold!
	dinosaur [ˈdaɪnəsɔː]	der Dinosaurier	**!** Betonung auf der 1. Silbe: **dinosaur** [ˈdaɪnəsɔː] 

Background file

▶ p. 129	**decade** [ˈdekeɪd]	das Jahrzehnt	a **decade** = ten years
	pavement [ˈpeɪvmənt]	der Gehweg, der Bürgersteig	▶▶ *AE* **sidewalk** The **pavement/sidewalk** at the side of a road is for people to walk on.
	a couple (of ...) [ˈkʌpl]	ein Paar; ein paar (...)	They're a nice **couple**. (= two people who are together) We ate **a couple of** sandwiches. (= some, several)

recognizable (by) ['rekəgnaɪzəbl]	(wieder)erkennbar (an)	Students from the local school are **recognizable** by their uniforms. (= you can recognize them when you see their uniforms.) adj: **recognizable** – verb: (to) **recognize**
(to) **host sth.** [həʊst]	etwas veranstalten, ausrichten	verb: (to) **host** (to) **host** a festival / a sports event noun: **host** **1.** der/die Gastgeber/in; **2.** der/die (Radio-/TV-)Moderator/in
importance [ɪm'pɔːtns]	die Bedeutung, die Wichtigkeit	noun: **importance** – adj: **important**
fascinating ['fæsɪneɪtɪŋ]	faszinierend	I find these huge old trees really **fascinating**.

Story

▸ p. 130	**wildfire** ['waɪldfaɪə]	der Waldbrand; der Großbrand, der Flächenbrand	a very big fire, e.g. in a forest
	(to) **burn** [bɜːn]	brennen	• What's that smell? Is something **burning**? (= Is there a fire?) • (to) **burn** sth. = etwas verbrennen • (to) **burn** sth. **down** = etwas abbrennen, etwas niederbrennen
	pit [pɪt]	die Grube	**fire pit** = die Feuergrube, die Feuerstelle *(z. B. für Lagerfeuer)* 
	temperature ['temprətʃə]	die Temperatur; das Fieber	**Temperatures** are very high. = It is very hot.

Temperatures

degree [dɪ'griː]	der Grad	*You write:* **25 °C / 77 °F** *You say:* **25 degrees Celsius / 77 degrees Fahrenheit**
Celsius (C) ['selsiəs]	Celsius	**Water starts to freeze at 0 °C. That's 32 °F.** (Wasser beginnt bei 0 °C zu gefrieren. Das sind 32 °F.)
Fahrenheit (F) ['færənhaɪt]	Fahrenheit	(to) **freeze** [friːz], **froze** [frəʊz], **frozen** ['frəʊzn] (ge)frieren; zufrieren; erstarren

tiny ['taɪni]	winzig	►► very small **tiny** ◄► **huge**
(to) **yawn** [jɔːn]	gähnen	verb: (to) **yawn** – noun: **yawn** (das Gähnen) "I'm so tired!" she said and **yawned**. / ... she said with a **yawn**.
(to) **wake up** [weɪk 'ʌp], **woke up** [wəʊk], **woken up** ['wəʊkən]	aufwachen	• I **wake up** early every morning. • (to) **wake** sb. **(up)** = jn. (auf)wecken My phone alarm **wakes me (up)** at 6.30 in the morning.

	smoke [sməʊk]	der Rauch	 **smoke** noun: **smoke** – verb: (to) **smoke** (rauchen)
	(to) **be on fire**	brennen	• (to) **be on fire** ►► (to) **burn** • (to) **catch fire** = Feuer fangen, in Brand geraten • (to) **set** sth. **on fire** = etwas in Brand setzen, etwas anzünden
► p. 131	**spark**		noun: **spark** The forest is very dry. A single **spark** can start a fire. verb: (to) **spark** sth. Be careful, or you might **spark** a fire. (entfachen, entzünden, auslösen) How can we **spark** people's interest in a healthy lifestyle? (*(Interesse)* wecken)
	further [ˈfɜːðə]	weiter (entfernt)	**further (from)** ◄► **closer (to)** Let's not walk **further** into the forest. There might be bears. For **further** information, click here.
	(to) **report** sth./sb. **(to)** [rɪˈpɔːt]	etwas/jn. melden, anzeigen (bei) *(z. B. bei der Polizei)*	

(to) **report** – **report**

verbs:	(to) **report on** sth.	über etwas berichten	Most papers **reported on** the accident.
	(to) **report** sth./sb. **(to)**	etwas/jn. melden, anzeigen (bei)	You should **report** this **to** the police. The car **was reported** stolen. (... wurde als gestohlen gemeldet)
nouns:	**report (on)**	der Bericht (über)	Have you read the **reports on** the accident?
	reporter	der Reporter, die Reporterin	She works as a **reporter** for the local paper.

	thick [θɪk]	dick; dicht	a **thick** book; **thick** dark hair **thick** ◄► **thin**
	(to) **tie** [taɪ]	binden, schnüren	• When it's hot, I always **tie** my hair back. • (to) **tie** sb./sth. **to** sth. = jn./etwas an etwas festbinden **!** (to) **tie** *(verb)* = binden, schnüren **tie** *(noun)* = die Krawatte Can you **tie** a **tie**?
► p. 132	**OMG (Oh my God!)** [əʊ em ˈdʒiː]	Oh mein Gott!	**OMG** I can't believe it! Wow, you did it!
	crowdfunding [ˈkraʊdfʌndɪŋ]	das Crowdfunding *(Schwarmfinanzierung)*	noun: **crowdfunding** – Could **crowdfunding** be a way to get enough money for our project? verb: (to) **crowdfund** sth. – Could we **crowdfund** our project? (etwas durch Crowdfunding finanzieren)

	exhibition [eksɪˈbɪʃn]	die Ausstellung; die Messe	• I want to see the Van Gogh **exhibition** at the museum. (die Ausstellung) • This new machine was presented at last year's technology **exhibition**. (die Messe)
	choir [ˈkwaɪə]	der Chor	 a **choir**

Viewing

▶ p. 133	**inch** [ɪntʃ]	der Zoll *(Längenmaß = 2,54 cm)*	
	(to) **be set in …**	spielen in … *(Film, Geschichte)*	The film **is set in** Mexico, but was filmed in Spain.
	bottled (water) [ˈbɒtld]	(Wasser) in Flaschen	**bottled** water = water which you can buy in bottles
	well [wel]	die Quelle, der Brunnen	Many years ago people had to get water from **wells**. 
	climate [ˈklaɪmət]	das Klima	Is this weather normal or is it because of **climate change**? (der Klimawandel)

Study skills

▶ p. 134	**acre** [ˈeɪkə]	*britisches/amerikanisches Flächenmaß, entspricht 0,405 Hektar*	
	(to) **increase (by)** [ɪnˈkriːs]	steigern, (sich) erhöhen; steigen, zunehmen (um)	Our profits **increased by** 10%. (stiegen um) = We were able to **increase** our profits **by** 10%. (erhöhen) **!** Aussprache: (to) **increase** *(verb)* [ɪnˈkriːs] – **increase** *(noun)* [ˈɪŋkriːs] (der Anstieg, das Wachstum, die Zunahme)
	(to) **decrease (by)** [dɪˈkriːs]	abnehmen, sinken, zurückgehen, (sich) verringern (um)	**!** Aussprache: (to) **decrease** *(verb)* [dɪˈkriːs] – **decrease** *(noun)* [ˈdiːkriːs] (die Abnahme, der Rückgang)
	(to) **brainstorm** [ˈbreɪnstɔːm]	Ideen (ungeordnet) sammeln	verb: (to) **brainstorm** – Let's **brainstorm** ideas first. noun: **brainstorming** – **Brainstorming** is a good way of collecting ideas. (das Brainstorming *(Sammeln spontaner/ungeordneter Ideen)*)

Unit 5 Canada: The northern neighbour

pp. 150/151	**ocean** [ˈəʊʃn]	der Ozean	the **Pacific (Ocean)** [pəˈsɪfɪk] = der Pazifik, der Pazifische Ozean the **Atlantic (Ocean)** [ətˈlæntɪk] = der Atlantik, der atlantische Ozean
	Arctic [ˈɑːktɪk]	die Arktis; arktisch	noun: **Arctic** – life in the **Arctic** adj: **Arctic / arctic** – the **Arctic** area; **arctic** winters (= very, very cold) the **Arctic Ocean** = der Arktische Ozean, das Nordpolarmeer
	First Nations (people) *(pl)* [fɜːst ˈneɪʃnz]	*die Ureinwohner/innen Kanadas*	The **First Nations people** are Native Canadians, but they're not Inuit or Metis. noun: **nation** (die Nation) – adj: **national**
	Inuit [ˈɪnjuɪt]	die Inuit *(kanadische Ureinwohner/innen)*	The **Inuit** are Native Canadians from Northern Canada, Greenland *(Grönland)* or Alaska.
	Metis [meɪˈtiː]	die Metis *(Nachfahren europäischer Einwanderer/Einwanderinnen in Kanada und kanadischer Ureinwohner/innen)*	The **Metis**'s roots are both Native Canadian and European.
	province [ˈprɒvɪns]	die Provinz, das Bundesland	! Betonung auf der 1. Silbe: **province** [ˈprɒvɪns]
	whale [weɪl]	der Wal	a **whale** 
	maple leaf [ˈmeɪpl liːf], *pl* **maple leaves** [ˈmeɪpl liːvz]	das Ahornblatt	a **maple leaf** **maple** = der Ahorn leaf, *pl* **leaves** = das Blatt *(Pflanze)* 
	moose [muːs], *pl* **moose**	der Elch	 a **moose**

Story

► p. 152	**log** [lɒg]	das Protokoll *(Aufzeichnungen)*	an official record of events during a certain period of time, e.g. a journey on a ship
	gold rush [ˈgəʊld rʌʃ]	der Goldrausch	noun: **rush** (die Eile; der Ansturm; der Stoß *(Flüssigkeit/Gas)*) – verb: (to) **rush** (eilen; hetzen; (schnell) fließen)
	(to) **reach** (sb./a place) [riːtʃ]	(jn./einen Ort) erreichen	If we leave now, we'll **reach** London before dinner. After careful thought I **reached the conclusion** not to buy a new car. (... kam ich zu dem Schluss ...)
	fox [fɒks]	der Fuchs	 a **fox**

	(to) **trick** sb. [trɪk]	jn. täuschen, hereinlegen	verb: (to) **trick** sb. You **trick** people by telling them some sad story to make them give you money. noun: **trick** (der Trick; das Kunststück) It's the oldest **trick** in the book.
	wolf [wʊlf], *pl* **wolves** [wʊlvz]	der Wolf	a **wolf** 
▸ p. 153	**current** [ˈkʌrənt]	die Strömung, der Strom	Don't swim in the river! There are dangerous **currents**. It's hard to swim **against the current**. (gegen den Strom schwimmen *(auch sinnbildlich)*)
	reception [rɪˈsepʃn]	der Empfang *(auch beim Telefon)*; die Rezeption	During my stay in the countryside I had very bad **reception** on my phone. We arrived at our hotel and checked in at **reception**.
	signal [ˈsɪgnəl]	das Signal	Reception here is very good. I have a strong **signal** on my phone. This flag is a warning **signal**: don't swim in the sea today!
	(to) **untie** [ʌnˈtaɪ]	losbinden, *(Knoten)* lösen, aufmachen	(to) **tie** ◀▶ (to) **untie** We **tied** the fallen tree to the car and pulled it from the road. Then we **untied** it again and drove on.
	Shoot! *(AE)* [ʃuːt]	Mist!	**Shoot!** I'll miss the bus!
	(to) **disappear** [dɪsəˈpɪə]	verschwinden	The clouds **disappeared** and the sun came out. (to) **appear** ◀▶ (to) **disappear**
	bush [bʊʃ]	der Busch	**!** Aussprache: [bʊʃ]  **bushes**
	beard [bɪəd]	der Bart	This man has a white **beard**. 
▸ p. 154	(to) **wonder** [ˈwʌndə]	sich fragen	Do you know that woman over there? I **wonder** who she is. *German:* Ich **frage mich**, wer ... *English:* I **wonder** who ...
	a grey-haired dog [heəd]	ein Hund mit grauem Fell	a white-**eyed** animal = ein Tier mit weißen Augen
	(to) **grab** [græb]	packen, greifen (nach), ergreifen	(to) take or hold sb./sth. suddenly/quickly I slipped on the snow, but Jill **grabbed** my arm and stopped me from **falling over**.
	(to) **fall over**	hinfallen, umkippen	

	(to) **splash** [splæʃ]	spritzen, platschen	verb: (to) **splash** The dog **splashed** around in the water. Don't **splash** me **with** water! (nass-spritzen mit ...) noun: **splash** He jumped into the water with a **splash**. (das Platschen; der Spritzer *(z. B. Matsch-)*)
	hook [hʊk]	der Haken, der Angelhaken	 **hooks** 
▸ p. 155	(to) **swing** [swɪŋ], **swung**, **swung** [swʌŋ]	schwingen	There were strong winds, and the plane **swung** from side to side as we were landing.
	(to) **crack** [kræk]	krachen, knallen, knacken	verb: (to) **crack** – She **cracked** a nut. / The ice **cracked** when I walked on it. noun: **crack** – We heard a **crack** of thunder. (das Krachen, das Knacken, der Knall)
	(to) **kick** [kɪk]	treten; *(Sport)* schießen	(to) **kick** sth. **up** = etwas aufwirbeln, hochschleudern verb: (to) **kick** – She **kicked** the ball. / I **kicked** the door open. noun: **kick** – I gave the door a good **kick**. (der Tritt, der Stoß, der Kick)
	whirlpool [ˈwɜːlpuːl]	der Strudel *(im Wasser)*	a **whirlpool** in the water 
	blade [bleɪd]	das (Rotor-)Blatt	This plane has a motor with two **blades**.
	(to) **drip** [drɪp]	tropfen	verb: (to) **drip** – The tap was **dripping**. noun: **drop** = **1.** der Tropfen The first **drops** of rain started to fall. **2.** der Fall; der Abwurf the famous ball **drop** on Times Square on New Year's Eve
	(to) **sniff (at)** [snɪf]	schnüffeln, schnuppern (an)	The dog **sniffed** the ground.
	tear [tɪə]	die Träne	'My cat is gone!' she said with **tears** in her eyes (= she was crying)
▸ p. 156	**paw** [pɔː]	die Pfote	cats' **paws** 
	(to) **drift** [drɪft]	treiben, sich bewegen, driften	Clouds can **drift** across the sky, and boats can **drift** across the sea.
	border [ˈbɔːdə]	die (Landes-)Grenze	We didn't even notice when we drove across the **border** between Holland and Germany.
	downriver [daʊnˈrɪvə]	flussabwärts	in the direction of the current of a river

	Say …	Sagen wir mal, … / … zum Beispiel …	Would you like to live abroad for a while, **say,** for a year or two?
	(to) **expect** [ɪk'spekt]	erwarten	verb: (to) **expect** – I'm surprised. I didn't **expect** this result. You can't **expect** the children **to do** this without help. noun: **expectation** [ekspek'teɪʃn] What are your **expectations** of your new job? (die Erwartung)
	nightfall ['naɪtfɔːl]	der Einbruch der Dunkelheit	the time in the evening when it gets dark
	(to) **paddle** ['pædl]	paddeln	Let's hire boats and **paddle** around the lake. verb: (to) **paddle** – noun: **paddle** (das Paddel)
	hell [hel]	die Hölle	**Get the hell out of here!** *(infml)* = Scher dich / Schert euch zum Teufel! / Verschwinde(t)!
	(to) **nod (your head)** [nɒd]	(mit dem Kopf) nicken	verb: (to) **nod (your head)** – noun: **nod (of your head)** (das Kopfnicken) • "You're right," he said and **nodded (his head)**. = You're right," he said with a **nod.** • (to) **nod to** sb. = jm. zunicken
	grim [grɪm]	grimmig	I don't like that **grim** look on your face. What's wrong?
► p. 157	**position** [pə'zɪʃn]	die Position, der Standort	►► place; location With this app I can send you my exact **position**. (= where exactly I am)
	(to) **give up** [gɪv 'ʌp]	aufgeben	Times may be hard, but I always try not to **give up**. She **gave up** smoking last year. (to) **give** sth. **up** = etwas aufgeben, aufhören mit etwas I always **give up my seat for/to** elderly people on the bus. (für jn. aufstehen)
	shore [ʃɔː]	das Ufer; die Küste	at the **shore** 
	(to) **watch for** sth.	Ausschau halten nach etwas	The dog was under the table, **watching for** bits of food to fall down. **Watch out!** There's an accident ahead. (Achtung! …) **Watch out for** snakes. They can be dangerous.
	glow [gləʊ]	das Leuchten, der Schein *(z. B. eines Feuers)*	noun: **glow** – We saw the **glow** of the fire in the dark. verb: (to) **glow** – We saw the campfire **glow** in the dark. (glühen, leuchten, strahlen)
	(to) **hang** [hæŋ], **hung, hung** [hʌŋ]	hängen	socks **hanging** on a **stick** 
	stick [stɪk]	der Stock; der Schläger *(Sport)*	

	pack (of wolves) [pæk]	das Rudel (von Wölfen)	a group of wolves which hunt together
	sense of humour [sens əv ˈhjuːmə]	der (Sinn für) Humor	**humour** = der Humor [ˈhjuːmə] *German:* Sie hat **(viel) Humor**. / Sie hat **keinen Humor**. *English:* She has **a good sense of humour**. / She has no **sense of humour**.
► p. 158	**mad** [mæd]	wahnsinnig, verrückt	Going out in this weather? Are you **mad**? ! **mad – madder – maddest**
	sarcastic [sɑːˈkæstɪk]	sarkastisch	"That certainly went well," he said **sarcastically**. (= meaning the opposite of what he said) adj: **sarcastic** – adv: **sarcastically** [sɑːˈkæstɪkli]
	nightmare [ˈnaɪtmeə]	der Albtraum	a very terrible/scary dream; a terrible/scary situation or experience After the accident I had **nightmares** for weeks. Everyone was panicking. It was a **nightmare**!
	landline [ˈlændlaɪn]	die Festnetzleitung, das Festnetztelefon	Her mobile is switched off. Let's call her on her **landline**. 
	worth [wɜːθ]	wert	*German:* Das war **es wert**. *English:* It was **worth it**. *German:* Es lohnt sich, den Film **anzuschauen**. *English:* The film is **worth watching**.
	(to) **scratch** [skrætʃ]	kratzen; zerkratzen	verb: (to) **scratch** Who **scratched** my car? noun: **scratch** (der Kratzer) See those **scratches** on my car? 
	ash [æʃ]	die Asche	When a fire stops burning, **ash** is left.
	(to) **rub** [rʌb]	reiben, scheuern	Bears sometimes **rub** their backs **against** trees. (reiben ... an)
	fur [fɜː]	das Fell *(Tiere)*	I love my cat's soft **fur**.
	(to) **set off** [set ˈɒf]	aufbrechen *(sich auf den Weg machen)*	►► (to) leave, (to) begin a drive/walk/journey
	trail [treɪl]	der Weg, der Pfad, die Spur	We have great **trails** for hiking near here. Sometimes you can see white **trails** made by planes in the blue sky.
► p. 159	**pessimist** [ˈpesɪmɪst]	der Pessimist, die Pessimistin	nouns: **pessimism** [ˈpesɪmɪzəm] ◄► **optimism** [ˈɒptɪmɪzəm] *(persons)* **pessimist** [ˈpesɪmɪst] ◄► **optimist** [ˈɒptɪmɪst] adj: **pessimistic** [pesɪˈmɪstɪk] ◄► **optimistic** [ɒptɪˈmɪstɪk]
	according to ... [əˈkɔːdɪŋ tə]	laut ...; ... zufolge	**According to** Alex, it's a great show. (= Alex says it's a great show.)
	extract [ˈekstrækt]	der Auszug *(aus einem Buch, Film)*	a short part of a book which gives you an impression of what the whole book is like ! Betonung auf der 1. Silbe: **extract** [ˈekstrækt]

Im *English-German Dictionary* kannst du nachschlagen, was ein Wort bedeutet oder wie es ausgesprochen wird.

Es werden folgende **Abkürzungen und Symbole** verwendet:

AE = American English | *BE = British English*
infml = informal (umgangssprachlich) | *pl = plural* (Mehrzahl)
sb. = somebody (jemand) | *sth. = something* (etwas)
jd. = jemand jm. = jemandem | jn. = jemanden

° Mit diesem Kringel sind Wörter markiert, die nicht zum Lernwortschatz gehören.

Die **Fundstellenangaben** zeigen, wo ein Wort zum ersten Mal vorkommt.
Die Ziffern in Klammern bezeichnen Seitenzahlen.
1 = Lighthouse 1 2 = Lighthouse 2 3 = Lighthouse 4: 1 (18) = Lighthouse 4, Unit 1, Seite 18

A

a [ə] ein, eine 1 **once a month** einmal pro Monat 2
abbreviation (of/for) [əbriːviˈeɪʃn] die Abkürzung (für) 3
ability [əˈbɪləti] die Fähigkeit 4: 2 (59)
able [ˈeɪbl]: **be able to do sth.** etwas tun können, in der Lage sein etwas zu tun 4: 2 (59)
about [əˈbaʊt]:
1. ungefähr 3
2. **be about to do sth.** im Begriff sein, etwas zu tun 4: 3 (96)
3. **out and about** unterwegs 4: 1 (18)
4. **about me/you/...** über mich/dich/... 1 **How about ... ?** Wie wäre es mit ... ? 2 **What about a ... ?** Wie wäre es mit einer/einem ... ? 1 **What about you?** Und du?/Was ist mit dir? 1
above [əˈbʌv] über, oberhalb (von); oben 2
abroad [əˈbrɔːd] im/ins Ausland 3
absolute [ˈæbsəluːt] absolut 3
absolutely [ˈæbsəluːtli] absolut, vollkommen, total *(Adv.)* 3
accent [ˈæksent] der Akzent 4: 2 (52)
accept [əkˈsept] akzeptieren, annehmen 4: 1 (25)
accident [ˈæksɪdənt]:
1. der Unfall 2
2. der Zufall 2
by accident zufällig 2
accommodation [əkɒməˈdeɪʃn] die Unterkunft; die Wohnung, das (Fremden-)Zimmer 3
according to [əˈkɔːdɪŋ tə] laut, zufolge 4: 5 (159)
account [əˈkaʊnt] das (Bank-)Konto; der Account 2
accusation [ækjuˈzeɪʃn] der Vorwurf, die Anschuldigung 4: 3 (97)
accuse sb. of sth. [əˈkjuːz] jn. einer Sache beschuldigen, jm. etwas vorwerfen 4: 3 (97)
acoustic [əˈkuːstɪk] akustisch 2
acre [ˈeɪkə] *britisches/amerikanisches Flächenmaß, entspricht 0,405 Hektar* 4: 4 (134)
acrobat [ˈækrəbæt] der Akrobat, die Akrobatin 3
across [əˈkrɒs] über *(quer über)* 2
act [ækt]:
1. die Tat, die Handlung 2
2. handeln, sich verhalten 2
3. Theater spielen, schauspielern 2
4. aufführen, spielen 1
act sth. out etwas vorspielen, aufführen 1
acting [ˈæktɪŋ] die Schauspielerei 1
action [ˈækʃn] die Action *(z. B. Film)*; die Aktion, die Handlung 2 **take action** Maßnahmen ergreifen 4: 2 (58)
active [ˈæktɪv] aktiv 1
activism [ˈæktɪvɪzəm] der Aktivismus 2
activist [ˈæktɪvɪst] der Aktivist, die Aktivistin 2
activity [ækˈtɪvəti] die Aktivität, die Tätigkeit 1
actor [ˈæktə] der Schauspieler, die Schauspielerin 2
actually [ˈæktʃuəli] tatsächlich; eigentlich 3
ad [æd] *(infml) siehe* **advertisement**
adapt [əˈdæpt] adaptieren, (sich) anpassen; *(Text)* bearbeiten 4: 4 (118)
adaptation [ædæpˈteɪʃn] die Anpassung, die Adaption; *(Text)* die Bearbeitung 4: 4 (118)
add [æd] hinzufügen, addieren 1
addicted (to) [əˈdɪktɪd] süchtig (nach), abhängig (von) 4: 1 (21)
addiction (to) [əˈdɪkʃn] die Sucht (nach), die Abhängigkeit (von) 4: 1 (21)
addition [əˈdɪʃn]: **in addition(to)** außerdem; zusätzlich (zu) 3
additional [əˈdɪʃənl] zusätzliche(r, s) 3
additional time [əˈdɪʃənl taɪm] die Nachspielzeit *(Fußball)* 3
address [əˈdres] die Adresse 1
administration [ədmɪnɪˈstreɪʃn] die Verwaltung; die Schulleitung 4: 3 (96)
administrator [ədˈmɪnɪstreɪtə] der/die Verwaltungsangestellte; der/die Verwalter/in 4: 3 (96) **school administrator** *(AE)* das Mitglied der Schulleitung 4: 3 (96)
admire [ədˈmaɪə] bewundern 3
adopt [əˈdɒpt] adoptieren 4: 2 (66)
adoption [əˈdɒpʃn] die Adoption 4: 2 (66)
adult [ˈædʌlt] die/der Erwachsene 4: 1 (32)
advanced [ədˈvɑːnst] fortgeschritten 3
advantage [ədˈvɑːntɪdʒ] der Vorteil 3
adventure [ədˈventʃə] das Abenteuer 2
adventurer [ədˈventʃərə] der/die Abenteurer/in 3
adventurous [ədˈventʃərəs] abenteuerlustig 3
advert [ˈædvɜːt] *(infml) siehe* **advertisement**
advertise sth. [ˈædvətaɪz] Werbung machen für etwas, etwas inserieren 3
advertisement [ədˈvɜːtɪsmənt] *infml auch* **ad, advert** die Anzeige, das Inserat; der Werbespot 3
advice *(no pl)* [ədˈvaɪs] der Rat(schlag), Ratschläge 3 **give sb. advice** jm. Rat geben 3 **take sb.'s advice** auf js. Rat hören 3
advice column [ədˈvaɪs kɒləm] der Kummerkasten, die Ratgeber-Spalte *(z. B. in Zeitschriften)* 3
advise [ədˈvaɪz] empfehlen; (be)raten 4: 3 (85)
adviser [ədˈvaɪzə] der Berater, die Beraterin 4: 3 (85)
affect [əˈfekt] beeinflussen, betreffen, sich auswirken auf 4: 1 (24)
affected (by) [əˈfektɪd] betroffen, beeinflusst (von) 4: 1 (24)
after [ˈɑːftə]:
1. **after (school)** nach (der Schule) 1
2. **after (you read)** nachdem (du liest) 1
after-school activity [ɑːftə skuːl ækˈtɪvəti] die freiwillige Veranstaltung in der Schule nach Unterrichtsschluss 4: 3 (101)
afternoon [ɑːftəˈnuːn] der Nachmittag 1 **in the afternoon** nachmittags, am Nachmittag 1
afternoon tea [ɑːftənuːn ˈtiː] der Nachmittagstee, der Fünfuhrtee 1
afterwards [ˈɑːftəwədz] nachher, danach 2
again [əˈgen] wieder, noch einmal 1
against [əˈgenst] gegen 2
age [eɪdʒ] das Alter, die Altersgruppe 3 **at the age of 12** im Alter von 12

(Jahren) 3 **for ages** *(infml)* eine Ewigkeit (lang) 3 **people of all ages** Menschen aller Altersklassen 3
aged 12 [eɪdʒd] im Alter von 12 Jahren 4: 3 (95)
agency [ˈeɪdʒənsi] die Agentur, die Organisation 3
agent [ˈeɪdʒənt] der/die Agent/in 2
ago [əˈɡəʊ]: **a long time ago** vor langer Zeit 2
agree [əˈɡriː ɒn]: **agree on** sich einigen auf 2 **agree to do sth.** einwilligen, etwas zu tun; sich bereit erklären, etwas zu tun 3 **agree to sth.** in etwas einwilligen, einer Sache zustimmen 3 **agree with sb./sth.** jm. zustimmen; mit etwas einverstanden sein 2
°**agreement** [əˈɡriːmənt] die Zustimmung, die Übereinstimmung
ahead [əˈhed] voran, voraus 4: 3 (95)
aim [eɪm] das Ziel 3
air [eə] die Luft 3
air pollution [eə] die Luftverschmutzung 3
airport [ˈeəpɔːt] der Flughafen 2
alarm [əˈlɑːm] der Wecker; der Alarm; die Alarmanlage 2
album [ˈælbəm] das Album 3
alien [ˈeɪliən]:
1. außerirdisch 2
2. der/die Außerirdische 2
all [ɔːl] alle(s) 1 **all over the world** überall auf der Welt, auf der ganzen Welt 2 **all the family** die ganze Familie 1 **all the time** die ganze Zeit, ständig 1 **all weekend** das ganze Wochenende 1 **not ... at all** überhaupt nicht(s), gar nicht(s); überhaupt kein/e, gar kein/e 2 °**all in all** alles in allem
allergic (to) [əˈlɜːdʒɪk] allergisch (gegen) 1
alley [ˈæli] die Gasse 4: 3 (85)
alligator [ˈælɪɡeɪtə] der Alligator 4: (10/11)
allow sb. to do sth. [əˈlaʊ] jm. erlauben, etwas zu tun 3
allowed [əˈlaʊd] erlaubt 3 **be allowed to do sth.** etwas tun dürfen 3
almost [ˈɔːlməʊst] fast, nahezu, beinahe 3
alone [əˈləʊn] allein 1
along the road [əˈlɒŋ] die Straße entlang 3
alphabet [ˈælfəbet] das Alphabet 1
already [ɔːlˈredi] schon 1
also [ˈɔːlsəʊ] auch 1
alternative [ɔːlˈtɜːnətɪv]:
1. die Alternative 2
2. alternativ 2
although [ɔːlˈðəʊ] obwohl 3
always [ˈɔːlweɪz] immer 1
am [æm]: **I am (= I'm)** ich bin 1
a.m. [eɪˈem]: **4 a.m.** 4 Uhr (früh)morgens 1 **9 a.m.** 9 Uhr vormittags 1
amazing [əˈmeɪzɪŋ] erstaunlich; großartig 1
ambulance [ˈæmbjələns] der Krankenwagen 2
an [ən] ein/e *(vor Vokalen)* 1
analyse [ˈænəlaɪz] analysieren, untersuchen 3
ancestor [ˈænsestə] der Vorfahre, die Vorfahrin 4: 4 (122)
and [ænd], [ənd] und 1 **harder and harder** immer schwerer/schwieriger 4: 4 (119)
°**anger sb.** [ˈæŋɡə] jn. (ver)ärgern
angry [ˈæŋɡri] wütend 1 **angry at sb.** wütend auf jn. 2
animal [ˈænɪml] das Tier 1
animal charity [ˈænɪml tʃærəti] die wohltätige Organisation, die Tiere unterstützt 2
ankle [ˈæŋkl] der Knöchel, das Fußgelenk 2
announce [əˈnaʊns] verkünden, bekanntgeben; durchsagen 2
announcement [əˈnaʊnsmənt]:
1. die Durchsage, die Ansage 2
2. die Bekanntgabe, die Ankündigung 2
annoy sb. [əˈnɔɪ] jn. ärgern 2
annoyance [əˈnɔɪəns] der Ärger, die Verärgerung 4: 3 (98)
annoyed (about) [əˈnɔɪd] verärgert (über) 2
annoying [əˈnɔɪɪŋ] ärgerlich 2
°**anonymous** [əˈnɒnɪməs] anonym
another [əˈnʌðə] ein/e andere/r/s; noch ein/e 1
answer [ˈɑːnsə]:
1. die Antwort 1
No answer. Er/Sie geht/ging nicht ans Telefon. 4: 2 (65)
2. (be)antworten 1
answer the door aufmachen, zur/an die Tür gehen 4: 2 (65) **answer the phone** ans Telefon gehen 4: 2 (65)
°**antonym** [ˈæntənɪm] das Antonym *(Gegenteil)*
any [ˈeni] jegliche/r/s, jede/r/s beliebige 2 **(at) any time** zu jeder Zeit, jederzeit 2 **Do you have any questions?** Habt ihr / Hast du (irgendwelche) Fragen? 1 **not (...) any more** nicht mehr 2 **there aren't any ...** es gibt keine ... 1
anybody [ˈenibɒdi] irgendjemand; jede/r (beliebige) 2 **Can you see anybody?** Kannst du (irgend)jemanden sehen? 2 **not ... anybody** niemand 2
anyone [ˈeniwʌn] irgendjemand; jede/r (beliebige) 2 **Can you see anyone?** Kannst du (irgend)jemanden sehen? 2 **not ... anyone** niemand 2
anything [ˈeniθɪŋ] (irgend)etwas; alles; egal, was 2 **Can you see anything?** Kannst du (irgend)etwas sehen? 2 **not ... anything** nichts 2
anywhere [ˈeniweə] irgendwo(hin); überall 2
apartment [əˈpɑːtmənt] die Wohnung 2
appear [əˈpɪə] erscheinen; auftauchen 3 **appear to be/do** zu sein/zu tun scheinen 3
appearance [əˈpɪərəns] die Erscheinung, das Erscheinungsbild, das Aussehen 3
apple [ˈæpl] der Apfel 1
applicant [ˈæplɪkənt] der/die Bewerber/in, der Antragsteller, die Antragstellerin 4: 3 (94)
application [æplɪˈkeɪʃn] die Bewerbung; der Antrag 4: 3 (94)
apply (to sb. for sth.) [əˈplaɪ] sich (bei jm. um etwas) bewerben; etwas beantragen 4: 3 (94)
apprentice [əˈprentɪs] der Lehrling, der/die Auszubildende 4: 3 (92)
apprenticeship [əˈprentɪʃɪp] die Ausbildung, die Lehre 4: 3 (92)
°**approach** [əˈprəʊtʃ] sich nähern, näher kommen
appropriate [əˈprəʊpriət] angemessen, passend, geeignet 4: 3 (96)
April [ˈeɪprəl] der April 1
apron [ˈeɪprən] die (Koch-)Schürze 3
°**aquarium** [əˈkweəriəm] das Aquarium
°**Arabic** [ˈærəbɪk] arabisch; Arabisch
architect [ˈɑːkɪtekt] der Architekt, die Architektin 2
Arctic [ˈɑːktɪk]:
1. die Arktis 4: 5 (150/151)
2. arktisch 4: 5 (150/151)
Arctic Ocean der Arktische Ozean, das Nordpolarmeer 4: 5 (150/151)
are [ɑː]: **The books are £2.** Die Bücher kosten 2 Pfund. 2 **we/they are** wir/sie sind 1 **you are** du bist / ihr seid 1
area [ˈeəriə] die Gegend, der Bereich 2
argue [ˈɑːɡjuː]:
1. argumentieren 3
argue an opinion eine Meinung vertreten 3 **argue for/against sth.** sich für/gegen etwas aussprechen 3
2. **argue (about)** (sich) streiten (über/wegen) 3
argument [ˈɑːɡjumənt]:
1. das Argument 3
2. der Streit 3
arm [ɑːm] der Arm 2
armadillo [ɑːməˈdɪləʊ], *pl* **armadillos** das Gürteltier 4: 3 (82/83)
army [ˈɑːmi] die Armee 4: 3 (92)
around [əˈraʊnd]:
1. **around ...** um (... herum), in ... umher 2
(all) around the globe auf der ganzen Welt 2 **(all) around the world** überall auf der Welt, auf der ganzen Welt 2
°2. **I haven't seen you around.** Ich habe dich hier noch nie gesehen.
arrest [əˈrest]:
1. die Festnahme 4: 2 (57)
2. **arrest sb. (for sth.)** jn. (wegen etwas) festnehmen, verhaften 4: 2 (57)
arrival [əˈraɪvl] die Ankunft 2
arrive [əˈraɪv] ankommen 2

art [ɑːt] die Kunst 1
article [ˈɑːtɪkl] der Artikel 1
artificial [ɑːtɪˈfɪʃl] künstlich; unecht 4: 4 (116/117)
artificial intelligence (AI) [ɑːtɪfɪʃl ɪnˈtelɪdʒəns] die künstliche Intelligenz (KI) 4: 4 (118)
artist [ˈɑːtɪst] der/die Künstler/in 2
artistic [ɑːˈtɪstɪk] kunstvoll, künstlerisch 2
artwork [ˈɑːtwɜːk] das Kunstwerk 3
as [æz], [əz]:
1. als, während *(Konjunktion)* 2
2. als *(Präposition)* 1
as the winner als Gewinner/in 1
3. wie *(Präposition)* 2
as well auch 3 **(not) as good as** (nicht) so gut wie 2 **... as well as ...** sowohl ... als auch ... 3
as if [əz ˈɪf] als ob, als wenn 2
ash [æʃ] die Asche 4: 5 (158)
ask [ɑːsk]:
1. fragen 1
ask a question eine Frage stellen 1
2. **ask sb. for sth.** jn. um etwas bitten 1
ask sb. to do sth. jn. bitten, etwas zu tun 1
asleep [əˈsliːp]: **be asleep** schlafen 1 **fall asleep** einschlafen 2
assembly [əˈsembli] die Schulversammlung 1
assistant [əˈsɪstənt]:
1. der/die Assistent/in 2
2. *(= shop assistant)* der/die Verkäufer/in 2
assistant principal [əsɪstənt ˈprɪnsəpl] *(AE)* der/die stellvertretende Schulleiter/in 4: 3 (96)
association [əsəʊʃiˈeɪʃn] der Verband, die Vereinigung 4: 1 (26)
astronaut [ˈæstrənɔːt] der/die Astronaut/in 4: 4 (124)
at [æt], [ət] an; in; bei; auf 1 **at 8 o'clock** um 8 Uhr 1 **at a place** an einem Ort 2 **at last** schließlich, endlich 3 **at least** wenigstens, zumindest 2 **at night** nachts, in der Nacht 1 **at the age of 12** im Alter von 12 (Jahren) 3 **at the cinema** im Kino 1 **at work** bei der Arbeit, am Arbeitsplatz 1 **angry at sb.** wütend auf jn. 2 **be good at sth. / at doing sth.** etwas gut können; gut in etwas sein 1 **Open your books at page 10.** Schlagt eure Bücher auf Seite 10 auf. 1
ate [eɪt], [et] *siehe* eat
athlete [ˈæθliːt] der/die (Leicht-) Athlet/in 4: 2 (59)
Atlantic [ətˈlæntɪk]:
1. atlantisch 4: 5 (150/151)
2. **the Atlantic (Ocean)** der Atlantik, der atlantische Ozean 4: 5 (150/151)
°**atmosphere** [ˈætməsfɪə] die Atmosphäre
attack [əˈtæk]:
1. angreifen 4: 4 (127)
2. der Angriff 4: 4 (127)
attend [əˈtend] (hin)gehen zu, teilnehmen (an); besuchen 3
attention [əˈtenʃn] die Aufmerksamkeit 2 **get sb.'s attention** js. Aufmerksamkeit erregen, gewinnen 2 **keep sb.'s attention** js. Aufmerksamkeit aufrecht erhalten 2 **pay attention (to)** aufpassen (auf), aufmerksam sein; Beachtung schenken, zuhören 2
attract [əˈtrækt] anziehen, anlocken 3
attraction [əˈtrækʃn] die Attraktion, der Anziehungspunkt 3
attractive [əˈtræktɪv] attraktiv 3
aubergine [ˈəʊbəʒiːn] die Aubergine 3
audience [ˈɔːdiəns] das Publikum; die Zuschauer/innen, die Zuhörer, die Zuhörerinnen 1
audio [ˈɔːdiəʊ] Audio-, Ton- 2
August [ˈɔːgəst] der August 1
aunt [ɑːnt] die Tante 1
°**author** [ˈɔːθə] der/die Autor/in
autumn [ˈɔːtəm] der Herbst 1
average [ˈævərɪdʒ]:
1. durchschnittlich 4: 3 (95)
2. der Durchschnitt 4: 3 (95)
on average im Durchschnitt, durchschnittlich 4: 3 (95)
avoid [əˈvɔɪd] (ver)meiden; verhindern 4: 1 (35)
awake [əˈweɪk] wach 2
award [əˈwɔːd] der Preis *(die Auszeichnung)* 2
award-winner [əˈwɔːd wɪnə] der/die Preisträger/in 2
award-winning [əˈwɔːd wɪnɪŋ] preisgekrönt 2
away [əˈweɪ] weg, fort 1
awesome [ˈɔːsəm] *(infml)* klasse, stark, großartig 2
axes [ˈæksiːz] *Plural von axis*
axis [ˈæksɪs], *pl* **axes** die Achse 2

B

baby [ˈbeɪbi] das Baby 2
babysat [ˈbeɪbisæt] *siehe* **babysit**
babysit [ˈbeɪbisɪt], **babysat, babysat** babysitten 2
babysitting [ˈbeɪbisɪtɪŋ] das Babysitten 2
back [bæk]:
1. zurück 1
back at home wieder zu Hause 1
2. der Rücken; die Rückseite, der hintere Teil 2
at the back (of your book) hinten (in deinem Buch) 2 **have sb.'s back** jm. den Rücken freihalten *(jn. unterstützen/schützen)* 4: 2 (52) **on the back of the card** auf der Rückseite der Karte 2
background [ˈbækgraʊnd] der Hintergrund 3
backpack [ˈbækpæk] der Rucksack 4: 1 (28)
bad [bæd] schlecht; schlimm 1 **do badly** schlecht abschneiden, keinen Erfolg haben 3 **Too bad!** *(infml)* Schade! / Pech gehabt! 4: 3 (86)
bag [bæg] die Tasche 1
baggy [ˈbægi] weit (geschnitten), sackig *(Kleidung)* 3
baggy trousers *(pl)* [bægi ˈtraʊzəz] die Schlabberhose *(weit geschnittene Hose)* 3
bagpipes *(pl)* [ˈbægpaɪps] der Dudelsack 3
bake [beɪk] backen 1
baked beans *(pl)* [beɪkt ˈbiːnz] die weißen Bohnen in Tomatensoße 2
baker [ˈbeɪkə] der/die Bäcker/in 2
bakery [ˈbeɪkəri] die Bäckerei 2
baking powder [ˈbeɪkɪŋ paʊdə] das Backpulver 1
balcony [ˈbælkəni] der Balkon 1
ball [bɔːl] der Ball 1
ball drop [ˈbɔːl drɒp] das Herablassen des Zeitballs *(am Times Square zum Jahreswechsel)* 4: 1 (21)
balloon [bəˈluːn] der Ballon 1
ban [bæn]:
1. verbieten 4: 2 (57)
be banned verboten sein/werden 4: 2 (57)
2. **ban (on)** das Verbot (von) 4: 2 (57)
banana [bəˈnɑːnə] die Banane 1
bank [bæŋk]:
1. die Bank *(Geldinstitut)* 1
2. das (Fluss-)Ufer 3
banknote [ˈbæŋknəʊt] der Geldschein 4: 2 (57)
bar [bɑː] die Säule, die Stange *(z. B. Eisen-)* 2
bar chart [ˈbɑː tʃɑːt] das Säulendiagramm 2
barbecue [ˈbɑːbɪkjuː] das Grillfest, das Grillen 1
bark [bɑːk]:
1. das Bellen 1
2. **bark (at sb.)** (jn. an)bellen 1
°**base** [beɪs] die Base *(Teil des Baseballfelds)*
bat [bæt] der Schläger *(Sport)* 1
bath [bɑːθ] das (Wannen-)Bad; die Badewanne 2
bathrobe [ˈbɑːθrəʊb] der Bademantel 4: 3 (98)
bathroom [ˈbɑːθruːm]:
1. das Bad(ezimmer) 1
2. *(AE)* die Toilette *(in privaten Häusern/Wohnungen)* 4: 1 (29)
be [biː], **was/were, been** sein 1
I want to be a nurse. Ich möchte Krankenpfleger/in werden. 2
beach [biːtʃ] der Strand 1 **on the beach** am Strand 1 **to the beach** zum Strand, an den Strand 1
bean [biːn] die Bohne 2 **baked beans** *(pl)* die weißen Bohnen in Tomatensoße 2
bear [beə] der Bär 4: 4 (126)
beard [bɪəd] der Bart 4: 5 (153)
beast [biːst] das Tier; die Bestie; das Biest 2
beat [biːt]:
1. der Schlag *(z. B. Herzschlag)*; der

Beat, der Rhythmus *(Musik)* 4: 2 (63)
2. beat, beat, beaten schlagen, besiegen 3
beaten [ˈbiːtn] *siehe* **beat**
beautiful [ˈbjuːtɪfl] wunderschön 1
beauty [ˈbjuːti] die Schönheit 2
°beaver [ˈbiːvə] der Biber
became [bɪˈkeɪm] *siehe* **become**
because [bɪˈkɒz] weil 1
because of [bɪˈkɒz əv] wegen 3
become [bɪˈkʌm], **became, become** werden 2
bed [bed] das Bett 1 **go to bed** ins Bett gehen 1
bed and breakfast (B&B) [bed ən ˈbrekfəst] das Zimmer mit Frühstück; die Frühstückspension 3
bedroom [ˈbedruːm] das Schlafzimmer 1
beef [biːf] das Rindfleisch 2
been [biːn] *siehe* **be**
before [bɪˈfɔː]:
1. zuvor; vorher; schon einmal 3
2. **before (the lesson)** vor (der Unterrichtsstunde) 1
3. **before (you take a photo)** bevor (du ein Foto machst) 1
beg [beg] flehen, (eindringlich) bitten; betteln 4: 1 (31) **beg for sth. (from sb.)** (bei jm.) um etwas betteln 4: 1 (31) **beg sb. to do sth.** jn. anflehen, etwas zu tun 4: 1 (31)
began [bɪˈgæn] *siehe* **begin**
beggar [begə] der/die Bettler/in 4: 1 (31)
begin [bɪˈgɪn], **began, begun** anfangen, beginnen 2 **To begin with ...** Zunächst (einmal) ...; anfangs 3
beginning [bɪˈgɪnɪŋ] der Anfang 2
begun [bɪˈgʌn] *siehe* **begin**
behaviour [bɪˈheɪvjə] das Verhalten; das Benehmen 4: 2 (54)
behind [bɪˈhaɪnd]:
1. hinter 1
2. dahinter 2
°beignet [ˈbenjeɪ] der Beignet *(gefüllter Krapfen)*
belief [bɪˈliːf] der Glaube, die Überzeugung 2
believe (in) [bɪˈliːv] glauben (an) 2
bell [bel] die Klingel, die Glocke 4: 3 (96)
belong [bɪˈlɒŋ] (hin)gehören 4: 1 (31) **belong to sb./sth.** jm./zu etwas gehören 3
below [bɪˈləʊ] unter(halb von); unten 2
bench [bentʃ] die Bank *(zum Sitzen)* 3
berry [ˈberi] die Beere 3
best [best] beste(r, s); am besten 1 **Best wishes** Viele Grüße *(Briefschluss)* 2 **like sth. best** etwas am liebsten mögen 1
better [ˈbetə] besser 1 **for better or (for) worse** was auch immer geschieht, in guten wie in schlechten Zeiten *(beim Ehegelöbnis)* 2 **Get better soon!** Gute Besserung! 2 **like sth. better** etwas lieber mögen 1
between [bɪˈtwiːn] zwischen 1
big [bɪg]:
1. groß 1
2. schwer, dick *(Person)* 2
big wheel [bɪg ˈwiːl] das Riesenrad 3
biggest [ˈbɪgɪst] der/die/das größte; am größten 1
bike [baɪk] das Fahrrad 1
bike lane [ˈbaɪk leɪn] der Radweg 3
°bilingual [baɪˈlɪŋgwəl] zweisprachig
bill [bɪl] *(AE)* der Geldschein 4: 2 (57)
billion [ˈbɪliən] die Milliarde 3
bin [bɪn] der (Müll-)Eimer 1
bio [ˈbaɪəʊ] *siehe* **biography**
biography [baɪˈɒgrəfi] *kurz auch* **bio** die Biografie 3
biology [baɪˈɒlədʒi] die Biologie 1
bird [bɜːd] der Vogel 2
birthday [ˈbɜːθdeɪ] der Geburtstag 1 **Happy birthday!** Herzlichen Glückwunsch zum Geburtstag! 1 **My birthday is in April.** Ich habe im April Geburtstag. 1 **on my birthday** an meinem Geburtstag 1 **When's your birthday?** Wann hast du Geburtstag? 1
biscuit [ˈbɪskɪt] der Keks, das Plätzchen 2
bisexual [baɪˈsekʃuəl]:
1. der/die Bisexuelle 2
2. bisexuell 2
bit [bɪt] das Teil, das Stück(chen) 3 **a bit** ein bisschen, ein wenig 2
bitter [ˈbɪtə] bitter; verbittert 3
black [blæk] schwarz 1
blade [bleɪd] das (Rotor-)Blatt 4: 5 (155)
bland [blænd] fade (schmeckend); nichtssagend, farblos 4: 2 (61)
blanket [ˈblæŋkɪt] die Decke *(zum Zudecken u. Ä.)* 2
°bled [bled] *siehe* **bleed**
°bleed [bliːd], **bled, bled** bluten
blew [bluː] *siehe* **blow**
blind [blaɪnd] blind 2
block [blɒk]:
1. blocken, sperren; blockieren, (ver)sperren, verstopfen 3
2. der (Wohn-)Block 1
block of flats das Mehrfamilienhaus 1
blonde [blɒnd] blond 2
blow [bləʊ], **blew, blown** pusten, blasen; wehen 2 **blow sth. up** etwas aufblasen *(z. B. Ballon)* 2
blown [bləʊn] *siehe* **blow**
blue [bluː] blau 1
blueberry [ˈbluːbəri] die Blaubeere, die Heidelbeere 3
bluegrass [ˈbluːgrɑːs] der Bluegrass *(Musikrichtung innerhalb der Country-music)* 4: 2 (63)
board [bɔːd] die Tafel 1
boarding school [ˈbɔːdɪŋ skuːl] das Internat 4: 4 (122)
boat [bəʊt] das Boot; das Schiff 3
body [ˈbɒdi] der Körper 2
boil [bɔɪl] kochen *(in Wasser)*; sieden 1
°bone [bəʊn] der Knochen; die (Fisch-)Gräte
bonfire [ˈbɒnfaɪə] das *(große Freuden-)* Feuer 2
Bonfire Night [ˈbɒnfaɪə naɪt] der Abend des 5. November *(GB)* 2
book [bʊk]:
1. das Buch 1
2. buchen; reservieren 2
booking [ˈbʊkɪŋ] die Buchung, die Reservierung 2
bookshop [ˈbʊkʃɒp] der Buchladen 2
boot [buːt] der Boot, der Stiefel 2
border [ˈbɔːdə] die (Landes-)Grenze 4: 5 (156)
bored [bɔːd] gelangweilt 2 **be bored / get bored** sich langweilen 2 **I'm bored** mir ist langweilig 2
boring [ˈbɔːrɪŋ] langweilig 1
born [bɔːn]: **he was born** er wurde geboren 2
borough [ˈbʌrə], [ˈbɜːrəʊ] *(AE)* der (Stadt-)Bezirk 4: 1 (18)
borrow [ˈbɒrəʊ] (aus)leihen, sich borgen 2
botanical [bəˈtænɪkl] botanisch 4: 1 (20)
botanical garden [bətænɪkl ˈgɑːdn] der botanische Garten 4: 1 (20)
both [bəʊθ] beide 2 **both ... and ...** sowohl ... als auch ... 2
bottle [ˈbɒtl] die Flasche 2
bottled (water) [ˈbɒtld] (Wasser) in Flaschen 4: 4 (133)
bottom [ˈbɒtəm] das untere Ende 2
bought [bɔːt] *siehe* **buy**
bowl [bəʊl] die Schüssel, die Schale 2
bowling alley [ˈbəʊlɪŋ æli] die Bowlingbahn 4: 3 (85)
box [bɒks] die Box, der Kasten 2
box [bɒks] boxen 1
boxing [ˈbɒksɪŋ] das Boxen 1
boxing ring [ˈbɒksɪŋ rɪŋ] der Boxring 4: 1 (30)
boy [bɔɪ] der Junge 1
boyfriend [ˈbɔɪfrend] der (feste) Freund 2
braces *(pl)* [ˈbreɪsɪz] die Zahnspange, die Zahnklammer 2
°bracket [ˈbrækɪt] die Klammer
brainstorm [ˈbreɪnstɔːm] Ideen (ungeordnet) sammeln 4: 4 (134)
brainstorming [ˈbreɪnstɔːmɪŋ] das Brainstorming *(Sammeln spontaner/ ungeordneter Ideen)* 4: 4 (134)
brand [brænd] die (Produkt-)Marke 2
brave [breɪv] mutig 1
bravery [ˈbreɪvəri] der Mut, die Tapferkeit 2
bread [bred] das Brot 1
break [breɪk] die Pause 1 **at break** in der Pause 1
break [breɪk], **broke, broken: break sth.** etwas zerbrechen 1 **break the fast** das Fasten brechen 2
breakfast [ˈbrekfəst] das Frühstück 1 **cooked breakfast** *ein warmes Frühstück, z. B. mit gebratenem Speck und Spiegeleiern* 3 **full cooked breakfast** *ein reichhaltiges warmes Frühstück mit allem, was dazugehört* 3
breath [breθ] der Atem(zug) 3

breathe (in/out) [briːð] (ein-/aus-) atmen 2
bred [bred] *siehe* **breed**
breed [briːd]:
1. die (Tier-)Rasse, die Unterart; die Züchtung 4: 4 (123)
2. **breed, bred, bred** brüten, Junge bekommen, sich vermehren; züchten; hervorrufen 4: 4 (123)
bride [braɪd] die Braut 2
bridegroom [ˈbraɪdgruːm] der Bräutigam 2
bridesmaid [ˈbraɪdzmeɪd] die Brautjungfer 2
bridge [brɪdʒ] die Brücke 2
bright [braɪt] hell, freundlich; leuchtend 3
bring [brɪŋ], **brought, brought** bringen, mitbringen 1 **bring sth. in** etwas (neu) einführen; etwas hereinbringen 4: 1 (21)
Britain [ˈbrɪtn] Großbritannien 1
British [ˈbrɪtɪʃ] britisch 1
British Isles *(pl)* [brɪtɪʃ ˈaɪlz] die Britischen Inseln 3
°**brochure** [ˈbrəʊʃə] die Broschüre, der Prospekt
broke [brəʊk] *siehe* **break**
broken [ˈbrəʊkən] *siehe* **break**
be broken kaputt, sein; zerbrochen sein 2
brother [ˈbrʌðə] der Bruder 1
brought [brɔːt] *siehe* **bring**
brown [braʊn] braun 1
brush [brʌʃ]:
1. die Bürste 1
2. bürsten 1
brush your teeth (sich) die Zähne putzen 1
°**bubble** [ˈbʌbl] die Blase *(Sprechblase, Seifenblase etc.)*
buffalo [ˈbʌfələʊ], *pl* **buffalo** *or* **buffaloes** der Büffel; der/das Bison 4: 4 (122)
buffet [ˈbʊfeɪ] das Büfett 3
bug [bʌg]:
1. das Insekt, der Käfer; der Fehler *(Programmfehler, Gerätefehler)* 4: 4 (119)
2. **bug sb.** *(infml)* jn. nerven, beunruhigen 4: 4 (119)
build [bɪld], **built, built** bauen 2
builder [ˈbɪldə]:
1. der/die Bauarbeiter/in 2
2. der/die Konstrukteur/in 4: 4 (132)
building [ˈbɪldɪŋ] das Gebäude 1
built [bɪlt] *siehe* **build**
bully [ˈbʊli]:
1. der/die Mobber/in; der/die Tyrann/in 1
2. tyrannisieren, mobben 1
°**bureau** [ˈbjʊərəʊ] das Büro; *(AE:)* die Behörde
burger [ˈbɜːgə] der Hamburger *(Frikadelle)* 1
burn [bɜːn] brennen 4: 4 (130) **burn sth.** etwas verbrennen 4: 4 (130) **burn sth. down** etwas abbrennen, niederbrennen 4: 4 (130)
bus [bʌs] der Bus 1 **by bus** mit dem Bus 1 **double-decker bus** der Doppeldeckerbus 3 **on the bus** im Bus 1
bus stop [ˈbʌs stɒp] die Bushaltestelle 1
bush [bʊʃ] der Busch 4: 5 (153)
business [ˈbɪznəs] das Geschäft, der Betrieb 2 **start a business** ein Geschäft aufmachen, einen Betrieb gründen/eröffnen 2
business card [ˈbɪznəs kɑːd] die Visitenkarte, die Geschäftskarte 2
business owner [ˈbɪznəs əʊnə] der/die Geschäftsinhaber/in 4: 4 (122)
business people [ˈbɪznəs piːpl] *Plural von* **business person**
business person [ˈbɪznəs pɜːsn], *pl* **business people** die Geschäftsperson 4: 2 (59)
businessman [ˈbɪznəsmən], *pl* **businessmen** der Geschäftsmann 4: 2 (59)
businessmen [ˈbɪznəsmən] *Plural von* **businessman**
businesswoman [ˈbɪznəswʊmən], *pl* **businesswomen** die Geschäftsfrau 4: 2 (59)
businesswomen [ˈbɪznəswɪmɪn] *Plural von* **businesswoman**
busy [ˈbɪzi]:
1. hektisch, belebt 1
2. (viel)beschäftigt 1
be busy (viel)beschäftigt sein, (viel) zu tun haben 1 **keep (yourself) busy** sich beschäftigen, auf Trab bleiben 3 **keep sb. busy** jn. beschäftigen, auf Trab halten 3
but [bʌt], [bət] aber 1
butter [ˈbʌtə] die Butter 1
buy [baɪ], **bought, bought** kaufen 1
by [baɪ]:
1. **by Omar** von Omar (geschrieben) 3
2. **by bus** mit dem Bus 1
by email per E-Mail 3 **by phone** per Telefon, telefonisch 1 **know sb./sth. by ...** jn./etwas erkennen an ... 2
pay by card mit Karte (be)zahlen *(z. B. Bankkarte)* 2
3. **by the river** am Fluss 2
by the sea am Meer, an der See 1
Bye. [baɪ] Tschüs. / Auf Wiedersehen. 1

C

cab [kæb] das Taxi 3
cabin [ˈkæbɪn] die Hütte; die Kabine 4: (14/15)
cable car [ˈkeɪbl kɑː]:
1. die Seilbahn 3
°2. die Kabelstraßenbahn *(in San Francisco)*; die Seilbahn
cafe [ˈkæfeɪ] das Café 1
cafeteria [kæfəˈtɪəriə] *(AE)* die Cafeteria; die Mensa *(an Schule, College, Universität)* 4: 3 (88)
cake [keɪk] der Kuchen, die Torte 1
calendar [ˈkælɪndə] der Kalender 2
call [kɔːl]:
1. nennen; rufen; anrufen 1
call sb. names jn. beschimpfen 3
called ... mit Namen ..., der/die ... heißt 1 **be called** heißen 1
2. der Ruf 1
3. *(kurz für:* **phone call)** der (Telefon-) Anruf 1
make a call telefonieren, einen (Telefon-)Anruf tätigen 4: 5 (153)
calm [kɑːm]:
1. ruhig, besonnen 2
2. **calm (down)** sich beruhigen 3
calm sb. down jn. beruhigen 3
came [keɪm] *siehe* **come**
camera [ˈkæmərə] die Kamera 2
camp [kæmp]:
1. das (Zelt-)Lager 4: (14/15)
2. campen, zelten 4: 4 (126)
camper [ˈkæmpə] der/die Camper/in; der/die Teilnehmer/in am *summer camp* 4: (14/15)
campfire [ˈkæmpfaɪə] das Lagerfeuer 4: (14/15)
campground [ˈkæmpgraʊnd] *(AE)* der Campingplatz 4: 4 (126)
campsite [ˈkæmpsaɪt] der Campingplatz 2
can [kæn], [kən] können 1
can [kæn] die Dose 4: 1 (31)
canal [kəˈnæl] der Kanal 3
candle [ˈkændl] die Kerze 2
candy [ˈkændi] *(AE)* die Süßigkeiten 4: (12/13)
canned (fruit etc.) [kænd] (Obst etc.) in Dosen, Dosen-(Obst etc.) 4: 1 (31)
can't [kɑːnt]: **I can't (= cannot) see ...** Ich kann ... nicht sehen. 1
canteen [kænˈtiːn] die Kantine, die (Schul-)Mensa 1
canyon [ˈkænjən] der Cañon 4: (10/11)
cap [kæp] die (Schirm-)Mütze, die Kappe 1
capital [ˈkæpɪtl]:
1. **capital (city)** die Hauptstadt 2
2. **capital (letter)** der Großbuchstabe 2
capsule [ˈkæpsjuːl] die Kapsel; die Raumkapsel; die Kabine (auf einem Riesenrad) 3
captain [ˈkæptɪn] der/die Kapitän/in 4: 3 (90) **team captain** der/die Mannschaftskapitän/in 4: 3 (90)
caption [ˈkæpʃn] die Bildunterschrift 3
car [kɑː] das Auto 1
car light [ˈkɑː laɪt] der Autoscheinwerfer 1
car park [ˈkɑː pɑːk] der Parkplatz 4: 1 (30)
card [kɑːd]:
1. die Karte 1
playing card die Spielkarte 1
2. die (Bank-/Kredit-)Karte 2
pay by card mit Karte (be)zahlen *(z. B. Bankkarte)* 2
cardigan [ˈkɑːdɪgən] die Strickjacke 3

care [keə]:
1. **care about sth.** etwas wichtig nehmen 3
care for betreuen, pflegen; sich kümmern um; aufpassen auf 3 **I don't care.** Es ist mir egal. 3 **Who cares?** Wen interessiert das? / Was soll's? / Na und? 3
2. die Sorgfalt, die Vorsicht 3
Take care. Pass auf dich auf. 3
3. die Versorgung, die Betreuung; die Pflege 3
take care of sich kümmern um 3
°**career** [kəˈrɪə] die Karriere; der (schulische/berufliche) Werdegang
careful [ˈkeəfl] vorsichtig 1
careless [ˈkeələs] leichtsinnig, unvorsichtig 3
carer [ˈkeərə] die Pflegekraft; der/die Betreuer/in 3
°**caribou** [ˈkærɪbuː], *pl* **caribou** der/das Karibu *(kanadisches Rentier)*
carnival [ˈkɑːnɪvl] der Karneval 2
carpet [ˈkɑːpɪt] der Teppich 4: 3 (90)
carrot [ˈkærət] die Möhre, die Karotte 1
carry [ˈkæri] tragen; befördern; bei sich haben 3
carton [ˈkɑːtn] der (Papp-)Karton; die Packung 2
cartoon [kɑːˈtuːn] der Zeichentrickfilm; der/das Comic; der Cartoon 2
case [keɪs] das Etui, der Behälter, der Kasten 1
cash [kæʃ] das Cash, das Bargeld 2
pay (in) cash bar bezahlen 2
cash machine [ˈkæʃ məʃiːn] der Geldautomat 2
castle [ˈkɑːsl] die Burg 2
cat [kæt] die Katze 1 **rain cats and dogs** stark regnen 1
catch [kætʃ], **caught, caught** (ein)fangen; erwischen; einholen; nehmen *(z. B. einen Zug, einen Bus)* 3 **catch fire** Feuer fangen, in Brand geraten 4: 4 (130)
catchy [ˈkætʃi] eingängig *(Lied, Slogan)* 4: 3 (89)
category [ˈkætəgəri] die Kategorie 4: 3 (89)
catfish [ˈkætfɪʃ], *pl* **catfish** der Wels *(Fisch)* 3
Catholic [ˈkæθlɪk]:
1. der/die Katholik/in 3
2. katholisch 3
cattle *(pl)* [ˈkætl] das Vieh, die Rinder 4: (10/11)
caught [kɔːt] *siehe* catch
°**'cause** [kɔːz] *(infml)* weil (= because)
°**cause sth.** [kɔːz] etwas bewirken, verursachen
°**Caution!** [ˈkɔːʃn] Vorsicht!, Warnung!
cave [keɪv] die Höhle 3
celebrate [ˈselɪbreɪt] feiern 2
celebration [selɪˈbreɪʃn] die Feier, das Fest 2
°**celebrity** [səˈlebrəti] der/die Prominente, der/die Promi
°**census** [ˈsensəs], *pl* **censuses** die (Daten-)Erhebung, die (Volks-) Zählung
cent [sent] der Cent 1
centimetre (= cm) [ˈsentɪmiːtə] der Zentimeter 3
central [ˈsentrəl] zentral 3
centre [ˈsentə] das Zentrum; die Mitte 1
century [ˈsentʃəri] das Jahrhundert 4: 2 (55)
cereals *(pl)* [ˈsɪəriəlz] die Getreide-/Frühstücksflocken 3
ceremony [ˈserəməni] die Feier, die Zeremonie 2
certain [ˈsɜːtn] gewiss, bestimmt; sicher 3
certainly [ˈsɜːtnli] sicher(lich), gewiss *(Adv.)* 3
chain [tʃeɪn]:
1. die Kette 1
2. die Einzelhandelskette 3
chain store die Filiale (einer Einzelhandelskette) 3
chair [tʃeə] der Stuhl 1
challenge [ˈtʃælɪndʒ]:
1. die Herausforderung 2
take on a challenge eine Herausforderung annehmen, sich einer Herausforderung stellen 2
2. **challenge sb. (to sth.)** jn. (zu etwas) herausfordern 2
challenging [ˈtʃælɪndʒɪŋ] anspruchsvoll, (heraus)fordernd 2
champion [ˈtʃæmpiən] der/die Meister/in *(in einer Sportart)*, der Champion 3
championship [ˈtʃæmpiənʃɪp] die Meisterschaft 4: 1 (27)
chance [tʃɑːns]:
1. das Risiko 3
2. die Chance, die Gelegenheit 3
change [tʃeɪndʒ]:
1. sich umziehen *(die Kleidung wechseln)* 2
2. **change (into)** (sich) (ver)ändern (zu/in); wechseln; (sich) verwandeln (in), werden (zu) 1
change (trains) umsteigen 2
Changing of the Guards die Wachablösung 3 **change your mind** seine Meinung ändern 4: 4 (120)
3. die Veränderung, der Wechsel, die Verwandlung 1
4. das Wechselgeld 2
5. **change of clothes** die (frische) Kleidung zum Wechseln 2
changing room [ˈtʃeɪndʒɪŋ ruːm] der Umkleideraum; die Anprobe *(im Geschäft)* 2
channel [ˈtʃænl] der Sender, der (TV-) Kanal 3 **the (English) Channel** der Ärmelkanal 3
°**chapter** [ˈtʃæptə] das Kapitel
character [ˈkærəktə] der Charakter; die Figur *(aus einer Geschichte)* 1
charge (e.g. a phone) [tʃɑːdʒ] aufladen *(z. B. ein Telefon)* 3
charger [ˈtʃɑːdʒə] das Ladegerät 3
charity [ˈtʃærəti] die wohltätige Organisation 2 **animal charity** die wohltätige Organisation, die Tiere unterstützt 2
charity shop [ˈtʃærəti ʃɒp] *das Geschäft, das gespendete Waren für wohltätige Zwecke verkauft* 2
chart [tʃɑːt] das Diagramm; die Tabelle 2 **bar chart** das Säulendiagramm 2 **column chart** das Säulendiagramm 4: 4 (134) **line chart** das Liniendiagramm 4: 4 (134) **pie chart** das Tortendiagramm 2
chase [tʃeɪs]:
1. verfolgen, jagen 4: 2 (67)
2. die Verfolgung(sjagd) 4: 2 (67)
chat [tʃæt]:
1. die Unterhaltung; der Chat 2
have a chat eine Unterhaltung führen, sich unterhalten 2
2. **chat (with)** chatten (mit); sich unterhalten (mit) 2
chatty [ˈtʃæti] gesprächig 2
cheap [tʃiːp] billig, preiswert 2
cheat [tʃiːt]:
1. der Betrug, der Schwindel, die Mogelei 4: 4 (120)
2. **cheat (at/on sth.)** betrügen, mogeln, schummeln (bei etwas) 4: 4 (120)
cheater [ˈtʃiːtə] der Betrüger, die Betrügerin 4: 4 (120)
check [tʃek]:
1. die (Über-)Prüfung, die Kontrolle 1
2. (über)prüfen, kontrollieren 1
check on sb./sth. nach jm./etwas schauen, sich um jn./etwas kümmern 4: 2 (66) **check sb./sth. out** *(infml)* sich jn./etwas anschauen, anhören; etwas ausprobieren 2
checklist [ˈtʃeklɪst] die Checkliste 2
checkpoint [ˈtʃekpɔɪnt] der Kontrollpunkt 3
cheek [tʃiːk] die Wange 4: 1 (30)
cheer [tʃɪə] jubeln, *(Sportler/innen)* anfeuern 3
cheese [tʃiːz] der Käse 1
cheesy [ˈtʃiːzɪ] kitschig 2
chemical [ˈkemɪkl]:
1. Chemikalie 2
2. chemisch 2
chemistry [ˈkemɪstri] die Chemie 4: 3 (96)
chew [tʃuː] kauen 4: 1 (30) **chew at/on sth.** an etwas kauen, auf etwas (herum)kauen 4: 1 (30)
chewing gum [ˈtʃuːɪŋ gʌm] der/das Kaugummi 4: 1 (30)
chicken [ˈtʃɪkɪn] das Huhn; das (Brat-) Hähnchen 1
child [tʃaɪld], *pl* **children** das Kind 2
children [ˈtʃɪldrən] *Plural von child*
chill out [tʃɪl ˈaʊt] *(infml)* sich entspannen, abhängen 4: 2 (62)
chips *(pl)* [tʃɪps]:
1. die Pommes frites 1
fish and chips der Fisch mit Pommes Frites 1
2. *(AE)* die (Kartoffel-)Chips 4: 1 (27)

chocolate [ˈtʃɒklət]:
1. die Praline 2
2. die Schokolade 1
hot chocolate der Kakao, die heiße (Trink-)Schokolade 1

choice [tʃɔɪs] die (Aus-)Wahl; die Entscheidung 3 **you have no choice but to do sth.** dir bleibt nichts anderes übrig, als etwas zu tun 4: 3 (95)

choir [ˈkwaɪə] der Chor 4: 4 (132)

choose [tʃuːz], **chose, chosen** (aus)wählen 1 **choose to do sth.** sich entscheiden, beschließen etwas zu tun 3

chore [tʃɔː] die (Haus-)Arbeit, die *(lästige)* Pflicht 2 **do chores** (Haus-)Arbeiten erledigen 2

chorus [ˈkɔːrəs] der Chor (mehrstimmiges Gesangsstück); der Refrain *(Lied)* 4: 3 (97) **a chorus of "I'm sorrys" / complaints / ...** *(etwa)* Bekundungen von Mitgefühl / Beschwerderufe / ... 4: 3 (97) **speak in chorus** im Chor sprechen 4: 3 (97)

chose [tʃəuz] *siehe* choose

chosen [ˈtʃəuzn] *siehe* choose

christening [ˈkrɪsnɪŋ] die Taufe 2

Christmas [ˈkrɪsməs] (das) Weihnachten 1 **Father Christmas** der Weihnachtsmann 4: 1 (31)

Christmas Day [krɪsməs ˈdeɪ] der 1. Weihnachtstag (25. 12.) 1

church [tʃɜːtʃ] die Kirche 3

cinema [ˈsɪnəmə] das Kino 1 **at the cinema** im Kino 1

cinnamon [ˈsɪnəmən] der Zimt 4: 2 (60)

circle [ˈsɜːkl] der Kreis 1

circus [ˈsɜːkəs] der Zirkus 1

citizen [ˈsɪtɪzn] der/die (Staats-)Bürger/in 2

city [ˈsɪti] die City, die (Groß-)Stadt 1

city council [sɪti ˈkaunsl] der Stadtrat 4: 3 (85)

clap (your hands) [klæp] (in die Hände) klatschen 3

class [klɑːs] die Klasse; der Unterricht; der Kurs 1 **in class** im Unterricht 1

class teacher [ˈklɑːs tiːtʃə] der/die Klassenlehrer/in 1

classic [ˈklæsɪk]:
1. der Klassiker 3
2. klassisch 3

classical [ˈklæsɪkl] klassisch 2

classical music [klæsɪkl ˈmjuːzɪk] klassische Musik 2

°classmate [ˈklɑːsmeɪt] der Mitschüler, die Mitschülerin

classroom [ˈklɑːsruːm] das Klassenzimmer 1

clean [kliːn]:
1. sauber 1
2. sauber machen, putzen 1
clean out the stables ausmisten 4: 3 (93) **clean sth. up** etwas aufräumen, sauber machen 1

clean-up [ˈkliːn ʌp] das Säubern, das Saubermachen 1

clean-up day [ˈkliːn ʌp deɪ] der Dreck-weg-Tag *(Aktionstag zum Müllsammeln)* 1

cleaner [ˈkliːnə] die Reinigungskraft 1

clear [klɪə] klar, deutlich 1

clever [ˈklevə] schlau, klug 1

click [klɪk]:
1. der Klick, das Klicken 2
2. **click (on)** klicken (auf), anklicken 2

cliff [klɪf] die Klippe 3

cliff jumping [ˈklɪf dʒʌmpɪŋ] das Klippenspringen 3

climate [ˈklaɪmət] das Klima 4: 4 (133)

climate change [ˈklaɪmət tʃeɪndʒ] der Klimawandel 4: 4 (133)

climb [klaɪm]:
1. der Aufstieg, die Klettertour; der Anstieg 2
2. klettern (auf) 2

climber [ˈklaɪmə] der Kletterer, die Kletterin 2

clip [klɪp] der (Video-)Clip 4: 2 (62)

clock [klɒk] die (Wand-, Stand-, Turm-)Uhr 1

close [kləuz] schließen, zumachen 1 **close sth. off** etwas absperren 4: 1 (21)

close (to) [kləus] knapp; nahe (bei, an) 3

closed [kləuzd] geschlossen 1

clothes *(pl)* [kləuðz] die Kleidung, die Kleidungsstücke 1

clothes swap [ˈkləuðz swɒp] der Kleidertausch, die Kleidertauschparty 1

clothing *(no pl)* [ˈkləuðɪŋ] die Kleidung 3 **piece of clothing** das Kleidungsstück 3

clotted cream [klɒtɪd ˈkriːm] die besonders dicke Sahne, der Streichrahm 1

cloud [klaud] die Wolke 1 **have your head in the clouds** in Gedanken verloren oder unrealistisch sein 1

cloudless [ˈklaudləs] wolkenlos 3

cloudy [ˈklaudi] wolkig, bewölkt 1

club [klʌb] der Klub, der Verein 1 **join a club** bei einer AG mitmachen, in einen Klub eintreten 1 **school club** die AG *(in der Schule)* 1

clue [kluː] der (Lösungs-)Hinweis; der Anhaltspunkt 3 **I don't have a clue. / I have no clue.** *(infml)* Ich habe keine Ahnung. / Keine Ahnung. 3

coach [kəutʃ] der (Reise-)Bus 3

coal [kəul] die Kohle 3

coast [kəust] die Küste 3

coastal [ˈkəustl] Küsten- 4: 4 (116/117)

coat [kəut] der Mantel; die Jacke 4: 1 (31)

cocoa [ˈkəukəu] der Kakao 1

code [kəud]:
1. der Code 1
2. die Vorwahl(nummer) 1
3. programmieren *(Computer)*; kodieren 1

coding [ˈkəudɪŋ] das Programmieren 1

coffee [ˈkɒfi] der Kaffee 1

coin [kɔɪn] die Münze 2

cold [kəuld]:
1. kalt 1
be cold frieren 1
2. die Kälte 1
3. die Erkältung 1
have a cold erkältet sein 1

cold meat [kəuld ˈmiːt] der (Braten-/Wurst-)Aufschnitt 3 **cold meats** *(pl)* die Aufschnittsorten 3

collect [kəˈlekt] (ein)sammeln 1

collection [kəˈlekʃn] die Sammlung 2

college [ˈkɒlɪdʒ] die Hochschule 4: 3 (89)

colon [ˈkəulən] der Doppelpunkt 4: 1 (22)

colonization [kɒlənaɪˈzeɪʃn] die Kolonisation 4: 4 (122)

colonize [ˈkɒlənaɪz] besiedeln, aus etwas eine Kolonie machen 4: 4 (122)

colony [ˈkɒləni] die Kolonie 4: 2 (55)

colour [ˈkʌlə] die Farbe 1 **people/actors of colour** die nicht-weißen Menschen/Schauspieler/innen 4: 1 (25) **What colour is ...?** Welche Farbe hat ...? 1

colourful [ˈkʌləfl] farbig, bunt 2

colourless [ˈkʌlələs] farblos 3

column [ˈkɒləm] die Säule; die Spalte *(in Texten)* 3 **advice column** der Kummerkasten, die Ratgeber-Spalte *(z. B. in Zeitschriften)* 3

column chart [ˈkɒləm tʃɑːt] das Säulendiagramm 4: 4 (134)

come [kʌm], **came, come:**
1. (mit)kommen 1
come after sb. hinter jm. herkommen 3 **come off (sth.)** abgehen (von etwas), (herunter)fallen (von etwas), sich lösen (von etwas) 2 **Come on!** Komm(t) (schon)! Na los! 3 **come rain or shine** bei jedem Wetter; was auch (immer) geschieht 1 **come round (to)** vorbeikommen, vorbeischauen (bei) 2 **come up** (Sonne) aufgehen 2
2. **come true** wahr werden 2

comedy [ˈkɒmədi] die Comedyshow; die Komödie 3

comfortable [ˈkʌmftəbl] bequem, gemütlich 2

comma [ˈkɒmə] das Komma 4: 1 (22)

comment (about/on sth.) [ˈkɒment]:
1. der Kommentar (über/zu etwas) 3
2. (etwas) kommentieren 3

common [ˈkɒmən] häufig, weit verbreitet, gewöhnlich 4: 3 (95)

°common sense [kɒmən ˈsens] der gesunde Menschenverstand

communicate [kəˈmjuːnɪkeɪt] kommunizieren 3

communication [kəmjuːnɪˈkeɪʃn] die Kommunikation, die Verständigung 3

community [kəˈmjuːnəti] die Gemeinschaft, die Gemeinde 3

company [ˈkʌmpəni] die Firma, die Gesellschaft 3

compare sth. (to / with sth.) [kəmˈpeə] etwas vergleichen (mit etwas) 2

competition [kɒmpəˈtɪʃn] der Wettbewerb 1 **hold a competition** einen Wettbewerb veranstalten, abhalten 4: 4 (132)
complain (to sb. about sth.) [kəmˈpleɪn] sich (bei jm. über etwas) beschweren, beklagen; jammern 4: 2 (53)
complete [kəmˈpliːt]:
1. vollständig, komplett 3
2. vervollständigen 3
3. abschließen, fertigstellen 4: 1 (34)
completely [kəmˈpliːtli] völlig, absolut *(Adv.)* 3
compliment [ˈkɒmplɪmənt] das Kompliment 3 **(to) pay sb. a compliment** jm. ein Kompliment machen 3
computing [kəmˈpjuːtɪŋ] die Informatik 1
concert [ˈkɒnsət] das Konzert 2
conclusion [kənˈkluːʒn] der Schluss; die Schlussfolgerung 4: 3 (85) **draw a conclusion** einen Schluss / eine Schlussfolgerung ziehen 4: 3 (85) **reach a conclusion** zu einem Schluss kommen 4: 3 (85)
condition [kənˈdɪʃn] die Bedingung; der Zustand 3 **conditions** *(pl)* die Bedingungen, die Verhältnisse 3
condor [ˈkɒndɔː] der Kondor *(Vogel)* 4: 4 (123)
°conference [ˈkɒnfərəns] die Konferenz, die Besprechung
confidence [ˈkɒnfɪdəns] das (Selbst-)Vertrauen, die Zuversicht 2
confident [ˈkɒnfɪdənt] (selbst)sicher; zuversichtlich 2
conflict [ˈkɒnflɪkt] der Konflikt, die Auseinandersetzung, der Streit 3
confuse [kənˈfjuːz] verwirren; durcheinanderbringen 3 **°get confused about sth.** mit etwas durcheinanderkommen
confusion [kənˈfjuːʒn] die Verwirrung; das Durcheinander 3
connect (with/to) [kəˈnekt] (sich) verbinden (mit) 2
connection [kəˈnekʃn] die Verbindung; der Anschluss 2
cons *(pl)* [kɒnz]: **the pros and cons** das Pro und Kontra; das Für und Wider 4: 3 (84)
console [kənˈsəʊl] die Konsole 1
contact [ˈkɒntækt]:
1. der Kontakt 4: 3 (100)
in contact in Kontakt 4: 3 (100)
2. **contact sb.** Kontakt aufnehmen mit jm., sich in Verbindung setzen mit jm. 4: 3 (100)
°contain [kənˈteɪn] enthalten
continue [kənˈtɪnjuː] fortfahren, weitermachen; (sich) fortsetzen, weitergehen 1 **continue to do sth.** etwas weiterhin tun, (mit) etwas weitermachen, fortfahren 1
contrast [kənˈtrɑːst] vergleichen, (einander) gegenüberstellen 3
contrast [ˈkɒntrɑːst] der Kontrast, der Gegensatz 3
control [kənˈtrəʊl]:
1. kontrollieren, regulieren 4: 3 (98)
2. **control (of/over)** die Kontrolle (über) 4: 3 (98)
be in control of/over die Kontrolle haben (über) 4: 3 (98) **lose control (of/over)** die Kontrolle verlieren (über) 4: 3 (98)
conversation [kɒnvəˈseɪʃn] das Gespräch 2
°convince sb. of sth. [kənˈvɪns] jn. von etwas überzeugen
cook [kʊk]:
1. der Koch, die Köchin 1
2. kochen 1
cooked breakfast [kʊkt ˈbrekfəst] *ein warmes Frühstück, z. B. mit gebratenem Speck und Spiegeleiern* 3 **full cooked breakfast** *ein reichhaltiges warmes Frühstück mit allem, was dazugehört* 3
cooking [ˈkʊkɪŋ]:
1. das Kochen 1
2. das *(gekochte)* Essen 1
coordinate [kəʊˈɔːdɪneɪt] koordinieren 4: 1 (34)
coordination [kəʊˈɔːdɪneɪʃn] die Koordination, die Koordinierung 4: 1 (34)
cop [kɒp] *(infml)* der Cop *(amerikanische umgangssprachliche Bezeichnung für Polizist/in)* 4: 2 (52)
copy [ˈkɒpi]:
1. die Kopie; das Exemplar 3
2. kopieren, abschreiben 3
corn [kɔːn]:
1. das Korn, das Getreide 4: 2 (61)
2. *(AE)* der Mais 4: 2 (61)
cornbread [ˈkɔːnbred] das Maisbrot 4: 2 (61)
corner [ˈkɔːnə] die Ecke 2
corner shop [ˈkɔːnə ʃɒp] der Eckladen, der Tante-Emma-Laden 2
cornflake crumbs *(pl)* [ˈkɔːnfleɪk krʌmz] die zerbröselten Cornflakes 1
correct [kəˈrekt]:
1. korrekt 2
2. korrigieren 2
corridor [ˈkɒrɪdɔː] der Korridor 1
cost [kɒst]:
1. die Kosten; der Preis 1
2. **cost, cost, cost** kosten 1
costume [ˈkɒstjuːm] das Kostüm, die Verkleidung 2
cosy [ˈkəʊzi] gemütlich 3
cottage [ˈkɒtɪdʒ] das Häuschen, das Cottage *(kleines Haus, meist auf dem Land)* 1
cotton [ˈkɒtn] die Baumwolle 3
cotton mill [ˈkɒtn mɪl] die Baumwollfabrik, die Baumwollspinnerei 3
cough [kɒf]:
1. der Husten 2
2. husten 2
could [kʊd]:
1. **I could** ich konnte 2
2. **Could you ...?** Könntest du ...? / Könnten Sie ...? 2
council [ˈkaʊnsl] der Rat *(z. B. Gemeinderat)* 4: 3 (85) **city council** der Stadtrat 4: 3 (85) **town council** der Stadtrat 4: 3 (85)
counsellor [ˈkaʊnsələ] der/die Berater/in; der/die Betreuer/in 4: (14/15)
°count (to ten) [kaʊnt] (bis zehn) zählen
country [ˈkʌntri]:
1. das Land, *(auch:)* die ländliche Gegend 1
2. **country (music)** die Countrymusic *(Musikstil)* 4: 2 (62)
countryside [ˈkʌntrisaɪd] das Land *(ländliche Gegend)*, die Landschaft; die Natur 3
couple [ˈkʌpl] das Paar 4: 4 (129)
a couple (of ...) ein Paar; ein paar (...) 4: 4 (129)
course [kɔːs]:
1. der Kurs 2
2. **main course** das Hauptgericht 1
court [kɔːt]:
1. der Platz, der Court *(Tennis, Basketball)* 4: 1 (26)
2. das Gericht, der Gerichtshof 4: 2 (56)
cousin [ˈkʌzn] der Cousin, die Cousine 1
cover [ˈkʌvə]:
1. bedecken, abdecken, zudecken 4: 2 (61)
2. die Abdeckung, der Deckel 4: 2 (61)
3. das Cover *(Hülle von Musikalben)* 3
cow [kaʊ] die Kuh 2
crack [kræk]:
1. lösen *(z. B. Problem)*, knacken *(z. B. Code)* 1
2. krachen, knallen, knacken 4: 5 (155)
3. das Krachen, das Knacken, der Knall 4: 5 (155)
crafts *(pl)* [krɑːfts] das Kunsthandwerk, das Basteln 1
crater [ˈkreɪtə] der Krater 4: 4 (124)
crazy [ˈkreɪzi] verrückt 2 **crazy about sth.** wild auf etwas, versessen auf etwas 2
cream [kriːm] die Sahne 1
creamy [ˈkriːmi] cremig; sahnig 4: 2 (61)
create [kriˈeɪt] (er)schaffen 2
creative [kriˈeɪtɪv] kreativ 2
creativity [kriːeɪˈtɪvəti] die Kreativität 2
creator [kriˈeɪtə] der/die Autor/in, der/die Zeichner/in, der/die Schöpfer/in 4: 1 (33)
creature [ˈkriːtʃə] das Geschöpf, das (Lebe-)Wesen 3
cricket [ˈkrɪkɪt]:
1. das Kricket *(Mannschaftssportart)* 1
2. die Grille *(Insekt)* 1
crime [kraɪm] das Verbrechen; die Kriminalität 4: 1 (21)
criminal [ˈkrɪmɪnl]:
1. der/die Verbrecher/in 4: 1 (21)
2. kriminell 4: 1 (21)
crisps *(pl)* [krɪsps] die (Kartoffel-)Chips 4: 1 (27)

criticism [ˈkrɪtɪsɪzəm] die Kritik 4: 3 (85)
criticize sb. for sth. [ˈkrɪtɪsaɪz] jn. wegen etwas kritisieren 4: 3 (85)
crocodile [ˈkrɒkədaɪl] das Krokodil 4: (10/11)
crop top [ˈkrɒp tɒp] das Crop Top *(bauchfreies Top)* 4: 3 (96)
cross [krɒs]:
1. das Kreuz 3
2. kreuzen, überqueren 3
cross your fingers die Daumen drücken/halten *(jm. Glück / gutes Gelingen wünschen)* 3
°3. mit einem Kreuz versehen
crowd [kraʊd] die (Menschen-)Menge 4: 1 (21)
crowded [ˈkraʊdɪd] überfüllt, voll *(von Menschen)* 4: 1 (21)
crowdfund sth. [ˈkraʊdfʌnd] etwas durch Crowdfunding finanzieren 4: 4 (132)
crowdfunding [ˈkraʊdfʌndɪŋ] das Crowdfunding *(Schwarmfinanzierung)* 4: 4 (132)
crumb [krʌm] die Flocke, der Krümel 1 **cornflake crumbs** *(pl)* die zerbröselten Cornflakes 1
crunchy [ˈkrʌntʃi] knusprig, knackig 4: 2 (61)
crush [krʌʃ]:
1. die Schwärmerei, das Verliebtsein 3
have a crush (on sb.) in jn. verliebt sein 3
2. der Schwarm *(jd., in den/die man verliebt ist)* 3
cry [kraɪ]:
1. der Schrei, der Ruf 3
2. weinen; rufen, schreien 3
cub [kʌb] das (Löwen-, Bären-)Junge 4: 4 (127)
cucumber [ˈkjuːkʌmbə] die Gurke *(Salatgurke)* 3
cultural [ˈkʌltʃərəl] kulturell 3
culture [ˈkʌltʃə] die Kultur 1
cup [kʌp]: **World Cup** die Weltmeisterschaft 3
curious (about) [ˈkjʊəriəs] neugierig (auf) 2
curl [kɜːl] die Locke 2
curly [ˈkɜːli] lockig 2
current [ˈkʌrənt] die Strömung, der Strom 4: 5 (153)
curtain [ˈkɜːtn] der Vorhang, die Gardine 3
cushion [ˈkʊʃn] das Kissen 1
custard [ˈkʌstəd] der Custard *(Vanillesoße)* 1
customer [ˈkʌstəmə] der Kunde, die Kundin 2
cut [kʌt]:
1. der Schnitt 1
2. **cut, cut, cut** schneiden 1 ausschneiden 3 **cut sth. out** etwas ausschneiden 1 **cut sth. up** etwas in Stücke schneiden, klein schneiden 3
cute [kjuːt] niedlich, süß 1
cyberbullying [ˈsaɪbəbʊliŋ] das Cybermobbing 3
cycle [ˈsaɪkl] Rad fahren 1
cycle lane [ˈsaɪkl leɪn] der Radweg 3
cycling [ˈsaɪklɪŋ] das Radfahren 1

D

dad [dæd] der Papa, der Vati 1
daddy [ˈdædi] der Vati, der Papa 4: 1 (31)
°**dam** [dæm] der (Stau-)Damm
damage [ˈdæmɪdʒ]:
1. (be)schädigen, schaden 4: 4 (127)
2. **damage (to)** *(no pl)* der Schaden, die Schäden (an) 4: 4 (127)
dance [dɑːns]:
1. tanzen 1
2. der Tanz 1
do a dance einen Tanz tanzen 1
dancer [ˈdɑːnsə] der/die Tänzer/in 1
dancing [ˈdɑːnsɪŋ] das Tanzen 1
danger [ˈdeɪndʒə] die Gefahr 2
dangerous [ˈdeɪndʒərəs] gefährlich 2
dare [deə]:
1. wagen, sich trauen 2
2. die Mutprobe 2
for a dare als Mutprobe 2
dark [dɑːk]:
1. dunkel 2
2. das Dunkel, die Dunkelheit 2
darkness [ˈdɑːknəs] die Dunkelheit 2
data [ˈdeɪtə] die Daten 4: 4 (119)
date [deɪt]:
1. das Datum 1
date of birth das Geburtsdatum 1
2. die Verabredung, das Date *(auch die Person, mit der man ausgeht)* 2
3. **date sb.** mit jm. gehen, eine Beziehung haben 2
daughter [ˈdɔːtə] die Tochter 1
day [deɪ] der Tag 1 **one day** eines Tages 4: 1 (26) **work long days** lange arbeiten, lange Arbeitstage haben 1
dead [ded] tot 1 **My phone is dead.** Mein Telefon-Akku ist leer. 3
deal [diːl] das Geschäft; die Vereinbarung 4: 3 (89)
deal with [ˈdiːl wɪð], **dealt, dealt:**
1. klarkommen mit, fertigwerden mit, umgehen mit 3
2. sich befassen mit, behandeln *(z. B. Thema)* 3
dealt [delt] *siehe* **deal with**
dear [dɪə] der Liebling, der Schatz *(BE: auch als Anrede)* 4: 1 (31) **Dear ...** Liebe/r ... 1
death [deθ] der Tod 4: 2 (57)
debate [dɪˈbeɪt]:
1. debattieren 3
2. die Debatte 3
hold/have a debate eine Debatte führen 3
decade [ˈdekeɪd] das Jahrzehnt 4: 4 (129)
December [dɪˈsembə] der Dezember 1
decide [dɪˈsaɪd] beschließen, sich entscheiden beschließen, sich entscheiden (etwas zu tun) 3 **decide on sth.** etwas beschließen, sich für etwas entscheiden 3 **decide to do sth.** beschließen, sich entscheiden etwas zu tun 3
decision [dɪˈsɪʒn] die Entscheidung 4: 4 (119)
decorate [ˈdekəreɪt] dekorieren, schmücken 1
decoration [dekəˈreɪʃn] die Dekoration, der Schmuck, die Verzierung 1
decrease (by) [dɪˈkriːs] abnehmen, sinken, zurückgehen, (sich) verringern (um) 4: 4 (134)
decrease (in) [ˈdiːkriːs] die Abnahme, der Rückgang (an/von) 4: 4 (134)
deep [diːp] tief 3
deer [dɪə], *pl* **deer** das Reh; der Hirsch 3
definite [ˈdefɪnət] klar, deutlich, sicher 3
definitely [ˈdefɪnətli] auf jeden Fall; ganz bestimmt *(Adv.)* 3
°**definition** [defɪˈnɪʃn] die Definition
degree (°) [dɪˈgriː] das/der Grad 1
delete [dɪˈliːt] löschen 3
°**deli** [ˈdeli] das Feinkostgeschäft
delicious [dɪˈlɪʃəs] köstlich, lecker 1
°**deliver** [dɪˈlɪvə] (aus)liefern
demo [ˈdeməʊ] *siehe* **demo version**
demo version [ˈdeməʊ vɜːʃn] *kurz auch* **demo** die Demoversion 4: 4 (118)
demonstrate [ˈdemənstreɪt] demonstrieren, vorführen 4: 4 (118)
demonstration [demənˈstreɪʃn] die Vorführung, die Demonstration 4: 4 (118)
department [dɪˈpɑːtmənt] die Abteilung 3
°**department** [dɪˈpɑːtmənt] *(AE)* das Ministerium, das Amt
department store [dɪˈpɑːtmənt stɔː] das Kaufhaus 3
dependent (on) [dɪˈpendənt] abhängig (von), angewiesen (auf) 2
describe [dɪˈskraɪb] beschreiben 1
description [dɪˈskrɪpʃn] die Beschreibung 1
desert [ˈdezət] die Wüste 4: 3 (87)
desert island [dezət ˈaɪlənd] die einsame Insel 4: 3 (87)
design [dɪˈzaɪn]:
1. die Gestaltung, das Design 1
2. entwerfen, gestalten 1
design and technology [dɪzaɪn ən tekˈnɒlədʒi] das Werken, der Werkunterricht 1
desk [desk]:
1. der Schreibtisch 1
2. der Schalter *(z. B. Verkaufs-, Postschalter)* 3
dessert [dɪˈzɜːt] die Nachspeise, das Dessert 1 **for dessert** zum/als Nachtisch 1
destination [destɪˈneɪʃn] das Ziel, der Bestimmungsort 2
destroy [dɪˈstrɔɪ] zerstören, vernichten 4: 2 (65)
detached home/house [dɪˈtætʃt] das frei stehende Haus 1

detail [ˈdiːteɪl] das Detail, die Einzelheit 4: 4 (120)
detective [dɪˈtektɪv] der Detektiv, die Detektivin 3
detention [dɪˈtenʃn] das Nachsitzen *(in der Schule)* 4: 4 (120)
°detour [ˈdiːtʊə] *(AE)* die Umleitung
develop [dɪˈveləp] entwickeln; sich entwickeln 3
developer [dɪˈveləpə] der/die Entwickler/in *(z. B. Software)* 3
device [dɪˈvaɪs] das Gerät, der Apparat 3
dialect [ˈdaɪəlekt] der Dialekt 4: 2 (52)
°dialogue [ˈdaɪəlɒg] der Dialog
diary [ˈdaɪəri] der Kalender; das Tagebuch 3 **keep a diary** Tagebuch führen 3
dictation [dɪkˈteɪʃn] das Diktat 3
dictionary [ˈdɪkʃənri] das Wörterbuch, das *(alphabetische)* Wörterverzeichnis 2
did [dɪd] *siehe* **do** **they didn't go ... (= did not)** sie gingen nicht / sie sind nicht gegangen 2
die (of) [daɪ] sterben (an) 2
difference [ˈdɪfrəns] der Unterschied 1 **make a difference** etwas bewirken, etwas ausmachen 3
different (to) [ˈdɪfrənt] verschieden; anders (als) 1
difficult [ˈdɪfɪkəlt] schwierig, schwer 1
dig [dɪg], **dug, dug** graben 1
digital [ˈdɪdʒɪtl] digital 3
dignity [ˈdɪgnəti] die Würde 4: 1 (30)
dime [daɪm] *(AE)* das Zehncentstück 4: 1 (19)
°diner [ˈdaɪnə] *(AE)* der Diner *(einfaches Schnell- Restaurant)*
dining room [ˈdaɪnɪŋ ruːm] das Esszimmer 1
dinner [ˈdɪnə] das Abendessen 1 **for dinner** zum Abendessen 1
dinosaur [ˈdaɪnəsɔː] der Dinosaurier 4: 4 (128)
direct [dəˈrekt] direkt, unmittelbar 3
direction [dəˈrekʃn] die Richtung 2
directions *(pl)* [dəˈrekʃnz] die Wegbeschreibung(en) 2 **ask for directions** nach dem Weg fragen 2 **give directions** den Weg beschreiben 2
dirt [dɜːt] der Dreck 4: 3 (97)
dirty [ˈdɜːti] schmutzig 1
disability [dɪsəˈbɪləti] die Behinderung 3
disabled [dɪsˈeɪbld] (körper)-behindert 3
disadvantage [dɪsədˈvɑːntɪdʒ] der Nachteil 3
disagree [dɪsəˈgriː] nicht zustimmen, widersprechen 2
disappear [dɪsəˈpɪə] verschwinden 4: 5 (153)
disappoint sb. [dɪsəˈpɔɪnt] jn. enttäuschen 2
disappointed (in/with) [dɪsəˈpɔɪntɪd] enttäuscht (von) 2

disappointing [dɪsəˈpɔɪntɪŋ] enttäuschend 2
disappointment [dɪsəˈpɔɪntmənt] die Enttäuschung 2
disaster [dɪˈzɑːstə] die Katastrophe, das Unglück 4: 4 (121)
discover [dɪˈskʌvə] entdecken 2
discoverer [dɪsˈkʌvərə] der/die Entdecker/in 2
discovery [dɪˈskʌvəri] die Entdeckung 2
discriminate against sb. [dɪˈskrɪmɪneɪt] jn. diskriminieren 4: 2 (53)
discrimination (against sb.) [dɪskrɪmɪˈneɪʃn] die Diskriminierung (eines Menschen) 4: 2 (53)
discuss [dɪˈskʌs] diskutieren 2
discussion [dɪˈskʌʃn] die Diskussion 2
disease [dɪˈziːz] die Krankheit 2
dish [dɪʃ]:
1. die Schüssel, die Schale 1
2. das Gericht *(Mahlzeit)* 1
main dish das Hauptgericht 1
dishwasher [ˈdɪʃwɒʃə] die Geschirrspülmaschine 2
disorganized [dɪsˈɔːgənaɪzd] schlecht organisiert, chaotisch 2
display [dɪˈspleɪ]:
1. zeigen, zur Schau stellen 4: 3 (97)
2. die Ausstellung, die Vorführung, die Schau; die Schaufensterauslage 4: 3 (97)
be on display ausgestellt sein 4: 3 (97)
distract [dɪˈstrækt] ablenken 4: 3 (97)
distraction [dɪˈstrækʃn] die Ablenkung 4: 3 (97)
diverse [daɪˈvɜːs] unterschiedlich, vielfältig 4: 1 (22)
diversity [daɪˈvɜːsəti] die Vielfalt 4: 1 (22)
divide (up) (into) [dɪˈvaɪd] auf-/einteilen (in) 3
do [duː], **did, done** machen, tun 1 **do your homework** Hausaufgaben machen 1 **If anyone does come ...** Falls wirklich/tatsächlich jemand ... kommt, ... 4: 5 (158)
doctor (Dr) [ˈdɒktə] der Arzt, die Ärztin 2
document [ˈdɒkjumənt] das Dokument; die Textdatei 3
dog [dɒg] der Hund 1 **rain cats and dogs** stark regnen 1 **walk the dog** mit dem Hund rausgehen, mit dem Hund Gassi gehen 2
dog walker [ˈdɒg wɔːkə] der/die Hundeausführer/in 2
dog walking [ˈdɒg wɔːkɪŋ] Hunde ausführen 2
doll [dɒl] die Puppe 4: 3 (97)
dollar ($) [ˈdɒlə] der Dollar 4: (12/13)
dolphin [ˈdɒlfɪn] der Delfin 2
done [dʌn] *siehe* **do** **Well done.** Gut gemacht! 1
door [dɔː] die Tür 1 **answer the door** aufmachen, zur/an die Tür gehen 4: 2 (65)

doorkeeper [ˈdɔːkiːpə] der/die Pförtner/in 3
double [ˈdʌbl] doppelt, Doppel- 3
double-decker (bus) [dʌbl ˈdekə] der Doppeldecker(bus) 3
double room [dʌbl ˈruːm] das Doppelzimmer 3
dough [dəʊ] der Teig 1
down [daʊn]:
1. hinunter, herunter 1
down a hill einen Hügel hinunter, herunter 2
2. **be down** außer Betrieb sein, zusammengebrochen sein 4: 2 (65)
The phone lines are down. Die Telefonleitungen sind zusammengebrochen. 4: 2 (65)
download [ˈdaʊnləʊd]:
1. der/das Download 3
2. herunterladen 3
downriver [daʊnˈrɪvə] flussabwärts 4: 5 (156)
downstairs [daʊnˈsteəz] (nach) unten *(die Treppe hinunter)* 2
downtown [daʊnˈtaʊn] *(AE)* im/ins Stadtzentrum 4: 1 (30)
dragon [ˈdrægən] der Drache 2
drama [ˈdrɑːmə] das Schauspiel, die darstellende Kunst 1
dramatic [drəˈmætɪk] dramatisch 2
drank [dræŋk] *siehe* **drink**
draw [drɔː], **drew, drawn** zeichnen 1
drawing [ˈdrɔːɪŋ]:
1. die Zeichnung 1
2. das Zeichnen 1
drawn [drɔːn] *siehe* **draw**
dream [driːm]:
1. der Traum 1
2. **dream (of/about sth.)** träumen (von etwas) 1
dress [dres]:
1. das Kleid 2
2. sich kleiden, sich anziehen 2
get dressed sich anziehen 1 **She was dressed in a shirt.** Sie trug ein Shirt. / Sie war mit einem Shirt bekleidet. 4: 3 (97)
dress code [ˈdres kəʊd] der Dresscode *(Kleiderordnung)* 4: 3 (96)
drew [druː] *siehe* **draw**
drift [drɪft] treiben, sich bewegen, driften 4: 5 (156)
drink [drɪŋk]:
1. das Getränk 1
2. **drink, drank, drunk** trinken 1
drip [drɪp] tropfen 4: 5 (155)
drive [draɪv], **drove, driven** *(mit dem Auto)* fahren 2
driven [ˈdrɪvn] *siehe* **drive**
driver [ˈdraɪvə] der/die Fahrer/in 2
°driver's license [ˈdraɪvəz laɪsns] *(AE)* der Führerschein
driving licence [ˈdraɪvɪŋ laɪsns] der Führerschein 4: 3 (95) **provisional driving licence** die vorläufige Fahrerlaubnis 4: 3 (95)
driving test [ˈdraɪvɪŋ test] die Fahrprüfung 3
drone [drəʊn] die Drohne 1

drop [drɒp]:
1. fallen, sinken; fallen lassen 4: 1 (21)
2. der Tropfen 4: 5 (155)
3. der Fall; der Abwurf 4: 1 (21)
ball drop das Herablassen des Zeitballs *(am Times Square zum Jahreswechsel)* 4: 1 (21)
drove [drəʊv] *siehe* **drive**
drug [drʌg] die Droge, das Rauschgift 4: 1 (21)
drum [drʌm] die Trommel 4: 2 (63)
drums *(pl)* das Schlagzeug 4: 2 (63)
drummer [ˈdrʌmə] der/die Trommler/in 4: 2 (63)
drunk [drʌŋk] *siehe* **drink**
dry [draɪ]:
1. (ab)trocknen 4: 2 (64)
2. trocken 4: 2 (64)
dude [du:d] *(infml)* Mann, Alter *(Anrede)* 4: 2 (52)
°dug [dʌg] *siehe* **dig**
duke [dju:k] der Herzog 1
dungeon [ˈdʌndʒən] der Kerker, das Verlies *(in einer Burg)* 2
during [ˈdjʊərɪŋ] während *(Präposition)* 2

E

each [i:tʃ] jede(r, s) (einzelne), jeweils 1
each other [i:tʃ ˈʌðə] einander, sich (gegenseitig) 2
ear [ɪə] das Ohr 2
earbuds *(pl)* [ˈɪəbʌdz] der Ohrhörer, der In-Ear-Kopfhörer 4: 1 (32)
earlier [ˈɜ:liə] vorhin; vorher, früher 3
early [ˈɜ:li] früh 2
earn [ɜ:n] verdienen *(Geld)* 2
earth [ɜ:θ] die Erde 2
east [i:st] der Osten; östlich; Ost- 3
eastern [ˈi:stən] östlich, Ost- 3
easy [ˈi:zi] einfach, leicht 2
eat [i:t], **ate, eaten** essen; fressen 1
eaten [ˈi:tn] *siehe* **eat**
ed [ed] *siehe* **education**
edge [edʒ] der Rand, die Kante 3
edit [ˈedɪt] bearbeiten, editieren 3
editor [ˈedɪtə] der Editor *(Text-/Bildbearbeitungsprogramm)* 3
educate sb. [ˈedʒukeɪt] jn. ausbilden, unterrichten, erziehen 4: 3 (95)
education [edʒuˈkeɪʃn] *infml auch* **ed** die Erziehung, die (Schul-)Bildung 4: 3 (95)
educational [edʒuˈkeɪʃənl] Erziehungs-, Bildungs- 4: 3 (95)
eel [i:l] der Aal 3
effect (on) [ɪˈfekt] die (Aus-)Wirkung (auf), der Einfluss (auf); der Effekt 2
effective [ɪˈfektɪv] effektiv, wirksam 2
effort [ˈefət] die Anstrengung, die Mühe 4: 1 (34) **make an effort** sich Mühe geben 4: 1 (34)
e.g. [i: ˈdʒi:] *(aus dem Lateinischen)* z. B. (zum Beispiel) 3
egg [eg] das Ei 1
eight [eɪt] acht 1
eighteen [eɪˈti:n] achtzehn 1
eighties [ˈeɪti:z]: **the 1980s** die Neunzehnhundertachtzigerjahre 3
eighty [ˈeɪti] achtzig 1
either [ˈaɪðə]:
1. beide; eine/r/s *(von zweien)* 4: 3 (92)
not … either auch nicht 3
2. **either … or …** entweder … oder … 4: 1 (19)
elderly [ˈeldəli]:
1. ältere(r, s) 4: 1 (31)
2. **the elderly** die Älteren, ältere Menschen 4: 1 (31)
electric [ɪˈlektrɪk] elektrisch, Elektro- 1
electricity [ɪlekˈtrɪsəti] der Strom, die Elektrizität 4: 1 (21)
electro [ɪˈlektrəʊ] der Electro, die Elektromusik 2
electronic [ɪlekˈtrɒnɪk] elektronisch 2
electronics *(pl)* [ɪlekˈtrɒnɪks] die Elektronik; die elektronischen Geräte 2
elementary school [elɪˈmentri sku:l] *(AE)* die Grundschule 4: 3 (88)
elephant [ˈelɪfənt] der Elefant 1
elevator [ˈelɪveɪtə] *(AE)* der Lift *(Aufzug)* 4: 1 (20)
eleven [ɪˈlevən] elf 1
else [els]: **everybody/everyone else** alle anderen; jede/r andere 2 **no one else** niemand anders, niemand sonst 2 **somebody/someone else** jemand anders 2 **What else?** Was sonst noch? 1
email [ˈi:meɪl]:
1. die E-Mail 3
2. **email sb.** jm. mailen, eine E-Mail schicken 3
embarrass sb. [ɪmˈbærəs] jn. in Verlegenheit bringen, jn. bloßstellen, jm. peinlich sein 2
embarrassed [ɪmˈbærəst] verlegen, peinlich berührt 2
embarrassing [ɪmˈbærəsɪŋ] peinlich 2
emigrant [ˈemɪgrənt] der Auswanderer, die Auswanderin 4: 1 (24)
emigrate [ˈemɪgreɪt] auswandern, emigrieren 4: 1 (24)
emigration [emɪˈgreɪʃn] die Auswanderung 4: 1 (24)
emotion [ɪˈməʊʃn] die Emotion, das Gefühl 3
emotional [ɪˈməʊʃənl] emotional 3
employ sb. [ɪmˈplɔɪ] jn. anstellen, beschäftigen 4: 3 (94)
employee [ɪmˈplɔɪi:] der/die Arbeitnehmer/in 4: 3 (94)
employer [ɪmˈplɔɪə] der/die Arbeitgeber/in 4: 3 (94)
employment [ɪmˈplɔɪmənt] die Arbeit, die Anstellung 4: 3 (94)
empty [ˈempti]:
1. leer 2
2. leeren 2
encourage [ɪnˈkʌrɪdʒ] ermutigen, ermuntern; unterstützen 4: 3 (100)
encouragement [ɪnˈkʌrɪdʒmənt] die Ermunterung, die Ermutigung; die Unterstützung 4: 3 (100)
encouraging [ɪnˈkʌrɪdʒɪŋ] ermutigend 4: 3 (100)
end [end]:
1. enden; beenden 1
2. das Ende, der Schluss 1
at the end (of) am Ende (von) 1 **in the end** schließlich; zum Schluss 1
endangered [ɪnˈdeɪndʒəd] gefährdet, vom Aussterben bedroht 4: 4 (123)
ending [ˈendɪŋ] die Endung; das Ende *(Text, Geschichte)* 2
endless [ˈendləs] endlos 3
enemy [ˈenəmi] der/die Feind/in 3
energetic [enəˈdʒetɪk] aktiv, tatkräftig, energiegeladen 2
energy [ˈenədʒi] die Energie 2
enjoy [ɪnˈdʒɔɪ] genießen 1 **enjoy doing sth.** es genießen, etwas zu tun 1 **Enjoy yourselves.** Viel Spaß! Amüsiert euch gut! 3 **Enjoy!** Viel Vergnügen! / Guten Appetit! 1
enough [ɪˈnʌf] genug 1
enter [ˈentə] eintreten, betreten; einreisen *(in ein Land)*, hineinfahren *(in eine Straße)* 4: 3 (97)
entertain sb. [entəˈteɪn] jn. unterhalten 4: 1 (21)
entertaining [entəˈteɪnɪŋ] unterhaltsam 4: 1 (21)
entertainment [entəˈteɪnmənt] das Entertainment, die Unterhaltung 4: 1 (21)
enthusiastic (about) [ɪnθju:ziˈæstɪk] begeistert (von) 4: 1 (35)
entrance [ˈentrəns] der Eingang; der Zutritt 4: 3 (97) **gain entrance (to)** sich Zutritt verschaffen (zu/nach/in) 4: 3 (97)
environment [ɪnˈvaɪrənmənt] die Umwelt; das Umfeld, die Umgebung 3
equal [ˈi:kwəl] gleich(berechtigt) 4: 3 (99)
equality [iˈkwɒləti] die Gleichberechtigung, die Gleichheit 4: 3 (99)
equipment *(no pl)* [ɪˈkwɪpmənt] die Ausrüstung 2
escalator [ˈeskəleɪtə] die Rolltreppe 3
especially [ɪˈspeʃəli] insbesondere 2
essay (on/about) [ˈeseɪ] der Aufsatz (über) 4: 4 (120)
estate [ɪˈsteɪt] die Wohnsiedlung; das Gewerbegebiet 1
°etc. [etˈsetərə] *(aus dem Lateinischen)* usw. (und so weiter)
ethnic [ˈeθnɪk] ethnisch, Volks- 4: 1 (22)
EU (= European Union) [i: ˈju:] die EU (Europäische Union) 3
euro [ˈjʊərəʊ], *pl* **euros** der Euro 1
European Union [jʊərəpi:ən ˈju:niən] die Europäische Union 3
even [ˈi:vn] sogar, selbst 2 **even if** selbst wenn, sogar wenn 2 **not even** nicht einmal 2 **°even though** auch wenn, obwohl *(betont)*
evening [ˈi:vnɪŋ] der Abend 1 **in the evening** abends, am Abend 1
event [ɪˈvent] das Ereignis 2

eventually [ɪ'ventʃuəli] letztendlich, schließlich 3
ever ['evə] jemals, schon einmal 2 **the best son ever** der beste Sohn überhaupt / der beste Sohn, den man sich wünschen kann 1
every ['evri] jede(r, s) 1 **every 30 minutes** alle 30 Minuten 1
everybody ['evribɒdi] jeder; alle 1 **Hello everybody!** Hallo allerseits! 1
everyday ['evrideɪ] alltäglich, Alltags- 4: 2 (52)
everyday life [evrideɪ 'laɪf] der Alltag 4: 2 (52)
everyone ['evriwʌn] jeder, alle 1
everything ['evriθɪŋ] alles 2
everywhere ['evriweə] überall 1
exact [ɪg'zækt] genau, exakt 3
exam [ɪg'zæm] *siehe* **examination**
examination [ɪgzæmɪ'neɪʃn] *infml auch* **exam** die Prüfung 4: 3 (99) **take/do an exam(ination)** eine Prüfung machen 4: 3 (99)
example [ɪg'zɑːmpl] das Beispiel 1 **for example** zum Beispiel 1
excellent ['eksələnt] ausgezeichnet, hervorragend 3
except (for) [ɪk'sept] außer, bis auf 3
exchange [ɪks'tʃeɪndʒ]:
1. der Schüleraustausch; der Austausch, der Wechsel 3
2. tauschen, austauschen 3
exchange class [ɪks'tʃeɪndʒ klɑːs] *die Schulklasse, die am Schüleraustausch teilnimmt* 3
exchange partner [ɪks'tʃeɪndʒ pɑːtnə] der/die Austauschpartner/in 3
exchange student [ɪks'tʃeɪndʒ stjuːdnt] der/die Austauschschüler/in 3
excited [ɪk'saɪtɪd] aufgeregt, gespannt 2
exciting [ɪk'saɪtɪŋ] aufregend 1
exclamation mark [ekskləˈmeɪʃn mɑːk] das Ausrufezeichen 4: 1 (22)
Excuse me, ... [ɪks'kjuːz miː] Entschuldigung, ... / Entschuldigen Sie, ... 1
exercise ['eksəsaɪz] die Übung, die Aufgabe 1
exercise book ['eksəsaɪz bʊk] das Schulheft, das Übungsheft 1
exhibition [eksɪ'bɪʃn] die Ausstellung; die Messe 4: 4 (132)
exit ['eksɪt]:
1. der Ausgang; der Austritt; die Ausfahrt 3
2. aussteigen; hinausgehen, *(einen Ort)* verlassen 3
expect [ɪk'spekt] erwarten 4: 5 (156)
expectation [ekspek'teɪʃn] die Erwartung 4: 5 (156)
expensive [ɪk'spensɪv] teuer 1
experience [ɪk'spɪəriəns]:
1. die Erfahrung; das Erlebnis 2
2. **experience sth.** etwas erfahren; erleben 2
expert ['ekspɜːt] der Experte, die Expertin 2
explain sth. to sb. [ɪk'spleɪn] jm. etwas erklären 1
explanation [ekspləˈneɪʃn] die Erklärung 2
exploration [ekspləˈreɪʃn] die Erforschung, die Erkundung 3
explore [ɪk'splɔː] erforschen, erkunden 3
explorer [ɪk'splɔːrə] der/die Forschungsreisende, der/die Entdecker/in 3
express [ɪk'spres] ausdrücken, zum Ausdruck bringen 4: 4 (125)
expression [ɪk'spreʃn] der Ausdruck 4: 4 (125)
extra ['ekstrə] Extra-, zusätzliche(r, s) 2
°extra-terrestrial [ekstrətəˈrestriəl]:
1. das außerirdische Lebewesen
2. außerirdisch
extract ['ekstrækt] der Auszug *(aus einem Buch, Film)* 4: 5 (159)
extreme [ɪk'striːm]:
1. das Extrem 4: 2 (60)
2. extrem 4: 2 (60)
eye [aɪ] das Auge 2
eyed [eɪd]: **a white-eyed animal** ein Tier mit weißen Augen 4: 5 (154)

F

face [feɪs] das Gesicht 1
fact [fækt] die Tatsache 2 **in fact** tatsächlich, in Wirklichkeit, genau genommen 2
factory ['fæktri] die Fabrik 3
fairly ['feəli] ziemlich, recht 4: 2 (60)
fake [feɪk]:
1. falsch, gefälscht 3
2. der/das Fake, die Fälschung 3
3. **fake sth.** etwas faken, fälschen, vortäuschen 3
fall [fɔːl], **fell, fallen** fallen; hinfallen 2 **fall asleep** einschlafen 2 **fall off** herunterfallen 2 **fall over** hinfallen, umkippen 4: 5 (154)
fallen ['fɔːlən] *siehe* **fall**
falls *(pl)* [fɔːlz] der Wasserfall *(besonders in Namen)* 4: 5 (150/151)
false [fɔːls] falsch, unrichtig 1
false friend [fɔːls 'frend] der „falsche Freund" *(Übersetzungsfalle)* 2
fame [feɪm] der Ruhm 2
family ['fæməli] die Familie 1
family name ['fæməli neɪm] der Familienname, der Nachname 1
famous (for) ['feɪməs] berühmt (für, wegen) 2
fancy ['fænsi] ausgefallen, extravagant, schick 4: 4 (125)
fantastic [fæn'tæstɪk] fantastisch 4: 2 (69)
fantasy ['fæntəsi] die Fantasie; die Fantasy *(Literatur-, Filmgattung)* 4: 2 (69)
far [fɑː] weit (entfernt) 2 **so far** bis jetzt, bis hierher 2
farm [fɑːm] der Bauernhof, die Farm 2
farmer ['fɑːmə] der Bauer, die Bäuerin; der/die Landwirt/in 4: 1 (16/17)
fascinating ['fæsɪneɪtɪŋ] faszinierend 4: 4 (129)
fashion ['fæʃn] die Mode, die Fashion 3
fast [fɑːst] schnell 1
fast [fɑːst]:
1. fasten 2
2. das Fasten, die Fastenzeit 2 **break the fast** das Fasten brechen 2
fast fashion [fɑːst 'fæʃn] die Fast Fashion *(„schnelle Mode", die zu niedrigen Preisen verkauft und nur kurz getragen wird)* 3
fat [fæt]:
1. das Fett 4: 2 (60)
2. dick, fett 4: 2 (60)
father ['fɑːðə] der Vater 2
fault [fɔːlt] der Fehler; die Schuld 3
favourite ['feɪvərɪt]:
1. Lieblings- 1
2. der Liebling, der/die Favorit/in 1
feather ['feðə] die Feder *(eines Vogels)* 4: 4 (123)
feature ['fiːtʃə] das Merkmal, die Eigenschaft 3
February ['februəri] der Februar 1
fed [fed] *siehe* **feed**
fee [fiː] die Gebühr; das Honorar; der (Mitglieds-)Beitrag 4: 3 (92)
feed [fiːd], **fed, fed** füttern; ernähren 2
feel [fiːl]:
1. die Stimmung, die Atmosphäre, das „Feeling" 4: 3 (85) **small-town feel** die Kleinstadt-Atmosphäre 4: 3 (85)
2. **feel, felt, felt** sich fühlen; fühlen 1 **feel sorry for sb.** Mitleid haben mit jm. 1
feeling ['fiːlɪŋ] das Gefühl 2
feet [fiːt] *Plural von* **foot**
fell [fel] *siehe* **fall**
felt [felt] *siehe* **feel**
female ['fiːmeɪl]:
1. weiblich 4: 3 (98)
2. die Frau 4: 3 (98)
ferry ['feri] die Fähre 2
festival ['festɪvl] das Fest(ival) 2
few [fjuː] wenige 3 **a few** ein paar, einige 2 **in the last few weeks** in den letzten paar Wochen 2
field [fiːld]:
1. das Feld; die Weide; die Wiese 1 **in the field** auf der Weide 1
2. das Spielfeld, der Platz *(im Sport, z. B. Fußballplatz)* 1 **on the field** auf dem Spielfeld, auf dem Platz 1
fifteen [fɪf'tiːn] fünfzehn 1
fifth [fɪfθ]: **one fifth** ein Fünftel 4: 4 (122)
fifty ['fɪfti] fünfzig 1
fight [faɪt]:
1. der Kampf; der Streit 2 **have a fight** sich prügeln; sich streiten 2
2. **fight, fought, fought** kämpfen, bekämpfen 2 **fight back** sich wehren 4: 3 (98)

fighter ['faɪtə] der/die Kämpfer/in 2
figure ['fɪgə] die Figur 3
°figure sth. out [fɪgər 'aʊt] etwas (heraus)finden, durchschauen, aus etwas schlau werden
file [faɪl] die Datei; der Ordner, die Liste 1
fill [fɪl]: **fill (up)** (auf)füllen; sich füllen 4: 1 (31) **it fills back up** er/es füllt sich wieder, er/es wird wieder voll 4: 1 (31)
film [fɪlm]:
1. der Film 1
2. **film sth.** etwas filmen 3
filter ['fɪltə]:
1. der Filter 3
2. filtern 3
final ['faɪnl] endgültige(r, s), letzte(r, s), End-, Abschluss- 4: 1 (34) **final product** das Endprodukt 4: 1 (34)
finally ['faɪnəli] schließlich, endlich 1
find [faɪnd], **found, found** finden 1 **find out (about)** herausfinden; sich informieren (über) 1
fine [faɪn]: **I'm fine.** Mir geht es gut. 1
finger ['fɪŋgə] der Finger 1 **cross your fingers** die Daumen drücken/halten *(jm. Glück / gutes Gelingen wünschen)* 3 **tap your fingers** mit den Fingern klopfen 3
finish ['fɪnɪʃ]:
1. das Ende, das Ziel (*(z. B. beim Sport)*) 2
2. enden; beenden, zu Ende machen 2
fire ['faɪə] das Feuer 2 **be on fire** brennen 4: 4 (130) **catch fire** Feuer fangen, in Brand geraten 4: 4 (130) **set sth. on fire** etwas in Brand setzen, etwas anzünden 4: 4 (130) **stop a fire** ein Feuer löschen 2
fire engine ['faɪər endʒɪn] das Feuerwehrauto 2
fire pit ['faɪə pɪt] die Feuergrube, die Feuerstelle *(z. B. für Lagerfeuer)* 4: 4 (130)
firefighter ['faɪəfaɪtə] der Feuerwehrmann, die Feuerwehrfrau 2
°firefighting ['faɪəfaɪtɪŋ] die Brandbekämpfung
firework ['faɪəwɜːk] der Feuerwerkskörper 2 **fireworks** *(pl)* das Feuerwerk 2
first [fɜːst]:
1. erste(r, s) 1
2. zuerst, als Erstes 1
at first zuerst, am Anfang 1
first name ['fɜːst neɪm] der Vorname 1
First Nations (people) *(pl)* [fɜːst 'neɪʃnz] *die Ureinwohner/innen Kanadas* 4: 5 (150/151)
°first-timer [fɜːst 'taɪmə] *jd., der etw. zum ersten Mal macht*
Firstly, ... ['fɜːstli] Erstens ... 4: 4 (119)
fish [fɪʃ]:
1. fischen, angeln 3
2. *pl* **fish** der Fisch 1

fish and chip shop [fɪʃ ən 'tʃɪp ʃɒp] *die Imbissstube, die Fisch mit Pommes Frites verkauft* 1
fishing ['fɪʃɪŋ] das Fischen, das Angeln; die Fischerei 3
fit [fɪt]:
1. passen (zu); sitzen *(Kleidung)* 4: (12/13)
2. die Passform, der Sitz *(Kleidung)* 4: (12/13)
five [faɪv] fünf 1
fix sth. [fɪks] *(infml)* etwas in Ordnung bringen; reparieren 4: 1 (31)
flag [flæg] die Fahne, die Flagge 2
°flambé ['flɒmbeɪ] flambiert
flash [flæʃ]:
1. der Blitz *(Kamera)*; das Aufblitzen; das Blinklicht 3
2. blinken, blitzen (mit); *(Telefon)* mit Blitz fotografieren 3
flat [flæt] die Wohnung 1 **block of flats** das Mehrfamilienhaus 1
flat [flæt] flach, eben; *(Reifen)* platt 4: 4 (116/117)
flew [fluː] *siehe* **fly**
flexible ['fleksəbl] flexibel 4: 3 (93)
flood [flʌd]:
1. die Überschwemmung, das Hochwasser; die Flut 4: 2 (64)
2. überschwemmen, überfluten 4: 2 (64)
be flooded unter Wasser stehen 4: 2 (64)
floor [flɔː]:
1. der Fußboden 1
2. die Etage, der Stock, das Stockwerk 1
flour ['flaʊə] das Mehl 1
flow [fləʊ]:
1. der Fluss; der Strom 3
2. fließen; strömen 3
flower ['flaʊə] die Blume; die Blüte 2
flowerpot ['flaʊəpɒt] der Blumentopf 2
flown [fləʊn] *siehe* **fly**
fly [flaɪ], **flew, flown** fliegen 1
focus (on) ['fəʊkəs]:
1. sich konzentrieren (auf) 4: 1 (27)
2. der Mittelpunkt, der Hauptpunkt, der Schwerpunkt (auf) 4: 1 (27)
focus of attention Zentrum der Aufmerksamkeit 4: 1 (27)
fold [fəʊld] falten 2
folder ['fəʊldə] die Mappe, der Ordner 1
folks [fəʊks] *(pl, infml)* die Leute 4: 1 (30)
follow ['fɒləʊ] (be)folgen; verfolgen 2
food [fuːd] das Essen, das Lebensmittel; das Futter 1
foot [fʊt], *pl* **feet**:
1. der Fuß *(Körperteil)* 2
2. der Fuß *(Längenmaß; ca. 30 cm)* 2
football ['fʊtbɔːl] der Fußball 1
footballer ['fʊtbɔːlə] der/die Fußballspieler/in 2
for [fɔː] für 1 **for 30 seconds** für 30 Sekunden, 30 Sekunden lang 1 **for 30 years** 30 Jahre (lang); seit 30 Jahren 3 **for a dare** als Mutprobe 2 **for a long time** seit langem; lange *(für eine lange Zeit)* 2 **for hours** seit Stunden, stundenlang 2 **for once** ausnahmsweise, dieses eine Mal 3 **for the first time** zum ersten Mal 2 **What's for homework?** Was haben wir als Hausaufgabe(n) auf? 1
force [fɔːs]:
1. der Zwang; die Gewalt; die Kraft 4: 4 (122)
2. **force sth.** etwas erzwingen 4: 4 (122)
force sb. to do sth. jn. zwingen, etwas zu tun 4: 4 (122)
foreground ['fɔːgraʊnd] der Vordergrund 3
°forehead ['fɔːhed] die Stirn
forest ['fɒrɪst] der Wald 2
°forestry ['fɒrɪstri] die Forstwirtschaft
forget [fə'get], **forgot, forgotten** vergessen 1 **Don't forget.** Vergiss (es) nicht. / Denk dran! 1
forgot [fə'gɒt] *siehe* **forget**
forgotten [fə'gɒtn] *siehe* **forget**
fork [fɔːk] die Gabel 1
form [fɔːm]:
1. (sich) formen, (sich) bilden 3
2. die Form, die Art 3
form of transport die Fortbewegungsart, die Art der Beförderung 3
3. das Formular 3
complete a form ein Formular ausfüllen 3
formal ['fɔːml] förmlich, formell 3
format ['fɔːmæt]:
1. das Format 3
2. formatieren 3
fortunately ['fɔːtʃənətli] zum Glück, glücklicherweise 3
forty ['fɔːti] vierzig 1
forward ['fɔːwəd]:
1. **forward sth. to sb.** etwas an jn. weiterleiten; jm. etwas nachsenden 3
2. **look forward to doing sth.** sich darauf freuen, etwas zu tun 2
look forward to sth. sich auf etwas freuen 2
fought [fɔːt] *siehe* **fight**
found [faʊnd]:
1. *siehe* **find**
2. gründen 4: 1 (25)
founder ['faʊndə] der/die Gründer/in 4: 1 (25)
four [fɔː] vier 1
fourteen [fɔː'tiːn] vierzehn 1
fox [fɒks] der Fuchs 4: 5 (152)
free [friː]:
1. kostenlos 1
for free kostenlos 2
2. frei 1
free time die Freizeit, die freie Zeit 1 **Are you free after school?** Hast du nach der Schule Zeit? 1
freedom ['friːdəm] die Freiheit 4: 1 (16/17)
freeze [friːz], **froze, frozen** (ge)frieren; erstarren 1

freeze-frame ['friːz freɪm] das Standbild *(Film)* 1
French fries [frentʃ 'fraɪz] *(pl, AE)* die Pommes frites 4: 1 (19)
frenemy ['frenəmi] der/die falsche Freund/in 3
frequent ['friːkwənt] häufig 4: 2 (64)
fresh [freʃ] frisch 3
freshman ['freʃmən], *pl* **freshmen** der/die Studienanfänger/in; der/die Anfänger/in in der High School 4: 3 (88)
Friday ['fraɪdeɪ], ['fraɪdi] der Freitag 1
fridge [frɪdʒ] der Kühlschrank 4: 1 (31)
fried [fraɪd] frittiert, gebraten 1
friend [frend] der/die Freund/in 1 **make friends** Freunde/-innen finden 2
friendly ['frendli] freundlich, nett 1
friendship ['frendʃɪp] die Freundschaft 3
fries *(pl)* [fraɪz]: **French fries** *(AE)* die Pommes frites 4: 1 (19)
fringe [frɪndʒ] der Rand, das Randgebiet 3
from [frɒm] von, aus 1 **Where are you from?** Wo kommst du her? 1
front [frʌnt] der vordere Teil, die Vorderseite 2 **at the front** vorne 2 **in front of** vor 1
froze [frəʊz] *siehe* **freeze**
frozen ['frəʊzn] *siehe* **freeze**
fruit [fruːt] das Obst 1
frustrate sb. [frʌ'streɪt] jn. frustrieren 4: 3 (98)
frustrated [frʌ'streɪtɪd] frustriert 4: 3 (98)
frustrating [frʌ'streɪtɪŋ] frustrierend 4: 3 (98)
frustration [frʌ'streɪʃn] die Frustration 4: 3 (98)
fry [fraɪ] braten; frittieren 1
full [fʊl]:
1. voll 2
full of ... voller ... 2
2. satt 2
full stop [fʊl 'stɒp] der Punkt *(Satzzeichen)* 4: 1 (22)
full-time [fʊl 'taɪm] Vollzeit-, Ganztags- 4: 3 (93)
fun [fʌn] der Spaß 1 **be fun** Spaß machen; lustig sein 1 **have fun** Spaß haben 1
fun run ['fʌn rʌn] der Volkslauf *(z. B. zum Geldsammeln für wohltätige Zwecke)* 2
°**function** ['fʌŋkʃn] die Funktion
funeral ['fjuːnərəl] die Beerdigung, das Begräbnis 4: 2 (62)
funk [fʌŋk] der Funk *(Musikstil)* 4: 2 (62)
funny ['fʌni]:
1. seltsam 1
2. witzig, lustig 1
What's funny about ...? Was ist lustig an ...? 1
fur [fɜː] das Fell *(Tiere)* 4: 5 (158)
furniture ['fɜːnɪtʃə] die Möbel(stücke) 1
further ['fɜːðə] weiter (entfernt) 4: 4 (131)
future ['fjuːtʃə]:
1. die Zukunft 2
2. zukünftige(r, s) 2

G

Gaelic ['geɪlɪk] Gälisch *(Sprache)* 3
game [geɪm]:
1. das Spiel 1
2. Computerspiele spielen 2
gap [gæp] die Lücke, der Abstand 3
garage ['gærɑːʒ] die Garage 1
garden ['gɑːdn] der Garten 1
garlic ['gɑːlɪk] der Knoblauch 1
gas [gæs]:
1. das Gas 4: 3 (85)
2. *(AE:)* das Benzin 4: 3 (85)
gate [geɪt] das Tor, das Gatter 1
gather ['gæðə] sammeln; (sich) versammeln; *(Sturm)* sich zusammenbrauen 4: 2 (64)
gave [geɪv] *siehe* **give**
gay [geɪ]:
1. der Schwule 2
2. schwul 2
general ['dʒenrəl] allgemein 4: 1 (18) **in general** im Allgemeinen, generell 4: 1 (18)
generate ['dʒenəreɪt] erzeugen, generieren 3
generation [dʒenə'reɪʃn] die Erzeugung, die Generierung 3
generator ['dʒenəreɪtə] der Generator 3
generous ['dʒenərəs] großzügig 2
gentlemen ['dʒentlmən]: **ladies and gentlemen** sehr geehrte Damen und Herren 3
°**geographical** [dʒiːə'græfɪkl] geographisch
geography [dʒi'ɒgrəfi] die Geografie, die Erdkunde 1
get [get], **got, got**:
1. bekommen 1
get sth. *(sich etwas)* holen/besorgen 1
2. werden 1
Get better/well soon! Gute Besserung! / Werde bald gesund! 2 **get dressed** sich anziehen 1 **get ready (for)** sich fertig machen (für), sich vorbereiten (auf) 2 **get warm** warm werden 1
3. **get (to)** gelangen, (hin)kommen (nach) 2
get around sich fortbewegen *(mobil sein)* 4: 3 (85) **get away with sth.** mit etwas durchkommen, mit etwas (ungestraft) davonkommen 4: 2 (57) **get in touch (with)** (sich) in Verbindung setzen (mit), Kontakt aufnehmen (zu) 3 **get off a train/bus** aus einem Zug/Bus aussteigen 2 **get off your bike/your horse** vom Fahrrad / vom Pferd absteigen 2 **get on a train/bus** in einen Zug/Bus einsteigen 2 **get up** aufstehen 1
4. **get sth.** etwas verstehen, mitbekommen 3
Don't get me wrong. Versteh(t) mich nicht falsch. 3
ghost [gəʊst] der Geist, das Gespenst 2
ghost tour ['gəʊst tʊə] die Geistertour *(Stadtführung mit gruseligen Themen/Elementen)* 2
gift [gɪft] das Geschenk, die Gabe; das Talent 2
gift shop ['gɪft ʃɒp] der Geschenk(artikel)laden, der Souvenirladen 2
girl [gɜːl] das Mädchen 1
girlfriend ['gɜːlfrend] die (feste) Freundin 2
give [gɪv], **gave, given** geben 1 **give sth. up** etwas aufgeben, aufhören mit etwas 4: 5 (157) **give up** aufgeben 4: 5 (157) **give up your seat for/to sb.** für jn. aufstehen *(z. B. im Bus)* 4: 5 (157)
°**giveaway** ['gɪvəweɪ] *(infml)* die die Lebensmitteltafel, die Kleiderkammer *(wo Dinge an Bedürftige verschenkt werden)*
given ['gɪvn] *siehe* **give**
glad [glæd]: **be glad** froh sein 2
glass [glɑːs] das Glas 1 **a glass of milk** ein Glas Milch 1
glasses *(pl)* ['glɑːsɪz] die Brille 2
global ['gləʊbl] global, weltweit 2
globe [gləʊb] der Globus; die Kugel 2 **across the globe** auf der ganzen Welt 2 **all (a)round the globe** auf der ganzen Welt 2
glove [glʌv] der Handschuh 2
glow [gləʊ]:
1. glühen, leuchten, strahlen 4: 5 (157)
2. das Leuchten, der Schein *(z. B. eines Feuers)* 4: 5 (157)
glue [gluː] der Kleber, der Klebstoff 1
glue stick ['gluː stɪk] der Klebestift 1
go [gəʊ], **went, gone**:
1. gehen, fahren 1
go back to zurückführen nach/in, zurückgehen auf/zu 3 **go down** (Sonne) untergehen 2 **go on (about sb./sth.)** die ganze Zeit (über jn./etwas) reden 4: 1 (30) **go out** rausgehen, weggehen; ausgehen 3 **go up** aufgehen *(Sonne)*; hochgehen; (an)steigen 1 **How's it going?** *(infml)* Wie geht's? / Wie läuft's? 2 **I must go.** Ich muss Schluss machen. *(am Telefon/Briefschluss)* 1 **There you go.** Hier, bitte schön.; *(auch:)* Da hast du's! / Na siehst du! 3
2. werden 1
go green grün/umweltfreundlich werden 1
3. **I'm going to ...** ich werde ... *(Plan, Vorhaben)* 2
goal [gəʊl] das Ziel *(Absicht, Lebensziel)*; das Tor *(im Sport)* 3
goalkeeper ['gəʊlkiːpə] der Torwart, die Torhüterin 3
goat [gəʊt] die Ziege 1

god [gɒd] der Gott 2
gold [gəʊld]:
1. das Gold 1
2. goldfarben 1
gold rush ['gəʊld rʌʃ] der Goldrausch 4: 5 (152)
golden ['gəʊldn] golden, aus Gold 3
gone [gɒn] *siehe* **go** **be gone** weg sein 2
good [gʊd]:
1. brav 1
2. gut 1
be good with ... gut umgehen können mit ... 1 **too much of a good thing** zu viel des Guten 2
Goodbye. [gʊd'baɪ] Auf Wiedersehen! 1
goods *(pl)* [gʊdz] die Waren, die Güter 4: 1 (31)
got [gɒt] *siehe* **get** °**have got** haben
°**gotten** ['gɒtn] *(AE)* *3. Form von* (to) get
govern ['gʌvn] regieren 4: 2 (57)
government ['gʌvənmənt] die Regierung 3
governor ['gʌvənə] der/die Gouverneur/in 4: 2 (57)
grab [græb] packen, greifen (nach), ergreifen 4: 5 (154)
grade [greɪd] *(AE)* die Klasse, das Schuljahr 4: 3 (88)
graduate ['grædʒuət] der/die Hochschulabsolvent/in 4: 2 (57)
graduate (from) ['grædʒueɪt] den Abschluss machen (an) *(Schule, Hochschule)* 4: 2 (57)
graduation [grædʒu'eɪʃn] der (Schul-/Universitäts-)Abschluss 4: 2 (57)
gram (g) [græm] das Gramm 1
grammar ['græmə] die Grammatik 3
grandfather ['grænfɑːðə] der Großvater 4: 1 (23)
grandma ['grænmɑː] die Oma 1
grandmother ['grænmʌðə] die Großmutter 4: 1 (23)
grandpa ['grænpɑː] der Opa 1
grandparents *(pl)* ['grænpeərənts] die Großeltern 2
°**graphic novel** [græfɪk 'nɒvl] der Bildroman, der Comicroman
grass [grɑːs] das Gras; der Rasen 3
grateful ['greɪtfl]: **be grateful (to sb. for doing sth.)** (jm. für etwas) dankbar sein 2
°**gray** [greɪ] *(AE)* grau
great [greɪt]:
1. großartig, toll 1
2. groß *(bedeutend, angesehen)* 2
Great Britain [greɪt 'brɪtn] Großbritannien 1
great-grandfather [greɪt 'grænfɑːðə] der Urgroßvater 4: 4 (122)
great-grandmother [greɪt 'grænmʌðə] die Urgroßmutter 4: 4 (122)
great-great-grandfather [greɪt greɪt 'grænfɑːðə] der Ururgroßvater 4: 4 (122)
great-great-grandmother [greɪt greɪt 'grænmʌðə] die Ururgroßmutter 4: 4 (122)
green [griːn]:
1. grün 1
2. umweltbewusst 1
go green grün/umweltfreundlich werden 1
greet [griːt] begrüßen 1
greeting ['griːtɪŋ] die Begrüßung; der Gruß 1
grew [gruː] *siehe* **grow**
grey [greɪ] grau 1
grim [grɪm] grimmig 4: 5 (156)
groan [grəʊn]:
1. stöhnen 4: 3 (96)
2. das Stöhnen 4: 3 (96)
groom [gruːm] der Bräutigam 2
groomsman ['gruːmzmən], *pl* **groomsmen** der Trauzeuge *(des Bräutigams)* 2
gross [grəʊs] *(infml)* widerlich 4: 3 (97)
ground [graʊnd] der (Erd-)Boden 1
ground floor [graʊnd 'flɔː] das Erdgeschoss 1
Ground Zero [graʊnd 'zɪərəʊ] *hier: das Gelände des am 11. September 2001 zerstörten World Trade Centers in New York City* 4: 1 (20)
group [gruːp]:
1. die Gruppe 1
2. gruppieren 1
grow [grəʊ], **grew, grown**:
1. anbauen 4: 4 (122)
2. werden 4: 4 (122)
3. wachsen 2
grow up aufwachsen; erwachsen werden 2
grown [grəʊn] *siehe* **grow**
guard [gɑːd]:
1. schützen, bewachen 3
2. der/die Wärter/in; die Wache 3
Changing of the Guards die Wachablösung 3 **security guard** der/die Sicherheitsbedienstete 4: 2 (52)
guess [ges]:
1. die Vermutung 1
Make/Have/Take a guess! Rate mal! 1
2. (er)raten 1
Guess what! Stell dir / Stellt euch (mal) vor! 1 **I guess** ich glaube, ich nehme an 1
guest [gest] der Gast 3
guide [gaɪd]:
1. führen, leiten 1
2. *(kurz für* **tour guide**) der/die Reiseleiter/in; der/die Fremdenführer/in 1
guide dog ['gaɪd dɒg] der Blindenhund 1
guitar [gɪ'tɑː] die Gitarre 1
°**gumbo** ['gʌmbəʊ] *der Eintopf mit Huhn bzw. Meeresfrüchten und Okra*
gun [gʌn] die Schusswaffe, die Pistole 4: 3 (88)
gun licence ['gʌn laɪsns] der Waffenschein 4: 3 (95)
guy [gaɪ] der Typ, der Kerl 2 **guys** *(pl, infml)* Leute *(Anrede)* 1
gym [dʒɪm] *siehe* **gymnasium**
gymnasia [dʒɪm'neɪziə] *Plural von* **gymnasium**
gymnasium [dʒɪm'neɪziəm], *pl* **gymnasiums** *or* **gymnasia** *kurz auch* **gym** die Turnhalle, die Sporthalle; das Fitnessstudio 4: 1 (31)
gymnast ['dʒɪmnæst] der/die Turner/in 3
gymnastics [dʒɪm'næstɪks] die Gymnastik, das Turnen 3

H

habit ['hæbɪt] die (An-)Gewohnheit 3
had [hæd] *siehe* **have**
hail [heɪl]:
1. der Hagel 4: 2 (64)
2. hageln 4: 2 (64)
hailstone ['heɪlstəʊn] das Hagelkorn 4: 2 (64)
hair [heə] das Haar, die Haare 2
haircut ['heəkʌt] der Haarschnitt, die Frisur; das Haareschneiden 4: 3 (93)
hairdresser ['heədresə] der/die Friseur/in 2
hairdresser's ['heədresəz] der Friseursalon 2
haired [heəd]: **a grey-haired dog** ein Hund mit grauem Fell 4: 5 (154)
half [hɑːf]:
1. halbe(r, s) 3
half a lemon / an orange / an hour eine halbe Zitrone/Orange/Stunde 2
half full halb voll 3 **half past 6** halb 7 2
2. *pl* **halves** die Hälfte; *(Fußball)* die Halbzeit 3
half-time [hɑːf 'taɪm] die Halbzeit(pause) 3
halfway [hɑːf'weɪ] auf halbem Wege, halb(wegs) 3
hall [hɔːl]:
1. der Flur, die Diele 1
2. die Halle, der Saal 1
sports hall die Sporthalle 1
halves [hɑːvz] *Plural von* **half**
ham [hæm] der Schinken 1
hamster ['hæmstə] der Hamster 1
hand [hænd] die Hand 1 **On the one hand ...** Einerseits ... 4: 3 (85) **On the other hand ...** Andererseits ... 4: 3 (85)
put your hand up / put up your hand sich melden, aufzeigen 1 **shake sb.'s hand / shake sb. by the hand** jm. die Hand schütteln/geben 3
handle ['hændl]:
1. der Griff, der Handgriff 3
2. **handle sth.** mit etwas umgehen, etwas handhaben 3
hang [hæŋ], **hung, hung** hängen 4: 5 (157) **hang out** rumhängen, abhängen 1
happen (to sb.) ['hæpən] (jm.) geschehen, passieren 1
happiness ['hæpinəs] das Glück, die Zufriedenheit 2

happy [ˈhæpi] glücklich, froh 1 **Happy birthday!** Herzlichen Glückwunsch zum Geburtstag! 1 **be happy to do sth.** gerne etwas tun 4: 3 (93)
harbour [ˈhɑːbə] der Hafen 4: 1 (20)
hard [hɑːd] schwer, schwierig; hart 1 **think hard** scharf nachdenken 2
hard-working [hɑːd ˈwɜːkɪŋ] fleißig 2
hardly [ˈhɑːdli] kaum 4: 1 (30)
has [hæz], [həz]: **he/she/it has** er/sie/es hat 1
hashtag [ˈhæʃtæg] das/der Hashtag *(Rautezeichen in einem elektronischen Text)* 4: 2 (52)
hat [hæt] der Hut, die Mütze 1
hate [heɪt]:
1. hassen 1
2. der Hass 1
°**hate on sb.** über jn. herziehen, jn. haten *(in sozialen Medien)*
have [hæv], **had, had** haben 1 **have (food)** (Nahrung/etwas) essen; *(im Restaurant:)* nehmen 2 **have to do sth.** etwas tun müssen 2 **I have to go.** Ich muss Schluss machen. *(am Telefon/Briefschluss)* 2 **I'll have ...** Ich nehme ... *(beim Essen, z. B. im Restaurant)* 3 °**have got** haben
he [hiː] er 1 **he's (= he is)** er ist 1
head [hed] der Kopf 1 **have your head in the clouds** in Gedanken verloren oder unrealistisch sein 1 **shake your head** den Kopf schütteln 3
head student [hed ˈstjuːdnt] der/die Schulsprecher/in; der/die Vertrauensschüler/in 2
head teacher [ˈhed tiːtʃə] der/die Schulleiter/in; der/die Direktor/in 2
headache [ˈhedeɪk] die Kopfschmerzen 2 **have a headache** Kopfschmerzen haben 2
headdress [ˈheddres] der Kopfschmuck 4: 4 (124)
heading [ˈhedɪŋ] die Überschrift 1
headline [ˈhedlaɪn] die Überschrift 4: 3 (87)
headphones *(pl)* [ˈhedfəʊnz] der Kopfhörer 1
headpiece [ˈhedpiːs] der Kopfschmuck 3
health [helθ] die Gesundheit 1 **in sickness or in health** wenn man krank oder gesund ist 2
healthcare [ˈhelθkeə] die Gesundheitsfürsorge; die Gesundheitsversorgung 4: 3 (92)
healthy [ˈhelθi] gesund 1
hear [hɪə], **heard, heard** hören 1
heard [hɜːd] *siehe* **hear**
heart [hɑːt] das Herz 4: 2 (65) **by heart** auswendig 4: 2 (65)
heat [hiːt]:
1. die Hitze, die Wärme 1
2. erwärmen, erhitzen 1
heather [ˈheðə] das Heidekraut *(Pflanze)* 3
heavy [ˈhevi] schwer *(Gewicht; Mahlzeit)* 4: 2 (61)
height [haɪt] die Höhe, die Größe *(bei Menschen)* 2
held [held] *siehe* **hold**
helicopter [ˈhelɪkɒptə] der Hubschrauber 3
hell [hel] die Hölle 4: 5 (156) **Get the hell out of here** *(infml)*! Scher dich / Schert euch zum Teufel! / Verschwinde(t)! 4: 5 (156)
Hello. [həˈləʊ] Hallo. 1 **Hello everybody!** Hallo allerseits! 1
helmet [ˈhelmɪt] der Helm 2
help [help]:
1. die Hilfe 1
2. helfen 1
helper [ˈhelpə] der/die Helfer/in 3
helpful [ˈhelpfl] hilfsbereit; hilfreich, nützlich 1
helpless [ˈhelpləs] hilflos 3
her [hɜː], [hə]:
1. sie; ihr 1
like her wie sie 2
2. **her friends** ihre Freunde/Freundinnen 1
here [hɪə] hier; hierher 1 **Here you are.** Bitte schön. / Hier, bitte. 1
hero [ˈhɪərəʊ], *pl* **heroes** der/die Held/in 2
hers [hɜːz] ihrer, ihre, ihres *(zu „she")* 3
herself [hɜːˈself] sich (selbst) *(zu „she")* 3
Hi. [haɪ] Hallo. 1
hid [hɪd] *siehe* **hide**
hidden [ˈhɪdn] *siehe* **hide**
hide [haɪd], **hid, hidden** verstecken; sich verstecken 4: 1 (31)
high [haɪ] hoch 2
high school [ˈhaɪ skuːl] *(AE) die Schule für 14- bis 18-Jährige* 4: 2 (57)
highlight [ˈhaɪlaɪt]:
1. das Highlight *(Höhepunkt)* 1
2. hervorheben, markieren, unterstreichen 1
highway [ˈhaɪweɪ] *(AE)* die Fernstraße *(oft mit vier oder mehr Spuren)* 4: 3 (95)
hike [haɪk] wandern 1
hiker [ˈhaɪkə] der Wanderer, die Wanderin 3
hiking [ˈhaɪkɪŋ] das Wandern 1
hill [hɪl] der Hügel 2
him [hɪm] ihm, ihn 1
himself [hɪmˈself] sich (selbst) *(zu „he")* 2
hip-hopper [ˈhɪp hɒpə] der/die Hip-Hopper/in 4: 1 (20)
hire [ˈhaɪə]:
1. der Verleih, die Vermietung 3
2. mieten, leihen; *(Person:)* einstellen 3
his [hɪz]:
1. seiner, seine, seins *(zu „he")* 3
2. **his room** sein Zimmer 1
Hispanic [hɪˈspænɪk] hispanisch *(spanischer oder lateinamerikanischer Herkunft)* 4: 1 (25)
history [ˈhɪstri] die Geschichte *(vergangene Zeiten)* 1
hit [hɪt]:
1. der Hit 4: 1 (32)
2. **hit, hit, hit** stoßen gegen, zusammenstoßen mit; treffen auf 2
hold [həʊld], **held, held** halten 2 **hold a competition** einen Wettbewerb veranstalten, abhalten 4: 4 (132) °**hold sb. over** jn. über Wasser halten
holiday [ˈhɒlədeɪ] der Urlaub 1 **holidays** die Ferien 1 **on holiday** im/in den Urlaub 1
home [həʊm]:
1. das Heim, das Zuhause 1
at home zu Hause 1 **be home to (sb./sth.)** Heimat für jn./etwas sein, etwas beheimaten 3
2. nach Hause 1
go home nach Hause gehen 1
homeless [ˈhəʊmləs] obdachlos 3
homelessness [ˈhəʊmləsnəs] die Obdachlosigkeit 4: 1 (21)
hometown [həʊmˈtaʊn] die Heimatstadt 3
homework [ˈhəʊmwɜːk] die Hausaufgabe(n) 1 **do your homework** Hausaufgaben machen 1 **What's for homework?** Was haben wir als Hausaufgabe(n) auf? 1
honest [ˈɒnɪst] ehrlich 2
honesty [ˈɒnəsti] die Ehrlichkeit 2
honey [ˈhʌni] der Honig 1
hook [hʊk] der Haken, der Angelhaken 4: 5 (154)
hoop [huːp] der Korb *(Basketball)* 4: 1 (31)
hope [həʊp]:
1. hoffen 2
2. die Hoffnung 2
hopeful [ˈhəʊpfl] zuversichtlich, hoffnungsvoll 3
horizontal [hɒrɪˈzɒntl] waagerecht, horizontal 2
horoscope [ˈhɒrəskəʊp] das Horoskop 2
horrible [ˈhɒrəbl] schrecklich 1
horse [hɔːs] das Pferd 1
hospital [ˈhɒspɪtl] das Krankenhaus 1
host [həʊst]:
1. der/die Gastgeber/in 4: 1 (23)
2. der/die (Radio-/TV-)Moderator/in 4: 4 (129)
3. **host sth.** etwas veranstalten, ausrichten 4: 4 (129)
host dad [ˈhəʊst dæd] der Gastvater 4: 1 (23)
host family [ˈhəʊst fæməli] die Gastfamilie 4: 1 (23)
host mum [ˈhəʊst mʌm] die Gastmutter 4: 1 (23)
hostel [ˈhɒstl] das Hostel *(günstige Unterkunft für Reisende)* 2
hot [hɒt] heiß, warm 1
hot chocolate [hɒt ˈtʃɒklət] der Kakao, die heiße (Trink-)Schokolade 1
hot meal [hɒt ˈmiːl] die warme Mahlzeit 1
hotel [həʊˈtel] das Hotel 2

hour ['aʊə] die Stunde 1 **a two-hour class** ein zweistündiger Kurs 2 **opening hours** *(pl)* die Öffnungszeiten 4: 3 (85) **per hour** pro Stunde 1 **work long hours** lange arbeiten, Überstunden machen 4: 3 (85) **working hours** *(pl)* die Arbeitszeit(en) 4: 3 (85)
house [haʊs] das Haus 1
house-warming (party) ['haʊs wɔ:mɪŋ] die Einzugsfeier 2
household ['haʊshəʊld] der Haushalt; Haushalts- 4: 1 (31)
how [haʊ] wie 1 **How about ... ?** Wie wäre es mit ... ? 2 **How are you?** Wie geht's? / Wie geht es dir/euch/Ihnen? 1 **How much is/are ...?** Was (Wie viel) kostet/kosten ...? 2 **how to do sth.** wie man etwas tut / tun kann / tun soll 1
however [haʊ'evə]:
1. wie (auch) immer; egal, wie 4: 3 (97)
2. allerdings, jedoch 3
hug [hʌg]:
1. die Umarmung 2
2. **hug (sb.)** (jn.) umarmen; einander umarmen 2
huge [hju:dʒ] riesig, Riesen- 4: 3 (95)
human ['hju:mən]:
1. der Mensch 4: 2 (58)
2. menschlich 4: 2 (58)
human rights *(pl)* [hju:mən 'raɪts] Menschenrechte 4: 2 (58)
humanity [hju:'mænəti] die Menschheit; die Menschlichkeit 4: 2 (58)
humour ['hju:mə] der Humor 4: 5 (157) **sense of humour** der (Sinn für) Humor 4: 5 (157)
hundred ['hʌndrəd]: **a/one hundred** (ein)hundert 1 **in the 1700s (= the seventeen hundreds)** im 18. Jahrhundert 3
hung [hʌŋ] *siehe* **hang**
hungry ['hʌŋgri] hungrig 1 **I'm hungry.** Ich habe Hunger. 1
hunt [hʌnt]:
1. die Jagd 3
2. jagen 3
hunter ['hʌntə] der/die Jäger/in 3
hurricane ['hʌrɪkən] der Hurrikan, der Orkan 4: 2 (64)
hurry ['hʌri]:
1. sich beeilen; eilen 3
Hurry up! Beeil dich! / Beeilt euch! 3
2. die Eile 3
in a hurry in Eile 3
hurt [hɜ:t], **hurt, hurt** verletzen; wehtun 2 **be hurt** verletzt sein 2 **get hurt** sich verletzen 2
husband ['hʌzbənd] der (Ehe-)Mann 1
hyphen ['haɪfn] der Bindestrich; der Trennstrich 4: 1 (22)

I

I [aɪ] ich 1 **I'm (= I am)** ich bin 1
ice [aɪs] das Eis *(gefrorenes Wasser)* 4: 2 (64)
ice cream [aɪs 'kri:m] das (Speise-) Eis 1
ice rink ['aɪs rɪŋk] die Schlittschuhbahn 1
icing ['aɪsɪŋ] die Glasur, der Zuckerguss 1
icing sugar ['aɪsɪŋ ʃʊgə] der Puderzucker 1
icy ['aɪsi] eiskalt, eisig, vereist 4: 2 (64)
ID card [aɪ 'di kɑ:d] *siehe* **identity card**
idea [aɪ'dɪə] die Idee 1
identical (with) [aɪ'dentɪkl] identisch (mit) 3
identify [aɪ'dentɪfaɪ] (sich) identifizieren; erkennen 3 **identify (yourself) (as)** sich identifizieren (als); sich zu erkennen geben (als) 3
identity [aɪ'dentəti] die Identität 4: 4 (122)
identity card [aɪ'dentəti kɑ:d] *kurz auch* **ID card** der Personalausweis 3
if [ɪf]:
1. ob 1
2. wenn, falls 1
even if selbst wenn, sogar wenn 2
What if ...? Was wäre, wenn ...? 1
ignore [ɪg'nɔ:] nicht beachten, ignorieren 4: 1 (31)
ill [ɪl] krank 1
illness ['ɪlnəs] die Krankheit 1
image ['ɪmɪdʒ] das Bild, die Abbildung 3
°imaginary [ɪ'mædʒɪnəri] imaginär *(nur in der Vorstellung vorhanden)*
imaginative [ɪ'mædʒɪnətɪv] fantasievoll, einfallsreich, kreativ 2
imagine sth. [ɪ'mædʒɪn] sich etwas vorstellen 2 **imagine being/doing sth.** sich vorstellen, etwas zu sein / etwas zu tun 2
immigrant ['ɪmɪgrənt] der Einwanderer, die Einwanderin 4: 1 (24)
immigrate ['ɪmɪgreɪt] einwandern, immigrieren 4: 1 (24)
immigration [ɪmɪ'greɪʃn] die Einwanderung 4: 1 (24)
impatience [ɪm'peɪʃns] die Ungeduld 2
impatient [ɪm'peɪʃnt] ungeduldig 2
importance [ɪm'pɔ:tns] die Bedeutung, die Wichtigkeit 4: 4 (129)
important [ɪm'pɔ:tnt] wichtig 1 **What's important to you in a friend?** Was ist dir an/bei einem Freund / einer Freundin wichtig? 2
impossible [ɪm'pɒsəbl] unmöglich 3
impress [ɪm'pres] beeindrucken 4: 3 (88)
impression [ɪm'preʃn] der Eindruck 4: 3 (88)
improve [ɪm'pru:v] verbessern; sich verbessern 4: 2 (63)
in [ɪn] in; auf 1 **in a place** an einem Ort 2 **in English** auf Englisch 1 **in the afternoon** nachmittags, am Nachmittag 1 **in the country** auf dem Land 1 **in the evening** abends, am Abend 1 **in the field** auf der Weide 1 **in the morning** morgens, am Morgen 1 **in the photo** auf dem Foto 1 **in the picture** auf dem Bild 1 **in the sky** am Himmel 3 **in town** in der Stadt 1 **one in five** eine/r von fünf(en), jede/r fünfte 3 **What's important to you in a friend?** Was ist dir an/bei einem Freund / einer Freundin wichtig? 2
inappropriate [ɪnə'prəʊpriət] unangemessen, unpassend, ungeeignet 4: 3 (96)
inch [ɪntʃ] der Zoll *(Längenmaß = 2,54 cm)* 4: 4 (133)
include [ɪn'klu:d] (mit) einschließen 3
including [ɪn'klu:dɪŋ] einschließlich, inklusive 3
increase (by) [ɪn'kri:s] steigern, (sich) erhöhen; steigen, zunehmen (um) 4: 4 (134)
increase (in) ['ɪŋkri:s] der Anstieg, das Wachstum, die Zunahme (an/von) 4: 4 (134)
independent (of/from) [ɪndɪ'pendənt] unabhängig (von) 2
indirect [ɪndə'rekt] indirekt 3
indoor ['ɪndɔ:] im Haus/Gebäude, drinnen stattfindend 4: 3 (82/83)
indoors [ɪn'dɔ:z] drinnen; in einem Haus/Gebäude 4: 3 (82/83)
industrial [ɪn'dʌstriəl] Industrie-, industriell 3
industry ['ɪndəstri] die Industrie 3
inequality [ɪnɪ'kwɒləti] die Ungleichheit 4: 3 (99)
influence ['ɪnfluəns]:
1. beeinflussen 4: 2 (55)
2. **influence (on)** der Einfluss (auf) 4: 2 (55)
info ['ɪnfəʊ] *(infml)* die Info *(kurz für „Information")* 4: 4 (132)
informal [ɪn'fɔ:ml] informell, locker 3
information [ɪnfə'meɪʃn] die Information(en) 1
informative [ɪn'fɔ:mətɪv] informativ 3
inhabit (a place) [ɪn'hæbɪt] (einen Ort) bewohnen 4: 4 (128)
injustice [ɪn'dʒʌstɪs] die Ungerechtigkeit; das Unrecht 4: 2 (56)
°inning ['ɪnɪŋ] das Inning *(Spielabschnitt beim Baseballspiel)*
insect ['ɪnsekt] das Insekt 2
insensitive ['sensətɪv] gefühllos, unsensibel, taktlos 4: 4 (125)
inside [ɪn'saɪd]:
1. (dr)innen; nach (dr)innen *(Adv.)* 1
2. innerhalb (von) *(Präp.)* 1
inside the house im Haus 1
install [ɪn'stɔ:l] installieren; einbauen 3
installation [ɪnstə'leɪʃn] die Installation, der Einbau 3
instead [ɪn'sted] stattdessen 3
instead of [ɪn'sted əv] anstatt, anstelle von 3
instruction [ɪn'strʌkʃn] die Anweisung 1
instrument ['ɪnstrəmənt] das Instrument 2

intelligence [ɪnˈtelɪdʒəns] die Intelligenz 4: 4 (118) **artificial intelligence (AI)** die künstliche Intelligenz (KI) 4: 4 (118)

intelligent [ɪnˈtelɪdʒənt] intelligent 4: 4 (118)

interest [ˈɪntrəst]:
1. **interest sb. (in)** jn. interessieren (für) 2
2. **interest (in)** das Interesse (an) 2 **take/show an interest (in)** Interesse zeigen (an) 2

interested (in) [ˈɪntrəstɪd] interessiert (an) 2

interesting [ˈɪntrəstɪŋ] interessant 1

interestingly [ˈɪntrəstɪŋli] interessanterweise 3

international [ɪntəˈnæʃnəl] international 2

interrupt [ɪntəˈrʌpt] unterbrechen 3

interruption [ɪntəˈrʌpʃn] die Unterbrechung 3

interview [ˈɪntəvjuː]:
1. das Interview 3
2. interviewen, befragen 3

into [ˈɪntu], [ˈɪntə] in (... hinein) 1

intolerant (of) [ɪnˈtɒlərənt] intolerant (gegenüber) 2

intro [ˈɪntrəʊ] (*kurz für* **introduction**) die Einführung, die Einleitung 3

introduce sb. to sb./sth. [ɪntrəˈdjuːs] jm. jn./etwas vorstellen, jn. mit jm./etwas bekanntmachen 3

introduction [ɪntrəˈdʌkʃn] die Einführung, die Einleitung 1

Inuit [ˈɪnjuɪt] die Inuit (*kanadische Ureinwohner/innen*) 4: 5 (150/151)

invent [ɪnˈvent] erfinden 3

invention [ɪnˈvenʃn] die Erfindung 3

invisible [ɪnˈvɪzəbl] unsichtbar 2

invitation (to) [ɪnvɪˈteɪʃn] die Einladung (zu, nach) 1

invite (to) [ɪnˈvaɪt] einladen (zu, nach) 1

irregular [ɪˈregjələ] unregelmäßig; ungleichmäßig 3

is [ɪz] (*er/sie/es*) ist 1 **he isn't (= is not)** er ist nicht 1 **The football is £3.** Der Fußball kostet 3 Pfund. 2

island [ˈaɪlənd] die Insel 1

isle [aɪl] die Insel, das Eiland (*kurz für „island"*) 3 **British Isles** (*pl*) die Britischen Inseln 3

°issue [ˈɪʃuː] die (Streit-)Frage, das Problem, das Thema

it [ɪt] es (*bei Sachen und Tieren auch: er; sie*) 1 **it's (= it is)** es ist 1

its [ɪts]:
1. sein/seine, ihr/ihre (*besitzanzeigend: Dinge und Tiere*) 1
2. seiner, seine, seins; ihrer, ihre, ihres (*zu „it"*) 3

itself [ɪtˈself] sich (selbst) (zu *„it"*) 3

J

jacket [ˈdʒækɪt] die Jacke; das Jackett 2 **rain jacket** die Regenjacke 2

jam [dʒæm] die Marmelade 1

January [ˈdʒænjuəri] der Januar 1

jar [dʒɑː] das Glas(gefäß) 2

°jaywalk [ˈdʒeɪwɔːk] eine Straße regelwidrig überqueren, bei Rot über die Straße gehen

jealous (of) [ˈdʒeləs] neidisch (auf); eifersüchtig 3

jelly [ˈdʒeli] das Gelee; der Wackelpudding 1

Jew [dʒuː] der Jude, die Jüdin 4: 1 (22)

jewellery [ˈdʒuːəlri] der Schmuck 4: (14/15)

jewelry [ˈdʒuːəlri] (*AE*) der Schmuck 4: (14/15)

Jewish [ˈdʒuːɪʃ] jüdisch 4: 1 (22)

jigsaw (puzzle) [ˈdʒɪgsɔː] das Puzzle 1

job [dʒɒb] der Job, die (Arbeits-)Stelle; die Aufgabe 2

join sb./sth. [dʒɔɪn] sich jm. anschließen; bei etwas mitmachen 1 **join a club** bei einer AG mitmachen, in einen Klub eintreten 1

joke [dʒəʊk]:
1. der Witz, der Scherz 2
2. Witze machen, scherzen 2 **You're joking!** Du machst wohl Witze! 2

journey [ˈdʒɜːni] die Reise, die Fahrt; der Weg 1

Jr. [ˈdʒuːniə] *siehe* **junior**

judge [dʒʌdʒ] der/die Richter/in 3

judo [ˈdʒuːdəʊ] das Judo 3 **do judo** Judo machen 3

juggle [ˈdʒʌgl] jonglieren 1

juice [dʒuːs] der Saft 2

July [dʒuˈlaɪ] der Juli 1

jump [dʒʌmp]:
1. der Sprung, das Hindernis 2
2. springen 2
3. (*vor Schreck*) zusammenzucken 4: 3 (97)

June [dʒuːn] der Juni 1

jungle [ˈdʒʌŋgl] der Dschungel 3

junior [ˈdʒuːniə]:
1. der/die Junior/in; Junior (*als Namensteil*) 4: 2 (58)
2. (*AE*) *der/die Schüler/in im vorletzten Schuljahr* 4: 3 (88)

°Jurassic [dʒʊˈræsɪk] den Jura betreffend (*erdgeschichtliche Epoche vor ca. 200 Millionen Jahren*)

just [dʒʌst]:
1. nur, bloß; einfach 1
2. gerade (eben) 2
3. (*adj.*) gerecht 4: 2 (56)

justice [ˈdʒʌstɪs] die Gerechtigkeit 3 **bring sb. to justice** jn. vor Gericht bringen 3 **do justice to sb.** jm. Gerechtigkeit bringen, jm. gerecht werden 3

K

karaoke [kæriˈəʊki] das Karaoke 1

karate [kəˈrɑːti] das Karate 2

kayak [ˈkaɪæk] das Kajak 3

kayaker [ˈkaɪækə] der/die Kajakfahrer/in 3

kayaking [ˈkaɪækɪŋ] das Kajakfahren 3

keep [kiːp], **kept, kept**:
1. halten; behalten; aufbewahren 2 **keep (yourself) busy** sich beschäftigen, auf Trab bleiben 3 **keep in touch (with)** in Verbindung/Kontakt bleiben (mit) 3 **keep sb. busy** jn. beschäftigen, auf Trab halten 3
2. **keep doing sth.** etwas dauernd/immer wieder tun 2 **keep going** (immer) weiter gehen 2

kept [kept] *siehe* **keep**

kettle [ˈketl] der Wasserkocher (*elektrisch*) 3

key [kiː]:
1. der Schlüssel; Schlüssel- 2
2. die Taste (*auf einer Tastatur*) 3

key ring [ˈkiː rɪŋ] das Schlüsselbund, der Schlüsselring 3

keyboard [ˈkiːbɔːd] die Tastatur 3

keyword [ˈkiːwɜːd] das Stichwort, das Schlagwort 2

kick [kɪk]:
1. treten; (*Sport*) schießen 4: 5 (155) **kick sth. up** etwas aufwirbeln, hochschleudern 4: 5 (155)
2. der Tritt, der Stoß, der Kick 4: 5 (155)

kid [kɪd] das Kind, der/die Jugendliche 1

kill [kɪl] töten 2

killer [ˈkɪlə] der/die Mörder/in 2

kilometre (km) [ˈkɪləmiːtə] der Kilometer 1

kind [kaɪnd] freundlich, nett 1

kind (of) [kaɪnd] die Art (von), die Sorte (von) 1

kindness [ˈkaɪndnəs] die Güte, die Freundlichkeit 3

king [kɪŋ] der König 3

Kingdom [ˈkɪŋdəm]: **the United Kingdom (the UK)** das Vereinigte Königreich 1

kiosk [ˈkiːɒsk] der Kiosk, die Verkaufsbude, der Verkaufsstand 1

kiss [kɪs]:
1. der Kuss 4: 1 (30)
2. (sich) küssen 4: 1 (30)

kitchen [ˈkɪtʃɪn] die Küche 1

kneel [niːl], **knelt, knelt** knien 4: 2 (59)

knelt [nelt] *siehe* **kneel**

knew [njuː] *siehe* **know**

knife [naɪf], *pl* **knives** das Messer 1

knit [nɪt] stricken 2

knives [naɪvz] *Plural von* **knife**

knock [nɒk]:
1. der Stoß, der Schlag, das Klopfen 4: 3 (96)
2. stoßen, klopfen 4: 3 (96) **knock at** (an)klopfen (an) (*z. B. Tür*) 4: 3 (96) **knock sth. over** etwas umstoßen 4: 3 (96)

know [nəʊ], **knew, known** wissen; kennen 1 **know sb./sth. by ...** jn./etwas erkennen an ... 2 **you know** nämlich, weißt du 3

known [nəʊn] *siehe* **know**

L

lab [læb] *siehe* **laboratory**
laboratory [lə'bɒrətri] *infml auch* **lab** das Labor 1
lacrosse [lə'krɒs] das Lacrosse *(Ballspiel, ähnlich wie Hockey)* 4: 5 (150/151)
ladies and gentlemen [leɪdi:z ənd 'dʒentlmən] sehr geehrte Damen und Herren 3
lady ['leɪdi] die Dame 4: 1 (31)
lain [leɪn] *siehe* **lie**
lake [leɪk] der (Binnen-)See 3
lamb [læm] das Lamm(fleisch) 2
lamp [læmp] die Lampe 1
land [lænd]:
1. das Land *(Grund und Boden)* 2
2. landen 2
landline ['lændlaɪn] die Festnetzleitung, das Festnetztelefon 4: 5 (158)
landscape ['lændskeɪp] die Landschaft; das Landschaftsbild 3
lane [leɪn] die Gasse 3 **bike lane** der Radweg 3 **cycle lane** der Radweg 3
language ['læŋgwɪdʒ] die Sprache 1
large [lɑ:dʒ] groß 2
last [lɑ:st] letzte(r, s); als letztes 2 **last week** letzte/vorige Woche 2 **last week/year/month** letzte/vorige Woche, letztes/voriges Jahr, letzten/vorigen Monat 2 **at last** schließlich, endlich 3
last (for) [lɑ:st] (an)dauern; halten *(von Bestand sein)* 3
late [leɪt] (zu) spät 1 **I'm late.** Ich habe mich verspätet. 1
later ['leɪtə] später 1 **Speak later.** Tschüs. / Bis später. 1
latest ['leɪtɪst] neueste/r/s, aktuelle/r/s 3
laugh [lɑ:f]:
1. das Lachen 2
2. **laugh (at)** lachen (über) 2
laugh out loud laut auf-/loslachen 2
launch [lɔ:ntʃ]:
1. der Start; die Einführung 4: 4 (119)
2. starten; einführen *(z. B. Produkt auf den Markt bringen)* 4: 4 (119)
law [lɔ:] das Gesetz; Jura *(Studium)* 4: 1 (23) **by law** per Gesetz, gesetzlich 4: 1 (23) **pass a law** ein Gesetz verabschieden 4: 1 (24)
lawyer ['lɔ:jə] der/die (Rechts-)Anwalt/Anwältin 4: 2 (54)
lay [leɪ] *siehe* **lie**
lazy ['leɪzi] faul 2
lead [li:d], **led**, **led** führen, leiten 3
leader ['li:də] der/die Leiter/in; der/die (An-)Führer/in 3
leaf [li:f], *pl* **leaves** das Blatt *(Pflanze)* 4: 5 (150/151)
league [li:g] dir Liga *(Sport)* 4: 1 (26)
learn [lɜ:n] lernen 1
least [li:st] *(der/die/das)* wenigste, am wenigsten 3 **at least** wenigstens, zumindest 2
leave [li:v], **left**, **left** lassen; zurücklassen 2 **leave sb. alone** jn. allein lassen; jn. in Ruhe lassen 2
leaves [li:vz] *Plural von* **leaf**
led [led] *siehe* **lead**
left [left] *siehe* **leave**
left [left] links; nach links 2 **on the left** auf der linken Seite 2 **to the left of ...** links von ... 2
°left-hand side ['left hænd saɪd] die linke Seite
leg [leg] das Bein 2
legend ['ledʒənd] die Legende, die Sage 3
lemon ['lemən] die Zitrone 1
lemonade [lemə'neɪd] die Limonade 1
lesbian ['lezbiən]:
1. die Lesbe 2
2. lesbisch 2
less [les] weniger 3
lesson ['lesn] die (Unterrichts-)Stunde 1
let [let], **let**, **let** lassen 3 **let's (= let us)** lass(t) uns 1
letter ['letə]:
1. der Brief 1
2. der Buchstabe 1
level ['levl]:
1. der Grad, die Stufe; das Niveau, die Ebene 2
2. das Stockwerk, die Etage, die Ebene 4: 1 (29)
LGBTQ [el dʒi bi ti: 'kju:] LGBTQ 2
liberty ['lɪbəti] die Freiheit 4: 1 (16/17)
library ['laɪbrəri] die Bücherei, die Bibliothek 1
licence ['laɪsns] die Genehmigung, die Lizenz 4: 3 (95) **driving licence** Führerschein 4: 3 (95) **gun licence** der Waffenschein 4: 3 (95)
°license ['laɪsns] *(AE)* die Genehmigung, Lizenz **driver's license** *(AE)* der Führerschein
lie [laɪ]:
1. die Lüge 3
tell a lie / lies lügen 3
2. **lie (to sb.)** (jn. an)lügen 3
lie [laɪ], **lay**, **lain** liegen 1 **lie down** sich hinlegen 2
life [laɪf], *pl* **lives** das Leben 2
°life skills *(pl)* ['laɪf skɪlz] die Alltagskompetenzen, die lebenswichtigen Fertigkeiten
lifeguard ['laɪfgɑ:d] der/die Rettungsschwimmer/in; der/die Bademeister/in 3
lift [lɪft]:
1. der Lift *(Aufzug)* 3
2. heben, hochheben 3
light [laɪt]:
1. hell 3
2. leicht 3
light [laɪt] das Licht; die Lampe 1 **car light** der Autoscheinwerfer 1
lighting ['laɪtɪŋ] die Beleuchtung 3
lightning ['laɪtnɪŋ] der Blitz / die Blitze *(bei Gewitter)* 4: 2 (64)
like [laɪk]:
1. mögen 1
I'd (= I would) like ... Ich hätte gern ... / Ich möchte ... 1 **I'd (= I would) like to meet ...** Ich würde mich gerne mit ... treffen. 1 **Would you like ...?** Möchtest du ...? 1 **Would you like me to ...?** Möchtest du, dass ich ...? 3
2. liken *(in sozialen Netzwerken: positiv bewerten)* 3
3. der Like *(positive Rückmeldung / „Gefällt mir" in sozialen Netzwerken)* 3
like:
1. als ob, als wenn 4: 1 (31)
2. wie; wie zum Beispiel 1
like *(infml)* irgendwie, halt *(bedeutungsloses Füllwort)* 4: 3 (97) **like this** so, auf diese Art 1 **a story like this** so/solch eine Geschichte 1 **It looks like rain.** Es sieht nach Regen aus. 1 **something like that** so etwas 2 **What does it look like?** Wie sieht es aus? 1 **What's ... like?** Wie ist ...? / Wie sieht ... aus? 1
likely ['laɪkli] wahrscheinlich 4: 3 (86)
limit ['lɪmɪt]:
1. **limit (for/to)** die Grenze (für), die Begrenzung, die Beschränkung (auf) 4: 3 (95)
speed limit die Geschwindigkeitsbegrenzung 4: 3 (95)
2. **limit sth. (to)** etwas beschränken, begrenzen (auf); etwas einschränken 4: 3 (95)
limo ['lɪməʊ] *(kurz für* **limousine***)* die Limousine, der Straßenkreuzer 4: 3 (90)
limousine ['lɪməzi:n] *kurz auch* **limo** die Limousine, der Straßenkreuzer 4: 3 (90)
line [laɪn]:
1. die Linie 3
2. die Reihe 1
3. die Zeile 1
4. die (U-Bahn-)Linie, die (Zug-)Strecke 3
5. *(AE)* die (Warte-)Schlange 4: 1 (30)
get in line sich (in einer Schlange) anstellen 4: 1 (30)
6. die Leitung 4: 2 (64)
phone line die Telefonleitung 4: 2 (64) **power line** die (Stark-)Stromleitung 4: 2 (64)
line chart ['laɪn tʃɑ:t] das Liniendiagramm 4: 4 (134)
lingua franca [lɪŋgwə 'fræŋkə] die Lingua Franca *(Verkehrssprache)* 2
link [lɪŋk]:
1. die Verbindung; der Link 2
2. **link (to/with)** verbinden (mit) 2
lion ['laɪən] der Löwe 1
lip [lɪp] die Lippe 4: 1 (30)
lipstick ['lɪpstɪk] der Lippenstift 4: 1 (30)
list [lɪst]:
1. die Liste 1
2. (auf)listen 1
listen (to) ['lɪsn] zuhören; (sich etwas) anhören 1

listener ['lɪsənə] der/die Zuhörer/in 3
litre ['li:tə] der Liter 3 **a one-litre bottle** eine Einliterflasche 3
little ['lɪtl]:
1. klein 1
2. **a little** ein wenig, ein bisschen 1
live [lɪv] leben, wohnen 1
live [laɪv] aktiv *(Vulkan)*; lebend, lebendig *(Lebewesen)*; live *(z. B. Show)* 3
lives [laɪvz] *Plural von* **life**
living room ['lɪvɪŋ ru:m] das Wohnzimmer 1
lizard ['lɪzəd] die Eidechse 1
local ['ləʊkl] einheimisch, am/vom Ort 3
local train [ləʊkl 'treɪn] der Nahverkehrszug, die S-Bahn 3
location [ləʊ'keɪʃn] der Ort *(Standort; Einsatzort, Drehort)* 3
loch [lɒx] der See *(schottisches Wort für „lake")* 3
lock [lɒk]:
1. das Schloss *(Türschloss)* 2
2. abschließen *(z. B. Tür)* 2
be locked out ausgesperrt sein 2
log [lɒg] das Protokoll *(Aufzeichnungen)* 4: 5 (152)
°**lone** [ləʊn] einzeln, einsam
long [lɒŋ] lang 1 **(for) a long time** lange 1 **work long days** lange arbeiten, lange Arbeitstage haben 1
look [lʊk]:
1. aussehen 1
It looks like rain. Es sieht nach Regen aus. 1
2. sehen, schauen 1
look after sich kümmern um; aufpassen auf 1 **look at sth.** sich etwas anschauen 1 **look for** suchen; Ausschau halten nach 2 **look forward to doing sth.** sich darauf freuen, etwas zu tun 2 **look forward to sth.** sich auf etwas freuen 2 **look sth. up** etwas nachschlagen, nachschauen 1
3. der Look, das Aussehen 2
looks *(pl)* das Aussehen 2
4. der Blick 4: 1 (31)
have/take a (good) look at sth. sich etwas (gut) anschauen 4: 1 (31)
lookout ['lʊkaʊt] der Wachposten, der Ausguck 4: 4 (116/117)
loose [lu:s] locker (sitzend), lose 3
lose [lu:z], **lost, lost** verlieren 2 **lose touch (with)** den Kontakt verlieren (zu) 3
lost [lɒst] *siehe* **lose** **Are you lost?** Hast du dich verlaufen/verirrt? 1 **be lost** sich verlaufen/verirrt haben 1 **get lost** sich verlaufen, sich verirren 1
lot [lɒt]:
1. **a lot (of) / lots (of)** viel/e 1
2. **a lot** sehr 1
°**lottery** ['lɒtəri:] die Lotterie **win the lottery** im Lotto / in der Lotterie gewinnen
loud [laʊd] laut 1 **laugh out loud** laut auf-/loslachen 2

love [lʌv]:
1. der Liebling 1
2. die Liebe 1
be in love (with sb.) verliebt sein (in jn.) 3 **fall in love (with sb.)** sich verlieben (in jn.) 3
3. lieben, sehr mögen 1
I'd (= I would) love ... Ich hätte liebend gern ... / Ich möchte liebend gern ... 1 **I'd (= I would) love to meet ...** Ich würde mich liebend gerne mit ... treffen. 1
lovely ['lʌvli]:
1. (wunder)schön, herrlich 3
2. *(Person)* nett, lieb 3
lover ['lʌvə]: **(music) lover** der/die (Musik-)Liebhaber/in 4: 4 (129)
loving ['lʌvɪŋ] liebevoll 3
low [ləʊ] niedrig, tief 3
lower ['ləʊə] hinunterlassen, herunterlassen; sinken (lassen) 3
luck [lʌk]: **Good luck.** Viel Glück! 3
luckily ['lʌkɪli] glücklicherweise 2
lucky ['lʌki] Glücks-, glücklich 1 **lucky number** die Glückszahl 1 **be lucky** Glück haben 1
luggage ['lʌgɪdʒ] das Gepäck 3
lunch [lʌntʃ] das Mittagessen 1 **at lunch** beim Mittagessen 1 **What's for lunch?** Was gibt es zum Mittagessen? 1
lunchtime ['lʌntʃtaɪm] die Mittagszeit 1 **at lunchtime** zur Mittagszeit 1
lyrics *(pl)* ['lɪrɪks] der Liedtext 2

M

ma'am [mæm] *(AE)* meine Dame, gnädige Frau 4: 3 (84)
machine [mə'ʃi:n] der Automat, die Maschine 2 **cash machine** der Geldautomat 2 **ticket machine** der Fahrkartenautomat 2
mad [mæd]
1. wahnsinnig, verrückt 4: 5 (158)
2. **mad (about)** *(AE, infml)* wütend (wegen) 4: 2 (52)
madam ['mædəm] meine Dame, gnädige Frau 4: 3 (84) **Dear Sir or Madam** Sehr geehrte Damen und Herren 4: 3 (84)
made [meɪd] *siehe* **make** **a made-up character/story/...** eine erfundene Figur/Geschichte/... 4: 2 (62)
mag [mæg] *siehe* **magazine**
magazine [mægə'zi:n] *infml auch* **mag** die Zeitschrift 2
magic ['mædʒɪk]:
1. magisch 1
2. die Zauberei 1
do magic zaubern 1
magic set ['mædʒɪk set] der Zauberkasten 1
magic trick ['mædʒɪk trɪk] der Zaubertrick 1
main [meɪn] Haupt-, wichtigste(r, s) 1 **main course/dish** das Hauptgericht 1

mainly ['meɪnli] hauptsächlich, vorwiegend *(Adv.)* 4: (14/15)
make [meɪk], **made, made** machen, herstellen 1 **make (money)** (Geld) verdienen 2 **make friends** Freunde/-innen finden 2 **make it** es schaffen *(mit etwas Erfolg haben)* 4: 3 (86) **make sb. do sth.** jn. dazu bringen, etwas zu tun 2 **make sb. sth.** jn. zu etwas machen 3 **make sb./sth. into sb./sth.** jn./etwas zu jm./etwas machen 3 **make sth. up** etwas bilden, ausmachen 4: 2 (62) **make sth. up** etwas erfinden, sich etwas ausdenken 4: 2 (62) **make sure that ...** sicherstellen, dass ...; dafür sorgen, dass ... 3
male [meɪl]:
1. männlich 4: 3 (98)
2. der Mann 4: 3 (98)
mall [mɔ:l] Einkaufszentrum 4: 2 (50/51)
man [mæn], *pl* **men** der Mann 1
manage sth. ['mænɪdʒ] etwas verwalten, regeln, leiten 2
manager ['mænɪdʒə] der/die Manager/in 2
mango ['mæŋgəʊ], *pl* **mangoes** die Mango 3
many ['mæni] viele 1 **how many?** wie viele? 1
map [mæp] die Landkarte, der Stadtplan 1
maple ['meɪpl] der Ahorn 4: 5 (150/151)
maple leaf ['meɪpl li:f], *pl* **maple leaves** das Ahornblatt 4: 5 (150/151)
maple leaves ['meɪpl li:vz] *Plural von* **maple leaf**
°**maple syrup** [meɪpl 'sɪrəp] der Ahornsirup
marathon ['mærəθən] der Marathon(lauf) 4: 1 (26)
March [mɑ:tʃ] der März 1
°**Mardi Gras** [mɑ:di 'grɑ:] der Faschingsdienstag *(auch: die Karnevalsfeiern in New Orleans)*
marina [mə'ri:nə] der Jachthafen 1
mark [mɑ:k]:
1. der Fleck; der Abdruck *(z. B. Lippenstift)*; die Spur 4: 1 (30)
2. die Markierung; das Zeichen 2
3. die (Schul-)Note, die Zensur 2
4. kennzeichnen, markieren 2
market ['mɑ:kɪt] der Markt 1
married (to) ['mærid] verheiratet (mit) 1 **get married (to sb.)** jn. heiraten 2
marry ['mæri] heiraten 1
mask [mɑ:sk] die Maske 2
match [mætʃ]:
1. das Spiel, der Wettkampf 1
2. das Gegenstück, das (zusammenpassende) Paar 4: 1 (31)
be a good match gut zusammenpassen 4: 1 (31)
3. (passend) zusammenfügen 2
match (sth.) zueinander passen; passen zu (etwas), übereinstimmen mit

(etwas); (passend) zusammenfügen 4: 1 (31) **match to** zuordnen 2
material [məˈtɪəriəl] der Stoff; das Material 3
°math [mæθ] *(AE)* die Mathe(matik)
maths [mæθs] die Mathe(matik) 1
matter [ˈmætə] von Bedeutung sein, wichtig sein 4: 2 (57) **It doesn't matter.** Es/Das ist egal. 4: 2 (57)
May [meɪ] der Mai 1
may [meɪ] dürfen 2 **May I ...?** Darf ich ...? 2 **he may find out ...** er findet vielleicht heraus; er kann herausfinden 3
maybe [ˈmeɪbi] vielleicht 1
me [mi:] mich; mir 1 **Me, too.** Ich auch. 1 **It's me.** Ich bin's. 1 **Not me!** Ich nicht! (= Ich bin/war/habe/... es/das nicht!) 1
meal [mi:l] die Mahlzeit, das Essen 1 **hot meal** die warme Mahlzeit 1
mean [mi:n] gemein, fies 1
mean [mi:n], **meant, meant** bedeuten; sagen wollen 1 **mean to do sth.** etwas mit Absicht tun, etwas tun wollen 3
meaning [ˈmi:nɪŋ] die Bedeutung 1
meant [ment] *siehe* **mean**
measure [ˈmeʒə] (aus)messen 4: 1 (20)
measurement [ˈmeʒəmənt] die Abmessung, das Maß, die Maßeinheit 4: 1 (20)
meat [mi:t] das Fleisch 1 **meats** *(pl)* die Fleischsorten 3 **cold meat** der (Braten-/Wurst-)Aufschnitt 3
mechanic [mɪˈkænɪk] der/die Mechaniker/in 2
media [ˈmi:diə] die Medien 2 **social media** soziale Medien 2
mediate [ˈmi:dieɪt] vermitteln *(inhaltlich wiedergeben)* 3
mediation [mi:diˈeɪʃn] die Vermittlung, die Sprachmittlung 3
medium [ˈmi:diəm] medium *(Kleidergröße: mittelgroß/M)* 2
meet [mi:t], **met, met** kennenlernen; (sich) treffen 1 **meet up (with sb.)** sich treffen (mit jm.) 4: 3 (97) **Nice to meet you.** Freut mich, dich/euch/Sie kennenzulernen. 1
meeting [ˈmi:tɪŋ] das Meeting *(Treffen, Zusammenkunft)* 2
melody [ˈmelədi] die Melodie 3
melon [ˈmelən] die Melone 1
melt [melt] schmelzen 4: 4 (126) **melt sth.** etwas zerlassen, auflösen, schmelzen lassen 4: 4 (126)
member [ˈmembə] das Mitglied 2
men [men] *Plural von* **man**
°mention [ˈmenʃn] erwähnen
menu [ˈmenju:] die Speisekarte 1
mermaid [ˈmɜ:meɪd] die Nixe, die Meerjungfrau 3
merman [ˈmɜ:mən], *pl* **mermen** der Nix, der Wassermann, der Meermann 3
mess [mes] das Chaos, die Unordnung 1
message [ˈmesɪdʒ]:
1. die Botschaft, die Aussage 1
2. die Nachricht, die Mitteilung 1
3. **message (sb.)** (jm.) Nachrichten schicken, Nachrichten austauschen (mit jm.) 1
messy [ˈmesi] unordentlich 1
met [met] *siehe* **meet**
metal [ˈmetl]:
1. das Metall 2
2. Metall-, aus Metall 2
Metis [meɪˈti:] die Metis *(Nachfahren europäischer Einwanderer/Einwanderinnen und kanadischer Ureinwohner/innen in Kanada)* 4: 5 (150/151)
metre [ˈmi:tə] der Meter 1
mice [maɪs] *Plural von* **mouse**
microphone [ˈmaɪkrəfəʊn] das Mikrofon 3
microplastic [ˈmaɪkrəʊplæstɪk] das Mikroplastik 3
middle [ˈmɪdl] die Mitte 2 **in the middle (of)** in der Mitte (von) 2
midnight [ˈmɪdnaɪt] die Mitternacht 1
might [maɪt]: **it might help ...** es könnte ... helfen, vielleicht hilft es ... 3
mile [maɪl] die Meile *(ca. 1,6 km)* 1
miles per hour (mph) [maɪlz pər ˈaʊə] Meilen pro Stunde 1 **at 30 miles per hour** mit 30 Meilen pro Stunde 1
milk [mɪlk] die Milch 1
milkshake [ˈmɪlkʃeɪk] der Milchshake 3
mill [mɪl] die Mühle; die Fabrik *(besonders Textil-)* 3 **cotton mill** die Baumwollfabrik, die Baumwollspinnerei 3
millilitre (ml) [ˈmɪlili:tə] der Milliliter 1
million [ˈmɪljən] die Million 3
mind [maɪnd] der Geist, der Verstand; die Gedanken; der Kopf *(im übertragenen Sinn)* 4: 4 (120) **change your mind** seine Meinung ändern 4: 4 (120) **make up your mind** sich entscheiden, sich entschließen 4: 4 (120)
mind map [ˈmaɪnd mæp] die Gedankenkarte, das Wörternetz, die Mindmap 1
mind sth. [maɪnd]:
1. auf etwas achten, auf etwas aufpassen 3
Mind the gap. Achten Sie auf den Abstand zwischen Zug und Bahnsteigkante. 3 **Mind the step.** Vorsicht Stufe! 3 **Mind your head.** Vorsicht, niedrige Decke! 3
2. **I don't mind doing sth.** Es macht mir nichts aus, etwas zu tun. 2
mine [maɪn] meine, meiner, meins 3
mine [maɪn]:
1. das Bergwerk 3
2. **mine sth.** etwas abbauen, fördern *(Bergbau)* 3
mini-drone [ˈmɪni drəʊn] die Minidrohne 1
mining [ˈmaɪnɪŋ] der Bergbau 3
mint [mɪnt] die (Pfeffer-)Minze 3
minus [ˈmaɪnəs] minus 4: 3 (93)
minute [ˈmɪnɪt] die Minute 1 **Just a minute.** Einen Moment. / Moment mal. 3 **Wait a minute.** Warte mal. / Einen Moment. 2
mirror [ˈmɪrə] der Spiegel 1
miss [mɪs]:
1. vermissen 2
2. verpassen 2
miss a penalty einen Elfmeter verschießen *(= nicht treffen)* 3
3. versäumen, auslassen 2
missing [ˈmɪsɪŋ] vermisst 1
mistake [mɪˈsteɪk] der Fehler 2 **by mistake** aus Versehen 2
mix [mɪks]:
1. der Mix, die Mischung 4: 1 (35)
2. (ver)mischen 1
mixture [ˈmɪkstʃə] die Mischung 1
mobile phone [məʊbaɪl ˈfəʊn] das Handy, das Telefon 1
modern [ˈmɒdn] modern 1
mom [mɒm] *(AE)* die Mutti, die Mama 4: 1 (31)
moment [ˈməʊmənt] der Moment 1 **at the moment** im Moment, zurzeit 1 **have a moment in the sun** kurz im Mittelpunkt stehen 1
momma [ˈmɒmə] *(AE)* die Mutti, die Mama 4: 1 (31)
Monday [ˈmʌndeɪ], [ˈmʌndi] der Montag 1
money [ˈmʌni] das Geld 1 **pocket money** das Taschengeld 2
monkey [ˈmʌŋki] der Affe 1
month [mʌnθ] der Monat 1
moon [mu:n] der Mond 2 **be over the moon** *(infml)* ganz aus dem Häuschen sein (= hocherfreut sein) 2
moose [mu:s], *pl* **moose** der Elch 4: 5 (150/151)
more [mɔ:] mehr, weitere 1 **three more** noch drei, drei weitere 1
morning [ˈmɔ:nɪŋ] der Morgen 1 **in the morning** morgens, am Morgen 1
mosque [mɒsk] die Moschee 2
most [məʊst] die meisten, am meisten 1 **most schools** die meisten Schulen 1
mostly [ˈməʊstli] hauptsächlich *(Adv.)* 4: (14/15)
mother [ˈmʌðə] die Mutter 2
motivate [ˈməʊtɪveɪt] motivieren 3
motivation [məʊtɪˈveɪʃn] die Motivation 3
motorboat [ˈməʊtəbəʊt] das Motorboot 4: 5 (152)
mountain [ˈmaʊntən] der Berg 2
mountainous [ˈmaʊntənəs] bergig, gebirgig 4: 4 (116/117)
mouse [maʊs], *pl* **mice** die Maus 1
move [mu:v]:
1. (sich) bewegen 1
move (sth.) *(etwas)* verschieben; aus dem Weg räumen 4: 4 (131)
2. **move (to)** (um)ziehen (nach) 2
movement [ˈmu:vmənt] die Bewegung 4: 2 (57)

movie [ˈmuːvi] *(AE)* der Film, der Spielfilm 4: 1 (20)
movie theater [ˈmuːvi θɪətə] *(AE)* das Kino 4: 1 (20)
°moxie [ˈmɒksi] *(AE, infml)* der Mumm *(Mut, Entschlossenheit)*
Mr Lee [ˈmɪstə] Herr Lee 1
Mrs Lee [ˈmɪsɪz] Frau Lee *(Anrede für verheiratete Frauen)* 1
Ms Lee [mɪz] Frau Lee 1
much [mʌtʃ] viel; sehr 1 **How much is/are ...?** Was (Wie viel) kostet/kosten ...? 2 **Thank you very much.** Vielen Dank. / Danke vielmals. 1 **too much of a good thing** zu viel des Guten 2
multicultural [mʌltiˈkʌltʃərəl] multikulturell 2
mum [mʌm] die Mama, die Mutti 1
mural [ˈmjʊərəl] das Wandgemälde 3
museum [mjuˈziːəm] das Museum 1
music [ˈmjuːzɪk] die Musik 1 **classical music** klassische Musik 2
music clip [ˈmjuːzɪk klɪp] der Musikclip 4: 2 (62)
musical [ˈmjuːzɪkl] musikalisch, Musik- 2
musician [mjuˈzɪʃn] der/die Musiker/in 2
Muslim [ˈmʊzlɪm]:
1. muslimisch 2
2. der/die Muslim/Muslima 2 **a practising Muslim** ein/e praktizierende/r Muslim/Muslima *(gläubig)* 2
must [mʌst]:
1. müssen 1 **I must go.** Ich muss Schluss machen. *(am Telefon/Briefschluss)* 1
2. **a must** *(infml)* ein Muss, eine Notwendigkeit 4: 2 (62) **a must-do** *(infml)* ein Muss; etwas, was man unbedingt tun muss 4: 2 (62) **a must-have** *(infml)* etwas, was man unbedingt haben muss 4: 2 (62) **a must-read** *(infml)* etwas, was man unbedingt lesen muss 4: 2 (62) **a must-see** *(infml)* ein Muss; etwas, was man unbedingt sehen muss 4: 2 (62)
°mustard [ˈmʌstəd] der Senf
mustn't do [ˈmʌsnt] nicht tun dürfen 2
my [maɪ] mein/e 1
myself [maɪˈself] mich/mir (selbst) 3
mystery [ˈmɪstri] das Geheimnis, das Rätsel 3

N

name [neɪm]:
1. der Name 1 **call sb. names** jn. beschimpfen 3 **family name** der Familienname, der Nachname 1 **first name** der Vorname 1 **What's your name?** Wie heißt du? 1
2. (be)nennen 3
name day [ˈneɪm deɪ] der Namenstag 2
narrator [nəˈreɪtə] der/die Erzähler/in 4: 3 (96)
narrow [ˈnærəʊ] eng, schmal 3
nasty [ˈnɑːsti] gemein, fies; schlimm, scheußlich 3
nation [ˈneɪʃn] die Nation 4: 5 (150/151)
national [ˈnæʃnəl] national 2
national anthem [næʃnəl ˈænθəm] die Nationalhymne 4: 2 (59)
national park [næʃnəl ˈpɑːk] der Nationalpark 4: 4 (116/117)
native [ˈneɪtɪv] einheimisch 4: 2 (55)
Native American [neɪtɪv əˈmerɪkən]:
1. der/die amerikanische Ureinwohner/in 4: 2 (55)
2. *zur indigenen Bevölkerung Nordamerikas gehörend oder sie betreffend* 4: 2 (55)
natural [ˈnætʃrəl] natürlich, Natur- 3
natural history [nætʃrəl ˈhɪstri] die Naturkunde 3
nature [ˈneɪtʃə] die Natur 3
near [nɪə] nahe (bei), in der Nähe von 1
nearest [ˈnɪərəst]: **the nearest ...** der/die/das nächstgelegene ... 3
nearly [ˈnɪəli] fast 2
°necessary [ˈnesəsəri] notwendig, nötig, erforderlich
neck [nek] der Hals, der Nacken 2
necklace [ˈnekləs] die (Hals-)Kette 4: 2 (60)
need [niːd] brauchen 1 **need to do sth.** etwas tun müssen 1 **you needn't do it** du musst es nicht tun; du brauchst es nicht zu tun 3
negative [ˈnegətɪv] negativ 2
neighbour [ˈneɪbə] der/die Nachbar/in 1
neighbourhood [ˈneɪbəhʊd] die Nachbarschaft, die Gegend, das Viertel 1
neither [ˈnaɪðə] keine/r/s *(von zweien)* 4: 3 (92)
nephew [ˈnefjuː] der Neffe 2
nerdy [ˈnɜːdi]: **be nerdy** ein Nerd sein *(absonderlich, streberhaft)* 3
nervous [ˈnɜːvəs] nervös, aufgeregt 3
net [net] das Netz *(Sport)* 3
network [ˈnetwɜːk] das Netz(werk) 3 **social network** das soziale Netzwerk 3
never [ˈnevə] nie, niemals 1
new [njuː] neu 1
New Year's Eve [njuː jɪəz ˈiːv] der/das Silvester 4: 1 (21)
news [njuːz] die Nachrichten 1
newsagent [ˈnjuːzeɪdʒənt] der/die Zeitungshändler/in 2
newsagent's [ˈnjuːzeɪdʒənts] der Zeitschriftenladen, der Zeitungskiosk 2
newspaper [ˈnjuːspeɪpə] die (Tages-)Zeitung 1
next [nekst]:
1. nächste(r, s) 1 **the next day** am nächsten Tag 1
2. **Next ...** Als Nächstes ... 1
next to [ˈnekst tə] neben 1
nice [naɪs] nett, schön 1 **Nice to meet you.** Freut mich, dich/euch/Sie kennenzulernen. 1
nickel [ˈnɪkl] *(AE)* das Fünfcentstück 4: 1 (19)
niece [niːs] die Nichte 2
night [naɪt] die Nacht 1 **at night** nachts, in der Nacht 1
nightfall [ˈnaɪtfɔːl] der Einbruch der Dunkelheit 4: 5 (156)
nightmare [ˈnaɪtmeə] der Albtraum 4: 5 (158)
nine [naɪn] neun 1
nineteen [naɪnˈtiːn] neunzehn 1
ninety [ˈnaɪnti] neunzig 1
no [nəʊ]:
1. nein 1
2. kein, keine; verboten 1
no one [ˈnəʊ wʌn] niemand 2
nobody [ˈnəʊbədi] niemand 2
nod [nɒd]:
1. **nod (of your head)** das Kopfnicken 4: 5 (156)
2. **nod (your head)** (mit dem Kopf) nicken 4: 5 (156)
noise [nɔɪz] das Geräusch; der Lärm 1
none [nʌn] keine(r, s) 4: 3 (97)
noodles *(pl)* [nuːdlz] die Nudeln 1
noon [nuːn] der Mittag; 12 Uhr mittags 1
normal [ˈnɔːml] normal 2
normally [ˈnɔːməli] normalerweise 3
north [nɔːθ] der Norden; nördlich; Nord- 1
north-east [nɔːθˈiːst] der Nordosten, nordöstlich; Nordost- 3
north-west [nɔːθˈwest] der Nordwesten, nordwestlich; Nordwest- 3
northern [ˈnɔːðən] Nord-, nördlich 3
nose [nəʊz] die Nase 2
not [nɒt] nicht 1 **I'm not a boy.** Ich bin kein Junge. 1
note [nəʊt]:
1. die Notiz; der kurze Brief 1 **make notes** (sich) Notizen machen *(zur Vorbereitung)* 1 **take notes** (sich) Notizen machen *(beim Lesen oder Zuhören)* 3 **°sticky note** die Haftnotiz, der Klebezettel
2. **(= banknote)** der Geldschein 4: 2 (57)
°3. **note sth. down** sich etwas aufschreiben, notieren
nothing [ˈnʌθɪŋ] nichts 2
notice [ˈnəʊtɪs]:
1. (be)merken 1
2. der Anschlag, die Bekanntmachung *(an einem Schwarzen Brett)* 1
°novel [ˈnɒvl] der Roman **graphic novel** der Bildroman, der Comicroman
November [nəʊˈvembə] der November 1
now [naʊ] nun, jetzt 1
nowhere [ˈnəʊweə] nirgendwo(hin) 2
number [ˈnʌmbə]:
1. die Anzahl 2
2. die Zahl, die Ziffer, die Nummer 1

nurse [nɜːs] der/die Krankenpfleger/in 2
nut [nʌt] die Nuss 4: 2 (61)

O

object [ˈɒbdʒɪkt] das Objekt, der Gegenstand 2
ocean [ˈəʊʃn] der Ozean 4: 5 (150/151)
o'clock [əˈklɒk]**: at 8 o'clock** um 8 Uhr 1
October [ɒkˈtəʊbə] der Oktober 1
of [ɒv], [əv] von 1 **a glass of milk** ein Glas Milch 1 **bags of rubbish** Tüten/Säcke (mit/voller) Müll 1 **the first of April (1st April)** der erste April 1
of course [əv ˈkɔːs] natürlich, selbstverständlich 1
off [ɒf]**:**
1. weg von; hinunter von 2
come off (sth.) abgehen (von etwas), (herunter)fallen (von etwas), sich lösen (von etwas) 2 **fall off** herunterfallen 2 **get off (a train/bus)** aussteigen (aus einem Zug/Bus) 2 **get off your bike/your horse** vom Fahrrad/vom Pferd absteigen 2 **run off** weglaufen 3
2. **be off** aus sein *(ausgeschaltet sein)* 2
offer [ˈɒfə]**:**
1. das Angebot 3
2. (an)bieten 3
office [ˈɒfɪs] das Büro 1
officer [ˈɒfɪsə] der Beamte, die Beamtin 2
official [əˈfɪʃl] offiziell 3
official language [əfɪʃl ˈlæŋgwɪdʒ] die Amtssprache 3
often [ˈɒfn], [ˈɒftən] oft 1
oh [əʊ] Null *(im gesprochenen Englisch)* 1
oil [ɔɪl] das Öl 1
OK [əʊˈkeɪ]**: I'm OK.** Es geht mir gut. 1 **That's OK.** Schon gut./Kein Problem. 1
old [əʊld] alt 1 **How old are you?** Wie alt bist du? 1
old-fashioned [əʊld ˈfæʃənd] altmodisch 3
olive [ˈɒlɪv] die Olive 3
Olympic [əˈlɪmpɪk] olympisch 3
Olympics [əˈlɪmpɪks] die olympischen Spiele 3
OMG (= Oh my God!) [əʊ em ˈdʒiː] Oh mein Gott! 4: 4 (132)
on [ɒn]**:**
1. auf 1
on holiday im/in den Urlaub 1 **on Monday** am Montag 1 **on Mondays** an jedem Montag, montags 1 **on my birthday** an meinem Geburtstag 1 **on the beach** am Strand 1 **on the bus** im Bus 1 **on the field** auf dem Spielfeld, auf dem Platz 1 **on the phone** am Telefon 1 **get on (a train/bus)** einsteigen (in einen Zug/Bus) 2
2. **be on** gezeigt werden, „laufen" *(Kino, Fernsehen)*, stattfinden; an sein (eingeschaltet sein) 2
What's on? Was läuft?/Was findet statt? *(Kino, Theater)* 2
3. **walk/run/drive on** weitergehen/-laufen/-fahren 3
once [wʌns] einmal; einst 2 **for once** ausnahmsweise, dieses eine Mal 3
one [wʌn]**:**
1. eins 1
one day eines Tages 4: 1 (26) **one way** eine Strecke *(= ohne Rückfahrt/Rückflug)* 2 **one-way ticket** die einfache Fahrkarte *(= ohne Rückfahrt)* 2 °**one way** nur in eine(r) Richtung
2. **the last one** der/die/das Letzte 2
onion [ˈʌnjən] die Zwiebel 1
online [ɒnˈlaɪn] online, Online- 1
only [ˈəʊnli]**:**
1. nur, bloß; erst 1
2. **the only person/people** die einzige Person/die einzigen Leute 3
onto the platform [ˈɒntu], [ˈɒntə] auf den Bahnsteig 2
open [ˈəʊpən]**:**
1. öffnen; aufschlagen *(Buch)* 1
2. eröffnet werden; sich öffnen, aufgehen 3
3. offen, geöffnet 1
open to offen für 4: 3 (85)
opening hours *(pl)* [ˈəʊpənɪŋ aʊəz] die Öffnungszeiten 4: 3 (85)
opinion (of) [əˈpɪnjən] die Meinung (zu/bezüglich) 1 **in my opinion** meiner Meinung nach 1
opposite [ˈɒpəzɪt]**:**
1. das Gegenteil 2
2. gegensätzlich, entgegengesetzt 2
3. gegenüber (von) 2
optimism [ˈɒptɪmɪzəm] der Optimismus 4: 5 (159)
optimist [ˈɒptɪmɪst] der/die Optimist/in 4: 5 (159)
optimistic [ɒptɪˈmɪstɪk] optimistisch 4: 5 (159)
optimize [ˈɒptɪmaɪz] optimieren 4: 4 (118)
option [ˈɒpʃn] die Wahl(möglichkeit), die Option 4: 3 (95) **you have no option but to do sth.** dir bleibt nichts anderes übrig, als etwas zu tun 4: 3 (95)
or [ɔː] oder; sonst 1
orange [ˈɒrɪndʒ]**:**
1. orange(farben) 1
2. die Orange 1
orbit [ˈɔːbɪt] der Orbit *(Umlaufbahn z. B. eines Satelliten)* 3
orca [ˈɔːkə] der Orca *(Schwertwal)* 4: 5 (150/151)
order [ˈɔːdə]**:**
1. ordnen, anordnen 3
2. die Reihenfolge 2
in order in eine(r) Reihenfolge 2
put in the right order in die richtige Reihenfolge bringen 2
order [ˈɔːdə]**:**
1. die Bestellung 3
2. **order sth.** etwas bestellen 3
order [ˈɔːdə]**: in order to** um ... zu 3
organization [ɔːgənaɪˈzeɪʃn] die Organisation 2
organize [ˈɔːgənaɪz] organisieren 2 **(well) organized** (gut) organisiert 2
original [əˈrɪdʒənl]**:**
1. das Original 4: (14/15)
2. original, ursprünglich 4: (14/15)
other [ˈʌðə] andere(r, s) 1 **each other** einander, sich (gegenseitig) 2 **the others** die anderen 1
otherwise [ˈʌðəwaɪz] anderenfalls, ansonsten, sonst; anders 4: 1 (31)
our [ˈaʊə] unser/e 1
ours [ɑːz], [ˈaʊəz] unserer, unsere, unseres 3
ourselves [aʊəˈselvz] uns (selbst) 3
out (of ...) [aʊt]**:**
1. **out** heraus, hinaus, nach draußen 2
out and about unterwegs 4: 1 (18)
out of ... aus ... (heraus/hinaus) 2
go out rausgehen, weggehen; ausgehen 3 **put your hands out** die Hände ausstrecken 2 **stay out** *(abends)* fortbleiben, wegbleiben 3
2. **The power is out.** Der Strom ist ausgefallen. 4: 2 (65)
°**outboard (motor)** [aʊtbɔːd ˈməʊtə] der Außenbordmotor
outdoor [ˈaʊtdɔː] Outdoor- 3
outdoor activity [ˈaʊtdɔː] die Outdoor-Aktivität; die Aktivität für draußen/im Freien 3
outdoors [aʊtˈdɔːz] im Freien, draußen 3
°**outline** [ˈaʊtlaɪn] der Entwurf, die Übersicht
outside [aʊtˈsaɪd]**:**
1. draußen; nach draußen *(Adv.)* 1
2. außerhalb (von) *(Präp.)* 1
outside the house außerhalb des Hauses 1
oven [ˈʌvn] der Backofen 1
over [ˈəʊvə]**:**
1. über; mehr als 1
over a period of time im Laufe eines Zeitraums 4: 2 (54) **over here** hier herüber; hier drüben 1 **over there** da drüben, dort drüben 1 **over time/over the years** im Laufe der Zeit/im Lauf der Jahre 4: 2 (54) **all over the world** überall auf der Welt, auf der ganzen Welt 2
2. **be over** vorbei sein, zu Ende sein 4: 2 (64)
own [əʊn]**:**
1. eigene/r/s 1
your own room dein/ein eigenes Zimmer 1
2. **own sth.** etwas besitzen 4: 4 (122)
owner [ˈəʊnə] der/die Besitzer/in 4: 4 (122) **business owner** der/die Geschäftsinhaber/in 4: 4 (122)

P

Pacific [pəˈsɪfɪk]:
1. pazifisch 4: 5 (150/151)
2. **the Pacific (Ocean)** der Pazifik, der Pazifische Ozean 4: 5 (150/151)

pack [pæk] packen, einpacken 3
pack (of wolves) [pæk] das Rudel (von Wölfen) 4: 5 (157)
packet [ˈpækɪt] die Packung, das Päckchen 1
paddle [ˈpædl]:
1. das Paddel 4: 5 (156)
2. paddeln 4: 5 (156)

paddleboarding [ˈpædlbɔːdɪŋ] das Stand-up Paddeln *(Stehpaddeln)* 3
page (= p.) [peɪdʒ] die (Buch-/Heft-)Seite 1
paid [peɪd] *siehe* **pay**
paint [peɪnt]:
1. die Farbe, der Lack 2
2. (an)malen; lackieren, (an)streichen 2

pair [peə]:
1. das Paar 2
2. **pair sth. (with sth.)** etwas (mit etwas) koppeln *(z. B. Geräte)* 3

palace [ˈpæləs] der Palast, das Schloss 1
pancake [ˈpænkeɪk] der Pfannkuchen 2
panic [ˈpænɪk]:
1. die Panik 4: 2 (65)
2. in Panik geraten 4: 2 (65)
Don't panic. Keine Panik. / Immer mit der Ruhe. 4: 2 (65)

pants [pænts] *(pl, AE)* die Hose 4: 1 (19)
paper [ˈpeɪpə]:
1. die (Tages-)Zeitung 1
2. das Papier 1
piece of paper das Stück Papier, der Zettel 1

parade [pəˈreɪd] die Parade, der Umzug 2
paragraph [ˈpærəgrɑːf] der (Text-)Abschnitt 3
paramedic [pærəˈmedɪk] der/die Rettungssanitäter/in 3
parents *(pl)* [ˈpeərənts] die Eltern 1
park (a car) [pɑːk] parken 4: 1 (30)
parking lot [ˈpɑːkɪŋ lɒt] *(AE)* der Parkplatz 4: 1 (30)
parking space [ˈpɑːkɪŋ speɪs] der Parkplatz *(die Parklücke für 1 Auto)* 4: 1 (30)
parkour [pɑːˈkʊə] der Parkour *(akrobatischer Hindernislauf in der Stadt)* 1
parliament [ˈpɑːləmənt] das Parlament 3 **the Houses of Parliament** *(pl)* das Parlamentsgebäude in London 3
parrot [ˈpærət] der Papagei 1
part (of) [pɑːt] der Teil (von) 1 **take part (in)** teilnehmen (an), mitmachen (bei) 3
part-time [pɑːt ˈtaɪm] Teilzeit-, Halbtags- 4: 3 (93)
party [ˈpɑːti] (Partys) feiern 4: 2 (60)
pass [pɑːs] vorbeigehen/-ziehen; vorübergehen *(Zeit, Moment, Gelegenheit)* 4: 2 (64) **pass a law** ein Gesetz verabschieden 4: 1 (24) **pass sb./sth.** an jm./etwas vorbeigehen, vorbeifahren 4: 2 (64) **pass through (a village)** fahren/reisen durch (ein Dorf) 4: 2 (64)
passenger [ˈpæsɪndʒə] der/die Passagier/in, der Fahrgast 4: 3 (95)
passive [ˈpæsɪv] passiv 1
passport [ˈpɑːspɔːt] der (Reise-)Pass 3
past [pɑːst]:
1. die Vergangenheit 2
2. vergangene(r, s) 2

past [pɑːst]:
1. vorbei, vorüber 3
2. vorbei an, vorüber an 2
3. nach *(bei Uhrzeitangaben)* 2
half past 6 halb 7 2

path [pɑːθ] der Weg, der Pfad 3
patience [ˈpeɪʃns] die Geduld 2
patient [ˈpeɪʃnt] geduldig 2
pattern [ˈpætn] das *(wiederkehrende)* Muster, das Schema 3
patterned [ˈpætnd] gemustert 3
°pause [pɔːz] die Pause
pavement [ˈpeɪvmənt] der Gehweg, der Bürgersteig 4: 4 (129)
paw [pɔː] die Pfote 4: 5 (156)
pay [peɪ]:
1. die Bezahlung *(Lohn)* 4: 3 (93)
2. **pay (for sth.), paid, paid** zahlen; (etwas) bezahlen 1
pay (in) cash bar bezahlen 2 **pay attention (to)** aufpassen (auf), aufmerksam sein; Beachtung schenken, zuhören 2 **pay by card** mit Karte (be)zahlen *(z. B. Bankkarte)* 2

PE (= physical education) [piː ˈiː] der (Schul-)Sport 1
pea [piː] die Erbse 1
peace [piːs] der Frieden 2
peaceful [ˈpiːsfl] friedlich, friedfertig 3
°peer [pɪər] *der/die Angehörige derselben Alters oder Berufsgruppe*
pelican [ˈpelɪkən] der Pelikan 3
pen [pen] der Kugelschreiber, der Stift; der Füller 1
penalty [ˈpenəlti] der Strafstoß; der Elfmeter *(Fußball)* 3
pence [pens] *Plural von* **penny**
pencil [ˈpensl] der Bleistift 1
pencil case [ˈpensl keɪs] das Federmäppchen 1
pencil sharpener [ˈpensl ʃɑːpnə] der Bleistift(an)spitzer 1
penny (p) [ˈpeni], *pl* **pence**:
1. der Penny *(kleinste britische Münze)* 1
2. *(AE)* der Cent 4: 1 (19)

people [ˈpiːpl]:
1. *(pl)* die Leute, die Menschen 1
2. man 3
3. *pl* **peoples** das Volk 4: 4 (122)

pepper [ˈpepə]:
1. der Pfeffer 1
2. die Paprika, die Peperoni 1

pepper spray das Pfefferspray 4: 4 (127)
per [pɜː], [pə] pro 1 **miles per hour (mph)** Meilen pro Stunde 1
per cent (%) [pə ˈsent] das Prozent 2
percentage [pəˈsentɪdʒ] der Anteil, der Prozentsatz 3
perfect [ˈpɜːfɪkt] perfekt 1
perfectly (still) [ˈpɜːfɪktli] ganz/völlig (still) 1
perform [pəˈfɔːm] auftreten *(Künstler/in)*; aufführen 3
performance [pəˈfɔːməns] die Vorstellung, die Aufführung 3
performer [pəˈfɔːmə] der/die Künstler/in *(der/die etwas aufführt)* 3
period (of time) [ˈpɪəriəd] der Zeitraum, die (Zeit-)Periode 3
period [ˈpɪəriəd] *(AE)* die (Unterrichts-)Stunde 4: 3 (88)
person [ˈpɜːsn] die Person 1 **in person** persönlich 4: 3 (93)
personal [ˈpɜːsənl] persönlich 2
personality [pɜːsəˈnæləti] die Persönlichkeit; der Charakter 2
pessimism [ˈpesɪmɪzəm] der Pessimismus 4: 5 (159)
pessimist [ˈpesɪmɪst] der/die Pessimist/in 4: 5 (159)
pessimistic [pesɪˈmɪstɪk] pessimistisch 4: 5 (159)
pet [pet] das (Haus-)Tier 1
petition [pəˈtɪʃn] der Antrag, die Petition *(Unterschriftensammlung)* 4: 2 (59)
petrol [ˈpetrəl] das Benzin 4: 3 (85)
philosophy [fəˈlɒsəfi] die Philosophie 2
phone [fəʊn]:
1. anrufen; telefonieren 1
2. das Handy, das Telefon 1
answer the phone ans Telefon gehen 4: 2 (65) **by phone** per Telefon, telefonisch 1 **on the phone** am Telefon 1

phone call [ˈfəʊn kɔːl] der (Telefon-)Anruf 1
phone number [ˈfəʊn nʌmbə] die Telefonnummer 1
photo [ˈfəʊtəʊ] das Foto 1 **in the photo** auf dem Foto 1 **take photos** Fotos machen 1
photograph [ˈfəʊtəgrɑːf]:
1. das Foto 2
2. fotografieren 2

photographer [fəˈtɒgrəfə] der/die Fotograf/in 1
photography [fəˈtɒgrəfi] die Fotografie *(Hobby)*, das Fotografieren 2
phrase [freɪz] die Ausdruck, die (Rede-)Wendung 1
physical education (PE) [fɪzɪkl edʒuˈkeɪʃn] der (Schul-)Sport 1
piano [piˈænəʊ] das Klavier 2 **play the piano** Klavier spielen 2
pick [pɪk] pflücken; (aus)wählen, aussuchen 2 **pick sth. up** etwas aufheben *(vom Boden)*, etwas hochheben 2 **pick up (the phone)** ans Telefon

gehen; zum (Telefon-)Hörer greifen 4: 2 (65)
picker [ˈpɪkə] die Greifzange *(z. B. für Müll)*; der/die Pflücker/in 2
°**picklock** [pɪklɒk] der Dietrich *(Werkzeug zum Öffnen von Schlössern ohne Schlüssel)*
picnic [ˈpɪknɪk] das Picknick 1 **have a picnic** ein Picknick machen 1
picture [ˈpɪktʃə] das Bild 1
pie chart [ˈpaɪ tʃɑːt] das Tortendiagramm 2
piece [piːs] das Stück, der/das Teil 1 **piece of paper** das Stück Papier 1
pier [pɪə] der Pier, die Seebrücke 1
pig [pɪg] das Schwein 2
piggy bank [ˈpɪgi bæŋk] das Sparschwein 2
pineapple [ˈpaɪnæpl] die Ananas 3
ping [pɪŋ] pingen *(elektronisch anklopfen)* 3
pink [pɪŋk] rosa 1
piper [ˈpaɪpə] der/die Dudelsackspieler/in 3
pit [pɪt] die Grube 4: 4 (130) **fire pit** die Feuergrube, die Feuerstelle *(z. B. für Lagerfeuer)* 4: 4 (130)
pitch [pɪtʃ] der Platz *(Sport)*, das Spielfeld 3
pity [ˈpɪti]:
1. **pity (for)** das Mitleid (mit) 4: 1 (31) **That's a pity.** Das ist schade. 4: 1 (31)
2. **pity sb.** jn. bemitleiden 4: 1 (31)
pizza [ˈpiːtsə] die Pizza 2
place [pleɪs]:
1. der Ort, der Platz 1 **at/in a place** an einem Ort 2 **in this place** an diesem Ort 1 **take place** stattfinden 2
°2. stellen, legen, setzen, platzieren
°**placemat** [ˈpleɪsmæt] die Placemat *(Übungsformname)*; das Set, das Platzdeckchen
plain [pleɪn] einfach, schlicht; „ohne alles" 3
plan [plæn]:
1. der Plan 1
2. planen 1 **plan to do sth.** planen, etwas zu tun 1
plane [pleɪn] das Flugzeug 2
planet [ˈplænɪt] der Planet 2
plant [plɑːnt]:
1. die Pflanze 3
2. pflanzen 3
plastic [ˈplæstɪk] das Plastik, der Kunststoff 2
plate [pleɪt] der Teller 3
platform [ˈplætfɔːm] der Bahnsteig 2 **at platform 4** auf Gleis 4 2
play [pleɪ]:
1. spielen 1 **play the piano** Klavier spielen 2
2. das Spiel 3
3. das Theaterstück 4: 4 (128)
player [ˈpleɪə] der/die Spieler/in 1
playground [ˈpleɪgraʊnd] der Schulhof; der Spielplatz 1
playing card [ˈpleɪɪŋ kɑːd] die Spielkarte 1
please [pliːz] bitte 1
°**Pledge of Allegiance** [pledʒ əv əˈliːdʒəns] das Treuegelöbnis
plug [plʌg]:
1. der Stecker 4: 1 (32)
2. **plug sth. in** etwas einstecken, anschließen 4: 1 (32)
plus [plʌs] plus 4: 3 (93)
p.m. [piːˈem]: **4 p.m.** 4 Uhr nachmittags, 16 Uhr 1 **9 p.m.** 9 Uhr abends, 21 Uhr 1
°**po'boy** [ˈpəʊ bɔɪ] das Po'Boy-Sandwich *(reichhaltig gefülltes Stück Baguette)*
pocket [ˈpɒkɪt] die Tasche *(an Kleidungsstücken)* 2
pocket money [ˈpɒkɪt mʌni] das Taschengeld 2
point [pɔɪnt]:
1. der Punkt 1 **point in time** der Zeitpunkt 3
2. das Komma *(Dezimalzeichen)* 1 **1.6 (one point six)** 1,6 (eins Komma sechs) 1
3. das Argument, der Standpunkt 3 **I take your point.** Ich verstehe, was du sagen willst. 3 **make a/your point** ein Argument vortragen/vorbringen 3 **Make your point.** Leg deinen Standpunkt dar. / Sag, wie du darüber denkst. 3 **take a point** einen Standpunkt verstehen 3 **That's a good point.** Das ist ein gutes Argument. 3
point (at/to) [pɔɪnt] zeigen, deuten (auf) 4: 3 (85) **point sth. out** auf etwas hinweisen, aufmerksam machen 4: 3 (85)
police *(pl)* [pəˈliːs] die Polizei 2
police officer [pəˈliːs ɒfɪsə] der Polizeibeamte, die Polizeibeamtin 2
polite [pəˈlaɪt] höflich 1
politician [pɒləˈtɪʃn] der/die Politiker/in 4: 3 (87)
pollution [pəˈluːʃn] die (Umwelt-)Verschmutzung 3
pony [ˈpəʊni] das Pony 3
ponytail [ˈpəʊniteɪl] der Pferdeschwanz *(Frisur)* 4: 1 (30)
poor [pɔː], [pʊə] arm 2 **Poor George!** Der arme George! / Armer George! 2
pop (music) [ˈpɒp mjuːzɪk] der Pop, die Popmusik 1
popular [ˈpɒpjələ] beliebt, populär 1
population [pɒpjuˈleɪʃn] die Bevölkerung, die Einwohner(zahl) 4: (12/13)
porcupine [ˈpɔːkjupaɪn] das Stachelschwein 4: 4 (126)
pork [pɔːk] das Schweinefleisch 2
pose [pəʊz] die Pose, die Haltung 3 **power pose** die Machtpose 3
position [pəˈzɪʃn] die Position, der Standort 4: 5 (157)
positive [ˈpɒzətɪv] positiv 2
possible [ˈpɒsəbl] möglich 3
post [pəʊst]:
1. die Post *(Briefe etc.)* 3
2. der Post *(Teil eines Blogs)* 1
3. posten *(im Internet veröffentlichen)* 1
postbox [ˈpəʊstbɒks] der Briefkasten 3
postcard [ˈpəʊstkɑːd] die Postkarte 2
pot [pɒt] der Topf; die Kanne *(z. B. Tee-, Kaffeekanne)* 2
potato [pəˈteɪtəʊ], *pl* **potatoes** die Kartoffel 1
pound (£) [paʊnd] das Pfund *(britische Währung)* 1
poverty [ˈpɒvəti] die Armut 3
powder [ˈpaʊdə] das Pulver 1
power [ˈpaʊə] die Kraft, die Macht, die Energie; der (elektrische) Strom 2
power pose [ˈpaʊə pəʊz] die Machtpose 3
°**powerful** [ˈpaʊəfl] kräftig, stark, mächtig
°**powwow** [ˈpaʊwaʊ] die Versammlung *(amerik. Ureinwohner/innen)*, der Kriegsrat
practical [ˈpræktɪkl] praktisch 2 **play a practical joke on sb.** jm. einen Streich spielen 2
practice [ˈpræktɪs] die Übung(en) 1
practise [ˈpræktɪs] üben 1 **a practising doctor** ein/e praktizierende/r Arzt/Ärztin *(seinen/ihren Beruf ausübend)* 2 **a practising Muslim** ein/e praktizierende/r Muslim/Muslima *(gläubig)* 2
°**praline** [ˈprɑːliːn], [ˈpreɪliːn] der Krokant *(aus dem Französischen)*
pray [preɪ] beten 2
prayer [preə] das Gebet 2
prediction [prɪˈdɪkʃn] die Vorhersage, die Voraussage 2
prefer sth. to sth. [prɪˈfɜː] etwas einer Sache vorziehen, etwas lieber tun/haben als etwas 3 **I'd prefer ...** Ich würde ... vorziehen. 3
preheat (the oven to ...) [priːˈhiːt] (den Backofen) vorheizen (auf) 1
preparation [prepəˈreɪʃn] die Vorbereitung; die Zubereitung 2
prepare (for) [prɪˈpeə] vorbereiten, zubereiten; sich vorbereiten (auf) 2
present [ˈpreznt] das Geschenk 1
°**present** [ˈpreznt] die Gegenwart
present sth. (to sb.) [prɪˈzent] (jm.) etwas präsentieren, vorstellen 1
presentation [preznˈteɪʃn] das Referat, die Präsentation 1 **give a presentation** ein Referat halten 1
presenter [prɪˈzentə] der/die Moderator/in 2
president [ˈprezɪdənt] der/die Präsident/in 4: (12/13)
press [pres] drücken 3
pretty [ˈprɪti]:
1. hübsch 3
2. **pretty busy/old/cool/...** ziemlich hektisch/alt/cool/... 4: 2 (60)
price [praɪs] der (Kauf-)Preis 2
pride [praɪd] der Stolz 2
primary school [ˈpraɪməri skuːl] die Grundschule 3

prime minister [praɪm ˈmɪnɪstə] der/die Premierminister/in 3
prince [prɪns] der Prinz 3
princess [prɪnˈses] die Prinzessin 3
principal [ˈprɪnsəpl] *(AE)* der/die Schulleiter/in 4: 3 (96) **assistant principal** der/die stellvertretende Schulleiter/in 4: 3 (96)
print sth. (out) [prɪnt] etwas (aus-)drucken 3
printer [ˈprɪntə] der Drucker 3
prison [ˈprɪzn] das Gefängnis 3
privacy [ˈprɪvəsi] die Privatsphäre 4: 3 (85)
private [ˈpraɪvət] privat; persönlich 3
prize [praɪz] der Preis, der Gewinn 1
prize ceremony [ˈpraɪz serəməni] die Preisverleihung 2
pro [prəʊ] *siehe* **professional**
probably [ˈprɒbəbli] wahrscheinlich 2
problem [ˈprɒbləm] das Problem 1
problem-solving [ˈprɒbləm sɒlvɪŋ] das Lösen von Problemen, die Problemlösung 4: 4 (132)
produce [prəˈdjuːs] produzieren 3
product [ˈprɒdʌkt] das Produkt 3 **final product** das Endprodukt 4: 1 (34)
professional [prəˈfeʃənl]:
1. professionell, Profi- 2
2. *infml auch* **pro** der Fachmann, die Fachfrau, der Profi 2
profile [ˈprəʊfaɪl] das Profil; die Beschreibung, das Portrait 3
program [ˈprəʊgræm]:
1. das (Computer-)Programm 2
2. programmieren 2
programme [ˈprəʊgræm] das (Fernseh-)Programm, die Sendung 2
programmer [ˈprəʊgræmə] der/die Programmierer/in 2
project [ˈprɒdʒekt] das Projekt 1
prom [prɒm] *(AE)* der Schul(abschluss)ball 4: 3 (90)
promise [ˈprɒmɪs]:
1. versprechen 2
2. das Versprechen 2
keep a promise ein Versprechen halten 2
promo [ˈprəʊməʊ] *siehe* **promotion**
promote [prəˈməʊt] Werbung machen für; fördern, unterstützen 4: 1 (33) **promote sb.** jn. befördern 4: 1 (33)
promotion [prəˈməʊʃn] *kurz auch* **promo** die Werbung; die Förderung; der *(berufliche)* Aufstieg 4: 1 (33)
°**promposal** [prɒmˈpəʊzl] *(AE) Einladung, als Partner/in mit jm. zum Schulball zu gehen*
pronounce [prəˈnaʊns] aussprechen 2
pronunciation [prənʌnsiˈeɪʃn] die Aussprache 2
°**prop** [prɒp] die Requisite
property [ˈprɒpəti] das Eigentum; die Immobilie; das Gelände 4: 3 (82/83)
proposal [prəˈpəʊzl] der Vorschlag, der Antrag; der Heiratsantrag 4: 3 (90)
pros *(pl)* [prəʊz]: **the pros and cons** das Pro und Kontra; das Für und Wider 4: 3 (84)
protect (from/against) [prəˈtekt] (be)schützen (vor) 2
°**protection (from/against)** [prəˈtekʃn] der Schutz (vor)
protest [ˈprəʊtest] der Protest, die Protestdemonstration 4: 2 (53)
protest [prəˈtest] protestieren 4: 2 (53)
Protestant [ˈprɒtɪstənt]:
1. der/die Protestant/in 3
2. protestantisch, evangelisch 3
protester [prəˈtestə] der/die Demonstrant/in 4: 2 (53)
proud (of) [praʊd] stolz (auf) 2
province [ˈprɒvɪns] die Provinz, das Bundesland 4: 5 (150/151)
provisional [prəˈvɪʒənl] vorläufig 4: 3 (95) **provisional driving licence / driver's license** die vorläufige Fahrerlaubnis 4: 3 (95)
pub [pʌb] der/das Pub, die Kneipe 3
public [ˈpʌblɪk] öffentlich 3
public transport *(no pl)* [pʌblɪk ˈtrænspɔːt] die öffentlichen Verkehrsmittel 3
public transportation [pʌblɪk trænspɔːˈteɪʃn] *(AE, no pl)* die öffentlichen Verkehrsmittel 4: 3 (85)
pull [pʊl]:
1. das Ziehen, der Ruck 3
2. ziehen 3
pull sb. out (of sth.) jn. aus etwas herausholen, abziehen *(z. B. Truppen)* 4: 3 (96)
°**pumpkin pie** [ˈpʌmpkɪn paɪ] *(AE)* die Kürbistorte *(traditionelle herbstliche Nachspeise in den USA)*
punctuation [pʌŋktʃuˈeɪʃn] die Zeichensetzung 4: 1 (22)
purchase [ˈpɜːtʃəs] *(fml)*:
1. der (Ein-)Kauf, der Erwerb 4: 2 (55)
2. **purchase sth.** etwas kaufen, erwerben 4: 2 (55)
purple [ˈpɜːpl] violett, lila 1
purpose [ˈpɜːpəs] die Absicht; der Sinn, der Zweck 3 **on purpose** mit Absicht 3
push [pʊʃ]:
1. der Stoß, der Schubs 3
2. schieben, stoßen, schubsen 3
put [pʊt], **put, put** *(etwas wohin)* tun, legen, stellen, stecken 1 **put in the right order** in die richtige Reihenfolge bringen 2 **put out a fire** ein Feuer löschen 4: 4 (130) **put sth. on** etwas anziehen *(Kleidung)*, aufsetzen *(z. B. Hut, Brille)* 2 **put sth. up** etwas aufhängen *(an der Wand)* 1 **put sth. up** etwas aufstellen *(z. B. Schild)*, etwas aufbauen *(z. B. Zelt)* 1 **put your hand up / put up your hand** sich melden, aufzeigen 1 **put your hands out** die Hände ausstrecken 2
puzzle [ˈpʌzl] das Rätsel 1
puzzled [ˈpʌzld] verwundert 2

Q

quality [ˈkwɒləti]:
1. hochwertig, von hoher Qualität 4: 3 (99)
2. die Qualität, Qualitäts-; die Eigenschaft 4: 3 (99)
be better quality von besserer Qualität sein 4: 3 (99)
quarter [ˈkwɔːtə]:
1. das Viertel 2
quarter to 3 viertel vor 3 2
2. *(AE)* das 25-Cent-Stück 4: 1 (19)
queen [kwiːn] die Königin 2
queer [kwɪə] queer *(= durch den Ausdruck der sexuellen Orientierung oder geschlechtlichen Identität von der gesellschaftlichen Norm abweichend)* 2
question [ˈkwestʃən] die Frage 1 **ask a question** eine Frage stellen 1
question mark [ˈkwestʃən mɑːk] das Fragezeichen 4: 1 (22)
queue [kjuː]:
1. die (Warte-)Schlange 3
2. sich *(in einer Warteschlage)* anstellen, Schlange stehen 3
quick [kwɪk] schnell 3
°**quicksand** [ˈkwɪksænd] der Treibsand
quiet [ˈkwaɪət] ruhig, still, leise 1
quite [kwaɪt] ziemlich, ganz 1
quiz [kwɪz], *pl* **quizzes** das Quiz, das Ratespiel; der Test 1 **do a quiz** ein Quiz / ein Ratespiel / einen Test machen 1
quizzes [ˈkwɪzɪz] *Plural von* **quiz**
quote [kwəʊt]:
1. das Zitat 4: 1 (25)
2. zitieren 4: 1 (25)

R

rabbit [ˈræbɪt] das Kaninchen 1
raccoon [rəˈkuːn] der Waschbär 4: 4 (126)
°**race** [reɪs] das (Wett-)Rennen
racism [ˈreɪsɪzəm] der Rassismus 3
racist [ˈreɪsɪst]:
1. der/die Rassist/in 3
2. rassistisch 3
radio [ˈreɪdiəʊ] das Radio 3
rail [reɪl] die Bahn; die Schiene, das Gleis 3
rail service [ˈreɪl sɜːvɪs] die Bahnverbindung 3
rain [reɪn]:
1. der Regen 1
come rain or shine bei jedem Wetter; was auch (immer) geschieht 1
2. regnen 1
rain cats and dogs stark regnen 1
rain jacket [ˈreɪn dʒækɪt] die Regenjacke 2
rainbow [ˈreɪnbəʊ] der Regenbogen 2
rainforest [ˈreɪnfɒrɪst] der Regenwald 3
rainy [ˈreɪni] regnerisch 1
°**rally** [ˈræli] sich versammeln, sich zusammenscharen; demonstrieren
ran [ræn] *siehe* **run**

ranch [rɑːntʃ], [ræntʃ] die Ranch *(Viehfarm in USA)* 4: 3 (82/83)
random ['rændəm] zufällig, beliebig 4: 3 (97)
rang [ræŋ] *siehe* **ring**
ranger ['reɪndʒə] *der/die Aufseher/in in einem Nationalpark* 4: 4 (126)
rare [reə] selten *(Adj.)* 1
rarely ['reəli] selten *(Adv.)* 1
°rat [ræt] die Ratte
rate sth. [reɪt] bewerten, beurteilen, einstufen 2
rather ['rɑːðə]: **I'd rather ... (than ...)** Ich würde lieber ... (als ...) 4: 3 (97)
rating ['reɪtɪŋ] die Bewertung, die Beurteilung 2
reach (sb./a place) [riːtʃ] (jn./einen Ort) erreichen 4: 5 (152) **reach a conclusion** zu einem Schluss kommen 4: 5 (152) **reach for sth.** nach etwas greifen 4: 3 (97) **reach out (your hand)** die Hand ausstrecken 4: 3 (97) **reach over** die Hand ausstrecken, (hinüber)greifen 4: 3 (97)
react (to) [ri'ækt] reagieren (auf) 4: 2 (53)
reaction (to) [ri'ækʃn] die Reaktion (auf) 4: 2 (53)
read [red] *siehe* **read**
read [riːd], **read, read** lesen 1 **°read out** (laut) vorlesen
reader ['riːdə] der/die Leser/in 1
ready ['redi] fertig, bereit 1 **get ready (for)** sich fertig machen (für), sich vorbereiten (auf) 2
real [rɪəl] echt, wirklich 2 **for real** echt, wirklich *(Adv.)* 4: 1 (32)
real-life [rɪəl 'laɪf] real *(aus dem echten Leben)* 4: 4 (128)
realization [riːəlaɪ'zeɪʃn] die Erkenntnis 4: 2 (68)
realize sth. ['rɪəlaɪz] etwas erkennen, sich einer Sache bewusst werden 4: 2 (68)
really ['riːəli], ['rɪəli] wirklich 1
reason ['riːzn] der Grund, die Begründung 1 **for this reason** aus diesem Grund 1
receipt [rɪ'siːt] der (Kauf-)Beleg, die Quittung, der Kassenzettel 2
°receive [rɪ'siːv] erhalten, empfangen
recent ['riːsnt] aktuell, jüngst 3 **in recent years** in den letzten Jahren 3
recently ['riːsntli] in letzter Zeit, kürzlich, neuerdings 3
reception [rɪ'sepʃn] der Empfang *(auch beim Telefon)*; die Rezeption 4: 5 (153)
recipe ['resəpi] das (Koch-)Rezept 1
recipe book ['resəpi bʊk] das Kochbuch 1
recognizable (by) ['rekəgnaɪzəbl] (wieder)erkennbar (an) 4: 4 (129)
recognize ['rekəgnaɪz] (wieder)erkennen 3
recommend sth. (to sb.) [rekə'mend] (jm.) etwas empfehlen 3
recommendation [rekəmən'deɪʃn] die Empfehlung 4: 2 (63)
record [rɪ'kɔːd] aufnehmen, aufzeichnen 1
record ['rekɔːd] die Schallplatte 4: 3 (89)
record deal ['rekɔːd diːl] der Plattenvertrag 4: 3 (89)
recording [rɪ'kɔːdɪŋ] die Aufnahme *(Ton-, Bild-)* 2
recycle [riː'saɪkl] recyceln, wiederverwerten 3
red [red] rot 1
°redhead ['redhed] der Rotschopf *(rothaariger Mensch)*
reduce (by) [rɪ'djuːs] reduzieren, verringern (um) 4: 3 (95)
reduction [rɪ'dʌkʃn] die Reduzierung, die Verringerung 4: 3 (95)
°redwood (tree) ['redwʊd] der Mammutbaum
refrigerator [rɪ'frɪdʒəreɪtə] der Kühlschrank 4: 1 (31)
region ['riːdʒən] die Region 3
regional ['riːdʒənl] regional 3
registration [redʒɪ'streɪʃn]:
1. *die Anwesenheitskontrolle und Ankündigung aktueller Ereignisse vor dem Unterricht* 1
°2. die Anmeldung, die Registrierung
regular ['regjələ] regelmäßig; gewohnt, normal 3
relax [rɪ'læks] sich entspannen 2
reliable [rɪ'laɪəbl] verlässlich, zuverlässig 2
relief [rɪ'liːf] die Erleichterung; die Linderung 4: 2 (65)
relieve [rɪ'liːv] erleichtern; lindern 4: 2 (66)
relieved [rɪ'liːvd] erleichtert 4: 2 (66)
religion [rɪ'lɪdʒən] die Religion 1
religious [rɪ'lɪdʒəs] religiös 1
remain [rɪ'meɪn] (ver)bleiben 3
remember [rɪ'membə]:
1. daran denken, nicht vergessen 1
remember to do sth. daran denken, etwas zu tun 1
2. sich erinnern an 1
remember doing sth. sich daran erinnern, etwas getan zu haben 1
rent [rent]:
1. die Miete 3
2. mieten; leihen 3
rent-a-cop [rent ə 'kɒp] *(infml)* die private uniformierte Sicherheitskraft 4: 2 (52)
repair [rɪ'peə]:
1. die Reparatur 3
2. reparieren 3
repeat [rɪ'piːt] wiederholen 2
report [rɪ'pɔːt]:
1. der Bericht 2
2. **report (on)** berichten (über) 2
3. **report sth./sb. (to)** etwas/jn. melden, anzeigen (bei) *(z. B. bei der Polizei)* 4: 4 (131)
republic [rɪ'pʌblɪk] die Republik 3
reputation [repju'teɪʃn] der Ruf *(Ansehen)* 4: 1 (21)
rescue ['reskjuː]:
1. retten 3
2. die Rettung 3
rescuer ['reskjuːə] der/die Retter/in 3
research [rɪ'sɜːtʃ]:
1. erforschen, untersuchen, recherchieren 1
2. die Forschung(en), die Recherche(n) 1
do research recherchieren 1
reservation [rezə'veɪʃn] das Reservat, die Reservation *(der indigenen Bevölkerung Nordamerikas zugewiesenes Gebiet)* 4: (14/15)
resource [rɪ'sɔːs] das (Hilfs-)Mittel, die Ressource 4: 2 (55)
resources *(pl)* [rɪ'sɔːsɪz] die Ressourcen, die (finanziellen) Mittel 4: 2 (55)
respect [rɪ'spekt]:
1. respektieren, achten 2
2. **respect (for)** der Respekt (vor) 2
responsible (for) [rɪ'spɒnsəbl] verantwortlich (für); verantwortungsbewusst 4: 2 (57)
rest [rest]:
1. ruhen; sich ausruhen 1
2. die Ruhe, die Pause, die Erholung 1
take a rest Pause machen 1
3. der Rest 2
restaurant ['restrɒnt] das Restaurant 1
restroom ['restruːm] *(AE)* die Toilette *(in öffentlichen Gebäuden)* 4: 1 (29)
result [rɪ'zʌlt]:
1. das Ergebnis 3
as a result folglich, demzufolge 3
2. **result in** führen zu 3
return [rɪ'tɜːn]:
1. zurückkehren, zurückkommen 2
2. **return sth.** etwas zurückgeben, zurückbringen 4: 4 (122)
3. die Rückkehr 2
4. die Rückgabe 4: 4 (122)
5. **return ticket** *kurz auch* **return** die (Hin- und) Rückfahrkarte 2
reuse [riː'juːz] wiederverwenden 3
reuse [riː'juːs] die Wiederverwendung 3
review [rɪ'vjuː]:
1. der Bericht, die Rezension *(kritische Besprechung)* 4: 2 (69)
2. besprechen, rezensieren; überprüfen 4: 2 (69)
°revision [rɪ'vɪʒn] die Wiederholung *(von Lernstoff)*
rewrite [riː'raɪt], **rewrote, rewritten** neu schreiben, umschreiben 3
rewritten [riː'rɪtn] *siehe* **rewrite**
rewrote [riː'rəʊt] *siehe* **rewrite**
rhino ['raɪnəʊ] *(infml), pl* **rhinos** das Nashorn 3
rhinoceros [raɪ'nɒsərəs], *pl* **rhinoceros** *or* **rhinoceroses** das Nashorn 3
rhythm ['rɪðəm] der Rhythmus 3
rice [raɪs] der Reis 1
rich [rɪtʃ] reich 4: 3 (94)
ridden ['rɪdn] *siehe* **ride**
ride [raɪd]:
1. die Fahrt; das Fahrgeschäft *(auf Volksfesten, in Vergnügungsparks)* 3
2. die Mitfahrgelegenheit 4: 2 (64)
ask sb. for a ride jn. um eine Mitfahrgelegenheit bitten 4: 2 (64) **Do you**

need a ride? Soll ich dich (im Auto) mitnehmen? 4: 2 (64) **give sb. a ride** jn. *(im Auto)* mitnehmen 4: 2 (64)
3. **ride, rode, ridden** reiten; fahren *(z. B. Fahrrad)* 1
ride a bike mit dem Fahrrad fahren 1
ride a horse ein Pferd reiten 1

ride-sharing ['raɪd ʃeərɪŋ] die Fahrgemeinschaft(en), die Mitfahrgelegenheiten 4: 3 (95)
ridge [rɪdʒ] der Bergkamm, der Grat 3
right [raɪt]:
1. richtig *(Adj.)* 1
be right Recht haben 1
2. das Recht 2
3. *(adv.)* genau, gerade, direkt 3
right after school gleich/direkt nach der Schule 3 **right by the sea** direkt am Meer 3 **right from the start** gleich/direkt von Anfang an 3 **right now** genau/gerade jetzt 3 **right then** genau/gerade dann 3

right [raɪt] rechts; nach rechts 2
on the right rechts, auf der rechten Seite 2 **to the right of ...** rechts von ... 2
°right-hand side ['raɪt hænd saɪd] die rechte Seite
ring [rɪŋ] der Ring 1 **boxing ring** der Boxring 4: 1 (30) **key ring** das Schlüsselbund, der Schlüsselring 3 **wedding ring** der Ehering 1
ring [rɪŋ], **rang, rung** läuten, klingeln 4: 2 (65)
rise [raɪz]:
1. die Erhöhung, der Anstieg 4: 2 (65)
2. **rise, rose, risen** sich erheben; (an)steigen 4: 2 (65)
Panic was rising inside him. In ihm stieg Panik auf. / Er bekam Panik. 4: 2 (65)

risen ['rɪzən] *siehe* **rise**
risk [rɪsk] das Risiko 3 **at risk** in Gefahr 3 **at the risk of ...** auf die Gefahr hin ... 3 **take a risk** ein Risiko eingehen 3
risky ['rɪski] riskant 3
river ['rɪvə] der Fluss 2 **by the river** am Fluss 2
°riverside ['rɪvəsaɪd] das Flussufer
road [rəʊd] die Straße *(in oder zwischen Orten)* 3
road trip ['rəʊd trɪp] die Autoreise 3
robot ['rəʊbɒt] der Roboter 1
rock [rɒk]:
1. der Rock *(die Rockmusik)* 2
2. der Fels(en), der Stein 3

rock pool ['rɒk puːl] der Gezeitentümpel *(Wasser, das sich bei Ebbe zwischen Felsen bildet)* 3
rocky ['rɒki] felsig, steinig 3
rode [rəʊd] *siehe* **ride**
role [rəʊl] die Rolle *(Film, Theater)* 2
role model ['rəʊl mɒdl] das Vorbild 3
role-play ['rəʊlpleɪ]:
1. das Rollenspiel 2
2. **role-play sth.** etwas in einem Rollenspiel darstellen 2

roll [rəʊl]:
1. das Brötchen 4: 2 (60)
2. die Rolle 4: 2 (60)
3. rollen 4: 2 (60)
roll (out) rollen; ausrollen *(Teig)* 1

roller coaster ['rəʊlə kəʊstə] die Achterbahn 3
romance [rəʊ'mæns], ['rəʊmæns] die Romanze, die Liebesgeschichte, die Romantik *(Stimmung)* 4: 2 (69)
romantic [rəʊ'mæntɪk] romantisch 2
roof [ruːf] das Dach 4: 2 (65)
room [ruːm] der Raum, das Zimmer
1 **double room** das Doppelzimmer
3 **single room** das Einzelzimmer 3
twin room das Zweibettzimmer 3

rope [rəʊp] das Seil 3
rose [rəʊz] *siehe* **rise**
round [raʊnd]:
1. rund *(Adj.)* 1
2. die Runde 1
3. **round ...** um (... herum), in ... umher 1
all round the globe auf der ganzen Welt 2 **come round (to)** vorbeikommen, vorbeischauen (bei) 2

roundabout ['raʊndəbaʊt] der Kreisverkehr 3
route [ruːt] die Route, der Weg 3
routine [ruː'tiːn] die (Tanz-)Nummer, die Choreographie; die Routine 3
row [rəʊ] die Reihe, die (Häuser-)Zeile 2
royal ['rɔɪəl] königlich 3
rub [rʌb] reiben, scheuern 4: 5 (158)
rubber ['rʌbə] das Radiergummi 1
rubbish ['rʌbɪʃ] der (Haus-)Müll, der Abfall 1
rucksack ['rʌksæk] der Rucksack 1
rude [ruːd] unhöflich, frech 1
rug [rʌg] der Teppich, der Läufer 3
rule [ruːl]:
1. die Herrschaft 3
2. herrschen (über) 3

rule [ruːl] die Regel 2
ruler ['ruːlə] das Lineal 1
run [rʌn]:
1. der Lauf, das Rennen 2
fun run der Volkslauf *(z. B. zum Geldsammeln für wohltätige Zwecke)* 2
°2. der Run *(Punktegewinn einer Mannschaft im Baseball)*

run [rʌn], **ran, run**:
1. rennen, laufen 1
2. fahren, verkehren *(Bus, Bahn)* 4: 1 (28)
3. **run on sth.** laufen, fahren mit etwas *(betrieben werden mit)* 4: 1 (28)
My car runs on ... Mein Auto fährt mit ... (= wird betrieben mit ...) 4: 1 (28)
4. **run sth.** etwas betreiben, leiten 4: 1 (28)
family-run business der Familienbetrieb 4: 1 (28)

rung [rʌŋ] *siehe* **ring**
running ['rʌnɪŋ] das Laufen *(Sport)* 1
rural ['rʊərəl] ländlich, Land- 4: 3 (82/83)
rush [rʌʃ]:
1. die Eile; der Ansturm; der Stoß *(Flüssigkeit/Gas)* 4: 5 (152)
2. eilen; hetzen; (schnell) fließen 4: 5 (152)

S

sacred ['seɪkrɪd] heilig 4: 4 (123)
sad [sæd] traurig 1
safe [seɪf] sicher *(gefahrlos)* 2 **to be on the safe side** um auf der sicheren Seite sein, sicherheitshalber 4: 5 (158)
safety ['seɪfti] die Sicherheit 2
said [sed] *siehe* **say**
Saint (= St) [seɪnt] Sankt (St) 3
salad ['sæləd] der Salat *(als Gericht oder Beilage)* 1
sale [seɪl] der Verkauf 3 **for sale** zu verkaufen 3
salmon ['sæmən], *pl* **salmon** der Lachs 4: 4 (124)
salt [sɔːlt] das Salz 1
salty ['sɔːlti] salzig 3
same [seɪm]: **the same** gleich; derselbe/dieselbe/dasselbe; dieselben 1
sand [sænd] der Sand 3
sandcastle ['sændkɑːsl] die Sandburg 3
sang [sæŋ] *siehe* **sing**
Santa ['sæntə] *siehe* **Santa Claus**
Santa Claus ['sæntə klɔːz] *kurz auch* **Santa** der Weihnachtsmann 4: 1 (31)
sarcastic [sɑː'kæstɪk] sarkastisch 4: 5 (158)
sari ['sɑːri] der Sari *(Kleid/Gewand indischer Frauen)* 2
sat [sæt] *siehe* **sit**
Saturday ['sætədeɪ], ['sætədi] der Samstag 1
sauce [sɔːs] die Soße 1
sausage ['sɒsɪdʒ] das (Brat-, Bock-)Würstchen, die Wurst 1
save [seɪv]:
1. retten 2
2. sparen 2
3. sichern *(Daten)* 2

savings *(pl)* ['seɪvɪŋz] die Ersparnisse 2
savings account ['seɪvɪŋz əkaʊnt] das Sparkonto 2
savoury ['seɪvəri] herzhaft, salzig 1
saw [sɔː] *siehe* **see**
say [seɪ], **said, said** sagen 1 **Say ...** Sagen wir mal, ... / ... zum Beispiel ... 4: 5 (156) **say sorry to sb.** sich bei jm. entschuldigen 3
scan (a text for) [skæn] (einen Text) überfliegen (nach), absuchen (nach) 3
scare sb. [skeə] jn. erschrecken, jm. Angst machen 2
scared [skeəd]: **be scared (of)** Angst haben (vor) 1
scarf [skɑːf], *pl* **scarves** der Schal 2
scarves [skɑːvz] *Plural von* **scarf**
scary ['skeəri] unheimlich, beängstigend, gruselig 2
scene [siːn] die Szene 1

scholarship [ˈskɒləʃɪp] das Stipendium 4: 3 (92)
school [skuːl] die Schule 1 **at school** in der Schule 1
school administrator [skuːl ədˈmɪnɪstreɪtə] *(AE)* das Mitglied der Schulleitung 4: 3 (96)
school club [ˈskuːl klʌb] die AG *(in der Schule)* 1
school uniform [skuːl ˈjuːnɪfɔːm] die Schuluniform 1
schoolchild [ˈskuːltʃaɪld], *pl* **schoolchildren** das Schulkind 2
schoolchildren [ˈskuːltʃɪldrən] *Plural von* **schoolchild**
schoolwork [ˈskuːlwɜːk] die Arbeit für die / in der Schule 4: 4 (134)
sci-fi [ˈsaɪ faɪ] *siehe* **science fiction**
science [ˈsaɪəns] die Naturwissenschaft 1
science fiction [saɪəns ˈfɪkʃn] *infml auch* **sci-fi** die Science-Fiction 2
scientist [ˈsaɪəntɪst] der/die (Natur-)Wissenschaftler/in 2
scone [skɒn] *das kleine runde Milchbrötchen, leicht süß, oft mit Rosinen* 1
°scoop neck [ˈskuːp nek] der U-Ausschnitt *(Kleidung)*
scooter [ˈskuːtə] der (Tret-)Roller 1
score [skɔː]:
1. der Spiel-/Punktestand; der *(im Spiel/Sport erzielte)* Punkt 2
2. *(einen Punkt / ein Tor / einen Treffer)* erzielen 2
scoreboard [ˈskɔːbɔːd] die Anzeigetafel *(z. B. f. Spielstand beim Sport)* 3
Scots [skɒts] Schottisch *(Sprache)*; schottisch 3
scratch [skrætʃ]:
1. der Kratzer 4: 5 (158)
2. kratzen; zerkratzen 4: 5 (158)
scream [skriːm]:
1. der Schrei 2
2. schreien 2
screen [skriːn] der Bildschirm; die Leinwand *(Kino)* 2
script [skrɪpt] das Skript, das Drehbuch 4: 1 (34)
sculpture [ˈskʌlptʃə] die Skulptur 3
sea [siː] das Meer, die See 1 **by the sea** am Meer, an der See 1
sea level [ˈsiː levl] der Meeresspiegel 2
seagull [ˈsiːgʌl] die Möwe 1
°seal [siːl] die Robbe, der Seehund
search (for) [sɜːtʃ]:
1. die Suche (nach) 3
2. **search (for sth.)** (etwas/nach etwas) suchen 3
search sb. jn. durchsuchen 4: 2 (54)
season [ˈsiːzn] die Jahreszeit; die Saison 1
seat [siːt] der (Sitz-)Platz 2 **take a seat** Platz nehmen 2
second [ˈsekənd]:
1. die Sekunde 1
2. **(2nd)** zweite(r, s) 1
second-hand [sekənd ˈhænd] second-hand *(gebraucht, aus zweiter Hand)* 2
second-hand shop [sekənd hænd ˈʃɒp] der Secondhandladen 2
secondary school [ˈsekəndri skuːl] die weiterführende Schule 1
Secondly, ... [ˈsekəndli] Zweitens ... 4: 4 (119)
secret [ˈsiːkrət]:
1. das Geheimnis 1
2. geheim 1
security [sɪˈkjʊərəti] die Sicherheit 4: 2 (52)
security guard [sɪˈkjʊərəti gɑːd] der/die Sicherheitsbedienstete 4: 2 (52)
see [siː], **saw, seen** sehen 1 **see sb.** zu jm. gehen, jn. aufsuchen 2 **See you soon.** Bis bald! 1 **See you.** Bis dann. / Tschüs. 1 **go and see sb. / go to see sb. (about sth.)** jn. besuchen (gehen/fahren); jn. (wegen etwas) aufsuchen 2
seem (to be/do) [siːm] erscheinen; (zu sein / zu tun) scheinen 3
seen [siːn] *siehe* **see**
segregation [segrɪˈgeɪʃn] die Trennung *(nach Hautfarbe/Religion/Geschlecht)* 4: 2 (56)
self-pity [self ˈpɪti] das Selbstmitleid 4: 1 (31)
sell [sel], **sold, sold** verkaufen 2
semi-detached home/house [semi dɪˈtætʃt] die Doppelhaushälfte 1
send [send], **sent, sent** senden, schicken 1
senior [ˈsiːniə] *(AE) der/die Schüler/in im letzten Schuljahr der amerikanischen High School* 4: 3 (88)
sense [sens] der Sinn 3 **sense of humour** der (Sinn für) Humor 4: 5 (157) **sense of smell** der Geruchssinn 3 **sense of touch** der Tastsinn 3 **make sense** Sinn ergeben 3
sensitive (to) [ˈsensətɪv] einfühlsam (gegenüber), sensibel; heikel *(z. B. Thema)* 4: 4 (125)
sent [sent] *siehe* **send**
sentence [ˈsentəns] der Satz 1
separate [ˈsepəreɪt] trennen 4: (12/13)
separate [ˈseprət] getrennt, separat 4: (12/13)
September [sepˈtembə] der September 1
°sequoia (tree) [sɪˈkwɔɪə] der Mammutbaum
series [ˈsɪəriːz], *pl* **series** die Serie, die Sendereihe 3
serious [ˈsɪəriəs] ernst(haft) 3 **Are you serious?** Meinst du das ernst? 3 **take sth. seriously** etwas ernst nehmen 3
service [ˈsɜːvɪs] die (Zug-/Bus-)Verbindung; der Service 3
service station [ˈsɜːvɪs steɪʃn] die Tankstelle; die (Autobahn-)Raststätte 3
sesame [ˈsesəmi] der Sesam 3
set [set], **set, set** stellen, legen, setzen 2 **set off** aufbrechen *(sich auf den Weg machen)* 4: 5 (158) **set sth. on fire** etwas in Brand setzen, etwas anzünden 4: 4 (130) **set sth. up** etwas einrichten; etwas aufbauen 3 **set the alarm** (sich) den Wecker stellen 2 **set the table** den Tisch decken 2 **be set (in)** spielen (in) *(Film, Geschichte)* 4: 4 (133)
settle [ˈsetl] sich niederlassen, sich ansiedeln 4: 4 (122)
settlement [ˈsetlmənt] die (Be-)Siedlung 4: 4 (122)
settler [ˈsetlə] der/die Siedler/in 4: 4 (122)
seven [ˈsevn] sieben 1
seventeen [sevnˈtiːn] siebzehn 1
seventy [ˈsevnti] siebzig 1
several [ˈsevrəl] mehrere, einige 3
sew [səʊ], **sewed, sewn** nähen 3
sewing machine [ˈsəʊɪŋ məʃiːn] die Nähmaschine 3
sewn [səʊn] *siehe* **sew**
sexism [ˈseksɪzəm] der Sexismus 4: 3 (97)
sexist [ˈseksɪst]:
1. der/die Sexist/in 4: 3 (97)
2. sexistisch *(diskriminierend aufgrund des Geschlechts)* 4: 3 (97)
shake [ʃeɪk], **shook, shaken** schütteln 3 **shake sb.'s hand / shake sb. by the hand** jm. die Hand schütteln/geben 3 **shake your head** den Kopf schütteln 3
shaken [ˈʃeɪkən] *siehe* **shake**
shaky [ˈʃeɪki] zittrig, wacklig, schwach 4: 3 (97)
Shall I ...? [ʃæl], [ʃəl] Soll ich ...? 3
shame [ʃeɪm]:
1. **a shame** schade; eine Schande 1
2. **shame sb. (publicly)** jn. (öffentlich) anprangern, bloßstellen; jn. beschämen 4: 3 (97)
shaming [ˈʃeɪmɪŋ]: **public shaming** das öffentliche Anprangern, das öffentliche Bloßstellen 4: 3 (97)
shape [ʃeɪp]:
1. die Form, die Gestalt 4: (10/11)
2. **shape (sth. into sth.)** (etwas zu etwas) formen 4: (10/11)
share [ʃeə]:
1. der (An-)Teil 1
2. teilen 1
sharpener [ˈʃɑːpnə] der Anspitzer 1
she [ʃiː] sie *(weibliche Person)* 1 **she's (= she is)** sie ist 1
sheep [ʃiːp], *pl* **sheep** das Schaf 2
shelf [ʃelf], *pl* **shelves** das Regal(brett) 1
shelves [ʃelvz] *Plural von* **shelf**
shine [ʃaɪn]:
1. der (Sonnen-)Schein; der Glanz 1 **come rain or shine** bei jedem Wetter; was auch (immer) geschieht 1
2. **shine, shone, shone** scheinen *(Sonne)*; leuchten, strahlen, glänzen 1
shiny [ˈʃaɪni] glänzend 3
ship [ʃɪp] das Schiff 3
shipbuilding [ˈʃɪpbɪldɪŋ] der Schiffbau 3
shirt [ʃɜːt] das Hemd 1

shock [ʃɒk]:
1. der Schock 2
2. **shock sb.** jn. schockieren 2

shocked [ʃɒkt] schockiert 2
shocking [ˈʃɒkɪŋ] schockierend 2
shoe [ʃuː] der Schuh 1 **be in sb's shoes** in js. Haut stecken 4: 2 (53) **put yourself in sb.'s shoes** sich in js. Lage versetzen 4: 2 (53)
shone [ʃɒn] *siehe* **shine**
shook [ʃʊk] *siehe* **shake**
shoot [ʃuːt], **shot, shot** (er)schießen 4: 2 (57)
shooting [ˈʃuːtɪŋ] die Schießerei 4: 2 (57)
shop [ʃɒp]:
1. der Laden, das Geschäft 1
2. (ein)kaufen, „shoppen" 2

shop for sth. etwas kaufen (gehen) 2
shop assistant [ˈʃɒp əsɪstənt] der/die Verkäufer/in 2
shopper [ˈʃɒpə] der Kunde, die Kundin; der/die Einkäufer/in 2
shopping [ˈʃɒpɪŋ] das Einkaufen; die Einkäufe 1 **do the shopping** die Einkäufe erledigen, einkaufen gehen 1 **go shopping** einkaufen gehen 1
shopping centre [ˈʃɒpɪŋ sentə] das Einkaufszentrum 1
shopping list [ˈʃɒpɪŋ lɪst] die Einkaufsliste 1
shopping mall [ˈʃɒpɪŋ mɔːl] Einkaufszentrum 4: 2 (50/51)
shore [ʃɔː] das Ufer; die Küste 4: 5 (157)
short [ʃɔːt]:
1. kurz 1
2. klein *(Person; Körpergröße)* 1

shorts *(pl)* [ʃɔːts] die kurze Hose, die Shorts 2
shot [ʃɒt]:
1. der Schuss; der Wurf *(Sport)* 4: 2 (57)
2. *siehe* **shoot**

should [ʃʊd]: **it should ...** es sollte ... 2
shoulder [ˈʃəʊldə] die Schulter 4: 3 (96)
shout [ʃaʊt]:
1. der Ruf, der Schrei 3
2. rufen, schreien 3

shout at sb. jn. anschreien 3
show [ʃəʊ]:
1. die Show, die Aufführung; die Ausstellung 1
2. **show, showed, shown** zeigen 1

shower [ˈʃaʊə] die Dusche 1 **have a shower** (sich) duschen 1
shown [ʃəʊn] *siehe* **show**
shrug [ʃrʌg]:
1. das Achselzucken 4: 3 (96)
2. **shrug (your shoulders)** mit den Achseln/Schultern zucken 4: 3 (96)

shy [ʃaɪ] scheu, schüchtern 2
sick [sɪk] krank 2 **be sick** sich übergeben 2 **I feel sick.** Mir ist schlecht 2
sickness [ˈsɪknəs] die Krankheit 2 **in sickness or in health** wenn man krank oder gesund ist 2
side [saɪd] die Seite *(z. B. Straßenseite)* 2
sidewalk [ˈsaɪdwɔːk] *(AE)* der Gehweg, der Bürgersteig 4: 4 (129)
sigh [saɪ]:
1. der Seufzer 3
2. seufzen 3

sight [saɪt]:
1. der Anblick, die Sicht(weite), die Sehkraft 2
2. die Sehenswürdigkeit 2

sightseeing [ˈsaɪtsiːɪŋ] das Sightseeing *(Besichtigung von Sehenswürdigkeiten)* 3
sign [saɪn]:
1. das Schild; das Zeichen 2
2. **sign sth.** etwas unterschreiben 4: 2 (59)

sign language [ˈsaɪn læŋgwɪdʒ] die Zeichensprache, die Gebärdensprache 4: 4 (133)
signal [ˈsɪgnəl] das Signal 4: 5 (153)
silence [ˈsaɪləns] die Stille; das Schweigen 2
silent [ˈsaɪlənt] still, lautlos 2 **fall/go silent** still werden, verstummen 2
°silicon [ˈsɪlɪkən] das Silizium
silk [sɪlk] die Seide 3
silver [ˈsɪlvə]:
1. das Silber 1
2. silberfarben 1

similar (to sb./sth.) [ˈsɪmələ] (jm./einer Sache) ähnlich 3
simple [ˈsɪmpl] einfach 3
simulation [sɪmjuˈleɪʃn] die Simulation 2
since [sɪns]: **since 2010** seit 2010 3 **since then** seitdem 3
sing [sɪŋ], **sang, sung** singen 1
singer [ˈsɪŋə] der/die Sänger/in 1
singing [ˈsɪŋɪŋ] das Singen 1
single [ˈsɪŋgl] Einzel-, einzelne(r, s) 2
single room [sɪŋgl ˈruːm] das Einzelzimmer 3
single ticket [sɪŋgl ˈtɪkɪt] die einfache Fahrkarte *(= ohne Rückfahrt)* 2
sir [sɜː] mein Herr, gnädiger Herr 4: 3 (84) **Dear Sir or Madam** Sehr geehrte Damen und Herren 4: 3 (84)
sister [ˈsɪstə] die Schwester 1
sit [sɪt], **sat, sat** sitzen; sich setzen 1 **sit down** sich hinsetzen 1
site [saɪt] die Stelle, der Ort, die Stätte 3 *(kurz für* **website***)* die Website 3
situation [sɪtʃuˈeɪʃn] die Situation 2
six [sɪks] sechs 1
sixteen [sɪksˈtiːn] sechzehn 1
sixty [ˈsɪksti] sechzig 1
size [saɪz] die Größe 2 **What size are you / do you take?** Welche Größe hast du? 2
ski [skiː] Ski laufen, Ski fahren 3
skill [skɪl] die Fähigkeit, die Fertigkeit 1 **°life skills** die Alltagskompetenzen, die lebenswichtigen Fertigkeiten **°study skills** die Lerntechniken
skim a text [skɪm] einen Text überfliegen *(um den Inhalt grob zu erfassen)* 3
skin [skɪn] die Haut; die Schale *(z. B. Banane)* 3
skirt [skɜːt] der Rock 1
sky [skaɪ] der Himmel 3 **in the sky** am Himmel 3
skydiving [ˈskaɪdaɪvɪŋ] das Fallschirmspringen 3
skyscraper [ˈskaɪskreɪpə] der Wolkenkratzer 3
slam [slæm]:
1. der Knall 4: 3 (97)
2. (hin)knallen, zuschlagen *(Tür)* 4: 3 (97)

slave [sleɪv] der Sklave, die Sklavin 4: 2 (56)
slavery [ˈsleɪvəri] die Sklaverei 4: 2 (56)
sleep [sliːp]:
1. der Schlaf 1
2. **sleep, slept, slept** schlafen 1

sleep late lange schlafen 2
slept [slept] *siehe* **sleep**
slid [slɪd] *siehe* **slide**
slide [slaɪd]:
1. das Dia; die Folie *(Präsentationssoftware)* 2
2. die Rutsche, die Rutschbahn 3
3. **slide, slid, slid** schieben, rutschen; gleiten (lassen) 3

slide show [ˈslaɪd ʃəʊ] die Slideshow, die Bildschirmpräsentation 1
slip [slɪp] (aus)rutschen 3
slippers *(pl)* [slɪpə] die Hausschuhe 2
slouch [slaʊtʃ] sich lümmeln, in krummer Haltung stehen/sitzen 3
slow [sləʊ]:
1. langsam 1
2. **slow (down)** (sich) verlangsamen, langsamer werden/machen, 4: 2 (65)

slow sb. down jn. langsamer machen, aufhalten 4: 2 (65) **slow sth. down** etwas langsamer machen, verlangsamen 4: 2 (65)
small [smɔːl] klein 1
smart [smɑːt]:
1. schick 1
2. intelligent, clever 1

smell [smel]:
1. der Geruch; der Gestank 1
2. riechen; schlecht riechen 1

smile [smaɪl]:
1. das Lächeln 1
2. lächeln 1

smile at sb. jn. anlächeln 1
smoke [sməʊk]:
1. der Rauch 4: 4 (130)
2. rauchen 4: 4 (130)

°s'more [smɔː] *der Doppelkeks mit Schokolade und Marshmallows, gegrillt*
snake [sneɪk] die Schlange 1
sneaker [ˈsniːkə] *(AE)* der Sportschuh, der Turnschuh 4: 1 (19)
sniff (at) [snɪf] schnüffeln, schnuppern (an) 4: 5 (155)
snow [snəʊ]:
1. der Schnee 1
2. schneien 1

snowboarding [ˈsnəʊbɔːdɪŋ] das Snowboardfahren 3
snowmobile [ˈsnəʊməbiːl] das Schneemobil 4: (10/11)
snowy [ˈsnəʊi] schneebedeckt; verschneit 1
so [səʊ]:
1. so 1
so good so gut 1
2. also, daher 1
3. **so (that)** sodass 1
4. **He said so.** Das hat er gesagt. 2 **I don't think so.** Das glaube/denke ich nicht. 2 **I hope so.** Das hoffe ich. 2 **I think so.** Ich glaube/denke ja. 2 **If so, ...** Wenn ja, ... 2
so far [səʊ ˈfɑː] bis jetzt, bis hierher 2
soccer [ˈsɒkə] der Fußball 4: 1 (24)
sociable [ˈsəʊʃəbl] kontaktfreudig, gesellig 2
social [ˈsəʊʃl] sozial 2
social media [səʊʃl ˈmiːdiə] die sozialen Medien 2 **on social media** in den sozialen Medien 2
social network [səʊʃl ˈnetwɜːk] das soziale Netzwerk 3
socials [ˈsəʊʃlz] (*kurz für* **social media**) die sozialen Medien 4: 2 (54)
sock [sɒk] die Socke 1
sofa [ˈsəʊfə] das Sofa 1
soft [sɒft] weich; *(Stimme)* leise 3 **in a soft voice** mit leiser Stimme 3
soft drink [ˈsɒft drɪŋk] das alkoholfreie Getränk 3
sold [səʊld] *siehe* **sell**
soldier [ˈsəʊldʒə] der/die Soldat/in 3
solution (to a problem) [səˈluːʃn] die Lösung (eines Problems) 1
solve [sɒlv] lösen *(Rätsel, Problem)*, lüften *(Geheimnis)* 2
some [sʌm], [səm] einige, ein paar; etwas, ein wenig 1
somebody [ˈsʌmbədi] jemand 1
someone [ˈsʌmwʌn] jemand 1
something [ˈsʌmθɪŋ] etwas 1
sometimes [ˈsʌmtaɪmz] manchmal 1
somewhere [ˈsʌmweə] irgendwo(hin) 2
son [sʌn] der Sohn 1
sonar [ˈsəʊnɑː] Sonar-, das Sonargerät 3
song [sɒŋ] das Lied 1
songwriter [ˈsɒŋraɪtə] der/die Songwriter/in *(Liedermacher/in)* 4: 1 (25)
soon [suːn] bald 1 **°soon enough** schon bald
sophomore [ˈsɒfəmɔː] *(AE) der/die Schüler/in im 2. Schuljahr der amerikanischen High School* 4: 3 (88)
sorry [ˈsɒri]: **Sorry. / I'm sorry.** Tut mir leid. / Entschuldigung. 1 **be/feel sorry for sb.** Mitleid haben mit jm. 1 **I'm / I feel sorry for him.** Er tut mir leid. 1 **say sorry to sb.** sich bei jm. entschuldigen 3
sort (of) [sɔːt] die Art (von) 2
sound [saʊnd]:
1. das Geräusch; der Klang, der Laut 1
2. klingen *(sich ... anhören)* 1
soup [suːp] die Suppe 2
sour [saʊr] sauer, säuerlich 3
source [sɔːs] die Quelle *(z. B. Website, Text)* 3
south [saʊθ] der Süden; südlich; Süd- 3
south-east [saʊθˈiːst] der Südosten, südöstlich; Südost- 3
south-west [saʊθˈwest] der Südwesten; südwestlich; Südwest- 3
southern [ˈsʌðən] südlich, Süd- 3
space [speɪs] der Raum, der Platz; der Weltraum 2
spacesuit [ˈspeɪssuːt] der Raumanzug 4: 4 (124)
spark [spɑːk]:
1. der Funke 4: 4 (131)
2. **spark sth.** etwas entfachen, entzünden, auslösen; *(Interesse)* wecken 4: 4 (131)
sparkling [ˈspɑːklɪŋ] kohlensäurehaltig 3
sparkling water [spɑːklɪŋ ˈwɔːtə] der Sprudel 3
spat [spæt] *siehe* **spit**
speak (to) [spiːk], **spoke, spoken** sprechen (mit) 1 **Speak later.** Tschüs. / Bis später. 1 **speak out** (deutlich) seine Meinung sagen, seine Stimme erheben 4: 2 (59)
speaker [ˈspiːkə] der Sprecher, die Sprecherin 4: 2 (52)
speaking [ˈspiːkɪŋ] das Sprechen 1
special [ˈspeʃl] besondere(r, s) 1
special effects *(pl)* [speʃl ɪˈfekts] die Special Effects *(in Filmen)* 2
species [ˈspiːʃiːz], *pl* **species** die Art *(Biologie)* 4: 4 (123)
specific [spəˈsɪfɪk] bestimmte(r, s), spezifische(r, s) 3
spectacular [spekˈtækjələ] spektakulär, aufsehenerregend 3
sped [sped] *siehe* **speed**
speech [spiːtʃ] die Rede, die Ansprache; die Sprache 4: 2 (52) **give a speech** eine Rede halten 4: 2 (52)
speech bubble [ˈspiːtʃ bʌbl] die Sprechblase 1
speed [spiːd]:
1. die Geschwindigkeit 4: 3 (95)
at a speed of ... mit einer Geschwindigkeit von ... 4: 3 (95)
2. **speed, sped, sped** rasen, zu schnell fahren 4: 3 (95)
speed limit [ˈspiːd lɪmɪt] die Geschwindigkeitsbegrenzung 4: 3 (95)
spell [spel] buchstabieren 1
spellchecker [ˈspeltʃekə] der Spellchecker *(Programm zur Rechtschreibüberprüfung)* 3
spelling [ˈspelɪŋ] die Schreibweise, die Rechtschreibung 1
spend [spend], **spent, spent: spend money (on ...)** Geld ausgeben (für ...) 2 **spend time** Zeit verbringen 2
spent [spent] *siehe* **spend**
spice [spaɪs] das Gewürz 1
spicy [ˈspaɪsi] würzig, scharf 1
°spin (around) [spɪn], **spun, spun** (sich) (herum)drehen
spit (sth. out) [spɪt], **spat, spat** (etwas aus)spucken; etwas zischen/fauchen *(in gereiztem Ton sagen)* 4: 3 (97)
splash [splæʃ]:
1. das Platschen; der Spritzer *(z. B. Matsch-)* 4: 5 (154)
2. spritzen, platschen 4: 5 (154)
spoke [spəʊk] *siehe* **speak**
spoken [ˈspəʊkən] *siehe* **speak**
spoon [spuːn] der Löffel 1
sport [spɔːt] der Sport; die Sportart 1 **do sport** Sport machen/treiben 1 **play sport(s)** Sport machen/treiben 4: 1 (27)
sports hall [ˈspɔːts hɔːl] die Sporthalle 1
sportspeople [ˈspɔːtspiːpl] *Plural von* **sportsperson**
sportsperson [ˈspɔːtspɜːsn], *pl* **sportspeople** der/die Sportler/in 2
sporty [ˈspɔːti] sportlich 2
spot [spɒt]:
1. die Stelle, der Punkt; der Fleck 3 **on the spot** auf der Stelle *(ohne sich fortzubewegen)* 4: 5 (157)
2. **spot sth.** etwas entdecken 4: 3 (97)
spotlight [ˈspɒtlaɪt] das Spotlight, der Scheinwerfer; die Aufmerksamkeit 2 **in/under the spotlight** im Rampenlicht, im Blickpunkt des Interesses 2 **turn the spotlight on sb./sth.** den Scheinwerfer / die Aufmerksamkeit auf jn./etwas richten 2
spray [spreɪ]:
1. (be)sprühen 4: 4 (127)
2. das Spray 4: 4 (127)
pepper spray das Pfefferspray 4: 4 (127)
spring [sprɪŋ] der Frühling 1
°spun [spʌn] *siehe* **spin**
square [skweə]:
1. rechteckig; quadratisch 2
2. der Platz *(in der Stadt)* 2
3. das Quadrat, Quadrat- 4: 1 (20)
square kilometre(s) (km²) Quadratkilometer 4: 1 (20)
squeeze [skwiːz] (zusammen)drücken; (sich) zwängen, (sich) quetschen 4: 3 (97)
St = Saint [seɪnt] St = Sankt 3
stable [ˈsteɪbl] der Stall 4: 3 (93) **clean out the stables** ausmisten 4: 3 (93)
stadium [ˈsteɪdiəm] das Stadion 1
stage [steɪdʒ] die Bühne 2
stain [steɪn]:
1. der Fleck 4: 3 (97)
2. Flecken bekommen 4: 3 (97)
stain sth. auf etwas Flecken machen/hinterlassen 4: 3 (97)
stairs *(pl)* [steəz] die Treppe; die (Treppen-)Stufen 2
stall [stɔːl] der (Markt-)Stand, die Bude 3

stamp [stæmp] die Marke; die Briefmarke 4: 1 (32)
stand [stænd]:
1. der (Markt-)Stand, die Bude 3
2. der Standpunkt, die Haltung 4: 2 (54)
take a stand (against sth.) Stellung beziehen (gegen etwas) 4: 2 (54)
3. **stand, stood, stood** stehen; sich (hin)stellen 1
stand out (against/from) auffallen, sich abheben (gegen/von) 3 **stand up** (auf)stehen 1
star [stɑː]:
1. der (Film-/Pop-)Star 1
2. der Stern 2
star sign [ˈstɑː saɪn] das Sternzeichen 2
stare [steə]:
1. das Starren, der starre Blick 1
2. **stare (at)** (an)starren 1
start [stɑːt]:
1. der Anfang, der Start 1
2. beginnen, anfangen (mit) 1
start a business ein Geschäft aufmachen, einen Betrieb gründen/eröffnen 2 **To start with ...** Zunächst (einmal) ...; anfangs 3
state [steɪt]:
1. der Zustand 3
2. der (Bundes-)Staat 4: (10/11)
statement [ˈsteɪtmənt] die Aussage; der Aussagesatz 4: 4 (125)
station [ˈsteɪʃn]:
1. der Bahnhof 1
2. die Station; die Stelle, die Position 4: 3 (85)
car-charging station die (Auto-)Ladestation 4: 3 (85) **service station** die Tankstelle; die (Autobahn-)Raststätte 3
statistic [stəˈtɪstɪk] die statistische Tatsache, die statistische Größe 3
statistics *(pl)* die Statistik(en) 3
statue [ˈstætʃuː] die Statue 3
stay [steɪ]:
1. der Aufenthalt 2
2. bleiben; übernachten 2
stay in touch (with) in Verbindung/Kontakt bleiben (mit) 3 **stay out** *(abends)* fortbleiben, wegbleiben 3 **stay up** aufbleiben *(nicht ins Bett gehen)* 2
steal [stiːl], **stole, stolen** stehlen, rauben 2
step [step] die Stufe; der Schritt 1
stepbrother [ˈstepbrʌðə] der Stiefbruder 1
stepdad [ˈstepdæd] der Stiefvater 1
stepdaughter [ˈstepdɔːtə] die Stieftochter 1
stepfather [ˈstepfɑːðə] der Stiefvater 1
stepmother [ˈstepmʌðə] die Stiefmutter 1
stepmum [ˈstepmʌm] die Stiefmutter 1
stepsister [ˈstepsɪstə] die Stiefschwester 1
stepson [ˈstepsʌn] der Stiefsohn 1
stereotype [ˈsteriətaɪp] der Stereotyp, das Klischee, die Klischeevorstellung 4: 4 (124)
stick [stɪk] der Stock; der Schläger *(Sport)* 4: 5 (157)
°**sticky note** [stɪki ˈnəʊt] die Haftnotiz, der Klebezettel
still [stɪl] (immer) noch; trotzdem 1
stir [stɜː] (um)rühren 1
stir-fry [ˈstɜː fraɪ]:
1. *das Gericht aus kurz angebratenen Zutaten, z. B. kleinen Stücken Fleisch, Fisch und/oder Gemüse* 1
2. (Gemüse- oder Fleischstücke) unter Rühren scharf anbraten 1
stole [stəʊl] *siehe* **steal**
stolen [ˈstəʊlən] *siehe* **steal**
stone [stəʊn] der Stein 4: 2 (64)
stop [stɒp]:
1. der Halt, der Haltepunkt; die Unterbrechung 1
bus stop die Bushaltestelle 1
2. (an)halten; stoppen; aufhören (mit) 1
stop a fire ein Feuer löschen 2
store [stɔː] das Geschäft 3
storm [stɔːm] der Sturm; das Gewitter 3
storm chaser [ˈstɔːm tʃeɪsə] der/die Sturmjäger/in 4: 2 (67)
stormy [ˈstɔːmi] stürmisch 3
story [ˈstɔːri] die Geschichte *(Erzählung)* 1
storyteller [ˈstɔːri telə] der/die (Geschichten-)Erzähler/in 2
straight [streɪt]:
1. gerade; *(Haare)* glatt 2
2. direkt, gleich, geradewegs 3
straight on geradeaus (weiter) 2
strange [streɪndʒ] seltsam, sonderbar 2
stranger [ˈstreɪndʒə] der/die Fremde 2
strap [stræp] der Träger *(z. B. am Top/Kleid)*; der Gurt, der Riemen 4: 3 (96)
strategy [ˈstrætədʒi] die Strategie 4: 1 (34) **problem-solving strategy** die Strategie zur Problemlösung 4: 1 (34)
strawberry [ˈstrɔːbəri] die Erdbeere 1
stream [striːm] streamen 2
streamer [ˈstriːmə] der/die Streamer/in *(Person, die etwas streamt)* 2
street [striːt] die Straße *(in Ortschaften)* 1 **in the street** auf der Straße 1 **on a quiet street** an einer ruhigen Straße 1
street music [ˈstriːt mjuːzɪk] die Straßenmusik 1
street musician [ˈstriːt mjuzɪʃn] der/die Straßenmusiker/in 2
strength [streŋθ] die Stärke, die Kraft 2
stress [stres]:
1. der Stress 3
2. **stress sb.** jn. stressen, (über)belasten 3
stressed [strest] gestresst 1
stressful [ˈstresfl] stressig 3
strict [strɪkt] streng 3
strike [straɪk] der Streik 4: 2 (61)
be on strike streiken 4: 2 (61) **go on strike** in den Streik treten 4: 2 (61)
strong [strɒŋ] stark 2
structure [ˈstrʌktʃə]:
1. die Struktur 2
2. strukturieren, aufbauen 2
student [ˈstjuːdnt] der/die Schüler/in; der/die Student/in 1
studio [ˈstjuːdiəʊ] das Studio 2
study [ˈstʌdi] studieren; lernen *(z. B. für Prüfungen)* 2
°**study skills** *(pl)* [ˈstʌdi skɪlz] die Lerntechniken
stuff [stʌf] *(infml)* das Zeug, der Kram; die Sachen 4: 1 (30)
stupid [ˈstjuːpɪd] dumm, blöd; albern 2
style [staɪl] der Stil; die Mode; die Art 3 **(be) in style** in Mode (sein) 3 **(be/go) out of style** aus der Mode (sein/kommen) 3 **...-style** im Stil von ..., nach ...-Art, ...-mäßig 4: 1 (26)
subject [ˈsʌbdʒɪkt] das (Schul-)Fach 1
submarine [sʌbməˈriːn] das U-Boot 3
subscribe to sth. [səbˈskraɪb] etwas abonnieren 3
subway [ˈsʌbweɪ] *(AE)* die U-Bahn 4: 1 (16/17)
success [səkˈses] der Erfolg 2
successful [səkˈsesfl] erfolgreich 2
such (a) [sʌtʃ] so(lch) (ein/e) 2
such as [ˈsʌtʃ əz] wie (zum Beispiel) 3
sudden [ˈsʌdn] plötzliche(r, s) 3
suddenly [ˈsʌdənli] plötzlich, auf einmal 2
sugar [ˈʃʊgə] der Zucker 1
suggest sth. (to sb.) [səˈdʒest] (jm.) etwas vorschlagen 2
suggestion [səˈdʒestʃən] der Vorschlag 2
suit [suːt] der (Herren-)Anzug; das (Damen-)Kostüm 2
°**suitable** [ˈsuːtəbl] passend, geeignet
sum sth. up [sʌm ˈʌp] etwas zusammenfassen 3 **To sum up, ...** Um (es) zusammenzufassen, .../Zusammenfassend kann man sagen, ... 3
summarize sth. [ˈsʌməraɪz] etwas zusammenfassen 3
summary [ˈsʌməri] die Zusammenfassung 3
summer [ˈsʌmə] der Sommer 1
summer camp [ˈsʌmə kæmp] Ferienlager *(im Sommer)* 4: (14/15)
sun [sʌn] die Sonne 1 **have a moment in the sun** kurz im Mittelpunkt stehen 1
sunbathe [ˈsʌnbeɪð] sonnenbaden 2
Sunday [ˈsʌndeɪ], [ˈsʌndi] der Sonntag 1
sung [sʌŋ] *siehe* **sing**
sunglasses *(pl)* [ˈsʌnglɑːsɪz] die Sonnenbrille 2
sunny [ˈsʌni] sonnig 1 **It's sunny.** Die Sonne scheint. 1
sunrise [ˈsʌnraɪz] der Sonnenaufgang 2

sunset [ˈsʌnset] der Sonnenuntergang 2
super [ˈsu:pə] super 1
superhero [ˈsu:pəhɪərəʊ], *pl* **superheroes** der/die Superheld/in 1
supermarket [ˈsu:pəmɑ:kɪt] der Supermarkt 1
superpower [ˈsu:pəpaʊə] die Superkraft 2
support [səˈpɔ:t]:
1. die Unterstützung 2
2. unterstützen 2
supporter [səˈpɔ:tə] der/die Anhänger/in, der Fan 2
suppose [səˈpəʊz] glauben, annehmen, vermuten 4: 3 (98)
supposedly [səˈpəʊzɪdli] vermeintlich, angeblich *(Adv.)* 4: 3 (98)
sure [ʃʊə], [ʃɔ:] sicher 1 **make sure that ...** sicherstellen, dass ...; dafür sorgen, dass ... 3
surf [sɜ:f] surfen 2 **surf the web** im Internet surfen 2
surprise [səˈpraɪz]:
1. die Überraschung 2
2. überraschen 2
surprised [səˈpraɪzd] überrascht 1
surprisingly [səˈpraɪzɪŋli] überraschenderweise, überraschend *(Adv.)* 3
survey [ˈsɜ:veɪ] die Umfrage 4: 3 (85) **do a survey** eine Umfrage durchführen 4: 3 (85)
suspicious (of) [səˈspɪʃəs] verdächtig; misstrauisch (gegenüber) 4: 2 (57)
sustainable [səˈsteɪnəbl] nachhaltig, umweltverträglich; zukunftsfähig 3
swallow [ˈswɒləʊ] (ver)schlucken 4: 1 (32)
swam [swæm] *siehe* **swim**
swap [swɒp]:
1. tauschen 1
2. der Tausch 1
clothes swap der Kleidertausch, die Kleidertauschparty 1
swear [sweə], **swore, sworn** fluchen; schwören 4: 3 (96)
swear word [ˈsweə wɔ:d] das Schimpfwort 4: 3 (96)
sweet [swi:t]:
1. süß 1
2. das Bonbon 1
sweets *(pl)* die Süßigkeiten 1
sweet shop [ˈswi:t ʃɒp] das Süßwarengeschäft 2
swim [swɪm]:
1. der Schwimmgang, das Bad *(z. B. im Meer)* 3
go for a swim schwimmen gehen 3
2. **swim, swam, swum** schwimmen 1
swimmer [ˈswɪmə] der/die Schwimmer/in 1
swimming [ˈswɪmɪŋ] das Schwimmen 1
swimsuit [ˈswɪmsu:t] der Badeanzug 2
swing [swɪŋ], **swung, swung** schwingen 4: 5 (155)
swipe [swaɪp] wischen *(auf Touchscreen)*; durchziehen, einlesen *(z. B. Kreditkarte)* 3
switch [swɪtʃ]:
1. der Schalter 3
2. **switch sth. on/off** etwas einschalten / ausschalten 3
swore [swɔ:] *siehe* **swear**
sworn [swɔ:n] *siehe* **swear**
swum [swʌm] *siehe* **swim**
swung [swʌŋ] *siehe* **swing**
symbol [ˈsɪmbl] das Symbol 3
sympathetic [sɪmpəˈθetɪk] verständnisvoll, mitfühlend 4: 1 (31)
sympathy [ˈsɪmpəθi] das Mitgefühl, das Verständnis; die Sympathie 4: 1 (31)
°**synonym** [ˈsɪnənɪm] das Synonym *(Wort mit gleicher Bedeutung)*
system [ˈsɪstəm] das System 3

T

table [ˈteɪbl]:
1. der Tisch 1
set the table den Tisch decken 2
°2. die Tabelle
table tennis [ˈteɪbl tenɪs] das Tischtennis 1
tablespoon [ˈteɪblspu:n] der Esslöffel 1
take [teɪk], **took, taken**:
1. dauern, *(Zeit)* brauchen, in Anspruch nehmen 1
2. (mit)nehmen; bringen 1
take a test einen Test machen, ablegen 3 **take action** Maßnahmen ergreifen 4: 2 (58) **take notes** sich Notizen machen 3 **take out the rubbish** den Müll rausbringen 2 **take part (in)** teilnehmen (an), mitmachen (bei) 3 **take photos** Fotos machen 1 **take place** stattfinden 2 **take sb.'s advice** auf js. Rat hören 3 **take sth. down** etwas abreißen *(Gebäude)* 3 **take sth. off** etwas ausziehen *(Kleidung)*, ablegen *(Hut, Brille)* 2 **take sth. seriously** etwas ernst nehmen 3 °**take sth. in** etwas (in sich) aufnehmen, etwas wahrnehmen
taken [ˈteɪkn] *siehe* **take**
talk [tɔ:k]:
1. das Gespräch; die Rede, der Vortrag 1
2. **talk (to)** sprechen, reden (mit) 1
talk about sprechen, reden über 1
tall [tɔ:l] groß *(Person)*; hoch *(Gebäude)* 2
tap [tæp]:
1. der Wasserhahn 3
2. das (leise) Klopfen 3
3. **tap sth.** tippen an/auf etwas; (leise) klopfen 3
tap your fingers mit den Fingern klopfen 3
tap water [ˈtæp wɔ:tə] das Leitungswasser 3
task [tɑ:sk] die Aufgabe 1
taste [teɪst]:
1. der Geschmack 1
2. schmecken; kosten, probieren 1
tasteful [ˈteɪstfl] geschmackvoll 3
tasteless [ˈteɪstləs] geschmacklos 3
tasty [ˈteɪsti] schmackhaft, lecker 1
taught [tɔ:t] *siehe* **teach**
taxi [ˈtæksi] das Taxi 2
tea [ti:] der Tee 1
teach [ti:tʃ], **taught, taught** lehren, unterrichten 1 **teach sb. to do sth.** jm. beibringen, etwas zu tun 1
teacher [ˈti:tʃə] der/die Lehrer/in 1
team [ti:m] das Team, die Mannschaft 1
team captain [ˈti:m kæptɪn] der/die Mannschaftskapitän/in 4: 3 (90)
teamwork [ˈti:mwɜ:k] das Teamwork, die Zusammenarbeit 2
teapot [pɒt] die Teekanne 2
tear [tɪə] die Träne 4: 5 (155)
teaspoon [ˈti:spu:n] der Teelöffel 1
tech [tek] *siehe* **technology**
technical [ˈteknɪkl] technisch 4: 1 (34)
technology [tekˈnɒlədʒi] *infml auch* **tech** die Technik, der Technikunterricht; die Technologie 1
teen [ti:n] der Teenager 2
teeth [ti:θ] *Plural von* **tooth** **brush your teeth** (sich) die Zähne putzen 1
tell [tel], **told, told** erzählen, sagen 1 **tell sb. (not) to do sth.** jn. auffordern, etwas (nicht) zu tun; jm. sagen, dass er/sie etwas (nicht) tun soll 3
temperature [ˈtemprətʃə] die Temperatur; das Fieber 4: 4 (130)
ten [ten] zehn 1 **tens of thousands of people** zehntausende Menschen 3
ten thousand [ten ˈθaʊznd] zehntausend (10000) 2
tennis [ˈtenɪs] das Tennis 1
tent [tent] das Zelt 3
terms *(pl)* [tɜ:mz] die (Vertrags-)Bedingungen, die Konditionen 3
terraced home/house [ˈterəst] das Reihenhaus 1
terrarium [teˈreəriəm] das Terrarium 1
terrible [ˈterəbl] schrecklich, fürchterlich 1
territory [ˈterətri] das Gebiet, das Territorium; das Revier *(z. B. bei Tieren)* 4: 2 (55)
test [test]:
1. testen 1
2. der Test; die Klassenarbeit 1
driving test die Fahrprüfung 3 **take a test** einen Test machen, ablegen 3
text [tekst]:
1. der Text 1
2. **text (message)** die SMS 1
3. **text sb.** jm. eine SMS schicken 1
textbook [ˈtekstbʊk] das Schulbuch, das Lehrbuch 4: 3 (99)
textile [ˈtekstaɪl]:
1. Textil- 3
2. der Stoff 3
textiles *(pl)* die Textilien 3
than [ðən]: **louder/older than ...** lauter/älter als ... 2

thank sb. [θæŋk] sich bei jm. bedanken 2
thank you [ˈθæŋk juː] danke (schön) 1 **Thank you very much.** Vielen Dank./ Danke vielmals. 1
thankful [ˈθæŋkfl] dankbar 4: 1 (31)
thanks [θæŋks] danke (schön) 1
°Thanksgiving (Day) [θæŋksˈɡɪvɪŋ] das Erntedankfest
that [ðæt]:
1. das (dort) 1
that's (= that is) das (da) ist 1 **That's when they're useful.** Dann/Genau dann sind sie nützlich. 2
2. dass 1
I'm happy that ... Ich bin froh, dass ... 1 **so that** sodass 1
3. der, die, das *(Relativpronomen)* 1
4. **that bad** so schlecht 4: 1 (32)
the [ðə] der, die, das 1 **the harder ..., the more ...** je härter/schwieriger ..., desto mehr... 4: 1 (30)
theatre [ˈθɪətə] das Theater 1
their [ðeə] ihr/e *(zu „they")* 1
theirs [ðeəz] ihrer, ihre, ihrs *(zu „they")* 3
them [ðem], [ðəm] sie, ihnen 1
theme [θiːm] das Thema 3
theme park [ˈθiːm pɑːk] der Themenpark *(Freizeitpark mit Attraktionen zu einem bestimmten Thema)* 3
themselves [ðəmˈselvz] sich (selbst) (zu *„they"*) 3
then [ðen]:
1. dann, danach 1
2. **(back) then** damals 4: 1 (24)
there [ðeə] da, dort; dahin, dorthin 1 **there are** es sind .../es gibt ... 1 **there's (= there is)** es ist .../es gibt ... 1
therefore [ˈðeəfɔː] daher, deshalb 3
these [ðiːz] diese (hier) 1 **These are my friends.** Das hier sind meine Freunde/Freundinnen. 1
they [ðeɪ]:
1. sie *(Plural)* 1
they're (= they are) sie sind 1
2. man 3
3. er/sie *(geschlechtsneutral)* 3
thick [θɪk] dick; dicht 4: 4 (131)
thin [θɪn] dünn; schlank 4: 3 (96)
thing [θɪŋ] das Ding, die Sache 1 **How are things?** Wie geht's (so)? 3
think [θɪŋk], **thought, thought** denken, meinen, glauben 1 **think about** nachdenken über 1 **think of sb./sth.** an jn./etwas denken 2 **think of sth.** sich etwas überlegen, ausdenken 2 **I think ...** Ich denke/meine/glaube/ finde, ... 1
third (3rd) [θɜːd] dritte(r, s) 1
Thirdly, ... [ˈθɜːdli] Drittens ... 4: 4 (119)
thirsty [ˈθɜːsti]: **be thirsty** durstig sein, Durst haben 2
thirteen [θɜːˈtiːn] dreizehn 1
thirty [ˈθɜːti] dreißig 1
this [ðɪs]:
1. dies; diese(r, s) 1
this morning/afternoon/evening heute Morgen/Nachmittag/ Abend 2
2. **this good** so gut 4: 1 (32)
those [ðəʊz] die dort, jene (dort) 1
though [ðəʊ] obwohl 3 **°even though** auch wenn, obwohl *(betont)*
thought [θɔːt]:
1. der Gedanke 4: 2 (65)
2. *siehe* **think**
thousand [ˈθaʊznd] tausend 2 **tens of thousands of people** zehntausende Menschen 3
three [θriː] drei 1
threw [θruː] *siehe* **throw**
through [θruː] durch 2
throw [θrəʊ], **threw, thrown** werfen 3 **throw sth. away** etwas wegwerfen 3
thrown [θrəʊn] *siehe* **throw**
thunder [ˈθʌndə] der Donner *(z. B. bei Gewitter)* 4: 2 (64)
thunderstorm [ˈθʌndəstɔːm] das Gewitter 4: 2 (64)
Thursday [ˈθɜːzdeɪ], [ˈθɜːzdi] der Donnerstag 1
°tick [tɪk] ankreuzen, abhaken
ticket [ˈtɪkɪt] die Eintrittskarte, die Fahrkarte, das Ticket 1 **one-way ticket** die einfache Fahrkarte *(= ohne Rückfahrt)* 2 **single ticket** die einfache Fahrkarte *(= ohne Rückfahrt)* 2
ticket machine [ˈtɪkɪt məʃiːn] der Fahrkartenautomat 2
tidy [ˈtaɪdi]:
1. ordentlich 1
2. aufräumen 1
tie [taɪ]:
1. die Krawatte 1
2. binden, schnüren 4: 4 (131)
tie sb./sth. (to sth.) jn./etwas (an etwas) festbinden 4: 4 (131)
tight [taɪt] knapp, eng (anliegend) *(Kleidung)* 3
tights *(pl)* [taɪts] die Strumpfhose 3
till [tɪl] bis 2 **not ... till** erst, wenn ... 2
time [taɪm]:
1. die Zeit; die Uhrzeit 1
have a great/good time (viel) Spaß haben, sich vergnügen 2 **in time** rechtzeitig 4: 3 (99) **on time** pünktlich 2 **opening times** *(pl)* die Öffnungszeiten 4: 3 (85) **What time is it?** Wie spät ist es? 1 **What time?** Um wie viel Uhr? 1 **What's the time?** Wie spät ist es? 1
2. das Mal 2
for the first time zum ersten Mal 2 **lots of times** viele Male, oft 2 **three times** dreimal 2
°timeline [ˈtaɪmlaɪn] die Zeitachse, die Chronik
times [taɪmz] mal 3
timetable [ˈtaɪmteɪbl] der Stundenplan 1
tin [tɪn] die Dose, die Büchse 2
tiny [ˈtaɪni] winzig 4: 4 (130)
tip [tɪp]:
1. das Trinkgeld 3
2. **tip sb.** jm. Trinkgeld geben 3
tip [tɪp] der Tipp 1
tired [ˈtaɪəd] müde 1
title [ˈtaɪtl] der Titel, die Überschrift 1
to [tu], [tə]:
1. bis 1
(from) A to Z (von) A bis Z 1
2. (um) zu 1
how to do sth. wie man etwas tut/ tun kann/tun soll 1 **things to eat** Dinge zum Essen 1
3. vor *(bei Uhrzeitangaben)* 2
quarter to 7 viertel vor 7 2
4. zu, nach 1
different to you anders als du 1 **the answer to the question** die Antwort auf die Frage 1
today [təˈdeɪ] heute 1 **today's letter** der Brief von heute 1
together [təˈɡeðə] zusammen 1
toilet [ˈtɔɪlət] die Toilette 1
told [təʊld] *siehe* **tell**
tolerant (of) [ˈtɒlərənt] tolerant (gegenüber) 2
tomato [təˈmɑːtəʊ], *pl* **tomatoes** die Tomate 1
tomato sauce [təˈmɑːtəʊ sɔːs] die Tomatensoße 1
tomorrow [təˈmɒrəʊ] morgen 2
tonight [təˈnaɪt] heute Nacht, heute Abend 2
too [tuː]:
1. auch 1
from York too auch aus York 1
2. **too slow** zu langsam 1
took [tʊk] *siehe* **take**
tool [tuːl] das Werkzeug; das (Hilfs-) Mittel 3
tooth [tuːθ], *pl* **teeth** der Zahn 1
top [tɒp]:
1. die Spitze, das obere Ende 1
2. oberste(r, s), höchste(r, s) 2
the top shelf das oberste/höchste Regal 2 **the top six films** die sechs besten Filme 1
top floor [tɒp ˈflɔː] das Dach-/Obergeschoss, das oberste Stockwerk, die oberste Etage 1
topic [ˈtɒpɪk] das Thema 1
tornado [tɔːˈneɪdəʊ] der Tornado *(Wirbelsturm)* 4: 2 (64)
total [ˈtəʊtl]:
1. die Gesamtmenge, die Gesamtzahl 4: 2 (65)
2. Gesamt-; total 4: 2 (65)
totally [ˈtəʊtəli] völlig, total *(Adv.)* 4: 2 (65)
touch [tʌtʃ]:
1. anfassen, berühren 2
2. die Berührung 2
3. der Kontakt, die Verbindung 3
get in touch (with) (sich) in Verbindung setzen (mit), Kontakt aufnehmen (zu) 3 **in touch with** in Kontakt mit 3 **keep/stay in touch (with)** in Verbindung/Kontakt

bleiben (mit) 3 **lose touch (with)** den Kontakt verlieren (zu) 3
tour (of) [tʊə] die Tour, die Reise, der Rundgang / die Rundfahrt 1
tour guide [ˈtʊə gaɪd] der/die Reiseleiter/in; der/die Fremdenführer/in 1
tourist [ˈtʊərɪst] der/die Tourist/in 1
°tow [təʊ] ziehen, schleppen **tow away** (Auto) abschleppen **tow-away zone** *der Bereich, in dem falsch geparkte Autos abgeschleppt werden*
°toward [təˈwɔːd] *(AE)* nach, auf ... zu, in Richtung (von)
towards [təˈwɔːdz] nach, auf ... zu, in Richtung (von) 3
tower [ˈtaʊə] der Turm 2
town [taʊn] die Stadt 1
town centre [taʊn ˈsentə] das Stadtzentrum 1
town council [taʊn ˈkaʊnsl] der Stadtrat 4: 3 (85)
toy [tɔɪ] das Spielzeug 1
track [træk] *(AE)* das (Bahn-)Gleis 4: 3 (95)
trade [treɪd]:
1. der Handel 4: 1 (16/17)
2. handeln, Handel (be)treiben 4: 1 (16/17)
trader [ˈtreɪdə] der/die Händler/in 4: 1 (16/17)
tradition [trəˈdɪʃn] die Tradition 1
traditional [trəˈdɪʃənl] traditionell 1
traffic [ˈtræfɪk] der (Straßen-)Verkehr 3
trail [treɪl] der Weg, der Pfad, die Spur 4: 5 (158)
train [treɪn] der Zug, die Eisenbahn 1 **local train** der Nahverkehrszug, die S-Bahn 3
train driver [ˈtreɪn draɪvə] der/die Lokomotivführer/in 2
train sb. [treɪn] jn. trainieren; ausbilden 2
train station [ˈtreɪn steɪʃn] der Bahnhof 1
trainer [ˈtreɪnə]:
1. der/die Trainer/in 1
2. der Sportschuh, der Turnschuh 3
°trait [treɪt] der Wesenszug, die Eigenschaft
tram [træm] die Straßenbahn 3
trampoline [ˈtræmpəliːn] das Trampolin 1
trampolining [ˈtræmpəliːnɪŋ] das Trampolinspringen/-turnen 1
transgender [trænzˈdʒendə] transgender 2
translate [trænsˈleɪt] übersetzen 3
translation [trænsˈleɪʃn] die Übersetzung 3
transport [trænˈspɔːt] transportieren, befördern 2
transport *(no pl)* [ˈtrænspɔːt] das Fortbewegungsmittel, das Verkehrsmittel; die Beförderung 2 **form of transport** die Fortbewegungsart, die Art der Beförderung 3 **public transport** die öffentlichen Verkehrsmittel 3
transportation [trænspɔːˈteɪʃn] *(AE, no pl)* das Fortbewegungsmittel; die Beförderung 4: 3 (85) **public transportation** die öffentlichen Verkehrsmittel 4: 3 (85)
trash [træʃ] *(AE)* der Abfall, der Müll 4: 1 (31)
trauma [ˈtrɔːmə] das Trauma 4: 4 (122)
travel [ˈtrævl]:
1. das Reisen 1
2. reisen, fahren 1
Travelcard [ˈtrævlkɑːd] die Ein- oder Mehrtagesfahrkarte *(London)* 3
treat [ˈtriːt]:
1. der Hochgenuss, das besondere Vergnügen; die (besondere) Leckerei 2
2. **treat sb. (to sth.)** jn. (zu etwas) einladen 2
3. **treat sb.** jn. behandeln 4: 2 (58)
tree [triː] der Baum 1
trendy [ˈtrendi] modisch, trendy, „angesagt" 3
triathlon [traɪˈæθlən] der Triathlon *(Sportart, Dreikampf bestehend aus Schwimmen, Radfahren und Laufen)* 3
tribal [ˈtraɪbl] Stammes- 4: 4 (122)
tribe [traɪb] der (Volks-)Stamm 4: 4 (122)
trick [trɪk]:
1. der Trick, das Kunststück 1 **the oldest trick in the book** der älteste Trick der Welt 4: 3 (98)
2. **trick sb.** jn. täuschen, hereinlegen 4: 5 (152)
trifle [ˈtraɪfl] das Trifle *(britischer Nachtisch)* 1
trip [trɪp] der Ausflug; die Reise 2 **class trip** der Klassenausflug 2 **school trip** der Schulausflug 2
troll [trəʊl] der Troll *(Provokateur/in in Online-Medien)* 3
trophy [ˈtrəʊfi] die Trophäe; der Pokal 2
trouble [ˈtrʌbl] der Ärger, die Schwierigkeiten 1 **be in trouble** Ärger haben, in Schwierigkeiten sein 1 **the Troubles** *(pl)* der Nordirlandkonflikt (*wörtlich:* die Unruhen) 3
trousers *(pl)* [ˈtraʊzəz] die Hose 1 **baggy trousers** die Schlabberhose *(weit geschnittene Hose)* 3
truck [trʌk] der Last(kraft)wagen, der LKW 4: 4 (133)
true [truː] wahr, richtig 1 **come true** wahr werden 2
trumpet [ˈtrʌmpɪt] die Trompete 4: 2 (52)
trust [trʌst]:
1. das Vertrauen 3
2. **trust sb.** jm. vertrauen 3
truth [truːθ] die Wahrheit 3 **tell the truth** die Wahrheit sagen 3 **To tell the truth, ...** Ehrlich gesagt, ... 3
try [traɪ]:
1. der Versuch 2 **Have a try! / Give it a try!** Versuch's/Probier's doch mal! 2
2. versuchen, (aus)probieren 2 **try sth. on** etwas anprobieren *(Kleidung)* 2 **try to do sth.** versuchen, etwas zu tun 2
tube [tjuːb] *(infml)* die Londoner U-Bahn 3
Tuesday [ˈtjuːzdeɪ], [ˈtjuːzdi] der Dienstag 1
tuition [tjuˈɪʃn] der Unterricht, die Anleitung; die Studiengebühren 4: 3 (92)
tuition fees *(pl)* [tjuˈɪʃn fiːz] die Studiengebühren 4: 3 (92)
tunnel [ˈtʌnl] der Tunnel 3
turkey [ˈtɜːki] der Truthahn, die Pute; das Putenfleisch 4: 4 (122)
turn [tɜːn]:
1. (sich) (um)drehen 1 **Turn it upside down.** Dreh/Stell es auf den Kopf. 1 **turn out** sich herausstellen; sich erweisen (als) 4: 3 (96) **turn right/left** (nach) rechts/links abbiegen 2 **turn sth. (over)** etwas umdrehen 1
2. gehen nach, sich wenden nach 4: 1 (32) **His lips turn up.** Seine Mundwinkel gehen nach oben. (= Er lächelt.) 4: 1 (32)
turn [tɜːn]: **it is sb.'s turn (to do sth.)** jd. ist dran / an der Reihe (etwas zu tun) 1 **take turns / take it in turns (to do sth)** sich abwechseln; sich dabei abwechseln, etwas zu tun 1 **When is (it) my turn (to do sth.)?** Wann bin ich dran / an der Reihe (etwas zu tun)? 1
twelfth (12th) [twelfθ] zwölfte(r, s) 1
twelve [twelv] zwölf 1
twenty [ˈtwenti] zwanzig 1
twice [twaɪs] zweimal 3
twin beds *(pl)* [ˈtwɪn bedz] zwei einzelne Betten *(z. B. im Hotelzimmer)* 3
twin room [twɪn ˈruːm] das Zweibettzimmer 3
two [tuː] zwei 1
type (in) [taɪp] (ein)tippen 3
type (of) [taɪp] die Art (von), die Sorte (von) 3
typical (of) [ˈtɪpɪkl] typisch (für) 2
tyre [ˈtaɪə] der Reifen 3

U

ugly [ˈʌgli] hässlich 3
UK (= United Kingdom) [juː ˈkeɪ] das Vereinigte Königreich 1
umbrella [ʌmˈbrelə] der (Regen-)Schirm 1
unable [ʌnˈeɪbl]: **be unable to do sth.** etwas nicht tun können, nicht in der Lage sein etwas zu tun 4: 2 (59)
uncertain [ʌnˈsɜːtn] unsicher 4: 3 (96)
uncle [ˈʌŋkl] der Onkel 1
uncomfortable [ʌnˈkʌmftəbl] unbequem, ungemütlich 2
uncommon [ʌnˈkɒmən] selten, ungewöhnlich, unüblich 4: 3 (95)
uncool [ʌnˈkuːl] uncool 2
under [ˈʌndə] unter 1

underground [ˈʌndəgraʊnd] die U-Bahn 2
underground [ʌndəˈgraʊnd] unterirdisch, unter die Erde 2
understand [ʌndəˈstænd], **understood, understood** verstehen 1
understood [ʌndəˈstʊd] *siehe* **understand**
underwater [ʌndəˈwɔːtə] unter Wasser, Unterwasser- 2
unemployed [ʌnɪmˈplɔɪd] arbeitslos 4: 3 (94)
unemployment [ʌnɪmˈplɔɪmənt] die Arbeitslosigkeit 4: 3 (94)
unequal [ʌnˈiːkwəl] ungleich 4: 3 (99)
°unexpected [ʌnɪkˈspektɪd] unerwartet
unfair [ʌnˈfeə] unfair 2
unfortunately [ʌnˈfɔːtʃənətli] unglücklicherweise, leider 3
unfriendly [ʌnˈfrendli] unfreundlich 1
unhappiness [ʌnˈhæpinəs] die Unzufriedenheit, die Traurigkeit 2
unhappy [ʌnˈhæpi] unglücklich, unzufrieden 2
unhealthy [ʌnˈhelθi] ungesund 2
unhelpful [ʌnˈhelpfl] wenig hilfreich 2
uniform [ˈjuːnɪfɔːm] die Uniform 1
United Kingdom (UK) [junaɪtɪd ˈkɪŋdəm] das Vereinigte Königreich 1
university [juːnɪˈvɜːsəti] die Universität 4: 3 (92)
unjust [ʌnˈdʒʌst] ungerecht 4: 2 (56)
unkind [ʌnˈkaɪnd] unfreundlich, herzlos 2
unknown [ʌnˈnəʊn] unbekannt 3
unless [ənˈles] es sei denn; außer (wenn) 4: 4 (127)
unlikely [ʌnˈlaɪkli] unwahrscheinlich 4: 3 (86)
unlock [ʌnˈlɒk] aufschließen, entsperren 2
unlucky [ʌnˈlʌki]: **be unlucky** Pech haben 3
unpack [ʌnˈpæk] auspacken 3
unplug sth. [ʌnˈplʌg] den Stecker von etwas herausziehen, etwas ausstöpseln 4: 1 (32)
untidy [ʌnˈtaɪdi] unordentlich 2
untie [ʌnˈtaɪ] losbinden, *(Knoten)* lösen, aufmachen 4: 5 (153)
until [ənˈtɪl] bis *(zeitlich)* 2 **not … until** erst, wenn … 2
untrue [ʌnˈtruː] unwahr, falsch 4: 3 (96)
unusual [ʌnˈjuːʒuəl] ungewöhnlich 3
up [ʌp] hinauf, hoch 1 **up a hill** einen Hügel hinauf, hoch 2 **What's up?** Was ist los? / Was gibt's (Neues)? 4: 2 (52)
upbeat [ˈʌpbiːt] *(infml)* optimistisch, zuversichtlich, fröhlich 4: 2 (63)
upcycle [ˈʌpsaɪkl] upcyceln *(gebrauchte Gegenstände als höherwertige Waren weiterverwenden)* 3
upload [ʌpˈləʊd]:
1. der/das Upload 3
2. uploaden, hochladen 3
upset [ʌpˈset]:
1. bestürzt; aufgebracht, verärgert 2
2. **upset sb., upset, upset** jn. erschüttern; jn. aufregen, ärgern, 2
upside down [ʌpsaɪd ˈdaʊn] verkehrt herum, auf dem Kopf 1
upstairs [ʌpˈsteəz] (nach) oben *(die Treppe hinauf)* 2
urban [ˈɜːbən] städtisch, urban 4: 4 (116/117)
us [ʌs], [əs] uns 1
use [juːz] benutzen, verwenden 1
use [juːs] der Gebrauch, die Verwendung 4: 1 (24)
useful [ˈjuːsfl] nützlich, hilfreich 1
useless [ˈjuːsləs] nutzlos 3
user [ˈjuːzə] der/die (Be-)Nutzer/in 1
usual [ˈjuːʒuəl] üblich, gewöhnlich 3
usually [ˈjuːʒuəli] normalerweise, meistens 1

V

vacation [vəˈkeɪʃn] *(AE)* der Urlaub 4: 1 (19)
vacuum [ˈvækjuəm] Staub saugen 2
vacuum cleaner [ˈvækjuəm kliːnə] der Staubsauger 2
valley [ˈvæli] das Tal 3
valuable [ˈvæljuəbl] wertvoll 4: 1 (25)
value [ˈvæljuː] der Wert 4: 1 (19)
value for money das Preis-Leistungs-Verhältnis, der Gegenwert 4: 1 (19)
It's good value (for money). Es ist sein Geld wert. / Es ist preiswert. 4: 1 (19)
vampire [ˈvæmpaɪə] der Vampir 2
van [væn] der Kleinbus; der Lieferwagen 4: 1 (30)
vanilla [vəˈnɪlə] die Vanille 1
veg [vedʒ], *pl* **veg** *siehe* **vegetables**
vegan [ˈviːgən]:
1. der/die Veganer/in 1
2. vegan 1
vegetables *(pl)* [ˈvedʒtəblz] *infml auch* **veg** das/die Gemüse 1
vegetarian [vedʒəˈteəriən] *infml auch* **veggie:**
1. der/die Vegetarier/in 1
2. vegetarisch 1
veggie [ˈvedʒi] *siehe* **vegetarian**
°vehicle [ˈviːəkl] das Fahrzeug
°version [ˈvɜːʃn] die Version
versus (v; vs) [ˈvɜːsəs] gegen *(bei Wettkämpfen)*; gegenüber 3
vertical [ˈvɜːtɪkl] senkrecht, vertikal 2
very [ˈveri] sehr 1
vet [vet] der Tierarzt, die Tierärztin 1
via Ellis Island [ˈvaɪə] über Ellis Island 4: 1 (24)
vibrant [ˈvaɪbrənt] dynamisch, voller Leben 4: 2 (55)
victim [ˈvɪktɪm] das Opfer 3
°Vieux Carré [vjɜː kəˈreɪ] das French Quarter *(der älteste Stadtteil von New Orleans)*
view [vjuː]:
1. der (An-)Blick, die (Aus-)Sicht 1
2. der Aufruf *(eines Online-Videos)* 4: 2 (53)
3. **view sth.** etwas anschauen 1
village [ˈvɪlɪdʒ] das Dorf 1
villain [ˈvɪlən] der/die Verbrecher/in; der Schurke, die Schurkin 2
violence [ˈvaɪələns] die Gewalt; die Gewalttätigkeit 4: 2 (57)
violent [ˈvaɪələnt] gewalttätig; gewaltsam 4: 2 (57)
violin [vaɪəˈlɪn] die Geige, die Violine 4: 2 (63)
viral [ˈvaɪrəl] Virus-, viral 4: 2 (57) **go viral** sich *(im Internet)* rasend schnell verbreiten 4: 2 (57)
virtual [ˈvɜːtʃuəl] virtuell 3
virus [ˈvaɪrəs], *pl* **viruses** der/das Virus 4: 2 (57)
viruses [ˈvaɪrəsɪz] *Plural von* **virus**
°visa [ˈviːzə] das Visum
°visible [ˈvɪzəbl] sichtbar
visit [ˈvɪzɪt]:
1. der Besuch 1
2. besuchen 1
visitor [ˈvɪzɪtə] der/die Besucher/in; der Gast 1
visitor information centre [vɪzɪtər ɪnfəˈmeɪʃn sentə] die Touristeninformation, das Fremdenverkehrsbüro 1
visual [ˈvɪʒuəl] visuell, optisch 2
vocab [ˈvəʊkæb] *siehe* **vocabulary**
vocabulary [vəˈkæbjələri] *infml auch* **vocab** der Wortschatz, das Vokabular; das Vokabelverzeichnis 1
vocational [vəʊˈkeɪʃənl] beruflich, Berufs- 4: 3 (92)
vocational school [vəʊkeɪʃənl ˈskuːl] die berufsbildende Schule 4: 3 (92)
vocational training [vəʊkeɪʃənl ˈtreɪnɪŋ] die Berufsausbildung 4: 3 (92)
voice [vɔɪs] die Stimme 3
voice message [ˈvɔɪs mesɪdʒ] die Sprachnachricht 3
voice-over [ˈvɔɪs əʊvə] der Filmkommentar, die Off-Stimme 3
volcano [vɒlˈkeɪnəʊ], *pl* **volcanoes** *or* **volcanos** der Vulkan 3
volunteer [vɒlənˈtɪə]:
1. der/die Freiwillige; der/die ehrenamtliche Mitarbeiter/in 3
2. freiwillig/ehrenamtlich arbeiten *(unbezahlt)* 3
vote [vəʊt]:
1. die Abstimmung, das Votum 3
have a vote (on) abstimmen (über) 3
2. **vote (on sth.)** wählen; abstimmen (über etwas) 3
vote for/against sb./sth. für/gegen jn./etwas stimmen 3

W

°waffle ['wɒfl] die Waffel
waistcoat ['weɪskəʊt] die Weste 3
wait (for) [weɪt] warten (auf) 2 **Wait a minute.** Warte mal./Einen Moment. 2 **I can't wait!** Ich kann es kaum erwarten! 2 **°wait up (for)** aufbleiben, wachbleiben (wegen)
waiter ['weɪtə] der Kellner 3
waitress ['weɪtrəs] die Kellnerin 3
wake [weɪk], **woke, woken: wake sb. (up)** jn. (auf)wecken 4: 4 (130) **wake up** aufwachen 4: 4 (130)
walk [wɔ:k]:
1. der Spaziergang 1
2. (zu Fuß) gehen, wandern 1
walk around umhergehen (in) 2
walk into sb. mit jm. (beim Gehen) zusammenstoßen 3 **walk the dog** mit dem Hund rausgehen, mit dem Hund Gassi gehen 2
°walker ['wɔ:kə] die Gehhilfe, der Rollator
walking ['wɔ:kɪŋ] das Wandern 1
walking boot ['wɔ:kɪŋ bu:t] der Wanderstiefel 2
wall [wɔ:l] die Wand, die Mauer 1 **on the wall** an die Wand; an der Wand 1
wander ['wɒndə] (umher)wandern, schlendern 4: 1 (25) **wander off** weggehen, sich absetzen 4: 1 (25)
want [wɒnt] wollen 1 **want sb. to do sth.** wollen, dass jd. etwas tut 3 **want to do sth.** etwas tun wollen 1
wanted ['wɒntɪd] gesucht; polizeilich gesucht 2
war [wɔ:] der Krieg 2
wardrobe ['wɔ:drəʊb] der Kleiderschrank 1
warm [wɔ:m] warm 1
warn sb. (about/against/of) [wɔ:n] jn. warnen (vor) 4: 2 (64)
warning (about/against/of) ['wɔ:nɪŋ] die Warnung (vor) 4: 2 (64)
was [wɒz], [wəz] *siehe* **be**
wash [wɒʃ]:
1. (sich) waschen 2
2. die Wäsche, das (Sich-)Waschen 3
washing ['wɒʃɪŋ] die Wäsche 2 **do the washing** die Wäsche erledigen, Wäsche waschen 2
waste [weɪst]:
1. verschwenden 3
2. die Verschwendung 3
watch [wɒtʃ] die Armbanduhr 3
watch (sth.) [wɒtʃ] (sich etwas) anschauen; (etwas) beobachten 1 **watch for sth.** Ausschau halten nach etwas 4: 5 (157) **watch out for** aufpassen auf; sich hüten vor, sich in Acht nehmen vor 4: 5 (157)
water ['wɔ:tə] das Wasser 1
water sports *(pl)* ['wɔ:tə spɔ:ts] der Wassersport 3
waterfall ['wɔ:təfɔ:l] der Wasserfall 3
watermelon ['melən] die Wassermelone 1
waterskiing ['wɔ:təski:ɪŋ] das Wasserskifahren 3
wave [weɪv]:
1. die Welle 3
2. das Winken 1
give sb. a wave jm. zuwinken 1
3. **wave (to sb.)** (jm. zu)winken 1
wax [wæks] das Wachs 3
way [weɪ]:
1. der Weg 1
one-way ticket die einfache Fahrkarte *(= ohne Rückfahrt)* 2
2. die Art und Weise 1
Way to go! *(AE, infml)* Gut gemacht! 4: 2 (52) **(in) this way** auf diese Art/Weise 1 **in different ways** unterschiedlich *(Adv.)*, auf unterschiedliche Art/Weise 1 **No way!** Auf keinen Fall! 3
3. die Richtung 2
that way da entlang, in jene(r) Richtung 2 **the wrong way** (in) die falsche Richtung 2 **this way** hier entlang, in diese(r) Richtung 2
we [wi:] wir 1 **we're (= we are)** wir sind 1
weapon ['wepən] die Waffe 4: 3 (82/83)
wear [weə], **wore, worn** tragen, anhaben *(Kleidung)* 1
weather ['weðə] das Wetter, die Witterung 1
web [web] das Netz; das Internet 2 **surf the web** im Internet surfen 2
wedding ['wedɪŋ] die Hochzeit 1
wedding present ['wedɪŋ preznt] das Hochzeitsgeschenk 1
wedding ring ['wedɪŋ rɪŋ] der Ehering 1
Wednesday ['wenzdeɪ], ['wenzdi] der Mittwoch 1
week [wi:k] die Woche 1
weekday ['wi:kdeɪ] der Werktag, der Wochentag 1
weekend [wi:k'end] das Wochenende 1 **at the weekend** am Wochenende 1
weird [wɪəd] seltsam, komisch 1
welcome ['welkʌm]:
1. der Empfang; das Willkommen 4: 1 (24)
Welcome to ... Willkommen in/an ... 1 **get a warm/great welcome** herzlich begrüßt werden 4: 1 (24) **give sb. a warm/great welcome** jn. herzlich begrüßen 4: 1 (24)
2. **welcome sb. (to)** jn. begrüßen (in), jn. willkommen heißen (in) 4: 1 (24)
3. **You're welcome.** Bitte, gern geschehen./Nichts zu danken. 1
welfare ['welfeə] die Sozialhilfe; die Wohlfahrt, die Fürsorge; das Wohl(ergehen) 4: 1 (30)
well [wel]:
1. gut *(Adv.)* 1
Well done. Gut gemacht! 1 **... as well as ...** sowohl ... als auch ... 3 **as well** auch 3 **do well** es gut machen; gut abschneiden, erfolgreich sein 3
2. gesund 2
Get well soon! Gute Besserung! 2
3. **Well, ...** Nun, .../ Also, .../ Na ja, ... 1
well [wel] die Quelle, der Brunnen 4: 4 (133)
well-being ['wel bi:ɪŋ] das Wohl(ergehen) 3
well-known [wel 'nəʊn] bekannt 3
went [went] *siehe* **go**
were [wɜ:], [wə] *siehe* **be**
werewolf ['weəwʊlf], *pl* **werewolves** der Werwolf 4: 5 (157)
werewolves ['weəwʊlvz] *Plural von* **werewolf**
west [west] der Westen; westlich; West- 3
western ['westən] westlich, West- 3
wet [wet] nass 3
whale [weɪl] der Wal 4: 5 (150/151)
what [wɒt]:
1. was 1
2. welche(r, s) 1
What about a ... ? Wie wäre es mit einer/einem ... ? 1 **What about you?** Und du?/Was ist mit dir? 1 **What's your name?** Wie heißt du? 1
whatever [wɒt'evə] was (auch) (immer) 4: 3 (97)
wheel [wi:l]:
1. das Rad 3
big wheel das Riesenrad 3
2. fahren; schieben; ziehen 3
wheelchair ['wi:ltʃeə] der Rollstuhl 1
when [wen]:
1. wann 1
2. wenn *(zeitlich)* 1
3. als *(zeitlich)* 2
whenever [wen'evə] wann (auch) immer 3
where [weə] wo; wohin 1 **Where are you from?** Wo kommst du her? 1
whereas [weər'æz] während, wohingegen 4: 4 (116/117)
wherever [weər'evə] wo/wohin (auch) immer; egal, wo(hin) 3
°whether ['weðə] ob
which [wɪtʃ]:
1. welche(r, s) 1
Which clubs ...? Welche AGs ...? 1
2. der, die, das; die *(Relativpronomen)* 3
a charity which helps ... eine Hilfsorganisation, die ... hilft 3
while [waɪl]:
1. während 2
2. **a while** eine Weile, einige Zeit 2
whipped cream [wɪpt 'kri:m] die Schlagsahne, die geschlagene Sahne 1
whirlpool ['wɜ:lpu:l] der Strudel *(im Wasser)* 4: 5 (155)
whisper ['wɪspə]:
1. das Flüstern, das Geflüster 4: 3 (97)
2. flüstern 4: 3 (97)
white [waɪt] weiß 1

who [huː]:
1. wer 1
2. wen; wem 2
3. der, die *(Relativpronomen)* 3
people who ... Menschen, die ... 3
whoever [huːˈevə] wer/wen/wem auch immer 4: 3 (97)
whole [həʊl] ganze(r, s) 3
whom [huːm] wem/wen *(Fragepronomen)* 3
whose [huːz]:
1. wessen 2
2. dessen, deren *(Relativpronomen)* 3
why [waɪ] warum 1 **that's why** deswegen, darum 2
Wi-Fi [ˈwaɪ faɪ] das WLAN, die kabellose Datenübertragung 3
wife [waɪf], *pl* **wives** die (Ehe-)Frau 1
wild [waɪld] wild 3
°**wilderness** [ˈwɪldənəs] die Wildnis
wildfire [ˈwaɪldfaɪə] der Waldbrand; der Großbrand, der Flächenbrand 4: 4 (130)
wildlife *(no pl)* [ˈwaɪldlaɪf] die Tiere *(in freier Wildbahn)*, die Tierwelt 4: 4 (126)
will [wɪl]: **I'll (= I will) be ...** ich werde ... sein 2
win [wɪn]:
1. der Sieg 3
°**win the lottery** im Lotto / in der Lotterie gewinnen
2. **win, won, won** gewinnen 1
wind [wɪnd] der Wind 1
window [ˈwɪndəʊ] das Fenster 1
windy [ˈwɪndi] windig 1
°**wink (at sb.)** [wɪŋk] (jm. zu-)zwinkern
winner [ˈwɪnə] der/die Gewinner/in; der/die Sieger/in 1
winter [ˈwɪntə] der Winter 1
wipe [waɪp] (ab)wischen 4: 1 (30)
wish [wɪʃ]:
1. (sich) wünschen 2
2. der Wunsch 2
Best wishes Viele Grüße *(Briefschluss)* 2 **make a wish** sich etwas wünschen 2
with [wɪð]:
1. mit 1
2. bei 1
with me/us/... bei mir/uns/... 1
without [wɪˈðaʊt] ohne 3
wives [waɪvz] *Plural von* **wife**
woke [wəʊk] *siehe* **wake up**
woken [ˈwəʊkən] *siehe* **wake up**
wolf [wʊlf], *pl* **wolves** der Wolf 4: 5 (152)
wolves [wʊlvz] *Plural von* **wolf**
woman [ˈwʊmən], *pl* **women** die Frau 1
women [ˈwɪmɪn] *Plural von* **woman**
won [wʌn] *siehe* **win**
wonder [ˈwʌndə] sich fragen 4: 5 (154)
wonderful [ˈwʌndəfl] wunderbar 2
won't [wəʊnt]: **they won't (= will not) believe ...** sie werden ... nicht glauben 2
wood [wʊd] das Holz; der Wald 3
wooden [ˈwʊdn] Holz-, hölzern 3
word [wɜːd] das Wort 1 **words (of a song)** *(pl)* der (Song-)Text 2
°**wordbank** [ˈwɜːdbæŋk] die Wortbank *(Sammlung von Wörtern zu einem Thema)*
wore [wɔː] *siehe* **wear**
work [wɜːk]:
1. die Arbeit 1
at work bei der Arbeit, am Arbeitsplatz 1
2. arbeiten; funktionieren 1
work long days lange arbeiten, lange Arbeitstage haben 1 **work on sth.** an etwas arbeiten 4: 3 (99) **work sth. out** etwas herausfinden, etwas erarbeiten, etwas verstehen 2
worker [ˈwɜːkə] der/die Arbeiter/in; die Arbeitskraft 3
world [wɜːld] die Welt 2 **the best place in the world** der beste Ort der Welt / auf der Welt 2
World Cup [wɜːld ˈkʌp] die Weltmeisterschaft 3
world-famous [wɜːld ˈfeɪməs] weltberühmt 3
world war [wɜːld ˈwɔː] der Weltkrieg 2
worn [wɔːn] *siehe* **wear**
worried (about) [ˈwʌrid] beunruhigt, besorgt (wegen) 1
worry [ˈwʌri]:
1. die Sorge 1
2. **worry (about)** sich Sorgen machen (wegen, um) 1
Don't worry. Mach dir keine Sorgen. 1
worse [wɜːs] schlechter, schlimmer 2
for better or (for) worse was auch immer geschieht, in guten wie in schlechten Zeiten *(beim Ehegelöbnis)* 2
worst [wɜːst] der/die/das Schlechteste, Schlimmste; am schlechtesten, am schlimmsten 2
worth [wɜːθ] wert 4: 5 (158)
would [wʊd]: **Would you like ...?** Möchtest du ...? 1 **I'd (= I would) like/love ...** Ich hätte (liebend) gern ... / Ich möchte (liebend gern) ... 1 **I'd (= I would) love/like to meet ...** Ich würde mich (liebend) gerne mit ... treffen. 1
write [raɪt], **wrote, written** schreiben 1 **write sth. down** etwas aufschreiben 3
writer [ˈraɪtə] der/die Autor/in; der/die Verfasser/in 2
writing [ˈraɪtɪŋ] das Geschriebene, das Schreiben, das Werk / die Werke 4: 2 (52)
written [ˈrɪtn] *siehe* **write**
wrong [rɒŋ] falsch 1 **be wrong** Unrecht haben 1 **Something is wrong.** Irgendetwas ist nicht in Ordnung. / Irgendetwas stimmt nicht. 2 **What's wrong?** Was ist los? / Was/Wo ist das Problem? 2
wrote [rəʊt] *siehe* **write**

Y

yard [jɑːd] *(AE)*: **yard** der Garten 4: 2 (66)
yawn [jɔːn]:
1. das Gähnen 4: 4 (130)
2. gähnen 4: 4 (130)
°**yeah** [jeə] *(infml)* ja
year [jɪə] das Jahr; der Jahrgang 1 **year-round** ganzjährig, das ganze Jahr über 4: 4 (129) **a five-year-old** ein/e Fünfjährige/r 4: 3 (93) **a five-year-old kid** ein fünf Jahre altes Kind 4: 3 (93)
year-round [jɪə ˈraʊnd] ganzjährig, das ganze Jahr über 4: 4 (129)
yellow [ˈjeləʊ] gelb 1
yes [jes] ja 1
yesterday [ˈjestədeɪ] gestern 2
yet [jet]: **... yet?** ... schon ...? 2 **not ... yet** noch nicht ... 2
°**Yiddish** [ˈjɪdɪʃ] jiddisch; Jiddisch
yoghurt [ˈjɒgət] der Joghurt 2
you [juː]:
1. du; dich; dir; ihr; euch; Sie; Ihnen 1
2. man 2
young [jʌŋ] jung 3
your [jɔː], [jə] dein/e; euer/eure; Ihr/e 1
yours [jɔːz] deine, deiner, deins; eurer, eure, eures; Ihrer, Ihre, Ihres 1
yourself [jəˈself] du/dir/dich (selbst) 2
yourselves [jɔːˈselvz] ihr/euch (selbst) 3 **Enjoy yourselves.** Viel Spaß! Amüsiert euch gut! 3
youth [juːθ] die Jugend; der Jugendliche 1
youth centre [ˈjuːθ sentə] das Jugendzentrum 1

Z

zero [ˈzɪərəʊ], *pl* **zeros** die Null, die Nullen 1
zine [ziːn] *siehe* **magazine**
zip wire [ˈzɪp waɪə] die Seilrutsche 2
°**zone** [zəʊn] die Zone **tow-away zone** *der Bereich, in dem falsch geparkte Autos abgeschleppt werden*
zoo [zuː] der Zoo 1

Infinitive	Simple past	Past participle	
(to) **babysit**	**babysat**	**babysat**	babysitten
(to) **be**	**was; were**	**been**	sein
(to) **beat**	**beat**	**beaten**	schlagen, besiegen
(to) **become**	**became**	**become**	werden
(to) **begin**	**began**	**begun**	anfangen, beginnen
(to) **bleed**	**bled**	**bled**	bluten
(to) **blow**	**blew** [uː]	**blown**	pusten, blasen; wehen
(to) **break**	**broke**	**broken**	zerbrechen
(to) **breed**	**bred**	**bred**	züchten; brüten, Junge bekommen, sich vermehren
(to) **bring**	**brought**	**brought**	(mit)bringen
(to) **build** [ɪ]	**built** [ɪ]	**built** [ɪ]	bauen
(to) **buy**	**bought**	**bought**	kaufen
(to) **catch**	**caught** [ɔː]	**caught** [ɔː]	(ein)fangen; erwischen
(to) **choose**	**chose**	**chosen**	(aus)wählen
(to) **come**	**came**	**come**	(mit)kommen
(to) **cost**	**cost**	**cost**	kosten
(to) **cut**	**cut**	**cut**	(aus)schneiden
(to) **deal with** [iː]	**dealt** [e]	**dealt** [e]	sich befassen mit; klarkommen (mit)
(to) **do**	**did**	**done** [ʌ]	tun, machen
(to) **draw**	**drew**	**drawn**	zeichnen
(to) **drink**	**drank**	**drunk**	trinken
(to) **drive** [aɪ]	**drove** [əʊ]	**driven** [ɪ]	fahren
(to) **eat** [iː]	**ate** [et, eɪt]	**eaten** [iː]	essen; fressen
(to) **fall**	**fell**	**fallen**	(hin)fallen
(to) **feed**	**fed**	**fed**	füttern; ernähren
(to) **feel**	**felt**	**felt**	fühlen, sich fühlen
(to) **fight**	**fought**	**fought**	(be)kämpfen
(to) **find**	**found**	**found**	finden
(to) **fly**	**flew**	**flown**	fliegen
(to) **forget**	**forgot**	**forgotten**	vergessen
(to) **freeze**	**froze**	**frozen**	(ge)frieren; erstarren
(to) **get**	**got**	**got**	bekommen; (sich etw.) holen; werden
(to) **give** [ɪ]	**gave**	**given** [ɪ]	geben
(to) **go**	**went**	**gone**	gehen, fahren
(to) **grow (up)**	**grew (up)**	**grown (up)**	(auf)wachsen; anbauen; werden
(to) **hang (out)**	**hung (out)** [ʌ]	**hung (out)**	(rum)hängen, (ab)hängen
(to) **have**	**had**	**had**	haben; etw. essen
(to) **hear** [ɪə]	**heard** [ɜː]	**heard**	hören
(to) **hide**	**hid**	**hidden**	(sich) verstecken
(to) **hit**	**hit**	**hit**	treffen auf, schlagen, stoßen gegen
(to) **hold**	**held**	**held**	halten
(to) **hurt**	**hurt**	**hurt**	verletzen; wehtun
(to) **keep**	**kept**	**kept**	(be)halten; aufbewahren
(to) **kneel**	**knelt**	**knelt**	knien
(to) **know** [nəʊ]	**knew** [njuː]	**known** [nəʊn]	wissen; kennen
(to) **lead** [iː]	**led** [e]	**led** [e]	führen, leiten

Infinitive	Simple past	Past participle	
(to) **leave**	**left**	**left**	lassen, zurücklassen, verlassen
(to) **let**	**let**	**let**	lassen
(to) **lie**	**lay**	**lain**	liegen
(to) **lose** [uː]	**lost**	**lost**	verlieren
(to) **make**	**made**	**made**	machen, herstellen
(to) **mean**	**meant**	**meant**	bedeuten, meinen
(to) **meet**	**met**	**met**	treffen; (sich) treffen
(to) **pay**	**paid**	**paid**	(be)zahlen
(to) **put**	**put**	**put**	legen, stellen, stecken
(to) **read** [iː]	**read** [e]	**read** [e]	lesen
(to) **rewrite**	**rewrote**	**rewritten**	neu schreiben, umschreiben
(to) **ride** [aɪ]	**rode**	**ridden** [ɪ]	reiten; *(Rad)* fahren
(to) **ring**	**rang**	**rung**	läuten, klingeln
(to) **rise**	**rose**	**risen**	(an)steigen; sich erheben
(to) **run**	**ran**	**run**	rennen, laufen
(to) **say**	**said** [sed]	**said** [sed]	sagen
(to) **see**	**saw**	**seen**	sehen
(to) **sell**	**sold**	**sold**	verkaufen
(to) **send**	**sent**	**sent**	senden, schicken
(to) **set**	**set**	**set**	stellen, legen, setzen
(to) **sew** [əʊ]	**sewed** [əʊ]	**sewn** [əʊ]	nähen
(to) **shake**	**shook**	**shaken**	schütteln; zittern
(to) **shine**	**shone** [ʃɒn]	**shone** [ʃɒn]	scheinen *(Sonne)*; strahlen, glänzen
(to) **shoot**	**shot**	**shot**	(er)schießen
(to) **show**	**showed**	**shown**	zeigen
(to) **sing**	**sang**	**sung**	singen
(to) **sink**	**sank**	**sunk**	sinken
(to) **sit**	**sat**	**sat**	sitzen; sich setzen
(to) **sleep**	**slept**	**slept**	schlafen
(to) **slide**	**slid**	**slid**	rutschen; schieben; gleiten (lassen)
(to) **speak** [iː]	**spoke**	**spoken**	sprechen
(to) **speed**	**sped**	**sped**	rasen, zu schnell fahren
(to) **spend**	**spent**	**spent**	*(Geld)* ausgeben, *(Zeit)* verbringen
(to) **spin (around)**	**spun (around)**	**spun (around)**	(sich) (herum)drehen
(to) **spit**	**spat**	**spat**	(aus)spucken; zischen/fauchen *(in gereiztem Ton sagen)*
(to) **split**	**split**	**split**	(sich) (auf)teilen, sich (auf)spalten
(to) **stand**	**stood**	**stood**	stehen; sich (hin)stellen
(to) **steal**	**stole**	**stolen**	stehlen, rauben
(to) **stick**	**stuck**	**stuck**	kleben; stecken
(to) **swear**	**swore**	**sworn**	fluchen; schwören
(to) **swim**	**swam**	**swum**	schwimmen
(to) **swing**	**swung**	**swung**	schwingen
(to) **take**	**took**	**taken**	(mit)nehmen; bringen; dauern
(to) **teach**	**taught**	**taught**	lehren, unterrichten
(to) **tell**	**told**	**told**	sagen; erzählen, berichten
(to) **think**	**thought**	**thought**	denken, glauben, meinen

Infinitive	Simple past	Past participle	
(to) **throw**	**threw** [uː]	**thrown**	werfen
(to) **understand**	**understood**	**understood**	verstehen
(to) **upset**	**upset**	**upset**	jn. erschüttern; jn. aufregen, ärgern
(to) **wake (up)**	**woke (up)**	**woken (up)**	aufwachen; jn. (auf)wecken
(to) **wear** [eə]	**wore** [ɔː]	**worn** [ɔː]	tragen, anhaben *(Kleidung)*
(to) **win**	**won** [ʌ]	**won** [ʌ]	gewinnen
(to) **write** [aɪ]	**wrote**	**written** [ɪ]	schreiben

Um dir das Lernen zu erleichtern, kannst du die unregelmäßigen Verben in Gruppen einteilen.

Alle drei Formen gleich:	*put, put, put*	→ **chicken verbs**
Zwei Formen gleich:	*bring,* brought, brought	→ **echo verbs**
	become, became, *become*	→ **sandwich verbs**
Alle drei Formen verschieden:	*sing, sang, sung*	→ **cat verbs** (miau)

Lernst du diese Formen in ähnlichen Zweiergruppen, behältst du sie besser: *be, was, been* und *see, saw, seen* oder *break, broke, broken* und *speak, spoke, spoken*

Finde zu jeder Gruppe weitere Beispiele in der Übersicht auf den Seiten 300–302.

Ähnliche Wörter im Englischen und Deutschen

Viele englische Wörter ähneln deutschen Wörtern: *a cowboy* = ein Cowboy
Beachte aber die Unterschiede 1–3!

(1) Nomen werden im Deutschen großgeschrieben, aber im Englischen klein.
(2) Manche Wörter haben im Deutschen andere Endungen, aber einen ähnlichen Stamm, z. B. planen – *(to) plan*.
(3) Oft unterscheidet sich die Aussprache. Höre dir die blau markierten Wörter in der App an und sprich sie nach.

active / activity
address
allergic (to)
alphabet
alternative
anonymous
April
article
August
balcony
ball
banana
barbecue
bass
biology
blues
bowling
Brexit
(to) bring
British
browser
bus
butter
cafe
camera
card
character
chocolate
circus
class
classroom
clever
club
coffee
comic
computer
console
cool
corridor
cost / (to) cost
cousin
creative
crown
culture
curry
dance / (to) dance
December
decoration
definition
detail
dialogue
drama
drink / (to) drink
electric
elephant
end / (to) end
England / English
experiment
family
February
film
(to) find
fish
football
friend / friendly
gallery
garage
garden
gold
group
guest
hamster
happy
hello
highlight
horn
house
hungry
idea
information
insect
January
jewels
July
June
karaoke
kebab
kilometre (km)
kiosk
lamp
market
maths
melon
milk
millilitre
minute
modern
moment
museum
music
name
negative
November
number
object
October
online
open
orange
parallel
partner
pasta
pause
perfect
person
photo
picnic
plan / (to) plan
pool
post
poster
problem
project
pronoun
rafting
respect
restaurant
ring
robot
room
rucksack
salad
sandwich
sauce
scene
school
(to) send
September
shopping centre
silver
(to) sink
skateboard
smart
sofa
software
song
sport
star
stop
story
student
summer
supermarket
surfing
sweatshirt
(to) swim
synagogue
test / (to) test
text / (to) text
title
toilet
tomato
top
tourist
tradition
trainer
trick
uniform
vanilla
vegan
vegetarian / veggie
video
warm
website
wind
winner
winter
word
yoghurt
zoo

Typical tasks	Häufige Arbeitsanweisungen
Act out the conversation / song / story.	Führt das Gespräch / das Lied / die Geschichte vor.
Add more ideas / points / ...	Füge weitere Ideen / Punkte / ... hinzu.
Answer the questions / partner B's questions.	Beantworte die Fragen / Partner Bs Fragen.
Ask and answer questions.	Stelle und beantworte Fragen.
What's the book / film / ... about?	Worum geht es in dem Buch / Film / ...?
Before you read / listen / watch (a film / ...) / ...	Bevor du liest / (zu)hörst / (einen Film / ...) anschaust / ...
Brainstorm ideas.	Sammle spontane Einfälle / Gedanken.
Check the spelling / your answers / ideas (with a partner).	Überprüfe deine Rechtschreibung / Antworten / Ideen (mit einem Partner / einer Partnerin).
Choose the correct answer / word.	Wähle die richtige Antwort / das richtige Wort aus.
Collect ideas / words / phrases / information.	Sammle Ideen / Wörter / Ausdrücke / Informationen.
Compare the pictures / your answers / ideas / ... with a partner.	Vergleiche die Bilder / deine Antworten / Ideen / ... mit einem Partner / einer Partnerin.
Complete the table / list / sentences / conversation / rule / ...	Vervollständige die Tabelle / Liste / Sätze / Unterhaltung / Regel / ...
Copy (and complete) the table / list / notes.	Schreibe die Tabelle / die Liste / Notizen ab (und vervollständige sie).
Correct the false / wrong sentences / answers.	Berichtige die falschen Sätze / Antworten.
Describe the picture / your room / ...	Beschreibe das Bild / dein Zimmer / ...
Describe (one of the tours) in one sentence.	Beschreibe (eine der Touren) in einem Satz.
Discuss your reasons / your ideas / your opinion / ... with a partner.	Diskutiere deine Gründe / deine Ideen / deine Meinung / ... mit einem Partner / einer Partnerin.
Explain what ... means.	Erkläre was ... bedeutet.
Find (a partner).	Suche (eine Partnerin / einen Partner).
Find the answers / the correct / right / wrong words / information / images / ...	Finde die Antworten / die richtigen / falschen Wörter / Informationen / Bilder / ...
Find reasons for and against ...	Finde Gründe, die für und gegen ... sprechen.
Finish the sentences.	Vervollständige die Sätze.
Give advice / feedback.	Gib Ratschläge / eine Rückmeldung.
Give reasons.	Begründe (deine Antwort).
Give short answers.	Antworte in Stichworten.
Give your opinion.	Sag / Äußere deine Meinung.
Have a conversation with (two partners).	Unterhalte dich mit (zwei Partner/-innen).
In your own words, ...	In deinen eigenen Worten, ...
Listen and check / practise / repeat / guess / take notes / match.	Höre zu und überprüfe / übe / wiederhole / rate / mache Notizen / ordne zu.
Listen for information on / about ...	Höre zu und achte auf Informationen zu ...
Look at the photos / pictures /map / title (and answer the questions).	Sieh dir die Fotos / Bilder / Karte / Überschrift an (und beantworte die Fragen).
Make a poster / quiz / list / ...	Erstelle ein Poster / ein Quiz / eine Liste / ...

Typical tasks	Häufige Arbeitsanweisungen
Make groups (of six / ... students).	Bildet Gruppen (zu je sechs / ... Schüler/-innen).
Make sentences / notes / lists / a mind map.	Fertige Sätze / Notizen / Listen / eine Mindmap an.
Match the sentence parts / the words to ... the correct (pictures).	Verbinde die Satzhälften / die Wörter mit ... den richtigen (Bildern).
Name ...	Nenne ...
Present ...	Präsentiere ...
Put the sentences / dialogue / events in the correct order.	Bringe die Sätze / den Dialog / die Ereignisse in die richtige Reihenfolge.
Read the conversation / text / story / article.	Lies den Dialog / den Text / die Geschichte / den Artikel.
Rewrite your message / ...	Überarbeite deine Nachricht / ...
Say what you think of / about ...	Sage, was du über ... denkst.
Say why.	Begründe.
Scan the text / ...	Überfliege den Text / ...
Skim the story.	Durchsuche die Geschichte nach bestimmten Informationen.
Swap cards / roles.	Tauscht die Karten / die Rollen.
Take notes (about ...).	Mache dir Notizen (zu ...).
Take turns.	Wechselt euch ab.
Talk to a partner / in groups.	Sprich mit einem Partner / einer Partnerin / deiner Gruppe.
Tell your partner / the class.	Erzähle / Sage es deinem/r Partner/-in / der Klasse.
There are ... extra headings / words / answers.	Es gibt ... extra Überschriften / Wörter / Antworten.
Think of (ideas / reasons for) ...	Überlege dir (Ideen / Gründe für) ...
True, false or not in the text? Correct the false sentences.	Richtig, falsch oder nicht im Text? Korrigiere die falschen Sätze.
Use your notes / the words in a) / keywords / the information (in the table) / the words in brackets.	Benutze deine Notizen / die Wörter aus Aufgabe a) / Stichworte / die Informationen (aus der Tabelle) / die Wörter in Klammern.
Watch part 1 / scene 1 / the whole film / the video (and answer the questions).	Sieh dir Teil 1 / Szene 1 / den ganzen Film / das Video an (und beantworte die Fragen).
What's the book / film / ... about?	Worum geht es in dem Buch / Film / ...?
Work alone / in pairs / in groups.	Arbeite allein / in Partnerarbeit / in Gruppen.
Work out the meaning of (the words).	Finde die Bedeutung (der Wörter) heraus.
Write the correct answers / sentences / questions / words.	Schreibe die richtigen Antworten / Sätze / Fragen / Wörter (auf).
Write a short description / a blog post / an ending to the story / ...	Schreibe eine kurze Beschreibung / einen Blogeintrag / ein Ende für die Geschichte / ...
Write more information for each ...	Schreibe mehr Informationen zu jedem / jeder ...

Cover
Statue: stock.adobe.com/Oleksandr Dibrova; Kinder: Chocolate Films; Hintergrund: stock.adobe.com/wajan

Illustrationen
Cornelsen/Harald Ardeias: S. 19/o., S. 20/o. Brücke, Stadion, Köpfe; S. 28, S. 29, S. 30, S. 31, S. 38, S. 46/o., S. 48, S. 52/m.r., S. 55/o.r., S. 77, S. 86, S. 96, S. 97, S. 98, S. 103, S. 104/o.r., S. 106/u., S. 107, S. 108, S. 109, S. 112/u., S. 114, S. 125, S. 126/o.r., S. 147/u., S. 148/m.r., S. 149/o.r.; **Cornelsen/Inhouse/Josephine Bienert-Köhler:** S. 172; **Cornelsen/Carlos Borrell Eiköter:** S. 128, S. 150/o.r.; Umschlaginnenseite hinten (U3); **Cornelsen/Irina Zinner:** S. 181, S. 182, S. 183, S. 186, S. 190, S. 191, S. 193, S. 194, S. 195, S. 205, S. 208, S. 209, S. 210; **Cornelsen/Peter Kast bearbeitet von Carlos Borrell Eiköter:** S. 312; **Cornelsen/Till Nachtmann:** S. 152/m.r., S. 152/u.l., S. 152/u.r., S. 153, S. 154, S. 155, S. 156, S. 157, S. 158; **Cornelsen/Till Nachtmann/action Press/Everett Collection, Inc.:** S. 152/m.l.; **Eric Gira:** S. 47; **Zweiband/Eric Gira:** S. 34/u.r.

Abbildungen
S. 4: stock.adobe.com/f11photo; **S. 5:** stock.adobe.com/SeanPavonePhoto; **S. 6:** Shutterstock.com/Daniel M Ernst; **S. 7:** stock.adobe.com/Aerial Film Studio; **S. 8:** Shutterstock.com/Michal Sarauer; **S. 10/A:** stock.adobe.com/KBDESIGN-PHOTO; **S. 10/B:** mauritius images/Cavan Images; **S. 10/C:** mauritius images/Maxim Kalitvintsev/Alamy/Alamy Stock Photos; **S. 10/D:** Shutterstock.com/Jakub Maculewicz; **S. 10/Hintergrund:** stock.adobe.com/ii-graphics; **S. 11/E:** stock.adobe.com/oscity; **S. 11/F:** Shutterstock.com/Photomika-com; **S. 11/G:** stock.adobe.com/Terri Cage; **S. 12/1:** stock.adobe.com/ii-graphics; **S. 12/2:** Shutterstock/Lucky-photographer; **S. 12/3:** Shutterstock.com/Dave Primov; **S. 12/4:** stock.adobe.com/rdnzl; **S. 13/5 Deutschland:** Shutterstock.com/vectorlight; **S. 13/5 USA:** stock.adobe.com/ii-graphics; **S. 13/6:** stock.adobe.com/alexlmx; **S. 13/7:** Shutterstock.com/Svet foto; **S. 13/8:** Shutterstock.com/Prostock-studio; **S 13/9:** Shutterstock.com/MR.Silaphop Pongsai; **S. 13/10:** stock.adobe.com/Olga Yastremska and Leonid Yastremskiy/New Africa; **S. 14/o.l.:** Cornelsen/Chocolate Films; **S. 14/m.r.:** Shutterstock.com/Drazen Zigic; **S. 15/o.r.:** Shutterstock.com/SNEHIT PHOTO; **S. 15/m.l.:** Shutterstock.com/MJTH; **S. 15/m.r.:** Cornelsen/Chocolate Films; **S. 16/o.:** stock.adobe.com/f11photo; **S. 16/D:** stock.adobe.com/dell; **S. 16/E:** stock.adobe.com/f11photo; **S. 17:** Cornelsen/Digital Learning Ass. Ltd.; **S. 18/o.l. u. m.:** Chocolate Films; **S. 18/o.r.:** stock.adobe.com/Krakenimages.com; **S. 18/A:** stock.adobe.com/magann; **S. 18/B:** stock.adobe.com/khalid; **S. 18/C:** stock.adobe.com/Corrado; **S. 18/D:** Shutterstock.com/Christian Mueller; **S. 18/E:** Shutterstock.com/David W. Leindecker; **S. 19/u./1:** stock.adobe.com/BillionPhotos.com; **S. 19/u.2.l.:** stock.adobe.com/Spiroview Inc.; **S. 19/u./2.r.:** stock.adobe.com/BillionPhotos.com; **S. 19/u./3:** stock.adobe.com/BillionPhotos.com; **S. 19/u.4.l.:** stock.adobe.com/Andrey_Lobachev; **S. 19/u./4.r.:** stock.adobe.com/BillionPhotos.com; **S. 20/o. Karte:** stock.adobe.com/lesniewski; **S. 20/m.l.:** mauritius images/Valentin Wolf/imageBROKER; **S. 21/o.r.:** Imago Stock & People GmbH; **S. 21/m.r.:** stock.adobe.com/Benjamin Huang; **S. 22/m.l.u.m:** stock.adobe.com/Krakenimages.com; **S. 22/m.r.:** Chocolate Films; **S. 23:** Bridgeman Images/PVDE; **S. 24:** imago sport; **S. 25/l.:** dpa Picture-Alliance/CJ Rivera/Invision/AP; **S. 25/r.:** imago sport/@guelbergoes; **S. 26/A:** stock.adobe.com/steven hendricks; **S. 26/B:** stock.adobe.com/Julianna Olah; **S. 26/C:** stock.adobe.com/CreativePhotography; **S. 27:** stock.adobe.com/Tixel; **S. 33:** Cornelsen/Digital Learning Ass. Ltd.; **S. 34/o.r.:** CartoonStock/Hagen; **S. 35:** Shutterstock.com/Ground Picture; **S. 36/o.:** Cornelsen/Chocolate Films; **S. 36/m.:** Cornelsen/Chocolate Films; **S. 36/u.:** stock.adobe.com/Krakenimages.com; **S. 37/o.:** Shutterstock.com/Ground Picture; **S. 37/u.:** mauritius images/Robertharding/Alamy/Alamy Stock Photos; **S. 39/A:** stock.adobe.com/pyzata; **S. 39/B:** Shutterstock.com/NATNN; **S. 39/C:** Shutterstock.com/Pond Saksit; **S. 39/D:** Shutterstock.com/Billion Photos; **S. 39/E:** Shutterstock.com/4 PM production; **S. 39/u.l.:** stock.adobe.com/f11photo; **S. 40 o.l.:** stock.adobe.com/valvectors; **S. 40/o.r.:** Cornelsen/Chocolate Films; **S. 40/m.:** mauritius images/alamy stock photo/John Muggenborg; **S. 41/o.l.:** mauritius images/Richard Levine/Alamy Stock Photos; **S. 41/o.r.:** mauritius images/ZUMA Press, Inc./Alamy Stock Photos; **S. 41/u.m.:** mauritius images/Sergey Yatunin/Alamy Stock Photos; **S. 41/u.r.:** mauritius images/Michael Marquand/Alamy Stock Photos; **S. 42/m.l.:** Shutterstock.com/Nagel Photography; **S. 42/m.2.v.l.:** Shutterstock.com/Michael Rosskothen; **S. 42/m.:** Bridgeman Images; **S. 42/m.r.:** Bridgeman Images/Currier, N. (1813–88) and Ives, J.M. (1824–95)/Private Collection/J. T. Vintage; **S. 42/o.r.:** Shutterstock.com/Neil Phillip Mey; **S. 42/A:** Shutterstock.com/Reshetnikov_art; **S. 42/B:** Shutterstock.com/Todd Taulman Photography; **S. 42/C:** Shutterstock.com/gary718; **S. 42/D:** interfoto e.k.; **S. 43/m.l.:** Shutterstock.com/Inger Eriksen; **S. 43/m.o.:** interfoto e.k.; **S. 43/m.r.:** Shutterstock.com/Thomas Hengge; **S 43/E:** Shutterstock.com/eurobanks; **S. 43/F:** Shutterstock.com/Natthawon Chaosakun; **S. 43/G:** mauritius images/United Archives; **S 43/H:** Shutterstock.com/Eric Isselee; **S. 44/o.:** Imago Stock & People GmbH; **S. 44/m.o.:** stock.adobe.com/pio3; **S. 44/m.u.:** stock.adobe.com/Linda Harms; **S. 44/u.:** mauritius images/Richard Levine/Alamy/Alamy Stock Photos; **S. 45/o.r.:** Shutterstock.com/P Maxwell Photography; **S. 45/m.r.:** stock.adobe.com/Markus Mainka; **S. 46/u.r.:** stock.adobe.com/Mariana Ianovska; **S. 49/o.r.:** Shutterstock.com/DUSAN ZIDAR; **S. 49/m.r.:** Shutterstock.com/kintomo; **S. 50/A:** Cornelsen/Digital Learning Ass. Ltd.; **S. 50/B:** stock.adobe.com/Brian Swanson; **S. 50/C:** stock.adobe.com/Joe O'Neill; **S. 50/D:** Shutterstock.com/f11photo; **S. 51/E:** stock.adobe.com/SeanPavonePhoto; **S. 51/F:** stock.adobe.com/Sean PavonePhoto; **S. 51/G:** Imago Stock & People GmbH/USA TODAY Network; **S. 51/H:** Cornelsen/Digital Learning Ass. Ltd.;

S. 52/o.r.: Shutterstock.com/fizkes; **S. 53:** Shutterstock.com/Pressmaster; **S. 54:** Shutterstock.com/Drazen Zigic; **S. 55/m.l.:** Shutterstock.com/f11photo; **S. 56:** dpa Picture-Alliance/ASSOCIATED PRESS; **S. 57:** Imago Stock & People GmbH/TT; **S. 58:** mauritius images/JT Vintage; **S. 59/l.:** Depositphotos/Leonard Zhukovsky; **S. 59/r.:** imago sport/imago images/ZUMA Wire; **S. 60/o.r.:** Shutterstock.com/GTS Productions; **S. 60/m.r.:** stock.adobe.com/Lynne Ann Mitchell; **S. 61/A:** Shutterstock.com/Food Via Lenses; **S. 61/B:** Shutterstock.com/Foodio; **S. 61/C:** Shutterstock.com/Brent Hofacker; **S. 61/D:** Shutterstock.com/Brent Hofacker; **S. 62/o.l.:** Imago Stock & People GmbH/imago/ZUMA Press; **S. 62/m.r.:** mauritius images/Paul Wood/Alamy/Alamy Stock Photos; **S. 63:** Shutterstock.com/Kaspars Grinvalds; **S. 64/A:** Shutterstock.com/Rasica; **S. 64/B:** Shutterstock.com/John D Sirlin; **S. 64/C:** Shutterstock.com/Suzanne Tucker; **S. 64/D:** stock.adobe.com/MIKHAIL; **S. 64/E:** NASA; **S. 64/u.l.:** stock.adobe.com/Jan H. Andersen; **S. 64/u.r.:** stock.adobe.com/Geber86; **S. 65:** stock.adobe.com/jetcityimage; **S. 67:** Cornelsen/Digital Learning Ass. Ltd.; **S. 69:** Shutterstock.com/Caftor; **S. 70/A:** stock.adobe.com/Jeffery; **S. 70/B:** stock.adobe.com/rmbarricarte; **S. 70/C:** Shutterstock.com/Chantal Schoenherz; **S. 70/D:** stock.adobe.com/Patrick Civello; **S. 70/E:** Shutterstock.com/Sean Pavone; **S. 70/F:** mauritius images/Goddard on the Go/Alamy/Alamy Stock Photos; **S. 71/o.:** Shutterstock.com/Vovatol; **S. 71/u.:** mauritius images/Tribune Content Agency LLC/Alamy/Alamy Stock Photos; **S. 72/Icon Tickets:** Shutterstock.com/M-vector; **S. 72/Icon Ski u. Schlittschuh:** Shutterstock.com/popicon; **S. 72/Icon Tasse:** Shutterstock.com/Sereda Serhii; **S. 72/Icon Tasche:** Shutterstock.com/Turac Novruzova;**S. 72/m.l.:** Shutterstock.com/Elena Efimova;**S. 72/u.r.:** Imago Stock & People GmbH/ZUMA Wire; **S. 72/2.v.u.r.:** Shutterstock.com/Artiom Photo; **S. 73/o.r.:** stock.adobe.com/cherryandbees; **S. 74 o.l.:** stock.adobe.com/valvectors; **S. 74/o.r.:** Shutterstock.com/fizkes; **S. 74/2.v.o.r.:** Shutterstock.com/Dapitart; **S. 74/2.v.u.r.:** stock.adobe.com/EmmaStock; **S. 74/u.r.:** mauritius images/William Morgan/Alamy/Alamy Stock Photos; **S. 75/o.r.:** Shutterstock.com/Drazen Zigic; **S. 75/m.l.:** mauritius images/John Warburton-Lee; **S. 75/u.r.:** mauritius images/Cinema Legacy Collection; **S. 76/o.:** Shutterstock.com/Drazen Zigic; **S. 76/u.:** Imago Stock & People GmbH/imago images/ZUMA Wire; **S. 78/m.r.:** dpa Picture-Alliance/ASSOCIATED PRESS; **S. 78/u.r.:** mauritius images/World Book Inc.; **S. 79:** dpa Picture-Alliance/Pacific Press; **S. 80:** Shutterstock.com/Andriy Blokhin; **S. 81/o.r.:** Imago Stock & People GmbH/piemags; **S. 82/A:** Shutterstock.com/Marcelo Morena; **S. 82/B:** NASA/Sheri Locke; **S. 82/C:** stock.adobe.com/Speedfighter; **S. 82/D:** mauritius images/Bob Daemmrich/Alamy; **S. 82/E:** stock.adobe.com/Natallia; **S. 83:** Cornelsen/Digital Learning Ass. Ltd.; **S. 84/o.l. Hintergrund:** stock.adobe.com/GCapture; **S. 84/o.l. Jacob:** Shutterstock.com/morrowlight; **S. 84/o.l. Diego:** Shutterstock.com/MUTH; **S. 84/o.r.:** mauritius images/Joerg Hackemann/Alamy/Alamy Stock Photos; **S. 84/u.r.:** Shutterstock.com/Moab Republic; **S. 85:** mauritius images/Danita Delimont; **S. 87:** Shutterstock.com/PeopleImages.com – Yuri A; **S. 88/o.:** Imago Stock & People GmbH/USA TODAY Network; **S. 88/u.:** mauritius images/Bob Daemmrich/Alamy/Alamy Stock Photos; **S. 89/o.:** Shutterstock.com/FiledIMAGE; **S. 89/u.:** Shutterstock.com/Everett Collection; **S. 90/o.:** mauritius images/Guoqiang Xue/Alamy/Alamy Stock Photos; **S. 90/u.r.:** stock.adobe.com/digitalskillet1; **S. 91:** Shutterstock.com/melitas; **S. 92/o.r.:** Shutterstock.com/morrowlight; **S. 92/m.r.:** Shutterstock.com/MJTH; **S. 93/o.:** Shutterstock.com/Ann Kosolapova; **S. 93/m.l.:** Shutterstock.com/morrowlight; **S. 93/m.r.:** Shutterstock.com/MJTH; **S. 95/o.r.:** Shutterstock.com/antoniodiaz; **S. 95/A:** stock.adobe.com/Sandika; **S. 95/B:** stock.adobe.com/Anthony; **S. 95/C:** Shutterstock.com/pisaphotography; **S. 95/D:** stock.adobe.com/theerakit; **S. 95/E:** stock.adobe.com/Ricochet64; **S. 95/F:** stock.adobe.com/jojoo64; **S. 99:** Cornelsen/Digital Learning Ass. Ltd.; **S. 100:** stock.adobe.com/fizkes; **S. 101/o.r.:** Shutterstock.com/Billion Photos; **S. 101/m.r.:** Shutterstock.com/Kokoulina; **S. 102:** Shutterstock.com/BrigitteT; **S. 104/m.r.:** stock.adobe.com/digitalskillet1; **S. 106/o.l.:** stock.adobe.com/valvectors; **S. 106/o.r.:** Shutterstock.com/MJTH; **S. 110/o.:** stock.adobe.com/soupstock; **S. 110/m.:** stock.adobe.com/imtmphoto; **S. 110/u.:** Shutterstock.com/BearFotos; **S. 111:** mauritius images/ZUMA Press, Inc./Alamy/Alamy Stock Photos; **S. 112/o.:** Shutterstock.com/LongJon; **S. 112/m.:** Shutterstock.com/melissamn; **S. 116/A:** Shutterstock.com/Sean Pavone; **S. 116/B:** Imago Stock & People GmbH; **S. 116/C:** stock.adobe.com/Sergii Figurnyi; **S. 116/D:** stock.adobe.com/Hanyun; **S. 117/E:** mauritius images/Nick Fox/Alamy/Alamy Stock Photos; **S. 117/F:** stock.adobe.com/Hakan Ozturk; **S. 117/G:** mauritius images/Phil Bird/imageBROKER; **S. 117/H:** Shutterstock.com/kropic1; **S. 118/l.:** stock.adobe.com/auremar; **S. 118/m.:** stock.adobe.com/Krakenimages.com; **S. 118/r.:** stock.adobe.com/Pixel-Shot; **S. 119/o.:** Shutterstock.com/sdecoret; **S. 119/u.:** Shutterstock.com/Frame Stock Footage; **S. 120/A:** Shutterstock.com/kylepost-photography; **S. 120/B:** stock.adobe.com/Llama-World-studio/generiert mit KI; **S. 120/o.r.:** Cornelsen/Chocolate Films; **S. 120/o.l.:** stock.adobe.com/Krakenimages.com; **S. 121/o.l.:** stock.adobe.com/Pixel-Shot; **S. 121/o.r.:** stock.adobe.com/auremar; **S. 121/m.r.:** Shutterstock.com/BearFotos; **S. 122/o.l.:** Cornelsen/Chocolate Films; **S. 122/o.r.:** stock.adobe.com/Krakenimages.com; **S. 122/m.r.:** Imago Stock & People GmbH/ZUMA Press Wire; **S. 123:** Shutterstock.com/FRAYN; **S. 124/o.l.:** mauritius images/Terray Sylvester/VWPics/Alamy/Alamy Stock Photos; **S. 124/o.r.:** stock.adobe.com/Hanna Tor; **S. 124/m.r.:** CartoonStock/Jon Carter; **S. 126/2.v.o.:** stock.adobe.com/KseniaJoyg; **S. 126/3.v.o.:** stock.adobe.com/Photographer owns all copyright to the photograph. You have downloaded this photograph from 500px. Your use of the Image is gove/221554545/photo/500px.com/Photographer owns all copyright to the photograph. You have downloaded this photograph from 500px. Your use of the Image is governed by 500px's terms and conditions. Terms and availability are liable to change; it is your responsibility to check before you use an image. Please check on https:/Alexander; **S. 126/2.v.u.:** stock.adobe.com/Dan; **S. 126/u.:** stock.adobe.com/Andy Dean; **S. 127/o.r.:** stock.adobe.com/elvis901; **S. 127/m.r.:** stock.adobe.com/duaneups; **S. 127/u.r.:** Shutterstock.com/Drazen Zigic; **S. 129/o.:** Shutterstock.com/Larry Gibson; **S. 129/u.:** Shutterstock.com/f11photo; **S. 130/o. Amy:** Cornelsen/Chocolate Films;

S. 130/o. Troy: Shutterstock.com/Drazen Zigic; **S. 130/o. Diego:** Shutterstock.com/MJTH; **S. 130/o. Tiana:** Cornelsen/Chocolate Films; **S. 130/u.r.:** stock.adobe.com/AkuAku; **S. 131/o.r.:** Shutterstock.com/Gorodenkoff; **S. 131/u.l.:** stock.adobe.com/Maurice; **S. 132/Amy:** Cornelsen/Chocolate Films; **S. 132/Tiana:** Cornelsen/Chocolate Films; **S. 132/Diego:** Shutterstock.com/MJTH; **S. 132/Troy:** Shutterstock.com/Drazen Zigic; **S. 133:** "Swimming in the desert" by Alvaro Ron, USA, 2017, 18 Min/interfilmBerlin Management GmbH; **S. 135/o.l.:** Shutterstock.com/Alliance Images; **S. 135/o.m.:** mauritius images/Jeffrey Isaac Greenberg 19+/Alamy/Alamy Stock Photos; **S. 135/o.r.:** stock.adobe.com/© James Baker 2007/James Baker 2007/James; **S. 136/A:** stock.adobe.com/Aerial Film Studio; **S. 136/B:** stock.adobe.com/Michal; **S. 136/C:** Shutterstock.com/Tint Media; **S. 136/D:** Shutterstock.com/lunamarina; **S. 136/E:** Shutterstock.com/frank_peters; **S. 136/F:** Shutterstock.com/frank_peters; **S. 137/m.r.:** mauritius images/World Book Inc.; **S. 137/u.r.:** Cornelsen/Chocolate Films; **S. 138/m.r.:** stock.adobe.com/Olga; **S. 140/o.l.:** stock.adobe.com/valvectors; **S. 140/o.r.:** Cornelsen/Chocolate Films; **S. 140/m.l.:** Shutterstock.com/Richard Thornton; **S. 140/m.r.:** Shutterstock.com/Simone Hogan; **S. 140/u.l.:** stock.adobe.com/René Stevens; **S. 141/m.l.:** Shutterstock.com/Ebtikar; **S. 141/u.r.:** Shutterstock.com/Sudowoodo; **S. 142:** mauritius images/Science Source; **S. 144/m.r.:** stock.adobe.com/shishiga; **S. 145/A:** stock.adobe.com/Martin M303; **S. 145/B:** stock.adobe.com/f11photo; **S. 145/C:** Shutterstock.com/Image Source Trading Ltd; **S. 145/D:** Imago Stock & People GmbH/imago images/ZUMA Press; **S. 145/E:** stock.adobe.com/JFL Photography; **S. 146/o.:** stock.adobe.com/Krakenimages.com; **S. 147/o.r.:** mauritius images/ZUMA Press, Inc./Alamy/Alamy Stock Photos; **S. 148/o.r.:** stock.adobe.com/fotomaster; **S. 150/A:** stock.adobe.com/slowmotiongli; **S. 150/B:** Shutterstock.com/Topuria Design; **S. 150/C:** Shutterstock.com/Sahara Prince; **S. 151/D:** Shutterstock.com/Cavan-Images; **S. 151/E:** Shutterstock.com/Peter Dean; **S. 151/F:** stock.adobe.com/peteleclerc; **S. 151/G:** Cornelsen/Digital Learning Ass. Ltd; **S. 152/m.r.:** Shutterstock.com/Paisit Teeraphatsakool; **S. 160/o.l.:** mauritius images/Yvette Cardozo/Alamy/Alamy Stock Photos; **S. 160/o.r.:** Shutterstock.com/Ghost Bear; **S. 160/m.r.:** stock.adobe.com/Dolores Harvey; **S. 161/o.r.:** Shutterstock.com/Daniel M Ernst; **S. 161/m.r.:** stock.adobe.com/Tharanga; **S. 163/u.r.:** Shutterstock.com/Elsa Nur Afiana; **S. 165:** Shutterstock.com/Red Vector; **S. 168:** CartoonStock/Jon Carter; **S. 170:** Shutterstock.com/Kateryna Onyshchuk; **S. 171:** "Swimming in the desert" by Alvaro Ron, USA, 2017, 18 Min/interfilmBerlin Management GmbH; **S. 176:** stock.adobe.com/babimu; **S. 177:** Shutterstock.com/Iakov Filimonov; **. 198/o.r.:** Shutterstock.com/greenpic.studio; **S. 198/m.l.:** Shutterstock.com/Laurie Barr; **S. 199/o.l.:** Shutterstock.com/Iryna Inshyna; **S. 199/o.r.:** stock.adobe.com/isarawut; **S. 199/m.:** stock.adobe.com/cherryandbees; **S. 199/u.l.:** stock.adobe.com/Zamrznuti tonovi; **S. 199/u.r.:** stock.adobe.com/Antonioguillem; **S. 200/m.l.:** stock.adobe.com/Athena; **S. 200/m.:** stock.adobe.com/ValentinValkov; **S. 200/m.r.:** stock.adobe.com/klikk; **S. 200/u.l.:** stock.adobe.com/PNG Aom.WingWon; **S. 200/u.m.:** stock.adobe.com/AGCuesta; **S. 200/u.r.:** stock.adobe.com/Dimitrius; **S. 201/flood:** stock.adobe.com/bilanol; **S. 201/tsunami wave:** Shutterstock.com/FOTOKITA; **S. 201/landslide:** stock.adobe.com/Fotograf; **S. 201/volcanic eruption** stock.adobe.com/oleg525; **S. 201/drought:** stock.adobe.com/Generative AI; **S. 201/wildfire:** Shutterstock.com/Alaskagirl8821; **S. 201/blizzard:** stock.adobe.com/ugljesaras; **S. 201/freezing rain:** Shutterstock.com/FedBul; **S. 202/catering:** Shutterstock.com/Drazen Zigic; **S. 202/childcare:** stock.adobe.com/Halfpoint; **S. 202/plumbing.:** stock.adobe.com/Rido; **S. 202/agriculture:** stock.adobe.com/photoschmidt 2017/photoschmidt; **S. 202/construction:** stock.adobe.com/Gorodenkoff; **S. 202/motor service:** stock.adobe.com/Minerva Studio; **S. 202/computing:** Shutterstock.com/Gorodenkoff; **S. 202/hairdressing:** stock.adobe.com/Monkey Business; **S. 202/hospitality:** Shutterstock.com/DC Studio; **S. 202/retirement home:** Shutterstock.com/belushi; **S. 202/laboratory.:** stock.adobe.com/StockPhotoPro; **S. 202/factory.:** stock.adobe.com/Unique Vision; **S. 202/call centre:** stock.adobe.com/Atstock Productions; **S. 202/beauty salon:** stock.adobe.com/New Africa; **S. 202/influencer.:** stock.adobe.com/oneinchpunch; **S. 214/o.:** stock.adobe.com/buraratn; **S. 214/m.o.:** stock.adobe.com/Eastman Arts; **S. 214/m.u.:** stock.adobe.com/New Africa; **S. 214/u.:** Shutterstock.com/Sara Winter; **S. 215:** Shutterstock.com/a2l; **S. 217:** stock.adobe.com/Valentina; **S. 220/m.:** stock.adobe.com/dbvirago; **S. 220/u.:** Shutterstock.com/Tobik; **S. 221/o.:** Shutterstock/Dawid Rojek; **S. 221/m.:** stock.adobe.com/cineberg; **S. 222/o.:** stock.adobe.com/nfuru; **S. 222/m.o.:** stock.adobe.com/Sergio; **S. 222/m.u.:** stock.adobe.com/Hafiez Razali; **S. 222/u.:** Shutterstock.com/CoolKengzz; **S. 223/o.:** stock.adobe.com/Cavid; **S. 223/m.:** Shutterstock.com/mikeledray; **S. 224/o.:** Shutterstock.com/Africa Studio; **S. 224/u.:** stock.adobe.com/tputman151; **S. 225:** stock.adobe.com/paseven; **S. 226/m.:** stock.adobe.com/drummatra; **S. 226/u.:** stock.adobe.com/Wattana; **S. 229:** Shutterstock.com/foto-lite; **S. 230/m.l:** stock.adobe.com/MissesJones; **S. 230/m.r.:** stock.adobe.com/GalleryGlider; **S. 230/u.:** stock.adobe.com/Denis Gladkiy; **S. 231/o.:** stock.adobe.com/Iryna; **S. 231/u.:** Shutterstock.com/sumire8; **S. 232/m.:** Shutterstock.com/mike_expert; **S. 232/u.:** stock.adobe.com/Vladimir Melnikov; **S. 233/o.:** Shutterstock.com/stockcreations; **S. 233/o.r.:** Shutterstock.com/Surasak Klinmontha; **S. 234/o.:** Shutterstock.com/Iasha; **S. 234/m.:** Shutterstock.com/iconim; **S. 235/o.:** Shutterstock.com/tatiana80; **S. 235/u.:** Shutterstock.com/Motimo; **S. 236:** Shutterstock.com/Nynke van Holten; **S. 237:** Shutterstock.com/Pressmaster; **S. 238:** stock.adobe.com/Skórzewiak; **S. 239/m.:** stock.adobe.com/Andrey Popov; **S. 239/o.:** stock.adobe.com/guruXOX; **S. 240:** stock.adobe.com/Savo Ilic; **S. 242/o.:** Shutterstock.com/NayaDadara; **S. 242/u.l.:** stock.adobe.com/thanasak; **S. 242/u.r.:** Shutterstock.com/Nieuwland Photography; **S. 243/m.:** Shutterstock.com/Daxiao Productions; **S. 243/u.l.:** Shutterstock.com/Olga Gutyria; **S. 243/u.r.:** Shutterstock.com/Atstock Productions; **S. 244/o.:** Shutterstock.com/SPF; **S. 244/u.:** Shutterstock/Amelia Martin; **S. 246:** Shutterstock.com/baltskars; **S. 248:** stock.adobe.com/methinee; **S. 250/o.:** stock.adobe.com/Papugrat; **S. 250/m.:** stock.adobe.com/James Steidl; **S. 251/m.:** stock.adobe.com/blueringmedia; **S. 251/u.:** stock.adobe.com/EmmaStock; **S. 252/o.:** NASA/JSC;

S. 252/m.o.: stock.adobe.com/Chingiz; **S. 252/m.:** stock.adobe.com/KalininStudios; **S. 252/u.:** stock.adobe.com/ding; **S. 253/o.:** stock.adobe.com/yod67; **S. 253/m.o.:** stock.adobe.com/Jeronimo Contreras; **S. 253/m.:** Shutterstock.com/Eric Isselee; **S. 253/u.:** Shutterstock.com/Hedzun Vasyl; **S. 254:** stock.adobe.com/angel_nt; **S. 255:** stock.adobe.com/leszekglasner; **S. 256/o.:** stock.adobe.com/Monkey Business; **S. 256/m.:** stock.adobe.com/LimeSky; **S. 257/o.:** stock.adobe.com/Mr image; **S. 257/m.o.:** stock.adobe.com/Carlos Caetano; **S. 257/m.u.:** stock.adobe.com/Dan; **S. 257/u.:** stock.adobe.com/Pawel; **S. 258/o.:** stock.adobe.com/Renato; **S. 258/m.:** stock.adobe.com/Artranq; **S. 258/u.:** stock.adobe.com/C Davids/peopleimages.com; **S. 259/o.:** Shutterstock.com/Passatic; **S. 259/m.:** stock.adobe.com/olrat; **S. 259/u.:** stock.adobe.com/ponprachan; **S. 260/m.:** stock.adobe.com/Mike; **S. 260/u.:** stock.adobe.com/Murphy44; **S. 261/o.:** stock.adobe.com/BillionPhotos.com; **S. 261/u.:** stock.adobe.com/Irina

Allgemeiner Hinweis zu den in diesem Lehrwerk verwendeten Glyphen der „Noto Color Emoji": Das Schulbuch verwendet Glyphen aus der Schriftart „Noto Color Emoji" für die Darstellung von Emojis. Die Nutzung der Glyphen ist im Rahmen der The SIL Open Font License gewährleistet. Link: https://fonts.google.com/noto/specimen/Noto+Color+Emoji/about?noto.query=noto+color+emoji

Datenquellen

S. 22: Das Diagramm basiert auf Daten des Unites States Census Bureau, U.S. Department of Commerce: B16001 Language Spoken at Home by Ability to Speak English for the Population 5 Years and Over, https://data.census.gov/table/ACSDT1Y2022.B16001?t=Language%20Spoken%20at%20Home&g=160XX00US3651000 (Zugriff29.7.2024); **S. 47:** Das Diagramm basiert auf Daten von NYC Open Data, Bilingual Program per program type and language per school, https://data.cityofnewyork.us/Education/2021-2022-Bilingual-Program-List/6iwb-7euj/about_data, Zugriff 5.2.2024; **S. 81:** Das Diagramm basiert auf Daten von The Data Center, https:www.datacenterresearch.org/data-resources/who-lives-in-new-orleans-now (Zugriff 28.11.24); **S. 134:** Das Diagramm basiert auf Daten des Frontline Wildfire Defense, https://www.frontlinewildfire.com/wildfire-news-and-resources/california-wildfires-history-statistics (Zugriff 10.10.2024); **S. 138:** Das Diagramm basiert auf Daten des U.S. Fish and Wildlife Service, https://www.fws.gov/media/condor-population-graph (Zugriff 3.9.2024), Photo By/Credit: Olivia Beitelspacher/USFWS; **S. 144:** Das Diagramm basiert auf Daten des National Opinion Research Center (NORC) at the University of Chicago (survey for Hopelab and Common Sense Media, conducted October 4–November 14, 2023), https://www.commonsensemedia.org/sites/default/files/research/report/teen-and-young-adult-perspectives-on-generative-ai.pdf (Zugriff 22.8.2024); **S. 149:** Das Diagramm basiert auf Daten des United States Census Bureau (2020 Census), https://www.census.gov/library/stories/2023/10/2020-census-dhc-a-aian-population.html (Zugriff 22.8.2024); **S. 150:** Die Zahlen basieren auf Daten von Statistics Canada: www.statcan.gc.ca: Population of Canada (41 million): Canada's population clock (real-time model; statcan.gc.ca; Zugriff 10.9.2024); Born abroad (23%): Immigration and ethnocultural – Canada at a Glance, 2023 (statcan.gc.ca; Zugriff 10.9.2024); Native people (5%): Canada's Indigenous population – Statistics Canada (statcan.gc.ca; Zugriff 10.9.2024); French spoken as a first language (22%): Language – 2021 Census promotional material (statcan.gc.ca; Zugriff 10.9.2024); French spoken as a first language in the province of Quebec (84,1%): Statistics on official languages in Canada – Canada.ca (Zugriff 10.9.2024); Native languages (about 70): Indigenous languages across Canada (statcan.gc.ca; Zugriff 10.9.2024)

Liedquellen

S. 25/m.l.: 'Cheering For Me Now': 5001 Broadway Music/Neue Welt Musikverlag GmbH, Hamburg. Text: Lin-Manuel Miranda/John Kander; **S. 58:** 'Black Lives Matter': Daniel Dax Entertainment/Sony Music Publishing (Germany) GmbH, Berlin. Text: Daniel jr Nwosu; **S. 113:** 'Fifteen': Universal/MCA Music Publishing GmbH, Berlin. Text: Taylor Swift

Textquellen

S. 30–32: *On the Come Up* by Angela Thomas, HarperCollins Children's Books 2019 (S. 157–169); Ausschnitt gekürzt und leicht verändert;
S. 40: *Helaina's story: What the 20 years since 9/11 have been like for a survivor* by Helaina Hovitz in Teen Vogue: https://www.teenvogue.com/story/what-the-20-years-since-911-have-been-like-for-a-survivor, September 10, 2021; gekürzt und leicht verändert; **S. 96–98:** *Moxie* by Jennifer Mathieu, Hodder Children's Books 2017 (S. 94–101); Ausschnitt, gekürzt und leicht verändert; **S. 106–109:** *Hartford Moves* (chapter 14): Marc Proulx, Cornelsen 2022; **S. 153–158:** *The Amazing Adventures of Jack London. Book 3: Forty Mile* (chapters 8 & 9) by David Fermer & Till Nachtmann, Cornelsen 2019

Continent / Country / Region	Adjective	Person	People
Afghanistan [af'gænɪstan] *Afghanistan*	Afghan ['afgan]	an Afghan	the Afghans
Africa ['æfrɪkə] *Afrika*	African ['æfrɪkən]	an African	the Africans
Alaska [ə'læskə] *Alaska*	Alaskan [ə'læskən]	an Alaskan	the Alaskans
Albania [al'beɪniə] *Albanien*	Albanian [al'beɪniən]	an Albanian	the Albanians
America [ə'merɪkə] *Amerika*	American [ə'merɪkən]	an American	the Americans
Asia ['eɪʒə] *Asien*	Asian ['eɪʒn]	an Asian	the Asians
Austria ['ɒstriə] *Österreich*	Austrian ['ɒstriən]	an Austrian	the Austrians
the Bahamas [bə'hɑːməz] *die Bahamas*	Bahamian [bə'heɪmiən]	a Bahamian	the Bahamians
Bangladesh [bæŋglə'deʃ] *Bangladesch*	Bangladeshi [bæŋglə'deʃi]	a Bangladeshi	the Bangladeshis
Bolivia [bə'lɪviə] *Bolivien*	Bolivian [bə'lɪviən]	a Bolivian	the Bolivians
California [kælə'fɔːniə] *Kalifornien*	Californian [kælə'fɔːniən]	a Californian	the Californians
Canada ['kænədə] *Kanada*	Canadian [kə'neɪdiən]	a Canadian	the Canadians
Caribbean [kærɪ'biːən] *die Karibik*	Caribbean [kærɪ'biːən]	a Carib ['kærɪb]	the Caribs
China ['tʃaɪnə] *China*	Chinese [tʃaɪ'niːz]	a Chinese	the Chinese
Cuba ['kjuːbə] *Kuba*	Cuban ['kjuːbən]	a Cuban	the Cubans
Czechia ['tʃekiə] *Tschechien,* the Czech Republic [ˌtʃek rɪ'pʌblɪk] *die Tschechische Republik*	Czech [tʃek]	a Czech	the Czechs
Denmark ['denmɑːk] *Dänemark*	Danish ['deɪnɪʃ]	a Dane [deɪn]	the Danes
(the) Dominican Republic [dəmɪnɪkən rɪ'pʌblɪk] *die Dominikanische Republik*	Dominican [də'mɪnɪkən]	a Dominican	the Dominicans
England ['ɪŋglənd] *England*	English ['ɪŋglɪʃ]	an Englishman / -woman	the English
Europe ['jʊərəp] *Europa*	European [ˌjʊərə'piːən]	a European	the Europeans
France [frɑːns] *Frankreich*	French [frentʃ]	a Frenchman / -woman	the French
Germany ['dʒɜːməni] *Deutschland*	German ['dʒɜːmən]	a German	the Germans
Great Britain ['brɪtn] *Großbritannien*	British ['brɪtɪʃ]	a Briton ['brɪtn]	the British
Haiti ['heɪti] *Haiti*	Haitian ['heɪʃn]	a Haitian	the Haitians
India ['ɪndiə] *Indien*	Indian ['ɪndiən]	an Indian	the Indians
Ireland ['aɪələnd] *Irland*	Irish ['aɪrɪʃ]	an Irishman / -woman	the Irish
Italy ['ɪtəli] *Italien*	Italian [ɪ'taliən]	an Italian	the Italians
Jamaica [dʒə'meɪkə] *Jamaika*	Jamaican [dʒə'meɪkən]	a Jamaican	the Jamaicans
Japan [dʒə'pæn] *Japan*	Japanese [dʒæpə'niːz]	a Japanese	the Japanese
Kenya ['kenjə] *Kenia*	Kenyan ['kenjən]	a Kenyan	the Kenyans
Korea [kə'riːə] *Korea*	Korean [kə'riːən]	a Korean	the Koreans
Latin America [latɪn ə'merɪkə] *Lateinamerika*	Latin American [latɪn ə'merɪkən]	a Latin American	the Latin Americans
Lebanon ['lebənən] *der Libanon*	Lebanese [lebə'niːz]	a Lebanese	the Lebanese
Lithuania [lɪθju'eɪniə] *Litauen*	Lithuanian [lɪθju'eɪniən]	a Lithuanian	the Lithuanians
Mexico ['meksɪkəʊ] *Mexiko*	Mexican ['meksɪkən]	a Mexican	the Mexicans
Morocco [mə'rɒkəʊ] *Marokko*	Moroccan [mə'rɒkən]	a Moroccan	the Moroccans
Nepal [nə'pɔːl] *Nepal*	Nepalese [nepə'liːz]	a Nepalese	the Nepalese
(the) Netherlands ['neðələndz] *die Niederlande, Holland*	Dutch [dʌtʃ]	a Dutchman / -woman	the Dutch

New Zealand [ˌnjuː ˈziːlənd] *Neuseeland*	New Zealand [ˌnjuː ˈziːlənd]	a New Zealander	the New Zealanders
Nicaragua [nɪkəˈrægjuə] *Nicaragua*	Nicaraguan [nɪkəˈrægjuən]	a Nicaraguan	the Nicaraguans
Nigeria [naɪˈdʒɪəriə] *Nigeria*	Nigerian [naɪˈdʒɪəriən]	a Nigerian	the Nigerians
Northern Ireland [nɔːðən ˈaɪələnd] *Nordirland*	Northern Irish [nɔːðən ˈaɪrɪʃ]	a Northern Irishman / -woman	the Northern Irish / Northern Irishmen / -women
Pakistan [pakɪˈstan] *Pakistan*	Pakistani [pakɪˈstani]	a Pakistani	the Pakistanis
Poland [ˈpəʊlənd] *Polen*	Polish [ˈpəʊlɪʃ]	a Pole [pəʊl]	the Poles
Portugal [ˈpɔːtʃʊgl] *Portugal*	Portuguese [pɔːtʃʊˈgiːz]	a Portuguese	the Portuguese
Puerto Rico [pwɜːtə ˈriːkəʊ] *Puerto Rico*	Puerto Rican [pwɜːtə ˈriːkən]	a Puerto Rican	the Puerto Ricans
Romania [ruˈmeɪniə] *Rumänien*	Romanian [ruˈmeɪniən]	a Romanian	the Romanians
Russia [ˈrʌʃə] *Russland*	Russian [ˈrʌʃn]	a Russian	the Russians
Scotland [ˈskɒtlənd] *Schottland*	Scottish [ˈskɒtɪʃ]	a Scot [skɒt]	the Scots
South Africa [saʊθ ˈæfrɪkə] *Südafrika*	South African [saʊθ ˈæfrɪkən]	a South African	the South Africans
South America [saʊθ əˈmerɪkə] *Südamerika*	South American [saʊθ əˈmerɪkən]	a South American	the South Americans
Spain [speɪn] *Spanien*	Spanish [ˈspænɪʃ]	Spaniard [ˈspænjəd]	the Spanish / the Spaniards
Syria [ˈsɪriə] *Syrien*	Syrian [ˈsɪriən]	a Syrian	the Syrians
Texas [ˈteksəs] *Texas*	Texan [ˈteksən]	a Texan	the Texans
Thailand [ˈtaɪlænd, ˈtaɪlənd] *Thailand*	Thai [taɪ]	a Thai	the Thais
Turkey [ˈtɜːki], Türkiye [ˈtʊəkijə] *die Türkei*	Turkish [ˈtɜːkɪʃ]	a Turk [tɜːk]	the Turks
the United Kingdom (the UK) [juˌnaɪtɪd ˈkɪŋdəm, ˌjuːˈkeɪ] *das Vereinigte Königreich (Großbritannien und Nordirland)*	British [ˈbrɪtɪʃ]	a Briton [ˈbrɪtn]	the British
Ukraine [juːˈkreɪn] *die Ukraine*	Ukrainian [juːˈkreɪniən]	a Ukrainian	the Ukrainians
the United States of America, the USA [juː es ˈeɪ], the US [juː ˈes] *die Vereinigten Staaten von Amerika*	American [əˈmerɪkən]	an American	the Americans
Vietnam [viːetˈnɑːm] *Vietnam*	Vietnamese [viːetnəˈmiːz]	a Vietnamese	the Vietnamese
Wales [weɪlz] *Wales*	Welsh [welʃ]	a Welshman / -woman	the Welsh

Unit 4

6 Listening Can you believe your eyes?

a) **Lösung:** Bild A zeigt einen kalifornischen Hirschen *(mule deer)*, Bild B wurde mit KI erstellt.

Cities and towns:
over 1,000,000 inhabitants
500,000 – 1,000,000 inhabitants
100,000 – 500,000 inhabitants
under 100,000 inhabitants
Ottawa National capital
Halifax Provincial/Territorial capital
International boundary
Provincial/Territorial boundary
Time zone boundary
–3h 30 Time difference to Greenwich Mean Time
0 100 200 300 400 500 miles
0 200 400 600 800 km
Canada
RUSSIA
Bering Strait
ICELAND
Greenland
(DENMARK)
Arctic Ocean
Beaufort Sea
Baffin Bay
Hudson Bay
Labrador Sea
Atlantic Ocean
Pacific Ocean
Gulf of Alaska
Alaska
(USA)
UNITED STATES OF AMERICA (USA)
Alaska Standard Time
7:00
–9 h
Pacific Standard Time
8:00
–8h
Mountain Standard Time
9:00
–7h
Central Standard Time
10:00
–6h
Eastern Standard Time
11:00
–5h
Atlantic Standard Time
12:00
–4h
Newfoundland Standard Time
12:30
–3h 30
Parry Islands
Queen Elizabeth Islands
Ellesmere Island
Melville Island
Devon Island
Banks Island
Victoria Island
Prince of Wales Island
Somerset Island
Baffin Island
Igloolik
Iqaluit
Southampton Island
Nunavut
Northwest Territories
Yukon Territory
British Columbia
Alberta
Saskatche-wan
Manitoba
Ontario
Québec
Nunavik
Newfoundland and Labrador
Labrador
Newfound-land
PEI
NB
Nova Scotia
Yukon
Klondike
Dawson City
Mt. Logan 5959
Whitehorse
Mackenzie Mountains
Mackenzie
Aklavik
Great Bear Lake
Yellowknife
Great Slave Lake
Glacier Bay National Park
Lower Post
Liard
Fort Nelson
Rocky Mountains
Peace
Queen Charlotte Islands
Mt. Waddington 4016
Mt. Robson 3954
Fraser
Vancouver Island
Vancouver
Victoria
Goodfish Lake
Edmonton
Calgary
Lake Athabasca
Saskatoon
Saskatchewan
Regina
Cowessess
Winnipeg
Lake Winnipeg
Churchill
Thunder Bay
Lake Superior
Great Lakes
Sault Sainte Marie
Lake Michigan
Lake Huron
Lake Ontario
Lake Erie
Windsor
Toronto
Niagara Falls
Ottawa
Montréal
Québec
Tadoussac
St. Lawrence
Kangiqsualujjuaq
Kuujjuaq
Lake Michikamau
Forteau
St. John's
Saint-Pierre & Miquelon
(FRANCE)
Sydney
Charlottetown
Fredericton
Saint John
Halifax
GERMANY
Hamburg
Munich
PEI = Prince Edward Island
NB = New Brunswick

l'éléphant
est une revue éditée par Scrineo
8, rue Saint-Marc 75002 Paris
01 82 09 95 74

Directeur de la publication
Jean-Paul Arif

Rédactrice en chef
Guénaëlle Le Solleu

Rédactrices
Marika Droneau, Mélina Juin

Conception graphique
Gilles Le Nozahic

Mise en pages
Julian Jeanne

Illustrations
Isabel Espanol, Julian Jeanne, Gwen Keraval, Léa Taillefert, Mathieu Ughetti

Cartographie
Allix Piot

Photos
Académie de France à Rome, Adobe Stock, AKG Images, Biosphoto, Bridgeman, V. Jacob, Leemage, NASA, Anita Quilès, Réa, RMN-GP, Roger Viollet, Science Photo Library, Sipa, Unsplash, Wikimedia Commons

Correction
Sandra Pizzo

Marketing et développement
Corinne Godichaud

Communication, relations presse
Emmanuelle Ribes

Relations lecteurs
Benjamin Cesbron

Ont collaboré à ce numéro
Étienne Augris, Antoine de Baecque, Marjorie Cessac, Valérie Denarnaud-Mayer, Émilie Dumarest, Alix Favre, Bénédicte de La Guérivière, Gaël Guillaumé, David Louapre, Audric Mazzietti, Isabelle Mimouni, Marie-Cécile Naves, Océane Pirez, Nicolas Prissette, Sara Quemener, Dorothée Schmid, Mélanie Semaine, Nathalie Vanfasse, Sophie Vo, Mathieu Ughetti

Diffusion
MLP / Interforum

Gestion des ventes au numéro
À Juste Titres - Julien Teissier
04 88 15 12 41

Gestion des abonnements
Sylvie Guichot
abonnement@lelephant-larevue.fr

Imprimeur
Aubin (86240 Ligugé)

Abonnement
64 € TTC par an
Publication trimestrielle

Dépôt légal
Janvier 2021
ISSN 2265-7371
Commission paritaire : 0423 K 91770

Fabriqué en France

La rumeur n'a pas attendu Internet pour salir les réputations. Marie-Antoinette en fit en son temps la douloureuse expérience. La moquerie devient soupçon, le soupçon devient mensonge, le mensonge accusation, l'accusation propage la haine, et la haine peut aller jusqu'à l'exécution. L'image désastreuse de cette reine incomprise a-t-elle suffi à la conduire à la guillotine ?

Aujourd'hui, ce sont les réseaux sociaux qui propagent la haine, sans se soucier de trier entre fantasme et réalité. Ils peuvent conduire à la mort, comme celle de Samuel Paty, sauvagement assassiné par un fanatique mal informé. Faut-il de nouvelles lois pour encadrer les réseaux sociaux ? Empêcher, par exemple, de diffuser des images de policiers ? Mais peut-on dans le même temps se battre pour la liberté d'expression et risquer de la compromettre par des lois dangereuses et inapplicables ? L'équilibre est toujours délicat entre tentations sécuritaires et préservation des libertés. Il est sain de rester vigilant.

Il est sain de rester vigilant car l'histoire sait être tragique, comme elle le fut en Argentine, frappée par une dictature sanglante construite sur la terreur entre 1976 et 1983. Il est sain de rester vigilant pour que le droit international, aujourd'hui balbutiant, s'impose à tous et que l'impunité des dirigeants malfaisants ne soit plus absolue.

Il est sain de rester vigilant, enfin, pour que l'action publique se concentre sur les vrais enjeux. La renaissance industrielle en est un. La compétition est rude et les choix stratégiques méritent de vrais débats. Notre capacité de recherche publique et privée en est un autre, et l'on peut regretter que le pays de Pasteur, pionnier dans la compréhension des mécanismes de l'immunité, ne figure pas dans le peloton de tête pour le vaccin contre le Covid-19. ●

GUÉNAËLLE LE SOLLEU ET JEAN-PAUL ARIF

C'est à quel sujet ?

Retrouvez les sept articles de ce numéro évoqués dans l'édito !

Réponse : Marie-Antoinette, loi de sécurité globale, liberté de la presse, Argentine, Philippe Sands, industrie, immunité.

22 LE GRAND TÉMOIN
Philippe Sands
▶ « En matière de droit international, nous en sommes encore au Moyen Âge. »

30 **Les réputations de Marie-Antoinette**
LA REINE DE FRANCE FUT AUTANT DÉTESTÉE QU'ADULÉE
▶ Du culte à la haine, de la curiosité au mimétisme, un foisonnement de représentations a rythmé son existence et a persisté bien après sa mort.

▶ Le *revival* de la « Marie-Antoinette-mania »

42 **L'eau : défis et batailles autour d'une ressource vitale**
LE FUTUR INQUIÉTANT DE L'ACCÈS À L'EAU DOUCE
▶ Alimentation, hygiène, géopolitique : la question de l'eau se pose avec une extrême complexité, de nombreuses contradictions et de criantes inégalités.

▶ Entretien avec JULIEN LECOLLINET, expert en irrigation internationale

56 **Le surréalisme, « machine à chavirer l'esprit »**
UN MOUVEMENT MAJEUR DES AVANT-GARDES DU XXe SIÈCLE
▶ Le surréalisme libère l'artiste de ses contraintes, de l'ordre établi, et laisse son inconscient s'exprimer librement.

▶ Quelques œuvres clés du surréalisme

70 **La France en quête d'une renaissance industrielle**
COMMENT RELANCER LE *MADE IN FRANCE* ?
▶ Stigmatisée pour son délitement depuis quarante ans, l'industrie retrouve quelques lettres de noblesse.

▶ Entretien avec DAVID COUSQUER, fondateur de Trendeo

86 **Qu'est-ce que la beauté ?**
FAUT-IL PRIVILIGIER NOTRE REGARD OU LA THÉORIE ?
▶ La beauté n'est pas un sujet de préoccupation aussi futile qu'il n'y paraît. Les philosophes s'y sont intéressés.

▶ À l'époque… l'œuvre d'art au fil du temps

104 **Le carbone 14, machine à remonter le temps**
UN INGRÉDIENT CENTRAL DU FONCTIONNEMENT DE LA VIE SUR TERRE
▶ Rouleaux de la mer Morte, suaire de Turin, peintures de la grotte Chauvet : autant de découvertes célèbres que l'on a pu dater grâce au carbone 14.

▶ Entretien avec ANITA QUILÈS, responsable du pôle archéométrie de l'Institut français d'archéologie orientale

COUVERTURE : ISABEL ESPANOL